COLLINS'
COLLECTORS' CHOICE

Collins' Collectors' Choice

Four Great Adventure Stories

WHEN EIGHT BELLS TOLL
THE GOLDEN GATE
CARAVAN TO VACCARÈS
CIRCUS

by

Alistair MacLean

Introduction by
Carl Foreman

COLLINS
St James's Place, London
1981

William Collins Sons and Co Ltd
London · Glasgow · Sydney · Auckland
Toronto · Johannesburg

First published 1981

MacLean, Alistair
Four great adventure stories.–
(Collins' Collectors' Choice)
I. Title
823'.914[F] PR6063.A248

ISBN 0-00-243347-8

Photoset in Baskerville by Unwin Brothers Ltd
Made and Printed in England by
Butler and Tanner Ltd, Frome, Somerset

CONTENTS

INTRODUCTION

When the legendary 'Mike' Frankovich, then head of Columbia Pictures, handed me a copy of Alistair MacLean's second book *The Guns of Navarone* and asked me to read it, with the suggestion that I might consider making it as a film, my first reaction was a negative one. First, there was the question of *amour propre*: all film-makers prefer the thrill of discovery to be their own. Perhaps more to the point, I had only recently, as film time is reckoned, written one war film, *The Bridge over the River Kwai*, and written and produced another, *The Key*, as Jan de Hartog's novel *Stella* was renamed for the cinema. I felt that I had had my fill of war stories, and I think I was afraid that Frankovich was 'type-casting' me as a writer and maker of war films. Nevertheless, I had great respect for his judgement and I read the book. That was, as I shall enlarge on later in this introduction, all too easy to do. I read it at one sitting – and recoiled from the manifest difficulties involved in translating it to the screen. It was, as I reported to 'the Squire' (our name for Frankovich), too big, too difficult, too potentially time-consuming, too expensive to consider as a film – at least for me. I wanted to do something smaller, more intimate, more socially realistic. Frankovich persisted gently, and made it clear that whilst he appreciated the difficulties he would not oppose a sensible and realistic approach to the eventual cost of a film based on this vast adventure story. He begged me to read the book again and to reconsider. I read it again. And I reconsidered. I made the film. And the rest, as they say, is history. It was, as I had feared, a tremendously difficult film to make, requiring two full years of dedicated effort by many others beside myself. But in the end it was magnificently worth it. Luck was with us, the film was a huge success, and it changed the lives of everyone connected with it, not least of Alistair MacLean. He was able to give up teaching and to become a full-time professional writer, which resulted in a spate of books that provide unequalled entertainment in every language that can be written and printed and in his name becoming the household word it is in every continent. I am very grateful to Squire Frankovich for his gentle persuasion. I think Alistair should be too, and very likely is, and so, indeed, should all his millions of readers; for if *The Guns of Navarone* made it all possible, in its way, it was an enlightened film mogul who first saw its possibilities as a film and patiently encouraged and supported its production.

When Ian Chapman, Alistair's discoverer and publisher, brought us together, I was taken aback. My image of the man who had written so robust, so dynamic, and so vast an adventure story was on the same scale: instead I met a rather small man, quiet, reserved, modest, his charm and erudition hidden, at least to me, behind an almost impenetrable Glasgow accent. Later I learned that his shy exterior belied unbounded courage and tenacity.

Alistair made it clear from the beginning that he had no intention of becoming involved in the writing or making of the film; he said, very pleasantly, that he felt his child was in the hands of a kind and intelligent foster parent and that he would stand by with his fingers crossed until it grew into a film. That was flattering. When the film was made and shown he was even more flattering; he requested a copy of the script for his own analysis and study, and asked me to autograph it for and to him. I was proud and happy to do so.

On my part, as I embarked on the screenplay, I learned that what had appeared to be deceptively simple and all too easy to write was in reality an example of masterly control of construction and consistently rising tension and suspense, leading from one breath-taking climax to another. Consequently, when we were preparing the credit titles for the film, I went beyond the contractual requirements and instead of simply stating, on the usual title card, that the film was 'based on a novel by Alistair MacLean', I emblazoned on the first and 'main' title the words: *Alistair MacLean's The Guns of Navarone*. He had received, and deserved in my opinion, what the super-stars of the cinema world crave and demand – his name *above* the title . . .

INTRODUCTION

There are two aspects of Alistair MacLean's work that I would like to mention in this introduction. First, he is a great, great story-teller, and all his books are compulsive reading. He has developed the question 'What happens next?' into a fine art. When you open an Alistair MacLean adventure story it is like leaping on to the back of a swift, strong, thoroughbred horse, a veritable Pegasus if you like, and embarking on a breathless ride through a countryside made magical by almost unparallelled imagination and inventiveness. You will always find it exceedingly difficult to put down a MacLean book, and sometimes impossible. I believe that Dumas would, if he could, or can, read MacLean with pleasure, with admiration and quite often a touch of honest and affectionate envy.

Second, although one may sometimes think of him as basically a writer of war stories, reconsideration, and this volume too, make it clear that he has a fantastically wide range. The impact of his early works, from *HMS Ulysses* and *The Guns of Navarone*, followed by *South of Java Head, Where Eagles Dare* and *Force Ten from Navarone* may tend to persuade the careless reviewer that this genre is the essential MacLean, whereas the fact is that Alistair MacLean provides a tremendous feast for the adventure story gourmet, with unlimited variety and change of locale, character, crisis, climax and conclusion. This collection is in itself proof of that mastery of medium and variety. Each story is completely different from the others, and yet each is a complete and individual trip on the MacLean roller-coaster. All the books have either been made into films, or will be, and I wish that I could have a hand in them. I wish, too, that *HMS Ulysses*, acknowledged to be his greatest book, had been made into a film; or that perhaps someday, rising costs and the death of the ships of that period notwithstanding, I may yet be the one who makes it.

But for now, like you, I intend to put the world around me with all its dullness and disappointments and boredom, away, to lose myself in sheer gluttony and pleasure, and to enjoy to the fullest four cracking good stories by one of the greatest story-tellers of our time.

CARL FOREMAN

November 1981

WHEN EIGHT BELLS TOLL

— 1 —

Dusk Monday – 3 a.m. Tuesday

THE PEACEMAKER Colt has now been in production, without change in design, for a century. Buy one today and it would be indistinguishable from the one Wyatt Earp wore when he was the Marshal of Dodge City. It is the oldest hand-gun in the world, without question the most famous and, if efficiency in its designated task of maiming and killing be taken as a criterion of its worth, then it is also probably the best hand-gun ever made. It is no light thing, it is true, to be wounded by some of the Peacemaker's more highly esteemed competitors, such as the Luger or Mauser: but the high-velocity, narrow-calibre, steel-cased shell from either of those just goes straight through you, leaving a small neat hole in its wake and spending the bulk of its energy on the distant landscape; whereas the large and unjacketed soft-nosed lead bullet from the Colt mushrooms on impact, tearing and smashing bone and muscle and tissue as it goes and expending all its energy on you.

In short when a Peacemaker's bullet hits you in, say, the leg, you don't curse, step into shelter, roll and light a cigarette one-handed then smartly shoot your assailant between the eyes. When a Peacemaker bullet hits your leg you fall to the ground unconscious, and if it hits the thigh-bone and you are lucky enough to survive the torn arteries and shock, then you will never walk again without crutches because a totally disintegrated femur leaves the surgeon with no option but to cut your leg off. And so I stood absolutely motionless, not breathing, for the Peacemaker Colt that had prompted this unpleasant train of thought was pointed directly at my right thigh.

Another thing about the Peacemaker: because of the very heavy and varying trigger pressure required to operate the semi-automatic mechanism, it can be wildly inaccurate unless held in a strong and steady hand. There was no such hope here. The hand that held the Colt, the hand that lay so lightly yet purposefully on the radio-operator's table, was the steadiest hand I've ever seen. It was literally motionless. I could see the hand very clearly. The light in the radio cabin was very dim, the rheostat of the angled table lamp had been turned down until only a faint pool of yellow fell on the scratched metal of the table, cutting the arm off at the cuff, but the hand was very clear. Rock-steady, the gun could have lain no quieter in the marbled hand of a statue. Beyond the pool of light I could half sense, half see the dark outline of a figure leaning back against the bulkhead, head slightly tilted to one side, the white gleam of unwinking eyes under the peak of a hat. My eyes went back to the hand. The angle of the Colt hadn't varied by a fraction of a degree. Unconsciously, almost, I braced my right leg to meet the impending shock. Defensively, this was a very good move, about as useful as holding up a sheet of newspaper in front of me. I wished to God that Colonel Sam Colt had gone in for inventing something else, something useful, like safety-pins.

Very slowly, very steadily, I raised both hands, palms outward, until they were level with my shoulders. The careful deliberation was so that the nervously inclined wouldn't be deceived into thinking that I was contemplating anything ridiculous, like resistance. It was probably a pretty superfluous precaution as the man behind that immobile pistol didn't seem to have any nerves and the last thought I had in my head was that of resistance. The sun was long down but the faint red after-glow of sunset still loomed on the north-west horizon and I was perfectly silhouetted against it through the cabin doorway. The lad behind the desk probably had his left hand on the rheostat switch ready to turn it up and blind me at an instant's notice. And there was that gun. I was paid to take chances. I was paid even to step, on occasion, into danger. But I wasn't paid to act the part of a congenital and suicidal idiot. I hoisted my hands a couple of inches higher and tried to look as peaceful and harmless as possible. The way I felt, that was no feat.

The man with the gun said nothing and did nothing. He

remained completely still. I could see the white blur of teeth now. The gleaming eyes stared unwinkingly at me. The smile, the head cocked slightly to one side, the negligent relaxation of the body – the aura in that tiny cabin of a brooding and sardonic menace was so heavy as to be almost palpable. There was something evil, something frighteningly unnatural and wrong and foreboding in the man's stillness and silence and cold-blooded cat-and-mouse indifference. Death was waiting to reach out and touch with his icy forefinger in that tiny cabin. In spite of two Scots grandparents I'm in no way psychic or fey or second-sighted, as far as extra-sensory perception goes I've about the same degree of receptive sensitivity as a lump of old lead. But I could smell death in the air.

'I think we're both making a mistake,' I said. 'Well, you are. Maybe we're both on the same side.' The words came with difficulty, a suddenly dry throat and tongue being no aids to clarity of elocution, but they sounded all right to me, just as I wanted them to sound, low and calm and soothing. Maybe he was a nut case. Humour him. Anything. Just stay alive. I nodded to the stool at the front corner of his desk. 'It's been a hard day. Okay if we sit and talk? I'll keep my hands high, I promise you.'

The total reaction I got was nil. The white teeth and eyes, the relaxed contempt, that iron gun in that iron hand. I felt my own hands begin to clench into fists and hastily unclenched them again, but I couldn't do anything about the slow burn of anger that touched me for the first time.

I smiled what I hoped was a friendly and encouraging smile and moved slowly towards the stool. I faced him all the time, the cordial smile making my face ache and the hands even higher than before. A Peacemaker Colt can kill a steer at sixty yards, God only knew what it would do to me. I tried to put it out of my mind, I've only got two legs and I'm attached to them both.

I made it with both still intact. I sat down, hands still high, and started breathing again. I'd stopped breathing but hadn't been aware of it, which was understandable enough as I'd had other things on my mind, such as crutches, bleeding to death and such-like matters that tend to grip the imagination.

The Colt was as motionless as ever. The barrel hadn't followed me as I'd moved across the cabin, it was still pointing rigidly at the spot where I'd been standing ten seconds earlier.

I moved fast going for that gun-hand, but it was no breakneck dive. I didn't, I was almost certain, even have to move fast, but I haven't reached the advanced age in which my chief thinks he honours me by giving me all the dirtiest jobs going by ever taking a chance: when I don't have to.

I eat all the right foods, take plenty of exercise and, even although no insurance company in the world will look at me, their medical men would pass me any time, but even so I couldn't tear that gun away. The hand that had looked like marble felt like marble, only colder. I'd smelled death all right, but the old man hadn't been hanging around with his scythe at the ready, he'd been and gone and left this lifeless shell behind him. I straightened, checked that the windows were curtained, closed the door noiselessly, locked it as quietly and switched on the overhead light.

There's seldom any doubt about the exact time of a murder in an old English country house murder story. After a cursory examination and a lot of pseudo-medical mumbo-jumbo, the good doctor drops the corpse's wrist and says, 'The decedent deceased at 11.57 last night' or words to that effect, then, with a thin deprecatory smile magnanimously conceding that he's a member of the fallible human race, adds, 'Give or take a minute or two.' The good doctor outside the pages of the detective novel finds it rather more difficult. Weight, build, ambient temperature and cause of death all bear so heavily and often unpredictably on the cooling of the body that the estimated time of death may well lie in a span of several hours.

I'm not a doctor, far less a good one, and all I could tell about the man behind the desk was that he had been dead long enough for rigor mortis to set in but not long enough for it to wear off. He was stiff as a man frozen to death in a Siberian winter. He'd been gone for hours. How many, I'd no idea.

He wore four gold bands on his sleeves, so that would seem to make him the captain. The captain in the radio cabin. Captains are seldom found in the radio cabin and never behind the desk. He was slumped back in his chair, his head to one side, the back of it resting against a jacket hanging from a hook on the bulkhead, the side of it against a wall cabinet. Rigor mortis kept him in that position but he should have slipped to the floor or at least slumped forward on to the table before rigor mortis had set in.

There were no outward signs of violence that I could see but on the assumption that it would be stretching the arm of coincidence a bit far to assume that he had succumbed from natural causes while preparing to defend his life with his Peacemaker I took a closer look. I tried to pull him upright but he wouldn't budge. I tried harder, I heard the sound of cloth ripping, then suddenly he was upright, then fallen over to the left of the table, the right arm pivoting stiffly around and upwards, the Colt an accusing finger pointing at heaven.

I knew now how he had died and why he hadn't fallen forward before. He'd been killed by a weapon that projected from his spinal column, between maybe the sixth and seventh vertebrae, I couldn't be sure, and the handle of this weapon had caught in the pocket of the jacket on the bulkhead and held him there.

My job was one that had brought me into contact with a fair number of people who had died from a fair assortment of unnatural causes, but this was the first time I'd ever seen a man who had been killed by a chisel. A half-inch wood chisel, apparently quite ordinary in every respect except that its wooden handle had been sheathed by a bicycle's rubber hand-grip, the kind that doesn't show fingerprints. The blade was imbedded to a depth of at least four inches and even allowing for an edge honed to a razor sharpness it had taken a man as powerful as he was violent to strike that blow. I tried to jerk the chisel free, but it wouldn't come. It often happens that way with a knife: bone or cartilage that has been pierced by a sharp instrument locks solid over the steel when an attempt is made to withdraw it. I didn't try again. The chances were that the killer himself had tried to move it and failed. He wouldn't have wanted to abandon a handy little sticker like that if he could help it. Maybe someone had interrupted him. Or maybe he had a large supply of half-inch wood chisels and could afford to leave the odd one lying around carelessly in someone's back.

Anyway, I didn't really want it. I had my own. Not a chisel but a knife. I eased it out of the plastic sheath that had been sewn into the inner lining of my coat, just behind the neck. It didn't look so much, a four-inch handle and a little double-edged three-inch blade. But that little blade could slice through a two-inch manila with one gentle stroke and the point was the point of a lancet. I looked at it and looked at the inner door behind the radio table, the one that led to the radio-operator's sleeping cabin, then I slid a little fountain-pen torch from my breast pocket, crossed to the outer door, switched off the overhead lamp, did the same for the table lamp and stood there waiting.

How long I stood there I couldn't be sure. Maybe two minutes, maybe as long as five. Why I waited, I don't know. I told myself I was waiting until my eyes became adjusted to the almost total darkness inside the cabin, but I knew it wasn't that. Maybe I was waiting for some noise, the slightest imagined whisper of stealthy sound, maybe I was waiting for something, anything, to happen – or maybe I was just scared to go through that inner door. Scared for myself? Perhaps I was. I couldn't be sure. Or perhaps I was scared of what I would find behind that door. I transferred the knife to my left hand – I'm right-handed but ambidextrous in some things – and slowly closed my fingers round the handle of the inner door.

It took me all of twenty seconds to open that door the twelve inches that was necessary for me to squeeze through the opening. In the very last half-inch the damned hinges creaked. It was a tiny sound, a sound you wouldn't normally have heard two yards away. With my steel-taut nerves in the state they were in, a six-inch naval gun going off in my ear would have sounded muffled by contrast. I stood petrified as any graven image; the dead man by my side was no more immobile than I. I could hear the thump of my accelerating heartbeat and savagely wished the damned thing would keep quiet.

If there was anyone inside waiting to flash a torch in my face and shoot me, knife me or do a little fancy carving up with a chisel, he was taking his time about it. I treated my lungs to a little oxygen, stepped soundlessly and sideways through the opening. I held the flash at the full outstretch extent of my right arm. If the ungodly are going to shoot at a person who is shining a torch at them they generally aim in the very close vicinity of the torch as the unwary habitually hold a torch in front of them. This, as I had learnt many years previously from a colleague who'd just had a bullet extracted from the lobe of his left lung because of this very unwariness, was a very unwise thing to do. So I held the torch as far from my body as possible, drew my left arm back with the knife ready to go, hoping fervently that the reactions of any person who might be in that cabin were slower than mine, and slid forward the switch of the torch.

There was someone there all right, but I didn't have to worry about his reactions. Not any more. He'd none left. He was lying face down on the bunk with that huddled shapeless look that belongs only to the dead. I made a quick traverse of the cabin with the pencil beam. The dead man was alone. As in the radio cabin, there was no sign of a struggle.

I didn't even have to touch him to ascertain the cause of death. The amount of blood that had seeped from that half-inch incision in his spine wouldn't have filled a teaspoon. I wouldn't have expected to find more; when the spinal column has been neatly severed the heart doesn't go on pumping long enough to matter a damn. There would have been a little more internal bleeding, but not much.

The curtains were drawn. I quartered every foot of the deck, bulkheads and furniture with my flash. I don't know what I expected to find: what I found was nothing. I went out, closed the door behind me and searched the radio cabin with the same results. There was nothing more for me here, I had found all I wanted to find, all I had never wanted to find. And I never once looked at the faces of the two dead men. I didn't have to, they were faces I knew as well as the face that looked back at me every morning out of my shaving mirror. Seven days previously they had dined with me and our chief in our favourite pub in London and they had been as cheerful and relaxed as men in their profession can ever be, their normal still watchfulness overlaid by the momentary savouring of the lighter side of life they knew could never really be for them. And I had no doubt they had gone on being as still and watchful as ever, but they hadn't been watchful enough and now they were only still. What had happened to them was what inevitably happened to people in our trade, which would inevitably happen to myself when the time came. No matter how clever and strong and ruthless you were, sooner or later you would meet up with someone who was cleverer and stronger and more ruthless than yourself. And that someone would have a half-inch wood chisel in his hand and all your hardly-won years of experience and knowledge and cunning counted for nothing for you never saw him coming, and you never saw him coming because you had met your match at last and then you were dead.

And I had sent them to their deaths. Not willingly, not knowingly, but the ultimate responsibility had been mine. This had all been my idea, my brain-child and mine alone, and I'd overridden all objections and fast-talked our very doubtful and highly sceptical chief into giving if not his enthusiastic approval at least his grudging consent. I'd told the two men, Baker and Delmont, that if they played it my way no harm would come to them so they'd trusted me blindly and played it my way and now they lay dead beside me. No hesitation, gentlemen, put your faith in me, only see to it that you make your wills first of all.

There was nothing more to be done here now. I'd sent two men to their deaths and that couldn't be undone. It was time to be gone.

I opened that outer door the way you'd open the door to a cellar you knew to be full of cobras and black widow spiders. The way *you* would open the door, that is: were cobras and black widow spiders all I had to contend with aboard that ship, I'd have gone through that door without a second thought; they were harmless and almost lovable little creatures compared to some specimens of *homo sapiens* that were loose on the decks of the freighter *Nantesville* that night.

With the door opened at its fullest extent I just stood there. I stood there for a long time without moving a muscle of body or limbs, breathing shallowly and evenly, and when you stand like that even a minute seems half a lifetime. All my being was in my ears. I just stood there and listened. I could hear the slap of waves against the hull, the occasional low metallic rumble as the *Nantesville* worked against wind and tide on its moorings, the low moan of the strengthening night wind in the rigging and, once, the far-off lonely call of a curlew. Lonesome sounds, safe sounds, sounds of the night and nature. Not the sounds I was listening for. Gradually, these sounds too became part of the silence. Foreign sounds, sounds of stealth and menace and danger, there were none. No sound of breathing, no slightest scrape of feet on steel decks, no rustle of clothing, nothing. If there was anyone waiting out there he was possessed of a patience and immobility that was superhuman and I wasn't worried about superhumans that night, just about humans, humans with knives and guns and chisels in their hands. Silently I stepped out over the storm sill.

I've never paddled along the night-time Orinoco in a dugout canoe and had a thirty-foot anaconda drop from a tree, wrap a coil around my neck and start constricting me to death and what's more I don't have to go there now to describe the experience, for I know exactly what it feels like. The sheer animal power, the feral ferocity of the pair of huge hands that closed round my neck from behind was terrifying, something I'd never known of, never dreamed of. After the first moment of blind panic and shocked paralysis, there was only one thought in my mind: it comes to us all and now it has come to me – someone who is cleverer and stronger and more ruthless than I am.

I lashed back with all the power of my right foot but the man behind me knew every rule in the book. His own right foot, travelling with even more speed and power than mine, smashed into the back of my swinging leg. It wasn't a man behind me, it was a centaur and he was shod with the biggest set of horseshoes I'd ever come across. My leg didn't just feel as if it had been broken, it felt as if it had been cut in half. I felt his left toe behind my left foot and stamped on it with every vicious ounce of power left me but when my foot came down his toe wasn't there any more. All I had on my feet was a pair of thin rubber swimming moccasins and the agonising jar from the steel deck plates shot clear to the top of my head. I reached up my hands to break his little fingers but he knew all about that too, for his hands were clenched into iron-hard balls with the second knuckle grinding into the carotid artery. I wasn't the first man he'd strangled and unless I did something pretty quickly I wasn't going to be the last either. In my ears I could hear the hiss of compressed air escaping under high pressure and behind my eyes the shooting lines and flashes of colour were deepening and brightening by the moment.

What saved me in those first few seconds were the folded hood and thick rubberized canvas neck ruff of the scuba suit I was wearing under my coat. But they weren't going to save me many seconds longer; the life's ambition of the character behind me seemed to be to make his knuckles meet in the middle of my neck. With the progress he was making that wouldn't take him too long, he was half-way there already.

I bent forward in a convulsive jerk. Half of his weight came on my back, that throttling grip not easing a fraction, and at the same time he moved his feet as far backwards as possible, the instinctive reaction to my move – he would have thought that I was making a grab for one of his legs. When I had him momentarily off-balance I swung round in a short arc till both our backs were towards the sea. I thrust backwards with all my strength, one, two, three steps, accelerating all the way. The *Nantesville* didn't boast of any fancy teak guard-rails, just small-section chain, and the small of the strangler's back took our combined charging weights on the top chain.

If I'd taken that impact I'd have broken my back or slipped enough discs to keep an orthopaedic surgeon in steady employment for months. But no shouts of agony from this lad. No gasps, even. Not a whisper of sound. Maybe he was a deaf mute – I'd heard of several deaf mutes possessed of this phenomenal strength – part of nature's compensatory process, I suppose.

But he'd been forced to break his grip, to grab swiftly at the upper chain to save us both from toppling over the side into the cold dark waters of Loch Houron. I thrust myself away and spun round to face him, my back against the radio office bulkhead. I needed that bulkhead, too – any support while my swimming head cleared and a semblance of life came back into my numbed right leg.

I could see him now as he straightened up from the guard-rail. Not clearly – it was too dark for that – but I could see the white blur of face and hands and the general outline of his body.

I'd expected some towering giant of a man, but he was no giant – unless my eyes weren't focusing properly, which was likely enough. From what I could see in the gloom he seemed a compact and well enough made figure, but that was all. He wasn't even as big as I was. Not that that meant a thing – George Hackenschmidt was a mere five foot nine and a paltry fourteen stone when he used to throw the Terrible Turk through the air like a football and prance around the training ring with eight hundred pounds of cement strapped to his back just to keep him in trim. I had no compunction or false pride about running from a smaller man and as far as this character was concerned the farther and faster the better. But not yet. My right leg wasn't up to it. I reached my hand behind my neck and brought the knife down, holding it in front of me, the blade in the palm of my hand so that he couldn't see the sheen of steel in the faint starlight.

He came at me calmly and purposefully, like a man who knew exactly what he intended to do and was in no doubt at all as to the outcome of his intended action. God knows I didn't doubt he had reason enough for his confidence. He came at me sideways so that my foot couldn't damage him, with his right hand extended at the full stretch of his arm. A one track mind. He was going for my throat again. I waited till his hand was inches from my face then jerked my own right hand violently upwards. Our hands smacked solidly together as the blade sliced cleanly through the centre of his palm.

He wasn't a deaf mute after all. Three short unprintable words, an unjustified slur on my ancestry, and he stepped quickly backwards, rubbed the back and front of his hand against his clothes then licked it in a queer, animal-like gesture. He peered closely at the blood, black as ink in the starlight, welling from both sides of his hand.

'So the little man has a little knife, has he?' he said softly. The voice was a shock. With this caveman-like strength I'd have expected a caveman-like intelligence and voice to match, but the words came in the calm, pleasant, cultured almost accentless speech of the well-educated southern Englishman. 'We shall have to take the little knife from him, shan't we?'

He raised his voice. 'Captain Imrie?' At least, that's what the name sounded like.

'Be quiet, you fool!' The urgent irate voice came from the direction of the crew accommodation aft. 'Do you want to—'

'Don't worry, captain.' The eyes didn't leave me. 'I have him. Here by the wireless office. He's armed. A knife. I'm just going to take it away from him.'

'You have him? You have him? Good, good, good!' It was the kind of a voice a man uses when he's smacking his lips and rubbing his hands together: it was also the kind of voice that a German or Austrian uses when he speaks English. The short guttural 'gut' was unmistakable. 'Be careful. This one I want alive. Jacques! Henry! Kramer! All of you. Quickly! The bridge. Wireless office.'

'Alive,' the man opposite me said pleasantly, 'can also mean not quite dead.' He sucked some more blood from the palm of his hand. 'Or will you hand over the knife quietly and peaceably? I would suggest—'

I didn't wait for more. This was an old technique. You talked to an opponent who courteously waited to hear you out, not appreciating that half-way through some well-turned phrase you were going to shoot him through the middle when, lulled into a sense of temporary false security, he least expected it. Not quite cricket, but effective, and I wasn't going to wait until it took effect on me. I didn't know how he was coming at me but I guessed it would be a dive, either head or feet first and that if he got me down on the deck I wouldn't be getting up again. Not without assistance. I took a quick step forward, flashed my torch a foot from his face, saw the dazzled eyes screw shut for the only fraction of time I'd ever have, and kicked him.

It wasn't as hard as it might have been, owing to the fact that my right leg still felt as if it were broken, nor as accurate, because of the darkness, but it was a pretty creditable effort in the circumstances and it should have left him rolling and writhing about the deck, whooping in agony. Instead he just stood there, unable to move, bent forward and clutching himself with his hands. He was more than human, all right. I could see the sheen of his eyes, but I couldn't see the expression in them, which was just as well as I don't think I would have cared for it very much.

I left. I remembered a gorilla I'd once seen in Basle Zoo, a big black monster who used to twist heavy truck tyres into figures of eight for light exercise. I'd as soon have stepped inside that cage as stay around that deck when this lad became more like his old self again. I hobbled forward round the corner of the radio office, climbed up a liferaft and stretched myself flat on the deck.

The nearest running figures, some with torches, were already at the foot of the companionway leading up to the bridge. I had to get right aft to the rope with the rubber-covered hook I'd swung up to swarm aboard. But I couldn't do it until the midship decks were clear. And then, suddenly, I couldn't do it at all: now that the need for secrecy and stealth was over someone had switched on the cargo loading lights and the midships and foredecks were bathed in a brilliant dazzle of white. One of the foredeck arc lamps was on a jumbo mast, just for'ard of and well above where I was lying. I felt as exposed as a fly pinned to a white ceiling. I flattened myself on that deck as if I were trying to push myself through it.

They were up the companionway and by the radio office now. I heard the sudden exclamations and curses and knew they'd found the hurt man: I didn't hear his voice so I assumed he wasn't able to speak yet.

The curt, authoritative German-accented voice took command.

'You cackle like a flock of hens. Be silent. Jacques, you have your machine-pistol?'

'I have my pistol, captain.' Jacques had the quiet competent sort of voice that I would have found reassuring in certain circumstances but didn't very much care for in the present ones.

'Go aft. Stand at the entrance to the saloon and face for'ard. Cover the midships decks. We will go to the fo'c'sle and then come aft in line abreast and drive him to you. If he doesn't surrender to you, shoot him in the legs. I want him alive.'

God, this was worse than the Peacemaker Colt. At least that fired only one shot at a time. I'd no idea what kind of machine-pistol Jacques had; probably it fired bursts of a dozen or more. I could feel my right thigh muscle begin to stiffen again, it was becoming almost a reflex action now.

'And if he jumps over the side, sir?'

'Do I have to tell you, Jacques?'

'No, sir.'

I was just as clever as Jacques was. He didn't have to tell me either. That nasty dry taste was back in my throat and mouth again. I'd a minute left, no more, and then it would be too late. I slid silently to the side of the radio office roof, the starboard side, the side remote from the spot where Captain Imrie was issuing curt instructions to his men, lowered myself soundlessly to the deck and made my way to the wheelhouse.

I didn't need my torch in there, the backwash of light from the big arc-lamps gave me all the illumination I wanted. Crouching down, to keep below window level, I looked around and saw what I wanted right away – a metal box of distress flares.

Two quick flicks of the knife severed the lashings that secured the flare-box to the deck. One piece of rope, perhaps ten feet in all, I left secured to a handle of the box. I pulled a plastic bag from the pocket of my coat, tore off the coat and the yachtsman's rubber trousers that I was wearing over my scuba suit, stuffed them inside and secured the bag to my waist. The coat and trousers had been essential. A figure in a dripping rubber diving suit walking across the decks of the *Nantesville* would hardly have been likely to escape comment whereas in the dusk and with the outer clothing I had on I could have passed for a crewman and, indeed, had done so twice at a distance: equally important, when I'd left the port of Torbay in my rubber dinghy it had been broad daylight and the sight of a scuba-clad figure putting to sea towards evening wouldn't have escaped comment either, as the curiosity factor of the inhabitants of the smaller ports of the Western Highlands and Islands did not, I had discovered, lag noticeably behind that of their mainland brethren. Some would put it even more strongly than that.

Still crouching low, I moved out through the wheelhouse door on to the starboard wing of the bridge. I reached the outer end and stood up straight. I had to, I had to take the risk, it was now or never at all, I could hear the crew already beginning to move forward to start their search. I lifted the flare-box over the side, eased it down the full length of the rope and started to swing it slowly, gently, from side to side, like a leadsman preparing to cast his lead.

The box weighed at least forty pounds, but I barely noticed the weight. The pendulum arc increased with every swing I made. It had reached an angle of about forty-five degrees on each swing now, pretty close to the maximum I could get and both time and my luck must be running out; I felt about as conspicuous as a trapeze artist under a dozen spotlights and just about as vulnerable too. As the box swung aft on its last arc I gave the rope a final thrust to achieve all the distance and momentum I could, opened my hands at the extremity of the arc and dropped down behind the canvas wind-dodger. It was as I dropped that I remembered I hadn't holed the damned box. I had no idea whether it would float or sink but I did have a very clear idea of what would happen to me if it didn't sink. One thing for sure – it was too late to worry about it now.

I heard a shout come from the main deck, some twenty or thirty feet aft of the bridge. I was certain I had been seen but I hadn't. A second after the shout came a loud and very satisfactory splash and a voice I recognized as Jacques's shouting: 'He's gone over the side. Starboard abaft the bridge. A torch, quick!' He must have been walking aft as ordered, seen this dark blur falling, heard the splash and come on the inevitable conclusion. A dangerous customer who thought fast, was Jacques. In three seconds he'd told his mates all they required to know: what had happened, where and what he wanted done as the necessary preliminary to shooting me full of holes.

The men who had been moving forward to start the sweep for me now came running aft, pounding along the deck directly beneath where I was crouching on the wing of the bridge.

'Can you see him, Jacques?' Captain Imrie's voice, very quick, very calm.

'Not yet, sir.'

'He'll be up soon.' I wished he wouldn't sound so damned confident. 'A dive like that must have knocked most of the breath out of him. Kramer, two men and into the boat. Take lamps and circle around. Henry, the box of grenades. Carlo, the bridge, quick. Starboard searchlight.'

I'd never thought of the boat, that was bad enough, but the grenades! I felt chilled. I knew what an underwater explosion, even a small explosion, can do to the human body; it was twenty times as deadly as the same explosion on land. And I had to, I just had to, be in that water in minutes. But at least I could do something about that searchlight, it was only two feet above my head. I had the power cable in my left hand, the knife in my right and had just brought the two into contact when my mind stopped thinking about those damned grenades and started working again. Cutting that cable would be about as clever as leaning over the wind-dodger and yelling 'Here I am, come and catch me' – a dead giveaway that I was still on board. Clobbering Carlo from behind as he came up the ladder would have the same effect. And I couldn't fool them twice. Not people like these. Hobbling as fast as I could I passed through the wheelhouse on to the port wing, slid down the ladder and ran towards the forepeak. The foredeck was deserted.

I heard a shout and the harsh chatter of some automatic weapon – Jacques and his machine-pistol, for a certainty. Had he imagined he'd seen something, had the box come to the surface, had he actually seen the box and mistaken it for me in the dark waters? It must have been the last of these – he wouldn't have wasted ammunition on anything he'd definitely recognized as a box. Whatever the reason, it had all my blessing. If they thought I was floundering about down there, riddled like a Gruyère cheese, then they wouldn't be looking for me up here.

They had the port anchor down. I swung over the side on a rope, got my feet in the hawse-pipe, reached down and grabbed the chain. The international athletics board should have had their stop-watches on me that night; I must have set a new world record for shinning down anchor chains.

The water was cold but my exposure suit took care of that. The sea was choppy, with a heavy tide running, both of which suited me well. I swam down the port side of the *Nantesville*, underwater for ninety per cent of the time and I saw no one and no one saw me: all the activity was on the starboard side of the vessel.

My aqualung unit and weights and flippers were where I had left them, tied to the top of the rudder post – the *Nantesville* was not much more than half-way down to her marks and the top of the post not far under water. Fitting on an aqualung in choppy seas with a heavy tide running isn't the easiest of tasks but the thought of Kramer and his grenades was a considerable help. Besides, I was in a hurry to be gone for I had a long way to go and many things to do when I arrived at my destination.

I could hear the engine note of the lifeboat rising and falling as it circled off the ship's starboard side but at no time did it come within a hundred feet of me. No more shots were fired and Captain Imrie had obviously decided against using the grenades. I adjusted the weights round my waist, dropped down into the dark safety of the waters, checked my direction on my luminous wrist compass and started to swim. After five minutes I came to the surface and after another five felt my feet ground on the shore of the rocky islet where I'd cached my rubber dinghy.

I clambered up on the rocks and looked back. The *Nantesville* was ablaze with light. A searchlight was shining down into the sea and the lifeboat still circling around. I could hear the steady clanking of the anchor being weighed. I hauled the dinghy into the water, climbed in, unshipped the two stubby oars and paddled off to the south-west. I was still within effective range of the searchlight but its chances of picking up a black-clad figure in a low-silhouette black dinghy on those black waters were remote indeed.

After a mile I shipped the oars and started up the outboard. Or tried to start it up. Outboards always work perfectly for me, except when I'm cold, wet and exhausted. Whenever I really need them, they never work. So I took to the stubby oars again and rowed and rowed and rowed, but not for what seemed any longer than a month. I arrived back at the *Firecrest* at ten to three in the morning.

— 2 —

Tuesday: 3 a.m. – dawn

'CALVERT?' Hunslett's voice was a barely audible murmur in the darkness.

'Yes.' Standing there above me on the *Firecrest*'s deck, he was more imagined than seen against the blackness of the night sky. Heavy clouds had rolled in from the south-west and the last of the stars were gone. Big heavy drops of cold rain were beginning to spatter off the surface of the sea. 'Give me a hand to get the dinghy aboard.'

'How did it go?'

'Later. This first.' I climbed up the accommodation ladder, painter in hand. I had to lift my right leg over the gunwale. Stiff and numb and just beginning to ache again, it could barely take my weight. 'And hurry. We can expect company soon.'

'So that's the way of it,' Hunslett said thoughtfully, 'Uncle Arthur *will* be pleased about this.'

I said nothing to that. Our employer, Rear-Admiral Sir Arthur Arnford-Jason, K.C.B. and most of the rest of the alphabet, wasn't going to be pleased at all. We heaved the dripping dinghy inboard, unclamped the outboard and took them both on to the foredeck.

'Get me a couple of waterproof bags,' I said. 'Then start getting the anchor chain in. Keep it quiet – leave the brake pawl off and use a tarpaulin.'

'We're leaving?'

'We would if we had any sense. We're staying. Just get the anchor up and down.'

By the time he'd returned with the bags I'd the dinghy deflated and in its canvas cover. I stripped off my aqualung and scuba suit and stuffed them into one of the bags along with the weights, my big-dialled waterproof watch and the combined wrist-compass and depth-gauge. I put the outboard in the other bag, restraining the impulse just to throw the damn thing overboard: an outboard motor was a harmless enough object to have aboard any boat, but we already had one attached to the wooden dinghy hanging from the davits over the stern.

Hunslett had the electric windlass going and the chain coming in steadily. An electric windlass is in itself a pretty noiseless machine: when weighing anchor all the racket comes from four sources – the chain passing through the hawse-pipe, the clacking of the brake pawl over the successive stops, the links passing over the drum itself and the clattering of the chain as it falls into the chain locker. About the first of these we could do nothing: but with the brake pawl off and a heavy tarpaulin smothering the sound from the drum and chain locker, the noise level was surprisingly low. Sound travels far over the surface of the sea, but the nearest anchored boats were almost two hundred yards away – we had no craving for the company of other boats in harbour. At two hundred yards, in Torbay, we felt ourselves uncomfortably close: but the sea-bed shelved fairly steeply away from the little town and our present depth of twenty fathoms was the safe maximum for the sixty fathoms of chain we carried.

I heard the click as Hunslett's foot stepped on the deck-switch. 'She's up and down.'

'Put the pawl in for a moment. If that drum slips, I'll have no hands left.' I pulled the bags right for'ard, leaned out under the pulpit rail and used lengths of heaving line to secure them to the anchor chain. When the lines were secure I lifted the bags over the side and let them dangle from the chain.

'I'll take the weight,' I said. 'Lift the chain off the drum – we'll lower it by hand.'

Forty fathoms is 240 feet of chain and letting that lot down to the bottom didn't do my back or arms much good at all, and the rest of me was a long way below par before we started. I was pretty close to exhaustion from the night's work, my neck ached fiercely, my leg only badly and I was shivering violently. I know of various ways of achieving a warm rosy glow but wearing only a set of underclothes in the middle of a cold, wet and windy autumn night in the Western Isles is not one of them. But at last the job was done and we were able to go below. If anyone wanted to investigate what lay at the foot of our anchor chain he'd need a steel articulated diving suit.

Hunslett pulled the saloon door to behind us, moved around in the darkness adjusting the heavy velvet curtains then switched on a small table lamp. It didn't give much light but we knew from experience that it didn't show up through the velvet, and advertising the fact that we were up and around in the middle of the night was the last thing I wanted to do.

Hunslett had a dark narrow saturnine face, with a strong jaw, black bushy eyebrows and thick black hair – the kind of face which is so essentially an expression in itself that it rarely shows much else. It was expressionless now and very still.

'You'll have to buy another shirt,' he said. 'Your collar's too tight. Leaves marks.'

I stopped towelling myself and looked in a mirror. Even in that dim light my neck looked a mess. It was badly swollen and discoloured, with four wicked-looking bruises where the thumbs and forefinger joints had sunk deep into the flesh. Blue and green and purple they were, and they looked as if they would be there for a long time to come.

'He got me from behind. He's wasting his time being a criminal, he'd sweep the board at the Olympic weight-lifting. I was lucky. He also wears heavy boots.' I twisted around and looked down at my right calf. The bruise was bigger than my fist and if it missed out any of the colours of the rainbow I couldn't offhand think which one. There was a deep red gash across the middle of it and blood was ebbing slowly along its entire length. Hunslett gazed at it with interest.

'If you hadn't been wearing that tight scuba suit, you'd have most like bled to death. I better fix that for you.'

'I don't need bandages. What I need is a Scotch. Stop wasting your time. Oh, hell, sorry, yes, you'd better fix it, we can't have our guests sloshing about ankle deep in blood.'

'You're very sure we're going to have guests?'

'I half expected to have them waiting on the doorstep when I got back to the *Firecrest*. We're going to have guests, all right. Whatever our pals aboard the *Nantesville* may be, they're no fools. They'll have figured out by this time that I could have approached only by dinghy. They'll know damn well that it was no nosey-parker local prowling about the ship – local lads in search of a bit of fun don't go aboard anchored ships in the first place. In the second place the locals wouldn't go near Beul nan Uamh – the mouth of the grave – in daylight, far less at night time. Even the *Pilot* says the place has an evil reputation. And in the third place no local lad would get aboard as I did, behave aboard as I did or leave as I did. The local lad would be dead.'

'I shouldn't wonder. And?'

'So we're not locals. We're visitors. We wouldn't be staying at any hotel or boarding-house – too restricted, couldn't move. Almost certainly we'll have a boat. Now, where would our boat be? Not to the north of Loch Houron for with a forecast promising a south-west Force 6 strengthening to Force 7, no boat is going to be daft enough to hang about a lee shore in that lot. The only holding ground and shallow enough sheltered anchorage in the other direction, down the Sound for forty miles, is in Torbay – and that's only four or five miles from where the *Nantesville* was lying at the mouth of Loch Houron. Where would you look?'

'I'd look in Torbay. Which gun do you want?'

'I don't want any gun. You don't want any gun. People like us don't carry guns.'

'Marine biologists don't carry guns,' he nodded. 'Employees of the Ministry of Agriculture and Fisheries don't carry guns. Civil Servants are above reproach. So we play it clever. You're the boss.'

'I don't feel clever any more. And I'll take long odds that I'm not your boss any more. Not after Uncle Arthur hears what I have to tell him.'

'You haven't told *me* anything yet.' He finished tying the bandage round my leg and straightened. 'How's that feel?'

I tried it. 'Better. Thanks. Better still when you've taken the cork from that bottle. Get into pyjamas or something. People found fully dressed in the middle of the night cause eyebrows to go up.' I towelled my head as vigorously as my tired arms would let me. One wet hair on my head and eyebrows wouldn't just be lifting, they'd be disappearing into hairlines. 'There isn't much to tell and all of it is bad.'

He poured me a large drink, a smaller one for himself, and added water to both. It tasted the way Scotch always does after you've swum and rowed for hours and damn near got yourself killed in the process.

'I got there without trouble. I hid behind Carrara Point till it was dusk and then paddled out to the Bogha Nuadh. I left the dinghy there and swam underwater as far as the stern of the ship. It was the *Nantesville* all right. Name and flag are different, a mast is gone and the white superstructure is now stone – but it was her all right. Near as dammit didn't make it – it was close to the turn of the tide but it took me thirty minutes against that current. Must be wicked at the full flood or ebb.'

'They say it's the worst on the West Coast – worse even than Coirebhreachan.'

'I'd rather not be the one to find out. I had to hang on to the stern post for ten minutes before I'd got enough strength back to shin up that rope.'

'You took a chance.'

'It was near enough dark. Besides,' I added bitterly, 'there are some precautions intelligent people don't think to take about crazy ones. There were only two or three people in the after accommodation. Just a skeleton crew aboard, seven or eight, no more. All the original crew have vanished completely.'

'No sign of them anywhere?'

'No sign. Dead or alive, no sign at all. I had a bit of bad luck. I was leaving the after accommodation to go to the bridge when I passed someone a few feet away. I gave a half-wave and grunted something and he answered back, I don't know what. I followed him back to the quarters. He picked up a phone in the crew's mess and I heard him talking to someone, quick and urgent. Said that one of the original crew must have been hiding and was trying to get away. I couldn't stop him – he faced the door as he was talking and he had a gun in his hand. I had to move quickly. I walked to the bridge structure—'

'You what? When you knew they were on to you? Mr Calvert, you want your bloody head examined!'

'Uncle Arthur will put it less kindly. It was the only chance I'd ever have. Besides, if they thought it was only a terrified member of the original crew they wouldn't have been so worried: if this guy had seen me walking around dripping wet in a scuba suit he'd have turned me into a colander. He wasn't sure. On the way for'ard I passed another bloke without incident – he'd left the bridge superstructure before the alarm had been given, I suppose. I didn't stop at the bridge. I went right for'ard and hid behind the winchman's shelter. For about ten minutes there was a fair bit of commotion and a lot of flash-light work around the bridge island then I saw and heard them moving aft – must have thought I was still in the after accommodation.

'I went through all the officers' cabins in the bridge island. No one. One cabin, an engineer's, I think, had smashed furniture and a carpet heavily stained with dry blood. Next door, the captain's bunk had been saturated with blood.'

'They'd been warned to offer no resistance.'

'I know. Then I found Baker and Delmont.'

'So you found them. Baker and Delmont.' Hunslett's eyes were hooded, gazing down at the glass in his hand. I wished to God he'd show some expression on that dark face of his.

'Delmont must have made a last-second attempt to send a call for help. They'd been warned not to, except in emergency, so they must have been discovered. He'd been stabbed in the back with a half-inch wood chisel and then dragged into the radio officer's cabin which adjoined the radio office. Some time later Baker had come in. He was wearing an officer's clothes – some desperate attempt to disguise himself, I suppose. He'd a gun in his hand, but he was looking the wrong way and the gun was pointing the wrong way. The same chisel in the back.'

Hunslett poured himself another drink. A much larger one. Hunslett hardly ever drank. He swallowed half of it in one gulp. He said: 'And they hadn't all gone aft. They'd left a reception committee.'

'They're very clever. They're very dangerous. Maybe we've moved out of our class. Or I have. A one-man reception committee, but when that one man was this man, two would have been superfluous. I know he killed Baker and Delmont. I'll never be so lucky again.'

'You got away. Your luck hadn't run out.'

And Baker's and Delmont's had. I knew he was blaming me. I knew London would blame me. I blamed myself. I hadn't much option. There was no one else to blame.

'Uncle Arthur,' Hunslett said. 'Don't you think—'

'The hell with Uncle Arthur! Who cares about Uncle Arthur? How in God's name do you think I feel?' I felt savage and I know I sounded it. For the first time a flicker of expression showed on Hunslett's face. I wasn't supposed to have any feelings.

'Not that,' he said. 'About the *Nantesville*. Now that she's been identified *as* the *Nantesville*, now we know her new name and flag – what were they, by the way?'

'*Alta Fjord*. Norwegian. It doesn't matter.'

'It does matter. We radio Uncle Arthur—'

'And have our guests find us in the engine room with earphones round our heads. Are you mad?'

'You seem damned sure they'll come.'

'I *am* sure. You too. You said so.'

'I agreed this is where they would come. *If* they come.'

'If they come! *If* they come! Good God, man, for all that they know I was aboard that ship for hours. I may have the names and full descriptions of all of them. As it happens I couldn't identify any of them and their names may or may not mean anything. But they're not to know that. For all they know I'm on the blower right now bawling out descriptions to Interpol. The chances are at least even that some of them are on file. They're too good to be little men. Some must be known.'

'In that case they'd be too late anyway. The damage would be done.'

'Not without the sole witness who could testify against them?'

'I think we'd better have those guns out.'

'No.'

'You don't blame me for trying?'

'No.'

'Baker and Delmont. Think of them.'

'I'm thinking of nothing else but them. You don't have to stay.'

He set his glass down very carefully. He was really letting

himself go tonight, he'd allowed that dark craggy face its second expression in ten minutes and it wasn't a very encouraging one. Then he picked up his glass and grinned.

'You don't know what you're saying,' he said kindly. 'Your neck – that's what comes from the blood supply to the brain being interrupted. You're not fit to fight off a teddybear. Who's going to look after you if they start playing games?'

'I'm sorry,' I said. I meant it. I'd worked with Hunslett maybe ten times in the ten years I'd known him and it had been a stupid thing for me to say. About the only thing Hunslett was incapable of was leaving your side in time of trouble. 'You were speaking of Uncle?'

'Yes. We know where the *Nantesville* is. Uncle could get a Navy boat to shadow her, by radar if—'

'I know where she was. She upped anchor as I left. By dawn she'll be a hundred miles away – in any direction.'

'She's gone? We've scared them off? They're going to love this.' He sat down heavily, then looked at me. 'But we have her new description—'

'I said that didn't matter. By tomorrow she'll have another description. The *Hokomaru* from Yokohama, with green topsides, Japanese flag, different masts—'

'An air search. We could—'

'By the time an air search could be organized they'd have twenty thousand square miles of sea to cover. You've heard the forecast. It's bad. Low cloud – and they'd have to fly under the low cloud. Cuts their effectiveness by ninety per cent. And poor visibility and rain. Not a chance in a hundred, not one in a thousand of positive identification. And if they do locate them – if – what then? A friendly wave from the pilot? Not much else he can do.'

'The Navy. They could call up the Navy—'

'Call up what Navy? From the Med? Or the Far East? The Navy has very few ships left and practically none in those parts. By the time any naval vessel could get to the scene it would be night again and the *Nantesville* to hell and gone. Even if a naval ship did catch up with it, what then? Sink it with gunfire – with maybe the twenty-five missing crew members of the *Nantesville* locked up in the hold?'

'A boarding party?'

'With the same twenty-five ex-crew members lined up on deck with pistols at their backs and Captain Imrie and his thugs politely asking the Navy boys what their next move was going to be?'

'I'll get into my pyjamas,' Hunslett said tiredly. At the doorway he paused and turned. 'If the *Nantesville* had gone, her crew – the new crew – have gone too and we'll be having no visitors after all. Had you thought of that?'

'No.'

'I don't really believe it either.'

II

They came at twenty past four in the morning. They came in a very calm and orderly and law-abiding and official fashion, they stayed for forty minutes and by the time they had left I still wasn't sure whether they were our men or not.

Hunslett came into my small cabin, starboard side forward, switched on the light and shook me. 'Wake up,' he said loudly. 'Come on. Wake up.'

I was wide awake. I hadn't closed an eye since I'd lain down. I groaned and yawned a bit without overdoing it then opened a bleary eye. There was no one behind him.

'What is it? What do you want?' A pause. 'What the hell's up? It's just after four in the morning.'

'Don't ask me what's up,' Hunslett said irritably. 'Police. Just come aboard. They say it's urgent.'

'Police? Did you say, "police"?'

'Yes. Come on, now. They're waiting.'

'Police? Aboard our boat? What—'

'Oh, for God's sake! How many more night-caps did you have last night after I went to bed? Police. Two of them and two customs. It's urgent, they say.'

'It better bloody well be urgent. In the middle of the bloody night. Who do they think we are – escaped train robbers? Haven't you told them who we are? Oh, all right, all right, all *right*! I'm coming.'

Hunslett left, and thirty seconds afterwards I joined him in the saloon. Four men sat there, two police officers and two customs officials. They didn't look a very villainous bunch to me. The older, bigger policeman got to his feet. A tall, burly, brown-faced sergeant in his late forties, he looked me over with a cold eye, looked at the near-empty whisky bottle with the two unwashed glasses on the table, then looked back at me. He didn't like wealthy yachtsmen. He didn't like wealthy yachtsmen who drank too much at night-time and were bleary-eyed, bloodshot and tousle-haired at the following crack of dawn. He didn't like wealthy effete yachtsmen who wore red silk dragon Chinese dressing-gowns with a Paisley scarf to match tied negligently round the neck. I didn't like them very much myself, especially the Paisley scarf, much in favour though it was with the yachting fraternity: but I had to have something to conceal those bruises on my neck.

'Are you the owner of this boat, sir?' the sergeant inquired. An unmistakable West Highland voice and a courteous one, but it took him all his time to get his tongue round the 'sir'.

'If you would tell me what makes it any of your damn business,' I said unpleasantly, 'maybe I'll answer that and maybe I won't. A private boat is the same as a private house, sergeant. You have to have a warrant before you shove your way in. Or don't you know the law?'

'He knows the law,' one of the customs men put in. A small dark character, smooth-shaven at four in the morning, with a persuasive voice, not West Highland. 'Be reasonable. This is not the sergeant's job. We got him out of bed almost three hours ago. He's just obliging us.'

I ignored him. I said to the sergeant: 'This is the middle of the night in a lonely Scottish bay. How would you feel if four unidentified men came aboard in the middle of the night?' I was taking a chance on that one, but a fair chance. If they were who I thought they might be and if I were who they thought I might be, then I'd never talk like that. But an innocent man would. 'Any means of identifying yourselves?'

'Identifying myself?' The sergeant stared coldly at me. 'I don't have to identify myself. Sergeant MacDonald. I've been in charge of the Torbay police station for eight years. Ask any man in Torbay. They all know me.' If he was who he claimed to be this was probably the first time in his life that anyone had asked him for identification. He nodded to the seated policeman. 'Police-Constable MacDonald.'

'Your son?' The resemblance was unmistakable. 'Nothing like keeping it in the family, eh, sergeant?' I didn't know whether to believe him or not, but I felt I'd been an irate householder long enough. A degree less truculence was in order. 'And customs, eh? I know the law about you, too. No search warrants for you boys. I believe the police would like your powers. Go anywhere you like and ask no one's permission beforehand. That's it, isn't it?'

'Yes, sir.' It was the younger customs man who answered. Medium height, fair hair, running a little to fat, Belfast accent, dressed like the other in blue overcoat, peaked hat, brown gloves, smartly creased trousers. 'We hardly ever do, though. We prefer co-operation. We like to ask.'

'And you'd like to ask to search this boat, is that it?' Hunslett said.

'Yes, sir.'

'Why?' I asked. Puzzlement now in my voice. And in my mind. I just didn't know what I had on my hands. 'If we're all going to be so courteous and co-operative, could we have any explanation?'

'No reason in the world why not, sir.' The older customs man was almost apologetic. 'A truck with contents valued at £12,000 was hi-jacked on the Ayrshire coast last night – night before last, that is, now. In the news this evening. From information received, we know it was transferred to a small boat. We think it came north.'

'Why?'

'Sorry, sir. Confidential. This is the third port we've visited and the thirteenth boat – the fourth in Torbay – that we've been on in the past fifteen hours. We've been kept on the run, I can tell you.' An easy friendly voice, a voice that said: 'You don't really think we suspect you. We've a job to do, that's all.'

'And you're searching all boats that have come up from the south. Or you think have come from there. Fresh arrivals, anyway. Has it occurred to you that any boat with hi-jacked goods on board wouldn't dare pass through the Crinan canal? Once you're in there, you're trapped. For four hours. So he'd have to come round the Mull of Kintyre. We've been here since this afternoon. It would take a pretty fast boat to get up here in that time.'

'You've got a pretty fast boat here, sir,' Sergeant MacDonald said. I wondered how the hell they managed it. From the Western Isles to the East London docks every sergeant in the country had the same wooden voice, the same wooden face, the same cold eye. Must be something to do with the uniform. I ignored him.

'What are we – um – supposed to have stolen?'

'Chemicals. It was an I.C.I. truck.'

'Chemicals?' I looked at Hunslett, grinned, then turned back to the customs officer. 'Chemicals, eh? We're loaded with them. But not £12,000 worth, I'm afraid.'

There was a brief silence. MacDonald said: 'Would you mind explaining, sir?'

'Not at all.' I lit a cigarette, the little mind enjoying its big moment, and smiled. 'This is a government boat, Sergeant MacDonald. I thought you would have seen the flag. Ministry of Agriculture and Fisheries. We're marine biologists. Our after cabin is a floating laboratory. Look at our library here.' Two shelves loaded with technical tomes. 'And if you've still any doubt left I can give you two numbers, one in Glasgow, one in London, that will establish our *bona fides*. Or phone the lock-master in the Crinan sea-basin. We spent last night there.'

'Yes, sir.' The lack of impression I had made on the sergeant was total. 'Where did you go in your dinghy this evening?'

'I beg your pardon, sergeant?'

'You were seen to leave this boat in a black rubber dinghy about five o'clock this evening.' I'd heard of icy fingers playing up and down one's spine but it wasn't fingers I felt then, it was a centipede with a hundred icy boots on. 'You went out into the Sound. Mr McIlroy, the postmaster, saw you.'

'I hate to impugn the character of a fellow civil servant but he must have been drunk.' Funny how an icy feeling could make you sweat. 'I haven't got a black rubber dinghy. I've never owned a black rubber dinghy. You just get out your little magnifying glass, sergeant, and if you can find a black rubber dinghy I'll make you a present of the brown wooden dinghy, which is the only one we have on the *Firecrest*.'

The wooden expression cracked a little. He wasn't so certain now. 'So you weren't out?'

'I *was* out. In our own dinghy. I was just round the corner of Garve Island there, collecting some marine samples from the Sound. I can show them to you in the after cabin. We're not here on holiday, you know.'

'No offence, no offence.' I was a member of the working classes now, not a plutocrat, and he could afford to thaw a little. 'Mr McIlroy's eyesight isn't what it was and everything looks black against the setting sun. You don't *look* the type, I must say, who'd land on the shores of the Sound and bring down the telephone wires to the mainland.'

The centipede started up again and broke into a fast gallop. Cut off from the mainland. How very convenient for somebody. I didn't spend any time wondering who had brought the wires down – it had been no act of God, I was sure of that.

'Did you mean what I thought you to mean, sergeant?' I said slowly. 'That you suspected me—'

'We can't take chances, sir.' He was almost apologetic now. Not only was I a working man, I was a man working for the Government. All men working for the Government are *ipso facto* respectable and trustworthy citizens.

'But you won't mind if we take a little look round?' The dark-haired customs officer was even more apologetic. 'The lines are down and, well, you know . . .' His voice trailed off and he smiled. 'If you were the hi-jackers – I appreciate now that it's a chance in a million, but still – and if we didn't search – well, we'd be out of a job tomorrow. Just a formality.'

'I wouldn't want to see that happen, Mr – ah—'

'Thomas. Thank you. Your ship's papers? Ah, thank you.' He handed them to the younger man. 'Let's see now. Ah, the wheelhouse. Could Mr Durran here use the wheelhouse to make copies? Won't take five minutes.'

'Certainly. Wouldn't he be more comfortable here?'

'We're modernized now, sir. Portable photo-copier. Standard on the job. Has to be dark. Won't take five minutes. Can we begin in this laboratory of yours?'

A formality, he'd said. Well, he was right there, as a search it was the least informal thing I'd ever come across. Five minutes after he'd gone to the wheelhouse Durran came aft to join us and he and Thomas went through the *Firecrest* as if they were looking for the Koh-i-noor. To begin with, at least. Every piece of mechanical and electrical equipment in the after cabin had to be explained to them. They looked in every locker and cupboard. They rummaged through the ropes and fenders in the large stern locker aft of the laboratory and I thanked God I hadn't followed my original idea of stowing the dinghy, motor and scuba gear in there. They even examined the after toilet. As if I'd be careless enough to drop the Koh-i-noor in there.

They spent most time of all in the engine room. It was worth examining. Everything looked brand new, and gleamed. Two big 100 h.p. diesels, diesel generator, radio generator, hot and cold water pumps, central heating plant, big oil and water tanks and the two long rows of lead-acid batteries. Thomas seemed especially interested in the batteries.

'You carry a lot of reserve there, Mr Petersen,' he said. He'd learnt my name by now, even though it wasn't the one I'd been christened with. 'Why all the power?'

'We haven't even got enough. Care to start those two engines by hand? We have eight electric motors in the lab. – and the only time they're used, in harbour, we can't run either the engines or generators to supply juice. Too much interference. A constant drain.' I was ticking off my fingers. 'Then there's the central heating, hot and cold water pumps, radar, radio, automatic steering, windlass, power winch for the dinghy, echo-sounder, navigation lights—'

'You win, you win.' He'd become quite friendly by this time. 'Boats aren't really in my line. Let's move forward shall we?'

The remainder of the inspection, curiously, didn't take long. In the saloon I found that Hunslett had persuaded the Torbay police force to accept the hospitality of the *Firecrest*. Sergeant MacDonald hadn't exactly become jovial, but he was much more human than when he'd come on board. Constable MacDonald, I noticed, didn't seem so relaxed. He looked positively glum. Maybe he didn't approve of his old man consorting with potential criminals.

If the examination of the saloon was cursory, that of the

two forward cabins was positively perfunctory. Back in the saloon, I said:

'Sorry I was a bit short, gentlemen. I like my sleep. A drink before you go?'

'Well.' Thomas smiled. 'We don't want to be rude either. Thank you.'

Five minutes and they were gone. Thomas didn't even glance at the wheelhouse – Durran had been there, of course. He had a quick look at one of the deck lockers but didn't bother about the others. We were in the clear. A civil good-bye on both sides and they were gone. Their boat, a big indeterminate shape in the darkness, seemed to have plenty of power.

'Odd,' I said.

'What's odd?'

'That boat. Any idea what it was like?'

'How could I?' Hunslett was testy. He was as short of sleep as I was. 'It was pitch dark.'

'That's just the point. A gentle glow in their wheelhouse – you couldn't even see what that was like – and no more. No deck lights, no interior lights, no navigation lights even.'

'Sergeant MacDonald has been looking out over this harbour for eight years. Do you need light to find your way about your own living-room after dark?'

'I haven't got twenty yachts and cruisers in my living-room swinging all over the place with wind and tide. And wind and tide doesn't alter my own course when I'm crossing my living-room. There are only three boats in the harbour carrying anchor lights. He'll have to use something to see where he's going.'

And he did. From the direction of the receding sound of engines a light stabbed out into the darkness. A five-inch searchlight, I would have guessed. It picked up a small yacht riding at anchor less than a hundred yards ahead of it, altered to starboard, picked up another, altered to port, then swung back on course again.

' "Odd" was the word you used,' Hunslett murmured. 'Quite a good word, too, in the circumstances. And what are we to think of the alleged Torbay police force?'

'You talked to the sergeant longer than I did. When I was aft with Thomas and Durran.'

'I'd like to think otherwise,' Hunslett said inconsequentially. 'It would make things easier, in a way. But I can't. He's a genuine old-fashioned cop and a good one, too. I've met too many. So have you.'

'A good cop and an honest one,' I agreed. 'This is not his line of country and he was fooled. It is our line of country and we were fooled. Until now, that is.'

'Speak for yourself.'

'Thomas made one careless remark. An off-beat remark. You didn't hear it – we were in the engine room.' I shivered, maybe it was the cold night wind. 'It meant nothing—not until I saw that they didn't want their boat recognized again. He said: "Boats aren't really in my line." Probably thought he'd been asking too many questions and wanted to reassure me. Boats not in his line – a customs officer and boats not in his line? They only spend their lives aboard boats, examining boats, that's all. They spend their lives looking and poking in so many odd corners and quarters that they know more about boats than the designers themselves. Another thing, did you notice how sharply dressed they were? A credit to Carnaby Street.'

'Customs officers don't usually go around in oil-stained overalls.'

'They've been living in those clothes for twenty-four hours. This is the what – the thirteenth boat they've searched in that time. Would you still have knife-edged creases to your pants after that lot? Or would you say they'd only just taken them from the hangers and put them on?'

'What else did they say? What else did they do?' Hunslett spoke so quietly that I could hear the note of the engines of the customs' boat fall away sharply as their searchlight lit up the low-water stone pier, half a mile away. 'Take an undue interest in anything?'

'They took an undue interest in everything. Wait a minute, though, wait a minute. Thomas seemed particularly intrigued by the batteries, by the large amount of reserve electrical power we had.'

'Did he now? Did he indeed? And did you notice how

lightly our two customs friends swung aboard their launch when leaving?'

'They'll have done it a thousand times.'

'Both of them had their hands free. They weren't carrying anything. They should have been carrying something.'

'The photo-copier. I'm getting old.'

'The photo-copier. Standard equipment my ruddy foot. So if our fair-haired pal wasn't busy photo-copying he was busy doing something else.'

We moved inside the wheelhouse. Hunslett selected the larger screw-driver from the tool-rack beside the echo-sounder and had the face-plate off our R.T.D./D.F. set inside sixty seconds. He looked at the interior for five seconds, looked at me for the same length of time, then started screwing the face-plate back into position. One thing was certain, we wouldn't be using that transmitter for a long time to come.

I turned away and stared out through the wheelhouse windows into the darkness. The wind was still rising, the black sea gleamed palely as the whitecaps came marching in from the south-west, the *Firecrest* snubbed sharply on her anchor chain and, with the wind and the tide at variance, she was beginning to corkscrew quite noticeably now. I felt desperately tired. But my eyes were still working. Hunslett offered me a cigarette. I didn't want one, but I took one. Who knew, it might even help me to think. And then I had caught his wrist and was staring down at his palm.

'Well, well,' I said. 'The cobbler should stick to his last.'

'He what?'

'Wrong proverb. Can't think of the right one. A good workman uses only his own tools. Our pal with the penchant for smashing valves and condensers should have remembered that. No wonder my neck was twitching when Durran was around. How did you cut yourself?'

'I didn't cut myself.'

'I know. But there's a smear of blood on your palm. He's been taking lessons from Peter Sellers, I shouldn't wonder. Standard southern English on the *Nantesville*, northern Irish on the *Firecrest*. I wonder how many other accents he has up his sleeve – behind his larynx, I should say. And I thought he was running to a little fat. He's running to a great deal of muscle. You noticed he never took his gloves off, even when he had that drink?'

'I'm the best noticer you ever saw. Beat me over the head with a club and I'll notice anything.' He sounded bitter. 'Why didn't they clobber us? You, anyway? The star witness?'

'Maybe we *have* moved out of our class. Two reasons. They couldn't do anything with the cops there, genuine cops as we've both agreed, not unless they attended to the cops too. Only a madman would deliberately kill a cop and whatever those boys may lack it isn't sanity.'

'But why cops in the first place?'

'Aura of respectability. Cops are above suspicion. When a uniformed policeman shoves his uniformed cap above your gunwale in the dark watches of the night, you don't whack him over the head with a marline-spike. You invite him aboard. All others you might whack, especially if we had the bad consciences we might have been supposed to have.'

'Maybe. It's arguable. And the second point?'

'They took a big chance, a desperate chance, almost, with Durran. He was thrown to the wolves to see what the reaction would be, whether either of us recognized him.'

'Why Durran?'

'I didn't tell you. I shone a torch in his face. The face didn't register, just a white blur with screwed-up eyes half-hidden behind an upflung hand. I was really looking lower down, picking the right spot to kick him. But they weren't to know that. They wanted to find out if we would recognize him. We didn't. If we had done we'd either have started throwing the crockery at him or yelped for the cops to arrest them – if we're against them then we're with the cops. But we didn't. Not a flicker of recognition. Nobody's as good as that. I defy any man in the world to meet up again in the same night with a man who has murdered two other people and nearly murdered himself without at least twitching an eyebrow. So the immediate heat is off, the urgent necessity to do us in has become less urgent. It's a safe bet that if we didn't recognize Durran, then we recognized nobody on the *Nantesville* and so we won't be burning up the lines to Interpol.'

'We're in the clear?'

'I wish to God we were. They're on to us.'

'But you said—'

'I don't know how I know,' I said irritably. 'I know. They went through the after end of the *Firecrest* like a Treble Chance winner hunting for the coupon he's afraid he's forgotton to post. Then half-way through the engine room search – click! – just like that and they weren't interested any more. At least Thomas wasn't. He'd found out something. You saw him afterwards in the saloon, the fore cabins and the upper deck. He couldn't have cared less.'

'The batteries?'

'No. He was satisfied with my explanation. I could tell. I don't know why, I only know I'm sure.'

'So they'll be back.'

'They'll be back.'

'I get the guns out now?'

'There's no hurry. Our friends will be sure we can't communicate with anyone. The mainland boat calls here only twice a week. It came today and won't be back for four days. The lines to the mainland are down and if I thought for a moment they would stay down I should be back in kindergarten. Our transmitter is out. Assuming there are no carrier pigeons in Torbay, what's the only remaining means of communication with the mainland?'

'There's the *Shangri-la*.' The *Shangri-la*, the nearest craft to ours, was white, gleaming, a hundred and twenty feet long and wouldn't have left her owner a handful of change from a quarter of a million pounds when he'd bought her. 'She'll have a couple of thousand quids' worth of radio equipment aboard. Then there are two, maybe three yachts big enough to carry transmitters. The rest will carry only receivers, if that.'

'And how many transmitters in Torbay harbour will still be in operating condition to-morrow?'

'One.'

'One. Our friends will attend to the rest. They'll have to. We can't warn anyone. We can't give ourselves away.'

'The insurance companies can stand it.' He glanced at his watch. 'This would be a nice time to wake up Uncle Arthur.'

'I can't put it off any longer.' I wasn't looking forward to talking to Uncle Arthur.

Hunslett reached for a heavy coat, pulled it on, made for the door and stopped. 'I thought I'd take a walk on the upper deck. While you're talking. Just in case. A second thought – I'd better have that gun now. Thomas said they'd already checked three boats in the harbour. MacDonald didn't contradict him, so it was probably true. Maybe there *are* no serviceable transmitters left in Torbay now. Maybe our friends just dumped the cops ashore and are coming straight back for us.'

'Maybe. But those yachts are smaller than the *Firecrest*. Apart from us, there's only one with a separate wheelhouse. The others will carry transmitters in the saloon cabin. Lots of them sleep in their saloon cabins. The owners would have to be banged on the head first before the radios could be attended to. They couldn't do that with MacDonald around.'

'You'd bet your pension on that? Maybe MacDonald didn't always go aboard.'

'I'll never live to collect my pension. But maybe you'd better have that gun.'

III

The *Firecrest* was just over three years old. The Southampton boatyard and marine-radio firm that had combined to build her had done so under conditions of sworn secrecy to a design provided by Uncle Arthur. Uncle Arthur had not designed her himself although he had never said so to the few people who knew of the existence of the boat. He'd pinched the idea from a Japanese-designed Indonesian-owned fishing craft that had been picked up with engine failure off the Malaysian coast. Only one engine had failed though two were installed, but still she had been not under command, an odd circumstance that had led the alert Engineer Lieutenant on the frigate that had picked her up to look pretty closely at her: the net result of his investigation, apart from giving this splendid inspiration to Uncle Arthur, was that the crew still languished in a Singapore prisoner of war camp.

The *Firecrest's* career had been chequered and inglorious. She had cruised around the Eastern Baltic for some time, without achieving anything, until the authorities in Memel and Leningrad, getting tired of the sight of her, had declared the *Firecrest persona non grata* and sent her back to England. Uncle Arthur had been furious, especially as he had to account to a parsimonious Under-Secretary for the considerable expense involved. The Waterguard had tried their hand with it at catching smugglers and returned it without thanks. No smugglers. Now for the first time ever it was going to justify its existence and in other circumstances Uncle Arthur would have been delighted. When he heard what I had to tell him he would have no difficulty in restraining his joy.

What made the *Firecrest* unique was that while she had two screws and two propeller shafts, she had only one engine. Two engine casings, but only one engine, even although that one engine was a special job fitted with an underwater by-pass exhaust valve. A simple matter of disengaging the fuel pump coupling and unscrewing four bolts on top – the rest were dummies – enabled the entire head of the diesel starboard engine to be lifted clear away, together with the fuel lines and injectors. With the assistance of the seventy-foot telescopic radio mast housed inside our aluminium foremast, the huge gleaming transmitter that took up eighty per cent of the space inside the starboard engine casing could have sent a signal to the moon, if need be: as Thomas had observed, we had power and to spare. As it happened I didn't want to send a signal to the moon, just to Uncle Arthur's combinex office and home in Knightsbridge.

The other twenty per cent of space was taken up with a motley collection of material that even the Assistant Commissioner in New Scotland Yard wouldn't have regarded without a thoughtful expression on his face. There were some packages of pre-fabricated explosives with amatol, primer and chemical detonator combined in one neat unit with a miniature timing device that ranged from five seconds to five minutes, complete with sucker clamps. There was a fine range of burglar's house-breaking tools, bunches of skeleton keys, several highly sophisticated listening devices, including one that could be shot from a Very-type pistol, several tubes of various harmless-looking tablets which were alleged, when dropped in some unsuspecting character's drink, to induce unconsciousness for varying periods, four pistols and a box of ammunition. Anyone who was going to use that lot in one operation was in for a busy time indeed. Two of the pistols were Lugers, two were 4.25 German Lilliputs, the smallest really effective automatic pistol on the market. The Lilliput had the great advantage that it could be concealed practically anywhere on your person, even upside down in a spring-loaded clip in your lower left sleeve – if, that was, you didn't get your suits cut in Carnaby Street.

Hunslett lifted one of the Lugers from its clamp, checked the loading indicator and left at once. It wasn't that he was imagining that he could already hear stealthy footsteps on the upper deck, he just didn't want to be around when Uncle Arthur came on the air. I didn't blame him. I didn't really want to be around then either.

I pulled out the two insulated rubber cables, fitted the powerfully spring-loaded saw-toothed metal clamps on to the battery terminals, hung on a pair of earphones, turned on the set, pulled another switch that actuated the call-up and waited. I didn't have to tune in, the transmitter was permanently preset, and pre-set on a V.H.F. frequency that would have cost the licence of any ham operator who dared wander anywhere near it for transmission purposes.

The red receiver warning light came on. I reached down and adjusted the magic eye control until the green fans met in the middle.

'This is station SPFX,' a voice came. 'Station SPFX.'

'Good morning. This is Caroline. May I speak to the manager, please?'

'Will you wait, please?' This meant that Uncle Arthur was in bed. Uncle Arthur was never at his best on rising. Three minutes passed and the earphones came to life again.

'Good morning, Caroline. This is Annabelle.'

'Good morning. Location 481, 281.' You wouldn't find those references in any Ordnance Survey Map, there weren't a dozen maps in existence with them. But Uncle Arthur had one. And so had I.

There was a pause, then: 'I have you, Caroline. Proceed.'

'I located the missing vessel this afternoon. Four or five miles north-west of here. I went on board tonight.'

'You did what, Caroline?'

'Went on board. The old crew has gone home. There's a new crew aboard. A smaller crew.'

'You located Betty and Dorothy?' Despite the fact that we both had scramblers fitted to our radio phones, making intelligible eavesdropping impossible, Uncle Arthur always insisted that we spoke in a roundabout riddle fashion and used code names for his employees and himself. Girls' names for our surnames, initials to match. An irritating foible, but one that we had to observe. He was Annabelle, I was Caroline, Baker was Betty, Delmont, Dorothy and Hunslett, Harriet. It sounded like a series of Caribbean hurricane warnings.

'I found them.' I took a deep breath. 'They won't be coming home again, Annabelle.'

'They won't be coming home again,' he repeated mechanically. He was silent for so long that I began to think that he had gone off the air. Then he came again, his voice empty, remote. 'I warned you of this, Caroline.'

'Yes, Annabelle, you warned me of this.'

'And the vessel?'

'Gone.'

'Gone where?'

'I don't know. Just gone. North, I suppose.'

'North, you suppose.' Uncle Arthur never raised his voice, when he went on it was as calm and impersonal as ever, but the sudden disregard of his own rules about circumlocution betrayed the savage anger in his mind. 'North where? Iceland? A Norwegian fjord? To effect a trans-shipment of cargo anywhere in a million squares miles between the mid-Atlantic and the Barents Sea? And you lost her. After all the time, the trouble, the planning, the expense, you've lost her!' He might have spared me that bit about the planning, it had been mine all the way. 'And Betty and Dorothy.' The last words showed he'd taken control of himself again.

'Yes, Annabelle, I've lost her.' I could feel the slow anger in myself. 'And there's worse than that, if you want to listen to it.'

'I'm listening.'

I told him the rest and at the end of it he said: 'I see. You've lost the vessel. You've lost Betty and Dorothy. And now our friends know about you, the one vital element of secrecy is gone for ever and every usefulness and effectiveness you might ever have had is completely negated.' A pause. 'I shall expect you in my office at 9 p.m. tonight. Instruct Harriet to take the boat back to base.'

'Yes, sir.' The hell with his Annabelle. 'I had expected that. I've failed. I've let you down. I'm being pulled off.'

'Nine o'clock tonight, Caroline. I'll be waiting.'

'You'll have a long wait, Annabelle.'

'And what might you mean by that?' If Uncle Arthur had had a low silky menacing voice then he'd have spoken those words in a low silky menacing voice. But he hadn't, he'd only this flat level monotone and it carried infinitely more weight and authority than any carefully modulated theatrical voice that had ever graced a stage.

'There are no planes to this place, Annabelle. The mailboat doesn't call for another four days. The weather's breaking down and I wouldn't risk our boat to try to get to the mainland. I'm stuck here for the time being, I'm afraid.'

'Do you take me for a nincompoop, sir?' Now he was at it. 'Go ashore this morning. An air-sea rescue helicopter will pick you up at noon. Nine p.m. at my office. Don't keep me waiting.'

This, then, was it. But one last try. 'Couldn't you give me another twenty-four hours, Annabelle?'

'Now you're being ridiculous. And wasting my time. Goodbye.'

'I beg of you, sir.'

'I'd thought better of you than that. Goodbye.'

'Goodbye. We may meet again sometime. It's not likely. Goodbye.'

I switched the radio off, lit a cigarette and waited. The call-up came through in half a minute. I waited another half-minute and switched on. I was very calm. The die was cast and I didn't give a damn.

'Caroline? Is that you, Caroline?' I could have sworn to a note of agitation in his voice. This was something for the record books.

'Yes.'

'What did you say? At the end there?'

'Goodbye. You said goodbye. I said goodbye.'

'Don't quibble with me, sir! You said—'

'If you want me aboard that helicopter,' I said, 'you'll have to send a guard with the pilot. An armed guard. I hope they're good. I've got a Luger, and you know I'm good. And if I have to kill anyone and go into court, then you'll have to stand there beside me because there's no single civil action or criminal charge that even you, with all your connections, can bring against me that would justify the sending of armed men to apprehend me, an innocent man. Further, I am no longer in your employment. The terms of my civil service contract state clearly that I can resign at any moment, provided that I am not actively engaged on an operation at that moment. You've pulled me off, you've recalled me to London. My resignation will be on your desk as soon as the mail can get through. Baker and Delmont weren't your friends. They were my friends. They were my friends ever since I joined the service. You have the temerity to sit there and lay all the blame for their deaths on my shoulders when you know damn well that every operation must have your final approval, and now you have the final temerity to deny me a one last chance to square accounts. I'm sick of your damned soulless service. Goodbye.'

'Now wait a moment, Caroline.' There was a cautious, almost placatory note to his voice. 'No need to go off half-cocked.' I was sure that no one had ever talked to Rear-Admiral Sir Arthur Arnford-Jason like that before but he didn't seem particularly upset about it. He had the cunning of a fox, that infinitely agile and shrewd mind would be examining and discarding possibilities with the speed of a computer, he'd be wondering whether I was playing a game and if so how far he could play it with me without making it impossible for me to retreat from the edge of the precipice. Finally he said quietly: 'You wouldn't want to hang around there just to shed tears. You're on to something.'

'Yes, sir, I'm on to something.' I wondered what in the name of God I was on to.

'I'll give you twenty-four hours, Caroline.'

'Forty-eight.'

'Forty-eight. And then you return to London. I have your word?'

'I promise.'

'And Caroline?'

'Sir?'

'I didn't care for your way of talking there. I trust we never have a repetition of it.'

'No, sir. I'm sorry, sir.'

'Forty-eight hours. Report to me at noon and midnight.' A click. Uncle Arthur was gone.

The false dawn was in the sky when I went on deck. Cold heavy slanting driving rain was churning up the foam-flecked sea. The *Firecrest*, pulling heavily on her anchor chain, was swinging slowly through an arc of forty degrees, corkscrewing quite heavily now on the outer arc of the swing, pitching in the centre of them. She was snubbing very heavily on the anchor and I wondered uneasily how long the lengths of heaving line securing the dinghy, outboard and scuba gear to the chain could stand up to this sort of treatment.

Hunslett was abaft the saloon, huddling in what little shelter it afforded. He looked up at my approach and said: 'What do you make of that?' He pointed to the palely gleaming shape of the *Shangri-la*, one moment on our quarter, the next dead astern as we swung on our anchor. Lights were burning brightly in the fore part of her superstructure, where the wheelhouse would be.

'Someone with insomnia,' I said. 'Or checking to see if the anchor is dragging. What do you think it is – our recent guests laying about the *Shangri-la* radio installation with crow-bars? Maybe they leave lights on all night.'

'Came on just ten minutes ago. And look, now – they're out. Funny. How did you get on with Uncle?'

'Badly. Fired me, then changed his mind. We have forty-eight hours.'

'Forty-eight hours? What are you going to do in forty-eight hours?'

'God knows. Have some sleep first. You too. Too much light in the sky for callers now.'

Passing through the saloon, Hunslett said, apropos of nothing: 'I've been wondering. What did you make of P.C. MacDonald? The young one.'

'What do you mean?'

'Well, glum, downcast. Heavy weight on his shoulders.'

'Maybe he's like me. Maybe he doesn't like getting up in the middle of the night. Maybe he has girl trouble and if he has I can tell you that P.C. MacDonald's love-life is the least of my concerns. Good night.'

I should have listened to Hunslett more. For Hunslett's sake.

— 3 —

Tuesday: 10 a.m. – 10 p.m.

I NEED MY sleep, just like anyone else. Ten hours, perhaps only eight, and I would have been my own man again. Maybe not exuding brightness, optimism and cheerfulness, the circumstances weren't right for that, but at least a going concern, alert, perceptive, my mind operating on what Uncle Arthur would be by now regarding as its customary abysmal level but still the best it could achieve. But I wasn't given that ten hours. Not even the eight. Exactly three hours after dropping off I was wide awake again. Well, anyway, awake. I would have had to be stone deaf, drugged or dead to go on sleeping through the bawling and thumping that was currently assailing my left ear from what appeared to be a distance of not more than twelve inches.

'Ahoy, there, *Firecrest*! Ahoy there!' Thump, thump, thump on the boat's side. 'Can I come aboard? Ahoy there! Ahoy, ahoy, ahoy!'

I cursed this nautical idiot from the depths of my sleep-ridden being, swung a pair of unsteady legs to the deck and levered myself out of the bunk. I almost fell down, I seemed to have only one leg left, and my neck ached fiercely. A glance at the mirror gave quick external confirmation of my internal decrepitude. A haggard unshaven face, unnaturally pale, and bleary bloodshot eyes with dark circles under them. I looked away hurriedly; there were lots of things I could put up with first thing in the morning, but not sights like that.

I opened the door across the passage. Hunslett was sound asleep and snoring. I returned to my own cabin and got busy with the dressing-gown and Paisley scarf again. The iron-lunged thumping character outside was still at it, if I didn't hurry he would be roaring out 'Avast there' any moment. I combed my hair into some sort of order and made my way to the upper deck.

It was a cold, wet and windy world. A grey, dreary, unpleasant world. Why the hell couldn't they have let me sleep on? The rain was coming down in slanting sheets, bouncing inches high on the decks, doubling the milkiness of the spume-flecked sea. The lonely wind mourned through the rigging and the lower registers of sound and the steep-sided wind-truncated waves, maybe three feet from tip to trough, were high enough to make passage difficult if not dangerous for the average yacht tender.

They didn't make things in the slightest difficult or dangerous for the yacht tender that now lay alongside us. It maybe wasn't as big – it looked it at first sight – as the *Firecrest*, but it was big enough to have a glassed-in cabin for'ard, a wheelhouse that bristled and gleamed with controls and instrumentation that would have been no disgrace to a VC-10 and, abaft that, a sunken cockpit that could have sunbathed a football team without overcrowding. There were three crewmen dressed in black oilskins and fancy French navy hats with black ribbons down the back, two of them each with a boathook round one of the *Firecrest*'s guard-rail stanchions. Half a dozen big inflated spherical rubber fenders kept the *Firecrest* from rubbing its plebeian paintwork against the whitely-varnished spotlessness of the tender alongside and it didn't require the name on the bows or the crew's hats to let me know that this was the tender that normally took up most of the after-deck space on the *Shangri-la*.

Amidships a stocky figure, clad in a white vaguely naval brass-buttoned uniform and holding above his head a golf umbrella that would have had Joseph green with envy, stopped banging his gloved fist against the *Firecrest*'s planking and glared up at me.

'Ha!' I've never actually heard anyone snort out a word but this came pretty close to it. 'There you are at last. Took your time about it, didn't you? I'm soaked, man, soaked!' A few spots of rain did show up quite clearly on the white seersucker. 'May I come aboard?' He didn't wait for any permission, just leaped aboard with surprising nimbleness for a man of his build and years and nipped into the *Firecrest*'s wheelhouse ahead of me, which was pretty selfish of him as he still had his umbrella and all I had was my dressing-gown. I followed and closed the door behind me.

He was a short, powerfully built character, fifty-five I would have guessed, with a heavily-tanned jowled face, close-cropped iron-grey hair with tufted eyebrows to match, long straight nose and a mouth that looked as if it had been closed with a zip-fastener. A good-looking cove, if you liked that type of looks. The dark darting eyes looked me up and down and if he was impressed by what he saw he made a heroic effort to keep his admiration in check.

'Sorry for the delay,' I apologized. 'Short of sleep. We had the customs aboard in the middle of the night and I couldn't get off after that.' Always tell everyone the truth if there's an even chance of that truth coming out anyway, which in this case there was: gives one a reputation for forthright honesty.

'The customs?' He looked as if he intended to say 'Pshaw' or 'Fiddlesticks' or something of that order, then changed his mind and looked up sharply. 'An intolerable bunch of busybodies. And in the middle of the night. Shouldn't have let them aboard. Sent them packing. Intolerable. What the deuce did they want?' He gave the distinct impression of having himself had some trouble with the customs in the past.

'They were looking for stolen chemicals. Stolen from some place in Ayrshire. Wrong boat.'

'Idiots!' He thrust out a stubby hand, he'd passed his final judgement on the unfortunate customs and the subject was now closed. 'Skouras. Sir Anthony Skouras.'

'Petersen.' His grip made me wince, less from the sheer power of it than from the gouging effects of the large number of thickly encrusted rings that adorned his fingers. I wouldn't have been surprised to see some on his thumbs but he'd missed out on that. I looked at him with new interest. 'Sir Anthony Skouras. I've heard of you, of course.'

'Nothing good. Columnists don't like me because they know I despise them. A Cypriot who made his shipping millions through sheer ruthlessness, they say. True. Asked by the Greek Government to leave Athens. True. Became a naturalized British citizen and bought a knighthood. Absolutely true. Charitable works and public services. Money can buy anything. A baronetcy next but the market's not right at the moment. Price is bound to fall. Can I use your radio transmitter? I see you have one.'

'What's that?' The abrupt switch had me off-balance, no great achievement the way I was feeling.

'Your radio transmitter, man! Don't you listen to the news? All those major defence projects cancelled by the Pentagon. Price of steel tumbling. Must get through to my New York broker at once!'

'Sorry. Certainly you may – but, your own radio-telephone? Surely—'

'It's out of action.' His mouth became more tight-lipped than ever and the inevitable happened: it disappeared. 'It's urgent, Mr Petersen.'

'Immediately. You know how to operate this model?'

He smiled thinly, which was probably the only way he was capable of smiling. Compared to the cinema-organ job he'd have aboard the *Shangri-la*, asking him if he could operate this was like asking the captain of a transatlantic jet if he could fly a Tiger Moth. 'I think I can manage, Mr Petersen.'

'Call me when you're finished. I'll be in the saloon.' He'd be calling me before he'd finished, he'd be calling me before he'd even started. But I couldn't tell him. Word gets around, I went down to the saloon, contemplated a shave and decided against it. It wouldn't take that long.

It didn't. He appeared at the saloon door inside a minute, his face grim.

'Your radio is out of order, Mr Petersen.'

'They're tricky to operate, some of those older jobs,' I said tactfully. 'Maybe if I—'

'I say it's out of order. I mean it's out of order.'

'Damned odd. It was working—'

'Would you care to try it, please?'

I tried it. Nothing. I twiddled everything I could lay hands on. Nothing.

'A power failure, perhaps,' I suggested. 'I'll check—'

'Would you be so good as to remove the face-plate, please?'

I stared at him in perplexity, switching the expression, after a suitable interval, to shrewd thoughtfulness. 'What do you know, Sir Anthony, that I don't?'

'You'll find out.'

So I found out and went through all the proper motions of consternation, incredulity and tight-lipped indignation. Finally I said: 'You knew. How did you know?'

'Obvious, isn't it?'

'Your transmitter,' I said slowly. 'It's more than just out of order. You had the same midnight caller.'

'And the *Orion*.' The mouth vanished again. 'The big blue ketch lying close in. Only other craft in the harbour apart from us with a radio transmitter. Smashed. Just come from there.'

'Smashed? Theirs as well? But who in God's name – it must be the work of a madman?'

'Is it? Is it the work of a madman? I know something of those matters. My first wife—' He broke off abruptly and gave an odd shake of the head, then went on slowly: 'The mentally disturbed are irrational, haphazard, purposeless, aimless in their behaviour patterns. This seems an entirely irrational act, but an act with a method and a purpose to it. Not haphazard. It's planned. There's a reason. At first I thought the reason was to cut off my connection with the mainland. But it can't be that. By rendering me temporarily incommunicado nobody stands to gain, I don't stand to lose.'

'But you said the New York Stock—'

'A bagatelle,' he said contemptuously. 'Nobody likes to lose money.' Not more than a few millions anyway. 'No, Mr Petersen, I am not the target. We have here an A and a B. A regards it as vital that he remains in constant communication with the mainland. B regards it as vital that A doesn't. So B takes steps. There's something damned funny going on in Torbay. And something big. I have a nose for such things.'

He was no fool but then not many morons have ended up

as multi-millionaires. I couldn't have put it better myself. I said: 'Reported this to the police yet?'

'Going there now. After I've made a phone call or two.' The eyes suddenly became bleak and cold. 'Unless our friend has smashed up the two public call boxes in the main street.'

'He's done better than that. He's brought down the lines to the mainland. Somewhere down the Sound. No one knows where.'

He stared at me, wheeled to leave, then turned, his face empty of expression. 'How did you know that?' The tone matched the face.

'Police told me. They were aboard with the customs last night.'

'The police? That's damned odd. What were the police doing here?' He paused and looked at me with his cold measuring eyes. 'A personal question, Mr Petersen. No impertinence intended. A question of elimination. What are you doing here? No offence.'

'No offence. My friend and I are marine biologists. A working trip. Not our boat – the Ministry of Agriculture and Fisheries.' I smiled. 'We have impeccable references, Sir Anthony.'

'Marine biology, eh? Hobby of mine, you might say. Layman, of course. Must have a talk sometime.' He was speaking absent-mindedly, his thoughts elsewhere. 'Could you describe the policeman, Mr Petersen?'

I did and he nodded. 'That's him all right. Odd, very odd. Must have a word with Archie about this.'

'Archie?'

'Sergeant MacDonald. This is my fifth consecutive season's cruising based on Torbay. The South of France and the Ægean can't hold a candle to these waters. Know quite a few of the locals pretty well by this time. He was alone?'

'No. A young constable. His son, he said. Melancholy sort of lad.'

'Peter MacDonald. He has reason for his melancholy, Mr Petersen. His two young brothers, sixteen years old, twins, died a few months back. At an Inverness school, lost in a late snow-storm in the Cairngorms. The father is tougher, doesn't show it so much. A great tragedy. I knew them both. Fine boys.'

I made some appropriate comment but he wasn't listening.

'I must be on my way, Mr Petersen. Put this damned strange affair in MacDonald's hands. Don't see that he can do much. Then off for a short cruise.'

I looked through the wheelhouse windows at the dark skies, the white-capped seas, the driving rain. 'You picked a day for it.'

'The rougher the better. No bravado. I like a mill-pond as well as any man. Just had new stabilizers fitted in the Clyde – we got back up here only two days ago – and it seems like a good day to try them out.' He smiled suddenly and put out his hand. 'Sorry to have barged in. Taken up far too much of your time. Seemed rude, I suppose. Some say I am. You and your colleague care to come aboard for a drink tonight? We eat early at sea. Eight o'clock, say? I'll send the tender.' That meant we didn't rate an invitation to dinner, which would have made a change from Hunslett and his damned baked beans, but even an invitation like this would have given rise to envious tooth-gnashing in some of the stateliest homes in the land: it was no secret that the bluest blood in England, from Royalty downwards, regarded a holiday invitation to the island Skouras owned off the Albanian coast as the conferment of the social cachet of the year or any year. Skouras didn't wait for an answer and didn't seem to expect one. I didn't blame him. It would have been many years since Skouras had discovered that it was an immutable law of human nature, human nature being what it is, that no one ever turned down one of his invitations.

II

'You'll be coming to tell me about your smashed transmitter and asking me what the devil I intend to do about it,' Sergeant MacDonald said tiredly. 'Well, Mr Petersen, I know all about it already. Sir Anthony Skouras was here half an hour ago. Sir Anthony had a lot to say. And Mr Campbell, the owner of the *Orion*, has just left. He'd a lot to say, too.'

'Not me, sergeant. I'm a man of few words.' I gave him

what I hoped looked like a self-deprecatory smile. 'Except, of course, when the police and customs drag me out of bed in the middle of the night. I take it our friends have left?'

'Just as soon as they'd put us ashore. Customs are just a damn nuisance.' Like myself, he looked as if he could do with some hours' sleep. 'Frankly, Mr Petersen, I don't know what to do about the broken radio-transmitters. Why on earth – who on earth would want to do a daft vicious thing like that?'

'That's what I came to ask you.'

'I can go aboard your boat,' MacDonald said slowly. 'I can take out my note-book, look around and see if I can't find any clues. I wouldn't know what to look for. Maybe if I knew something about fingerprinting and analysis and microscopy I might just find out something. But I don't. I'm an island policeman, not a one-man Flying Squad. This is CID work and we'd have to call in Glasgow. I doubt if they'd send a couple of detectives to investigate a few smashed radio valves.'

'Old man Skouras draws a lot of water.'

'Sir?'

'He's powerful. He has influence. If Skouras wanted action I'm damned sure he could get it. If the need arose and the mood struck him I'm sure he could be a very unpleasant character indeed.'

'There's not a better man or a kinder man ever sailed into Torbay,' MacDonald said warmly. That hard brown face could conceal practically anything that MacDonald wanted it to conceal but this time he was hiding nothing. 'Maybe his ways aren't my ways. Maybe he's a hard, aye, a ruthless businessman. Maybe, as the papers hint, his private life wouldn't bear investigation. That's none of my business. But if you were to look for a man in Torbay to say a word against him, you'll have a busy time on your hands, Mr Petersen.'

'You've taken me up wrongly, sergeant,' I said mildly. 'I don't even know the man.'

'No. But we do. See that?' He pointed through the side window of the police station to a large Swedish-style timber building upon the pier. 'Our new village hall. Town hall, they call it. Sir Anthony gave us that. Those six wee chalets up the hill there? For old folks. Sir Anthony again – every penny from his own pocket. Who takes all the schoolchildren to the

Oban Games – Sir Anthony on the *Shangri-la*. Contributes to every charity going and now he has plans to build a boatyard to give employment to the young men of Torbay – there's not much else going since the fishing-boats left.'

'Well, good for old Skouras,' I said. 'He seems to have adopted the place. Lucky Torbay. I wish he'd buy me a new radio-transmitter.'

'I'll keep my eyes and ears open, Mr Petersen. I can't do more. If anything turns up I'll let you know at once.'

I told him thanks, and left. I hadn't particularly wanted to go there, but it would have looked damned odd if I hadn't turned up to add my pennyworth to the chorus of bitter complaint.

I was very glad that I had turned up.

III

The midday reception from London was poor. This was due less to the fact that reception is always better after dark than to the fact that I couldn't use our telescopic radio mast: but it was fair enough and Uncle's voice was brisk and business-like and clear.

'Well, Caroline, we've found our missing friends,' he said.

'How many?' I asked cautiously. Uncle Arthur's ambiguous references weren't always as clear as Uncle Arthur imagined them to be.

'All twenty-five.' That made it the former crew of the *Nantesville*. 'Two of them are pretty badly hurt but they'll be all right.' That accounted for the blood I had found in the captain's and one of the engineers' cabins.

'Where?' I asked.

He gave me a map reference. Just north of Wexford. The *Nantesville* had sailed from Bristol; she couldn't have been more than a few hours on her way before she'd run into trouble.

'Exactly the same procedure as on the previous occasions,' Uncle Arthur was saying. 'Held in a lonely farmhouse for a couple of nights. Plenty to eat and drink and blankets to keep the cold out. Then they woke up one morning and found their guards had gone.'

'But a different procedure in stopping the – our friend?' I'd almost said *Nantesville* and Uncle Arthur wouldn't have liked that at all.

'As always. We must concede them a certain ingenuity, Caroline. After having smuggled men aboard in port, then using the sinking fishing-boat routine, the police launch routine and the yacht with the appendicitis case aboard, I thought they would be starting to repeat themselves. But this time they came up with a new one – possibly because it's the first time they've hi-jacked a ship during the hours of darkness. Carley rafts, this time, with about ten survivors aboard, dead ahead of the vessel. Oil all over the sea. A weak distress flare that couldn't have been seen a mile away and probably was designed that way. You know the rest.'

'Yes, Annabelle.' I knew the rest. After that the routine was always the same. The rescued survivors, displaying a marked lack of gratitude, would whip out pistols, round up the crew, tie black muslin bags over their heads so that they couldn't identify the vessel that would appear within the hour to take them off, march them on board the unknown vessel, land them on some lonely beach during the dark then march them again, often a very long way indeed, till they arrived at their prison. A deserted farmhouse. Always a deserted farmhouse. And always in Ireland, three times in the north and now twice in the south. Meantime the prize crew sailed the hi-jacked vessel to God alone knew where and the first the world knew of the disappearance of the pirated vessel was when the original crew, released after two or three days' painless captivity, would turn up at some remote dwelling and start hollering for the nearest telephone.

'Betty and Dorothy,' I said. 'Were they still in safe concealment when the crew were taken off?'

'I imagine so. I don't know. Details are still coming in and I understand the doctors won't let anyone see the captain yet.' Only the captain had known of the presence aboard of Baker and Delmont. 'Forty-one hours now, Caroline. What have you done?'

For a moment I wondered irritably what the devil he was talking about. Then I remembered. He'd given me forty-eight hours. Seven were gone.

'I've had three hours' sleep.' He'd consider that an utter waste of time, his employees weren't considered to need sleep. 'I've talked to the constabulary ashore. And I've talked to a wealthy yachtsman, next boat to us here. We're paying him a social call tonight.'

There was a pause. 'You're doing *what* tonight, Caroline?'

'Visiting. We've been invited. Harriet and I. For drinks.'

This time the pause was markedly longer. Then he said: 'You have forty-one hours, Caroline.'

'Yes, Annabelle.'

'We assume you haven't taken leave of your senses.'

'I don't know how unanimous informed opinion might be about that. I don't think I have.'

'And you haven't given up? No, not that. You're too damn' stiff-necked and – and—'

'Stupid?'

'Who's the yachtsman?'

I told him. It took me some time, partly because I had to spell out names with the aid of his damned code-book, partly because I gave him a very full account of everything Skouras had said to me and everything Sergeant MacDonald had said about Skouras. When his voice came again it was cagey and wary. As Uncle Arthur couldn't see me I permitted myself a cynical grin. Even Cabinet Ministers found it difficult to make the grade as far as Skouras's dinner-table, but the Permanent Under-Secretaries, the men with whom the real power of government lies, practically had their own initialled napkin rings. Under-Secretaries were the bane of Uncle Arthur's life.

'You'll have to watch your step very carefully here, Caroline.'

'Betty and Dorothy aren't coming home any more, Annabelle. Someone has to pay. I want someone to pay. You want someone to pay. We all do.'

'But it's inconceivable that a man in his position, a man of his wealth—'

'I'm sorry, Annabelle. I don't understand.'

'A man like that. Dammit all, I know him well, Caroline. We dine together. First-name terms. Know his present wife even better. Ex-actress. A philanthropist like that. A man who's spent five consecutive seasons there. Would a man like that, a millionaire like that, spend all that time, all that money, just to build up a front—'

'Skouras?' I used the code name. Interrogatory, incredulous, as if it had just dawned upon me what Uncle Arthur was talking about. 'I never said I suspected him, Annabelle. I have no reason to suspect him.'

'Ah!' It's difficult to convey a sense of heartfelt gladness, profound satisfaction and brow-mopping relief in a single syllable, but Uncle Arthur managed it without any trouble.

'Then why go?' A casual eavesdropper might have thought he detected a note of pained jealousy in Uncle Arthur's voice, and the casual eavesdropper would have been right. Uncle Arthur had only one weakness in his make-up – he was a social snob of monumental proportions.

'I want aboard. I want to see this smashed transmitter of his.'

'Why?'

'A hunch, let me call it, Annabelle. No more.'

Uncle Arthur was going in for the long silences in a big way today. Then he said: 'A hunch? A *hunch*? You told me this morning you were on to something.'

'There's something else. I want you to contact the Post Office Savings Bank, Head Office, in Scotland. After that the Records files of some Scottish newspapers. I suggest the *Glasgow Herald*, the *Scottish Daily Express* and, most particularly, the West Highland weekly, the *Oban Times*.'

'Ah!' No relief this time, just satisfaction. 'This is more like it, Caroline. What do you want and why?'

So I told him what I wanted and why, lots more of the fancy code work, and when I'd finished he said: 'I'll have my staff on to this straight away. I'll have all the information you want by midnight.'

'Then I don't want it, Annabelle. Midnight's too late for me. Midnight's no use to me.'

'Don't ask the impossible, Caroline.' He muttered something to himself, something I couldn't catch, then: 'I'll pull every string, Caroline. Nine o'clock.'

'Four o'clock, Annabelle.'

'Four o'clock this afternoon?' When it came to incredulity

he had me whacked to the wide. 'Four hours' time? You *have* taken leave of your senses.'

'You can have ten men on it in ten minutes. Twenty in twenty minutes. Where's the door that isn't open to you? Especially the door of the Assistant Commissioner. Professionals don't kill for the hell of it. They kill because they must. They kill to gain time. Every additional hour is vital to them. And if it's vital to them, how much more so is it to us? Or do you think we're dealing with amateurs, Annabelle?'

'Call me at four,' he said heavily. 'I'll see what I have for you. What's your next move, Caroline?'

'Bed,' I said. 'I'm going to get some sleep.'

'Of course. Time, as you said, is of the essence. You mustn't waste it, must you, Caroline?' He signed off. He sounded bitter. No doubt he was bitter. But then, insomnia apart, Uncle Arthur could rely on a full quota of sleep during the coming night. Which was more than I could No certain foreknowledge, no second sight, just a hunch, but not a small one, the kind of hunch you couldn't have hidden behind the Empire State Building. Just like the one I had about the *Shangri-la*.

IV

I only just managed to catch the last fading notes of the alarm as it went off at ten minutes to four. I felt worse than I had done when we'd lain down after a miserable lunch of corned beef and reconstituted powdered potatoes – if old Skouras had had a spark of human decency, he'd have made that invitation for dinner. I wasn't only growing old, I felt old. I'd been working too long for Uncle Arthur. The pay was good but the hours and working conditions – I'd have wagered that Uncle Arthur hadn't even set eyes on a tin of corned beef since World War II – were shocking. And all this constant worrying, chiefly about life expectancy, helped wear a man down.

Hunslett came out of his cabin as I came out of mine. He looked just as old as I did. If they had to rely on a couple of ageing crocks like us, I thought morosely, the rising generation must be a pretty sorry lot.

Passing through the saloon, I wondered bitterly about the

identity of all those characters who wrote so glibly about the Western Isles in general and the Torbay area in particular as being a yachtsman's paradise without equal in Europe. Obviously, they'd never been there. Fleet Street was their home and home was a place they never left, not if they could help it. An ignorant bunch of travel and advertising copy writers who regarded King's Cross as the northern limits of civilization. Well, maybe not all that ignorant, at least they were smart enough to stay south of King's Cross.

Four o'clock on an autumn afternoon, but already it was more night than day. The sun wasn't down yet, not by a very long way but it might as well have been for all the chance it had of penetrating the rolling masses of heavy dark cloud hurrying away to the eastwards to the inky blackness of the horizon beyond Torbay. The slanting sheeting rain that foamed whitely across the bay further reduced what little visibility there was to a limit of not more than four hundred yards. The village itself, half a mile distant and nestling in the dark shadow of the steeply-rising pine-covered hills behind, might never have existed. Off to the north-west I could see the navigation lights of a craft rounding the headland; Skouras returning from his stabilizer test run. Down in the *Shangri-la's* gleaming galley a master chef would be preparing the sumptuous evening meal, the one to which we hadn't been invited. I tried to put the thought of that meal out of my mind, but I couldn't so I just put it as far away as possible and followed Hunslett into the engine room.

Hunslett took the spare earphones and squatted beside me on the deck, note-book on his knee. Hunslett was as competent in shorthand as he was in everything else. I hoped that Uncle Arthur would have something to tell us, that Hunslett's presence there would be necessary. It was.

'Congratulations, Caroline,' Uncle Arthur said without preamble. 'You really are on to something.' As far as it is possible for a dead flat monotone voice to assume an overtone of warmth, then Uncle Arthur's did just that. He sounded positively friendly. More likely it was some freak of transmission or reception but at least he hadn't started off by bawling me out.

'We've traced those Post Office Savings books,' he went on.

He rattled off book numbers and details of times and amounts of deposits, things of no interest to me, then said: 'Last deposits were on 27 December. Ten pounds in each case. Present balance is £78 14s.6d. Exactly the same in both. And those accounts have not been closed.'

He paused for a moment to let me congratulate him, which I did, then continued.

'That's nothing, Caroline. Listen. Your queries about any mysterious accidents, deaths, disappearances off the west coasts of Inverness-shire or Argyll, or anything happening to people from that area. We've struck oil, Caroline, we've really struck oil. My God, why did we never think of this before? Have your pencil handy?'

'Harriet has.'

'Here we go. This seems to have been the most disastrous sailing season for years in the west of Scotland. But first, one from last year. The *Pinto*, a well-found sea-worthy forty-five foot motor cruiser left Kyle of Lochalsh for Oban at 8 a.m., 4 September. She should have arrived that afternoon. She never did. No trace of her has ever been found.'

'What was the weather at the time, Annabelle?'

'I thought you'd ask me that, Caroline.' Uncle Arthur's combination of modesty and quiet satisfaction could be very trying at times. 'I checked with the Met. Office. Force 1, variable. Flat calm, cloudless sky. Then we come to this year. 6 April and 26 April. The *Evening Star* and the *Jeannie Rose*. Two East Coast fishing boats – one from Buckie, the other from Fraserburgh.'

'But both based on the west coast?'

'I wish you wouldn't try to steal my thunder,' Uncle Arthur complained. 'Both were based on Oban. Both were lobster boats. The *Evening Star*, the first one to go, was found stranded on the rocks off Islay. The *Jeannie Rose* vanished without trace. No member of either crew was ever found. Then again on the 17 May. This time a well-known racing yacht, the *Cap Gris Nez*, an English-built and owned craft, despite her name, highly experienced skipper, navigator and crew, all of them long-time and often successful competitors in R.O.R.C. races. That class. Left Londonderry for the north of Scotland in fine weather. Disappeared. She was found almost a month later – or what was left of her – washed up on the Isle of Skye.'

'And the crew?'

'Need you ask? Never found. Then the last case, a few weeks ago – 8 August. Husband, wife, two teenage children, son and daughter. Converted lifeboat, the *Kingfisher*. By all accounts a pretty competent sailor, been at it for years. But he'd never done any night navigation, so he set out one calm evening to do a night cruise. Vanished. Boat and crew.'

'Where did he set out from?'

'Torbay.'

That one word made his afternoon. It made mine, too. I said: 'And do you still think the *Nantesville* is hell and gone to Iceland or some remote fjord in northern Norway?'

'I never thought anything of the kind.' Uncle's human relationship barometer had suddenly swung back from friendly to normal, normal lying somewhere between cool and glacial. 'The significance of the dates will not have escaped you?'

'No, Annabelle, the significance has not escaped me.' The Buckie fishing-boat, the *Evening Star*, had been found washed up on Islay three days after the S.S. *Holmwood* had vanished off the south coast of Ireland. The *Jeannie Rose* had vanished exactly three days after the M.V. *Antara* had as mysteriously disappeared in the St George's Channel. The *Cap Gris Nez*, the R.O.R.C. racer that had finally landed up on the rocks of the island of Skye, had vanished the same day as the M.V. *Headley Pioneer* had disappeared somewhere, it was thought, off Northern Ireland. And the converted lifeboat, *Kingfisher*, had disappeared, never to be seen again, just two days after the S.S. *Hurricane Spray* had left the Clyde, also never to be seen again. Coincidence was coincidence and I classed those who denied its existence with intellectual giants like the twentieth-century South African president who stoutly maintained that the world was flat and that an incautious step would take you over the edge with results as permanent as they would be disastrous: but this was plain ridiculous. The odds against such a perfect matching of dates could be calculated only in astronomical terms: while the complete disappearance of the crews of four small boats that had come to grief in so very limited an area was the final nail in the coffin of coincidence. I said as much to Uncle.

'Let us not waste time by dwelling upon the obvious, Caroline,' Uncle said coldly, which was pretty ungracious of him as the idea had never even entered his head until I had put it there fours hours previously. 'The point is – what is to be done? Islay to Skye is a pretty big area. Where does this get us?'

'How much weight can you bring to bear to secure the co-operation of the television and radio networks?'

There was a pause, then: 'What do you have in mind, Caroline?' Uncle at his most forbidding.

'An insertion of an item in their news bulletins.'

'Well.' An even longer pause. 'It was done daily during the war, of course. I believe it's been done once or twice since. Can't compel them, of course – they're a stuffy lot, both the BBC and the ITA.' His tone left little doubt as to his opinion of those diehard reactionaries who brooked no interference, an odd reaction from one who was himself a past-master of brookmanship of this nature. 'If they can be persuaded that it's completely apolitical and in the national interest there's a chance. What do you want?'

'An item that a distress signal has been received from a sinking yacht somewhere south of Skye. Exact position unknown. Signals ceased, the worst feared, an air-sea search to be mounted at first light to-morrow. That's all.'

'I may manage it. Your reason, Caroline?'

'I want to look around. I want an excuse to move around without raising eyebrows.'

'You're going to volunteer the *Firecrest* for this search and then poke around where you shouldn't?'

'We have our faults, Annabelle, Harriet and I, but we're not crazy. I wouldn't take this tub across the Serpentine without a favourable weather forecast. It's blowing a Force 7 outside. And a boat search would take a lifetime too long in those parts. What I had in mind was this. At the very eastern tip of Torbay Island, about five miles from the village, there's a small deserted sandy cove, semi-circular and well protected by steep bluffs and pine trees. Will you please arrange to have a long-range helicopter there exactly at dawn.'

'And now it's your turn to think I am crazy,' Uncle Arthur said coldly. That remark about the sea-keeping qualities of his own brain-child, the *Firecrest*, would have rankled badly. 'I'm supposed to snap my fingers and hey presto! a helicopter will be there at dawn.'

'That's fourteen hours from now, Annabelle. At five o'clock this morning you were prepared to snap your fingers and have a helicopter here by noon. Seven hours. Exactly half the time. But that was for something important, like getting me down to London to give me the bawling out of a lifetime before firing me.'

'Call me at midnight, Caroline. I hope to God you know what you are doing.'

I said: 'Yes, sir', and hung up. I didn't mean, Yes, sir, I knew what I was doing; I meant, Yes, sir, I hoped to God I knew what I was doing.

V

If the carpet in the *Shangri-la's* saloon had cost a penny under five thousand pounds then old Skouras must have picked it up second-hand somewhere. Twenty by thirty, bronze and russet and gold, but mainly gold, it flowed across the deck like a field of ripe corn, an illusion heightened both by its depth and the impediment it offered to progress. You had to wade through the damn thing. I'd never seen an item of furnishing like it in my life except for the curtains that covered two-thirds of the bulkhead space. The curtains made the carpet look rather shoddy. Persian or Afghanistan, with a heavy gleaming weave that gave a shimmering shot-silk effect with every little movement of the *Shangri-la*, they stretched all the way from deckhead to deck. What little of the bulkheads that could be seen, were sheathed in a satiny tropical hardwood, the same wood as was used for the magnificent bar that took up most of the after bulkhead of the saloon. The opulently upholstered settees and armchairs and bar-stools, dark green leather with gold piping, would have cost another fortune; even the trade-in value of the beaten copper tables scattered carelessly about the carpet would have fed a family of five for a year. At the Savoy Grill.

On the port bulkhead hung two Cézannes, on the starboard two Renoirs. The pictures were a mistake. In that room they didn't have a chance. They'd have felt more at home in the galley.

So would I. So, I was pretty sure, would Hunslett. It wasn't merely that our sports coats and Paisley scarves clashed violently with the décor in general and the black ties and dinner jackets of our host and his other guests in particular. It wasn't even that the general run of conversation might have been specifically designed to reduce Hunslett and myself to our proper status of artisans and pretty inferior artisans at that. All this talk about debentures and mergers and cross-options and takeovers and millions and millions of dollars has a pretty demoralizing effect on the lower classes, but you didn't need to have the IQ of a genius to realize that this line of talk wasn't being aimed specifically at us; to the lads with the black ties, debentures and takeovers were the stuff and staff of life and so a principal staple of conversation. Besides, this wish to be somewhere else obviously didn't apply only to us: at least two others, a bald-headed, goatee-bearded merchant banker by the name of Henri Biscarte and a big bluff Scots lawyer by the name of MacCallum were just as uncomfortable as I felt, but showed it a great deal more.

A silent movie picture of the scene would have given no clue as to what was wrong. Everything was so very comfortable, so very civilized. The deep armchairs invited complete relaxation. A blazing if superfluous log-fire burned in the hearth. Skouras was the smiling and genial host to the life. The glasses were never empty – the press of an unheard bell brought a white-jacketed steward who silently refilled glasses and as silently departed again. All so urbane, so wealthy, so pleasantly peaceful. Until you cut in the movie sound-track, that was. That was when you wished you were in the galley.

Skouras had his glass refilled for the fourth time in the forty-five minutes we had been there, smiled at his wife sitting in the armchair across the fire from him, lifted his glass in a toast.

'To you, my dear. To your patience with putting up with us all so well. A most boring trip for you, most boring. I congratulate you.'

I looked at Charlotte Skouras. Everybody looked at Charlotte Skouras. There was nothing unusual in that, millions of people had looked at Charlotte Skouras when she had been the most sought-after actress in Europe. Even in those days she'd been neither particularly young nor beautiful; she didn't have to be because she'd been a great actress and not a beautiful-but-boneheaded movie star. Now she was even older and less good-looking and her figure was beginning to go. But men still looked at her. She was somewhere in her late thirties, but they would still be looking at her when she was in her bath-chair. She had that kind of face. A worn face, a used face, a face that had been used for living and laughing and thinking and feeling and suffering, a face with brown tired wise-knowing eyes a thousand years old, a face that had more quality and character in every little line and wrinkle – and heaven only knew there was no shortage of these – than in a whole battalion of the fringe-haired darlings of contemporary society, the ones in the glossy magazines, the ones who week after week stared out at you with their smooth and beautiful faces, with their beautiful and empty eyes. Put them in the same room as Charlotte Skouras and no one would ever have seen them. Mass-produced carbon copies of chocolate boxes are no kind of competition at all for a great painter's original in oils.

'You are very kind, Anthony.' Charlotte Skouras had a deep slow slightly-foreign accented voice, and, just then, a tired strained smile that accorded well with the darkness under the brown eyes. 'But I am never bored. Truly. You know that.'

'With this lot as guests?' Skouras's smile was as broad as ever. 'A Skouras board meeting in the Western Isles instead of your blue-blooded favourites on a cruise in the Levant? Take Dollmann here.' He nodded to the man by his side, a tall thin bespectacled character with receding thin dark hair who looked as if he needed a shave but didn't. John Dollmann, the managing director of the Skouras shipping lines. 'Eh, John? How do you rate yourself as a substitute for young Viscount Horley? The one with sawdust in his head and fifteen million in the bank?'

'Poorly, I'm afraid, Sir Anthony.' Dollmann was as urbane

as Skouras himself, as apparently unconscious of anything untoward in the atmosphere. 'Very poorly. I've a great deal more brains, a great deal less money and I've no pretensions to being a gay and witty conversationalist.'

'Young Horley *was* rather the life and soul of the party, wasn't he? Especially when I wasn't around,' Skouras added thoughtfully. He looked at me. 'You know him, Mr Petersen?'

'I've heard of him. I don't move in those circles, Sir Anthony.' Urbane as all hell, that was me.

'Um.' Skouras looked quizzically at the two men sitting close by myself. One, rejoicing in the good Anglo-Saxon name of Hermann Lavorski, a big jovial twinkling-eyed man with a great booming laugh and an inexhaustible supply of risqué stories, was, I'd been told, his accountant and financial adviser. I'd never seen anyone less like an accountant and finance wizard, so that probably made him the best in the business. The other, a middle-aged, balding, Sphinx-faced character with a drooping handlebar moustache of the type once sported by Wild Bill Hickock and a head that cried out for a bowler hat, was Lord Charnley who, in spite of his title, found it necessary to work as a broker in the City to make ends meet. 'And how would you rate our two good friends here, Charlotte?' This with another wide and friendly smile at his wife.

'I'm afraid I don't understand.' Charlotte Skouras looked at her husband steadily, not smiling.

'Come now, come now, of course you do understand. I'm still talking about the poor company I provide for so young and attractive a woman as you.' He looked at Hunslett. 'She *is* a young and attractive woman, don't you think, Mr Hunslett?'

'Well, now.' Hunslett leaned back in his armchair, fingers judiciously steepled, an urbanely sophisticated man entering into the spirit of things. 'What is youth, Sir Anthony? I don't know.' He smiled across at Charlotte Skouras. 'Mrs Skouras will never be old. As for attractive – well, it's a bit superfluous to ask that. For ten million European men – and for myself – Mrs Skouras was the most attractive actress of her time.'

'*Was*, Mr Hunslett? *Was*?' Old Skouras was leaning forward in his chair now, the smile a shadow of its former self. 'But now, Mr Hunslett?'

'Mrs Skouras's producers must have employed the worst cameramen in Europe.' Hunslett's dark, saturnine face gave nothing away. He smiled at Charlotte Skouras. 'If I may be pardoned so personal a remark.'

If I'd had a sword in my hand and the authority to use it, I'd have knighted Hunslett on the spot. After, of course, having first had a swipe at Skouras.

'The days of chivalry are not yet over,' Skouras smiled. I saw MacCallum and Biscarte, the bearded banker, stir uncomfortably in their seats. It was damnably awkward. Skouras went on: 'I only meant, my dear, that Charnley and Lavorski here are poor substitutes for sparkling young company like Welshblood, the young American oil man, or Domenico, that Spanish count with the passion for amateur astronomy. The one who used to take you on the afterdeck to point out the stars in the Ægean.' He looked again at Charnley and Lavorski. 'I'm sorry, gentlemen, you just wouldn't do at all.'

'I don't know if I'm all that insulted,' Lavorski said comfortably. 'Charnley and I have our points. Um – I haven't seen young Domenico around for quite some time.' He'd have made an excellent stage feed man, would Lavorski, trained to say his lines at exactly the right time.

'You won't see him around for a very much longer time,' Skouras said grimly. 'At least not in my yacht or in any of my houses.' A pause. 'Or near anything I own. I promised him I'd see the colour of his noble Castilian blood if I ever clapped eyes on him again.' He laughed suddenly. 'I must apologize for even bringing that nonentity's name into the conversation. Mr Hunslett. Mr Petersen. Your glasses are empty.'

'You've been very kind, Sir Anthony. We've enjoyed ourselves immensely.' Bluff old, stupid old Calvert, too obtuse to notice what was going on. 'But we'd like to get back. It's blowing up badly tonight and Hunslett and I would like to move the *Firecrest* into the shelter of Garve Island.' I rose to a window, pulling one of his Afghanistan or whatever curtains to one side. It felt as heavy as a stage fire curtain, no wonder he needed stabilizers with all that topweight on. 'That's why we left our riding and cabin lights on. To see if we'd moved. She dragged a fair bit earlier this evening.'

'So soon? So soon?' He sounded genuinely disappointed.

'But of course, if you're worried—' He pressed a button, not the one for the steward, and the saloon door opened. The man who entered was a small weatherbeaten character with two gold stripes on his sleeves. Captain Black, the *Shangri-la's* captain. He'd accompanied Skouras when we'd been briefly shown around the *Shangri-la* after arriving aboard, a tour that had included an inspection of the smashed radio transmitter. No question about it, their radio was well and truly out of action.

'Ah, Captain Black. Have the tender brought alongside at once, will you. Mr Petersen and Mr Hunslett are anxious to get back to the *Firecrest* as soon as possible.'

'Yes, sir. I'm afraid there'll be a certain delay, Sir Anthony.'

'Delay?' Old Skouras could put a frown in his voice without putting one on his face.

'The old trouble, I'm afraid,' Captain Black said apologetically.

'Those bloody carburettors,' Skouras swore. 'You were right, Captain Black, you were right. Last tender I'll ever have with petrol engines fitted. Let me know as soon as she's all right. And detail one of the hands to keep an eye on the *Firecrest* to see that she doesn't lose position. Mr Petersen's afraid she'll drag.'

'Don't worry, sir.' I didn't know whether Black was speaking to Skouras or myself. 'She'll be all right.'

He left. Skouras spent some time in extolling diesel engines and cursing petrol ones, pressed some more whisky on Hunslett and myself and ignored my protests, which were based less on any dislike of whisky in general or Skouras in particular than on the fact that I didn't consider it very good preparation for the night that lay ahead of me. Just before nine o'clock he pressed a button by his arm rest and the doors of a cabinet automatically opened to reveal a 23-inch TV set.

Uncle Arthur hadn't let me down. The newscaster gave quite a dramatic account of the last message received from the T.S.D.Y. *Moray Rose*, reported not under command and making water fast somewhere to the south of the Island of Skye. A full-scale air and sea search, starting at dawn the next day, was promised.

Skouras switched the set off. 'The sea's crowded with damn

fools who should never be allowed outside a canal basin. What's the latest on the weather? Anyone know?'

'There was a Hebrides Force 8 warning on the 1758 shipping forecast,' Charlotte Skouras said quietly. 'South-west, they said.'

'Since when did you start listening to forecasts?' Skouras demanded. 'Or to the radio at all? But of course, my dear, I'd forgotten. Not so much to occupy your time these days, have you? Force 8 and south-west, eh? And the yacht would be coming down from the Kyle of Lochalsh, straight into it. They must be mad. And they have a radio – they sent a message. That makes them stark lunatics. Whether they didn't listen to the forecast or whether they listened and still set out, they must have been lunatics. Get them everywhere.'

'Some of those lunatics may be dying, drowning now. Or already drowned,' Charlotte Skouras said. The shadows under the brown eyes seemed bigger and darker than ever, but there was still life in those brown eyes.

For perhaps five seconds Skouras, face set, stared at her and I felt that if I snapped my fingers there would be a loud tinkling or crashing sound, the atmosphere was as brittle as that. Then he turned away with a laugh and said to me: 'The little woman, eh, Petersen? The little mother – only she has no children. Tell me, Petersen, are you married?'

I smiled at him while debating the wisdom of throwing my whisky glass in his face or clobbering him with something heavy, then decided against it. Apart from the fact that it would only make matters worse, I didn't fancy the swim back to the *Firecrest*. So I smiled and smiled, feeling the knife under the cloak, and said: 'Afraid not, Sir Arthur.'

'Afraid not? Afraid not?' He laughed his hearty good-fellowship laugh, the kind I can't stand, and went on cryptically: 'You're not so young to be sufficiently naïve to talk that way, come now, are you, Mr Petersen?'

'Thirty-eight and never had a chance,' I said cheerfully. 'The old story, Sir Anthony. The ones I'd have wouldn't have me. And vice-versa.' Which wasn't quite true. The driver of a Bentley with, the doctors had estimated, certainly not less than a bottle of whisky inside him, had ended my marriage before it was two months old – and also accounted for the savagely scarred left side of my face. It was then that Uncle Arthur had prised me from my marine salvage business and since then no girl with any sense would ever have contemplated marrying me if she'd known what my job was. What made it even more difficult was the fact that I couldn't tell her in the first place. And the scars didn't help.

'You don't look a fool to me,' Skouras smiled. 'If I may say so without giving offence.' That was rich, old Skouras worrying about giving offence. The zip-fastener of a mouth softened into what, in view of his next words, I correctly interpreted in advance as being a nostalgic smile. 'I'm joking, of course. It's not all that bad. A man must have his fun. Charlotte?'

'Yes?' The brown eyes wary, watchful.

'There's something I want from our stateroom. Would you—?'

'The stewardess. Couldn't she—?'

'This is personal, my dear. And, as Mr Hunslett has pointed out, at least by inference, you're a good deal younger than I am.' He smiled at Hunslett to show that no offence was intended. 'The picture on my dressing-table.'

'What!' She suddenly sat forward in her armchair, hands reaching for the fronts of the arm rests as if about to pull herself to her feet. Something touched a switch inside Skouras and the smiling eyes went bleak and hard and cold, changing their direction of gaze fractionally. It lasted only a moment because his wife had caught it even before I did, because she sat forward abruptly, smoothing down the short sleeves of her dress over sun-tanned arms. Quick and smooth, but not quite quick enough. For a period of not more than two seconds the sleeves had ridden nearly all the way up to her shoulders – and nearly four inches below those shoulders each arm had been encircled by a ring of bluish-red bruises. A continuous ring. Not the kind of bruises that are made by blows or finger pressure. The kind that are made by a rope.

Skouras was smiling again, pressing the bell to summon the steward. Charlotte Skouras rose without a further word and hurried quickly from the room. I could have wondered if I'd only imagined this momentary tableau I'd seen, but I knew damned well I hadn't. I was paid not to have an imagination of that kind.

She was back inside a moment, a picture frame maybe six by eight in her hand. She handed it to Skouras and sat down quickly in her own chair. This time she was very careful with the sleeves, without seeming to be.

'My wife, gentlemen,' Skouras said. He rose from his armchair and handed round a photograph of a dark-eyed, dark-haired woman with a smiling face that emphasized the high Slavonic cheek-bones. 'My first wife. Anna. We were married for thirty years. Marriage isn't all that bad. That's Anna, gentlemen.'

If I'd a gramme of human decency left in me I should have knocked him down and trampled all over him. For a man to state openly in company that he kept the picture of his former wife by his bedside and then impose upon his present wife the final and utter humiliation and degradation of fetching it was beyond belief. That and the rope-burns on his present wife's arms made him almost too good for shooting. But I couldn't do it, I couldn't do anything about it. The old coot's heart was in his voice and his eyes. If this was acting, it was the most superb acting I had ever seen, the tear that trickled down from his right eye would have rated an Oscar any year since cinema had begun. And if it wasn't acting then it was just the picture of a sad and lonely man, no longer young, momentarily oblivious of this world, gazing desolately at the only thing in this world that he loved, that he ever had loved or ever would love, something gone beyond recall. And that was what it was.

If it hadn't been for the other picture, the picture of the still, proud, humiliated Charlotte Skouras staring sightlessly into the fire, I might have felt a lump in my own throat. As it happened, I'd no difficulty in restraining my emotion. One man couldn't, however, but it wasn't sympathy for Skouras that got the better of him. MacCallum, the Scots lawyer, pale-faced with outrage, rose to his feet, said something in a thick voice about not feeling well, wished us good night and left. The bearded banker left on his heels. Skouras didn't see them go, he'd fumbled his way back to his seat and was staring before him, his eyes as sightless as those of his wife. Like his wife, he was seeing something in the depths of the flames. The picture lay face down on his knee. He didn't even look up when Captain Black came in and told us the tender was ready to take us back to the *Firecrest*.

VI

When the tender had left us aboard our own boat we waited till it was half-way back to the *Shangri-la*, closed the saloon door, unbuttoned the studded carpet and pulled it back. Carefully I lifted a sheet of newspaper and there, on the thin film of flour spread out on the paper below it, were four perfect sets of footprints. We tried our two for'ard cabins, the engineroom and the after cabin, and the silk threads we'd so laboriously fitted before our departure to the *Shangri-la* were all snapped.

Somebody, two at least to judge from the footprints, had been through the entire length of the *Firecrest*. They could have had at least a clear hour for the job, so Hunslett and I spent a clear hour trying to find out why they had been there. We found nothing, no reason at all.

'Well,' I said, 'at least we know now why they were so anxious to have us aboard the *Shangri-la*.'

'To give them a clear field here? That's why the tender wasn't ready – it was here.'

'What else?'

'There's something else. I can't put my finger on it. But there's something else.'

'Let me know in the morning. When you call Uncle at midnight, ask him to dig up what information he can on those characters on the *Shangri-la* and about the physician who attended the late Lady Skouras. There's a lot I want to know about the late Lady Skouras.' I told him what I wanted to know. 'Meantime, let's shift this boat over to Garve Island. I've got to be up at three-thirty – you've all the time for sleep in the world.'

I should have listened to Hunslett. Again I should have listened to Hunslett. And again for Hunslett's sake. But I didn't know then that Hunslett was to have time for all the sleep in the world.

— 4 —

Wednesday: 5 a.m. – dusk

AS THE SAYING went in those parts, it was as black as the earl of hell's waistcoat. The sky was black, the woods were black, and the icy heavy driving rain reduced what little visibility there was to just nothing at all. The only way to locate a tree was to walk straight into it, the only way to locate a dip in the ground was to fall into it. When Hunslett had woken me at three-thirty with a cup of tea he told me that when he'd been speaking to Uncle Arthur at midnight – I'd been asleep – he was left in no doubt that although the helicopter had been laid on Uncle had been most unenthusiastic and considered the whole thing a waste of time. It was a rare occasion indeed when I ever felt myself in total agreement with Uncle Arthur but this was one of those rare occasions.

It was beginning to look as if I'd never even find that damned helicopter anyway. I wouldn't have believed that it could have been so difficult to find one's way across five miles of wooded island at night-time. It wasn't even as if I had to contend with rivers or rushing torrents or cliffs or precipitous clefts in the ground or any kind of dense or tangled vegetation. Torbay was just a moderately wooded gently sloping island and crossing from one side to the other of it would have been only an easy Sunday afternoon stroll for a fairly active octogenarian. I was no octogenarian, though I felt like one, but then this wasn't a Sunday afternoon.

The trouble had started from the moment I'd landed on the Torbay shore opposite Garve Island. From the moment I'd tried to land. Wearing rubber-soled shoes and trying to haul a rubber dinghy over slippery seaweed-covered rocks, some as much as six feet in diameter, to a shore-line twenty interminable yards away is, even in broad daylight, a bone-breaking job: in pitch darkness it's almost as good a way as any for a potential suicide to finish off the job with efficiency and dispatch. The third time I fell I smashed my torch. Several bone-jarring bruises later my wrist-compass went the same way. The attached depth-gauge, almost inevitably, remained intact. A depth-gauge is a great help in finding your way through a trackless wood at night.

After deflating and caching the dinghy and pump I'd set off along the shore-line remote from the village of Torbay. It was logical that if I followed this long enough I'd be bound to come to the sandy cove at the far end of the island where I was to rendezvous with the helicopter. It was also logical that, if the tree line came right down to the shore, if that shore was heavily indented with little coves and if I couldn't see where I was going, I'd fall into the sea with a fair degree of regularity. After I'd hauled myself out for the third time I gave up and struck inland. It wasn't because I was afraid of getting wet – as I hadn't seen much point in wearing a scuba suit for walking through a wood and sitting in a helicopter I'd left it aboard and was already soaked to the skin. Nor was it because of the possibility that the hand distress flares I'd brought along for signalling the helicopter pilot, wrapped though they were in oilskin, might not stand up to this treatment indefinitely. The reason why I was now blundering my blind and painful way through the wood was that if I'd stuck to the shoreline my rate of progress there wouldn't have brought me to the rendezvous before midday.

My only guides were the wind-lashed rain and the lie of the land. The cove I was heading for lay to the east, the near-gale force wind was almost due west, so as long as I kept that cold stinging rain on the back of my neck I'd be heading in approximately the right direction: as a check on that, the Island of Torbay has a spinal hog's back, covered in pines to the top, running its east-west length and when I felt the land falling away to one side or the other it meant I was wandering. But the rain-laden wind swirled unpredictably as the wood alternately thinned and became dense again, the hog's back had offshoots and irregularities and as a result of the combination of the two I lost a great deal of time. Half an hour before dawn – by my watch, that was, it was still as black as the midnight hour – I was beginning to wonder if I could possibly make it in time.

And I was beginning to wonder if the helicopter could make it either. There was no doubt in my mind that it could land – that eastern cove was perfectly sheltered – but whether it could get there at all was another question. I had a vague idea that helicopters were unmanageable above certain wind speeds but had no idea what those wind speeds were. And if the helicopter didn't turn up, then I was faced with the long cold wet trudge back to where I had hidden the dinghy and then an even longer, colder and hungry wait until darkness fell at night and I could get out to the *Firecrest* unseen. Even now, I had only twenty-four hours left. By nightfall I would have only twelve. I began to run.

Fifteen minutes and God knows how many iron-hard tree trunks later I heard it, faint and intermittent at first, then gradually swelling in strength – the clattering roar of a helicopter engine. He was early, damn him, he was far too early, he'd land there, find the place deserted and take off for base again. It says much for my sudden desperate state of mind that it never occurred to me how he could even begin to locate, far less land in, that sandy cove in a condition of darkness that was still only a degree less than total. For a moment I even contemplated lighting a flare to let the pilot know that I was at least there or thereabouts and had the flare half-way out of my pocket before I shoved it back again. The arrangement had been that the flare would be lit only to show the landing strip in the sand: if I lit one there and then he might head for it, strike the tops of the pine trees and that would be the end of that.

I ran even faster. It had been years since I'd run more than a couple of hundred yards and my lungs were already wheezing and gasping like a fractured bellows in a blacksmith's shop. But I ran as hard as I could. I cannoned into trees, I tripped over roots, fell into gullies, had my face whipped time and again by low-spreading branches, but above all I cannoned into those damned trees. I stretched my arms before me but it did no good, I ran into them all the same. I picked up a broken branch I'd tripped over and held it in front of me but no matter how I pointed it the trees always seemed to come at me from another direction. I hit every tree in the Island of Torbay. I felt the way a bowling ball must feel after a hard season in a bowling alley, the only difference, and a notable one, being that whereas the ball knocked the skittles down, the trees knocked me down. Once, twice, three times I heard the sound of the helicopter engine disappearing away to the east, and the third time I was sure he was gone for good. But each time it came back. The sky was lightening to the east now, but still I couldn't see the helicopter: for the pilot, everything below would still be as black as night.

The ground gave way beneath my feet and I fell. I braced myself, arms outstretched, for the impact as I struck the other side of the gully. But my reaching hands found nothing. No impact. I kept on falling, rolling and twisting down a heathery slope, and for the first time that night I would have welcomed the appearance of a pine tree, any kind of tree, to stop my progress. I don't know how many trees there were on that slope; I missed the lot. If it was a gully, it was the biggest gully on the Island of Torbay. But it wasn't a gully at all it was the end of Torbay. I rolled and bumped over a sudden horizontal grassy bank and landed on my back in soft wet sand. Even while I was whooping and gasping and trying to get my knocked-out breath back into my lungs I still had time to appreciate the fortunate fact that kindly providence and a few million years had changed the jagged rocks that must once have fringed that shore into a nice soft yielding sandy beach.

I got to my feet. This was the place, all right. There was only one such sandy bay, I'd been told, in the east of the Isle of Torbay and there was now enough light for me to see that this was indeed just that, though a lot smaller than it appeared on the chart. The helicopter was coming in again from the east, not, as far as I could judge, more than three or four hundred feet up. I ran half-way down to the water's edge, pulled a hand flare from my pocket, slid away the waterproof covering and tore off the ignition strip. It flared into life at once, a dazzling blue-white magnesium light so blinding that I had to clap my free hand over my eyes. It lasted for only thirty seconds, but that was enough. Even as it fizzled and sputtered its acrid and nostril-wrinkling way to extinction the helicopter was almost directly overhead. Two vertically-downward pointing searchlights, mounted fore and aft on the helicopter, switched on simultaneously, interlocking pools of brilliance on the pale white sand. Twenty seconds later the skids sank into the soft sand, the rackety clangour of the motor died away and the blades idled slowly to a stop. I'd never been in a helicopter in my life but I'd seen plenty: in the half-darkness this looked like the biggest one I'd ever seen.

The right-hand door opened and a torch shone in my face as I approached. A voice, Welsh as the Rhondda Valley, said: 'Morning. You Calvert?'

'Me. Can I come aboard?'

'How do I know you're Calvert?'

'I'm telling you. Don't come the hard man, laddie. You've no authority to make an identification check.'

'Have you no proof? No papers?'

'Have you no sense? Haven't you enough sense to know that there are some people who *never* carry any means of identification? Do you think I just happened to be standing here, five miles from nowhere, and that I just happened to be carrying flares in my pocket? You want to join the ranks of the unemployed before sunset?' A very auspicious beginning to our assocation.

'I was told to be careful.' He was as worried and upset as a cat snoozing on a sun-warmed wall. Still a marked lack of cordiality. 'Lieutenant Scott Williams, Fleet Air Arm. Takes an admiral to sack me. Step up.'

I stepped up, closed the door and sat. He didn't offer to shake hands. He flicked on an overhead light and said:

'What the hell's happened to your face?'

'What's the matter with my face?'

'Blood. Hundreds of little scratches.'

'Pine needles.' I told him what had happened. 'Why a machine this size? You could ferry a battalion in this one.'

'Fourteen men, to be precise. I do lots of crazy things, Calvert, but I don't fly itsy-bitsy two-bit choppers in this kind of weather. Be blown out of the sky. With only two of us, the long-range tanks are full.'

'You can fly all day?'

'More or less. Depends how fast we go. What do you want from me?'

'Civility, for a start. Or don't you like early morning rising?'

'I'm an Air-Sea Rescue pilot, Calvert. This is the only machine on the base big enough to go out looking in this kind of weather. And I should be out looking, not out on some cloak-and-dagger joy-ride. I don't care how important it is, there's people maybe clinging to a life-raft fifty miles out in the Atlantic. That's my job. But I've got my orders. What do you want?'

'The *Moray Rose*?'

'You heard? Yes, that's her.'

'She doesn't exist. She never has existed.'

'What are you talking about? The news broadcasts—'

'I'll tell you as much as you need to know, lieutenant. It's essential that I be able to search this area without arousing suspicion. The only way that can be done is by inventing an ironclad reason. The foundering *Moray Rose* is that reason. So we tell the tale.'

'Phoney?'

'Phoney.'

'You can fix it?' he said slowly. 'You can fix a news broadcast?'

'Yes.'

'Maybe you could get me fired at that.' He smiled for the first time. 'Sorry, sir. Lieutenant Williams – Scotty to you – is now his normal cheerful willing self. What's on?'

'Know the coastlines and islands of this area well?'

'From the air?'

'Yes.'

'I've been here twenty months now. Air-Sea Rescue and in between army and navy exercises and hunting for lost climbers. Most of my work is with the Marine Commandos. I know this area at least as well as any man alive.'

'I'm looking for a place where a man could hide a boat. A fairly big boat. Forty feet – maybe fifty. Might be in a big boathouse, might be under over-hanging trees up some creek, might even be in some tiny secluded harbour normally invisible from the sea. Between Islay and Skye.'

'Well, now, is that all. Have you any idea how many hundreds of miles of coastline there is in that lot, taking in all the islands? Maybe thousands? How long do I have for this job? A month?'

'By sunset today. Now, wait. We can cut out all centres of population, and by that I mean anything with more than two or three houses together. We can cut out known fishing grounds. We can cut out regular steamship routes. Does that help?'

'A lot. What are we really looking for?'

'I've told you.'

'Okay, okay, so mine is not to reason why. Any idea where you'd like to start, any ideas for limiting the search?'

'Let's go due east to the mainland. Twenty miles up the coast, then twenty south. Then we'll try Torbay Sound and the Isle of Torbay. Then the islands farther west and north.'

'Torbay Sound has a steamer service.'

'Sorry, I should have said a daily service. Torbay has a bi-weekly service.'

'Fasten your seat-belt and get on those earphones. We're going to get thrown around quite a bit today. I hope you're a good sailor.'

'And the earphones?' They were the biggest I'd ever seen, four inches wide with inch-thick linings of what looked like sorbo rubber. A spring loaded swing microphone was attached to the headband.

'For the ears,' the lieutenant said kindly. 'So that you don't get perforated drums. And so you won't be deaf for a week afterwards. If you can imagine yourself inside a steel drum in the middle of a boiler factory with a dozen pneumatic chisels hammering outside, you'll have some idea of what the racket is like once we start up.'

II

Even with the earphone muffs on, it sounded exactly like being in a steel drum in a boiler factory with a dozen pneumatic chisels hammering on the outside. The earphones didn't seem to have the slightest effect at all, the noise came hammering and beating at you through every facial and cranial bone, but on the one and very brief occasion when I cautiously lifted one phone to find out what the noise was like without them and if they were really doing any good at all, I found out exactly what Lieutenant Williams meant about perforated drums. He hadn't been joking. But even with them on, after a couple of hours my head felt as if it were coming apart. I looked occasionally at the dark lean face of the young Welshman beside me, a man who had to stand this racket day in, day out, the year round. He looked quite sane to me. I'd have been in a padded cell in a week.

I didn't have to be in that helicopter a week. Altogether, I spent eight hours' flying time in it and it felt like a leap year.

Our first run northwards up the mainland coast produced what was to be the first of many false alarms that day. Twenty minutes after leaving Torbay we spotted a river, a small one but still a river, flowing into the sea. We followed it up-stream for a mile, then suddenly the trees, crowding down close to the banks on both sides, met in the middle where the river seemed to run through some rocky gorge.

I shouted into the microphone: 'I want to see what's there.'

Williams nodded. 'We passed a place a quarter of a mile back. I'll set you down.'

'You've got a winch. Couldn't you lower me?'

'When you know as much as I do about the effect of forty to fifty miles an hour winds in a steep-sided valley,' he said, 'you'll never talk about such things. Not even in a joke. I want to take this kite home again.'

So he turned back and set me down without much difficulty in the shelter of a bluff. Five minutes later I'd reached the beginning of the overhanging stretch. Another five minutes and I was back in the helicopter.

'What luck?' the lieutenant asked.

'No luck. An ancient oak tree right across the river, just at the entrance to the overhang.'

'Could be shifted.'

'It weighs two or three tons, it's imbedded feet deep in the mud and it's been there for years.'

'Well, well, we can't be right first time, every time.'

A few more minutes and another river mouth. It hardly looked big enough to take a boat of any size, but we turned up anyway. Less than half a mile from its mouth the river foamed whitely as it passed through rapids. We turned back.

By the time it was fully daylight we had reached the northern limit of possibility in this area. Steep-sided mountains gave way to precipitous cliffs that plunged almost vertically into the sea.

'How far does this go north?' I asked.

'Ten, twelve miles to the head of Loch Lairg.'

'Know it?'

'Flown up there a score of times.'

'Caves?'

'Nary a cave.'

I hadn't really thought that there would be. 'How about the other side?' I pointed to the west where the mountainous shore-line, not five miles away yet barely visible through the driving rain and low scudding cloud, ran in an almost sheer drop from the head of Loch Lairg to the entrance to Torbay Sound.

'Even the gulls can't find a foothold there. Believe me.'

I believed him. We flew back the way we had come as far as our starting point on the coast, then continued southwards. From the Isle of Torbay to the mainland the sea was an almost unbroken mass of foaming white, big white-capped rollers marching eastwards across the darkened firth, long creamy lines of spume torn from the wave-tops veining the troughs between. There wasn't a single craft in sight, even the big drifters had stayed at home, it was as bad as that. In that buffeting gale-force wind our big helicopter was having a bad time of it now, violently shaking and swaying like an out-of-control express train in the last moments before it leaves the track: one hour's flying in those conditions had turned me against helicopters for life. But when I thought of what it would be like down there in a boat in that seething maelstrom of a firth I could feel a positive bond of attachment growing between me and that damned helicopter.

We flew twenty miles south – if the way we were being jarred and flung through the air could be called flying – but covered sixty miles in that southing. Every little sound between the islands and the mainland, every natural harbour, every sea-loch and inlet had to be investigated. We flew very low most of the time, not much above two hundred feet: sometimes we were forced down to a hundred feet – so heavy was the rain and so powerful the wind now battering against the streaming windscreen that the wipers were almost useless and we had to get as low as possible to see anything at all. As it was, I don't think we missed a yard of the coastline of the mainland or the close in-shore islands. We saw everything. And we saw nothing.

I looked at my watch. Nine-thirty. The day wearing on and nothing achieved. I said: 'How much more of this can the helicopter stand?'

'I've been 150 miles out over the Atlantic in weather a damn sight worse than this.' Lieutenant Williams showed no signs of strain or anxiety or fatigue; if anything he seemed to be enjoying himself. 'The point is how much more can *you* stand?'

'Very little. But we'll have to. Back to where you picked me up and we'll make a circuit of the coast of Torbay. South coast first, then north up the west coast, then east past Torbay and down the southern shore of the Sound.'

'Yours to command.' Williams brought the helicopter round to the north-west in a swinging side-slipping movement that didn't do my stomach any good. 'You'll find coffee and sandwiches in that box there.' I left the sandwiches and coffee where they were.

It took us almost forty minutes to cover the twenty-five miles to the eastern tip of the Isle of Torbay, that wind took us two steps back for every three forward. Visibility was so bad that Williams flew on instruments the whole way and with that violent cross-wind blowing he should have missed our target by miles. Instead he hit that sandy cove right on the nose as if he'd been flying in on a radio beacon. I was beginning to have a very great deal of confidence in Williams, a man who knew exactly what he was doing: I was beginning to have no confidence at all in myself and to wonder if I had any idea in the world what I was doing. I thought about Uncle Arthur and quickly decided I'd rather think about something else.

'There,' Williams pointed. We were about half-way along the south coast of Torbay. 'A likely set-up, wouldn't you say?'

And a likely set-up it was. A large white three-storey stone-built Georgian house, set in a clearing about a hundred yards back from and thirty yards above the shore. There are dozens of such houses scattered in the most unlikely positions in some of the most barren and desolate islands in the Hebrides. Heaven only knew who built them, why or how. But it wasn't the house that was the focal point of interest in this case, it was the big boathouse on the edge of a tiny land-locked harbour. Without a further word from me Williams brought the big machine down neatly in the shelter of the trees behind the house.

I unwrapped the polythene bag I'd been carrying under my shirt. Two guns. The Luger I stuck in my pocket, the little German Lilliput I fixed to the spring clip in my left sleeve. Williams stared unconcernedly ahead and began to whistle to himself.

Nobody had lived in that house for years. Part of the roof had fallen in, years of salt air erosion had removed all paintwork and the rooms, when I looked in through the cracked and broken windows, were bare and crumbling with long strips of wall-paper lying on the floor. The path down to the little harbour was completely overgrown with moss. Every time my heel sunk into the path a deep muddy mark was left behind, the first made there for a long long time. The boatshed was big enough, at least sixty by twenty, but that was all that could be said for it. The two big doors had three hinges apiece and two huge padlocks where they met in the middle. Padlocks and hinges alike were almost eaten through by rust. I could feel the heavy tug of the Luger in my pocket and the weight made me feel faintly ridiculous. I went back to the helicopter.

Twice more in the next twenty minutes we came across almost identical situations. Big white Georgian houses with big boathouses at their feet. I knew they would be false alarms but I had to check them both. False alarms they were. The last occupants of those houses had been dead before I'd been born. People had lived in those houses once, people with families, big families, people with money and ambition and confidence and no fear at all of the future. Not if they had built houses as big as those. And now the people were gone and all that was left were those crumbling, mouldering monuments to a misplaced faith in the future. Some years previously I'd seen houses in plantations in South Carolina and Georgia, houses widely dissimilar but exactly the same, white-porticoed ante-bellum houses hemmed in by evergreen live oaks and overgrown with long grey festoons of Spanish moss. Sadness and desolation and a world that was gone for ever.

The west coast of the Isle of Torbay yielded nothing. We gave the town of Torbay and Garve Island a wide berth and flew eastwards down the southern shore of the Sound with the gale behind us. Two small hamlets, each with its disintegrating pier. Beyond that, nothing.

We reached the sandy cove again, flew north till we reached the northern shore of the Sound, then westwards along this shore. We stopped twice, once to investigate a tree-overhung land-locked harbour less than forty yards in diameter, and again to investigate a small complex of industrial buildings which had once, so Williams said, produced a fine-quality sand that had been one of the ingredients in a famous brand of toothpaste. Again, nothing.

At the last place we stopped for five minutes. Lieutenant Williams said he was hungry. I wasn't. I'd become used to the helicopter by now but I wasn't hungry. It was midday. Half our time gone and nothing accomplished. And it was beginning to look very much as if nothing was going to be accomplished. Uncle Arthur would be pleased. I took the chart from Williams.

'We have to pick and choose,' I said. 'We'll have to take a chance. We'll go up the Sound to Dolman Head, opposite Garve Island, then go up Loch Hynart.' Loch Hynart was a seven-mile-long loch, winding and many-islanded, that ran more or less due east, nowhere more than half a mile wide, deep into the heart of the mountain massif. 'Back to Dolman Point again then along the southern shore of the mainland peninsula again as far as Carrara Point. Then east along the southern shore of Loch Houron.'

'Loch Houron,' Williams nodded. 'The wildest waters and the worst place for boats in the West of Scotland. Last place I'd go looking Mr Calvert, that's for sure. From all accounts you'll find nothing there but wrecks and skeletons. There are more reefs and skerries and underwater rocks and overfalls and whirlpools and tidal races in twenty miles there than in the whole of the rest of Scotland. Local fishermen won't go near the place.' He pointed at the chart. 'See this passage between Dubh Sgeir and Ballara Island, the two islands at the mouth of Loch Houron? That's the most feared spot of all. You should see the grip the fishermen get on their whisky glasses when they talk about it. Beul nan Uamh, it's called. The mouth of the grave.'

'They're a cheery lot, hereabouts. It's time we were gone.'

The wind blew as strongly as ever, the sea below looked as wicked as ever, but the rain had stopped and that made our search all that much easier. The stretch of the Sound from the sand quarry to Dolman Point yielded nothing. Neither did Loch Hynart. Between Loch Hynart and Carrara Point, eight miles to the west, there were only two tiny hamlets crouched against the water's edge, their backs to the barren hills behind, their inhabitants – if there were any inhabitants – subsisting on God alone knew what. Carrara Point was storm-torn desolation itself. Great jagged broken fissured cliffs, huge fanged rocks rising from the sea, massive Atlantic breakers smashing in hundred foot high spray against the cliffs, the rocks and the tiny-seeming lighthouse at the foot of the cliffs. If I were Sir Billy Butlin looking for the site for my latest holiday camp, I wouldn't have spent too much time on Carrara Point.

We turned north now, then north-east, then east, along the southern shore of Loch Houron.

Many places have evil reputations. Few, at first seeing, live up to those reputations. But there are a few. In Scotland, the Pass of Glencoe, the scene of the infamous massacre, is one of them. The Pass of Brander is another. And Loch Houron was beyond all doubt another.

It required no imagination at all to see this as a dark and deadly and dangerous place. It looked dark and deadly and dangerous. The shores were black and rocky and precipitous and devoid of any form of vegetation at all. The four islands strung out in a line to the east were a splendid match for the hospitable appearance of the shores. In the far distance the northern and the southern shores of the loch came close together and vanished in a towering vertical cleft in the sinister brooding mountains. In the lee of the islands the loch was black as midnight but elsewhere it was a seething boiling white, the waters wickedly swirling, churning, spinning in evil-looking whirlpools as it passed across overfalls or forced its way through the narrow channels between the islands or between the islands and the shore. Water in torment. In the Beul nan Uamh – the mouth of the grave – between the first two islands the rushing leaping milk-white waters looked like floodwater in the Mackenzie river rapids in spring-time, when the snows melt. A yachtsman's paradise. Only a madman would take his boat into these waters.

Apparently there were still a few madmen around. We'd just left the first of the islands, Dubh Sgeir, to port, when I caught sight of a narrow break in the cliffs on the southern mainland. A small rock-girt bay, if bay it could be called, about the size of a couple of tennis courts, almost completely enclosed from the sea, the entrance couldn't have been more than ten yards wide. I glanced at the chart – Little Horseshoe Bay, it was called. Not original, but very apt. There was a boat in there, a fairly big one, a converted M.F.V. by the looks of her, anchored fore and aft in the middle of the bay. Behind the bay was a little plateau, mossy or grass-covered, I couldn't tell which, and, behind that, what looked like a dried-up river bed rising steeply into the hills behind. On the little plateau were four khaki-coloured tents, with men working at them.

'This could be it?' Williams said.

'This could be it.'

This wasn't it. A glance at the thin, wispy-bearded, pebble-bespectacled lad who came hurrying forward to greet me when I stepped onto the ground was all the proof I required that this was indeed not it. Another glance at the seven or eight bearded, scarved and duffel-coated characters behind him who had not, as I'd thought, been working but were struggling to prevent their tents from being blown away by the wind, was almost superfluous proof. That lot couldn't have hi-jacked a rowing boat. The M.F.V., I could see now, was down by the stern and listing heavily to starboard.

'Hallo, hallo, hallo,' said the character with the wispy beard. 'Good afternoon, good afternoon. By Jove, are we glad to see you!'

I looked at him, shook the outstretched hand, glanced at the listing boat and said mildly: 'You may be shipwrecked, but those are hardly what I'd call desperate straits. You're not on a deserted island. You're on the mainland. Help is at hand!'

'Oh, we know where we are all right.' He waved a deprecating hand. 'We put in here three days ago but I'm afraid out boat was holed in a storm during the night. Most unfortunate, most inconvenient.'

'Holed as she lay there? Just as she's moored now?'

'Yes, indeed.'

'Bad luck. Oxford or Cambridge?'

'Oxford, of course.' He seemed a bit huffed at my ignorance. 'Combined geological and marine biology party.'

'No shortage of rocks and sea-water hereabouts,' I agreed. 'How bad is the damage?'

'A holed plank. Sprung. Too much for us, I'm afraid.'

'All right for food?'

'Of course.'

'No transmitter?'

'Receiver only.'

'The helicopter pilot will radio for a shipwright and engineer to be sent out as soon as the weather moderates. Goodbye.'

His jaw fell about a couple of inches. 'You're off? Just like that?'

'Air-Sea Rescue. Vessel reported sinking last night.'

'Ah, that. We heard.'

'Thought you might be it. Glad for your sakes you're not. We've a lot of ground to cover yet.'

We continued eastwards towards the head of Loch Houron. Half-way there I said: 'Far enough. Let's have a look at those four islands out in the loch. We'll start with the most easterly one first of all – what's it called, yes, Eilean Oran – then make our way back towards the mouth of Loch Houron again.'

'You said you wanted to go all the way to the top.'

'I've changed my mind.'

'You're the man who pays the piper,' he said equably. He was a singularly incurious character, was young Lieutenant Williams. 'Northward ho for Eilean Oran.'

We were over Eilean Oran in three minutes. Compared to

Eilean Oran, Alcatraz was a green and lovely holiday resort. Half a square mile of solid rock and never a blade of grass in sight. But there was a house. A house with smoke coming from its chimney. And beside it a boatshed, but no boat. The smoke meant an inhabitant, at least one inhabitant, and however he earned his living he certainly didn't do it from tilling the good earth. So he would have a boat, a boat for fishing for his livelihood, a boat for transportation to the mainland, for one certain thing among the manifold uncertainties of this world was that no passenger vessel had called at Eilean Oran since Robert Fulton had invented the steamboat. Williams set me down not twenty yards from the shed.

I rounded the corner of the boathouse and stopped abruptly. I always stop abruptly when I'm struck in the stomach by a battering-ram. After a few minutes I managed to whoop enough air into my lungs to let me straighten up again.

He was tall, gaunt, grey, in his middle sixties. He hadn't shaved for a week or changed his collarless shirt in a month. It wasn't a battering-ram he'd used after all, it was a gun, none of your fancy pistols, just a good old-fashioned double-barrelled twelve-bore shotgun, the kind of gun that at close range – six inches in this case – can give points even to the Peacemaker Colt when it comes to blowing your head off. He had it aimed at my right eye. It was like staring down the Mersey tunnel. When he spoke I could see he'd missed out on all those books that laud the unfailing courtesy of the Highlander.

'And who the hell are you?' he snarled.

'My name's Johnson. Put that gun away. I—'

'And what the hell do you want here?'

'How about trying the "Ceud Mile Failte" approach?' I said. 'You see it everywhere in these parts. A hundred thousand welcomes—'

'I won't ask again, mister.'

'Air-Sea Rescue. There's a missing boat—'

'I haven't seen any boat. You can just get to hell off my island.' He lowered his gun till it pointed at my stomach, maybe because he thought it would be more effective there or make for a less messy job when it came to burying me. 'Now!'

I nodded to the gun. 'You could get prison for this.'

'Maybe I could and maybe I couldn't. All I know is that I don't like strangers on my island and that Donald MacEachern protects his own.'

'And a very good job you make of it, too, Donald,' I said approvingly. The gun moved and I said quickly: 'I'm off. And don't bother saying "haste ye back" for I won't be.'

As we rose from the island Williams said: 'I just caught a glimpse. That was a gun he had there?'

'It wasn't the outstretched hand of friendship they're always talking about in these parts,' I said bitterly.

'Who is he? What is he?'

'He's an undercover agent for the Scottish Tourist Board in secret training to be their goodwill ambassador abroad. He's not any of those I'm looking for, that I know. He's not a nut case, either – he's as sane as you are. He's a worried man and a desperate one.'

'You didn't look in the shed. You wanted to find out about a boat. Maybe there was someone pointing a gun at him.'

'That was one of the thoughts that accounted for my rapid departure. I could have taken the gun from him.'

'You could have got your head blown off.'

'Guns are my business. The safety catch was in the "On" position.'

'Sorry.' Williams's face showed how out of his depth he was, he wasn't as good at concealing his expression as I was. 'What now?'

'Island number two to the west here.' I glanced at the chart. 'Craigmore.'

'You'll be wasting your time going there.' He sounded very positive. 'I've been there. Flew out a badly injured man to a Glasgow hospital.'

'Injured how?'

'He'd cut himself to the thigh-bone with a flensing knife, infection had set in.'

'A flensing knife? For whales? I'd never heard—'

'For sharks. Basking sharks. They're as common as mackerel hereabouts. Catch them for their livers – you can get a ton of liver oil from a good-sized one.' He pointed to the chart, to a tiny mark on the north coast. 'Craigmore village. Been abandoned, they say, from before the First World War. We're coming up to it now. Some of those old boys built their homes in the damnedest places.'

Some of those old boys had indeed built their homes in the damnedest places. If I'd been compelled to build a home either there or at the North Pole I'd have been hard put to it to make a choice. A huddle of four small grey houses built out near the tip of a foreland, several wicked reefs that made a natural breakwater, an even more wicked-looking entrance through the reefs and two fishing-boats swinging and rolling wildly at anchor inside the reefs. One of the houses, the one nearest the shore, had had its entire seaward wall cut away. On the twenty or thirty feet of sloping ground that separated the house from the sea I could see three unmistakable sharks. A handful of men appeared at the open end of the house and waved at us.

'That's one way of making a living. Can you put me down?'

'What do you think, Mr Calvert?'

'I don't think you can.' Not unless he set his helicopter down on top of one of the little houses, that was. 'You winched this sick man up?'

'Yes. And I'd rather not winch you down, if you don't mind. Not in this weather and not without a crewman to help me. Unless you're desperate.'

'Not all that desperate. Would you vouch for them?'

'I'd vouch for them. They're a good bunch. I've met the boss, Tim Hutchinson, an Aussie about the size of a house, several times. Most of the fishermen on the west coast would vouch for them.'

'Fair enough. The next island is Ballara.'

We circled Ballara once. Once was enough. Not even a barnacle would have made his home in Ballara.

We were over the channel between Ballara and Dubh Sgeir now and the Beul nan Uamh was a sight to daunt even the stoutest-hearted fish. It certainly daunted me; five minutes in that lot whether in a boat or scuba suit and that would have been that. The ebb-tide and the wind were in head-on collision and the result was the most spectacular witches' cauldron I'd ever seen. There were no waves as such, just a bubbling swirling seething maelstrom of whirlpools, overfalls and races, running no way and every way, gleaming boiling white in the overfalls and races, dark and smooth and evil in the hearts of the whirlpools. Not a place to take Auntie Gladys out in a row-boat for a gentle paddle in the quiet even fall.

Oddly enough, close in to the east and south coast of Dubh Sgeir, one *could* have taken Auntie Gladys out. In those tidal races between islands a common but not yet clearly understood phenomenon frequently leaves an undisturbed stretch of water close in to one or other of the shores, calm and smooth and flat, a millpond with a sharply outlined boundary between it and the foaming races beyond. So it was here. For almost a mile between the most southerly and easterly headlands of Dubh Sgeir, for a distance of two or three hundred yards out from the shore, the waters were black and still. It was uncanny.

'Sure you really want to land here?' Williams asked.

'Is it tricky?'

'Easy. Helicopters often land on Dubh Sgeir. Not mine – others. It's just that you're likely to get the same reception here as you got on Eilean Oran. There are dozens of privately owned islands off the West Coast and none of them likes uninvited visitors. The owner of Dubh Sgeir hates them.'

'This world-famous Highland hospitality becomes positively embarrassing at times. The Scotsman's home is his castle, eh?'

'There *is* a castle here. The ancestral home of the Clan Dalwhinnie. I think.'

'Dalwhinnie's a town, not a clan.'

'Well, something unpronounceable.' That was good, considering that he like as not hailed from Rhosllanerchrugog or Pontrhydfendgaid. 'He's the clan chief. Lord Kirkside. Ex-Lord Lieutenant of the shire. Very important citizen but a bit of a recluse now. Seldom leaves the place except to attend Highland Games or go south about once a month to flay the Archbishop of Canterbury in the Lords.'

'Must be difficult for him to tell which place he's at, at times. I've heard of him. Used to have a very low opinion of the Commons and made a long speech to that effect every other day.'

'That's him. But not any more. Lost his older son – and his future son-in-law – in an air accident some time ago. Took the heart from the old boy, so they say. People in these parts think the world of him.'

We were round to the south of Dubh Sgeir now and suddenly the castle was in sight. Despite its crenellated battlements, round towers and embrasures, it didn't begin to rank with the Windsors and Balmorals of this world. A pocket castle. But the side had the Windsors and Balmorals whacked to the wide. It grew straight out of the top of a hundred and fifty foot cliff and if you leaned too far out of your bedroom window the first thing to stop your fall would be the rocks a long long way down. You wouldn't even bounce once.

Below the castle and a fair way to the right of it a cliff-fall belonging to some bygone age had created an artificial foreshore some thirty yards wide. From this, obviously at the cost of immense labour, an artificial harbour had been scooped out, the boulders and rubble having been used for the construction of a horseshoe breakwater with an entrance of not more than six or seven yards in width. At the inner end of this harbour a boathouse, no wider than the harbour entrance and less than twenty feet in length, had been constructed against the cliff face. A boathouse to berth a good-sized row-boat, no more.

Williams took his machine up until we were two hundred feet above the castle. It was built in the form of a hollow square with the landward side missing. The seaward side was dominated by two crenellated towers, one topped by a twenty-foot flagpole and flag, the other by an even taller TV mast. Aesthetically, the flagpole had it every time. Surprisingly the island was not as barren as it had appeared from the sea. Beginning some distance from the castle and extending clear to the cliff-bound northern shore of the island ran a two-hundred-yard wide stretch of what seemed to be flat smooth turf, not the bowling green standard but undoubtedly grass of the genuine variety as testified to by the heads down position of a handful of goats that browsed close to the castle. Williams tried to land on the grass but the wind was too strong to allow him to hold position: he finally put down in the eastern lee of the castle, close but not too close to the cliff edge.

I got out, keeping a wary eye on the goats, and was rounding the landward corner of the castle when I almost literally bumped into the girl.

I've always known what to look for in a suddenly-encountered girl in a remote Hebridean Island. A kilt, of course, a Hebridean girl without a kilt was unthinkable, a Shetland two-piece and brown brogues: and that she would be a raven-haired beauty with wild, green, fey eyes went without saying. Her name would be Deirdre. This one wasn't like that at all, except for the eyes, which were neither green nor fey but certainly looked wild enough. What little I could see of them, that was. Her blonde hair was cut in the uniform peekaboo scalloped style of the day, the one where the long side hair meets under the chin and the central fringe is hacked off at eyebrow level, a coiffure which in any wind above Force 1 allows no more than ten per cent of the face to be seen at any one time. Below hair level she wore a horizontally striped blue and white sailor's jersey and faded blue denim pants that must have been fixed on with a portable sewing machine as I didn't see how else she could have got into them. Her tanned feet were bare. It was comforting to see that the civilizing influence of television reached even the remoter outposts of empire.

I said: 'Good afternoon, Miss – um—'

'Engine failure?' she asked coldly.

'Well, no—'

'Mechanical failure? Of any kind? No? Then this is private property. I must ask you to leave. At once, please.'

There seemed to be little for me here. An outstretched hand and a warm smile of welcome and she'd have been on my list of suspects at once. But this was true to established form, the weary stranger at the gates receiving not the palm of the hand but the back of it. Apart from the fact that she lacked a blunderbuss and had a much better figure, she had a great deal in common with Mr MacEachern. I bent forward to peer through the windblown camouflage of blonde hair. She looked as if she had spent most of the night and half the morning down in the castle wine cellars. Pale face, pale lips, dark smudges under the blue-grey eyes. But clear blue-grey eyes.

'What the hell's the matter with you?' she demanded.

'Nothing. The end of a dream. Deirdre would never have talked like that. Where's your old man?'

'My old man?' The one eye I could see had the power

turned up to its maximum shrivelling voltage. 'You mean my father?'

'Sorry. Lord Kirkside.' It was no feat to guess that she was Lord Kirkside's daughter; hired help are too ignorant to have the execrable manners of their aristocratic betters.

'I'm Lord Kirkside.' I turned round to see the owner of the deep voice behind me, a tall rugged-looked character in his fifties, hawk nose, jutting grey eyebrows and moustache, grey tweeds, grey deer-stalker, hawthorn stick in hand. 'What's the trouble, Sue?'

Sue. I might have known. Exit the last vestige of the Hebridean dream. I said: 'My name is Johnson. Air-Sea Rescue. There was a boat, the *Moray Rose*, in bad trouble somewhere south of Skye. If she'd been not under command but still afloat she might have come drifting this way. We wondered—'

'And Sue was going to fling you over the cliff before you had a chance to open your mouth?' He smiled down affectionately at his daughter. 'That's my Sue. I'm afraid she doesn't like newspapermen.'

'Some do and some don't. But why pick on me?'

'When you were twenty-one could you, as the saying goes, tell a newspaperman from a human being? I couldn't. But I can now, a mile away. I can also tell a genuine Air-Sea Rescue helicopter when I see one. And so should you too, young lady. I'm sorry, Mr Johnson, we can't help you. My men and I spent several hours last night patrolling the cliff-tops to see if we could see anything. Lights, flares, anything. Nothing, I'm afraid.'

'Thank you, sir. I wish we had more voluntary co-operation of this kind.' From where I stood I could see, due south, the gently rocking masts of the Oxford field expedition's boat in Little Horseshoe Bay. The boat itself and the tents beyond were hidden behind the rocky eastern arm of the bay. I said to Lord Kirkside: 'But why newspapermen, sir? Dubh Sgeir isn't quite as accessible as Westminster.'

'Indeed, Mr Johnson.' He smiled, not with his eyes. 'You may have heard of – well, of our family tragedy. My elder boy, Jonathan, and John Rollinson – Sue's fiancé.'

I knew what was coming. And after all those months she

had those smudges under her eyes. She must have loved him a lot. I could hardly believe it.

'I'm no newspaperman, sir. Prying isn't my business.' It wasn't my business, it was my life, the *raison d'être* for my existence. But now wasn't the time to tell him.

'The air accident. Jonathan had his own private Beechcraft.' He waved towards the stretch of green turf running to the Northern cliffs. 'He took off from here that morning. They – the reporters – wanted on-the-spot reporting. They came by helicopter and boat – there's a landing stage to the west.' Again the mirthless smile. 'They weren't well received. Care for a drink? You and your pilot?' Lord Kirkside, for all the reputation Williams had given him, seemed to be cast in a different mould from his daughter and Mr Donald MacEachern: on the other hand, as the Archbishop of Canterbury knew to his cost, Lord Kirkside was a very much tougher citizen than either his daughter or Mr MacEachern.

'Thank you, sir. I appreciate that. But we haven't many hours of daylight left.'

'Of course, of course. How thoughtless of me. But you can't have much hope left by this time.'

'Frankly, none. But, well, you know how it is, sir.'

'We'll cross our fingers for that one chance in a million. Good luck, Mr Johnson.' He shook my hand and turned away. His daughter hesitated then held out her hand and smiled. A fluke of the wind had blown the hair off her face, and when she smiled like that, sooty eyes or not, the end of Deirdre and the Hebridean dream didn't seem to be of so much account after all. I went back to the helicopter.

'We're getting low on both fuel and time,' Williams said. 'Another hour or so and we'll have the dark with us. Where now, Mr Calvert?'

'North. Follow this patch of grass – seems it used to be used as a light aircraft runway – out over the edge of the cliff. Take your time.'

So he did, taking his time as I'd asked him, then continued on a northward course for another ten minutes. After we were out of sight of watchers on any of the islands we came round in a great half circle to west and south and east and headed back for home.

III

The sun was down and the world below was more night than day as we came in to land on the sandy cove on the eastern side of the Isle of Torbay. I could just vaguely distinguish the blackness of the tree-clad island, the faint silvery gleam of the sand and the semi-circular whiteness where the jagged reef of rocks fringed the seaward approach to the cove. It looked a very dicey approach indeed to me but Williams was as unworried as a mother at a baby show who has already slipped the judge a five pound note. Well, if he wasn't going to worry, neither was I: I knew nothing about helicopters but I knew enough about men to recognize a superb pilot when I sat beside one. All I had to worry about was that damned walk back through those Stygian woods. One thing, I didn't have to run this time.

Williams reached up his hand to flick on the landing lights but the light came on a fraction of a second before his fingers touched the switch. Not from the helicopter but from the ground. A bright light, a dazzling light, at least a five-inch searchlight located between the high-water line of the cove and the tree-line beyond. For a moment the light wavered, then steadied on the cockpit of the helicopter, making the interior bright as the light from the noon-day sun. I twisted my head to one side to avoid the glare. I saw Williams throw up a hand to protect his eyes, then slump forward wearily, dead in his seat, as the white linen of his shirt turned to red and the centre of his chest disintegrated. I flung myself forwards and downwards to try to gain what illusory shelter I could from the cannonading sub-machine shells shattering the windscreen. The helicopter was out of control, dipping sharply forwards and spinning slowly on its axis. I reached out to grab the controls from the dead man's hands but even as I did the trajectory of the bullets changed, either because the man with the machine-gun had altered his aim or because he'd been caught off-balance by the sudden dipping of the helicopter. An abruptly mad cacophony of sound, the iron clangour of steel-nosed bullets smashing into the engine casing mingled with the banshee ricochet of spent and mangled shells. The engine stopped, stopped as suddenly as if the ignition had been switched off. The helicopter was completely out of control, lifeless in the sky. It wasn't going to be in the sky much longer but there was nothing I could do about it. I braced myself for the jarring moment of impact when we struck the water, and when the impact came it was not just jarring, it was shattering to a degree I would never have anticipated. We'd landed not in the water but on the encircling reef of rocks.

I tried to get at the door but couldn't make it, we'd landed nose down and facing seawards on the outside of the reefs and from the position where I'd been hurled under the instrument panel the door was above and beyond my reach. I was too dazed, too weak, to make any real effort to get at it. Icy water poured in through the smashed windscreen and the fractured floor of the fuselage. For a moment everything was as silent as the grave, the hiss of the flooding waters seemed only to emphasize the silence; then the machine-gun started again. The shells smashed through the lower after part of the fuselage behind me and went out through the top of the windscreen above me. Twice I felt angry tugs on the right shoulder of my coat and I tried to bury my head even more deeply into the freezing waters. Then, due probably to a combination of an accumulation of water in the nose and the effect of the fusillade of bullets aft, the helicopter lurched forwards, stopped momentarily, then slid off the face of the reef and fell like a stone, nose first, to the bottom of the sea.

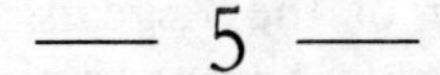

— 5 —

Wednesday: dusk – 8.40 p.m.

AMONG THE more ridiculous and wholly unsubstantiated fictions perpetuated by people who don't know what they are talking about is the particularly half-witted one that death by drowning is peaceful, easy and, in fact, downright pleasant. It's not. It's a terrible way to die. I know, because I was drowning and I didn't like it one little bit. My ballooning head felt as if it were being pumped full of compressed air, my ears and eyes ached savagely, my nostrils, mouth and stomach were full of sea water and my bursting lungs felt as if someone had filled them with petrol and struck a match. Maybe if I opened my mouth, maybe if to relieve that flaming agony that was my lungs I took that one great gasping breath that would be the last I would ever take, maybe then it would be quiet and pleasant and peaceful. On the form to date, I couldn't believe it.

The damned door was jammed. After the beating the fuselage had taken, first of all in smashing into the reef and then into the sea-bed it would be a miracle if it hadn't jammed. I pushed the door, I pulled at it, I beat at it with my clenched fists. It stayed jammed. The blood roared and hissed in my ears, the flaming vice around my chest was crushing my ribs and lungs, crushing the life out of me. I braced both feet on the instrument panel, laid both hands on the door handle. I thrust with my legs and twisted with my hands, using the power and the leverage a man can use only when he knows he is dying. The door handle sheared, the thrust of my legs carried me backwards and upwards toward the after end of the fuselage and suddenly my lungs could take no more. Death couldn't be worse than this agony. The air rushed out through my water-filled mouth and nostrils and I sucked in this one great gasping breath, this lungful of sea-water, this last I would ever take.

It wasn't a lungful of water, it was a lungful of air. Noxious compressed air laden with the fumes of petrol and oil, but air for all that. Not the tangy salt-laden air of the Western Isles, not the wine-laden air of the Ægean, the pine-laden air of Norway or the sparkling champagne air of the high Alps. All those I'd tasted and all of them put together were a thin and anaemic substitute for this marvellous mixture of nitrogen and oxygen and petrol and oil that had been trapped in an air pocket under the undamaged upper rear part of the helicopter's fuselage, the only part of the plane that hadn't been riddled by machine-gun bullets. This was air as it ought to be.

The water level was around my neck. I took half a dozen deep whooping breaths, enough to ease the fire in my lungs and the roaring and hissing and dizziness in my head to tolerable levels, then pushed myself backwards and upwards to the extreme limit of the fuselage. The water was at chest level now. I moved a hand around in the blind darkness to try to estimate the amount of air available to me. Impossible to judge accurately, but enough, I guessed, compressed as it was, to last for ten to fifteen minutes.

I moved across to the left of the fuselage, took a deep breath and pushed myself forwards and downwards. Eight feet behind the pilot's seat was the passenger door, maybe I could force that. I found it right away, not the door but the opening where the door had been. The impact that had jammed the door on the righthand side where I'd been had burst this door open. I pushed myself back to the upper part of the fuselage again and helped myself to a few more deep breaths of that compressed air. It didn't taste quite so good as it had done the first time.

Now that I knew I could go at any time, I was in no hurry to leave. Up above, guns in hand, those men would be waiting and if there was one outstanding attribute that characterized their attitude to work on hand, it was a single-minded thoroughness. Where those lads were concerned, a job half done was no job at all. They could only have come there by boat and that boat would have been very nearby. By this time it would be even nearer by; it would be sitting directly over the spot where the helicopter had gone down and the crew wouldn't be sitting around with drinks in their hands congratulating themselves on their success, they'd be lining the side with searchlights or flashes and waiting to see if anyone would break surface. With their guns in their hands.

If I ever got back to the *Firecrest* again, if I ever got in touch with Uncle Arthur again, I wondered dully what I would say to him. Already I'd lost the *Nantesville*, already I'd been responsible for the deaths of Baker and Delmont, already I'd given away to the unknown enemy the secret of my identity – if that hadn't been obvious after the fake customs officers had smashed our transmitter it was bitterly obvious now – and now I'd lost Lieutenant Scott Williams his life and the Navy a valuable helicopter. Of Uncle Arthur's forty-eight hours only twelve were left now, and nothing could be more certain than when Uncle Arthur had finished with me, I wouldn't be allowed even those twelve hours. After Uncle Arthur had finished with me my days as an investigator would be finished, and finished for ever; with the kind of references he'd give me I wouldn't even qualify as a store detective in a street barrow. Not that it would make any difference what Uncle Arthur thought now. Baker and Delmont and Williams were gone. There was a heavy debt that had to be paid and the matter was out of Uncle Arthur's hands now. On the form to date, I thought bleakly, there wasn't one bookmaker in the land who would have given odds of one in a thousand of that debt ever being repaid. Only a fool bets against a certainty.

I wondered vaguely how long the men up top would wait – my conviction that they would be waiting was absolute. And then I felt a dry salty taste in my mouth that had nothing to do with the steadily deteriorating quality of air. It was pretty foul by this time, but a man can survive a surprisingly long time in foul air and there was enough oxygen left in that heavily tainted atmosphere to last me for a good few minutes yet.

The question was not how long they would wait but how long I could wait. Or had I already waited too long? I could feel the panic in my throat like some solid lump in my windpipe completely obstructing my breathing and had to make a conscious physical effort to force it down.

I tried to recall all I could from my marine salvage days. How long had I been under water and how deep down was I? How long had that dive down from the surface of the sea to the bottom taken?

Under those conditions time loses all meaning. Say forty seconds. Just over half-way down I'd taken my last gulp of air before the water in the fuselage had flooded over my head. And then a minute, probably a minute and a half, fighting with that jammed door. Since then a minute to recover, half a minute to locate that open door, and then how long since? Six minutes, seven? Not less than seven. I couldn't reckon on a total of less than ten minutes. The lump was back in my throat again.

How deep was I? That was the life-or-death question. I could tell from the pressure that I was pretty deep. But how deep? Ten fathoms? Fifteen? Twenty? I tried to recall the chart of Torbay Sound. There were eighty fathoms in the deepest channel and the channel was pretty close to the southern shore at this point, so that the water was steep-to. God above, I might even be in twenty-five fathoms. If I was, well, that was it. Finish. How did the decompression tables go again? At thirty fathoms a man who has been under water for ten minutes requires to spend eighteen minutes for decompression stops on the way up. When you breathe air under pressure, the excess nitrogen is stored in the tissues: when you begin to surface this nitrogen is carried by the blood-stream to the lungs and is eliminated in respiration: and if you rise too rapidly respiration can't cope with it and nitrogen bubbles form in the blood, causing the agonizing and crippling diver's bends. Even at twenty fathoms I'd require a six-minute halt for decompression on the way up and if there was one certain fact in life it was that decompression stops were out for me. I'd be a broken man. What I did know for certain was that every additional second I remained there would make the bends all the more agonizing and crippling when they finally struck. All at once the prospect of surfacing beneath the steady guns and the pitiless eyes of the men above seemed positively attractive compared to the alternative. I took several deep breaths to get as much oxygen as possible into my blood-stream, exhaled to the fullest extent, took a long final breath to fill every last cubic millimetre in every last nook and cranny in my lungs, dived under the water, pushed my way out through the doorway and made for the surface.

I'd lost count of time on the way down and I now lost all count of time on the way up. I swam slowly and steadily using enough power to assist my progress through the water, but not so much as prematurely to use up all the stored oxygen. Every few seconds I let a little air escape from my mouth, not much, just enough to ease the pressure in my lungs. I looked up but the waters above me were as black as ink, there could have been fifty fathoms above my head for any trace of light I could see. And then suddenly, quite some time before the air supply was exhausted and before my lungs had begun to hurt again, the water was a shade less than pitch black and my head struck something hard and unyielding. I grabbed it, held on, surfaced, sucked in some lungfuls of that cold, salt, wonderful air and waited for the decompression pains to start, those sharply agonizing twinges in the joints of the limbs. But none came. I couldn't have been more than fifteen fathoms down and even then I should have felt something. It had probably been something nearer ten.

During the past ten minutes my mind had taken as much a beating as any other part of me but it would have to have been in very much poorer shape than it was for me not to recognize what I was clinging to. A boat's rudder, and if any confirmation had been required the milkily phosphorescent water being turned up by the two slowly turning screws a couple of feet ahead of me would have been all that was required. I'd surfaced right under their boat. I was lucky. I might have surfaced right under one of their propellers and had my head cut in half. Even now, if the man at the wheel suddenly decided to go astern I'd be sucked into the vortex of one or other of the screws and end up like something that had passed through a turnip-cutting machine. But I'd been through too much to cross any bridges before I came to them.

Off to port I could see, sharply illuminated by a couple of powerful lights from the boat's deck, the reef where we'd crashed. We were about forty yards away and, relative to the reefs, stationary in the water, the engines turning just enough to maintain the boat's position against the effect of wind and tide. Now and again a searchlight patrolled the dark waters all around. I couldn't see anything of the men on deck, but I didn't have to be told what they were doing; they were waiting and watching and the safety catches would be off. Nor could I see anything of the boat itself but I made up my mind that, even though I couldn't recognize it, I'd know it if I ever came across it again. I took out the knife from the sheath behind my neck and cut a deep vee notch in the trailing edge of the rudder.

For the first time, I heard voices. I heard four voices and I had no difficulty in the world in identifying any of them. If I lived to make Methuselah look a teenager I'd never forget any one of them.

'Nothing on your side, Quinn?' Captain Imrie, the man who had organized the manhunt for me aboard the *Nantesville*.

'Nothing on my side, captain.' I could feel the hairs rise on the nape of my neck. Quinn. Durran. The bogus customs officer. The man who had almost, but not quite, strangled me to death.

'Your side, Jacques?' Captain Imrie again.

'Nothing, sir.' The machine-pistol specialist. 'Eight minutes since we've been here, fifteen since they went under. A man would require pretty good lungs to stay down that long, captain.'

'Enough,' Imrie said. 'There'll be a bonus for all of us for this night's work. Kramer?'

'Captain Imrie?' A voice as guttural as Imrie's own.

'Full ahead. Up the Sound.'

I thrust myself backwards and dived deep. The waters above my head boiled into turbulent, phosphorescent life. I stayed deep, maybe ten feet down, heading for the reef. How long I swam like that, I don't know. Certainly less than a minute; my lungs weren't what they used to be, not even what they had been fifteen minutes ago: but when I was forced to the surface, I'd my dark oilskin over my head.

I needn't have bothered. I could see the faintly shimmering outline of the disappearing wake, no more. The searchlights were extinguished; when Captain Imrie decided a job was finished, then that job was finished. Predictably, the boat was in complete darkness with neither interior nor navigation lights showing.

I turned and swam slowly towards the reef. I reached a rock and clung to it until a measure of strength returned to my aching muscles, to my exhausted body. I would not have believed that fifteen minutes could have taken so much out of a man. I stayed there for five minutes. I could have stayed there for an hour. But time was not on my side. I slipped into deep water again and made for the shore.

II

Three times I tried and three times I failed to pull myself up from the rubber dinghy over the gunwale of the *Firecrest*. Four feet, no more. Just four feet. A Matterhorn. A ten-year-old could have done it. But not Calvert. Calvert was an old, old man.

I called out for Hunslett, but Hunslett did not come. Three times I called, but he did not come. The *Firecrest* was dark and still and lifeless. Where the hell was he? Asleep? Ashore? No, not ashore, he'd promised to stay aboard in case word came through at any time from Uncle Arthur. Asleep, then, asleep in his cabin. I felt the blind unreasoning anger rise. This was too much, after what I had been through this was too much. Asleep. I shouted at the top of my voice and hammered feebly on the steel hull with the butt of my Luger. But he didn't come.

The fourth time I made it. It was touch and go, but I made it. For a few seconds, dinghy painter in hand, I teetered on my stomach on the edge of the gunwale then managed to drag myself aboard. I secured the painter and went in search of Hunslett. There were words I wished to have with Hunslett.

I never used them. He wasn't aboard. I searched the *Firecrest* from forepeak to the after storage locker, but no Hunslett. No signs of a hasty departure, no remnants of a meal on the saloon table or unwashed dishes in the galley, no signs of any struggle, everything neat and in good order. Everything as it ought to have been. Except that there was no Hunslett.

For a minute or two I sat slumped on the saloon settee trying to figure out a reason for his absence, but only for a minute or two. I was in no condition to figure out anything. Wearily I made my way out to the upper deck and brought dinghy and outboard over the side. No fancy tricks about securing them to the anchor chain this time: apart from the fact that it was, the way I felt, physically impossible, the time for that was past. I deflated the dinghy and stowed it, along with the outboard, in the after locker. And if someone came aboard and started looking? If someone came aboard and started looking he'd get a bullet through him. I didn't care if he claimed to be a police superintendent or an assistant commissioner or the top customs official in the country, he'd get a bullet through him, in the arm or leg, say, and I'd listen to his explanations afterwards. If it was one of my friends, one of my friends from *Nantesville* or the reef back there, he got it through the head.

I went below. I felt sick. The helicopter was at the bottom of the sea. The pilot was down there with it, half his chest shot away by machine-gun bullets. I'd every right to feel sick. I stripped off my clothes and towelled myself dry and the very action of towelling seemed to drain away what little strength was left to me. Sure I'd had a hard time in the last hour, all this running and slipping and stumbling through the dark woods, locating and blowing up the dinghy and dragging it over those damned seaweed covered boulders had taken it out of me, but I was supposed to be fit, it shouldn't have left me like this. I was sick, but the sickness was in the heart and mind, not in the body.

I went into my cabin and laboriously dressed myself in fresh clothes, not forgetting the Paisley scarf. The rainbow coloured bruises that Quinn had left on my neck had now swollen and spread to such an extent that I had to bring the scarf right up to the lobes of my ears to hide them. I looked in the mirror. It might have been my grandfather staring back at me. My grandfather on his deathbed. My face had that drawn and waxy look that one normally associated with approaching dissolution. Not an all-over waxiness though; there was no blood on my face now but the pine needles had left their mark. I looked like someone with galloping impetigo. I felt like someone with galloping bubonic plague.

I checked that the Luger and the little Lilliput – I'd put them both back in their waterproof covering after leaving Dubh Sgeir – were still in working order. They were. In the saloon I poured myself a stiff three fingers of whisky. It went down my throat like a ferret down a burrow after a rabbit, one moment there, the next vanished in the depths. The weary old red corpuscles hoisted themselves to their feet and started trudging around again. It seemed a reasonable assumption that if I encouraged them with more of the same treatment they might even break into a slow gallop and I had just closed my hand around the bottle when I heard the sound of an approaching engine. I put the bottle back in the rack, switched out the saloon lights – although they would have been invisible from outside through the velvet curtains – and took up position behind the open saloon door.

I was pretty sure the precautions were unnecessary; ten to one this was Hunslett coming back from shore, but why hadn't he taken the dinghy, still slung on the davits aft? Probably someone, for what Hunslett had regarded as an excellent reason, had persuaded him to go ashore and was now bringing him back.

The motor-boat's engine slowed, went into neutral, astern, then neutral again. A slight bump, the murmur of voices, the sound of someone clambering aboard and then the engine opening up again.

The footfalls passed over my head as the visitor – there was only one set of footfalls – made his way towards the wheelhouse door. The springy confident step of a man who knew what he was about. There was only one thing wrong with that springy confident step. It didn't belong to Hunslett. I flattened myself against the bulkhead, took out the Luger, slid off the safety catch and prepared to receive my visitor in what I had now come to regard as the best traditions of the Highlands.

I heard the click as the wheelhouse door opened, the louder click as it was shut by a firm hand. A pool of light from a flashlamp preceded the visitor down the four steps from the wheelhouse to the saloon. He paused at the foot of the steps and the light moved away as he made to locate the light-switch. I stepped round the door and did three things at once – I hooked an arm around his neck, brought up a far from gentle knee into the small of his back and ground the muzzle of the Luger into his right ear. Violent stuff, but not unnecessarily violent stuff: it might have been my old friend Quinn. The gasp of pain was enough to show that it wasn't.

'This isn't a hearing aid you feel, friend. It's a Luger pistol. You're one pound pressure from a better world. Don't make me nervous.'

The better world seemed to have no appeal for him. He didn't make me nervous. He made an odd gurgling noise in his throat, he was trying either to speak or breathe, but he stood motionless, head and back arched. I eased the pressure a little.

'Put that light switch on with your left hand. Slowly. Carefully.'

He was very slow, very careful. The saloon flooded with light.

'Raise your hands above your head. As high as you can reach.'

He was a model prisoner, this one, he did exactly as he was told. I turned him round, propelled him into the centre of the room and told him to face me.

He was of medium height, nattily dressed in an astrakhan coat and a fur Cossack hat. He had a beautifully trimmed white beard and moustache, with a perfectly symmetrical black streak in the centre of the beard, the only one of its kind I had ever seen. The tanned face was red, either from anger or near-suffocation. From both, I decided. He lowered his hands without permission, sat on the settee, pulled out a monocle, screwed it into his right eye and stared at me with cold fury. I gave him look for look, stare for stare, pocketed the Luger, poured a whisky and handed it to Uncle Arthur. Rear-Admiral Sir Arthur Arnford-Jason, K.C.B. and all the rest of the alphabet.

'You should have knocked, sir,' I said reproachfully.

'I should have knocked.' His voice sounded half-strangled, maybe I had exerted more pressure than had been necessary. 'Do you always greet your guests this way?'

'I don't have guests, sir. I don't have friends, either. Not in the Western Isles. All I have is enemies. Anyone who comes through that door is an enemy. I didn't expect to see you here, sir.'

'I hope not. In view of that performance, I hope not.' He rubbed his throat, drank some whisky and coughed. 'Didn't expect to be here myself. Do you know how much bullion was aboard the *Nantesville*?'

'Close on a million, I understand.'

'That's what I understood. Eight millions! Think of it, eight million pounds' worth. All this gold that's being shovelled back from Europe into the vaults at Fort Knox usually goes in small lots, 108 lb. ingots at a time. For safety. For security. In case anything goes wrong. But the Bank knew that nothing could go wrong this time, they knew our agents were aboard, they were behind with their payments, so they cleverly loaded fourteen hundred and forty ingots without telling anyone. Eight million. The Bank is hopping mad. And everyone is taking it out on me.'

And he'd come up here to take it out on me. I said: 'You should have let me know. That you were coming.'

'I tried to. You failed to keep your noon-day schedule. The most elementary of crimes, Calvert, and the most serious. You failed to keep a schedule. You or Hunslett. Then I knew things were going from bad to worse. I knew I had to take over myself. So I came by plane and RAF rescue launch.' That would have been the high-speed launch I'd seen taking a bad battering in the Sound as we had headed down towards the cove. 'Where's Hunslett?'

'I don't know, sir.'

'You don't know?' He was using his quiet unemphatic tone, the one I didn't care for very much. 'You're out of your depth in this one, Calvert, aren't you?'

'Yes, sir. I'm afraid he's been removed by force. I'm not sure how. What have you been doing in the past two hours, sir?'

'Explain yourself.' I wished he'd stop screwing that damned monocle into his eye. It was no affectation, that monocle, he was nearly blind on that side, but it was an irritating mannerism. At that moment, anything would have irritated me.

'That RAF launch that dropped you off here just now. It should have been here at least two hours ago. Why didn't you come aboard then?'

'I did. We almost ran the *Firecrest* down in the darkness as we came round the headland. No one here. So I went and had some dinner. Nothing but baked beans aboard this damned boat as far as I could see.'

'The Columbia hotel wouldn't offer you much more. Toast below the beans, if you were lucky.' The Columbia was Torbay's only hotel.

'I had smoked trout, filet mignon and an excellent bottle of hock. I dined aboard the *Shangri-la*.' This with the slight hint of a smile. Uncle Arthur's Achilles' heel was showing again: Uncle Arthur loved a lord like nobody's business, and a knight with a seven-figure income was as good as a lord any day.

'The *Shangri-la*?' I stared at him, then remembered. 'Of course. You told me. You know Lady Skouras well. No, you said you knew her very well and her husband well. How is my old Sir Anthony?'

'Very well,' he said coldly. Uncle Arthur had as much humour as the next man, but discussing titled millionaires in tones of levity was not humorous.

'And Lady Skouras?'

He hesitated. 'Well—'

'Not so well. Pale, drawn, unhappy, with dark smudges under her eyes. Not unlike myself. Her husband mistreats her and mistreats her badly. Mentally and physically. He humiliated her in front of a group of men last night. And she had rope burns on her arms. Why would she have rope burns on her arms, Sir Arthur?'

'Impossible. Quite fantastic. I knew the former Lady Skouras, the one who died this year in hospital. She—'

'She was undergoing treatment in a mental hospital. Skouras as good as told me.'

'No matter. She adored him. He adored her. A man can't change like that. Sir Anthony – Sir Anthony's a gentleman.'

'Is he? Tell me how he made his last millions. You saw Lady Skouras, didn't you?'

'I saw her,' he said slowly. 'She was late. She arrived with the filet mignon.' He didn't seem to find anything funny in that. 'She didn't look very well and she'd a bruise on her right temple. She'd fallen climbing aboard from the tender and hit her head against a guard-rail.'

'Hit her head against her husband's fist, more like. To get back to the first time you boarded the *Firecrest* this evening. Did you search it?'

'I searched it. All except the after cabin. It was locked. I assumed there was something in there you didn't want chance callers to see.'

'There was something in there that callers, not chance, didn't want *you* to see,' I said slowly. 'Hunslett. Hunslett under guard. They were waiting for word of my death, then they'd have killed Hunslett or kept him prisoner. If word came through that I hadn't been killed, then they'd have waited until my return and taken me prisoner too. Or killed us both. For by then they would have known that I knew too much to be allowed to live. It takes time, a long time, to open up a strong-room and get all those tons of gold out and they know their time is running out. They're desperate now. But they still think of everything.'

'They were waiting for word of your death,' Uncle Arthur said mechanically. 'I don't understand.'

'That helicopter you laid on for me, sir. We were shot down tonight after sunset. The pilot's dead and the machine is at the bottom of the sea. They believe me to be dead also.'

'I see. You go from strength to strength, Calvert.' The absence of reaction was almost total, maybe he was getting punch-drunk by this time; more likely he was considering the precise phraseology that would return me to the ranks of the unemployed with economy and despatch. He lit a long, thin and very black cheroot and puffed meditatively. 'When we get back to London remind me to show you my confidential report on you.'

'Yes, sir.' So this was how it was coming.

'I was having dinner with the Under-Secretary just forty-eight hours ago. One of the things he asked me was which country had the best agents in Europe. Told him I'd no idea. But I told him who I thought, on the balance of probabilities, was the best agent in Europe. Philip Calvert.'

'That was very kind of you, sir.' If I could remove that beard, whisky, cheroot and monocle, at least three of which were obscuring his face at any given moment, his expression might have given me some faint clue as to what was going on in that devious mind. 'You were going to fire me thirty-six hours ago.'

'If you believe that,' Uncle Arthur said calmly, 'you'll believe anything.' He puffed out a cloud of foul smoke and went on: 'One of the comments in your report states: "Unsuitable for routine investigation. Loses interest and becomes easily bored. Operates at his best only under extreme pressure. At this level he is unique." It's on the files, Calvert. I don't cut off my right hand.'

'No, sir. Do you know what you are, sir?'

'A Machiavellian old devil,' Uncle Arthur said with some satisfaction. 'You know what's going on?'

'Yes, sir.'

'Pour me another whisky, my boy, a large one, and tell me what's happened, what you know and what you think you know.'

So I poured him another whisky, a large one, and told him what had happened, what I knew and as much of what I thought I knew as seemed advisable to tell him.

III

He heard me out, then said: 'Loch Houron, you think?'

'Loch Houron it must be. I spoke to no one else, anywhere else, and to the best of my knowledge no one else saw me. Someone recognized me. Or someone transmitted my description. By radio. It must have been by radio. The boat that was waiting for Williams and myself came from Torbay or somewhere near Torbay, a boat from Loch Houron could never have made it to the eastern end of the Sound of Torbay in five times the time we took. Somewhere near here, on land or sea, is a transceiver set. Somewhere out on Loch Houron there's another.'

'This University expedition boat you saw on the south shore of Loch Houron. This alleged University expedition. It would have a radio transmitter aboard.'

'No, sir. Boys with beards.' I rose, pulled back the saloon curtains on both sides, then sat down again. 'I told you their boat was damaged and listing. She'd been riding moored fore and aft in plenty of water. They didn't hole it themselves and it wasn't holed by any act of nature. Somebody kindly obliged. Another of those odd little boating incidents that occur with such profusion up and down the west coast.'

'Why did you pull those curtains back?'

'Another of those odd little boating incidents, sir. One that's about to happen. Some time tonight people will be coming aboard. Hunslett and I, those people think, are dead. At least, I'm dead and Hunslett is dead or a prisoner. But they can't leave an abandoned *Firecrest* at anchor to excite suspicion and invite investigation. So they'll come in a boat, up anchor, and take the *Firecrest* out into the Sound, followed by their own boat. Once there, they'll slice through the flexible salt-water cooling intake, open the salt-water cock, take to their own boat and lift their hats as the *Firecrest* goes down to join the helicopter. As far as the big wide innocent world is concerned, Hunslett and I will just have sailed off into the sunset.'

'And the gulfs will have washed you down,' Uncle Arthur nodded. 'You are very sure of this, Calvert?'

'You might say I'm absolutely certain.'

'Then why open those blasted curtains?'

'The scuttling party may be coming from anywhere and they may not come for hours. The best time to scuttle a boat in close waters is at slack tide, when you can be sure that it will settle exactly where you want it to settle, and slack tide is not until one o'clock this morning. But if someone comes panting hotfoot aboard soon after those curtains are opened, then that will be proof enough that the radio transmitter we're after, and our friends who are working the transmitter, are somewhere in this bay, ashore or afloat.'

'How will it be proof?' Uncle Arthur said irritably. 'Why should they come, as you say, panting hotfoot?'

'They know they have Hunslett. At least, I assume they have, I can't think of any other reason for his absence. They think they know I'm dead, but they can't be sure. Then they see the beckoning oil lamp in the window. What is this, they say to themselves, Calvert back from the dead? Or a third, or maybe even a third and a fourth colleague of Calvert and Hunslett that we wot not of? Whether it's me or my friends, they must be silenced. And silenced at once. Wouldn't you come panting hotfoot?'

'There's no need to treat the matter with levity,' Uncle Arthur complained.

'In your own words, sir, if you can believe that, you can believe anything.'

'You should have consulted me first, Calvert.' Uncle Arthur shifted in his seat, an almost imperceptible motion, though his expression didn't change. He was a brilliant administrator, but the more executive side of the business, the sand-bagging and pushing of people off high cliffs, wasn't exactly in his line. 'I've told you that I came to take charge.'

'Sorry, Sir Arthur. You'd better change that report, hadn't you? The bit about the best in Europe, I mean.'

'*Touché, touché, touché,*' he grumbled. 'And they're coming at us out of the dark, is that it? On their way now. Armed men. Killers. Shouldn't we – shouldn't we be preparing to defend ourselves? Dammit, man, I haven't even got a gun.'

'You won't need one. You may not agree with me.' I handed him the Luger. He took it, checked the indicator and that the safety catch moved easily, then sat there holding it awkwardly in his hand.

'Shouldn't we move, Calvert? We're sitting targets here.'

'They won't be here for some time. The nearest house or boat is a mile away to the east. They'll be pushing wind and tide and they daren't use a motor. Whether they're rowing a boat or paddling a rubber dinghy they have a long haul ahead of them. Time's short, sir. We have a lot to do tonight. To get back to Loch Houron. The expedition's out, they couldn't pirate a dinghy, far less five ocean-going freighters. Our friend Donald MacEachern acts in a highly suspicious fashion, he's got the facilities there, he's dead worried and he might have had half a dozen guns at his back while he had his in my front. But it was all too good to be true, professionals wouldn't lay it on the line like that.'

'Maybe that's how professionals would expect a fellow-professional to react. And you said he's worried.'

'Maybe the fish aren't biting. Maybe he's involved, but not directly. Then there's the shark-fishers. They have the boats, the facilities and, heaven knows, they're tough enough. Against that, they've been based there for years, the place is littered with sharks – it should be easy enough to check if regular consignments of liver oil are sent to the mainland – and they're well known and well thought of along the coast. They'll bear investigating. Then there's Dubh Sgeir. Lord Kirkside and his lovely daughter Sue.'

'Lady Susan,' Uncle Arthur said. It's difficult to invest an impersonal, inflectionless voice with cool reproach, but he managed it without any trouble. 'I know Lord Kirkside, of course' – his tone implied that it would be remarkable if he didn't – 'and while I may or may not be right about Sir Anthony, and I will lay you a hundred to one, in pounds, that I am, I'm convinced that Lord Kirkside is wholly incapable of any dishonest or illegal action.'

'Me, too. He's a very tough citizen, I'd say, but on the side of the angels.'

'And his daughter? I haven't met her.'

'Very much a girl of today. Dressed in the modern idiom, speaks in the modern idiom, I'm tough and I'm competent and I can take care of myself, thank you. She's not tough at all, just a nice old-fashioned girl in new-fashioned clothes.'

'So that clears them.' Uncle Arthur sounded relieved. 'That leaves us the expedition, in spite of your sneers, or MacEachern's place, or the shark-fishers. I go for the shark-fishers myself.'

I let him go for wherever he wanted to. I thought it was time I went to the upper deck and told him so.

'It won't be long now?'

'I shouldn't think so, sir. We'll put out the lights in the saloon here – it would look very odd if they peered in the windows and saw no one here. We'll put on the two sleeping-cabin lights and the stern light. That will destroy their nightsight. The after deck will be bathed in light. For'ard of that, as far as they are concerned, it will be pitch dark. We hide in the desk.'

'Where in the dark?' Uncle Arthur didn't sound very confident.

'You stand inside the wheelhouse. All wheelhouse doors are hinged for'ard and open outwards. Keep your hand on the inside handle. Lightly. When you feel it begin to turn, a very slow and stealthy turn, you can bet your boots, wait till the door gives a fraction, then kick the rear edge, just below the handle, with the sole of your right foot and with all the weight you have. If you don't break his nose or knock him overboard you'll at least set him in line for a set of false teeth. I'll take care of the other or others.'

'How?'

'I'll be on the saloon roof. It's three feet lower than the loom of the stern light even if they approach from the wheelhouse so they can't see me silhouetted against the loom of the stern light even if they approach from the bows.'

'But what are you going to do?'

'Clobber him or them. A nice big Stilson from the engine-room with a rag round it will do nicely.'

'Why don't we just dazzle them with torches and tell them to put their hands up?' Uncle Arthur clearly didn't care for my proposed *modus operandi.*

'Three reasons. These are dangerous and deadly men and you never give them warning. Not the true sporting spirit, but it helps you survive. Then there will almost certainly be night-glasses trained on the *Firecrest* at this very moment. Finally, sound carries very clearly over water and the wind is blowing towards Torbay. Shots, I mean.'

He said no more. We took up position and waited. It was still raining heavily with the wind still from the west. For once the rain didn't bother me, I'd a full set of oilskins on. I just lay there, spread-eagled on the saloon coach-roof, occasionally easing the fingers of my hands, the right round the Stilson, the left round the little knife. After fifteen minutes they came. I heard the gentle scuff of rubber on our starboard side – the side of the wheelhouse door. I pulled on the cord which passed through the rear window of the wheelhouse. The cord was attached to Uncle Arthur's hand.

There were only two of them. My eyes were perfectly tuned to the dark by this time and I could easily distinguish the shape of the first man coming aboard just below where I lay. He secured a painter and waited for his mate. They moved forward together.

The leading man gave a cough of agony as the door smashed, fair and square, as we later established, into his face. I wasn't so successful; the second man had cat-like reactions and had started to drop to the deck as the Stilson came down. I caught him on the back or shoulder, I didn't know which, and dropped on top of him. In one of his hands he'd have either a gun or knife and if I'd wasted a fraction of a second trying to find out which hand and what he had in it, I'd have been a dead man. I brought down my left hand and he lay still.

I passed the other man lying moaning in agony in the scuppers, brushed by Uncle Arthur, pulled the saloon curtains to and switched on the lights. I then went out, half-pulled, half-lifted the moaning man through the wheelhouse door, down the saloon steps and dropped him on the carpet. I didn't recognize him. That wasn't surprising, his own mother or wife wouldn't have recognized him. Uncle Arthur was certainly a man who believed in working with a will and he'd left the plastic surgeon a very tricky job.

'Keep your gun on him, sir,' I said. Uncle Arthur was looking down at his handiwork with a slightly dazed expression. What one could see of his face behind the beard seemed slightly paler than normal. 'If he breathes, kill him.'

'But – but look at his face, man. We can't leave—'

'You look at this, sir.' I stooped and picked up the weapon that had fallen from the man's hand as I'd dropped him to the floor. 'This is what is technically known to the United States' police departments as a whippet. A shot-gun with two-thirds of the barrel and two-thirds of the stock sawn off. If he'd got you first, you wouldn't have any face left at all. I mean that literally. Do you still feel like playing Florence Nightingale to the fallen hero?' That wasn't at all the way one should talk to Uncle Arthur, there would be a few more entries in the confidential report when we got back. If we got back. But I couldn't help myself, not then. I passed by Uncle Arthur and went out.

In the wheelhouse I picked up a small torch, went outside and shone it down into the water, hooding it with my hand so that the beam couldn't have been seen fifty yards away. They had a rubber dinghy, all right – and an outboard motor attached. The conquering heroes, bathed in that warm and noble glow of satisfaction that comes from the comforting realization of a worthwhile job well done, had intended to make it home the easy way.

Looping a heaving line round the outboard's cylinder head and hauling alternately on the heaving line and painter, I had both dinghy and outboard up and over in two minutes. I unclamped the outboard, lugged the dinghy round to the other side of the superstructure, the side remote from the inner harbour, and examined it carefully in the light of the torch. Apart from the manufacturer's name there was no mark on it, nothing to indicate to which craft it belonged. I sliced it to ribbons and threw it over the side.

Back in the wheelhouse, I cut a twenty-foot length from a roll of PVC electric wiring cable, went outside again and lashed the outboard to the dead man's ankles. I searched his pockets. Nothing, I'd known there would be nothing, I was dealing with professionals. I hooded the torch and looked at his face. I'd never seen him before. I took from him the pistol still clutched in his right hand, undid the spring clips holding the guard-chains in place above the gunwale slots for our companion-way ladder, then eased, first the outboard, and then the man, over the side. They vanished into the dark waters of Torbay harbour without the whisper of a splash. I went inside, closing wheelhouse and saloon doors behind me.

Uncle Arthur and the injured man had reversed positions by this time. The man was on his feet now, leaning drunkenly against the bulkhead, dabbing his face with a blood-stained towel Uncle Arthur must have found, and moaning from time to time. I didn't blame him; if I'd a broken nose, most of my front teeth displaced and a jaw that might or might not have been fractured, I'd have been moaning too. Uncle Arthur, gun in one hand and some of my Scotch in the other, was sitting on the settee and contemplating his bloody handiwork with an odd mixture of satisfaction and distaste. He looked at me as I came in, nodded towards the prisoner.

'Making a fearful mess of the carpet,' he complained. 'What do we do with him?'

'Hand him over to the police.'

'The police? You had your reservations about the police. I thought.'

'Reservations is hardly the word. We have to make the break some time.'

'Our friend outside, as well?'

'Who?'

'This fellow's – ah – accomplice.'

'I threw him over the side.'

Uncle Arthur made the mess on the carpet even worse. He spilt whisky all over it. He said: 'You what?'

'There's no worry.' I pointed downwards. 'Twenty fathoms and thirty pounds of metal attached to his ankles.'

'At – at the bottom of the sea?'

'What did you expect me to do with him? Give him a state funeral? I'm sorry, I didn't tell you, he was dead. I had to kill him.'

'Had to? Had to?' He seemed upset. 'Why, Calvert?'

'There's no "why." There's no justification needed. I killed him or he killed me, and then you, and now we'd both be where he is. Do you have to justify killing men who have murdered at least three times, probably oftener? And if that particular character wasn't a murderer, he came tonight to murder. I killed him with as little thought and compunction and remorse as I'd have tramped on a black widow spider.'

'But you can't go around acting like a public executioner.'

'I can and I will. As long as it's a choice between them and me.'

'You're right, you're right.' He sighed. 'I must confess that reading your reports of an operation is quite different from being with you on one. But I must also confess that it's rather comforting having you around at times like this. Well, let's put this man in cells.'

'I'd like to go to the *Shangri-la* first, sir. To look for Hunslett.'

'I see. To look for Hunslett. Has it occurred to you, Calvert, that if they are hostile to us, as you admit is possible, that they may not let you look for Hunslett?'

'Yes, sir. It's not my intention to go through the *Shangri-la*, a gun in each hand, searching for him. I wouldn't get five feet. I'm just going to ask for him, if anyone has seen him. Assuming they really are the bandits, don't you think it might be most instructive, sir, to observe their reactions when they see a dead man walking aboard, especially a dead man coming alongside from a boat to which they'd shortly beforehand dispatched a couple of killers? And don't you think it will become more and more instructive to watch them as time passes by with no sign of First and Second Murderers entering left?'

'Assuming they are the bandits, of course.'

'I'll know before we say goodbye to them.'

'And how do we account for our knowing one another?'

'If they're white as the driven snow, we don't have to account to them. If they're not, they won't believe a damned word either of us say anyway.'

I collected the roll of flex from the wheelhouse and led our prisoner to the cabin. I told him to sit down with his back to one of the bulkhead generators and he did. Resistance was the last thought in his mind. I passed a few turns of flex round his waist and secured him to the generator: his feet I secured to one of the stanchions. His hands I left free. He could move, he could use the towel and the bucket of cold fresh water I left to administer first aid to himself whenever he felt like it. But he was beyond reach of any glass or sharp instrument with which he could either free himself or do himself in. On the latter score I wasn't really worried one way or another.

I started the engines, weighed anchor, switched on the navigation lights and headed for the *Shangri-la*. Quite suddenly, I wasn't tired any more.

— 6 —

Wednesday: 8.40 p.m. – 10.40 p.m.

LESS THAN two hundred yards from the *Shangri-la* the anchor clattered down into fifteen fathoms of water. I switched off the navigation lights, switched on all the wheelhouse lights, passed into the saloon and closed the door behind me.

'How long do we sit here?' Uncle Arthur asked.

'Not long. Better get into your oilskins now, sir. Next really heavy shower of rain and we'll go.'

'They'll have had their night-glasses on us all the way across the bay, you think?'

'No question of that. They'll still have the glasses on us. They'll be worried stiff, wondering what the hell has gone wrong, what's happened to the two little playmates they sent to interview us. *If* they are the bandits.'

'They're bound to investigate again.'

'Not yet. Not for an hour or two. They'll wait for their two friends to turn up. They may think that it took them longer than expected to reach the *Firecrest* and that we'd upped anchor and left before they got there. Or they may think they'd trouble with their dinghy.' I heard the sudden drumming of heavy rain on the coach-roof. 'It's time to go.'

We left by the galley door, felt our way aft, quietly lowered the dinghy into the water and climbed down the transom ladder into it. I cast off. Wind and tide carried us in towards the harbour. Through the driving rain we could dimly see the *Shangri-la*'s riding light as we drifted by about a hundred yards from her port side. Half-way between the *Shangri-la* and the shore I started up the outboard motor and made back towards the *Shangri-la*.

The big tender was riding at the outer end of a boom which stretched out from the *Shangri-la*'s starboard side about ten feet for'ard of the bridge. The stern of the tender was about fifteen out from the illuminated gangway. I approached from astern, up-wind, and closed in on the gangway. An oilskinned figure wearing one of the *Shangri-la*'s crew's fancy French sailor hats came running down the gangway and took the painter.

'Ah, good evening, my man,' Uncle Arthur said. He wasn't putting on the style, it was the way he talked to most people. 'Sir Anthony is aboard?'

'Yes, sir.'

'I wonder if I could see him for a moment?'

'If you could wait a—' The sailor broke off and peered at Sir Arthur. 'Oh, it's – it's the admiral, sir.'

'Admiral Arnford-Jason. Of course – you're the fellow who ran me ashore to the Columbia after dinner.'

'Yes, sir. I'll show you to the saloon, sir.'

'My boat will be all right here for a few moments.' The unspoken implication was that I was his chauffeur.

'Perfectly, sir.'

They climbed the gangway and went aft. I spent ten seconds examining the portable lead that served the gangway light, decided that it would offer much resistance to a good hefty tug, then followed the two men aft. I passed by the passage leading to the saloon and hid behind a ventilator. Almost at once the sailor emerged from the passage and made his way for'ard again. Another twenty seconds and he'd be yelling his head off about the mysteriously vanished chauffeur. I didn't care what he did in twenty seconds.

When I reached the partly open saloon door I heard Sir Arthur's voice.

'No, no, I really am most sorry to break in upon you like

this. Well, yes, thank you, small one if you will. Yes, soda, please.' Uncle Arthur really was having a go at the whisky tonight. 'Thank you, thank you. Your health, Lady Skouras. Your health, gentlemen. Mustn't delay you. Fact is, I wonder if you can help us. My friend and I are most anxious, really most anxious. I wonder where he is, by the way? I thought he was right behind—'

Cue for Calvert. I turned down the oilskin collar that had been obscuring the lower part of my face, removed the souwester that had been obscuring most of the upper part of my face, knocked politely and entered. I said: 'Good evening, Lady Skouras. Good evening, gentlemen. Please forgive the interruption, Sir Anthony.'

Apart from Uncle Arthur there were six of them gathered round the fire at the end of the saloon. Sir Anthony standing, the others seated. Charlotte Skouras, Dollmann, Skouras's managing director, Lavorski, his accountant, Lord Charnley, his broker and a fifth man I didn't recognize. All had glasses in their hands.

Their reaction to my sudden appearance, as expressed by their faces, was interesting. Old Skouras showed a half-frowning, half-speculative surprise. Charlotte Skouras gave me a strained smile of welcome: Uncle Arthur hadn't been exaggerating when he spoke of that bruise, it was a beauty. The stranger's face was noncommittal, Lavorski's inscrutable, Dollmann's rigid as if carved from marble and Lord Charnley's for a fleeting moment that of a man walking through a country churchyard at midnight when someone taps him on the shoulder. Or so I thought. I could have imagined it. But there was no imagination about the sudden tiny snapping sound as the stem of the glass fell soundlessly on to the carpet. A scene straight from Victorian melodrama. Our aristocratic broker friend had something on his mind. Whether the others had or not it was difficult to say. Dollmann, Lavorski and, I was pretty sure, Sir Anthony could make their faces say whatever they wanted them to say.

'Good lord, Petersen!' Skouras's tone held surprise but not the surprise of a person welcoming someone back from the grave. 'I didn't know you two knew each other.'

'My goodness, yes. Petersen and I have been colleagues for

years, Tony. UNESCO, you know.' Uncle Arthur always gave out that he was a British delegate to UNESCO, a cover that gave him an excellent reason for his frequent trips abroad. 'Marine biology may not be very cultural, but it's scientific and educational enough. Petersen's one of my star performers. Lecturing, I mean. Done missions for me in Europe, Asia, Africa and South America.' Which was true, enough, only they weren't lecture missions. 'Didn't even know he was here until they told me at the hotel. But dear me, dear me, mustn't talk about ourselves. It's Hunslett. Petersen's colleague. And mine in a way. Can't find him anywhere. Hasn't been in the village. Yours is the nearest boat. Have you seen anything of him, anything at all?'

'Afraid I haven't,' Skouras said. 'Anybody here? No? Nobody?' He pressed a bell and a steward appeared. Skouras asked him to make inquiries aboard and the steward left. 'When did he disappear, Mr Petersen?'

'I've no idea. I left him carrying out experiments. I've been away all day collecting specimens. Jellyfish.' I laughed deprecatingly and rubbed my inflamed face. 'The poisonous type, I'm afraid. No sign of him when I returned.'

'Could your friend swim, Mr Petersen?' the stranger asked. I looked at him, a dark thickset character in his middle forties, with black snapping eyes deepset in a tanned face. Expressionless faces seemed to be the order of the day there, so I kept mine expressionless. It wasn't easy.

'I'm afraid not,' I said quietly. 'I'm afraid you're thinking along the same lines as myself. We've no guard-rails aft. A careless step—' I broke off as the steward re-entered and reported that no one had seen a sign of Hunslett, then went on: 'I think I should report this to Sergeant MacDonald at once.'

Everybody else seemed to think so, too, so we left. The cold slanting rain was heavier than ever. At the head of the gangway I pretended to slip, flung my arms about wildly for a bit then toppled into the sea, taking the gangway wandering lead with me. What with the rain, the wind and the sudden darkness there was quite a bit of confusion and it was the better part of a minute before I was finally hauled on to the landing stage of the companionway. Old Skouras was commiseration itself and offered me a change of clothes at once but I declined politely and went back to the *Firecrest* with Uncle Arthur. Neither of us spoke on the way back.

As we secured the dinghy I said: 'When you were at dinner on the *Shangri-la* you must have given some story to account for your presence here, for your dramatic appearance in an RAF rescue launch.'

'Yes. It was a good one. I told them a vital UNESCO conference in Geneva was being dead-locked because of the absence of a certain Dr Spenser Freeman. It happens to be true. In all the papers today. Dr Freeman is not there because it suits us not to have him there. No one knows that, of course. I told them that it was of vital national importance that he should be there, that we'd received information that he was doing field research in Torbay and that the Government had sent me here to get him back.'

'Why send the launch away? That would seem odd.'

'No. If he's somewhere in the wilds of Torbay I couldn't locate him before daylight. There's a helicopter, I said, standing by to fly him out. I've only to lift the phone to have it here in fifty minutes.'

'And of course, you weren't to know that the telephone lines were out of order. It might have worked if you hadn't called at the *Firecrest* in the rescue launch *before* you went to the *Shangri-la*. You weren't to know that our friends who were locked in the after cabin when you went aboard would report back that they'd heard an RAF rescue launch here at such and such a time. They might have seen it through a porthole, but even that wouldn't be necessary, the engines are unmistakable. So now our friends know you're lying like a trooper. The chances are that they've now a very shrewd idea as to who exactly you are. Congratulations sir. You've now joined the category I've been in for years – no insurance company in the world would issue you a life policy even on a ninety-nine per cent premium.'

'Our trip to the *Shangri-la* has removed your last doubts about our friends out there?'

'Yes, sir. You saw the reaction of our belted broker, Lord Charnley. And him an aristocrat to boot!'

'A small thing to base a big decision on, Calvert,' Uncle Arthur said coldly.

'Yes, sir.' I fished my scuba suit from the after locker and led the way below. 'I didn't fall into the water by accident. By accident on purpose. I didn't mention that when I was hanging on to the boat's rudder off the reef this evening I cut a notch in it. A deep vee notch. The *Shangri-la's* tender has a deep vee notch in it. Same notch, in fact. Same boat.'

'I see. I see indeed.' Uncle Arthur sat on the settee and gave me the combination of the cold blue eye and the monocle. 'You forgot to give me advance notification of your intentions.'

'I didn't forget.' I started to change out of my soaking clothes. 'I'd no means of knowing how good an actor you are, sir.'

'I'll accept that. So that removed your last doubts.'

'No, sir. Superfluous confirmation, really. I knew before then. Remember that swarthy character sitting beside Lavorski who asked me if Hunslett could swim. I'll bet a fortune to a penny that he wasn't at the *Shangri-la*'s dinner table earlier on.'

'You would win. How do you know?'

'Because he was in command of the crew of the boat who shot down the helicopter and killed Williams and hung around afterwards waiting to have a go at me. His name is Captain Imrie. He was the captain of the prize crew of the *Nantesville*.'

Uncle Arthur nodded, but his mind was on something else. It was on the scuba suit I was pulling on.

'What the hell do you think you're going to do with that thing?' he demanded.

'Advance notification of intentions, sir. Won't be long. I'm taking a little trip to the *Shangri-la*. The *Shangri-la*'s tender, rather. With a little homing device and a bag of sugar. With your permission, sir.'

'Something else you forgot to tell me, hey, Calvert? Like that breaking off the *Shangri-la*'s gangway light was no accident?'

'I'd like to get there before they replace it, sir.'

II

'I can't believe it, I can't believe it.' Uncle Arthur shook his head. For a moment I thought he was referring to the despatch with which I had made the uneventful return trip to the *Shangri-la*'s tender, but his next words showed that his mind was on higher and more important things. 'That Tony Skouras should be up to his neck in this. There's something far wrong. I just *can't* believe it. Good God, do you know he was up for a peerage in the next List?'

'So soon? He told me he was waiting for the price to come down.'

Uncle Arthur said nothing. Normally, he would have regarded such a statement as a moral insult, as he himself automatically collected a life peerage on retirement. But nothing. He was as shaken as that.

'I'd like nothing better than to arrest the lot of them,' I said. 'But our hands are tied. We're helpless. But now that I know what we do know I wonder if you would do me a favour before we go ashore, sir. There are two things I want to know. One is whether Sir Anthony really was down at some Clyde shipyard a few days ago having stabilizers fitted – a big job few yards would tackle in a yacht that size. Should find out in a couple of hours. People tell silly and unnecessary lies. Also I'd like to find out if Lord Kirkside has taken the necessary steps to have his dead son's title – he was Viscount somebody or other – transferred to his younger son.'

'You get the set ready and I'll ask them anything you like,' Uncle Arthur said wearily. He wasn't really listening to me, he was still contemplating with stunned disbelief the possibility that his future fellow peer was up to the neck in skullduggery on a vast scale. 'And pass me that bottle before you go below.'

At the rate Uncle Arthur was going, I reflected, it was providential that the home of one of the most famous distilleries in the Highlands was less than half a mile from where we were anchored.

III

I lowered the false head of the starboard diesel to the engine room deck as if it weighed a ton. I straightened and stood there for a full minute without moving. Then I went to the engine room door.

'Sir Arthur?'

'Coming, coming.' A few seconds and he was at the doorway, the glass of whisky in his hand. 'All connected up?'

'I've found Hunslett, sir.'

Uncle Arthur moved slowly forward like a man in a dream.

The transmitter was gone. All our explosives and listening devices and little portable transmitters were gone. That had left plenty of room. They'd had to double him up to get him in, his head was resting on his forearms and his arms on his knees, but there was plenty of room. I couldn't see his face. I could see no marks of violence. Half-sitting, half-lying there he seemed curiously peaceful, a man drowsing away a summer afternoon by a sun-warmed wall. A long summer afternoon because for ever was a long time. That's what I'd told him last night, he'd all the time in the world for sleep.

I touched his face. It wasn't cold yet. He'd been dead two to three hours, no more. I turned his face to see if I could find how he had died. His head lolled to one side like that of a broken rag doll. I turned and looked at Sir Arthur. The dream-like expression had gone, his eyes were cold and bitter and cruel. I thought vaguely of the tales I'd heard, and largely discounted, of Uncle Arthur's total ruthlessness. I wasn't so ready to discount them now. Uncle Arthur wasn't where he was now because he'd answered an advertisement in the *Daily Telegraph*; he'd have been hand-picked by two or three very clever men who would have scoured the country to find the one man with the extraordinary qualifications they required. And they had picked Uncle Arthur, the man with the extraordinary qualifications, and total ruthlessness must have been one of the prime requisites. I'd never really thought of it before.

He said: 'Murdered, of course.'

'Yes, sir.'

'How?'

'His neck is broken, sir.'

'His neck? A powerful man like Hunslett?'

'I know a man who could do it with one twist of his hands.

Quinn. The man who killed Baker and Delmont. The man who almost killed me.'

'I see.' He paused, then went on, almost absently: 'You will, of course, seek out and destroy this man. By whatever means you choose. You can reconstruct this, Calvert?'

'Yes, sir.' When it came to reconstruction when it was too damn late, I stood alone. 'Out friend or friends boarded the *Firecrest* very shortly after I had left this morning. That is, before daylight. They wouldn't have dared try it after it was light. They overpowered Hunslett and kept him prisoner. Confirmation that he was held prisoner all day comes from the fact that he failed to meet the noon-day schedule. They still held him prisoner when you came aboard. There was no reason why you should suspect that there was anyone aboard – the boat that put them aboard before dawn would have gone away at once. They couldn't leave one of the *Shangri-la*'s boats lying alongside the *Firecrest* all day.'

'There's no necessity to dot i's and cross t's.'

'No, sir. Maybe an hour or so after you departed the *Shangri-la*'s tender with Captain Imrie, Quinn and company aboard turns up: they report that I'm dead. That was Hunslett's death warrant. With me dead they couldn't let him live. So Quinn killed him. Why he was killed this way I don't know. They may have thought shots could be heard, they may not have wanted to use knives or blunt instruments in case they left blood all over the deck. They were intending to abandon the boat till they came back at night, at midnight, to take it out to the Sound and scuttle it and someone might have come aboard in the interim. My own belief is that he was killed this way because Quinn is a psychopath and compulsive killer and liked doing it this way.'

'I see. And then they said to themselves: "Where can we hide Hunslett till we come back at midnight? Just in case someone does come aboard." And then they said: "Ha! We know. We'll hide him in the dummy diesel." So they threw away the transmitter and all the rest of the stuff – or took it with them. It doesn't matter. And they put Hunslett inside.' Uncle Arthur had been speaking very quietly throughout and then suddenly, for the first time I'd ever known it, his voice became a shout. 'How in the name of God did they know this was a dummy diesel, Calvert? How *could* they have known?' His voice dropped to what was a comparative whisper. 'Someone talked, Calvert. Or someone was criminally careless.'

'No one talked, sir. Someone was criminally careless. I was. If I'd used my eyes Hunslett wouldn't be lying there now. The night the two bogus customs officers were aboard I knew that they had got on to something when we were in the engine room here. Up to the time that they'd inspected the batteries they'd gone through the place with a tooth-comb. After that they didn't give a damn. Hunslett even suggested that it was something to do with the batteries but I was too clever to believe him.' I walked to the work-bench, picked up a torch and handed it to Uncle Arthur. 'Do you see anything about those batteries that would excite suspicion?'

He looked at me, that monocled eye still ice-cold and bitter, took the torch and examined the batteries carefully. He spent all of two minutes searching, then straightened.

'I see nothing,' he said curtly.

'Thomas – the customs man who called himself Thomas – did. He was on to us from the start. He knew what he was looking for. He was looking for a powerful radio transmitter. Not the tuppence ha'penny job we have up in the wheelhouse. He was looking for signs of a power take-off from those batteries. He was looking for the marks left by screw clamps or by a pair of saw-toothed, powerfully spring-loaded crocodile clips.'

Uncle Arthur swore, very quietly, and bent over the batteries again. This time his examination took only ten seconds.

'You make your point well, Calvert.' The eyes were still bitter, but no longer glacial.

'No wonder they knew exactly what I was doing today,' I said savagely. 'No wonder they knew that Hunslett would be alone before dawn, that I'd be landing at that cove this evening. All they required was radio confirmation from someone out in Loch Houron that Calvert had been snooping around there and the destruction of the helicopter was a foregone conclusion. All this damned fol-de-rol about smashing up radio transmitters and making us think that we were the only craft left with a transmitter. God, how blind can you be?'

'I assume that there's some logical thought behind this outburst,' Uncle Arthur said coldly.

'That night Hunslett and I were aboard the *Shangri-la* for drinks. I told you that when we returned we knew that we'd had visitors. We didn't know why, then. My God!'

'You've already been at pains to demonstrate the fact that I was no brighter than yourself about the battery. It's not necessary to repeat the process—'

'Let me finish,' I interrupted. Uncle Arthur didn't like being interrupted. 'They came down to the engine room here. They knew there was a transmitter. They looked at that starboard cylinder head. Four bolts – the rest are dummies – with the paint well and truly scraped off. The port cylinder head bolts without a flake of paint missing. They take off this head, wire into the transceiver line on the output side of the scrambler and lead out to a small radio transmitter hidden, like as not, behind the battery bank there. They'd have all the equipment with them for they knew exactly what they wanted to do. From then on they could listen in to our every word. They knew all our plans, everything we intended to do, and made their own plans accordingly. They figured – and how right they were – that it would be a damn sight more advantageous for them to let Hunslett and I have our direct communication with you and so know exactly what was going on than to wreck this set and force us to find some other means of communication that they couldn't check on.'

'But why – but why destroy the advantage they held by – by—' He gestured at the empty engine casing.

'It wasn't an advantage any longer,' I said tiredly. 'When they ripped out that set Hunslett was dead and they thought Calvert was dead. They didn't need the advantage any more.'

'Of course, of course. My God, what a fiendish brew this is.' He took out his monocle and rubbed his eye with the knuckle of his hand. 'They're bound to know that we will find Hunslett the first time we attempt to use this radio. I am beginning to appreciate the weight of your remark in the saloon that we might find it difficult to insure ourselves. They cannot know how much we know, but they cannot afford to take chances. Not with, what is it now, a total of seventeen million pounds at stake. They will have to silence us.'

'Up and off is the only answer,' I agreed. 'We've been down here too long already, they might even be on their way across now. Don't let that Luger ever leave your hand, sir. We'll be safe enough under way. But first we must put Hunslett and our friend in the after cabin ashore.'

'Yes. Yes, we must put them ashore first.'

IV

At the best of times, weighing anchor by electric windlass is not a job for a moron, even an alert moron. Even our small windlass had a pull of over 1,400 pounds. A carelessly placed hand or foot, a flapping trouser leg or the trailing skirts of an oilskin, any of those being caught up between chain and drum and you can be minus a hand or foot before you can cry out, far less reach the deck switch which is invariably placed abaft the windlass. Doing this on a wet slippery deck is twice as dangerous. Doing it on a wet slippery deck, in total darkness, heavy rain and with a very unstable boat beneath your feet, not to mention having the brake pawl off and the winch covered by a tarpaulin, is a highly dangerous practice indeed. But it wasn't as dangerous as attracting the attention of our friends on the *Shangri-la*.

Perhaps it was because of my total absorption in the job on hand, perhaps because of the muffled clank of the anchor coming inboard, that I didn't locate and identify the sound as quickly as I might. Twice I'd thought I'd heard the far-off sound of a woman's voice, twice I'd vaguely put it down to late-night revelry on one of the smaller yachts in the bay – it would require an I.B.M. computer to work out the gallonage of gin consumed in British yacht harbours after the sun goes down. Then I heard the voice again, much nearer this time, and I put all thought of revelry afloat out of my mind. The only cry of desperation ever heard at a yacht party is when the gin runs out: this soft cry had a different quality of desperation altogether. I stamped on the deck switch, and all sound on the fo'c'sle ceased. The Lilliput was in my hand without my knowing how it had got there.

'Help me!' The voice was low and urgent and desperate. 'For God's sake, help me.'

The voice came from the water, amidships on the port side. I moved back silently to where I thought the voice had come from and stood motionless. I thought of Hunslett and I didn't move a muscle. I'd no intention of helping anyone until I'd made sure the voice didn't come from some dinghy – a dinghy with two other passengers, both carrying machine-guns. One word, one incautious flash of light, a seven-pound pull on a trigger and Calvert would be among his ancestors if, that was, they would have anything to do with such a bloody fool of a descendant.

'Please! Please help me! Please!'

I helped her. Not so much because the desperation in the voice was unquestionably genuine as because of the fact that it as unquestionably belonged to Charlotte Skouras.

I pushed through between the scuppers and the lowest guard-rail, a rubber tyre fender that was permanently attached to one of the guard-rail stanchions and lowered it to water-level. I said: 'Lady Skouras?'

'Yes, yes, it's me. Thank God, thank God!' Her voice didn't come just as easily as that, she was gasping for breath and she'd water in her mouth.

'There's a fender at the boat's side. Catch it.'

A moment or two, then: 'I have it.'

'Can you pull yourself up?'

More splashing and gasping, then: 'No. No, I can't do it.'

'No matter. Wait.' I turned round to go for Uncle Arthur but he was already by my side. I said softly in his ear: 'Lady Skouras is down there in the water. It may be a trap. I don't think so. But if you see a light, shoot at it.'

He said nothing but I felt his arm move as he took the Luger from his pocket. I stepped over the guard-rail and lowered myself till my foot came to rest on the lower part of the tyre. I reached down and caught her arm. Charlotte Skouras was no slender sylph-like figure, she had some bulky package tied to her waist, and I wasn't as fit as I'd been a long, long time ago, say about forty-eight hours, but with a helping hand from Uncle Arthur I managed to get her up on deck. Between us, we half-carried her to the curtained saloon and set her down on the settee. I propped a cushion behind her head and took a good look at her.

She'd never have made the front cover of *Vogue*. She looked terrible. Her dark slacks and shirt looked as if they had spent a month in the sea instead of probably only a few minutes. The long tangled auburn hair was plastered to her head and cheeks, her face was dead-white, the big brown eyes, with the dark half-circles, were wide open and frightened and both mascara and lipstick had begun to run. And she hadn't been beautiful to start with. I thought she was the most desirable woman I'd ever seen. I must be nuts.

'My dear Lady Skouras, my dear Lady Skouras!' Uncle Arthur was back among the aristocracy and showed it. He knelt by her side, ineffectually dabbing at her face with a handkerchief. 'What in God's name has happened? Brandy, Calvert, brandy! Don't just stand there, man. Brandy!'

Uncle Arthur seemed to think he was in a pub but, as it happened, I did have some brandy left. I handed him the glass and said: 'If you'll attend to Lady Skouras, sir, I'll finish getting the anchor up.'

'No, no!' She took a gulp of the brandy, choked on it and I had to wait until she had finished coughing before she went on. 'They're not coming for at least two hours yet. I know. I heard. There's something terrible going on, Sir Arthur. I had to come, I had to come.'

'Now, don't distress yourself, Lady Skouras, don't distress yourself,' Uncle Arthur said, as if she weren't distressed enough already. 'Just drink this down, Lady Skouras.'

'No, not that!' I got all set to take a poor view of this, it was damned good brandy, then I realized she was talking of something else. 'Not Lady Skouras. Never again! Charlotte. Charlotte Meiner. Charlotte.'

One thing about women, they always get their sense of priorities right. There they were on the *Shangri-la*, rigging up a home-made atom bomb to throw through our saloon windows and all she could think was to ask us to call her 'Charlotte.' I said: 'Why did you have to come?'

'Calvert!' Uncle Arthur's voice was sharp. 'Do you mind? Lady – I mean, Charlotte – has just suffered a severe shock. Let her take her time to—'

'No.' She struggled to an upright sitting position and forced a wan smile, half-scared, half-mocking. 'No, Mr Petersen, Mr Calvert, whatever your name, you're quite right. Actresses tend to over-indulge their emotions. I'm not an actress any longer.' She took another sip of the brandy and a little colour came back to her face. 'I've known for some time that something was very far wrong aboard the *Shangri-la*. Strange men have been aboard. Some of the old crew were changed for no reason. Several times I've been put ashore with the stewardess in hotels while the *Shangri-la* went off on mysterious journeys. My husband – Sir Anthony – would tell me nothing. He has changed terribly since our marriage – I think he takes drugs. I've seen guns. Whenever those strange men came aboard I was sent to my stateroom after dinner.' She smiled mirthlessly. 'It wasn't because of any jealousy on my husband's part, you may believe me. The last day or two I sensed that everything was coming to a climax. Tonight, just after you were gone, I was sent to my stateroom. I left, but stayed out in the passage. Lavorski was talking. I heard him saying: "If your admiral pal is a UNESCO delegate, Skouras, then I'm King Neptune. I know who he is. We all know who he is. It's too late in the day now and they know too much. It's them or us.' And then Captain Imrie – how I hate that man! – said: "I'll send Quinn and Jacques and Kramer at midnight. At one o'clock they'll open the sea-cocks in the Sound".'

'Charming friends your husband has,' I murmured.

She looked at me, half-uncertainly, half-speculatively and said: 'Mr Petersen or Mr Calvert – and I heard Lavorski call you Johnson—'

'It *is* confusing,' I admitted. 'Calvert, Philip Calvert.'

'Well, Philip,' – she pronounced it the French way and very nice it sounded too – 'you are one great bloody fool if you talk like that. You are in deadly danger.'

'Mr Calvert,' Uncle Arthur said sourly – it wasn't her language he disapproved of, it was this Christian name familiarity between the aristocracy and the peasants – 'is quite aware of the danger. He has unfortunate mannerisms of speech, that's all. You are a very brave woman, Charlotte.' Blue-bloods first-naming each other was a different thing altogether. 'You took a great risk in eavesdropping. You might have been caught.'

'I was caught, Sir Arthur.' The smile showed up the lines on either side of her mouth but didn't touch her eyes. 'That is another reason why I am here. Even without the knowledge of your danger, yes, I would have come. My husband caught me. He took me into my stateroom.' She stood up shakily, turned her back to us and pulled up the sodden dark shirt. Right across her back ran three great blue-red weals. Uncle Arthur stood stock-still, a man incapable of movement. I crossed the saloon and peered at her back. The weals were almost an inch wide and running half-way round her body. Here and there were tiny blood-spotted punctures. Lightly I tried a finger on one of the weals. The flesh was raised and puffy, a fresh weal, as lividly-genuine a weal as ever I'd clapped eyes on. She didn't move. I stepped back and she turned to face us.

'It is not nice, is it? It does not feel very nice.' She smiled and again that smile. 'I could show you worse than that.'

'No, no, no,' Uncle Arthur said hastily. 'That will not be necessary.' He was silent for a moment, then burst out: 'My dear Charlotte, what you must have suffered. It's fiendish, absolutely fiendish. He must be – he must be inhuman. A monster. A monster, perhaps under the influence of drugs. I would never have believed it!' His face was brick-red with outrage and his voice sounded as if Quinn had him by the throat. Strangled. 'No one would ever have believed it!'

'Except the late Lady Skouras,' she said quietly. 'I understand now why she was in and out of mental homes several times before she died.' She shrugged. 'I have no wish to go the same way. I am made of tougher stuff than Madeleine Skouras. So I pick up my bag and run away.' She nodded at the small polythene bag of clothes that had been tied to her waist. 'Like Dick Whittington, is it not?'

'They'll be here long before midnight when they discover you're gone,' I observed.

'It may be morning before they find out. Most nights I lock my cabin door. Tonight I locked it from the outside.'

'That helps,' I said. 'Standing about in those sodden clothes doesn't. There's no point in running away only to die of pneumonia. You'll find towels in my cabin. Then we can get you a room in the Columba Hotel.'

'I had hoped for better than that.' The fractional slump of the shoulders was more imagined than seen, but the dull defeat in the eyes left nothing to the imagination. 'You would put me in the first place they would look for me. There is no safe place for me in Torbay. They will catch me and bring me back and my husband will take me into that stateroom again. My only hope is to run away. Your only hope is to run away. Please. Can we not run away together?'

'No.'

'A man not given to evasive answers, is that it?' There was a lonely dejection, a proud humiliation about her that did very little for my self-respect. She turned towards Uncle Arthur, took both his hands in hers and said in a low voice: 'Sir Arthur. I appeal to you as an English gentleman.' Thumbs down on Calvert, that foreign-born peasant. 'May I stay? Please?'

Uncle Arthur looked at me, hesitated, looked at Charlotte Skouras, looked into those big brown eyes and was a lost man.

'Of course you may stay, my dear Charlotte.' He gave a stiff old-fashioned bow which, I had to admit, went very well with the beard and the monocle. 'Yours to command, my dear lady.'

'Thank you, Sir Arthur.' She smiled at me, not with triumph or satisfaction, just an anxious-to-be-friendly smile. 'It would be nice, Philip, to have the consent – what do you say? – unanimous.'

'If Sir Arthur wishes to expose you to a vastly greater degree of risk aboard this boat than you would experience in Torbay, that is Sir Arthur's business. As for the rest, my consent is not required. I'm a well-trained civil servant and I obey orders.'

'You are gracious to a fault,' Uncle Arthur said acidly.

'Sorry, sir.' I'd suddenly seen the light and a pretty dazzling beam it was too. 'I should not have called your judgement in question. The lady is very welcome. But I think she should remain below while we are alongside the pier, sir.'

'A reasonable request and a wise precaution,' Uncle Arthur said mildly. He seemed pleased at my change of heart, at my proper deference to the wishes of the aristocracy.

'It won't be for long.' I smiled at Charlotte Skouras. 'We leave Torbay within the hour.'

V

'What do I care what you charge him with?' I looked from Sergeant MacDonald to the broken-faced man with the wet blood-stained towel, then back to MacDonald again. 'Breaking and entering. Assault and battery. Illegal possession of a dangerous weapon with intent to create a felony – murder. Anything you like.'

'Well, now. It's just not quite as easy as that.' Sergeant MacDonald spread his big brown hands across the counter of the tiny police station and looked at the prisoner and myself in turn. 'He didn't break and enter, you know, Mr Petersen. He boarded. No law against that. Assault and battery? It looks as if he has been the victim and not the perpetrator. And what kind of weapon was he carrying, Mr Petersen?'

'I don't know. It must have been knocked overboard.'

'I see. Knocked overboard, was it? So we have no real proof of any felonious intent.'

I was becoming a little tired of Sergeant MacDonald. He was fast enough to co-operate with bogus customs officers but with me he was just being deliberately obstructive. I said: 'You'll be telling me next that it's all a product of my fevered imagination. You'll be telling me next that I just stepped ashore, grabbed the first passer-by I saw, hit him in the face with a four-by-two then dragged him up here inventing this tale as I went. Even you can't be so stupid as to believe that.'

The brown face turned red and, on the counter, the brown knuckles turned ivory. He said softly: 'You'll kindly not talk to me like that.'

'If you insist on behaving like a fool I'll treat you as such. Are you going to lock him up?'

'It's only your word against his.'

'No. I had a witness. He's down at the old pier now, if you want to see him. Admiral Sir Arthur Arnford-Jason. A very senior civil servant.'

'You had a Mr Hunslett with you last time I was aboard your boat.'

'He's down there, too.' I nodded at the prisoner. 'Why don't you ask a few questions of our friend here?'

'I've sent for the doctor. He'll have to fix his face first. I can't understand a word he says.'

'The state of his face doesn't help,' I admitted. 'But the main trouble is that he speaks Italian.'

'Italian, is it? I'll soon fix that. The owner of the Western Isles café is an Italian.'

'That helps. There are four little questions he might put to our pal here. Where is his passport, how he arrived in this country, who is his employer and where does he live.'

The sergeant looked at me for a long moment then said slowly: 'It's a mighty queer marine biologist that you are, Mr Petersen.'

'And it's a mighty queer police sergeant that you are, Mr MacDonald. Good night.'

I crossed the dimly-lit street to the sea-wall and waited in the shadow of a phone booth. After two minutes a man with a small bag came hurrying up the street and turned into the police station. He was out again in five minutes, which wasn't surprising: there was little a G.P. could do for what was plainly a hospital job.

The station door opened again and Sergeant MacDonald came hurrying out, long black mackintosh buttoned to the neck. He walked quickly along the sea-wall, looking neither to left nor right, which made it very easy for me to follow him, and turned down the old stone pier. At the end of the pier he flashed a torch, went down a flight of steps and began to haul in a small boat. I leaned over the pier wall and switched on my own torch.

'Why don't they provide you with a telephone or radio for conveying urgent messages?' I asked. 'You could catch your death of cold rowing out to the *Shangri-la* on a night like this.'

He straightened slowly and let the rope fall from his hands. The boat drifted out into the darkness. He came up the steps with the slow heavy tread of an old man and said quietly: 'What did you say about the *Shangri-la*?'

'Don't let me keep you, sergeant,' I said affably. 'Duty before the idle social chit-chat. Your first duty is to your masters. Off you go, now, tell them that one of their hirelings has been severely clobbered and that Petersen has very grave suspicions about Sergeant MacDonald.'

'I don't know what you are talking about,' he said emptily. 'The *Shangri-la* – I'm not going anywhere near the *Shangri-la*.'

'Where are you going, then? Do tell. Fishing? Kind of forgotten your tackle, haven't you?'

'And how would you like to mind your own damn business?' MacDonald said heavily.

'That's what I'm doing. Come off it, sergeant. Think I give a damn about our Italian pal? You can charge him with playing tiddley-winks in the High Street for all I care. I just threw him at you, together with a hint that you yourself were up to no good, to see what the reaction would be, to remove the last doubts in my mind. You reacted beautifully.'

'I'm maybe not the cleverest, Mr Petersen,' he said with dignity. 'Neither am I a complete idiot. I thought you were one of them or after the same thing as them.' He paused. 'You're not. You're a Government agent.'

'I'm a civil servant.' I nodded to where the *Firecrest* lay not twenty yards away. 'You'd better come to meet my boss.'

'I don't take orders from civil servants.'

'Suit yourself,' I said indifferently, turned away and looked out over the sea-wall. 'About your two sons, Sergeant MacDonald. The sixteen-year-old twins who, I'm told, died in the Cairngorms some time back.'

'What about my sons?' he said tonelessly.

'Just that I'm not looking forward to telling them that their own father wouldn't lift a finger to bring them back to life again.'

He just stood there in the darkness, quite still, saying nothing. He offered no resistance when I took his arm and led him towards the *Firecrest*.

VI

Uncle Arthur was at his most intimidating and Uncle Arthur in full intimidating cry was a sight to behold. He'd made no move to rise when I'd brought MacDonald into the saloon and he hadn't asked him to sit. The blue basilisk stare, channelled and magnified by the glittering monocle, transfixed the unfortunate sergeant like a laser beam.

'So your foot slipped, sergeant,' Uncle Arthur said without preamble. He was using his cold, flat, quite uninflected voice, the one that curled your hair. 'The fact that you stand here now indicates that. Mr Calvert went ashore with a prisoner and enough rope for you to hang yourself and you seized it with both hands. Not very clever of you, sergeant. You should not have tried to contact your friends.'

'They are no friends of mine, sir,' MacDonald said bitterly.

'I'm going to tell you as much as you need to know about Calvert – Petersen was a pseudonym – and myself and what we are doing.' Uncle Arthur hadn't heard him. 'If you ever repeat any part of what I say to anyone, it will cost you your job, your pension, any hope that you will ever again, in whatever capacity, get another job in Britain and several years in prison for contravention of the Official Secrets Act. I myself will personally formulate the charges.' He paused then added in a masterpiece of superfluity: 'Do I make myself clear?'

'You make yourself very clear,' MacDonald said grimly.

So Uncle Arthur told him all he thought MacDonald needed to know, which wasn't much, and finished by saying: 'I am sure we can now count on your hundred per cent co-operation, sergeant.'

'Calvert is just guessing at my part in this,' he said dully.

'For God's sake!' I said. 'You *knew* those customs officers were bogus. You *knew* they had no photo-copier with them. You *knew* their only object in coming aboard was to locate and smash that set – and locate any other we might have. You *knew* they couldn't have gone back to the mainland in that launch – it was too rough. The launch, was, in fact, the *Shangri-la*'s tender – which is why you left without lights – and no launch left the harbour after your departure. We'd have heard it. The only life we saw after that was when they switched on their lights in the *Shangri-la*'s wheelhouse to smash up their own radio – *one* of their own radios, I should have said. And how did you *know* the telephone lines were down in the Sound? You knew they were down, but why did you say the Sound? Because you *knew* they had been cut there. Then, yesterday morning, when I asked you if there was any hope of the lines being repaired, you said no. Odd. One would have thought that you would have told the customs boys going back to the mainland to contact the GPO at once. But you *knew* they weren't going back there. And your two sons, sergeant, the boys supposed to be dead, you forgot to close their accounts. Because you *knew* they weren't dead.'

'I forgot about the accounts,' MacDonald said slowly. 'And all the other points – I'm afraid I'm not good at this sort of thing.' He looked at Uncle Arthur. 'I know this is the end of the road for me. They said they would kill my boys, sir.'

'If you will extend us your full co-operation,' Uncle Arthur said precisely, 'I will personally see to it that you remain the Torbay police sergeant until you're falling over your beard. Who are "they"?'

'The only men I've seen is a fellow called Captain Imrie and the two customs men – Durran and Thomas. Durran's real name is Quinn. I don't know the others' names. I usually met them in my house, after dark. I've been out to the *Shangri-la* only twice. To see Imrie.'

'And Sir Anthony Skouras?'

'I don't know.' MacDonald shrugged helplessly. 'He's a good man, sir, he really is. Or I thought so. Maybe he is mixed up in this. Anyone can fall into bad company. It's very strange, sir.'

'Isn't it? And what's been your part in this?'

'There's been funny things happening in this area in the past months. Boats have vanished. People have vanished. Fishermen have had their nets torn, in harbour, and yacht engines have been mysteriously damaged, also in harbour. This is when Captain Imrie wants to prevent certain boats from going certain places at the wrong time.'

'And your part is to investigate with great diligence and a total lack of success,' Uncle Arthur nodded. 'You must be invaluable to them, sergeant. A man with your record and character is above suspicion. Tell me, sergeant, what are they up to?'

'Before God, sir, I have no idea.'

'You're totally in the dark?'

'Yes, sir.'

'I don't doubt it. This is the way the very top men operate. And you will have no idea where your boys are being held?'

'No, sir.'

'How do you know they're alive?'

'I was taken out to the *Shangri-la* three weeks ago. My sons had been brought there from God only knows where. They were well.'

'And are you really so naïve as to believe that your sons will be well and will be returned alive when all this is over? Even although your boys will be bound to know who their captors are and would be available for testimony and identification if the time came for that?'

'Captain Imrie said they would come to no harm. If I co-operated. He said that only fools ever used unnecessary violence.'

'You are convinced, then, they wouldn't go to the length of murder?'

'Murder! What are you talking about, sir?'

'Calvert?'

'Sir?'

'A large whisky for the sergeant.'

'Yes, sir.' When it came to lashing out with my private supplies Uncle Arthur was generous to a fault. Uncle Arthur paid no entertainment allowance. So I poured the sergeant a large whisky and, seeing that bankruptcy was inevitable anyway, did the same for myself. Ten seconds later the sergeant's glass was empty. I took his arm and led him to the engine room. When we came back to the saloon in a minute's time the sergeant needed no persuading to accept another glass. His face was pale.

'I told you that Calvert carried out a helicopter reconnaissance today,' Uncle Arthur said conversationally. 'What I didn't tell you was that his pilot was murdered this evening. I didn't tell you that two other of my best agents have been killed in the last sixty hours. And now, as you've just seen, Hunslett. Do you still believe, sergeant, that we are dealing with a bunch of gentlemanly law-breakers to whom human life is sacrosanct?'

'What do you want me to do, sir?' Colour was back in the

brown cheeks again and the eyes were cold and hard and a little desperate.

'You and Calvert will take Hunslett ashore to your office. You will call in the doctor and ask for an official post-mortem – we must have an official cause of death. For the trial. The other dead men are probably beyond recovery. You will then row out to the *Shangri-la* and tell Imrie that we brought Hunslett and the other man – the Italian – to your office. You will tell them that you heard us say that we must go to the mainland for new depth-sounding equipment and for armed help and that we can't be back for two days at least. Do you know where the telephone lines are cut in the Sound?'

'Yes, sir. I cut them myself.'

'When you get back from the *Shangri-la* get out there and fix them. Before dawn. Before dawn tomorrow you, your wife and son must disappear. For thirty-six hours. If you want to live. That is understood?'

'I understand what you want done. Not why you want it done.'

'Just do it. One last thing. Hunslett has no relations – few of my men have – so he may as well be buried in Torbay. Knock up your local undertaker during the night and make arrangements for the funeral on Friday. Calvert and I would like to be there.'

'But – but Friday? That's just the day after tomorrow.'

'The day after tomorrow. It will be all over then. You'll have your boys back home.'

MacDonald looked at him in long silence, then said slowly: 'How can you be sure?'

'I'm not sure at all.' Uncle Arthur passed a weary hand across his face and looked at me. 'Calvert is. It's a pity, sergeant, that the Secrets Act will never permit you to tell your friends that you once knew Philip Calvert. If it can be done, Calvert can do it. I think he can. I certainly hope so.'

'I certainly hope so, too,' MacDonald said sombrely.

Me too, more than either of them, but there was already so much despondency around that it didn't seem right to deepen it, so I just put on my confident face and led MacDonald back down to the engine room.

— 7 —

Wednesday: 10.40 p.m. – Thursday: 2 a.m.

THREE OF THEM came to kill us, not at midnight as promised, but at 10.40 p.m. that night. Had they come five minutes earlier then they would have got us because five minutes earlier we were still tied up to the old stone pier. And had they come and got us that five minutes earlier, then the fault would have been mine for, after leaving Hunslett in the police station, I had insisted that Sergeant MacDonald accompany me to use his authority in knocking up and obtaining service from the proprietor of the only chemist's shop in Torbay. Neither of them had been too keen on giving me the illegal help I wanted and it had taken me a full five minutes and the best part of my extensive repertoire of threats to extract from the very elderly chemist the minimum of reluctant service and a small green-ribbed bottle informatively labelled "The Tablets". But I was lucky and I was back aboard the *Firecrest* just after 10.30 p.m.

The west coast of Scotland doesn't go in much for golden Indian summers and that night was no exception. Apart from being cold and windy, which was standard, it was also black as sin and bucketing heavily, which if not quite standard was at least not so unusual as to excite comment. A minute after leaving the pier I had to switch on the searchlight mounted on the wheelhouse roof. The western entrance to the Sound from Torbay harbour, between Torbay and Garve Island, is a quarter of a mile wide and I could have found it easily on a compass course: but there were small yachts, I knew, between the pier and the entrance and if any of them was carrying a riding light it was invisible in that driving rain.

The searchlight control was on the wheelhouse deckhead. I moved it to point the beam down and ahead, then traversed it through a forty-degree arc on either side of the bows.

I picked up the first boat inside five seconds, not a yacht riding at its moorings but a rowing dinghy moving slowly through the water. It was fine on the port bow, maybe fifty yards away. I couldn't identify the man at the oars, the oars wrapped at their middle with some white cloth to muffle the sound of the rowlocks, because his back was towards me. A very broad back. Quinn. The man in the bows was sitting facing me. He wore oilskins and a dark beret and in his hand he held a gun. At fifty yards it's almost impossible to identify any weapon, but his looked like a German Schmeisser machine-pistol. Without a doubt Jacques, the machine-gun specialist. The man crouched low in the stern-sheets was quite unidentifiable, but I could see the gleam of a short gun in his hand. Messrs Quinn, Jacques and Kramer coming to pay their respects as Charlotte Skouras had said they would. But much ahead of schedule.

Charlotte Skouras was on my right in the darkened wheelhouse. She'd been there only three minutes, having spent all our time alongside in her darkened cabin with the door closed. Uncle Arthur was on my left, desecrating the clean night air with one of his cheroots. I reached up for a clipped torch and patted my right hand pocket to see if the Lilliput was still there. It was.

I said to Charlotte Skouras: 'Open the wheelhouse door. Put it back on the catch and stand clear.' Then I said to Uncle Arthur: 'Take the wheel, sir. Hard a-port when I call. Then back north on course again.'

He took the wheel without a word. I heard the starboard wheelhouse door click on its latch. We were doing no more than three knots through the water. The dinghy was twenty-five yards away, the men in the bows and stern holding up arms to shield their eyes from our searchlight. Quinn had stopped rowing. On our present course we'd leave them at least ten feet on our port beam. I kept the searchlight steady on the boat.

Twenty yards separated us and I could see Jacques lining up his machine-pistol on our light when I thrust the throttle lever right open. The note of the big diesel exhaust deepened and the *Firecrest* began to surge forward.

'Hard over now,' I said.

Uncle Arthur spun the wheel. The sudden thrust of our single port screw boiled back against the port-angled rudder, pushing the stern sharply starboard. Flame lanced from Jacques' machine-pistol; a silent flame, he'd a silencer on. Bullets ricocheted off our aluminium foremast but missed both light and wheelhouse. Quinn saw what was coming and dug his oars deep but he was too late. I shouted 'Midships, now,' pulled the throttle lever back to neutral and jumped out through the starboard doorway on to the deck.

We hit them just where Jacques was sitting, breaking off the dinghy's bows, capsizing it and throwing the three men into the water. The overturned remains of the boat and a couple of struggling figures came slowly down the starboard side of the *Firecrest*. My torch picked up the man closer in to our side. Jacques, with the machine-pistol held high above his head, instinctively trying to keep it dry though it must have been soaked when he had been catapulted into the water. I held gun-hand and torch-hand together, aiming down the bright narrow beam. I squeezed the Lilliput's trigger twice and a bright crimson flower bloomed where his face had been. He went down as if a shark had got him, the gun in the stiffly-upstretched arms. It was a Schmeisser machine-pistol all right. I shifted the torch. There was only one other to be seen in the water and it wasn't Quinn, he'd either dived under the *Firecrest* or was sheltering under the upturned wreck of the dinghy. I fired twice more at the second figure and he started to scream. The screaming went on for two or three seconds, then stopped in a shuddering gurgle. I heard the sound of someone beside me on the deck being violently sick over the side. Charlotte Skouras. But I'd no time to stay and comfort Charlotte Skouras, she'd no damned right to be out on deck anyway. I had urgent matters to attend to, such as preventing Uncle Arthur from cleaving Torbay's old stone pier in half. The townspeople would not have liked it. Uncle Arthur's idea of midships differed sharply from mine, he'd brought the *Firecrest* round in a three-quarter circle. He would have been the ideal man at the helm of one of those ram-headed Phoenician galleys that specialized in cutting the opposition in two, but as a helmsman in Torbay harbour he lacked something. I jumped into the wheelhouse, pulled the throttle all the way to astern and spun the wheel to port. I jumped out again and pulled Charlotte Skouras away before she got her head knocked off by one of the barnacle-encrusted piles that fronted the pier. Whether or not we grazed the pier was impossible to say but we sure as hell gave the barnacles a nasty turn.

I moved back into the wheelhouse, taking Charlotte Skouras with me. I was breathing heavily. All this jumping in and out through wheelhouse doors took it out of a man. I said: 'With all respects, sir, what the hell were you trying to do?'

'Me?' He was as perturbed as a hibernating bear in January. 'Is something up, then?'

I moved the throttle to slow ahead, took the wheel from him and brought the *Firecrest* round till we were due north on a compass bearing. I said: 'Keep it there, please,' and did some more traversing with the searchlight. The waters around were black and empty, there was no sign even of the dinghy. I'd expected to see every light in Torbay lit up like a naval review; those four shots, even the Lilliput's sharp, light-weighted cracks, should have had them all on their feet. But nothing, no sign, no movement at all. The gin bottle levels would be lower than ever. I looked at the compass: north-twenty-west. Like the honey-bee for the flower, the iron filing for the magnet, Uncle Arthur was determinedly heading straight for the shore again. I took the wheel from him, gently but firmly, and said: 'You came a bit close to the pier back there, sir.'

'I believe I did.' He took out a handkerchief and wiped his monocle. 'Damn glass misted up just at the wrong moment. I trust, Calvert, that you weren't just firing at random out there.' Uncle Arthur had become a good deal more bellicose in the past hour or so: he'd had a high regard for Hunslett.

'I got Jacques and Kramer. Jacques was the handy one with the automatic arms. He's dead. I think Kramer is too. Quinn got away.' What a set-up, I thought bleakly, what a set-up. Alone with Uncle Arthur on the high seas in the darkness of the night. I'd always known that his eyesight, even in optimum conditions, was pretty poor: but I'd never suspected that, when the sun was down, he was virtually blind as a bat. But unfortunately, unlike the bat, Uncle Arthur wasn't equipped with a built-in radar which would enable him to shy clear of rocks, headlands, islands and such-like obstructions of a similarly permanent and final nature with which we might go bump in the dark. To all intents and purposes I was single handed. This called for a radical revision in plans only I didn't see how I could radically revise anything.

'Not too bad,' Uncle Arthur said approvingly. 'Pity about Quinn, but otherwise not too bad at all. The ranks of the ungodly are being satisfactorily depleted. Do you think they'll come after us?'

'No. For four reasons. One, they won't know yet what has happened. Two, both their sorties this evening have gone badly and they won't be in a hurry to try any more boarding expeditions for some time. Three, they'd use the tender for this job, not the *Shangri-la* and if they get that tender a hundred yards I've lost all faith in demerara sugar. Four, there's mist or fog coming up. The lights of Torbay are obscured already. They can't follow us because they can't find us.'

Till that moment the only source of illumination we'd had in the wheelhouse had come from the reflected light of the compass lamp. Suddenly the overhead light came on. Charlotte Skouras's hand was on the switch. Her face was haggard and she was staring at me as if I were the thing from outer space. Not one of those admiring affectionate looks.

'What kind of man are you, Mr Calvert?' No 'Philip' this time. Her voice was lower and huskier than ever and it had a shake in it. 'You – you're not human. You kill two men and go on speaking calmly and reasonably as if nothing had happened. What in God's name are you, a hired killer? It's – it's unnatural. Have you no feelings, no emotions, no regrets?'

'Yes, I have. I'm sorry I didn't kill Quinn too.'

She stared at me with something like horror in her face, then switched her gaze to Uncle Arthur. She said to him and her voice was almost a whisper: 'I saw that man, Sir Arthur. I saw his face being blown apart by the bullets. Mr Calvert could have – could have arrested him, held him up and handed him over to the police. But he didn't. He killed him. And the other. It was slow and deliberate. Why, why, why?'

'There's no "why" about it, my dear Charlotte.' Sir Arthur

sounded almost irritable. 'There's no justification needed. Calvert killed them or they killed us. They came to kill us. You told us that yourself. Would you feel any compunction at killing a poisonous snake? Those men were no better than that. As for arresting them!' Uncle Arthur paused, maybe for the short laugh he gave, maybe because he was trying to recall the rest of the homily I'd delivered to him earlier that evening. 'There's no intermediate stage in this game. It's kill or be killed. These are dangerous and deadly men and you never give them warning.' Good old Uncle Arthur, he'd remembered the whole lecture, practically word for word.

She looked at him for a long moment, her face uncomprehending, looked at me then slowly turned and left the wheelhouse.

I said to Uncle Arthur: 'You're just as bad as I am.'

II

She reappeared again exactly at midnight, switching on the light as she entered. Her hair was combed and neat, her face was less puffy and she was dressed in one of those synthetic fibre dresses, white, ribbed and totally failing to give the impression that she stood in need of a good meal. From the way she eased her shoulders I could see that her back hurt. She gave me a faint tentative smile. She got none in return.

I said: 'Half an hour ago, rounding Carrara Point, I near as dammit carried away the lighthouse. Now I hope I'm heading north of Dubh Sgeir but I may be heading straight into the middle of it. It couldn't be any blacker if you were a mile down in an abandoned coal mine, the fog is thickening, I'm a not very experienced sailor trying to navigate my way through the most dangerous waters in Britain and whatever hope we have of survival depends on the preservation of what night-sight I've slowly and painfully built up over the past hour or so. *Put out that damned light!*'

'I'm sorry.' The light went out. 'I didn't think.'

'And don't switch on any other lights either. Not even in your cabin. Rocks are the least of my worries in Loch Houron.'

'I'm sorry,' she repeated. 'And I'm sorry about earlier on. That's why I came up. To tell you that. About the way I spoke and leaving so abruptly, I mean. I've no right to sit on judgement on others – and I think my judgement was wrong. I was just – well, literally shocked. To see two men killed like that, no, not killed, there's always heat and anger about killing, to see two men executed like that, because it wasn't kill or be killed as Sir Arthur said, and then see the person who did it not care . . .' Her voice faded away uncertainly.

'You might as well get your facts and figures right, my dear,' Uncle Arthur said. 'Three men, not two. He killed one just before you came on board tonight. He had no option. But Philip Calvert is not what any reasonable man would call a killer. He doesn't care in the way you say, because if he did he would go mad. In another way, he cares very much. He doesn't do this job for money. He's miserably paid for a man of his unique talents.' I made a mental note to bring this up next time we were alone. 'He doesn't do it for excitement, for – what is the modern expression? – kicks: a man who devotes his spare time to music, astronomy and philosophy does not live for kicks. But he cares. He cares for the difference between right and wrong, between good and evil, and when that difference is great enough and the evil threatens to destroy the good then he does not hesitate to take steps to redress the balance. And maybe that makes him better than either you or me, my dear Charlotte.'

'And that's not all of it either,' I said. 'I'm also renowned for my kindness to little children.'

'I'm sorry, Calvert,' Uncle Arthur said. 'No offence and no embarrassment, I hope. But if Charlotte thought it important enough to come up here and apologize, I thought it important enough to set the record straight.'

'That's not all Charlotte came up for,' I said nastily. '*If* that's what she came up for in the first place. She came up here because she's consumed with feminine curiosity. She wants to know where we are going.'

'Do you mind if I smoke?' she asked.

'Don't strike the match in front of my eyes.'

She lit the cigarette and said: 'Consumed with curiosity is right. What do you think? Not about where we're going, I know where we're going. You told me. Up Loch Houron. What I want to know is what is going on, what all this dreadful mystery is about, why all the comings and goings of strange men aboard the *Shangri-la*, what is so fantastically important to justify the deaths of three men in one evening, what you are doing here, what you are, who you are. I never really thought you were a UNESCO delegate, Sir Arthur. I know now you're not. Please. I have the right to know, I think.'

'Don't tell her,' I advised.

'Why ever not?' Uncle Arthur said huffily. 'As she says, she is deeply involved, whether she wants it or not. She does have the right to know. Besides, the whole thing will be public knowledge in a day or two.'

'You didn't think of that when you threatened Sergeant MacDonald with dismissal and imprisonment if he contravened the Official Secrets Act.'

'Merely because he could ruin things by talking out of turn,' he said stiffly. 'Lady – I mean, Charlotte – is in no position to do so. Not, of course,' he went on quickly, 'that she would ever dream of doing so. Preposterous. Charlotte is an old and dear friend, a *trusted* friend, Calvert. She *shall* know.'

Charlotte said quietly: 'I have the feeling that our friend Mr Calvert does not care for me overmuch. Or maybe he just does not care for women.'

'I care like anything,' I said. 'I was merely reminding the admiral of his own dictum: "Never, never, never – I forget how many nevers, I think there were four or five – tell anyone anything unless it's necessary, essential and vital." In this case it's none of the three.'

Uncle Arthur lit another vile cheroot and ignored me. His dictum was not meant to refer to confidential exchanges between members of the aristocracy. He said: 'This is the case of the missing ships, my dear Charlotte. Five missing ships, to be precise. Not to mention a fair scattering of very much smaller vessels, also missing or destroyed.

'Five ships, I said. On 5 April of this year the S.S. *Holmwood* disappeared off the south coast of Ireland. It was an act of piracy. The crew was imprisoned ashore, kept under guard for two or three days, then released unharmed. The *Holmwood* was never heard of again. On 24 April, the M.V. *Antara* vanished in St George's Channel. On 17 May, the M.V.

Headley Pioneer disappeared off Northern Ireland. On 6 August the S.S. *Hurricane Spray* disappeared after leaving the Clyde and finally, last Saturday, a vessel called the *Nantesville* vanished soon after leaving Bristol. In all cases the crews turned up unharmed.

'Apart from their disappearances and the safe reappearances of their crews, those five vessels all had one thing in common – they were carrying extremely valuable and virtually untraceable cargoes. The *Holmwood* had two and a half million pounds of South African gold aboard, the *Antara* had a million and a half pounds' worth of uncut Brazilian diamonds for industrial use, the *Headley Pioneer* had close on two million pounds' worth of mixed cut and uncut Andean emeralds from the Muzo mines in Columbia, the *Hurricane Spray*, which had called in at Glasgow *en route* from Rotterdam to New York, had just over three million pounds' worth of diamonds, nearly all cut, and the last one, the *Nantesville*,' – Uncle Arthur almost choked over this one – 'had eight million pounds in gold ingots, reserves being called in by the US Treasury.

'We had no idea where the people responsible for these disappearances got their information. Such arrangements as to the decision to ship, when, how and how much, are made in conditions of intense secrecy. They, whoever "they" are, had impeccable sources of information. Calvert says he knows those sources now. After the disappearance of the first three ships and about six million pounds' worth of specie it was obvious a meticulously organized gang was at work.'

'Do you mean to say – do you mean to say that Captain Imrie is mixed up in this?' Charlotte asked.

'Mixed up is hardly the word,' Uncle Arthur said dryly. 'He may well be the directing mind behind it all.'

'And don't forget old man Skouras,' I advised. 'He's pretty deep in the mire, too – about up to his ears, I should say.'

'You've no right to say that,' Charlotte said quickly.

'No right? Why ever not? What's he to you and what's all this defence of the maestro of the bull-whip? How's your back now?'

She said nothing. Uncle Arthur said nothing, in a different kind of way, then went on:

'It was Calvert's idea to hide two of our men and a radio

signal transmitter on most of the ships that sailed with cargoes of bullion or specie after the *Headley Pioneer* had vanished. We had no difficulty, as you can imagine, in securing the co-operation of the various exporting and shipping companies and governments concerned. Our agents – we had three pairs working – usually hid among the cargo or in some empty cabin or machinery space with a food supply. Only the masters of the vessels concerned knew they were aboard. They delivered a fifteen-second homing signal at fixed – very fixed – but highly irregular intervals. Those signals were picked up at selected receiving stations round the west coast – we limited our stations to that area for that was where the released crews had been picked up – and by a receiver aboard this very boat here. The *Firecrest*, my dear Charlotte, is a highly unusual craft in many respects.' I thought he was going to boast, quietly of course, of his own brilliance in designing the *Firecrest* but he remembered in time that I knew the truth.

'Between 17 May and 6 August nothing happened. No piracy. We believe they were deterred by the short, light nights. On 6 August, the *Hurricane Spray* disappeared. We had no one aboard that vessel – we couldn't cover them all. But we had two men aboard the *Nantesville*, the ship that sailed last Saturday. Delmont and Baker. Two of our best men. The *Nantesville* was forcibly taken just off the Bristol Channel. Baker and Delmont immediately began the scheduled transmissions. Cross-bearings gave us a completely accurate position at least every half-hour.

'Calvert and Hunslett were in Dublin, waiting. As soon—'

'That's right,' she interrupted. 'Mr Hunslett. Where is he? I haven't seen—'

'In a moment. The *Firecrest* moved out, not following the *Nantesville*, but moving ahead of its predicted course. They reached the Mull of Kintyre and had intended waiting till the *Nantesville* approached there but a south-westerly gale blew up out of nowhere and the *Firecrest* had to run for shelter. When the *Nantesville* reached the Mull of Kintyre area our radio beacon fixes indicated that she was still on a mainly northerly course and that it looked as if she might pass up the Mull of Kintyre on the outside — the western side. Calvert took a chance, ran up Loch Fyne and through the Crinan

Canal. He spent the night in the Crinan sea-basin. The sea-lock is closed at night. Calvert could have obtained the authority to have it opened but he didn't want to: the wind had veered to westerly late that evening and small boats don't move out of Crinan through the Dorus Mor in a westerly gusting up to Force 9. Not if they have wives and families to support – and even if they haven't.

'During the night the *Nantesville* turned out west into the Atlantic. We thought we had lost her. We think we know now why she turned out: she wanted to arrive at a certain place at a certain state of the tide in the hours of darkness, and she had time to kill. She went west, we believe, firstly because it was the easiest way to ride out the westerly gale and, secondly, because she didn't want to be seen hanging around the coast all of the next day and preferred to make a direct approach from the sea as darkness was falling.

'The weather moderated a fair way overnight. Calvert left Crinan at dawn, almost at the very minute the *Nantesville* turned back east again. Radio transmissions were still coming in from Baker and Delmont exactly on schedule. The last transmission came at 1022 hours that morning: after that, nothing.'

Uncle Arthur stopped and the cheroot glowed fiercely in the darkness. He could have made a fortune contracting out to the cargo shipping companies as a one-man fumigating service. Then he went on very quickly as if he didn't like what he had to say next, and I'm sure he didn't.

'We don't know what happened. They may have betrayed themselves by some careless action. I don't think so, they were too good for that. Some member of the prize crew may just have stumbled over their hiding-place. Again it's unlikely, and a man who stumbled over Baker and Delmont wouldn't be doing any more stumbling for some time to come. Calvert thinks, and I agree with him, that by the one unpredictable chance in ten thousand the prize crew's radio-operator happened to be traversing Baker and Delmont's wave-band at the very moment they were sending their fifteen-second transmission. At that range he'd about have his head blasted off and the rest was inevitable.

'A plot of the *Nantesville*'s fixes between dawn and the last transmission showed her course as 082° true. Predicted destination – Loch Houron. Estimated time of arrival – sunset. Calvert had less than a third of the *Nantesville*'s distance to cover. But he didn't take the *Firecrest* into Loch Houron because he was pretty sure that Captain Imrie would recognize a radio beacon transmitter when he saw one and would assume that we had his course. Calvert was also pretty sure that if the *Nantesville* elected to continue on that course – and he had a hunch that it would – any craft found in the entrance to Loch Houron would receive pretty short shrift, either by being run down or sunk by gunfire. So he parked the *Firecrest* in Torbay and was skulking around the entrance to Loch Houron in a frogman's suit and with a motorized rubber dinghy when the *Nantesville* turned up. He went aboard in darkness. The name was changed, the flag was changed, one mast was missing and the superstructure had been repainted. But it was the *Nantesville*.

'Next day Calvert and Hunslett were storm-bound in Torbay but on Wednesday Calvert organized an air search for the *Nantesville* or some place where she might have been hidden. He made a mistake. He considered it extremely unlikely that the *Nantesville* would still be in Loch Houron because Imrie knew that we knew that he had been headed there and therefore would not stay there indefinitely, because the chart showed Loch Houron as being the last place in Scotland where anyone in their sane minds would consider hiding a vessel and because, after Calvert had left the *Nantesville* that evening, she'd got under way and started to move out to Carrara Point. Calvert thought she'd just stayed in Loch Houron till it was dark enough to pass undetected down the Sound of Torbay or round the south of Torbay Island to the mainland. So he concentrated most of his search on the mainland and on the Sound of Torbay and Torbay itself. He thinks now the *Nantesville* is in Loch Houron. We're going there to find out.' His cheroot glowed again. 'And that's it, my dear. Now, with your permission, I'd like to spend an hour on the saloon settee. These nocturnal escapades . . .' He sighed, and finished: 'I'm not a boy any longer. I need my sleep.'

I liked that. I wasn't a boy any longer either and I didn't

seem to have slept for months. Uncle Arthur, I knew, always went to bed on the stroke of midnight and the poor man had already lost fifteen minutes. But I didn't see what I could do about it. One of my few remaining ambitions in life was to reach pensionable age and I couldn't make a better start than by ensuring that Uncle Arthur never laid hands on the wheel of the *Firecrest*.

'But surely that's not it,' Charlotte protested. 'That's not all of it. Mr Hunslett, where's Mr Hunslett? And you said Mr Calvert was aboard the *Nantesville*. How on earth did he—?'

'There are some things you are better not knowing, my dear. Why distress yourself unnecessarily? Just leave this to us.'

'You haven't had a good look at me recently, have you, Sir Arthur?' she asked quietly.

'I don't understand.'

'It may have escaped your attention but I'm not a child any more. I'm not even young any more. Please don't treat me as a juvenile. And if you want to get to that settee tonight—'

'Very well. If you insist. The violence, I'm afraid, has not all been one-sided. Calvert, as I said, was about the *Nantesville*. He found my two operatives, Baker and Delmont.' Uncle Arthur had the impersonal emotionless voice of a man checking his laundry list. 'Both men had been stabbed to death. This evening the pilot of Calvert's helicopter was killed when the machine was shot down in the Sound of Torbay. An hour after that Hunslett was murdered. Calvert found him in the *Firecrest*'s engine room with a broken neck.'

Uncle Arthur's cheroot glowed and faded at least half a dozen times before Charlotte spoke. The shake was back in her voice. 'They are fiends. Fiends.' A long pause, then: 'How can you cope with people like that?'

Uncle Arthur puffed a bit more then said candidly: 'I don't intend to try. You don't find generals slugging it out hand-to-hand in the trenches. Calvert will cope with them. Good night, my dear.'

He pushed off. I didn't contradict him. But I knew that Calvert couldn't cope with them. Not any more, he couldn't. Calvert had to have help. With a crew consisting of a myopic boss and a girl who, every time I looked at her, listened to her or thought of her, started the warning bells clanging away furiously in the back of my head, Calvert had to have a great deal of help. And he had to have it fast.

III

After Uncle Arthur had retired, Charlotte and I stood in silence in the darkened wheelhouse. But a companionable silence. You can always tell. The rain drummed on the wheelhouse roof. It was as dark as it ever becomes at sea and the patches of white fog were increasing in density and number. Because of them I had cut down to half speed and with the loss of steerage way and that heavy westerly sea coming up dead astern I'd normally have been hard put to it to control the direction of the *Firecrest*: but I had the auto-pilot on and switched to 'Fine' and we were doing famously. The auto-pilot was a much better helmsman than I was. And streets ahead of Uncle Arthur.

Charlotte said suddenly: 'What is it you intend to do tonight?'

'You *are* a gourmand for information. Don't you know that Uncle Arthur – sorry, Sir Arthur – and I are engaged upon a highly secret mission? Security is all.'

'And now you're laughing at me – and forgetting I'm along on this secret mission too.'

'I'm glad you're along and I'm not laughing at you, because I'll be leaving this boat once or twice tonight and I have to have somebody I can trust to look after it when I'm away.'

'You have Sir Arthur.'

'I have, as you say, Sir Arthur. There's no one alive for whose judgement and intelligence I have greater respect. But at the present moment I'd trade in all the judgement and intelligence in the world for a pair of sharp young eyes. Going by tonight's performance, Sir Arthur shouldn't be allowed out without a white stick. How are yours?'

'Well, they're not so young any more, but I think they're sharp enough.'

'So I can rely on you?'

'On me? I – well, I don't know anything about handling boats.'

'You and Sir Arthur should make a great team. I saw you star once in a French film about—'

'We never left the studio. Even in the studio pool I had a stand-in.'

'Well, there'll be no stand-in tonight.' I glanced out through the streaming windows. 'And no studio pool. This is the real stuff, the genuine Atlantic. A pair of eyes, Charlotte, that's all I require. A pair of eyes. Just cruising up and down till I come back and seeing that you don't go on the rocks. Can you do that?'

'Will I have any option?'

'Nary an option.'

'Then I'll try. Where are you going ashore?'

'Eilean Oran and Craigmore. The two innermost islands in Loch Houron. If,' I said thoughtfully, 'I can find them.'

'Eilean Oran and Craigmore.' I could have been wrong, but I thought the faint French accent a vast improvement on the original Gaelic pronunciation. 'It seems so wrong. So very wrong. In the middle of all this hate and avarice and killing. These names – they breathe the very spirit of romance.'

'A highly deceptive form of respiration, my dear.' I'd have to watch myself, I was getting as bad as Uncle Arthur. 'Those islands breathe the very spirit of bare, bleak and rocky desolation. But Eilean Oran and Craigmore hold the key to everything. Of that I'm very sure.'

She said nothing. I stared out through the high-speed Kent clear-view screen and wondered if I'd see Dubh Sgeir before it saw me. After a couple of minutes I felt a hand on my upper arm and she was very close to me. The hand was trembling. Wherever she'd come by her perfume it hadn't been bought in a supermarket or fallen out of a Christmas cracker. Momentarily and vaguely I wondered about the grievous impossibility of ever understanding the feminine mind: before fleeing for what she had thought to be her life and embarking upon a hazardous swim in the waters of Torbay harbour, she hadn't forgotten to pack a sachet of perfume in her polythene kit-bag. For nothing was ever surer than that any perfume she'd been wearing had been well and truly removed before I'd fished her out of Torbay harbour.

'Philip?'

Well, this was better than the Mr Calvert stuff. I was glad Uncle Arthur wasn't there to have his aristocratic feelings scandalized. I said: 'Uh-huh?'

'I'm sorry.' She said it as if she meant it and I supposed I should have tried to forget that she was once the best actress in Europe. 'I'm truly sorry. About what I said – about what I thought – earlier on. For thinking you were a monster. The men you killed, I mean. I – well, I didn't know about Hunslett and Baker and Delmont and the helicopter pilot. All your friends. I'm truly sorry, Philip. Truly.'

She was overdoing it. She was also too damn' close. Too damn' warm. You'd have required a pile-driver in top condition to get a cigarette card between us. And that perfume that hadn't fallen out of a cracker – intoxicating, the ad-boys in the glossies would have called it. And all the time the warning bells were clanging away like a burglar alarm with the St Vitus's dance. I made a manful effort to do something about it. I put my mind to higher things.

She said nothing. She just squeezed my arm a bit more and even the pile-driver would have gone on strike for piece-work rates. I could hear the big diesel exhaust thudding away behind us, a sound of desolate reassurance. The *Firecrest* swooped down the long overtaking combers then gently soared again. I was conscious for the first time of a curious meteorological freak in the Western Isles. A marked rise in temperature after midnight. And I'd have to speak to the Kent boys about their guarantee that their clearview screen wouldn't mist up under any conditions, but maybe that wasn't fair, maybe they'd never visualized conditions like this. I was just thinking of switching off the auto-pilot to give me something to do when she said: 'I think I'll go below soon. Would you like a cup of coffee first?'

'As long as you don't have to put on a light to do it. And as long as you don't trip over Uncle Arthur – I mean, Sir—'

'Uncle Arthur will do just fine,' she said. 'It suits him.' Another squeeze of the arm and she was gone.

The meteorological freak was of short duration. By and by

the temperature dropped back to normal and the Kent guarantee became operative again. I took a chance, left the *Firecrest* to its own devices and nipped aft to the stern locker. I took out my scuba diving equipment, together with air-cylinders and mask, and brought them for'ard to the wheelhouse.

It took her twenty-five minutes to make the coffee. Calor gas has many times the calorific efficiency of standard domestic coal gas and, even allowing for the difficulties of operating in darkness, this was surely a world record for slowness in making coffee at sea. I heard the clatter of crockery as the coffee was brought through the saloon and smiled cynically to myself in the darkness. Then I thought of Hunslett and Baker and Delmont and Williams, and I wasn't smiling any more.

IV

I still wasn't smiling when I dragged myself on to the rocks of Eilean Oran, removed the scuba equipment and set the big, rectangular-based, swivel-headed torch between a couple of stones with its beam staring out to sea. I wasn't smiling, but it wasn't for the same reason that I hadn't been smiling when Charlotte had brought the coffee to the wheelhouse just over half an hour ago, I wasn't smiling because I was in a state of high apprehension and I was in a state of high apprehension because for ten minutes before leaving the *Firecrest* I'd tried to instruct Sir Arthur and Charlotte in the technique of keeping a boat in a constant position relative to a fixed mark on the shore.

'Keep her on a due west compass heading,' I'd said. 'Keep her bows on to the sea and wind. With the engine at "Slow" that will give you enough steerage way to keep your head up. If you find yourselves creeping too far forwards, come round to the *south*' – if they'd come round to the north they'd have found themselves high and dry on the rock shores of Eilean Oran – 'head due east at half speed, because if you go any slower you'll broach to, come sharply round to the north then head west again at slow speed. You can see those breakers on the south shore there. Whatever you do, keep them at least two hundred yards away on the starboard hand when you're going west and a bit more when you're going east.'

They had solemnly assured me that they would do just that and seemed a bit chuffed because of what must have been my patent lack of faith in them both, but I'd reason for my lack of faith for neither had shown any marked ability to make a clear distinction between shore breakers and the north-south line of the foaming tops of the waves rolling eastwards towards the mainland. In desperation I'd said I'd place a fixed light on the shore and that that would serve as a permanent guide. I just trusted to God that Uncle Arthur wouldn't emulate the part of an eighteenth-century French sloop's skipper vis-à-vis the smugglers' lamp on a rock-girt Cornish shore and run the damned boat aground under the impression that he was heading for a beacon of hope. He was a very clever man, was Uncle Arthur, but the sea was not his home.

The boatshed wasn't quite empty, but it wasn't far off it. I flashed my small torch around its interior and realized that MacEachern's boatshed wasn't the place I was after. There was nothing there but a weather-beaten, gunwale-splintered launch, with, amidships, an unboxed petrol engine that seemed to be a solid block of rust.

I came to the house. On its northern side, the side remote from the sea, a light shone through a small window. A light at half-past one in the morning. I crawled up to this and hitched a wary eye over the window-sill. A neat, clean, well-cared-for small room, with lime-washed walls, mat-covered stone floor and the embers of a drift-wood fire smouldering in an ingle-nook in the corner. Donald MacEachern was sitting in a cane-bottomed chair, still unshaven, still in his month-old shirt, his head bent, staring into the dull red heart of the fire. He had the look of a man who was staring into a dying fire because that was all that was left in the world for him to do. I moved round to the door, turned the handle and went inside.

He heard me and turned around, not quickly, just the way a man would turn who knows there is nothing left on earth that can hurt him. He looked at me, looked at the gun in my hand, looked at his own twelve-bore hanging on a couple of nails on the wall then sank back into his chair again.

He said tonelessly: 'Who in the name of God are you?'

'Calvert's my name. I was here yesterday.' I pulled off my rubber hood and he remembered all right. I nodded to the twelve-bore. 'You won't be needing that gun tonight, Mr MacEachern. Anyway, you had the safety catch on.'

'You don't miss much,' he said slowly. 'There were no cartridges in the gun.'

'And no one standing behind you, was there?'

'I don't know what you mean,' he said tiredly. 'Who are you, man? What do you want?'

'I want to know why you gave me the welcome you did yesterday.' I put the gun away. 'It was hardly friendly, Mr MacEachern.'

'Who are you, sir?' He looked even older than he had done yesterday, old and broken and done.

'Calvert. They told you to discourage visitors, didn't they, Mr MacEachern?' No answer. 'I asked some questions tonight of a friend of yours. Archie MacDonald. The Torbay police sergeant. He told me you were married. I don't see Mrs MacEachern.'

He half rose from his cane chair. The old bloodshot eyes had a gleam to them. He sank back again and the eyes dimmed.

'You were out in your boat one night, weren't you, Mr MacEachern? You were out in your boat and you saw too much. They caught you and they took you back here and they took Mrs MacEachern away and they told you that if you ever breathed a word to anyone alive you would never see your wife that way again. Alive, I mean. They told you to stay here in case any chance acquaintances or strangers should call by and wonder why you weren't here and raise the alarm, and just to make sure that you wouldn't be tempted to go to the mainland for help – although heaven knows I would have thought there would be no chance in the world of you being as mad as that – they immobilized your engine. Salt-water impregnated sacks, I shouldn't wonder, so that any chance caller would think it was due to neglect and disuse, not sabotage.'

'Aye, they did that.' He stared sightlessly into the fire, his voice the sunken whisper of a man who is just thinking aloud and hardly aware that he is speaking. 'They took her away and they ruined my boat. And I had my life savings in the back room there and they took that too. I wish I'd had a million pounds to give them. If only they had left my Mairi. She's five years older than myself.' He had no defences left.

'What in the name of God have you been living on?'

'Every other week they bring me tinned food, not much, and condensed milk. Tea I have, and I catch a fish now and then off the rocks.' He gazed into the fire, his forehead wrinkling as if he were suddenly realizing that I brought a new dimension into his life. 'Who are you, sir? Who are you? You're not one of them. And you're not a policeman, I know you're not a policeman. I've seen them. I've seen policemen. But you are a very different kettle of fish.' There were the stirrings of life in him now, life in his face and in his eyes. He stared at me for a full minute, and I was beginning to feel uncomfortable under the gaze of those faded eyes, when he said: 'I know who you are. I know who you must be. You are a Government man. You are an agent of the British Secret Service.'

Well, by God, I took off my hat to the old boy. There I was, looking nondescript as anything and buttoned to the chin in a scuba suit, and he had me nailed right away. So much for the inscrutable faces of the guardians of our country's secrets. I thought of what Uncle Arthur would have said to him, the automatic threats of dismissal and imprisonment if the old man breathed a word. But Donald MacEachern didn't have any job to be dismissed from and after a lifetime in Eilean Oran even a maximum security prison would have looked like a hostelry to which Egon Ronay would have lashed out six stars without a second thought, so as there didn't seem to be much point in threatening him I said instead, for the first time in my life: 'I am an agent of the Secret Service, Mr MacEachern. I am going to bring your wife back to you.'

He nodded very slowly, then said: 'You will be a very brave man, Mr Calvert, but you do not know the terrible men who will wait for you.'

'If I ever earn a medal, Mr MacEachern, it will be a case of mistaken identification, but, for the rest, I know very well what I am up against. Just try to believe me, Mr MacEachern. It will be all right. You were in the war, Mr MacEachern.'

'You know. You were told?'

I shook my head. 'Nobody had to tell me.'

'Thank you, sir.' The back was suddenly very straight. 'I was a soldier for twenty-two years. I was a sergeant in the 51st Highland Division.'

'You were a sergeant in the 51st Highland Division,' I repeated. 'There are many people, Mr MacEachern, and not all of them Scots, who maintain that there was no better in the world.'

'And it is not Donald MacEachern who would be disagreeing with you, sir.' For the first time the shadow of a smile touched the faded eyes. 'There were maybe one or two worse. You make your point, Mr Calvert. We were not namely for running away, for losing hope, for giving up too easily.' He rose abruptly to his feet. 'In the name of God, what am I talking about? I am coming with you, Mr Calvert.'

I rose to my feet and touched my hands to his shoulders. 'Thank you, Mr MacEachern, but no. You've done enough. Your fighting days are over. Leave this to me.'

He looked at me in silence, then nodded. Again the suggestion of a smile. 'Aye, maybe you're right. I would be getting in the way of a man like yourself. I can see that.' He sat down wearily in his chair.

I moved to the door. 'Good night, Mr MacEachern. She will soon be safe.'

'She will soon be safe,' he repeated. He looked up at me, his eyes moist, and when he spoke his voice held the same faint surprise as his face. 'You know, I believe she will.'

'She will. I'm going to bring her back here personally and that will give me more pleasure than anything I've ever done in my life. Friday morning, Mr MacEachern.'

'Friday morning? So soon? So soon?' He was looking at a spot about a billion light years away and seemed unaware that I was standing by the open door. He smiled, a genuine smile of delight, and the old eyes shone. 'I'll not sleep a wink tonight, Mr Calvert. Nor a wink tomorrow night either.'

'You'll sleep on Friday,' I promised. He couldn't see me any longer, the tears were running down his grey unshaven cheeks, so I closed the door with a quiet hand and left him alone with his dreams.

— 8 —

Thursday: 2 a.m. – 4.30 a.m.

I HAD EXCHANGED Eilean Oran for the island of Craigmore and I still wasn't smiling. I wasn't smiling for all sorts of reasons. I wasn't smiling because Uncle Arthur and Charlotte Skouras together made a nautical combination that terrified the life out of me, because the northern tip of Craigmore was much more exposed and reef-haunted than the south shore of Eilean Oran had been, because the fog was thickening, because I was breathless and bruised from big combers hurling me on to unseen reefs on my swim ashore, because I was wondering whether I had any chance in the world of carrying out my rash promise to Donald MacEachern. If I thought a bit more I'd no doubt I could come up with all sorts of other and equally valid reasons why I wasn't smiling, but I hadn't the time to think any more about it, the night was wearing on and I'd much to do before the dawn.

The nearest of the two fishing boats in the little natural harbour was rolling quite heavily in the waves that curled round the reef forming the natural breakwater to the west so I didn't have to worry too much about any splashing sound I might make as I hauled myself up on deck. What I did have to worry about was that damned bright light in its sealed inverted glass by the flensing shed, it was powerful enough to enable me to be seen from the other houses on shore . . . But my worry about it was a little thing compared to my gratitude for its existence. Out in the wild blue yonder Uncle Arthur could do with every beacon of hope he could find.

It was a typical M.F.V., about forty-five feet long and with the general look of a boat that could laugh at a hurricane. I went through it in two minutes. All in immaculate condition, not a thing aboard that shouldn't have been there. Just a genuine fishing-boat. My hopes began to rise. There was no other direction they could go.

The second M.F.V. was the mirror image of the first, down to the last innocuous inch. It wouldn't be true to say that my hopes were now soaring, but at least they were getting up off the ground where they'd been for a long time.

I swam ashore, parked my scuba equipment above the high-water mark and made my way to the flensing shed, keeping its bulk between the light and myself as I went. The shed contained winches, steel tubs and barrels, a variety of ferocious weapons doubtless used for flensing, rolling cranes, some unidentifiable but obviously harmless machinery, the remains of some sharks and the most fearful smell I'd ever come across in my life. I left, hurriedly.

The first of the cottages yielded nothing. I flashed a torch through a broken window. The room was bare, it looked as if no one had set foot there for half a century, it was only too easy to believe Williams's statement that this tiny hamlet had been abandoned before the First World War. Curiously, the wall-paper looked as if it had been applied the previous day – a curious and largely unexplained phenomenon in the Western Isles. Your grandmother – in those days grandpa would have signed the pledge sooner than lift a finger inside the house – slapped up some wall-paper at ninepence a yard and fifty years later it was still there, as fresh as the day it had been put up.

The second cottage was as deserted as the first.

The third cottage, the one most remote from the flensing shed, was where the shark-fishers lived. A logical and very understandable choice, one would have thought, the farther away from the olfactory horror the better. Had I the option, I'd have been living in a tent on the other side of the island. But that was a purely personal reaction. The stench of that flensing shed was probably to the shark-fishers, as is the ammonia-laden, nostril-wrinkling, wholly awful *mist* – liquid manure – to Swiss farmers: the very breath of being. The symbol of success. One can pay too high a price for success.

I eased open the well-oiled – shark-liver oil, no doubt – door and passed inside. The torch came on again. Grandma wouldn't have gone very much on this front parlour but grandpa would cheerfully have sat there watching his beard turn white through the changing seasons without ever wanting to go down to the sea again. One entire wall was given up to food supplies, a miserable couple of dozen crates of whisky and score upon scores of crates of beer. Australians, Williams had said. I could well believe it. The other three walls – there was hardly a scrap of wall-paper to be seen – were devoted to a form of art, in uninhibited detail and glorious Technicolor, of a type not usually to be found in the better-class museums and art galleries. Not grandma's cup of tea at all.

I skirted the furniture which hadn't come out of Harrods and opened the interior door. A short corridor lay beyond. Two doors to the right, three to the left. Working on the theory that the boss of the outfit probably had the largest room to himself, I carefully opened the first door to the right.

The flash-light showed it to be a surprisingly comfortable room. A good carpet, heavy curtains, a couple of good arm-chairs, bedroom furniture in oak, a double bed and a bookcase. A shaded electric light hung above the bed. Those rugged Australians believed in their home comforts. There was a switch beside the door. I touched it and the overhead lamp came on.

There was only one person in the double bed but even at that he was cramped in it. It's hard to gauge a man's height when he's lying down but if this lad tried to stand up in a room with a ceiling height of less than six feet four inches, he'd finish up with concussion. His face was towards me but I couldn't see much of it, it was hidden by a head of thick black hair that had fallen over his brows and the most magnificently bushy black beard I'd ever clapped eyes on. He was sound asleep.

I crossed to the bed, prodded his ribs with the gun barrel and a pressure sufficient to wake a lad of his size and said: 'Wake up.'

He woke up. I moved a respectful distance away. He rubbed his eyes with one hairy forearm, got his hands under him and heaved himself to a sitting position. I wouldn't have been surprised to see him wearing a bearskin, but no, he was wearing a pair of pyjamas in excellent taste; I might have chosen the colour myself.

Law-abiding citizens woken in the dark watches of the night by a gun-pointing stranger react in all sorts of ways, varying from terror to apoplectically-purple outrage. The man in the beard didn't react in any of the standard ways at all. He just stared at me from under dark overhanging cliffs of eyebrows and the expression in the eyes was that of a Bengal tiger mentally tucking in his napkin before launching himself on the thirty-foot leap that is going to culminate in lunch. I stepped back another couple of paces and said: 'Don't try it.'

'Put that gun away, sonny boy,' he said. The deep rumbling voice seemed to come from the innermost recesses of the Carlsbad cavern. 'Put it away or I'll have to get up and clobber you and take it from you.'

'Don't be like that,' I complained, then added politely: 'If I put it away, will you clobber me?'

He considered this for a moment, then said: 'No.' He reached out for a big black cigar and lit it, his eyes on me all the time. The acrid fumes reached across the room and as it isn't polite for a guest in another's house to rush to open the nearest window without permission I didn't but it was a near thing. No wonder he'd never notice the stench from the flensing shed: compared to this, Uncle Arthur's cheroots came into the same category as Charlotte's perfume.

'My apologies for the intrusion. Are you Tim Hutchinson?'

'Yeah. And you, sonny boy?'

'Philip Calvert. I want to use one of your boat's transmitters to contact London. I also need your help. How urgently you can't imagine. A good many lives and millions of pounds can be lost in the next twenty-four hours.'

He watched a particularly noxious cloud of this Vesuvian poison gas drift up to the cringing ceiling, then bent his eyes on me again. 'Ain't you the little kidder, now, sonny boy.'

'I'm not kidding, you big black ape. And, while we're at it, we'll dispense with the "sonny boy", Timothy.'

He bent forward, the deep-set, coal-black eyes, not at all as friendly as I would have liked, then relaxed with a laugh. '*Touché*, as my French governess used to say. Maybe you ain't kidding at that. What are you, Calvert?'

In for a penny, in for a pound. This man would grant his co-operation for nothing less than the truth. And he looked like a man whose co-operation would be very well worth having. So, for the second time that night and the second time in my life, I said: 'I'm an agent of the British Secret Service.' I was glad that Uncle Arthur was out there fighting for his life on the rolling deep, his blood pressure wasn't what it ought to have been and a thing like this, twice in one night, could have been enough to see him off.

He considered my reply for some time, then said: 'The Secret Service. I guess you have to be at that. Or a nut case. But you blokes never tell.'

'I had to. It would have been obvious anyway when I tell you what I have to tell you.'

'I'll get dressed. Join you in the front room in two minutes. Help yourself to a Scotch there.' The beard twitched and I deduced from this that he was grinning. 'You should find some, somewhere.'

I went out, found some somewhere and was conducting myself on the grand tour of the Craigmore art gallery when Tim Hutchinson came in. He was dressed all in black, trousers, sailor's jersey, mackinaw and seaboots. Beds were deceptive, he'd probably passed the six foot four mark when he was about twelve and had just stopped growing. He glanced at the collection and grinned.

'Who would have thought it?' he said. 'The Guggenheim and Craigmore. Hot-beds of culture, both of them. Don't you think the one with the ear-rings looks indecently overdressed?'

'You must have scoured the great galleries of the world,' I said reverently.

'I'm no connoisseur. Renoir and Matisse are my cup of tea.' It was so unlikely that it had to be true. 'You look like a man in a hurry. Just leave out all the inessentials.'

I left out the inessentials, but not one of the essentials. Unlike MacDonald and Charlotte, Hutchinson got not only the truth but the whole truth.

'Well, if that isn't the most goddamned story any man ever heard. And right under our bloody noses.' It was hard to tell at times whether Hutchinson was Australian or American – I learnt later that he'd spent many years tuna-fishing in

Florida. 'So it was you in that chopper this afternoon. Brother, you've had a day and then some. I retract that "sonny boy" crack. One of my more ill-advised comments. What do you want, Calvert?'

So I told him what I wanted, his own personal assistance that night, the loan of his boats and crews for the next twenty-four hours and the use of a radio transmitter immediately. He nodded.

'Count on us. I'll tell the boys. You can start using that transmitter right away.'

'I'd rather go out with you to our boat right away,' I said, 'leave you there and come back in myself to transmit.'

'You lack a mite confidence in your crew, hey?'

'I'm expecting to see the bows of the *Firecrest* coming through that front door any minute.'

'I can do better than that. I'll roust out a couple of the boys, we'll take the *Charmaine* – that's the M.F.V. nearest the flensing shed – out to the *Firecrest*, I'll go aboard, we'll cruise around till you get your message off, then you come aboard the *Firecrest* while the boys take the *Charmaine* back again.'

I thought of the maelstrom of white breakers outside the mouth of the alleged harbour. I said: 'It won't be too dangerous to take an M.F.V. out on a night like this?'

'What's wrong with a night like this? It's a fine fresh night. You couldn't ask for better. This is nothing, I've seen the boys take a boat out there, six o'clock in a black December evening, into a full gale.'

'What kind of emergency was that?'

'A serious one, admittedly.' He grinned. 'We'd run out of supplies and the boys wanted to get to Torbay before the pubs shut. Straight up, Calvert.'

I said no more. It was obviously going to be a great comfort to have Hutchinson around with me for the rest of the night. He turned towards the corridor and hesitated: 'Two of the boys are married. I wonder—'

'There'll be no danger for them. Besides, they'll be well rewarded for their work.'

'Don't spoil it, Calvert.' For a man with such a deep rumbling voice he could make it very soft at times. 'We don't take money for this kind of work.'

'I'm not hiring you,' I said tiredly. I'd quite enough people fighting me already without Tim Hutchinson joining their ranks. 'There's an insurance reward. I have been instructed to offer you half.'

'Ah, now, that's very different indeed. I'll be delighted to relieve the insurance companies of their excess cash at any time. But not half, Calvert, not half. Not for a day's work, not after all you've done. Twenty-five per cent to us, seventy-five per cent to you and your friends.'

'Half is what you get. The other half will be used to pay compensation for those who have suffered hardship. There's an old couple on Eilean Oran, for instance, who are going to be wealthy beyond their dreams for the rest of their days.'

'You get nothing?'

'I get my salary, the size of which I'd rather not discuss, as it's a sore point. Civil servants are not permitted to accept gratuities.'

'You mean to say you get beaten up, shot down, half-drowned and suffered another couple of murder attempts just for a lousy pay cheque? What makes you tick, Calvert? Why the hell do you do it?'

'That's not an original question. I ask myself the same question about twenty times a day, rather more often recently. It's time we were gone.'

'I'll get the boys up. They'll be tickled pink by those gold watches or whatever the insurance boys will be handing over. Engraved, of course. We insist on that.'

'The reward will be in cash, not kind. Depends on how much of the stolen goods are recovered. We're pretty sure to recover all the *Nantesville's* cargo. Chances are that we'll recover the lot. The award is ten per cent. Yours will be five. The minimum you and your boys will pick up will be four hundred thousand pounds: the maximum will be eight hundred and fifty. Thousand pounds, I mean.'

'Say that in English.' He looked as if the London Post Office Tower had fallen on top of him. So I said it again, and after a time he looked as if only a telegraph pole had fallen on him and said carefully: 'At rates like that, a man might expect a fair bit of co-operation. Say no more. Put right out of your head any thoughts you had of advertising in the *Telegraph*. Tim Hutchinson is your man.'

II

And Tim Hutchinson was undoubtedly my man. On a night like that, dark as doomsday, rain sluicing down and a thickening mist making it impossible – for me, at least – to tell the difference between a naturally breaking sea and a wave foaming over a reef, Tim Hutchinson was my man. Cheap at half a million.

He was one of that rare breed, that very rare breed, of naturals to whom the sea is truly home. Twenty years' daily polishing and refining in every conceivable condition a rarely-bestowed gift with which you must be born in the first place and anyone can be like this. Just as the great Grand Prix drivers, the Carraciolas and Nuvolaris and Clarks, operate on a level incomprehensible to highly competent drivers of very fast cars, so Hutchinson operated on a level incomprehensible to the finest of amateur yachtsmen. Search your ocean racing clubs and Olympic yachting teams the world over and you will not find men like this. They are to be found, and even then so very seldom, only in the ranks of the professional deep-sea fishermen.

Those huge hands on throttle and wheel had the delicacy of a moth. He had the night-sight of a barn owl and an ear which could infallibly distinguish between waves breaking in the open sea, on reefs or on shores: he could invariably tell the size and direction of seas coming at him out of the darkness and mist and touch wheel or throttle as need be: he had an inbuilt computer which provided instant correlation of wind, tide, current and our own speed and always let him know exactly where he was. And I'll swear he could smell land, even on a lee shore and with the rest of us suffering olfactory paralysis from the fumes of the big black cigars which seemed to be an inseparable part of the man. It required only ten minutes beside him to realize that one's ignorance of the sea and ships was almost total. A chastening discovery.

He took the *Charmaine* out through the Scylla and Charybdis of that evil alleged harbour entrance under full throttle.

Foaming white-fanged reefs reached out at us, bare feet away, on either side. He didn't seem to notice them. He certainly didn't look at them. The two 'boys' he'd brought with him, a couple of stunted lads of about six foot two or thereabouts, yawned prodigiously. Hutchinson located the *Firecrest* a hundred yards before I could even begin to imagine I could see any shape at all and brought the *Charmaine* alongside as neatly as I could park my car by the kerb in broad daylight – on one of my better days, that was. I went aboard the *Firecrest* to the vast alarm of Uncle Arthur and Charlotte who'd heard no whisper of our arrival, explained the situation, introduced Hutchinson and went back aboard the *Charmaine*. Fifteen minutes later, the radio call over, I was back aboard the *Firecrest*.

Uncle Arthur and Tim Hutchinson were already thick as thieves. The bearded Australian giant was extremely courteous and respectful, calling Uncle Arthur 'Admiral' every other sentence while Uncle Arthur was plainly delighted and vastly relieved to have him on board. If I felt this was a slight on my own seaman-like qualities, I was undoubtedly correct.

'Where are we off to now?' Charlotte Skouras asked. I was disappointed to see that she was just as relieved as Uncle Arthur.

'Dubh Sgeir,' I said. 'To pay a call on Lord Kirkside and his charming daughter.'

'Dubh Sgeir!' She seemed taken aback. 'I thought you said the answer lay in Eilean Oran and Craigmore?'

'So I did. The answers to some essential preliminary questions. But the end of the road lies in Dubh Sgeir. And the foot of the rainbow.'

'You talk in riddles,' she said impatiently.

'Not to me, he doesn't,' Hutchinson said jovially. 'The foot of the rainbow, ma'am. That's where the pot of gold lies.'

'Here and now I'd settle for a pot of coffee,' I said. 'Coffee for four and I'll make it with my own fair hands.'

'I think I would rather go to bed,' Charlotte said. 'I am very tired.'

'You made me drink your coffee,' I said threateningly. 'Now you drink mine. Fair's fair.'

'If you are quick, then.'

I was quick. I'd four cups on a little tin tray in nothing flat, a powerful mixture of instant coffee, milk and sugar in all of them and a little something extra in one of them. There were no complaints about the coffee. Hutchinson drained his cup and said: 'Can't see why you three shouldn't get your heads down for a little. Unless you think I need help?'

No one thought he needed help. Charlotte Skouras was the first to go, saying she felt very sleepy, which I didn't doubt. She sounded it. Uncle Arthur and I left a moment later, Tim Hutchinson promising to call me when we neared the landing stage on the west side of Dubh Sgeir. Uncle Arthur wrapped himself in a rug on the saloon settee. I went to my own cabin and lay down.

I lay for three minutes then rose, picked up a three-cornered file, softly opened my cabin door and as softly knocked on Charlotte's door. There was no reply, so I opened the door, passed in, silently closed it and switched on the lights.

She was asleep all right, she was a million miles away. She hadn't even managed to make it to bed, she was lying on the carpet, still fully clothed. I put her on the bunk and pulled a couple of blankets over her. I pushed up a sleeve and examined the mark left by the rope burn.

It wasn't a very big cabin and it took me only a minute to find what I was looking for.

III

It made a pleasant change and a very refreshing one to transfer myself from the *Firecrest* to land without that damned clammy scuba suit impeding every stroke or step of the way.

How Tim Hutchinson located that old stone pier in the rain, the fog and the darkness was something that would have been for ever beyond me – if he hadn't told me later that night. He sent me to the bows with a torch in my hand and damned if the thing didn't loom out of the darkness as if he'd gone in on a radio bearing. He went into reverse, brought the bows, plunging heavily in the deep troughs, to within two feet of the pier, waited till I picked my moment to jump off then went full astern and disappeared into the fog and darkness. I tried to imagine Uncle Arthur executing that lot, but my imagination wasn't up to it. It boggled. Uncle Arthur, thank heaven, slept the sleep of the just. Drake was in his hammock and a thousand miles away, dreaming all the time of WC1.

The path from the landing stage to the plateau above was steep and crumbling and someone had carelessly forgotten to equip it with a handrail on the seaward side. I was in no way heavily burdened. All I was carrying apart from the weight of my own years was a torch, gun and coil of rope – I'd neither the intention nor the expectation of doing a Douglas Fairbanks on the outer battlements of the Dubh Sgeir castle, but experience had taught me that a rope was the most essential piece of equipment to carry along on a jaunt on a precipitously walled island – but even so I was breathing pretty heavily by the time I reached the top.

I turned not towards the castle but north along the grass strip that led to the cliff at the northern end of the island. The strip that Lord Kirkside's elder son had taken off from in his Beechcraft on the day when he and his brother-in-law to be had died, the strip that Williams and I had flown along less than twelve hours previously after our talk with Lord Kirkside and his daughter, the strip at the abrupt northern end of which I'd imagined I'd seen what I'd wanted to see, but couldn't be sure. Now I was going to make sure.

The strip was smooth and flat and I made good time without having to use the big rubber torch I had with me. I didn't dare use it anyway, not so close to the castle. There was no light to be seen from there but that was no guarantee that the ungodly weren't maintaining a sleepless watch on the battlements. If I were ungodly, I'd have been maintaining a sleepless watch on the battlements. I stumbled over something warm and soft and alive and hit the ground hard.

My nerves weren't what they had been forty-eight hours ago and my reactions were comparatively fast. I had the knife in my hand and was on to him before he could get to his feet. To his four feet. He had about him the pungent aroma of a refugee from Tim Hutchinson's flensing shed. Well might they say why stinks the goat on yonder hill who seems to dote on chlorophyll. I said a few conciliatory words to our four-footed friend and it seemed to work, for he kept his horns to himself. I went on my way.

This humiliating sort of encounter, I'd noticed, never happened to the Errol Flynns of this world. Moreover, if Errol Flynn had been carrying a torch a little fall like that would not have smashed it. Had he been carrying only a candle it would still have kept burning brightly in the darkness. But not my torch. Not my rubber encased, rubber mounted bulb, plexi-glass guaranteed unbreakable torch. It was kaput. I fished out the little pencil torch and tried it inside my jacket. I could have spared myself the caution, a glow-worm would have sneered at it. I stuck it back in my pocket and kept going.

I didn't know how far I was from the precipitous end of the cliff and I'd no intention of finding out the hard way. I dropped to my hands and knees and crawled forward, the glow-worm leading the way. I reached the cliff edge in five minutes and found what I was looking for almost at once. The deep score on the cliff edge was almost eighteen inches in width and four in depth in the centre. The mark was fresh but not too fresh. The grass had grown in again in most places. The time factor would be just about right. It was the mark that had been left by the tail fuselage of the Beechcraft plane when, with no one aboard, it had been started up, throttle opened and then the chocks removed. It hadn't had enough speed to become airborne and had fallen over the cliff edge, ripping this score in the earth as it had gone. That was all I needed, that and the holed hull of the Oxford expedition boat and the dark circles under the blue eyes of Susan Kirkside. Here was certainty.

I heard a slight noise behind me. A moderately fit five-year-old grabbing me by the ankles could have had me over the edge with nothing I could do to prevent it. Or maybe it was Billy the Kid back to wreak vengeance for the rude interruption of his night's sleep. I swung round with torch and gun at the ready. It *was* Billy the Kid, his yellow eyes staring balefully out of the night. But his eyes belied him, he was just curious or friendly or both. I moved back slowly till I was out of butting range, patted him weakly on the head and left. At this rate I'd die of heart failure before the night was out.

The rain had eased by this time and the wind fallen away quite a bit, but to compensate for this the mist was worse than ever. It swirled clammily around me and I couldn't see four feet in front of my face. I wondered grimly how Hutchinson was getting on in this lot, but put him quickly out of my mind. I'd no doubt he was a damned sight better at his job than I was at mine. I kept the wind on my right cheek and continued towards the castle. Under my rubber-canvas raincoat my last suit was sodden. The Civil Service was going to be faced with a cleaner's bill of some note.

I near as a toucher walked into the castle wall but saw its loom just in time. I didn't know whether I was to the right or the left of the entrance gate on the landward side, so I felt my way cautiously to the left to find out. After about ten feet the wall fell away at right angles to another wall. That meant I'd arrived at the left or eastern side of the gate. I began to feel my way to the right.

It was as well I had come upon the castle wall where I had done: had I arrived at the right-hand side, I'd have been upwind of the central gate and would never have smelled the tobacco smoke. It wasn't much as tobacco went, nothing like as robust as Uncle Arthur's cheroots and positively anaemic as compared to Tim Hutchinson's portable poison-gas factories, but tobacco smoke for all that. Someone at the entrance gate was smoking a cigarette. It was axiomatic that sentries should never smoke cigarettes. This I could deal with. They'd never trained me on how to handle billy goats on the edge of a precipice but on this subject they had become boringly repetitive.

I held the gun by the barrel and moved quietly forwards. He was leaning against the corner of the entrance, a hardly-seen shape, but his position outlined clearly enough by the movement of his cigarette end. I waited till he brought it to his mouth for the third time, and when it was glowing at its brightest and his night vision consequently most affected I took one step forward and brought the butt down where by extension of the curve and subsequent glow of the cigarette end the back of the head of a normal man ought to have been. Fortunately, he was a normal man.

He fell back against me. I caught him and something jabbed painfully into my ribs. I let him finish the trip down on his own and removed this item that had become stuck in my coat. A bayonet, and, what was more, a bayonet with a very nasty point to it. Attached to the bayonet was a Lee Enfield .303. Very military. It seemed unlikely that this was just a routine precaution. Our friends were becoming worried and I had no means of knowing how much they knew or guessed. Time was running very short for them, almost as short as it was for me. In a few hours it would be dawn.

I took the rifle and moved cautiously towards the edge of the cliff, the bayonet prodding the earth ahead of me as I went. By this time I was becoming quite adept at not falling over the edges of precipices and, besides, with a rifle and bayonet stretched out in advance you have five-feet notification of where eternity begins. I found the edge, stepped back, reversed the rifle, made two parallel scores in the sodden turf about a foot apart and eighteen inches in length, terminating on the very edge. I wiped the butt clean and placed the rifle on the ground. When the dawn came, the sentry changed and a search made, I trusted the proper conclusions would be drawn.

I hadn't hit him as hard as I'd thought, he was beginning to stir and moan feebly by the time I got back to him. This was all to the good; the alternative would have been to carry him and I was in no fit state to carry anyone. I stuffed a handkerchief into his mouth and the moaning stopped. Bad practice, I knew, for a gagged man with a head cold or nasal obstruction can die of suffocation in four minutes, but I hadn't the facilities to carry out a sinus examination, and, more importantly, it was his health or mine.

He was up on his feet in two minutes. He didn't try to run away or offer resistance, for by this time he had his ankles on a short hobble, his hands tied securely behind his back and the barrel of an automatic pressing into the side of his neck. I told him to walk, and he walked. Two hundred yards away, at the head of the path leading down to the landing stage, I led him off to one side, tied his wrists and ankles together and left him there. He seemed to be breathing without too much difficulty.

There were no other sentries, at least not on the main gate. I crossed the hollow square of a courtyard and came to the main door. It was closed but not locked. I passed inside and said a few hard things to myself about myself for not having searched that sentry for the torch he would almost certainly have been carrying. The window curtains must have been drawn and the darkness inside that hall was total. I didn't much fancy moving around a Scottish baronial hall in total darkness, the risk of bringing down a suit of armour with a resounding metallic crash or impaling oneself on targes, claymores or a royal set of antlers must be high. I took out my pencil flash but the glow-worm inside was breathing its last, even when hard-pressed against the face of my wrist-watch it was impossible to tell the time. It was impossible to see the wrist-watch.

From the air, yesterday, I'd seen that the castle had been built in perfect symmetry round three sides of a hollow square. It was a reasonable assumption then that if the main door was in the middle of the central of seaward-facing section then the main staircase would be directly opposite. It seemed likely that the middle of the hall would offer a passage unimpeded by either claymores or antlers.

It did. The stairs were where they should have been. Ten wide shallow steps and then the stairs branched both right and left. I chose the right-hand side because above me, on that side, I could see a faint loom of light. Six steps on the second flight of stairs, another right turn, eight more steps and then I was on the landing. Twenty-four steps and never a creak. I blessed the architect who had specified marble.

The light was much stronger now. I advanced towards its source, a door no more than an inch ajar, and applied a wary eye to the crack. All I could see was the corner of a wardrobe, a strip of carpet, the corner of the foot of a bed and, on the last, a muddy boot. A low-register cacophony of sound emerged, reminiscent of a boiler factory in the middle distance. I pushed the door and walked inside.

I'd come to see Lord Kirkside, and whoever this was it wasn't Lord Kirkside, for whatever Lord Kirkside was in the habit of doing I was fairly certain that he didn't go to bed in boots, braces and cloth cap, with a bayoneted rifle lying on the blankets beside him, which was what this character had done. I couldn't see his face, because the cloth cap reached as far as his nose. On the bedside beside him lay a torch and a half-empty whisky bottle. No glass, but from what little I could see of him I would have judged that he was, anyhow, one of those characters whose direct and simple enjoyment of life has not been impaired by the effete conventions of modern civilization. The faithful watchman prudently preparing himself for the rigours of the West Highland night before taking his turn at sentry-go. But he wouldn't be making it at the appointed hour for there was no one now to call him. From the look of it, he'd be lucky to make it for lunch.

It was just possible that he might wake himself up, those stentorian snores wouldn't have gone unremarked in a mortuary. He had about him the look of a man who, on regaining consciousness, would find himself in need of thirst-quenching nourishment, so I unscrewed the bottle top, dropped in half a dozen of the tablets supplied by my pharmaceutical friend in Torbay, replaced the top, took the torch and left.

Behind the next door to the left lay a bathroom. A filthy basin with, above it, a water-stained mirror, two shaving brushes covered with lather, a jar of shaving cream with the top off, two unwashed razors and, on the floor, two towels that might just possibly have been white at some distant aeon in the past. The interior of the bath was immaculate. Here was where the watchman performed his rudimentary ablutions.

The next room was a bedroom as dirty and disorderly as the watchman's. It was a fair guess that this was the home of the man I'd left lying out among the gorse and stones on the hillside.

I moved across to the left-hand side of the central block – Lord Kirkside would have his room somewhere in that block. He did, but he wasn't at home. The first room beyond the sleeping warrior's was his all right, a glance at the contents of the nearest wardrobe confirmed this. But his bed hadn't been slept in.

Predictably in this symmetrically designed house, the next room was a bathroom. The watchman wouldn't have felt at all at home in here, this antiseptic cleanliness was the hallmark of an effete aristocracy. A medicine cabinet was fixed to the wall. I took out a tin of Elastoplast and covered the face of the torch till I was left with a hole no more than the size of a sixpence. I put the tin in my pocket.

The next door was locked but locks, in the days when the Dubh Sgeir Castle had been built, were pretty rudimentary affairs. I took from my pocket the best skeleton key in the world – an oblong of stiff celluloid. I shoved it between door and jamb at bolt level, pulled the door handle back in the direction of the hinges, eased in the celluloid, released the handle, repeated the process and stood stock-still. That click might have wakened my watchman friend, it should certainly have wakened the person inside. But I heard no sound of movement.

I opened the door a fraction of an inch and went through the stock-still standing process once more. There was a light on inside the room. I changed the torch for the gun, went on my knees, crouched low and abruptly opened the door wide. I stood up, closed and locked the door and crossed over to the bed.

Susan Kirkside wasn't snoring but she was just as deep in sleep as the man I'd just left. She had a blue silk band round her hair, and all of her face was visible, a sight that must have been rare indeed during her waking hours. Twenty-one, her father had said she was, but lying there asleep, smudged eyes and all, she looked no older than seventeen. A magazine had slipped from her hands to the floor. On the bedside table was a half-empty glass of water and beside that a bottle containing a commercial brand of Nembutal tablets. Oblivion appeared to be a pretty hard thing to come by in Dubh Sgeir and I'd no doubt Susan Kirkside found it more difficult than most.

I picked up a towel from a basin in the corner of the room, removed the worst of the moisture and dirt from head and face, combed my hair into some semblance of order and gave my kindly reassuring smile a try-out in the mirror. I looked like someone from the pages of the *Police Gazette*.

It took almost two minutes to shake her awake or, at least, to pull her up from the dark depths of oblivion to a state of semi-awareness. Full consciousness took another minute, and it was probably this that saved me from a screaming match, she had time to adjust herself to the slow realization of the presence of a stranger in the middle of the night. Mind you, I had my kindly smile going full blast till my face ached, but I don't think it helped much.

'Who are you? Who *are* you?' Her voice was shaking, the blue eyes, still misted with sleep, wide open and scared. 'Don't you touch me! Don't you – I'll scream for help – I'll—'

I took her hands just to show her that there was touching and touching. 'I won't touch you, Sue Kirkside. And a fat lot of good screaming for help would do around these parts. Don't scream, there's a good girl. In fact, don't even talk above a whisper. I don't think it would be very wise or safe, do you?'

She stared at me for a few seconds, her lips moving as if she were about to speak, but the fear slowly leaving her eyes. Suddenly she sat bolt upright. 'You're Mr Johnson. The man from the helicopter.'

'You should be more careful,' I said reproachfully. 'They'd have you arrested for that in the Folies-Bergère.' Her free hand hauled the blankets up to her chin and I went on: 'My name is Calvert. I work for the Government. I'm a friend. I think you need a friend, don't you, Susan? You and your old man – Lord Kirkside, that is.'

'What do you want?' she whispered. 'What are you doing here?'

'I'm here to end your troubles,' I said. 'I'm here to cadge an invitation to your wedding to the Honourable John Rollinson. Make it about the end of next month, will you? I'm due some leave, then.'

'Go away from here.' Her voice was low and desperate. 'Go away from here or you'll ruin everything. Please, please, *please* go away. I'm begging you, I'm begging you. Go away. If you're a friend, go away. Please, oh please go away!'

It seemed that she wanted me to leave. I said: 'It appears that they have you pretty well brain-washed. If you believe their promise, you'll believe anything in the world. They won't let you go, they daren't let you go, they'll destroy every shred and trace of evidence that might ever point a finger at them. That includes anyone who has ever had anything to do with them.'

'They won't, they *won't*. I was with Mr Lavorski when he promised Daddy that no one would come to any harm. He said they were businessmen, and killing was no part of business. He meant it.'

'Lavorski, is it? It had to be.' I looked at the earnest scared face. 'He may have meant it when he said it. He wouldn't have mentioned that they've murdered four people in the last three days, or that they have tried to murder me four times in the last three days.'

'You're lying! You're making this up. Things like that – things like that don't happen any more. For pity's sake leave us alone!'

'There speaks the true daughter of the old Scottish clan chieftain.' I said roughly. 'You're no good to me. Where's your father?'

'I don't know. Mr Lavorski and Captain Imrie – he's another of them – came for him at eleven tonight. Daddy didn't say where he was going. He tells me nothing.' She paused and snatched her hands away. Faint red patches stained her cheeks. 'What do you mean, I'm no good to you?'

'Did he say when he would be back?'

'What do you mean I'm no good to you?'

'Because you're young and not very clever and you don't know too much about this world and you'll believe anything a hardened criminal will tell you. But most especially because you won't believe me. You won't believe the one person who can save you all. You're a stupid and pig-headed young fool, Miss Kirkside. If it wasn't that he was jumping from the frying-pan into the fire, I'd say the Honourable Rollinson has had a lucky escape.'

'What do you mean?' It is hard for a mobile young face to be expressionless, but hers was then.

'He can't marry you when he is dead,' I said brutally. 'And he is going to die. He's going to die because Sue Kirkside let him die. Because she was too blind to know truth when she saw it.' I had what was, for me, an inspiration. I turned down my collar and pulled my scarf away. 'Like it?' I asked.

She didn't like it at all. The red faded from her cheeks. I could see myself in her dressing-table mirror and I didn't like it either. Quinn's handiwork was in full bloom. The kaleidoscope of colour now made a complete ring round my neck.

'Quinn?' she whispered.

'You know his name. You know him?'

'I know them all. Most of them, anyway. Cook said that one night, after he'd too much to drink, he'd been boasting in the kitchen about how he'd once been the strong man in a stage act. He'd an argument one night with his partner. About a woman. He killed his partner. That way.' She had to make a physical effort to turn her eyes away from my neck. 'I thought – I thought it was just talk.'

'And do you still think our pals are unpaid missionaries for the Society for the Propagation of Christian Knowledge?' I sneered. 'Do you know Jacques and Kramer?'

She nodded.

'I killed them both tonight. After they had killed a friend of mine. They broke his neck. Then they tried to kill my boss and myself. And I killed another. He came out of the dark to murder us. I think his name was Henry. Do you believe me now? Or do you still think we're all dancing round the old maypole on the village green, singing ring-a-ring-o'-roses as we go?'

The shock treatment worked almost too well. Her face wasn't pale now, it was ashen. She said: 'I think I'm going to be sick.'

'Later,' I said coldly. What little self-regard I had was down among my shoe-laces, what I would have liked to do was to take her in my arms and say: 'There, there, now, don't you worry your pretty head, just you leave everything to your old Uncle Philip and all will be well at the end of the day.' In fact, it was damned hard not to do it. Instead, what I said, still in the same nasty voice, was: 'We've no time for those little fol-de-rols. You want to get married, don't you? Did your father say when he would be back?'

She looked at the wash-basin in the corner of the room as if she were still making up her mind whether to be sick or not then pulled her eyes back to me and whispered: 'You're just as bad as they are. You're a terrible man. You're a killer.'

I caught her shoulders and shook them. I said savagely: 'Did he say when he would be back?'

'No.' Her eyes were sick with revulsion. It was a long time since any woman had looked at me like that. I dropped my hands.

'Do you know what those men are doing here?'

'No.'

I believed her. Her old man would know, but he wouldn't

have told her. Lord Kirkside was too astute to believe that their uninvited guests would just up and leave them unharmed. Maybe he was just desperately gambling that if he told his daughter nothing and if he could swear she knew nothing then they would leave her be. If that was what he thought, he was in urgent need of an alienist. But that was being unjust, if I stood in his shoes – or, more accurately, was swimming in the murky waters he was in – I'd have grabbed at any straw.

'It's obvious that you know that your fiancé is still alive,' I went on. 'And your elder brother. And others. They're being held here, aren't they?'

She nodded silently. I wished she wouldn't look at me like that.

'Do you know how many?'

'A dozen. More than that. And I know there are children there. Three boys and a girl.'

That would be right. Sergeant MacDonald's two sons and the boy and the girl that had been aboard the converted lifeboat that had disappeared after setting off on the night cruise from Torbay. I didn't believe a word that Lavorski had said to Susan about their reverence for human life. But I wasn't surprised that the people in the boats who had accidentally stumbled across his illegal operations were still alive. There was a very good reason for this.

'Do you know where they are kept? There should be any amount of handy dungeons in Dubh Sgeir castle.'

'There are cellars deep underground. I've never been allowed to go near them in the past four months.'

'This is your big chance come at last. Get your clothes on and take me there.'

'Go down to the cellars?' Aghast was the word for her expression. 'Are you mad? Daddy tells me there are at least three men on guard duty all night long.' There were only two men now, but her opinion of me was low enough already, so I kept quiet. 'They're armed. You *must* be mad. I'm not going!'

'I didn't think you would. You'll let your boy friend die just because you're a contemptible little coward.' I could almost taste the self-loathing in my mouth. 'Lord Kirkside and the Honourable Rollinson. What a lucky father. What a fortunate fiancé.'

She hit me, and I knew I had won. I said without touching my face: 'Don't do that. You'll waken up the guard. Get your clothes on.'

I rose, sat on the footboard of the bed and contemplated the door and higher things while she changed. I was becoming tired of women telling me what a horrible character I was.

'I'm ready,' she said.

She was back in her uniform of pirate's jersey and the denims she'd outgrown when she was about fifteen. Thirty seconds flat and nary a sound of a portable sewing machine. Baffling, that's what it was.

— 9 —

Thursday: 4.30 a.m. – dawn

WE WENT DOWN the stairs hand in hand. I may have been the last man in the world she would have elected to be alone with on a desert island, but she clung on pretty tightly all the same.

At the foot of the steps we turned right. I flicked on the torch every few yards but it wasn't really necessary, Susan knew every yard of the way. At the end of the hall we turned left along the eastern wing. Eight yards and we stopped at a door on the right-hand side.

'The pantry,' she whispered. 'The kitchen is beyond that.'

I stooped and looked through the keyhole. Beyond was darkness. We passed through the doorway, then into an archway giving on to the kitchen. I flashed the tiny beam around the room. Empty.

There were three guards, Susan had said. The outside man, for whom I had accounted. The lad who patrolled the battlements. No, she didn't know what he did, but it was a good guess that he wasn't studying astronomy or guarding against parachutists. He'd have night glasses to his eyes and he'd be watching for fishing vessels, naval craft or fishery cruisers that might happen by and interrupt honest men at their work. He wouldn't see much on a night like this. And the third man, she said, guarded the back kitchen premises, the only entrance to the castle apart from the main gate – and the unfortunates in their cellars down below.

He wasn't in the kitchen premises, so he would be in the cellars down below.

A flight of steps led from the scullery beyond and kitchen down to a stone-flagged floor. To the right of this floor I could see the loom of light. Susan raised a finger to her lips and we made our way soundlessly down to the foot of the steps. I slid a cautious eye round the corner of this passageway.

It wasn't a passageway, it was the damnedest flight of steps I'd ever come across. They were lit by two or three far-spaced and very weak electric bulbs, the walls coming together towards the foot like a pair of railway lines disappearing into the distance. Maybe fifty feet – or seventy steps – down, where the first light was, another passageway branched off to the right. There was a stool at the corner of the small stone landing there, and sitting on the stool a man. Across his knees lay a rifle. They certainly went in for the heavy artillery.

I drew back. I murmured to Susan: 'Where in hell's name do those steps lead to?'

'The boathouse, of course.' A surprised whisper. 'Where else?'

Where else, indeed. Brilliant work, Calvert, brilliant work. You'd skirted the south side of the Dubh Sgeir in the helicopter, you'd seen the castle, you'd seen the boathouse, you'd seen nary a handhold on the sheer cliff separating them, and you'd never raised an eyebrow at the glaring obviousness of the fact that ne'er the twain did meet.

'Those are the cellars in that passage going off to the right?' She nodded. 'Why so far down? It's a long walk to collect the bubbly.'

'They're not really wine-cellars. They used to be used as water reservoirs.'

'No other way of getting down there?'

'No. Only this way.'

'And if we take five steps down this way he shoots us full of holes with his Lee Enfield. Know who it is?'

'Harry. I don't know his other name. He's an Armenian, Daddy says. People can't pronounce his real name. He's young and smooth and greasy – and detestable.'

'He had the effrontery to make a pass at the chieftain's daughter?'

'Yes. It was horrible.' She touched her lips with the back of her hand. 'He stank of garlic.'

'I don't blame him. I'd do it myself if I didn't feel my pension creeping up on me. Call him up and make amends.'

'What?'

'Tell him you're sorry. Tell him you misjudged his noble character. Tell him your father is away and this is the first chance you've had of speaking to him. Tell him anything.'

'No!'

'Sue!'

'He'll never believe me,' she said wildly.

'When he gets within two feet of you, he'll forget all about the reasoning why. He's a man, isn't he?'

'You're a man. And you're only six inches away.' The eternal female illogic.

'I've told you how it is, it's my pension coming between us. Quickly!'

She nodded reluctantly and I disappeared into the shadows of the nearest cellar, reversed gun in hand. She called and he came a-running, his rifle at the ready. When he saw who it was, he forgot all about his rifle. Susan started to speak her lines but she might have saved her breath. Harry, if nothing else, was an impetuous young man. That wild Armenian blood. I stepped forwards, arm swinging, and lowered him to the ground. I tied him up and, as I'd run out of handkerchiefs, ripped away part of his shirt-front and used it as a gag. Susan giggled, a giggle with a note of hysteria.

'What's up?' I asked.

'Harry. He's what they call a snappy dresser. That's a silk shirt. You're no respecter of persons, Mr Calvert.'

'Not persons like Harry. Congratulations. Wasn't so bad, was it?'

'It was still horrible.' Again the hand to the mouth. 'He's reeking of whisky.'

'Youngsters have odd tastes,' I said kindly. 'You'll grow out of it. At least it must have been an improvement on the garlic.'

II

The boathouse wasn't really a boathouse at all, it was a large vaulting cave formed in a cleft in a natural fault in the cliff strata. At the inner end of the cave longitudinal tunnels stretched away on either side paralleling the coastline, until they vanished beyond the reach of my torch. From the air, the boathouse in the small artificial harbour, a structure of about twenty feet by twenty, had seemed incapable of housing more than two or three fair-sized rowing boats. Inside it was big enough to berth a boat the size of the *Firecrest*, and then leave room to spare. Mooring bollards, four in number, lined the eastern side of the boathouse. There were signs of recent work where the inner end of the cave had been lengthened in the direction of the longitudinal tunnels to increase the berthing space and provide a bigger working platform, but otherwise it was as it must have been for hundreds of years. I picked up a boat-hook and tried to test the depth, but couldn't find bottom. Any vessel small enough to be accommodated inside could enter and leave at any state of the tide. The two big doors looked solid but not too solid. There was a small dry-land doorway on the eastern side.

The berth was empty, as I had expected to find it. Our friends were apprehensive and on piece-work rates. It wasn't difficult to guess what they were working at, the working platform was liberally stacked with the tools of their trade: an oil engine-driven air compressor with a steel reservoir with outlet valves, a manually-operated, two-cylinder double-acting air pump with two outlets, two helmets with attached corselets, flexible, non-collapsible air tubes with metal couplings, weighted boots, diving dresses, life-cum-telephone lines, lead weights and scuba equipment such as I had myself, with a stack of compressed air cylinders at the ready.

I felt neither surprise nor elation, I'd known this must exist for the past forty-eight hours although I'd become certain of the location only that night. I was faintly surprised perhaps, to see all this equipment here, for this would surely be only the spares. But I shouldn't have been even vaguely surprised. Whatever this bunch lacked, it wasn't a genius for organization.

III

I didn't see that night, nor did I ever see, the cellars where the prisoners were housed. After I'd huffed and puffed three-quarters of the way up that interminable flight of steps, I turned left along the passageway where we'd first seen Harry taking his ease. After a few yards the passageway broadened out into a low damp chamber containing a table made of beer-cases, some seats of the same and, in one corner, some furniture that hadn't yet been drunk. A bottle of whisky, nearly full, stood on the table: Harry's remedy for garlic halitosis.

Beyond this chamber was a massive wooden door secured by an equally massive-looking lock with the key missing. All the celluloid in the world wouldn't open this lot but a beehive plastic explosive would do a very efficient job indeed. I made another of the many mental notes I'd made that night and went up the stairs to rejoin Susan.

IV

Harry had come to. He was saying something in his throat which fortunately couldn't get past his silk-shirted gag to the delicate ears of the chieftain's young daughter, his eyes, to mint a phrase, spoke volumes and he was trying as best he could to do a Houdini with the ropes round his legs and arms. Susan Kirkside was pointing a rifle in his general direction and looking very apprehensive. She needn't have bothered, Harry was trussed like a turkey.

'These people down in the cellars,' I said. 'They've been there for weeks, some for months. They'll be blind as bats and weak as kittens by the time they get out.'

She shook her head. 'I think they'll be all right. They're taken out on the landing strip there for an hour and a half every morning under guard. They can't be seen from the sea.

We're not allowed to watch. Or not supposed to. I've seen them often. Daddy insisted on it. And Sir Anthony.'

'Well, good old Daddy.' I stared at her. 'Old man Skouras. He comes here?'

'Of course.' She seemed surprised at my surprise. 'He's one of them. Lavorski and this man Dollmann, the men that do all the arranging, they work for Sir Anthony. Didn't you know? Daddy and Sir Anthony are friends – were friends – before this. I've been in Sir Anthony's London home often.'

'But they're not friends now?' I probed keenly.

'Sir Anthony has gone off his head since his wife died,' Susan said confidently. I looked at her in wonder and tried to remember when I'd last been so authoritatively dogmatic on subjects I knew nothing about. I couldn't remember. 'He married again, you know. Some French actress or other. That wouldn't have helped. She's no good. She caught him on the rebound.'

'Susan,' I said reverently, 'you're really wonderful. I don't believe you'll ever understand what I mean by my pension coming between us. You know her well?'

'I've never met her.'

'You didn't have to tell me. And poor old Sir Anthony – he doesn't know what he's doing, is that it?'

'He's all mixed up,' she said defensively. 'He's sweet, really he is. Or was.'

'All mixed up with the deaths of four men, not to mention three of his own,' I said. Sergeant MacDonald thought him a good man. Susan thought him sweet. I wondered what she would say if she saw Charlotte Skouras's back. 'How do the prisoners do for food?'

'We have two cooks. They do it all. The food is brought down to them.'

'What other staff?'

'No other staff. Daddy was made to sack them all four months ago.'

That accounted for the state of the watchman's bathroom. I said: 'My arrival in the helicopter here yesterday afternoon was duly reported by radio to the *Shangri-la*. A man with a badly scarred face. Where's the radio transmitter?'

'You know everything, don't you?'

'Know-all Calvert. Where is it?'

'Off the hall. In the room behind the stairs. It's locked.'

'I have keys that'll open the Bank of England. Wait a minute.' I went down to the guard's room outside the prisoners' cellar, brought the whisky bottle back up to where Susan was standing and handed it to her. 'Hang on to this.'

She looked at me steadily. 'Do you really need this?'

'Oh my God, sweet youth.' I said nastily. 'Sure I need it. I'm an alcoholic.'

I untied the rope round Harry's ankles and helped him to his feet. He repaid this Samaritan gesture by swinging at me with his right foot but fifteen minutes on the floor hadn't helped his circulation or reactions any and I forestalled him with the same manoeuvre. When I helped him up the second time there was no fight left in him.

'Did you – did you really have to do that?' The revulsion was back in her eyes.

'Did I – did you see what he tried to do to me?' I demanded.

'You men are all the same,' she said.

'Oh, shut up!' I snarled. I was old and sick and tired and I'd run right out of the last of my witty ripostes.

V

The transceiver was a beauty, a big gleaming metallic RCA, the latest model as used in the naval vessels of a dozen nationalities. I didn't waste any time wondering where they had obtained it, that lot were fit for anything. I sat down and started tuning the set, then looked up at Susan. 'Go and fetch me one of your father's razor blades.'

'You don't want me to hear, is that it?'

'Think what you like. Just get it.'

If she'd been wearing a skirt she'd have flounced out of the room. With what she was wearing flouncing was out of the question. The set covered every transmission frequency from the bottom of the long wave to the top of the VHF It took only two minutes to raise SPFX. It was manned night and day the year round. It really was most considerate of the ungodly to provide me with such a magnificent instrument.

Sue Kirkside was back before I started speaking. I was ten

minutes on the microphone altogether. Apart from code-names and map references I used plain English throughout. I had to, I'd no book, and time was too short anyway. I spoke slowly and clearly, giving precise instructions about the movements of men, the alignment of radio frequencies, the minutest details of the layout of Dubh Sgeir castle and asking all-important questions about recent happenings on the Riviera. I didn't repeat myself once, and I asked for nothing to be repeated to me, because every word was being recorded. Before I was half-way through, Susan's eyebrows had disappeared up under the blonde fringe and Harry was looking as if he had been sandbagged. I signed off, reset the tuning band to its original position and stood up.

'That's it,' I said. 'I'm off.'

'You're *what*?' The grey-blue eyes were wide, the eyebrows still up under the fringe, but with alarm, this time, not astonishment. 'You're leaving? You're leaving me here?'

'I'm leaving. If you think I'd stay a minute longer in this damned castle than I have to, you must be nuts. I've played my hand far enough already. Do you think I want to be around here when the guards change over or when the toilers on the deep get back here?'

'Toilers on the deep? What do you mean?'

'Skip it.' I'd forgotten she knew nothing about what our friends were doing. 'It's Calvert for home.'

'You've got a gun,' she said wildly. 'You could – you could capture them, couldn't you?'

'Capture who?' The hell with the grammar.

'The guards. They're on the second floor. They'll be asleep.'

'How many?'

'Eight or nine. I'm not sure.'

'Eight or nine, she's not sure! Who do you think I am, Superman? Stand aside, do you want me to get killed? And, Susan, tell nothing to anybody. Not even Daddy. Not if you want to see Johnny-boy walk down that aisle. You understand?'

She put a hand on my arm and said quietly but with the fear still in her face: 'You could take me with you.'

'I could. I could take you with me and ruin everything. If I as much as fired a single shot at any of the sleeping warriors up top, I'd ruin everything. Everything depends on their never knowing that anybody was here tonight. If they suspected that, just had a hint of a suspicion of that, they'd pack their bags and take off into the night. Tonight. And I can't possibly do anything until tomorrow night. You understand, of course, that they wouldn't leave until after they had killed everyone in the cellar. And your father, of course. And they'd stop off at Torbay and make sure that Sergeant MacDonald would never give evidence against them. Do you want that, Susan? God knows I'd love to take you out of here, I'm not made of Portland cement, but if I take you the alarm bells will ring and then they'll pull the plug. Can't you see that? If they come back and find you gone, they'll have one thought and one thought only in their minds: our little Sue has left the island. With, of course, one thought in mind. You must not be missing.'

'All right.' She was calm now. 'But you're overlooking something.'

'I'm a great old overlooker. What?'

'Harry. He'll be missing. He'll have to be. You can't leave him to talk.'

'He'll be missing. So will the keeper of the gate. I clobbered him on the way in.' She started to get all wide-eyed again but I held up my hand, stripped off coat and wind-breaker, unwrapped the razor she'd brought me and nicked my forearm, not too deeply, the way I felt I needed all the blood I had, but enough to let me smear the bottom three inches of the bayonet on both sides. I handed her the tin of Elastoplast and without a word she stuck a strip across the incision. I dressed again and we left, Susan with the whisky bottle and torch, myself with the rifle, shepherding Harry in front of me. Once in the hall I relocked the door with the skeleton key I'd used to open it.

The rain had stopped and there was hardly any wind, but the mist was thicker than ever and the night had turned bitterly cold. The Highland Indian summer was in full swing. We made our way through the courtyard across to where I'd left the bayonet lying on the cliff edge, using the torch, now with the Elastoplast removed from its face, quite freely, but keeping our voices low. The lad maintaining his ceaseless vigil on the battlements couldn't have seen us five yards away with the finest night-glasses in the world, but sound in heavy mist has unpredictable qualities, it can be muffled, it can be distorted, or it can occasionally be heard with surprising clarity, and it was now too late in the day to take chances.

I located the bayonet and told Harry to lie face down in the grass; if I'd left him standing he just might have been tempted to kick me over the edge. I gouged the grass in assorted places with heel and toe, made a few more scores with the butt of a bayonet, stuck the blade of the gate-keeper's bayonet in the ground at a slight angle so that the rifle was just clear of the ground, laid Harry down so that the blood-stained bayonet tip was also just clear of the ground, so preventing the blood from running off among the wet grass, scattered most of the contents of the whisky bottle around and carefully placed the bottle, about a quarter full now, close to one of the bayonets. I said to Susan: 'And what happened here do you think?'

'It's obvious. They had a drunken fight and both of them slipped on the wet grass over the edge of the cliff.'

'And what did you hear?'

'Oh! I heard the sound of two men shouting in the hall. I went on to the landing and I heard them shouting at the tops of their voices. I heard the one tell Harry to get back to his post and Harry saying, no, by God, he was going to settle it now. I'll say both men were drunk, and I won't repeat the kind of language they were using. The last I heard they were crossing the courtyard together, still arguing.'

'Good girl. That's exactly what you heard.'

She came with us as far as the place where I'd left the gate-keeper. He was still breathing. I used most of what rope I'd left to tie them together at the waist, a few feet apart, and wrapped the end of it in my hand. With their arms lashed behind their backs they weren't going to have much balancing power and no holding power at all on the way down that steep and crumbling path to the landing stage. If either slipped or stumbled I might be able to pull them back to safety with a sharp tug. There was going to be none of this Alpine stuff with the rope around my waist also. If they were going to step out into the darkness they were going to do it without me.

I said: 'Thank you, Susan. You have been a great help.

Don't take any more of those Nembutal tablets tonight. They'd think it damn' funny if you were still asleep at midday tomorrow.'

'I wish it were midday the next day. I won't let you down, Mr Calvert. Everything is going to be all right, isn't it?'

'Of course.'

There was a pause, then she said: 'You could have pushed these two over the edge if you wanted to, couldn't you. But you didn't. You could have cut Harry's arm, but you cut your own. I'm sorry for what I said, Mr Calvert. About you being horrible and terrible. You do what you have to do.' Another pause. 'I think you're rather wonderful.'

'They all come round in the end,' I said, but I was talking to myself, she'd vanished into the mist. I wished drearily that I could have agreed with her sentiments, I didn't feel wonderful at all, I just felt dead tired and worried stiff for with all the best planning in the world there were too many imponderables and I wouldn't have bet a brass farthing on the next twenty-four hours. I got some of the worry and frustration out of my system by kicking the two prisoners to their feet.

We went slowly down that crumbling treacherous path in single file, myself last, torch in my left hand, rope tightly – but not too tightly – in my right hand. I wondered vaguely as we went why I *hadn't* nicked Harry instead of myself. It would have been so much more fitting, Harry's blood on Harry's bayonet.

VI

'You had a pleasant outing, I trust?' Hutchinson asked courteously.

'It wasn't dull. You would have enjoyed it.' I watched Hutchinson as he pushed the *Firecrest* into the fog and the darkness. 'Let me into a professional secret. How in the world did you find your way back into this pier tonight? The mist is twice as bad as when I left. You cruise up and down for hours, impossible to take any bearings, there's the waves, tide, fog, currents – and yet there you are, right on the nose, to the minute. It can't be done.'

'It was an extraordinary feat of navigation,' Hutchinson

said solemnly. 'There are such things as charts, Calvert, and if you look at that large-scale one for this area you'll see an eight-fathom bank, maybe a cable in length, lying a cable and a half out to the west of the old pier there. I just steamed out straight into wind and tide, waited till the depth-sounder showed I was over the bank and dropped the old hook. At the appointed hour the great navigator lifts his hook and lets wind and tide drift him ashore again. Not many men could have done it.'

'I'm bitterly disappointed,' I said. 'I'll never think the same of you again. I suppose you used the same technique on the way in?'

'More or less. Only I used a series of five banks and patches. My secrets are gone for ever. Where now?'

'Didn't Uncle Arthur say?'

'You misjudge Uncle Arthur. He says he never interferes with you in – what was it? – the execution of a field operation. "I plan," he said. "I co-ordinate. Calvert finishes the job".'

'He has his decent moments,' I admitted.

'He told me a few stories about you in the past hour. I guess it's a privilege to be along.'

'Apart from the four hundred thousand quid or whatever?'

'Apart, as you say, from the green men. Where to, Calvert?'

'Home. If you can find it in this lot.'

'Craigmore? I can find it.' He puffed at his cigar and held the end close to his eyes. 'I think I should put this out. It's getting so I can't even see the length of the wheelhouse windows, far less beyond them. Uncle Arthur's taking his time, isn't he?'

'Uncle Arthur is interrogating the prisoners.'

'I wouldn't say he'd get much out of that lot.'

'Neither would I. They're not too happy.'

'Well, it *was* a nasty jump from the pier to the foredeck. Especially with the bows plunging up and down as they were. And more especially with their arms tied behind their backs.'

'One broken ankle and one broken forearm,' I said. 'It could have been worse. They could have missed the foredeck altogether.'

'You have a point,' Hutchinson agreed. He stuck his head out the side window and withdrew it again. 'It's not the cigar,' he announced. 'No need to quit smoking. Visibility is zero, and I mean zero. We're flying blind on instruments. You may as well switch on the wheelhouse lights. Makes it all that easier to read the charts, depth-sounder and compass and doesn't affect the radar worth a damn.' He stared at me as the light came on. 'What the hell are you doing in that flaming awful outfit?'

'This is a dressing-gown,' I explained. 'I've three suits and all three are soaked and ruined. Any luck, sir?' Uncle Arthur had just come in to the wheelhouse.

'One of them passed out.' Uncle Arthur wasn't looking very pleased with himself. 'The other kept moaning so loudly that I couldn't make myself heard. Well, Calvert, the story.'

'The story, sir? I was just going to bed. I've told you the story.'

'Half a dozen quick sentences that I couldn't hear above their damned caterwauling,' he said coldly. 'The whole story, Calvert.'

'I'm feeling weak, sir.'

'I've rarely known a time when you weren't feeling weak, Calvert. You know where the whisky is.'

Hutchinson coughed respectfully. 'I wonder if the admiral would permit—'

'Certainly, certainly,' Uncle Arthur said in a quite different tone. 'Of course, my boy.' The boy was a clear foot taller than Uncle Arthur. 'And while you're at it, Calvert, you might bring one for me, too, a normal-sized one.' He had his nasty side to him, had Uncle Arthur.

I said 'good night' five minutes later. Uncle Arthur wasn't too pleased, I'd the feeling he thought I'd missed out on the suspense and fancy descriptions, but I was as tired as the old man with the scythe after Hiroshima. I looked in on Charlotte Skouras; she was sleeping like the dead. I wondered about that chemist back in Torbay, he'd been three parts asleep, myopic as a barn owl and crowding eighty. He could have made a mistake. He could have had only a minimal experience in the prescribing of sleep-inducing drugs for those who lived in the land of the Hebridean prayer: 'Would that the peats might cut themselves and the fish jump on the shore, that I upon my bed might lie, and sleep for ever more.'

VII

But I'd done the old boy an injustice. After what was, to me, our miraculous arrival in Craigmore's apology for a harbour it had taken me no more than a minute to shake Charlotte into something resembling wakefulness. I told her to get dressed – a cunning move this to make her think I didn't know she was still dressed – and come ashore. Fifteen minutes after that we were all inside Hutchinson's house and fifteen minutes still later, when Uncle Arthur and I had roughly splinted the prisoners' fractures and locked them in a room illuminated only by a sky-light that would have taken Houdini all his time to wriggle through, I was in bed in another tiny box-room that was obviously the sleeping-quarters of the chairman of the Craigmore's art gallery selection committee, for he'd kept all the best exhibits to himself. I was just dropping off to sleep, thinking that if the universities ever got around to awarding Ph.D.s to house agents, the first degree would surely go to the first man who sold a Hebridean hut within sniffing distance of a flensing shed, when the door opened and the lights came on. I blinked open exhausted eyes and saw Charlotte Skouras softly closing the door behind her.

'Go away,' I said. 'I'm sleeping.'

'May I come in?' she asked. She gazed around the art gallery and her lips moved in what could have been the beginnings of a smile. 'I would have thought you would have gone to sleep with the lights on tonight.'

'You should see the ones behind the wardrobe doors. Sorry, I'm tired. What can I do? I'm not at my best receiving lady callers in the middle of the night.'

'Uncle Arthur's next door. You can scream for help if you want.' She looked at a moth-eaten armchair. 'May I sit down?'

She sat down. She still wore that uncrushable white dress and her hair was neatly combed, but that was about all you could say for her. Attempts at humour there might have been in her voice, but there was none in her face and none in her eyes. Those brown, wise, knowing eyes, eyes that knew all about living and loving and laughter, the eyes that had once made her the most sought-after actress of her time now held only sadness and despair. And fear. Now that she had escaped from her husband and his accomplices, there should have been no need for fear. But it was there, half-buried in the tired brown eyes, but there. Fear was an expression I knew. The lines round the eyes and mouth that looked so right, so inevitable, when she smiled or laughed – in the days when she had smiled or laughed – looked as if they had been etched by time and suffering and sorrow and despair into a face that had never known laughter and love. Charlotte Skouras's face, without the Charlotte Meiner of old behind it, no longer looked as if it belonged to her. A worn, a weary and an alien face. She must have been about thirty-five, I guessed, but she looked a deal older. And yet when she sat in that chair, almost huddled in that chair, the Craigmore art gallery no longer existed.

She said flatly: 'You don't trust me, Philip.'

'What on earth makes you say that? Why shouldn't I?'

'You tell me. You are evasive, you will not answer questions. No, that is wrong, you will and you do answer questions, but I know enough of men to know that the answers you give me are the ones you want to give me and not the ones I should hear. Why should this be, Philip? What have I done that you should not trust me?'

'So the truth is not in me? Well, I suppose I do stretch it a bit at times, I may even occasionally tell a lie. Strictly in the line of business, of course. I wouldn't lie to a person like you.' I meant it and intended not to – unless I had to do it for her sake, which was different.

'Why should you not lie to a person like me?'

'I don't know how to say it. I could say I don't usually lie to lovely and attractive women for whom I have a high regard, and then you'd cynically say I was stretching the truth till it snapped, and you'd be wrong because it is the truth, if truth lies in the eye of the beholder. I don't know if that sounds like an insult, it's never meant to be. I could say it's because I hate to see you sitting there all washed up and with no place to go and no one to turn to at the one time in your life you need some place to go and someone to turn to, but I suppose again that might sound like an insult. I could say I don't lie to my friends, but that again would be an insult, the Charlotte Skourases of this world don't make friends with government hirelings who kill for their wages. It's no good. I don't know what to say, Charlotte, except that it doesn't matter whether you believe me or not as long as you believe no harm will come to you from me and, as long as I'm near you, no harm will come to you from anyone else either. Maybe you don't believe that, maybe your feminine intuition has stopped working.'

'It is working – what you say? – overtime. Very hard indeed.' The brown eyes were still and the face without expression. 'I do think I could place my life in your hands.'

'You might not get it back again.'

'It's not worth all that much. I might not want it back.'

She looked at me for a long moment when there was no fear in her eyes, then stared down at her folded hands. She gazed at them so long that I finally looked in the same direction myself, but there was nothing wrong with her hands that I could see. Finally she looked up with an almost timid half-smile that didn't belong to her at all.

'You are wondering why I came,' she asked.

'No. You've told me. You want me to tell you a story. Especially the beginning and end of the story.'

She nodded. 'When I began as a stage actress, I played very small parts, but I knew what the play was all about. In this real-life play, I'm still playing a very small part. Only, I no longer know what the play is all about. I come on for three minutes in Act 2, but I have no idea what has gone before. I'm back for another minute in Act 4, but I've no idea in the world what's happened between Acts 2 and 4. And I cannot begin to imagine how it will end. You cannot imagine how frustrating this can be for a woman.'

'You really know nothing of what has gone before this?'

'I ask you to believe me.'

I believed her. I believed her because I knew it to be true.

'Go to the front room and bring me, as they say in these parts, a refreshment,' I said. 'I grow weaker by the hour.'

So she rose obediently and went to the front room and brought me the refreshment which gave me just enough strength to tell her what she wanted to know.

VIII

'They were a triumvirate,' I said, which if not strictly accurate, was close enough to the truth for my explanation. 'Sir Anthony, Lavorski, who, I gather, was not only his public and private accountant, but his overall financial director as well, and John Dollmann, the managing director of the shipping companies – they were split up for tax reasons – associated with your husband's oil companies. I thought that MacCallum, the Scots lawyer, and Jules Biscarte, the lad with the beard who owns one of the biggest merchant banks in Paris, was in with them too. But they weren't. At least not Biscarte. I think he was invited aboard ostensibly to discuss business but actually to provide our triumvirate with information that would have given them the basis for their next coup, but he didn't like the way the wind was blowing and shied off. I know nothing about MacCallum.'

'I know nothing about Biscarte,' Charlotte said. 'Neither he nor Mr MacCallum stayed aboard the *Shangri-la*, they were at the Columba hotel for a few days and were invited out twice for dinner. They haven't been aboard since the night you were there.'

'Among other things they didn't care for your husband's treatment of you.'

'I didn't care for it myself. I know what Mr MacCallum was doing aboard. My husband was planning to build a refinery in the Clyde estuary this coming winter and MacCallum was negotiating the lease for him. My husband said that, by the end of the year, he expected to have a large account of uncommitted capital for investment.'

'I'll bet he did, that's as neat a phrase for the proceeds of grand larceny as ever I've come across. Lavorski, I think we'll find, was the instigator and guiding brain behind all this. Lavorski it would have been who discovered that the Skouras empire was badly in need of some new lifeblood in the way of hard cash and saw the way of putting matters right by using means they already had close to hand.'

'But – but my husband was never short of money,' Charlotte objected. 'He had the best of everything, yachts, cars, houses—'

'He was never short in that sense. Neither were half the

millionaires who jumped off the New York skyscrapers at the time of the stock market crash. Do be quiet, there's a good girl, you know nothing about high finance.' Coming from a character who eked out a bare living from an inadequate salary, I reflected, that was very good indeed. 'Lavorski struck upon the happy idea of piracy on a grand scale – vessels carrying not less than a million pounds' worth of specie at a time.'

She stared at me, her lips parted. I wished I had teeth like that, instead of having had half of them knocked out by Uncle Arthur's enemies over the years. Uncle Arthur, I mused bitterly, was twenty-five years older than I was and was frequently heard to boast that he'd still to lose his first tooth. She whispered: 'You're making all this up.'

'Lavorski made it all up. I'm just telling you, I wouldn't have the brains to think of something like that. Having thought up this splendid scheme for making money, they found themselves with three problems to solve: how to discover when and where large quantities of specie were being shipped, how to seize those ships and how to hide them while they opened the strong-room – a process which in ships fitted with the most modern strong-rooms can take anything up to a day – and removed said specie.

'Problem number one was easy. I have no doubt that they may have suborned high-ranking banking officials – the fact that they tried it on with Biscarte is proof of that – but I don't think it will ever be possible to bring those men to justice. But it will be possible to arrest and very successfully indict their ace informant, their trump card, our good friend and belted broker, Lord Charnley. To make a real good-going success of piracy you require the co-operation of Lloyd's. Well, that's an actionable statement, the co-operation of someone in Lloyd's. Someone like Lord Charnley. He is, by profession, a marine underwriter at Lloyd's. Stop staring at me like that, you're putting me off.

'A large proportion of valuable marine cargoes are insured at Lloyd's. Charnley would know of at least a number of those. He would know the amount, the firm or bank of dispatch, and possibly the date of dispatch and vessel.'

'But Lord Charnley is a wealthy man,' she said.

'Lord Charnley gives the appearance of being a wealthy man,' I corrected. 'Granted, he had to prove that he was a man of substance to gain admission to the old club, but he may have backed the wrong insurance horses or played the stock market. He either needed money or wanted money. He *may* have plenty but money is like alcohol, some people can take it and some can't, and with those who can't the more money they have the more they require.

'Dollmann solved problem two – the hi-jacking of the specie. I shouldn't imagine this strained his resources too far. Your husband ships his oil into some very odd and very tough places indeed and it goes without saying that he employs some very odd and very tough people to do it. Dollmann wouldn't have recruited the hi-jacking crew himself, he probably singled out our good friend Captain Imrie, who will prove to have a very interesting history, and gave him the authority to go through the Skouras fleets and hand-pick suitable men for the job. Once the hi-jacking crew was assembled and ready, Messrs Skouras, Lavorski and Dollmann waited till the victim was on the high seas, dumped you and the stewardess in a hotel, embarked the lads on the *Shangri-la*, intercepted the specie-carrying vessel and by one of a series of ruses I'll tell you about later, succeeded in boarding it and taking over. Then the *Shangri-la* landed the captured crew under guard while the prize crew sailed the hi-jacked vessel to the appointed hiding-place.'

'It can't be true, it can't be true,' she murmured. It was a long time since I'd seen any woman wringing her hands but Charlotte Skouras was doing it then. Her face was quite drained of colour. She knew that what I was saying was true and she'd never heard of any of it before. 'Hiding place, Philip? What hiding place?'

'Where would you hide a ship, Charlotte?'

'How should I know?' She shrugged tiredly. 'My mind is not very clear tonight. Up in the Arctic perhaps, or in a lonely Norwegian fjord or some desert island. I can't think any more, Philip. There cannot be many places. A ship is a big thing.'

'There are millions of places. You can hide a ship practically anywhere in the world. All you have to do is to open the bilge-valves and engine-room non-return valves to the bilges and detonate a couple of scuttling charges.'

'You mean – you mean that—'

'I mean just that. You send it to the bottom. The west side of the Sound to the east of Dubh Sgeir island, a cheery stretch of water rejoicing in the name of Beul nan Uamh – the mouth of the grave – must be the most densely packed marine graveyard in Europe today. At dead slack water the valves were opened at a very carefully selected spot in the Beul nan Uamh and down they went, all five of them, gurgle, gurgle, gurgle. Tide tables show that, coincidentally, most of them were sunk at or near midnight. Cease upon the midnight, as the poet says, only in this case with a very great deal of pain, at least for the underwriters involved. Beul nan Uamh. Odd, I never thought of it before. A very apt name indeed. The mouth of the grave. Damn place is printed far too large in the chart, it doesn't have to be very obvious to be too obvious for Calvert.'

She hadn't been listening to my meanderings. She said: 'Dubh Sgeir? But – but that's the home of Lord Kirkside.'

'It's not but, it's because. The hiding place was picked either by your husband, or, if someone else, then the arrangement was made through your husband. I never knew until recently that your husband was an old drinking pal of Lord Kirkside. I saw him yesterday, but he wouldn't talk. Nor would his charming daughter.'

'You do move around. I've never met the daughter.'

'You should. She thinks you're an old gold-digging hag. A nice kid really. But terrified, terrified for her life and those of others.'

'Why on earth should she be?'

'How do you think our triumvirate got Lord Kirkside to agree to their goings-on?'

'Money. Bribery.'

I shook my head. 'Lord Kirkside is a Highlander and a gentleman. It's a pretty fierce combination. Old Skouras could never lay hands on enough money to bribe Lord Kirkside to pass the uncollected fares box on a bus, if he hadn't paid. A poor illustration, Lord Kirkside wouldn't recognize a bus even if it ran over him, but what I mean is, the old boy is incorruptive. So your charming friends kidnapped old Kirkside's elder son – the younger lives in Australia – and just to make sure that Susan Kirkside wouldn't be tempted to do anything silly, they kidnapped her fiancé. A guess, but a damned good one. They're supposed to be dead.'

'No, no,' she whispered. Her hand was to her mouth and her voice was shaking. 'My God, no!'

'My God, yes. It's logical and tremendously effective. They also kidnapped Sergeant MacDonald's sons and Donald MacEachern's wife for the same reason. To buy silence and co-operation.'

'But – but people just can't disappear like that.'

'We're not dealing with street corner boys, we're dealing with criminal master-minds. Disappearances are rigged to look like accidental death. A few other people have disappeared also, people who had the misfortune to be hanging around in small private boats while our friends were waiting for the tide to be exactly right before opening the sea-cocks on the hijacked ships.'

'Didn't it arouse police suspicion? Having so many small boats disappear in the same place?'

'They sailed or towed two of those boats fifty or more miles away and ran them on the rocks. Another could have disappeared anywhere. The fourth did set sail from Torbay and disappeared, but the disappearance of one boat is not enough to arouse suspicion.'

'It must be true, I know it must be true.' She shook her head as if she didn't believe it was true at all. 'It all fits so well, it explains so many things and explains them perfectly. But – but what's the good of knowing all this now? They're on to you, they *know* you know that something is far wrong and that that something is in Loch Houron. They'll leave—'

'How do they know we suspect Loch Houron?'

'Uncle Arthur told me in the wheelhouse last night.' Surprise in her voice. 'Don't you remember?'

I hadn't remembered. I did now. I was half-dead from lack of sleep. A stupid remark. Perhaps even a give-away remark. I was glad Uncle Arthur hadn't heard that one.

'Calvert nears the sunset of his days,' I said. 'My mind's going. Sure they'll leave. But not for forty-eight hours yet.

They will think they have plenty of time, it's less than eight hours since we instructed Sergeant MacDonald to tell them that we were going to the mainland for help.'

'I see,' she said dully. 'And what did you do on Dubh Sgeir tonight, Philip?'

'Not much. But enough.' Another little white lie. 'Enough to confirm my every last suspicion. I swam ashore to the little harbour and picked the side door of the boathouse. It's quite a boathouse. Not only is it three times as big on the inside as it is from the outside, but it's stacked with diving equipment.'

'Diving equipment?'

'Heaven help us all, you're almost as stupid as I am. How on earth do you think they recover the stuff from the sunken vessels? They use a diving-boat and the Dubh Sgeir boathouse is its home.'

'Was – was that all you found out?'

'There was nothing more to find out. I had intended taking a look round the castle – there's a long flight of steps leading up to it from the boatyard inside the cliff itself – but there was some character sitting about three parts of the way up with a rifle in his hand. A guard of some sort. He was drinking out of some sort of bottle, but he was doing his job for all that. I wouldn't have got within a hundred steps of him without being riddled. I left.'

'Dear God,' she murmured. 'What a mess, what a terrible mess. And you've no radio, we're cut off from help. What are we going to do? What *are* you going to do, Philip?'

'I'm going there in the *Firecrest* this coming night, that's what I'm going to do. I have a machine-gun under the settee of the saloon in the *Firecrest* and Uncle Arthur and Tim Hutchinson will have a gun apiece. We'll reconnoitre. Their time is running short and they'll want to be gone tomorrow at the latest. The boathouse doors are ill-fitting and if there's no light showing that will mean they still haven't finished their diving. So we wait till they have finished and come in. We'll see the light two miles away when they open the door to let the diving-boat in to load up all the stuff they've cached from the four other sunken ships. The front doors of the boathouse will be closed, of course, while they load up. So we go in through the front doors. On the deck of the *Firecrest*.

The doors don't look all that strong to me. Surprise is everything. We'll catch them napping. A sub-machine-gun in a small enclosed space is a deadly weapon.'

'You'll be killed, you'll be killed!' She crossed to and sat on the bed-side, her eyes wide and scared. 'Please, Philip! Please, *please* don't. You'll be killed, I tell you. I beg of you, don't do it!' She seemed very sure that I would be killed.

'I have to, Charlotte. Time has run out. There's no other way.'

'Please.' The brown eyes were full of unshed tears. This I couldn't believe. 'Please, Philip. For my sake.'

'No.' A tear-drop fell at the corner of my mouth, it tasted as salt as the sea. 'Anything else in the world. But not this.'

She rose slowly to her feet and stood there, arms hanging limply by her side, tears trickling down her cheeks. She said dully: 'It's the maddest plan I've ever heard in my life,' turned and left the room, switching off the light as she went.

I lay there staring into the darkness. There was sense in what the lady said. It *was*, I thought, the maddest plan *I'd* ever heard in my life. I was damned glad I didn't have to use it.

— 10 —

Thursday: noon – Friday: dawn

'LET ME SLEEP.' I said. I kept my eyes shut. 'I'm a dead man.'

'Come on, come on.' Another violent shake, a hand like a power shovel. 'Up!'

'Oh, God!' I opened the corner of one eye. 'What's the time?'

'Just after noon. I couldn't let you sleep any more.'

'Noon! I asked to be shaken at five. Do you know—'

'Come here.' He moved to the window, and I swung my legs stiffly out of bed and followed him. I'd been operated on during my sleep, no anaesthetic required in the condition I was in, and someone had removed the bones from my legs. I felt awful. Hutchinson nodded towards the winow. 'What do you think of that?'

I peered out into the grey opaque world. I said irritably: 'What do you expect me to see in that damn fog?'

'The fog.'

'I see,' I said stupidly. 'The fog.'

'The 2 a.m. shipping forecast,' Hutchinson said. He gave the impression of exercising a very great deal of patience. 'It said the fog would clear away in the early morning. Well, the goddamned fog hasn't cleared away in the early morning.'

The fog cleared away from my befuddled brain. I swore and jumped for my least sodden suit of clothing. It was damp and clammy and cold but I hardly noticed these things, except subconsciously, my conscious mind was frantically busy with something else. On Monday night they'd sunk the *Nantesville* at slack water but there wasn't a chance in a thousand that they would have been able to get something done that night or the Tuesday night, the weather had been bad enough in sheltered Torbay harbour, God alone knew what it would have been like in Beul nan Uamh. But they could have started last night, they *had* started last night for there had been no diving-boat in the Dubh Sgeir boathouse, and reports from the *Nantesville*'s owners had indicated that the strongroom was a fairly antiquated one, not of hardened steel, that could be cut open in a couple of hours with the proper equipment. Lavorski and company would have the proper equipment. The rest of last night, even had they three divers and reliefs working all the time, they could have brought up a fair proportion of the bullion but I'd been damn sure they couldn't possibly bring up all eighteen tons of it. Marine salvage had been my business before Uncle Arthur had taken me away. They would have required another night or at least a good part of the night, because they only dared work when the sun was down. When no one could see them. But no one could see them in dense fog like this. This was as good as another night thrown in for free.

'Give Uncle Arthur a shake. Tell him we're on our way. In the *Firecrest*.'

'He'll want to come.'

'He'll have to stay. He'll know damn well he'll have to stay. Beul nan Uamh, tell him.'

'Not Dubh Sgeir? Not the boathouse?'

'*You* know damn well we can't move in against that until midnight.'

'I'd forgotten,' Hutchinson said slowly. 'We can't move in against it until midnight.'

II

The Beul nan Uamh wasn't living up to its fearsome reputation. At that time in the afternoon it was dead slack water and there was only the gentlest of swells running up from the south-west. We crossed over from Ballara to the extreme north of the eastern shore of Dubh Sgeir and inched our way southward with bare steerage way on. We'd cut the by-pass valve into the underwater exhaust and, even in the wheelhouse, we could barely hear the throb of the diesel. Even with both wheelhouse doors wide open, we could just hear it and no more. But we hadn't the wheelhouse doors open for the purpose of hearing our own engine.

By this time we were almost half-way down the eastern patch of miraculously calm water that bordered the normal mill-race of Beul nan Uamh, the one that Williams and I had observed from the helicopter the previous afternoon. For the first time, Hutchinson was showing something approaching worry. He never spared a glance through the wheelhouse windows, and only a very occasional one for the compass: he was navigating almost entirely by chart and depth-sounder.

'Are you sure it'll be this fourteen-fathom ledge, Calvert?'

'It has to be. It damn well has to be. Out to the seven fathom mark there the sea-bottom is pretty flat, but there's not enough depth to hide superstructure and masts at low tide. From there to fourteen it's practically a cliff. And beyond the fourteen-fathom ledge it does down to thirty-five fathom, steep enough to roll a ship down there. You can't operate at those depths without very special equipment indeed.'

'It's a damn narrow ledge,' he grumbled. 'Less than a cable.

How could they be sure the scuttled ship would fetch up where they wanted it to?'

'They could be sure. In dead slack water, you can always be sure.'

Hutchinson put the engine in neutral and went outside. We drifted on quietly through the greyly opaque world. Visibility didn't extend beyond our bows. The muffled beat of the diesel served only to enhance the quality of ghostly silence. Hutchinson came back into the wheelhouse, his vast bulk moving as unhurriedly as always.

'I'm afraid you're right. I hear an engine.'

I listened, then I could hear it too, the unmistakable thudding of an air compressor. I said: 'What do you mean afraid?'

'You know damn well.' He touched the throttle, gave the wheel a quarter turn to port and we began to move out gently into deeper water. 'You're going to go down.'

'Do you think I'm a nut case? Do you think I *want* to go down? I bloody well don't want to go down – and you bloody well know that I *have* to go down. And you know why. You want them to finish up here, load up in Dubh Sgeir and the whole lot to be hell and gone before midnight?'

'Half, Calvert. Take half of our share. God, man, we do nothing.'

'I'll settle for a pint in the Columba Hotel in Torbay. You just concentrate on putting this tub exactly where she ought to be. I don't want to spend the rest of my life swimming about the Atlantic when I come back up from the *Nantesville*.'

He looked at me, the expression in his eyes saying, 'if,' not 'when,' but kept quiet. He circled round to the south of the diving-boat – we could faintly hear the compressor all the way – then slightly to the west. He turned the *Firecrest* towards the source of the sound, manoeuvring with delicacy and precision. He said: 'About a cable length.'

'About that. Hard to judge in fog.'

'North twenty-two east true. Let go the anchor.'

I let go the anchor, not the normal heavy Admiralty type on the chain but a smaller CQR on the end of forty fathoms of rope. It disappeared silently over the side and the Terylene as silently slid down after it. I let out all forty fathoms and made fast. I went back to the wheelhouse and strapped the cylinders on my back.

'You won't forget, now,' Hutchinson said. 'When you come up, just let yourself drift. The ebb's just setting in from the nor'-nor'-east and will carry you back here. I'll keep the diesel ticking, you'll be able to hear the underwater exhaust twenty yards away. I hope to hell the mist doesn't clear. You'll just have to swim to Dubh Sgeir.'

'That *will* be ducky. What happens to you if it clears?'

'I'll cut the anchor rope and take off.'

'And if they come after you?'

'Come after me? Just like that? And leave two or three dead divers down inside the *Nantesville*?'

'I wish to God,' I said irritably, 'that you wouldn't talk about dead divers inside the *Nantesville*.'

III

There were three divers aboard the *Nantesville*, not dead but all working furiously, or as furiously as one can work in the pressurized slow-motion world of the undersea.

Getting down there had been no trouble. I'd swum on the surface towards the diving-boat, the compressor giving me a clear bearing all the time, and dived when only three yards away. My hands touched cables, life-lines and finally an unmistakable wire hawser. The wire hawser was the one for me.

I stopped my descent on the wire when I saw the dim glow of light beneath me. I swam some distance to one side then down until my feet touched something solid. The deck of the *Nantesville*. I moved cautiously towards the source of the light.

There were two of them, standing in their weighted boots at the edge of an open hatchway. As I'd expected, they were wearing not my self-contained apparatus, but regular helmet and corselet diving gear, with air-lines and life-lines, the life-lines almost certainly with telephone wires imbedded inside them. Self-contained diving equipment wouldn't have been much use down here, it was too deep for oxygen and compressed-air stores too limited. With those suits they could stay down an hour and a half, at least, although they'd have to spend thirty to forty minutes on decompression stops on the way up. I wanted to be gone in less than that, I wanted to be gone that very moment, my heart was banging away against my chest wall like a demented pop drummer with the ague but it was only the pressure of the water, I told myself, it couldn't be fear, I was far too brave for that.

The wire rope I'd used to guide me down to the *Nantesville*, terminated in a metal ring from which splayed out four chains to the corners of a rectangular steel mesh basket. The two divers were loading this basket with wire- and wood-handled steel boxes that they were hauling up from the hold at the rate of, I guessed, about one every minute. The steel boxes were small but obviously heavy: each held four 28-lb ingots of gold. Each box held a fortune. There were three hundred and sixty such fortunes aboard the *Nantesville*.

I tried to calculate the overall rate of unloading. The steel basket held sixteen boxes. Sixteen minutes to load. Another ten minutes to winch up to the diving-boat, unload and lower again. Say forty an hour. In a ninety-minute stretch, about sixty. But after ninety minutes they would have to change divers. Forty minutes, including two decompression stops of, say, twelve and twenty-four minutes, to get to the surface, then twenty minutes to change over and get other divers down. An hour at least. So, in effect, they were clearing sixty boxes every two and a half hours, or twenty-four an hour. The only remaining question was, how many boxes were left in the *Nantesville*'s strongroom?

I had to find out and I had to find out at once. I'd had only the two compressed air-cylinders aboard the *Firecrest* and already their two hundred atmospheres were seriously depleted. The wire hawser jerked and the full basket started to rise, the divers guiding it clear of the superstructure with a trailing guide rope. I moved forward from the corner of the partially opened hatch remote from where they were standing and cautiously wriggled over and down. With excessive caution, I supposed: their lamp cast only a small pool of light and they couldn't possibly have seen me from where I was standing.

I felt my hands – already puffed and numbed by the icy water – touch a life-line and air-line and quickly withdrew them. Below and to my right I could see another faint pool of light. A few cautious strokes and I could see the source of the light.

The light was moving. It was moving because it was attached to the helmet of a diver, angled so as to point down at an angle of forty-five degrees. The diver was inside the strongroom.

They hadn't opened that strongroom with any Yale key. They'd opened it with underwater torches cutting out a roughly rectangular section in the strongroom's side, maybe six feet by four.

I moved up to this opening and pushed my head round the side. Beyond the now stooping diver was another light suspended from the deckhead. The bullion boxes were neatly stacked in racks round the side and it was a five-second job to estimate their number. Of the three hundred and sixty bullion boxes, there were about one hundred and twenty left.

Something brushed my arm, pulled past my arm. I glanced down and saw that it was a rope, a nylon line, that the diver was pulling in to attach to the handle of one of the boxes. I moved my arm quickly out of the way.

His back was towards me. He was having difficulty in fastening the rope but finally secured it with two half hitches, straightened and pulled a knife from his waist sheath. I wondered what the knife was for.

I found out what the knife was for. The knife was for me. Stooped over as he had been, he could just possibly have caught a glimpse of me from the corner of his eye: or he might have felt the sudden pressure, then release of pressure, on the nylon rope: or his sixth sense was in better working condition than mine. I won't say he whirled round, for in a heavy diving suit at that depth the tempo of movement becomes slowed down to that of a slow-motion film.

But he moved too quickly for me. It wasn't my body that was slowing down as much as my mind. He was completely round and facing me, not four feet away, and I was still where I'd been when he'd first moved, still displaying all the lightning reactions and co-ordinated activity of a bag of cement. The six-inch-bladed knife was held in his lowered hand with thumb and forefinger towards me, which is the way that only nasty people with lethal matters on their minds hold knives, and I could see his face clearly. God knows what he wanted the knife for, it must have been a reflex action, he didn't require a knife to deal with me, he wouldn't have required a knife to deal with two of me.

It was Quinn.

I watched his face with a strangely paralysed intentness. I watched his face to see if the head would jerk down to press the telephone call-up buzzer with his chin. But his head didn't move, Quinn had never required any help in his life and he didn't require any now. My mask made it almost impossible for my face to be recognized but he knew whom he had, he knew whom he had without any doubt in the world. He had the face of a man in the moment of supreme religious ecstasy. He fell slowly forwards, his knees bending, till he was at an angle of almost forty-five degrees and launched himself forward, his right arm already swinging far behind his back.

The moment of thrall ended. I thrust off backwards from the strongroom's outer wall with my left foot, saw the air-hose come looping down towards me as Quinn came through the jagged hole, caught it and jerked down with all my strength to pull him off-balance. A sharp stinging pain burned its way upwards from my lower ribs to my right shoulder. I felt a sudden jerk in my right hand. I fell backwards on to the floor of the hold and then I couldn't see Quinn any more, not because the fall had dazed me nor because Quinn had moved, but because he had vanished in the heart of an opaque, boiling, mushrooming cloud of dense air-bubbles. A non-collapsible air-hose can, and often has to, stand up to some pretty savage treatment, but it can't stand up to the wickedly slicing power of a razor-sharp knife in the hands of the strongest man I'd ever known. Quinn had cut his own air-hose, had slashed it cleanly in two.

No power on earth could save Quinn now. With a pressure of forty pounds to the square inch on that severed air-line, he would be drowning already, his suit filling up with water and weighting him down so that he could never rise again. Almost without realizing what I was doing I advanced with the nylon rope still in my hands and coiled it any old way round the madly threshing legs, taking great care indeed to keep clear of those flailing arms, for Quinn could still have taken me with him, could have snapped my neck like a rotten stick. At the back of my mind I had the vague hope that when his comrades investigated, as they were bound to do immediately – those great clouds of bubbles must have already passed out through the hold on their way to the surface – they would think he'd become entangled and tried to cut himself free. I did not think it a callous action then nor do I now. I had no qualms about doing this to a dying man, and no compunction: he was doomed anyway, he was a psychopathic monster who killed for the love of it and, most of all, I had to think of the living who might die, the prisoners in the cellars of the Dubh Sgeir castle. I left him threshing there, dying there, and swam up and hid under the deck-head of the hold.

The two men who had been on deck were already on their way down, being slowly lowered on their life-lines. As soon as their helmets sunk below my level I came up through the hatchway, located the wire hawser and made my way up. I'd been down for just under ten minutes so when my wrist depth-gauge showed a depth of two fathoms I stopped for a three-minute decompression period. By now, Quinn would be dead.

I did as Hutchinson had told me, drifted my way back to the *Firecrest* – there was no hurry now – and located it without difficulty. Hutchinson was there to help me out of the water and I was glad of his help.

'Am I glad to see you, brother,' he said. 'Never thought the day would come when Tim Hutchinson would die a thousand deaths, but die a thousand deaths he did. How did it go?'

'All right. We've time. Five or six hours yet.'

'I'll get the hook up.' Three minutes later we were on our way and three minutes after that we were out near enough in the mid-channel of the Beul nan Uamh, heading north-north-east against the gathering ebb. I could hear the helm going on auto-pilot and then Hutchinson came through the door into the lit saloon, curtains tightly if, in that fog, unnecessarily drawn, where I was rendering some first aid to myself, just beginning to tape up a patch of gauze over the ugly gash that stretched all the way from lowest rib to shoulder. I couldn't see the expression behind the darkly-luxuriant foliage of that beard, but his sudden immobility was expression enough. He said, quietly: 'What happened, Calvert?'

'Quinn. I met him in the strongroom of the *Nantesville*.'

He moved forward and in silence helped me to tape up the gauze. When it was finished, and not until then, he said: 'Quinn is dead.' It wasn't a question.

'Quinn is dead. He cut his own air-hose.' I told him what had happened and he said nothing. He didn't exchange a dozen words all the way back to Craigmore. I knew he didn't believe me. I knew he never would.

Neither did Uncle Arthur. He'd never believe me till the day he died. But his reaction was quite different, it was one of profound satisfaction. Uncle Arthur was, in his own avuncular fashion, possessed of an absolute ruthlessness. Indeed, he seemed to take half the credit for the alleged execution. 'It's not twenty-four hours,' he'd announced at the tea-table, 'since I told Calvert to seek out and destroy this man by whatever means that came to hand. I must confess that I never thought the means would consist of the blade of a sharp knife against an air-hose. A neat touch, my boy, a very neat touch indeed.'

IV

Charlotte Skouras believed me. I don't know why, but she believed me. While she was stripping off my makeshift bandage, cleaning the wound and re-bandaging it very efficiently, a process I suffered with unflinching fortitude because I didn't want to destroy her image of a secret service agent by bellowing out loud at the top of my voice, I told her what had happened and there was no doubt that she believed me without question. I thanked her, for bandage and belief, and she smiled.

V

Six hours later, twenty minutes before our 11 p.m. deadline for taking off in the *Firecrest*, she was no longer smiling. She was looking at me the way women usually look at you when they have their minds set on something and can see that they are not going to get their own way: a rather less than affectionate look.

'I'm sorry, Charlotte,' I said. 'I'm genuinely sorry, but it's not on. You are not coming with us, and that's that.' She was dressed in dark slacks and sweater, like one who had – or had had – every intention of coming with us on a midnight jaunt. 'We're not going picnicking on the Thames. Remember what you said yourself this morning. There will be shooting. Do you think I want to see you killed?'

'I'll stay below,' she pleaded. 'I'll stay out of harm's way. Please, Philip, let me come.'

'No.'

'You said you'd do anything in the world for me. Remember?'

'That's unfair, and you know it. Anything to help you, I meant. Not anything to get you killed. Not you, of all people.'

'Of all people? You think so much of me?'

I nodded.

'I mean so much to you?'

I nodded again. She looked at me for a long time, her eyes wide and questioning, her lips moving as if about to speak and yet not speaking, then took a step forward, latched her arms around my neck and tried to break it. At least, that was the way it felt, the dead Quinn's handiwork was still with me, but it wasn't that at all, she was clinging to me as she might cling to a person she knew she would never see again. Maybe she was fey, maybe she had second sight, maybe she could see old Calvert floating, face down, in the murky waters of the Dubh Sgeir boathouse. When I thought about it I could see it myself, and it wasn't an attractive sight at all. I was beginning to have some difficulty with my breathing when she suddenly let me go, half-led, half-pushed me from the room and closed the door behind me. I heard the key turn in the lock.

VI

'Our friends are at home,' Tim Hutchinson said. We'd circled far to the south of Dubh Sgeir, close in to the southern shore of Loch Houron and were now drifting quickly on the flood tide, engines stopped, in an east by northerly direction past the little man-made harbour of Dubh Sgeir. 'You were right, Calvert. They're getting all ready for their moonlit flitting.'

'Calvert is usually right,' Uncle Arthur said in his best trained-him-myself voice. 'And now, my boy?'

The mist had thinned now, giving maybe a hundred yards' visibility. I looked at the T-shaped crack of light showing where the boathouse doors didn't quite meet each other in the middle and where the tops of the doors sagged away from the main structure.

'Now it is,' I said. I turned to Hutchinson. 'We've all of a fifteen foot beam. That entrance is not more than twenty wide. There's not a beacon or a mark on it. There's a four knot tide running. You really think it can be done – taking her through that entrance at four or five knots, fast enough to smash open those doors, without piling ourselves up on the rocks on the way in?'

'There's only one way to find out.' He pressed the starter button and the warm diesel caught fire at once, its underpass exhaust barely audible. He swung her round to the south on minimum revs, continued on this course for two cables, westwards for the same distance, curved round to the north, pushed the throttle wide open and lit a cigar. Tim Hutchinson preparing for action. In the flare of the match the dark face was quiet and thoughtful, no more.

For just over a minute there was nothing to be seen, just the darkness and patches of grey mist swirling past our bows. Hutchinson was heading a few degrees west of north, making allowance for the set of the tide. All at once we could see it, slightly off the starboard bow as it had to be to correct for the tide, that big T-shaped light in the darkness, fairly jumping at us. I picked up the sub-machine-guns, opened and latched back the port wheelhouse door and stood there, gun in left hand, door-jamb in right, with one foot on the outside deck and the other still in the wheelhouse. Uncle Arthur, I knew, was similarly positioned on the starboard side. We were as firmly braced as it was possible to be. When the *Firecrest* stopped, it would stop very suddenly indeed.

Forty yards away, Hutchinson eased the throttle and gave the wheel a touch to port. That bright T was even farther round on our starboard side now, but directly in line with us and the patch of dark water to the west of the almost phosphorescently foaming whiteness that marked the point where the flood tide ripped past the outer end of the eastern breakwater. Twenty yards away he pushed the throttle open again, we were heading straight for where the unseen west breakwater must be, we were far too far over to port, it was impossible now that we could avoid smashing bow first into it, then suddenly Hutchinson had the wheel spinning to starboard, the tide pushing him the same way, and we were through and not an inch of Uncle Arthur's precious paintwork had been removed. Hutchinson had the engine in neutral. I wondered briefly whether, if I practised for the rest of my life, I could effect a manoeuvre like that: I knew damned well that I couldn't.

I'd told Hutchinson that the bollards were on the starboard side of the boathouse, so that the diving-boat would be tied up on that side. He angled the boat across the tiny harbour towards the right-hand crack of light, spun the wheel to port till we were angling in towards the central crack of light and put the engine full astern. It was no part of the plan to telescope the *Firecrest*'s bows against the wall of the boathouse and send it – and us – to the bottom.

As an entrance it erred, if anything, on the spectacular side. The doors, instead of bursting open at their central hasps, broke off at the hinges and we carried the whole lot before us with a thunderous crash. This took a good knot off our speed. The aluminium foremast,with Uncle Arthur's fancy telescopic aerial inside, almost tore the tabernacle clear of the deck before it sheared off, just above wheelhouse level, with a most unpleasant metallic shrieking. That took another knot off. The screw, biting deep in maximum revs astern, took off yet another knot, but we still had a fair way on when, amid a crackling, splintering of wood, partly of our planking and mainly of the doors, and the screeching of the rubber tyres on our well-fendered bows, we stopped short with a jarring shock, firmly wedged between the port quarter of the diving-boat and the port wall of the boathouse. Uncle Arthur's feelings must have been almost as bruised and lacerated as the planking of his beloved *Firecrest*. Hutchinson moved the throttle to slow ahead to keep us wedged in position and switched on the five-inch searchlight, less to illuminate the already sufficiently well-lit shed than to dazzle bystanders ashore. I stepped out on the deck with the machine-pistol in my hands.

We were confronted, as the travel books put it, with a scene of bustling activity, or, more precisely, what had been a scene of bustling activity before our entrance had apparently paralysed them all in whatever positions they had been at the time. On the extreme right three faces stared at us over the edge of the hold of the diving-boat, a typical forty-five-foot M.F.V. about the same size as the *Charmaine*. Two men on deck were frozen in the act of lifting a box across to the hold. Another two were standing upright, one with his hands stretched above his head, waiting for another box swinging gently from a rope suspended from a loading boom. That box was the only moving thing in the boathouse. The winchman himself, who bore an uncommon resemblance to Thomas, the bogus customs officer, one lever against his chest and another held in his outstretched right hand, looked as if the lavas of Vesuvius had washed over him twenty centuries ago and left him frozen for ever. The others, backs bent, were standing on the wall at the head of the boathouse, holding a rope attached to a very large box which two frogmen were helping to lift clear of the water. When it came to hiding specie, they had one-track minds. On the extreme left stood Captain Imrie, presumably there to supervise operations, and, beside him, his patrons, Lavorski and Dollmann. This was the big day, this was the culmination of all their dreams, and they weren't going to miss a moment of it.

Imrie, Lavorski and Dollman were the ones for me. I moved forward until I could see the barrel of the machine-gun and until they could also see that it was pointing at them.

'Come close,' I said. 'Yes, you three. Captain Imrie, speak to your men. Tell them that if they move, if they try anything at all, I'll kill all three of you. I've killed four of you already. If I double the number, what then? Under the new laws you get only fifteen years. For murderous vermin, that is not enough. I'd rather you died here. Do you believe me, Captain Imrie?'

'I believe you.' The guttural voice was deep and sombre. 'You killed Quinn this afternoon.'

'He deserved to die.'

'He should have killed you that night on the *Nantesville*,' Imrie said. 'Then none of this would have happened.'

'You will come aboard our boat one at a time,' I said. 'In this situation, Captain Imrie, you are without question the most dangerous man. After you, Lavorski, then—'

'Please keep very still. Terribly still.' The voice behind me was totally lacking in inflection, but the gun pressed hard against my spine carried its own message, one not easily misunderstood. 'Good. Take a pace forward and take your right hand away from the gun.'

I took a pace forward and removed my right hand. This left me holding the machine-pistol by the barrel.

'Lay the gun on the deck.'

It obviously wasn't going to be much use to me as a club, so I laid it on the deck. I'd been caught like this before, once or twice, and just to show that I was a true professional I raised my hands high and turned slowly round.

'Why, Charlotte Skouras!' I said. Again I knew what to do, how to act, the correct tone for the circumvented agent, bantering but bitter. 'Fancy meeting you here. Thank you very much my dear.' She was still dressed in the dark sweater and slacks, only they weren't quite as spruce as the last time I'd seen them. They were soaking wet. Her face was dead white and without expression. The brown eyes were very still. 'And how in God's name did you get here?'

'I escaped through the bedroom window and swam out. I hid in the after cabin.'

'Did you indeed? Why don't you change out of those wet clothes?'

She ignored me. She said to Hutchinson: 'Turn off that searchlight.'

'Do as the lady says,' I advised.

He did as the lady said. The light went out and we were all now in full view of the men ashore. Imrie said: 'Throw that gun over the side, admiral.'

'Do as the gentleman says,' I advised.

Uncle Arthur threw the gun over the side. Captain Imrie and Lavorski came walking confidently towards us. They could afford to walk confidently, the three men in the hold, the two men who had suddenly appeared from behind the diving-boat's wheelhouse and the winch-driver – a nice round total of six – had suddenly sprouted guns. I looked over this show of armed strength and said slowly: 'You were waiting for us.'

'Certainly we were waiting for you,' Lavorski said jovially. 'Our dear Charlotte announced the exact time of your arrival. Haven't you guessed that yet, Calvert?'

'How do you know my name?'

'Charlotte, you fool. By heavens, I believe we have been greviously guilty of over-estimating you.'

'Mrs Skouras was a plant,' I said.

'A bait,' Lavorski said cheerfully. I wasn't fooled by his cheerfulness, he'd have gone into hysterics of laughter when I came apart on the rack. 'Swallowed hook, line, and sinker. A bait with a highly effective if tiny transmitter and a gun in a polythene bag. We found the transmitter in your starboard engine.' He laughed again until he seemed in danger of going into convulsions. 'We've known of every move you've made since you left Torbay. And how do you like that, Mr Secret Agent Calvert?'

'I don't like it at all. What are you going to do with us?'

'Don't be childish. What are you going to do with us, asks he naïvely. I'm afraid you know all too well. How did you locate this place?'

'I don't talk to executioners.'

'I think we'll shoot the admiral through the foot, to begin with,' Lavorski beamed. 'A minute afterwards through the arm, then the thigh—'

'All right. We had a radio-transmitter aboard the *Nantesville.*'

'We know that. How did you pin-point Dubh Sgeir?'

'The boat belonging to the Oxford geological expedition. It is moored fore and aft in a little natural harbour south of here. It's well clear of any rock yet it's badly holed. It's impossible that it would be holed naturally where it lay. It was holed unnaturally, shall we say. Any other boat you could have seen coming from a long way off, but that boat had only to move out to be in full sight of the boathouse – and the anchored diving-boat. It was very clumsy.'

Lavorski looked at Imrie, who nodded. 'He would notice that. I advised against it at the time. Was there more, Calvert?'

'Donald MacEachern on Eilean Oran. You should have taken him, not his wife. Susan Kirkside – you shouldn't have allowed her out and about, when did you last see a fit young twenty-one-year-old with blue shadows that size under her eyes? A fit young twenty-one-year-old with nothing in the world to worry about, that is? And you should have disguised that mark made by the tail fuselage of the Beechcraft belonging to Lord Kirkside's elder son when you ran it over the edge of the north cliff. I saw it from the helicopter.'

'That's all?' Lavorski asked. I nodded, and he looked again at Imrie.

'I believe him,' Imrie said. 'No one talked. That's all we need to know. Calvert first, Mr Lavorski?' They were certainly a brisk and business-like outfit.

I said quickly: 'Two questions. The courtesy of two answers. I'm a professional. I'd like to know. I don't know if you understand.'

'And two minutes,' Lavorski smiled. 'Make it quick. We have business on hand.'

'Where is Sir Anthony Skouras? He should be here.'

'He is. He's up in the castle with Lord Kirkside and Lord Charnley. The *Shangri-la*'s tied up at the west landing stage.'

'Is it true that you and Dollmann engineered the whole plan, that you bribed Charnley to betray insurance secrets, that you – or Dollmann, rather – selected Captain Imrie to pick his crew of cut-throats, and that you were responsible for the capture and sinking of the ships and the subsequent salvaging of the cargoes. And, incidentally, the deaths, directly or indirectly, of our men?'

'It's late in the day to deny the obvious.' Again Lavorski's booming laugh. 'We think we did rather well, eh, John?'

'Very well indeed,' Dollmann said coldly. 'We're wasting time.'

I turned to Charlotte Skouras. The gun was still pointing at me. I said: 'I have to be killed, it seems. As you will be responsible for my death, you might as well finish the job.' I reached down, caught the hand with the gun in it and placed it against my chest, letting my own hand fall away. 'Please do it quickly.'

There was no sound to be heard other than the soft throb of the *Firecrest*'s diesel. Every pair of eyes in that boatshed was on us, my back was to them all, but I knew it beyond any question. I wanted every pair of eyes in that boatshed on us. Uncle Arthur took a step inside the starboard door and said urgently: 'Are you mad, Calvert? She'll kill you! She's one of them.'

The brown eyes were stricken, there was no other expression for it, the eyes of one who knows her world is coming to an end. The finger came off the trigger, the hand opened slowly and the gun fell to the deck with a clatter that seemed to echo through the boatshed and the tunnels leading off on either side. I took her left arm and said: 'It seems Mrs Skouras doesn't feel quite up to it. I'm afraid you'll have to find someone else to—'

Charlotte Skouras cried out in sharp pain as her legs caught the wheelhouse sill and maybe I did shove her through that doorway with unnecessary force, but it was too late in the day to take chances now. Hutchinson had been waiting and caught her as she fell, dropping to his knees at the same time. I went through that door after her like an international rugby three-quarter diving for the line with a dozen hands reaching out for him, but even so Uncle Arthur beat me to it. Uncle Arthur had a lively sense of self-preservation. Even as I fell, my hand reached out for the loudhailer that had been placed in position on the wheelhouse deck.

'Don't fire!' The amplified voice boomed cavernously against the rock-faces and the wooden walls of the boatshed. 'If you shoot, you'll die! One shot, and you may all die. There's a machine-gun lined up on the back of every man in this boathouse. Just turn round, very very slowly, and see for yourselves.'

I half rose to my feet, hoisted a wary eye over the lower edge of a wheelhouse window, got the rest of the way to my feet, went outside and picked up the machine-gun on the deck.

Picking up that machine-gun was the most superfluous and unnecessary action I had performed for many a long day. If there was one thing that boathouse was suffering from at the moment it was a plethora of machine-guns. There were twelve of them in all, shoulder-slung machine-pistols, in twelve of the most remarkably steady pairs of hands I'd ever seen. The twelve men were ranged in a rough semi-circle round the inner end of the boathouse, big, quiet, purposeful-looking men dressed in woollen caps, grey-and-black camouflaged smocks and trousers and rubber boots. Their hands and faces were the colour of coal. Their eyes gleamed whitely, like performers in the Black and White Minstrel show, but with that every hint of light entertainment ended.

'Lower your hands to your sides and let your guns fall.' The order came from a figure in the middle of the group, a man indistinguishable from the others. 'Do please be very careful. Slowly down, drop the guns, utter stillness. My men are very highly trained commandos. They have been trained to shoot on suspicion. They know only how to kill. They have not been trained to wound or cripple.'

They believed him. I believed him. They dropped their guns and stood very still indeed.

'Now clasp your hands behind your necks.'

They did. All but one. Lavorski. He wasn't smiling any more and his language had little to recommend it.

That they were highly trained I could believe. No word or signal passed. The commando nearest Lavorski walked towards him on soundless soles, machine-pistol across his chest. The butt seemed to move no more than three inches. When Lavorski picked himself up the lower part of his face was covered in blood and I could see the hole where some teeth had been. He clasped his hands behind his neck.

'Mr Calvert?' the officer asked.

'Me,' I said.

'Captain Rawley, sir. Royal Marine Commandos.'

'The castle, captain?'

'In our hands.'

'The *Shangri-la*?'

'In our hands.'

'The prisoners?'

'Two men are on their way up, sir.'

I said to Imrie: 'How many guards?'

He spat and said nothing. The commando who had dealt

with Lavorski moved forward, machine-pistol high. Imrie said: 'Two.'

I said to Rawley: 'Two men enough?'

'I hope, sir, that the guards will not be so foolish as to offer resistance.'

Even as he finished speaking the flat rapid-fire chatter of a sub-machine-gun came echoing down the long flight of stone steps. Rawley shrugged.

'They'll never learn to be wise now. Robinson?' This to a man with a waterproof bag over his shoulder. 'Go up and open the cellar door. Sergeant Evans, line them up in two rows against the wall there, one standing, one sitting.'

Sergeant Evans did. Now that there was no danger of being caught in cross-fire we landed and I introduced Uncle Arthur, full military honours and all, to Captain Rawley. Captain Rawley's salute was something to see. Uncle Arthur beamed. Uncle Arthur took over.

'Capitally done, my boy!' he said to Rawley. 'Capitally. There'll be a little something for you in this New Year's List. Ah! Here come some friends.'

They weren't all exactly friends, this group that appeared at the bottom of the steps. There were four tough but dispirited looking characters whom I'd never seen before, but unquestionably Imrie's men, closely followed by Sir Anthony Skouras and Lord Charnley. They, in their turn, were closely followed by four commandos with the very steady hands that were a hallmark of Rawley's men. Behind them came Lord Kirkside and his daughter. It was impossible to tell what the black-faced commandos were thinking, but the other eight had the same expression on their faces, dazed and utter bewilderment.

'My dear Kirkside! My dear fellow!' Uncle Arthur hurried forward and shook him by the hand, I'd quite forgotten that they knew one another. 'Delighted to see you safe and sound, my dear chap. Absolutely delighted. It's all over now.'

'What in God's name is happening?' Lord Kirkside asked. 'You – you've got them? You have them all? Where is my boy? Where is Rollinson? What—?'

An explosive crack, curiously muffled, came down the flight of steps. Uncle Arthur looked at Rawley, who nodded. 'Plastic explosive, sir.'

'Excellent, excellent,' Uncle Arthur beamed. 'You'll see them any minute, Kirkside.' He crossed over to where old Skouras was lined up against the wall, hands clasped behind his neck, reached up both his own, pulled Skouras's arms down and shook his right hand as if he were attempting to tear it off.

'You're lined up with the wrong team, Tony, my boy.' This was one of the great moments of Uncle Arthur's life. He led him across to where Lord Kirkside was standing. 'It's been a frightful nightmare, my boy, a frightful nightmare. But it's all over now.'

'Why did you do it?' Skouras said dully. 'Why did you do it? God, oh God, you don't know what you've done.'

'Mrs Skouras? The *real* Mrs Skouras?' There is the ham actor in all of us, but more than most in Uncle Arthur. He pushed back his sleeve and studied his watch carefully. 'She arrived in London by air from Nice just over three hours ago. She is in the London Clinic.'

'What in God's name do you mean? You don't know what you are saying. My wife—'

'Your wife is in London. Charlotte here is Charlotte Meiner and always was.' I looked at Charlotte. A total incomprehension and the tentative beginnings of a dazed hope. 'Earlier this year, blazing the trail for many kidnappings that were to follow, your friends Lavorski and Dollmann had your wife seized and hidden away to force you to act with them, to put your resources at their disposal. I think they felt aggrieved, Tony, that you should be a millionaire while they were executives: they had it all worked out, even to having the effrontery of intending to invest the proceeds in your empire. However. Your wife managed to escape, so they seized her cousin and best friend, Charlotte – a friend upon whom, shall we say, your wife was emotionally very dependent – and threatened to kill her unless they got Mrs Skouras back again. Mrs Skouras surrendered immediately. This gave them the bright idea of having two swords of Damocles hanging over your head, so, being men of honour, they decided to keep Charlotte as well as your imprisoned wife. Then, they knew, you would do exactly as they wanted, when and as they wanted. To have a good excuse to keep both you and Charlotte under their surveillance at the same time, and to reinforce the idea that your wife was well and truly dead, they gave out that you had been secretly married.' Uncle Arthur was a kind man: no mention of the fact that it was common knowledge that, at the time of her alleged death, brain injuries sustained by Mrs Skouras in a car crash two years previously had become steadily worse and it was known that she would never leave hospital again.

'How on earth did you guess that?' Lord Kirkside asked.

'No guess. Must give my lieutenants their due,' Uncle Arthur said in his best magnanimous taught-'em-all-I-know voice. 'Hunslett radioed me at midnight on Tuesday. He gave me a list of names of people about whom Calvert wanted immediate and exhaustive inquiries made. That call was tapped by the *Shangri-la* but they didn't know what Hunslett was talking about because in our radio transmissions all proper names are invariably coded. Calvert told me later that when he'd seen Sir Anthony on Tuesday night he thought Sir Anthony was putting on a bit of an act. He said it wasn't all act. He said Sir Anthony was completely broken and desolated by the thought of his dead wife. He said he believed the original Mrs Skouras was still alive, that it was totally inconceivable that a man who so patently cherished the memory of his wife should have married again two or three months later, that he could only have pretended to marry again for the sake of the one person whom he ever and so obviously loved.

'I radioed France. Riviera police dug up the grave in Beaulieu where she had been buried near the nursing home where she'd died. They found a coffin full of logs. You knew this, Tony.'

Old Skouras nodded. He was a man in a dream.

'It took them half an hour to find out who had signed the death certificate and most of the rest of the day to find the doctor himself. They charged him with murder. This can be done in France on the basis of a missing body. The doctor wasted no time at all in taking them to his own private nursing home, where Mrs Skouras was in a locked room. The doctor, matron and a few others are in custody now. Why in God's name didn't you come to us before?'

'They had Charlotte and they said they would kill my wife out of hand. What – what would you have done?'

'God knows,' Uncle Arthur said frankly. 'She's in fair health, Tony. Calvert got radio confirmation at 5 a.m.' Uncle Arthur jerked a thumb upwards. 'On Lavorski's big transceiver in the castle.'

Both Skouras and Lord Kirkside had their mouths open. Lavorski, blood still flowing from his mouth, and Dollmann looked as if they had been sandbagged. Charlotte's eyes were the widest wide I'd ever seen. She was looking at me in a very peculiar way.

'It's true,' Susan Kirkside said. 'I was with him. He told me to tell nobody.' She crossed to take my arm and smiled up at me. 'I'm sorry again for what I said last night. I think you're the most wonderful man I've ever known. Except Rolly, of course.' She turned round at the sound of footsteps coming down the stairs and promptly forgot all about the second most wonderful man she'd ever known.

'Rolly!' she cried. 'Rolly!' I could see Rolly bracing himself.

They were all there, I counted them, Kirkside's son, the Hon. Rollinson, the policeman's sons, the missing members of the small boats and, behind them all, a small brown-faced old woman in a long dark dress with a black shawl over her head. I went forward and took her arm.

'Mrs MacEachern,' I said. 'I'll take you home soon. Your husband is waiting.'

'Thank you, young man,' she said calmly. 'That will be very nice.' She lifted her arm and held mine in a proprietorial fashion.

Charlotte Skouras came and held my other arm, not in quite so proprietorial a fashion, but there for everyone to see. I didn't mind. She said: 'You were on to me? You were on to me all the time?'

'He was,' Uncle Arthur said thoughtfully. 'He just said he knew. You never quite got round to explaining that bit, Calvert.'

'It wasn't difficult, sir – if you know all the facts, that is,' I added hastily. 'Sir Anthony put me on to you. That visit he paid me on the *Firecrest* to allay any suspicion we might have had about our smashed radio set only served, I'm afraid, to make me suspicious. You wouldn't have normally come to me, you'd have gone ashore immediately to the police or to a phone, sir. Then, in order to get me talking about the cut telephone wires, you wondered if the radio-wrecker, to complete our isolation from the mainland, had smashed the two public call boxes. From a man of your intelligence, such a suggestion was fatuous, there must be scores of houses in Torbay with their private phone. But you thought it might sound suspicious if you suggested cut lines, so you didn't. Then Sergeant MacDonald gave me a glowing report about you, said you were the most respected man in Torbay and your public reputation contrasted so sharply with your private behaviour in the *Shangri-la* on Tuesday night – well, I just couldn't buy it.

'That nineteenth-century late Victorian melodrama act that you and Charlotte put on in the saloon that night had me fooled for all of five seconds. It was inconceivable that any man so devoted to his wife could be vicious towards another obviously nice woman—'

'Thank you kindly, sir,' Charlotte murmured.

'It was inconceivable that he sent her for his wife's photograph, unless he had been ordered to do so. And you had been ordered to do so, by Lavorski and Dollmann. And it was inconceivable that she would have gone – the Charlotte Meiner I knew would have clobbered you over the head with a marline spike. Ergo, if you weren't what you appeared to be, neither were you, Charlotte.

'The villains, they thought, were laying a foundation for an excellent reason for your flight from the wicked baron to the *Firecrest*, where you could become their eyes and ears and keep them informed of all our plans and moves, because they'd no idea how long their secret little transmitter in the engine-room would remain undetected. After they knew we'd found Hunslett – they'd removed the transmitter by that time – it was inevitable that they would try to get you aboard the *Firecrest*. So they laid a little more groundwork by giving you a bruised eye – the dye is nearly off already – and some wicked weals across your back and dumped you into the water with your little polythene kitbag with the micro-transmitter and gun inside it. Do this, they said, or Mrs Skouras will get it.'

She nodded. 'They said that.'

'I have twenty-twenty eyesight. Sir Arthur hasn't – his eyes were badly damaged in the war. I had a close look at those weals on your back. Genuine weals. Also genuine pinpricks where the hypodermic with the anaesthetic had been inserted before the lashes were inflicted. To that degree at least, someone was humane.'

'I could stand most things,' Skouras said heavily. 'I couldn't stand the thought of – the thought of—'

'I guessed you had insisted on the anaesthetic, sir. No, I knew. The same way that I knew that you had insisted that the crews of all those small yachts be kept alive or the hell with the consequences. Charlotte, I ran a finger-nail down one of those weals. You should have jumped through the saloon roof. You never batted an eyelid. After submersion in salt water. After that, I knew.

'I have devious reasons for the things I do. You told us that you had come to warn us of our deadly danger – as if we didn't know. I told you we were leaving Torbay within the hour, so off you trotted to your little cabin and told them we were going to leave within the hour. So Quinn, Jacques and Kramer came padding across well in advance of the time you'd told us they would be coming, trusting we would have been lulled into a sense of false security. You must love Mrs Skouras very much, Charlotte. A clear-cut choice, she or us, and you made your choice. But I was waiting for them, so Jacques and Kramer died. I told you we were going to Eilean Oran and Craigmore, so off you trotted down to your little cabin and told them we were going to Eilean Oran and Craigmore, which wouldn't have worried them at all. Later on I told you we were going to Dubh Sgeir. So off you trotted down to your little cabin again, but before you could tell them anything you passed out on your cabin deck, possibly as a result of a little night-cap I'd put in your coffee. I couldn't have you telling your friends here that I was going to Dubh Sgeir, could I now? They would have had a reception committee all nicely organized.'

'You – you were in my cabin? You said I was on the floor?'

'Don Juan has nothing on me. I flit in and out of ladies' bedrooms like anything. Ask Susan Kirkside. You were on the floor. I put you to bed. I looked at your arms, incidentally, and the rope marks were gone. They'd used rubber bands, twisted pretty tightly, just before Hunslett and I had arrived?'

She nodded. She looked dazed.

'I also, of course, found the transmitter and gun. Then, back in Craigmore, you came and pumped me for some more information. And you did try to warn me, you were about torn in half by that time. I gave you that information. It wasn't the whole truth, I regret, but it was what I wanted you to tell Lavorski and company, which,' I said approvingly, 'like a good little girl you did. Off you trotted to your little white-washed bedroom—'

'Philip Calvert,' she said slowly, 'you are the nastiest, sneakingest, most low-down double-crossing—'

'There are some of Lavorski's men aboard the *Shangri-la*,' old Skouras interrupted excitedly. He had rejoined the human race. 'They'll get away—'

'They'll get life,' I said. 'They're in irons, or whatever Captain Rawley's men here are in the habit of using.'

'But how did you – how did you know where the *Shangri-la* was? In the darkness, in the mist, it's impossible—'

'How's the *Shangri-la*'s tender working?' I asked.

'The what? The *Shangri-la*'s – what the devil—?' He calmed down. 'It's not working. Engines out of order.'

'Demerara sugar has that effect upon them,' I explained. 'Any sugar has, in fact, when dumped in the petrol tanks, but demerara was all I could lay hands on that Wednesday night after Sir Arthur and I had left you but before we took the *Firecrest* in to the pier. I went aboard the tender with a couple of pounds of the stuff. I'm afraid you'll find the valves are ruined. I also took with me a homing signal transmitter, a transistorized battery-powered job, which I attached to the inner after bulkhead of the anchor locker, a place that's not looked at once a year. So, when you hauled the incapacitated tender aboard the *Shangri-la* – well, we knew where the *Shangri-la* was.'

'I'm afraid I don't follow, Calvert.'

'Look at Messrs Dollmann, Lavorski and Imrie. They

follow all right. I know the exact frequency that transmitter sends on – after all, it *was* my transmitter. One of Mr Hutchinson's skippers was given this frequency and tuned in to it. Like all M.F.V.s it has a loop aerial for direction finding, he just had to keep turning the loop till the signal was at full strength. He couldn't miss. He didn't miss.'

'Mr Hutchinson's skippers?' Skouras said carefully. 'M.F.V.s you said?'

It was as well, I reflected, that I wasn't overly troubled with self-conciousness, what with Mrs MacEachern on one hand, Charlotte on the other, and every eye, a large proportion of them hostile to a degree, bent upon me, it could have been embarrassing to a degree. 'Mr Hutchinson has two shark-fishing boats. Before I came to Dubh Sgeir last night I radioed from one of his boats asking for help – the gentlemen you see here. They said they couldn't send boats or helicopters in this weather, in almost zero visibility. I told them the last thing I wanted was their damned noisy helicopters, secrecy was everything, and not to worry about the sea transport, I knew some men for whom the phrase "zero visibility" was only a joke. Mr Hutchinson's skippers. They went to the mainland and brought Captain Rawley and his men back here. I didn't think they'd arrive until late at night, that's why Sir Arthur and I were afraid to move before midnight. What time did you get here, Captain Rawley?'

'Nine-thirty.'

'So early? I must admit it was a bit awkward without a radio. Then ashore in your little rubber boats, through the side door, waited until the diving-boat came back – and waited and waited.'

'We were getting pretty stiff, sir.'

Lord Kirkside cleared his throat. Maybe he was thinking of my nocturnal assignation with his daughter.

'Tell me this, Mr Calvert. If you radioed from Mr Hutchinson's boat in Craigmore, why did you have to radio again from here later that night?'

'If I didn't, you'd be down among the dead men by this time. I spent the best part of fifteen minutes giving highly detailed descriptions, of Dubh Sgeir externally and of the castle and boathouse layout internally. Everything that Captain Rawley and his men have done had to be done in total darkness. You'll keep an eye on our friends, Captain Rawley? A fishery cruiser will be off Dubh Sgeir shortly after dawn.'

The Marines herded them off into the left-hand cave, set three powerful lights shining into the prisoners' faces and mounted a four-man guard with machine-pistols at the ready. Our friends would undoubtedly keep until the fishery cruiser came in the morning.

Charlotte said slowly: 'That was why Sir Arthur remained behind this afternoon when you and Mr Hutchinson went to the *Nantesville*? To see that I didn't talk to the guards and find out the truth?'

'Why else?'

She took her arm away and looked at me without affection. 'So you put me through the hoop.' she said quietly. 'You let me suffer like this for thirty hours while you knew all the time.'

'Fair's fair. You were doing me down, I was doing you down.'

'I'm very grateful to you,' she said bitterly.

'If you aren't you damn well ought to be,' Uncle Arthur said coldly. This was one for the books, Uncle Arthur talking to the aristocracy, even if only the aristocracy by marriage, in this waspish tone. 'If Calvert won't speak for himself, I will.

'Point one: if you hadn't kept on sending your little radio messages, Lavorski would have thought that there was something damned fishy going on and might well have left the last ton or two of gold in the *Nantesville* and taken off before we got here. People like Lavorski have a highly attuned sixth sense of danger. Point two: they wouldn't have confessed to their crimes unless they thought we were finished. Point three: Calvert wanted to engineer a situation where all attention was on the *Firecrest* so that Captain Rawley and his men could move into position and so eliminate all fear of unnecessary bloodshed – maybe *your* blood, my dear Charlotte. Point four, and more important: if you hadn't been in constant radio contact with them, advising them of our impending arrival right up to the moment we came through those doors – we'd even left the saloon door open so that you could clearly overhear us and know all we were doing – there would have been a pitched battle, guns firing as soon as those doors were breached, and who knows how many lives would have been lost. But they *knew* they were in control, they *knew* the trap was set, they *knew* you were aboard with that gun to spring the trap. Point five, and most important of all: Captain Rawley here was hidden almost a hundred yards away along the cross tunnel and the detachment up above were concealed in a storeroom in the castle. How do you think *they* knew when to move in and move in simultaneously? Because, like all commandos, they had portable radio sets and were listening in to every word of your running commentary. Don't forget your transmitter was stolen from the *Firecrest*. It was *Calvert*'s transmitter, my dear. He knew the transmitting frequency to the mainland last night. That was after he had – um – given you a little something to drink and checked your transmitter before using the one up in the castle last night.'

Charlotte said to me: 'I think you are the most devious and detestable and untrustworthy man I've ever met.' Her eyes were shining, whether from tears or whatever I didn't know. I felt acutely embarrassed and uncomfortable. She put her hand on my arm and said in a low voice: 'You fool, oh, you fool! That gun might have gone off. I – I might have killed you, Philip!'

I patted her hand and said: 'You don't even begin to believe that yourself.' In the circumstances, I thought it better not to say if that gun had gone off I'd never have trusted a three-cornered file again.

VII

The grey mist was slowly clearing away and the dawn coming up on the quiet dark sea when Tim Hutchinson eased the *Firecrest* in towards Eilean Oran.

There were only four of us on the boat, Hutchinson, myself, Mrs MacEachern and Charlotte. I'd told Charlotte to find a bed in Dubh Sgeir castle for the night, but she'd simply ignored me, helped Mrs MacEachern on to the *Firecrest* and had made no move to go ashore again. Very self-willed, she was, and I could see that this was going to cause a lot of trouble in the years to come.

Uncle Arthur wasn't with us, a team of wild horses couldn't have dragged Uncle Arthur aboard the *Firecrest* that night. Uncle Arthur was having his foretaste of Paradise, sitting in front of a log fire in the Dubh Sgeir castle drawing-room, knocking back old Kirkside's superlative whisky and retailing his exploits to a breathless and spell-bound aristocracy. If I were lucky, maybe he'd mention my name a couple of times in the course of his recounting of the epic. On the other hand, maybe he wouldn't.

Mrs MacEachern wasn't having her foretaste of Paradise, she was there already, a calm dark old lady with a wrinkled brown face who smiled and smiled and smiled all the way to her home on Eilean Oran. I hoped to God old Donald MacEachern had remembered to change his shirt.

THE GOLDEN GATE

— 1 —

THE OPERATION had to be executed with a surgically military precision marked with a meticulousness that matched, in degree if not in scope, the Allied landings in war-time Europe. It was. The preparations had to be made in total stealth and secrecy. They were. A split-second co-ordination had to be achieved. It was. All the men had to be rehearsed and trained, over and over again until they played their parts perfectly and automatically. They were so trained. Every eventuality, every possible departure from the planned campaign had to be catered for. It was. And their confidence in their ability to carry out their plan, irrespective of reversals and departures from the norm, had to be total. It was.

Confidence was a quality exuded by their leader, Peter Branson. Branson was thirty-eight years old, just under six feet tall, strongly built, with black hair, pleasant features, lips that were curved in an almost perpetual smile and light blue eyes that had forgotten how to smile many years ago. He was dressed in a policeman's uniform but he was not a policeman. Neither was any of the eleven men with him in that disused trucker's garage not far from the banks of Lake Merced, half-way between Daly City to the south and San Francisco to the north, although three were attired in the same uniform as Branson.

The single vehicle there looked sadly out of place in what was, in effect, nothing more than an open-ended shed. It was a bus, but barely, by normal standards, qualified for the term. It was an opulently gleaming monster which above shoulder level was composed, except for the stainless steel cross-over struts, entirely of slightly tinted glass. There was no regular seating as such. There were about thirty swivel chairs, anchored to the floor but scattered seemingly at random, with deep arm-rests and aircraft-type swing-out dining-tables housed in each arm-rest. Towards the rear there was a cloakroom and a remarkably well-stocked bar. Beyond that there was a rear observation deck, the floor of which had for the moment been removed to reveal the cavernous baggage department. This was filled to near capacity but not with baggage. This enormous storage-space, seven and a half feet wide by the same in length, held, among other things, two petrol-driven electric generators, two twenty-inch searchlights, a variety of smaller ones, two very peculiar-looking missile-like weapons with mounting tripods, machine-pistols, a large crated unmarked wooden box and four smaller boxes, wooden but greased and a variety of other items of material, conspicuous among which were large coils of rope. Branson's men were still loading.

The coach, one of six ever made, had cost Branson ninety thousand dollars: for the purposes for which he intended to use it, he considered this figure a trifling investment. He was buying the coach, he had told the Detroit firm, as an agent for a publicity-shy millionaire, who was also an eccentric who wanted it painted yellow. And yellow it had been when it was delivered: it was now a gleaming, translucent white.

Two of the remaining five coaches had been bought by genuine and extrovert millionaires, both of whom intended them for luxurious, personal vacation travel. Both buses had rear ramps to accommodate their mini-cars. Both, presumably, would rest for about fifty weeks a year in their specially-built garages.

The other three buses had been bought by the government.

The dawn was not yet in the sky.

II

The other three buses were in a garage in down-town San Francisco. The big sliding doors were closed and bolted. In a canvas chair in a corner a man in plain clothes, a sawn-off riot gun held on his lap by flaccid hands, slept peacefully. He had been dozing when the two intruders arrived and was now blissfully unaware that he had sunk into an even deeper sleep because he'd inhaled the single-second squirt from the gas gun without being aware of the fact. He would wake up within the hour almost equally unaware of what had happened and would be extremely unlikely to admit to his superiors that his vigilance had been a degree less than eternal.

The three buses looked undistinguishable from Branson's, at least externally, although the centre one was markedly different in two respects, one visible, the other not. It weighed two tons more than its companions, for bullet-proof glass is a great deal heavier than ordinary plate glass, and those panoramic buses had an enormous glass area. And the interior of the coach was nothing less than a sybarite's dream, which was no less than what one would expect for the private transportation of the country's Chief Executive.

The presidential coach had two huge facing sofas, so deep, so soft and so comfortable that the overweight man possessed of prudent foresight would have thought twice about ensconcing himself in either of them for regaining the vertical would have called for an apoplectic amount of will-power or the use of a crane. There were four armchairs constructed along the same treacherously voluptuous lines. And that, in the way of seating accommodation, was that. There were cunningly concealed spigots for ice-water, scattered copper coffee tables and gleaming gold-plated vases awaiting their daily consignment of fresh flowers. Behind this section were the washroom and the bar, a bar whose capacious refrigerators, in this particular and unusual instance, were stocked largely with fruit juices and soft drinks in deference to the customs of the President's guests of honour, who were Arabs and Muslims.

Beyond this again, in a glassed-in compartment that extended the full width of the bus, was the communications centre, a maze of miniaturized electronic systems which was constantly manned whenever the President was aboard. It was said that this installation had cost considerably more than the coach itself. Besides incorporating a radio telephone system that could reach any place in the world, it had a small row of differently coloured buttons in a glass case which could be removed only with the aid of a special key. There were five such buttons. To press the first brought instant contact with the White House in Washington: the second was for the Pentagon: the third was for the airborne Strategic Air Command: the fourth was for Moscow and the fifth for London. Apart from the necessity of being in touch with his armed forces all the time, the President was an acute sufferer from telephonitis, even to the extent of an internal phone connecting him with his habitual seat on the bus and the communications compartment at the rear.

But it was not in this coach that the intruders were interested but in the one standing to its left. They entered by the front door and immediately removed a metal plate by the driver's seat. One of the men shone a torch downwards, appeared to locate what he wanted almost immediately, reached up and took from his companion something that looked like a polythene bag of putty to which there was attached a metal cylinder not more than three inches long and one in diameter. This he securely bound to a metal strut with adhesive tape. He seemed to know what he was doing – which he did, for the lean and cadaverous Reston was an explosives expert of some note.

They moved to the rear and went behind the bar. Reston climbed on to a stool, slid back an overhead cupboard door and looked at the liquor contents. Whatever the camp-followers in the Presidential motorcade were going to suffer from, it clearly wasn't going to be thirst. There were two rows of vertically stacked bottles, the first ten to the left, five in each row, being bourbon and scotch. Reston stooped and examined the upside down optics beneath the cupboard and saw that the bottles that interested him in the cupboard were duplicated in the ones below and that those were all full. It seemed unlikely that anyone was going to be interested in the contents of the cupboard for some little time to come.

Reston removed the ten bottles from their circular retaining holes in the cupboard and handed them down to his companion who stacked five of them on the counter and placed the other five in a canvas bag which had evidently been brought along for this purpose, then handed Reston a rather awkward piece of equipment which consisted of three parts: a small cylinder similar to the one that had been fitted forwards, a beehive-shaped device, no more than two inches high and the same in diameter, and a device which looked very like a car fire extinguisher, with the notable exception that it had a plastic head. Both this and the beehive were attached to the cylinder by wires.

The beehive had a rubber sucker at its base but Reston did

not seem to have any great faith in suckers for he produced a tube of quick-acting glue with which he liberally besmeared the base of the beehive. This done he pressed it firmly against the forward facing side of the cupboard, taped it securely to the large and small cylinders and then taped the three to the inner row of circular holes which retained the bottles. He replaced the five bottles in front. The device was completely hidden. He slid shut the door, replaced the stool and left the bus with his companion. The guard still slept peacefully. The two men left by the side door by which they had entered and locked it behind them. Reston produced a walkie-talkie. He said: 'P1?'

The amplified voice came through clearly on the fascia-mounted speaker in the bus in the garage north of Daly City. Branson made a switch.

'Yes?'

'Okay.'

'Good.' There was no elation in Branson's voice and no reason why there should have been: with six weeks of solid preparation behind him he would have been astonished if anything should have gone wrong. 'You and Mack get back to the apartment. Wait.'

III

Johnson and Bradley were curiously alike, good-looking, in their early thirties, almost identical in build and both with blond hair. They also bore a striking resemblance, both in build and colour, to the two men, newly wakened from sleep, who were propped up in the two beds in the hotel room, gazing at them with an understandable mixture of astonishment and outrage. One of them said: 'Who the hell are you and what the hell do you think you're doing here?'

'Kindly modulate your voice and mind your language,' Johnson said. 'It ill becomes a naval air officer. Who we are doesn't matter. We're here because we require a change of clothes.' He looked at the Beretta he was holding and touched the silencer with his left forefinger. 'I don't have to tell you what those things are.'

He didn't have to tell them what those things were. There

was a cold calm professionalism, a chilling surety about Johnson and Bradley that discouraged freedom of speech and inhibited even the very thought of action. While Johnson stood there, gun dangling in apparent negligence by his side, Bradley opened the valise they had brought with them, produced a length of thin rope and trussed up the two men with a speed and efficiency that indicated a long or intensive experience of such matters. When he had finished Johnson opened a cupboard, produced two suits, handed one to Bradley and said: 'Try them for size.'

Not only were the suits an almost perfect fit but so also were the hats. Johnson would have been surprised if they had been otherwise: Branson, that most meticulous of planners, almost never missed a trick.

Bradley surveyed himself in a full-length mirror. He said sadly: 'I should have stayed on the other side of the law. The uniform of a lieutenant in the US Naval Air Arm suits me very well indeed. Not that you look too bad yourself.'

One of the bound men said: 'Why do you want those uniforms?'

'I thought naval helicopter pilots were intelligent.'

The man stared at him. 'Jesus! You don't mean to stand there and tell us—'

'Yes. And we've both probably flown Sikorskys a damned sight more than either of you.'

'But uniforms? Why steal our uniforms? There's no trick in getting those made. Why do you—'

'We're parsimonious. Sure, we could get them made. But what we can't get made are all the documentation you carry about with you — identifications, licences, the lot.' He patted the pockets of his uniform. 'They're not here. Where?'

The other bound man said: 'Go to hell.' He looked as if he meant it, too.

Johnson was mild. 'This is off-season for heroes. Where?'

The other man said: 'Not here. The navy regard those as classified documents. They have to be deposited in the manager's safe.'

Johnson sighed. 'Oh, dear. Why make it difficult? We had a young lady stake-out in an armchair by the receptionist's last evening. Redhead. Beautiful. You may recall.' The two bound men exchanged the briefest of glances: it was quite clear that they did recall. 'She'd go on oath in a witness stand that neither of you deposited anything.' He smiled in a wintry fashion. 'A witness stand in court may be the last place on earth she'd want to go near, but if she says it's no deposit, it's no deposit. Let's not be silly. Three things you can do. Tell us. Have your mouths taped and after a little persuasion tell us. Or, if those don't work, we just search. You watch. If you're conscious, that is.'

'You going to kill us?'

'What on earth for?' Bradley's surprise was genuine.

'We can identify you.'

'You'll never see us again.'

'We can identify the girl.'

'Not when she removes her red wig, you can't.' He dug into the valise and came up with a pair of pliers. He had about him an air of gentle resignation. 'Time's a-wasting. Tape them up.'

Both bound men looked at each other. One shook his head, the other sighed. One smiled, almost ruefully: 'It does seem a gesture of useless defiance – *and* I don't want my good looks spoilt. Under the mattresses. At the foot.'

Under the mattresses they were. Johnson and Bradley flicked over the leaves of the two wallets, looked at each other, nodded, extracted the not inconsiderable dollar billfolds in each wallet and placed those by the bedside tables. One man said: 'Couple of crazy crooks you are.'

Johnson said: 'Maybe you'll be needing that more than us pretty soon.' He extracted money from his newly discarded suit and placed it in his uniform while Bradley did the same. 'Our suits you can have. Unthinkable for US officers to be running around the city in their striped underpants. And now, I'm afraid, we have to tape you.' He reached into the valise.

One man, a quick mixture of suspicion and apprehension in his eyes, tried, vainly, to sit up in bed. 'I thought you said—'

'Look, if we wanted to kill you, the noise from those silenced guns wouldn't even be heard in the corridor outside. Think we want you to start hollering the place down the moment we step outside that door? Besides, it would upset the neighbours.'

After they were taped Johnson said: 'And, of course, we don't want to have you jumping and wriggling around and making banging noises on the floor or walls. I'm afraid we can't have any bangs in the next couple of hours or so. Sorry.' He stooped, retrieved what looked like an aerosol can from the valise, and squirted it briefly in the faces of both bound men. They left, hanging up the no disturb notice outside. Johnson double-locked the door, produced his pliers, leaned on the key and snapped it leaving the head jammed in the lock.

Downstairs, they approached the clerk at reception, a cheerful youngster who gave a cheerful good morning.

Johnson said: 'You weren't on last night?'

'No, sir. The management wouldn't believe it but even a desk clerk requires a little sleep now and again.' He looked at them with interest. 'No offence, but aren't you the two gentlemen who're going to ride herd on the President this morning?'

Johnson smiled. 'I'm not sure if the President would care to have you put it quite that way, but yes. It's no secret. We phoned for an alarm call last night. Ashbridge and Martinez. Was it recorded?'

'Yes, sir.' The clerk put his pen through the names.

'Now, we've left one or two – ah – naval things in our room that we really shouldn't have done. Will you make certain that no one goes near our room until we return? Three hours, about.'

'You can depend on me, sir.' The clerk made a note. 'The no disturb sign—'

'We've already done that.'

They left and stopped at the first pay telephone on the street. Johnson went inside with the valise, fished inside and brought out a walkie-talkie. He was immediately through to Branson, waiting patiently in the dilapidated garage north of Daly City. He said: 'P1?'

'Yes?'

'Okay.'

'Good. Get down there.'

IV

The sun was coming up as the six men filed out of their cabin in the hills above Sausalito in Marin County, north across the bay from San Francisco. They made up a nondescript and not particularly attractive group, four of them in overalls and two in faded raincoats that might have been lifted from unsuspecting scarecrows. They all piled into a rather battered Chevrolet station wagon and headed down to the town. Before them stretched a stunning vista. To the south the Golden Gate and the staggering – if rather Manhattanized – skyline of San Francisco. To the south-east, lent a slightly spurious glamour by the early rays of the sun, Alcatraz Island, of unhappy history, lay to the north of the Fisherman's Wharf, in line of sight of Treasure Island, the Bay Bridge and Oakland on the far side of the bay. To the east lay Angel Island, the largest in the bay, while to the north-east lay Belvedere Island, Tiburon and, beyond that again, the wide reaches of San Pablo Bay vanishing into nothingness. There can be few more beautiful and spectacular vistas in the world – if such there so be – than that from Sausalito. On the basis that not to be moved by it would require a heart of stone, the six men in the station wagon had between them, it was clear, the makings of a fair-sized quarry.

They reached the main street, travelled along past the immaculate rows of sailing craft and the far from immaculate hodge-podge of boat-houses, until eventually the driver pulled off into a side-street, parked and stopped the engine. He and the man beside him got out and divested themselves of their coats, revealing themselves as clad in the uniforms of California State Patrolmen. The driver, a sergeant by the name of Giscard, was at least six feet three in height, burly, red-faced, tight-mouthed and, even to the cold, insolent eyes, was the conceptualized epitome of the dyed-in-the-wool tough cop. Policemen, admittedly, were part and parcel of Giscard's life but his frequent acquaintanceships with them he had kept to as limited a nature as possible on the numerous occasions when, hitherto without success, they had attempted to put him behind bars. The other, Parker, was tall, lean and of a nasty appearance and the best that could be said for him was that he might have passed for a cop if one were myopic or he were viewed at a considerable distance: his habitually wary bitter expression was probably attributable to the fact that he had experienced considerably less success than the sergeant in evading the long arm of the law.

They turned a corner and entered a local police precinct station. Two policemen were behind the counter, one very young, the other old enough to be his father. They looked rather tired and unenthusiastic as was natural for two men who were looking forward to some sleep, but they were polite, courteous.

'Good morning, good morning.' Giscard could be very brisk indeed as only befitted a man who had shown a clean pair of heels to half the police forces on the coast. 'Sergeant Giscard. Patrolman Parker.' He pulled from his pocket a paper with a long list of names. 'You must be Mahoney and Nimitz?'

'Indeed we are.' Mahoney, a guileless youth, would have found some difficulty in concealing his Hibernian ancestry. 'And how do you know?'

'Because I can read.' The niceties of salon conversation were not for Giscard. 'From this I take it that your station boss didn't advise you we were coming. Well, it's this damned motorcade this morning – and from what I've found out this morning maybe I'm not wasting all that much of my time in making this final check-up. You'd be surprised at the number of policemen in this state who are either illiterate or stone deaf.'

Nimitz was polite. 'If we were to know what we have done wrong, sergeant—'

'*You* haven't done anything wrong.' He consulted his sheet. 'Just four things. When do the day shift come on? How many? Where are the patrol cars? And the cells.'

'That's all?'

'All. Two minutes. And hurry. I've got to check every place from here across the bridge to Richmond.'

'Eight o'clock. Eight men – twice the usual. The cars—'

'Let me see them.'

Nimitz lifted a key from a board and led the two men round the corner of the block. He opened double doors. The two police cars, as was only proper on this auspicious occasion when a President, a King and a Prince were travelling through their precinct, had the impossible glitter of showroom models.

'Ignition keys?'

'In the ignition.'

Back in the station Giscard nodded to the entrance door, 'Keys?'

'I beg your pardon.'

Giscard was heavily patient. 'I know it's normally never locked. But you might *all* have to leave in a tearing hurry this morning. You want to leave the shop unattended?'

'I see.' Nimitz indicated the keys on the board.

'The cells.'

Nimitz led the way, taking keys with him. They were only a few feet away but round a corner out of sight of the more sensitive citizens who had reluctant occasion to enter the front office. Nimitz entered and Giscard unholstered his pistol and stuck it against his back. 'A dead policeman,' Giscard observed, 'is no good to anyone.' Parker joined them in ten seconds pushing a furious and flabbergasted Mahoney in front of him.

Both captives were gagged and left sitting on the floor, backs to the bars, arms thrust uncomfortably through them and wrists handcuffed. From the baleful expressions on their faces it was as well that they were so securely gagged. Giscard put the keys in his pocket, picked up two other sets from the board, ushered Parker out before him, locked the entrance door, pocketed that key too then went round and opened up the garage. He and Parker backed the cars out and while Giscard locked the doors – and, inevitably, pocketed the keys – Parker went to fetch the other four men from the station wagon. When they appeared they were not, surprisingly, any longer overalled working men but gleaming advertisements for the California State Patrol.

They drove north on the US 101, took the cut-off west to State I, passed by Muir Woods and its pre-Christian stands of two hundred and fifty feet high redwoods and finally stopped in the Mount Tamalpais State Park. Giscard brought out the walkie-talkie that went so well with his uniform and said: 'P1?'

Branson was still patiently waiting in the bus in the abandoned garage. 'Yes?'

'Okay.'

'Good. Stay.'

V

The forecourt and street outside the luxurious caravanserai atop Nob Hill were, understandably at that hour of the morning, practically deserted. There were, in fact, only seven people in sight. Six of those stood on the steps of the hotel which was that night housing more dollars on the hoof than it ever had remotely had in its long and illustrious career. The seventh of those, a tall, handsome man, aquiline-faced, youthful-looking despite his grey hair and clad in immaculate hounds-tooth, was pacing slowly up and down on the roadway. From the looks exchanged among the six men – two door-keepers, two policemen and two men in plain clothes whose coats fitted awkwardly under their left armpits – his presence appeared to be giving rise to an increasing degree of vexation. Finally, after a low-murmured conversation among them one of the uniformed men came down the steps and approached him.

He said: 'Morning, sir, No offence, sir, but do you mind moving on. We have a job to do.'

'How do you know I have not?'

'Sir. Please. You must understand we have some very important people in there.'

'Don't I know it. Don't I just know it.' The man sighed, reached inside his coat, produced and opened a wallet. The policeman looked at it, stiffened, unmistakably swallowed and deepened his complexion by two shades.

'I'm very sorry, sir. Mr Jensen, sir.'

'I'm sorry, too. Sorry for all of us. They can keep their damned oil as far as I'm concerned. Dear lord, what a circus.' He talked until the officer relaxed, then carried on his to-and-fro strolling. The policeman returned to the steps.

One of the plain-clothes men looked at him without a great deal of enthusiasm. He said: 'A great crowd mover-on you are.'

'Like to try?'

'If I must give you a demonstration,' he said wearily. He

walked down three steps, paused, looked back up. 'He flashed a card at you, didn't he?'

'Sort of.' The policeman was enjoying himself.

'Who?'

'Don't you recognize your own deputy director when you see him?'

'Jesus!' The FBI man's miraculous return to the top step could have been attributed to nothing other than sheer levitation.

'Are you not,' the policeman asked innocently, 'going to move him on?'

The plain-clothes man scowled then smiled. 'From now on, I think I'll leave those menial tasks to the uniformed branch.'

A bell-boy of great age appeared on the top step, hesitated, then went down to the street as Jensen gave him an encouraging wave. As he approached his wizened face was further creased in worry. He said: 'Aren't you taking a helluva chance, sir? FBI man up there.'

'No chance.' Jensen was unperturbed. 'He's California FBI. I'm Washington. Chalk and cheese. I doubt if he'd know the Director-General if he came and sat on his lap. What's the word, Willie?'

'They're all having breakfast in their rooms. No sleepers-in, all on schedule.'

'Let me know every ten minutes.'

'Yes, sir. Gee, Mr Jensen, aren't you taking one godawful chance? The place is swarming with fuzz and not only just inside. Those windows across there – there's a rifle behind a dozen of them and a man behind each rifle.'

'I know, Willie. I'm the man in the eye of the storm. Dead safe.'

'If you're caught—'

'I won't be. Even if I were, you're clear.'

'Clear! Everybody sees me talking to you—'

'Why? Because I'm FBI. I told you that. You've no reason to doubt it. There are six men on the top of the steps who believe the same thing. Anyway, Willie, you can always plead the Fifth Amendment.'

Willie departed. In full view of the six watchers Jensen pulled out his walkie-talkie. 'P1?'

'Yes?' Branson was as calm as ever.

'On schedule.'

'Fine. P1's moving now. Every ten minutes. Right?'

'Of course. How's my twin?'

Branson looked towards the rear of the coach. The bound and gagged man between the aisles bore an uncanny resemblance to Jensen.

'He'll live.'

— 2 —

VAN EFFEN eased the big coach on to the 280 and headed her north-east up the Southern Freeway. Van Effen was a short, stocky man, with close-cropped blond hair and a head that was almost a perfect cube. His ears were so close to his head that they appeared to have been pasted there, his nose had clearly been at odds with some heavy object in the past, he tended to wear a vacuous smile as if he'd decided it was the safest expression to cope with the numerous uncertain things that were going on in the uncertain world around him and the dreamy light blue eyes, which would never be accused of being possessed of any powers of penetration, served only to reinforce the overall impression of one overwhelmed by the insoluble complexities of life. Van Effen was a very very intelligent person whose knife-like intelligence could cope with an extremely wide variety of the world's problems and, although they had known each other for only two years, he had indisputably become Peter Branson's indispensable lieutenant.

Both men sat together in the front of the coach, both, for the nonce, dressed in long white coats which lent them, as drivers, a very professional appearance indeed: the State Department frowned on presidential motorcade drivers who opted for lumber jackets or rolled up sleeves. Branson himself generally drove and was good at it but, apart from the fact that he was not a San Franciscan and Van Effen had been born there, he wished that morning to concentrate his exclusive attention on his side of the coach's fascia which looked like a cross between the miniaturized flight instrumentation of a Boeing and those of a Hammond organ. As a communications system it could not compare to those aboard the presidential coach, but everything was there that Branson wanted. Moreover, it had one or two refinements that the presidential coach lacked. The President would not have considered them refinements.

Branson turned to the man in the seat behind him. Yonnie, a dark, swarthy and incredibly hirsute person who, on the rare occasions he could be persuaded to remove his shirt and approach a shower, looked more like a bear than a human being, had about him the general appearance – it was impossible to particularize – of an ex-pugilist who had taken not one but several hundred punches too many. Unlike many of Branson's associates Yonnie, who had been with Branson since he'd embarked upon his particular mode of life all of thirteen years ago, could not be classed among the intellectually gifted, but his patience, invariable good humour and total loyalty to Branson were beyond dispute.

Branson said: 'Got the plates, Yonnie?'

'The plates?' Yonnie wrinkled the negligible clearance between hairline and eyebrows, his customary indication of immense concentration, then smiled happily. 'Yeah, yeah, I got them.' He reached under his seat and brought up a pair of spring-clipped number plates. Branson's coach was, externally, exactly the same as the three in the presidential motorcade except for the fact that those were Washington DC plates while his were Californian. The plates that Yonnie held in his hand were Washington DC and, even better, exactly duplicated the numbers of one of the three waiting coaches in the garage.

Branson said: 'Don't forget. When I jump out the front door you jump out the back. And fix the *back* one first.'

'Leave it to me, chief.' Yonnie exuded confidence.

A buzzer on the fascia rang briefly, Branson made a switch. It was Jensen, the Nob Hill stake-out.

'P1?'

'Yes?'

'On schedule. Forty minutes.'

'Thanks.'

Branson closed the switch and flipped another.

'P4?'

'P4.'

'Move in.'

Giscard started up the stolen police car and moved up the Panoramic Highway followed by the second car. They didn't drive sufficiently quickly to attract attention but they didn't linger either and had reached the Mount Tamalpais radar stations in a matter of minutes. Those stations dominated the mountainous countryside for miles around and looked like nothing in the world as much as a couple of gigantic white golf balls. Giscard and his men had the entire lay-out committed to heart and memory and no trouble was envisaged.

Giscard said: 'There'll be no need to lean. We're cops, aren't we? The guardians of the people. You don't attack your guardians. No shooting, the boss says.'

One of them said: 'What if I *have* to shoot?'

'You'll lose half your cut.'

'No shooting.'

II

Branson flipped another switch.

'P3?' P3 was the code of the two men who had recently booby-trapped one of the motorcade buses.

'P3.'

'Anything?'

'Two drivers, is all.'

'Guards?'

'Okay. No suspicions.'

'Wait.'

Branson flipped a switch as another buzzer rang.

'P5,' the speaker said. 'On schedule. Thirty minutes.'

'Thank you.'

Branson made another switch.

'P2?' The code for Johnson and Bradley.

'Yes?'

'You can go now.'

'We go now.' The voice was Johnson's. He and Bradley, immaculate in their naval air uniforms, were sauntering casually along in the direction of the US Naval Air Station Alameda. Both men were carrying smooth shiny flight bags into which they had transferred the contents of the valise. As they approached the entrance they increased their pace. By the time they reached the two guards at the entrance they were giving the impression of two men who were in a considerable hurry. They showed their cards to one of the guards.

'Lieutenant Ashbridge, Lieutenant Martinez. Of course. You're very late, sir.'

'I know. We'll go straight to the choppers.'

'I'm afraid you can't do that, sir. Commander Eysenck wants you to report to his office at once.' The sailor lowered his voice confidentially. 'The commander doesn't sound very happy to me, sir.'

'Damn!' Johnson said, and meant it. 'Where's his office?'

'Second door on the left, sir.'

Johnson and Bradley hurried there, knocked and entered. A young petty officer seated behind his desk pursed his lips and nodded silently towards the door to his right. His demeanour indicated that he had no desire whatsoever to participate in the painful scene that was about to follow. Johnson knocked and entered, head down and apparently searching for something in his flight bag. The precaution was needless. In the well-known demoralization ploy of senior officers deepening their intimidation of apprehensive junior officers, Eysenck kept on making notes on a pad before him. Bradley closed the door. Johnson placed the flight bag on the edge of the desk. His right hand was concealed behind it. So was the aerosol gas can.

'So kind of you to turn up.' Eysenck spoke in a flat drawling accent: Annapolis had clearly failed to have any effect on his Boston upbringing. 'You had your strict orders.' He raised his head in what would normally have been a slow and effective gesture. 'Your explanations—' He broke off, eyes widening, but still not suspecting anything untoward. 'You're not Ashbridge and Martinez.'

'No, we're not, are we?'

It was clear that Eysenck had become suddenly aware that there was something very very far untoward. His hand stretched out for a desk button but Johnson already had his thumb on his. Eysenck slumped forward against his desk. Johnson nodded to Bradley who opened the door to the outer office and as he closed it behind him it could be seen that his hand was fumbling in the depths of his bag. Johnson moved behind the desk, studied the buttons below the phone, pressed one as he lifted the phone.

'Tower?'

'Sir?'

'Immediate clearance Lieutenants Ashbridge and Martinez.' It was a very creditable imitation of Eysenck's Boston accent. Branson again called P3, the two watchers by the garage.

'And now?'

'Filling up.'

The three buses inside the garage were indeed filling up. Two of them, indeed, had their complements of passengers and were ready to go. The coach that had been booby-trapped was given over mainly to newspapermen, wire service men and cameramen, among them four women, three of indeterminate age, the other young. On a platform at the rear of the bus were three mounted ciné cameras, for this was the coach that led the motorcade and the cameras would at all times have an excellent view of the presidential coach which was to follow immediately behind. Among the passengers in this coach were three men who wouldn't have recognized a typewriter or a camera if it had dropped on their toes but who would have had no difficulty whatsoever in differentiating between a Walther, Colt, Biretti, Smith & Wesson and other such paraphernalia generally regarded as superfluous to the needs of the communications media. This was known as the lead coach.

But there was one passenger in this coach who would have recognized a camera if he had seen it – he was, in fact, carrying a highly complicated apparatus – but who would also have had no difficulty at all in differentiating between a Walther, Colt, Biretti and Smith & Wesson, any of which he was legally entitled to carry and not infrequently did. On this occasion, however, he was unarmed – he considered it unnecessary; between them his colleagues constituted a veritable travelling arsenal – but he did carry a most unusual item of equipment, a beautifully miniaturized and transistorized transceiver radio concealed in the false bottom of his camera. His name was Revson and, as he had repeatedly proved in the past, in the service of his country although his country knew nothing of this – a man of quite remarkable accomplishments.

The rear coach was also well occupied, again by newspaper men and men with no interest in newspapers, although in this case the ratio was inversed. The greatly outnumbered journalists, although they realized that the presidential coach would soon, in terms of the realizable assets of its passengers, be nothing less than a rolling Fort Knox, wondered if it were necessary to have quite so many FBI agents around.

There were only three people aboard the Presidential coach, all crew members. The white-coated driver, his 'receive' switch depressed, was waiting for instructions to come through the fascia speaker. Behind the bar, an extraordinarily pretty brunette, who looked like an amalgam of all those 'Fly me' airline advertisements, was trying to look demure and inconspicuous and failing miserably. At the rear, the radio operator was already seated in front of his communications console.

III

A buzzer rang in Branson's coach.

'P5,' the speaker said. 'On schedule. Twenty minutes.'

A second buzzer rang.

'P4,' the speaker said. 'All okay.'

'Excellent.' For once Branson permitted himself a slight feeling of relief. The take-over of the Tamalpais radar stations had been essential to his plans. 'Scanners manned?'

'Affirmative.'

A third buzzer rang.

'P1?' Johnson's voice was hurried. 'P2. Can we go now?'

'No. Trouble?'

'Some.' Johnson, seated at the helicopter controls, engines still not started, watched a man emerge from Eysenck's office and break into a run, rounding the corner of the building. That could only mean, Johnson realized, that he was going to look through Eysenck's office window and that could only mean that he had failed to open the door which he and Bradley had locked behind them: the key was at that moment in Johnson's pocket. Not that looking through Eysenck's window was going to help him much because he and Bradley had dragged the unconscious Eysenck and petty officer into the windowless washroom leading off the Commander's office. The key of the washroom door was also in his pocket.

The man came into sight round the corner of the building. He wasn't running now. In fact, he stopped and looked around. It wasn't too hard to read what was going on in his mind. Eysenck and the petty officer might well be going about their lawful occasions and he was going to look pretty sick if he started to cry wolf. On the other hand if something had happened and he didn't report his suspicions he was going to make himself highly unpopular with his superiors. He turned and headed in the direction of the Station Commander's office, obviously with the intent of asking a few discreet questions. Half-way towards the office it became clear that his questions weren't going to be all that discreet: he had broken into a run.

Johnson spoke into the walkie-talkie.

'Bad trouble.'

'Hold on as long as possible. Leave in emergency. Rendezvous remains.'

In coach P1 Van Effen looked at Branson. 'Something wrong?'

'Yes. Johnson and Bradley are in trouble, want to take off. Imagine what's going to happen if they do, if they have to cruise around ten minutes waiting for us? A couple of hijacked helicopters with the President and half the oil in the Middle East in the city? Everybody's going to be as jittery as hell. They'll take no chances. Panic-stricken. They'll stop at nothing. The choppers will be shot out of the sky. They have Phantoms in a state of instant readiness on that base.'

'Well, now.' Van Effen eased the coach to a stop at the back of the garage which held the motorcade. 'Bad, but maybe not as bad as all that. If they have to take off before schedule, you could always instruct them to fly over the motorcade. It would take a pretty crazy air commander to instruct his pilots to fire machine-guns or rockets at a chopper hovering above the presidential coach. Bingo – no President, no Arabian oil kings and sheikhs, no Chief of Staff, no Mayor Morrison. Chopper might even crash down on to the top of the presidential coach. Not nice to be a sacked rear admiral without a pension. If, that is to say, he survives the court martial.'

'I hadn't thought of it that way.' Branson sounded half convinced, no more. 'You're assuming our air commander is as sane as you are, that he would react along your line of thinking. How are we to know that he is not certifiable? Extremely unlikely, I admit, but I have no option other than to accept your suggestion. And we've no option other than to go ahead.'

The buzzer rang. Branson made the appropriate switch.

'P1?'

'Yes?'

'P3.' It was Reston from the garage. 'Lead coach has just moved out.'

'Let me know when the presidential coach moves.'

Branson gestured to Van Effen, who started up the engine and moved slowly round the side of the garage.

The buzzer rang again.

'P5. On schedule. Ten minutes.'

'Fine. Get down to the garage.'

Again the buzzer rang. It was Reston. He said: 'Presidential coach is just moving out.'

'Fine.' Branson made another switch. 'Rear coach?'

'Yeah?'

'Hold it for a couple of minutes. We've a traffic jam here. Some nut has just slewed his articulated truck across the street. Pure accident, I'd say. But no chances. No panic, no need for anyone to leave their seats. We're coming back to the garage for a couple of minutes till they decide on a new route. Okay?'

'Okay.'

Van Effen drove slowly round to the front of the garage, nosed it past the front door until the first third of the coach was visible to the occupants of the rear coach inside, still parked where it had been. Branson and Van Effen descended unhurriedly from the opposite front seats, walked into the garage: Yonnie, unobserved by those inside exited via the back door and began to clamp the new number plate on top of the old.

The occupants of the rear coach watched the approach of the two white-coated figures curiously, but without suspicion, for endless frustrating delays were part and parcel of their lives. Branson walked around to the front door opposite the driver's side, while Van Effen wandered, aimlessly as it seemed, towards the rear. Had there been any cause for concern on the part of the occupants, it would have been allayed by the sight of two blue-overalled figures busily doing nothing by the main doors. They were not to know they were Reston and his friend.

Branson opened the front left-hand door and climbed up two steps. He said to the driver: 'Sorry about this. It happens. They're picking out a new route, a safe route, for us to go up to Nob Hill.'

The driver looked puzzled, no more. He said: 'Where's Ernie?'

'Ernie?'

'Lead coach driver.'

'Ah! That's his name. Taken sick, I'm afraid.'

'Taken sick?' Suspicion flared. 'Only two minutes ago—'

The driver twisted round in his seat as two minor explosions occurred in the rear of the coach, less explosions than soft plops of sound, to the accompanying sounds of breaking glass and a hiss as of air escaping under pressure. The rear of the coach was already enveloped in a dense, billowing and rapidly mushrooming cloud of grey smoke, so dense that it was impossible to see the now closed rear door and the figure of Van Effen leaning against it and making sure it stayed that way. Every man in the bus – or those who were still visible – had swung round in his seat, reaching for a gun in an automatic but useless reaction for there was nothing to be seen to fire at.

Branson held his breath, threw two of the grenade shaped gas bombs in rapid succession – one in the front aisle, one at the driver's feet – jumped to the garage floor, slammed the door and held the handle, a somewhat pointless precaution as he knew, for the first inhalation of that gas produced immediate unconsciousness. After ten seconds he left, walked round the front of the bus where he was joined by Van Effen Reston and his companion had already closed and bolted the main entrance. Now they were stripping off their overalls to reveal the conservative and well cut suits beneath.

Reston said: 'Over? So soon? Just like that?' Branson nodded. 'But if one whiff of that can knock a man out, surely it's going to kill them – if they keep on sitting there, I mean, inhaling the stuff all the time?'

They left via the side door, not too hurriedly, locking it behind them. Branson said: 'Contact with oxygen neutralizes the gas inside fifteen seconds. You could walk inside that bus now and be entirely unaffected. But it will be at least an hour before anyone in that bus comes to.'

Harriman stepped out of a taxi as they came round to the garage front. They boarded the coach – now the new rear coach of the motorcade – and Van Effen headed for Nob Hill. Branson made a switch in the fascia.

'P2?'

'Yes.'

'How are things?'

'Quiet. Too damned quiet. I don't like it.'

'What do you think is happening?'

'I don't know. I can just see someone on the phone asking for permission to launch a couple of guided missiles at us.'

'Permission from whom?'

'The highest military authority in the country.'

'Could take time to contact Washington.'

'Take damn-all time to contact Nob Hill.'

'Oh, my God!' Momentarily, even Branson's habitual massive calm was disturbed. The highest military authority in the country was, indeed, in the next suite to the President in the Mark Hopkins hotel. General Cartland, Chief of Staff and adviser extraordinary to the President, was indeed participating in that day's motorcade. 'You know what happens if they do contact him?'

'Yes. They'll cancel the motorcade.' Chief of the Armed Forces though the President might be, he could be over-ruled in matters of security by his Chief of Staff. 'Hold it a minute.' There was a pause then Johnson said: 'One of the guards at the gate is on the telephone. This could mean anything or nothing.'

Branson was conscious of a slight dampness in the region of his neck collar. Although he had given up the habit of prayer even before he'd left his mother's knee, he prayed it was nothing. Perhaps the call to the guard was perfectly innocuous: perhaps the outcome of the call might be innocuous: if it were not, the many months and the quarter million dollars he's spent in preparation for this *coup* was so much irrecoverable water under the bridge.

'P1?'

'Yes?' Branson was dimly aware that his teeth were clamped tightly together.

'You're not going to believe this but tower has just given us permission to lift off.'

Branson remained silent for a few moments while someone lifted the Golden Gate Bridge off his back. He was not one much given to brow-mopping but this, if ever, seemed a warranted occasion. He refrained. He said: 'Never look a gift horse in the mouth. How do you account for this?'

'The guards must have said that they'd checked our identity papers and that they were in order.'

'Start up, will you? I'd like to find out if I can hear you over the racket of the rotors.'

IV

Twin lines of security men, back to back at a distance of about six feet and facing outwards, formed a protective lane for the short distance between the hotel and the waiting presidential coach, which seemed rather superfluous as the streets had been barricaded off from the public for a hundred yards all around. The visiting dignitaries from the Arabian Gulf seemed to be in no way put out by this nor to be suffering from any claustrophobic sense of imprisonment: in their own homelands, where the fine art of assassination had reached peaks as yet undreamed of in the United States, this was part and parcel of their everyday lives: not only would they have felt naked without this overt show of protection, they would have been offended if not humiliated by the very concept that they were sufficiently unimportant not to merit the massive security precaution.

The President led the way, looking almost wistfully from side to side as if disappointed that there was no one there for him to wave at. He was a tall, rather portly figure, immaculately attired in a tan gaberdine suit, with a patrician face vaguely reminiscent of one of the better-fed Roman emperors and a splendid head of the purest silver hair which was widely supposed to be his especial pride and joy. One had but to look at him to appreciate that he had been doomed from the cradle to end up in the Oval Office: that anyone else should aspire to be – or be – the Chief Executive was quite unthinkable. Better brains there might be on Capitol Hill, but that magnificient presence was unique. As far as politicians went he was a man of the utmost probity – the fact that he was a multi-millionaire may have helped him in this – intelligent, humorous and was loved, liked, admired or held in genuine affection to an extent that had been achieved by no other President in the previous half century, a remarkable but far from impossible achievement. As always, he carried a stout cane, a relic from that occasion when he had required it for almost two days after tripping over the leash of his Labrador. That he had no need of the cane was quite indisputable. Perhaps he thought it rounded off his image, or lent him a slightly Rooseveltian aura. Whatever the reason, he was never seen in public or private without it.

He reached the coach, half-turned, smiled and bowed slightly as he ushered the first of his guests aboard.

Precedence and pride of place went inevitably to the King: his vast kingdom held as much oil as the rest of the world put together. He was a tall, imposing figure, a king from the floor-sweeping skirts of his dazzling white robes to the top of the equally dazzling burnous. He had an aquiline dark face, with a splendidly trimmed white beard and the hooded eyes of a brooding eagle. Supposedly the wealthiest man in all history, he could easily have been a tyrant and despot but was neither: against that his autocratic rule was absolute and the only laws he obeyed were those he made himself.

The Prince came next – his small sheikhdom had never rated and never had had a king. While his territorial holdings came to less than five per cent of the King's, his influence was almost as great: his sheikhdom, an arid and barren expanse of some of the world's most inhospitable sands, was literally afloat on a sea of oil. An extrovert and flamboyant personality, who owned a Cadillac for every four miles of his principality's hundred miles of road – it was said with some authority that if one of his cars had the slightest mechanical trouble it was regarded as obsolete and never used again, a fact which must have given some small satisfaction to General Motors – he was an excellent pilot, a remarkably gifted race-car driver and an assiduous patron of many of the most exclusive nightclubs in the world. He went to considerable lengths to cultivate his reputation as an international playboy, an exercise which deceived nobody: behind the façade lay the computerized mind of an outstanding businessman. He was of medium height, well built and wouldn't have been seen dead in the traditional Arab clothes. He was Savile Row's best customer. 'Dapper' was the only word to describe him, from the pointed crocodile shoes to the almost invisible hairline moustache.

They were followed by Sheikh Iman and Sheikh Kharan, the oil ministers respectively of the King and the Prince. They looked remarkably alike and were rumoured to have the same grandfather, which was not at all impossible. Both wore Western clothes, both were plump, smiling almost to the point of beaming and extremely shrewd indeed. The only way to tell them apart was while Iman sported a tiny black goatee beard Kharan was clean-shaven.

The next to board was General Cartland. Although wearing civilian clothes – an inconspicuous blue pin-stripe – he was unmistakably what he was. If he had been wearing only a bath towel he would still have been immediately recognizable as a general. The erect bearing, the precise movements, the clipped speech, the cool blue eyes that never asked a question twice – everything marked him out for the man he was. Even his grey hair was shorn. Although Cartland had more than a peripheral interest in oil – he did, after all, require some form of fuel for his ships, tanks and planes – he was not along because of any special expertise in the oil business. He was along primarily because the President refused to cross the street without him. The President – and he made no bones about it – was heavily dependent on Cartland for his advice, far-ranging width of experience and solid common sense, a fact which had given and still gave rise to considerable if wholly misplaced jealousy in Washington. Cooler judgements in that city regarded him as being virtually irreplaceable as presidential adviser, and although this duty left him with less and less time to run his army, navy and air force Cartland seemed to cope with both tasks effortlessly. He would have made an excellent politician or stateman but had unfortunately been cursed from birth with an unshakable incorruptibility and moral integrity.

The next man to board was Hansen, the President's energy czar. He was the latest appointee to the post and as yet a largely unknown quantity. His qualifications for the post were impeccable but his experience so far slight. Energy was one thing he appeared to possess in abundance. He was a darting, nervous, volatile individual, painfully thin, whose hands and dark eyes were never still. He was reputed to have a first-class brain. This was his biggest – indeed almost his only – confrontation with great oil barons and his awareness of being on trial was painful.

Muir went next. He was a very rubicund man, almost bald, and the number of his chins varied from two to four according to the angle of his neck. Unlike most fat men he had a permanently doleful expression. He had a positively bucolic appearance about him, an unsuccessful farmer who concentrated less on the production than the consumption of what he grew on his farm. This proposed deal with the Arab nations could raise as many political as physical problems, which was why Under-Secretary of State Muir was along. Although it was almost impossible to believe he was unquestionably the country's leading expert on the Middle East.

The President waved the last man aboard but John Morrison, waving his hand in turn, declined. The President acknowledged the gesture, smiled and preceded him up the steps. Morrison, a burly, genial man of unquestionably Italian ancestry, was not along for his energy expertise. Energy concerned him but not to the extent of causing him sleepless nights. He was along partly as a guide, partly because he conceived it to be his duty to accept the presidential invitation. Although the President was the official host to his guests, this was Morrison's parish and here he was both host and king. He was the Mayor of San Francisco.

V

In the rear coach, some fifty yards away, Branson saw the Presidential coach door close. He made a switch.

'P2?'

'Yes?' Johnson.

'We go now.'

'Now it is.'

VI

The motorcade moved off, led by a police car and motor-cycle outriders. They were followed by the lead coach, the presidential coach, the rear coach, a second police car and two more outriders. There was no attempt to make any scenic tour of the town, that had been attended to the previous afternoon soon after the Air Force One had landed at the International Airport. This was strictly a business trip. The motorcade went along California, right down Van Ness, left along Lombard, angled right up Richardson Avenue and so into the Presidio. From this point onwards the roads had been closed that morning to all normal traffic. They took the Viaduct Approach, curving right and to the north until at last, dead ahead, loomed the immensity of the Golden Gate Bridge.

— 3 —

THE GOLDEN Gate Bridge is unquestionably one of the engineering wonders of the world. To San Franciscans, inevitably, it is *the* engineering wonder of the world and as bridges go it must be at once the most spectacular and graceful in existence. To see the two great brick-red – or orange or ochre, according to the quality of the light – towers emerging from the dense banks of fog that so frequently billow in from the Pacific is to experience a profound sense of unreality and when the fog disperses completely the feeling changes to one of disbelief and a benumbment of the senses that men had not only the audacity to conceive of this epic poem in mechanical grandeur but also the technical expertise to bring it into being. Even while the evidence of the eyes is irrefutable it still remains difficult for the mind to accept that it actually is there.

That it is there at all is not, in fact, due to man but to one man, a certain Joseph B. Strauss, who, in the pig-headed fashion of considerable Americans, despite seemingly unsurmountable and political difficulties and the assurances of his architectural colleagues that his dream was a technical impossibility, just went ahead and built it anyway. The bridge was opened in May 1937.

Until the construction of the Varrazano-Narrows Bridge in 1964, it was the longest single-span suspension bridge in the world. Even now, it is only about twenty yards shorter. The two massive towers that support the bridge soar seven hundred and fifty feet above the waters of the Golden Gate: the bridge's total length is just under one and three-quarter miles. The cost of construction was $35,000,000: to replace it today something in the region of $200,000,000 would be needed.

The one sombre aspect about the bridge is that for Americans who find the burdens of life intolerable to bear this is unquestionably the most favoured point of departure. There have been at least five hundred known suicides: probably as many again have gone undetected. There have been eight known survivors. Among the rest, the possibility of survival seems extremely remote. If any did indeed survive the shattering impact of the two-hundred-foot drop to the water, the surging tides and vicious currents of the Golden Gate would swiftly have completed what the jump itself failed to do. Those dangerous tides and currents make their effect felt for some distance on either side of the bridge. Three miles to the east lies what used to be the forbidding prison-fortress of Alcatraz Island. No precise figures of those who attempted escape by swimming are available: but it is believed that only three of those who tried it ever survived.

It is idle to speculate upon the choice of the bridge as a springboard to eternity. Psychiatrists would have it that it is a spectacular and attention-riveting finale to a drab and unspectacular life dragged out in a grey anonymity. But it would seem that there is nothing either eye-catching or spectacular in jumping into the darkness in the middle of the night.

II

The procession made its stately way under the first of the giant towers. In the upholstered luxury of the presidential coach, the King, Prince and their two oil ministers gazed around them with a carefully controlled degree of regal and vice-regal appreciation, for although there was a marked absence of Golden Gate Bridges in their dusty homelands – and, indeed, no need for them – it would not have done to admit that there were some things better done in the West than in the Middle East. Nor did they enthuse overmuch about the scenery, for although a million square miles of drifting sands might not be without its attractions for a homesick Bedu, it could hardly be said to compare with the lush and fertile greenery of the farm land and forest land that stretched ahead of them across the Golden Gate. Indeed, the whole of the Bay area could not have looked better than it did on that splendid June morning, with the sun already climbing high to their right in a cloudless sky and sparkling iridescently off the blue-green waters below. It was the perfect story-book setting for a day which, the President and Hansen, his energy czar, devoutly hoped would have a story-book ending.

The Prince looked around the coach, this time in open admiration, for he was very much a man of his own generation and possessed of a passion for all things mechanical and said in his clipped Oxford accent: 'My word, Mr President, you do know how to travel in style. I wish I had one of these.'

'And so you shall,' the President said indulgently. 'My country would be honoured to present you with one such, as soon as possible after your return to your homeland. Equipped to your own specifications, of course.'

The King said drily: 'The Prince is accustomed to ordering his vehicles by the round dozen. No doubt, Achmed, you would like a couple of those to go with it.' He pointed upwards to where two naval helicopters were hovering overhead. 'You do take good care of us, Mr President.'

The President smiled non-committally. How could one comment upon the obvious? General Cartland said: 'For decorative purposes only, Your Highness. Apart from your own security men waiting on the other side and an occasional police car, you will see nothing between here and San Rafael. But the security is there all the same. Between here and San Rafael the motorcade will be under heavily armed surveillance literally every yard of the way. There are crack-pots everywhere, even in the United States.'

'Especially in the United States,' the President said darkly.

In mock seriousness the King said: 'So we are safe?'

The President regained his smiling composure. 'As in the vaults of Fort Knox.'

III

It was at this point, just after the lead coach had passed the half-way mark across the bridge, that five things happened in almost bewilderingly rapid succession. In the rear coach Branson pressed a button on the console in front of him. Two seconds later a small explosion occurred in the front of the lead coach, almost beneath the driver's feet. Although unhurt, the driver was momentarily shocked, then swore, recovered quickly and jammed his foot on the brake pedal. Nothing happened.

'Sweet Jesus!' It took him all of another second to realize that his hydraulic lines were gone. He jammed his hand-brake into the locked position and changed down into first gear. The coach began to slow.

Branson abruptly lifted his right arm, as abruptly lowered it again to reinforce the left in bracing himself against the fascia. Behind him his men did the same, outstretched arms, slightly bent at the elbows as they had learnt in frequent practices, braced against the backs of the seats in front: nobody sat in the front seats. Van Effen slipped the gear into neutral and kicked down on the brake pedal as if he were trying to thrust it through the floor.

The fact that Van Effen had recently and with malice aforethought seen fit to de-activate his rear brake lights did little to help the plight of the hapless driver of the police car behind. The motorcade was travelling slowly, about twenty-five miles an hour, and the rear police car was trailing the coach by about the same number of feet. The driver had no reason to suspect that anything might be amiss, for the bridge was closed to all traffic except the motorcade: there was no earthly reason to expect anything should interfere with the smooth and even tempo of their progress. He may even have spared a momentary side glance to admire the view. However it was, when he first realized that all was not what it should have been the distance between them had halved. An incredulous double-take cost him another few feet and, skilled police driver though he was, his reactions were no faster than those of the next man and by the time his foot had hit the brake the gap between himself and the now stationary coach had lessened to not more than five feet. The effect of a car's striking a solid and immovable object at twenty miles an hour has a less than humorous effect on the occupants of that car: the four officers in the car were no exception.

At the moment of impact Branson touched a second button on the fascia. The lead coach, slowing only by its hand-brake, was now doing no more than ten miles an hour when another small explosion occurred in the drinks cabinet at the rear, an explosion followed immediately by a pronounced hissing as if caused by compressed air escaping under very high pressure. Within seconds the entire compartment was filled with a dense, grey, obnoxious and noxious gas. The coach, almost immediately out of control as the driver slumped forward over the wheel, slewed slowly to the right and came to a rest less than two feet from the side of the road. Not that it would have mattered particularly if it had struck the safety barriers on the side of the bridge which were of a nature to withstand the assaults of anything less than a Chieftain tank.

The presidential coach came to no harm. The driver had seen the lead coach's brake warning lights come on, braked, pulled left to avoid the slewing coach ahead and came to a rest beside it. The expressions of the twelve occupants of the coach expressed varying degrees of unhappiness but not, as yet, of alarm.

The police car and two motor-cycle outriders leading the motorcade had been curiously slow to observe the confusion behind them. Only now had they spotted the slewed coach and were beginning to turn.

In the rear coach everything was taking place with the clockwork precision that stemmed from a score of practice runs that had covered all conceivable potentialities. Van Effen jumped down from the left-hand door, Yonnie from the right, just as the two motor-cycle outriders pulled up almost alongside. Van Effen said: 'You better get in there fast. Looks like we got a stiff on our hands.'

The two patrolmen propped their machines and jumped aboard the coach. They could now no longer be seen by the returning lead police car and outriders so it was safe to take swift and efficient action against them, which was done with considerable ease not least because their attention had immediately been caught up by the sight of the bound figure lying sprawled on the floor in the rear aisle.

Seven men emerged swiftly from the doors of the coach. Five of those joined Van Effen and Yonnie and ran towards the other coaches. Two more ran back towards the crashed police car. Two others inside the coach swung wide the rear door and mounted what appeared to be a relatively harmless length of steel tubing on a tripod stand. Branson and Jensen remained where they were: the bound man on the floor, whose identity Jensen had taken over, regarded them all severally with a baleful expression but, beyond that, the options open to him were rather limited.

The two men who had run back towards the crashed police car were called Kowalski and Peters. They didn't look like criminals, unless a couple of prosperous young commuters from the stockbroker belt could be called criminals. Yonnie apart, none of Branson's associates bore any resemblance whatever to the popular concept of those who habitually stepped outside the law. Both men, in fact, had killed a number of times, but then only legally – as far as the term 'legal' could be interpreted – as members of a highly specialized Marine commando unit in Vietnam. Disillusioned with civilian life they'd found their next best panacea with Branson, who had a splendid eye for the recruitment of such men. They had not killed since. Branson approved of violence if and when necessary: killing was not permitted except as a last resort. In his thirteen years of upsetting law officers in the United States, Canada and Mexico, Branson had not yet had to have recourse to the last resort. Whether this was due to moral scruples or not was unclear: what was clear was that Branson regarded it as bad business. The degree of intensity of police efforts to catch robbers as opposed to murderers differed quite appreciably.

The windows of both front doors of the car were wound down – obviously they had been so at the moment of the crash. The four uniformed men seated inside had not been seriously injured but clearly had been badly shaken and had suffered minor damage, the worst of which appeared to be a broken nose sustained by the man in the front seat next to the driver. For the most part they were just dazed, too dazed, in any effect to offer any resistance to the removal of their weapons. Working in smooth unison Kowalski and Peters wound up the front windows. Peters closed his door while Kowalski threw in a gas bomb and closed his in turn.

None of any of this action had been witnessed by the returning police car's crew or the motor-cycle outriders. The policemen left their cars and machines and were cautiously approaching the lead coach when Yonnie and Van Effen with the five others came running up. All had guns of one kind or another in their hands.

'Quickly!' Van Effen shouted. 'Take cover! There are a couple of crazy bastards back in that coach there, one with a bazooka, the other with a Schmeisser. Get behind the bus!'

Given time to consider the matter the policemen might have queried Van Effen's statements but they weren't given the time and the instinct for immediate if irrational self-preservation remains always paramount. Van Effen checked quickly to see if they were hidden from the view of the presidential coach. They were. Not that he feared anything from that source, he just wanted to be spared the chore of blasting open the lock of the door that would be surely locked against them if their actions were observed.

He nodded to Yonnie and walked away with another man towards the rear of the bus. Whatever might be said, and had unkindly been said, about Yonnie's cerebral limitations, this was the situation he had been born for, a basically elemental one in which action took precedence over thoughts. Long training had even given the vocabulary appropriate to the occasion. He said: 'Let's kinda put our hands up, huh?'

The six men turned round. Their expressions ran through the gamut of astonishment, anger and then resignation. Resignation was all that was left them. They had, with reason enough, not yet thought it time to produce their own weapons, and when the wise man is confronted at point-blank range with a pair of submachine-pistols he does what he is told and just kinda puts his hands up. Yonnie kept them covered while another man relieved them of their pistols. The remaining two men began to run back towards the rear coach as soon as they saw Van Effen and another climb aboard the presidential coach.

The reaction of those aboard this coach had, so far, amounted to no more than an amalgam of perplexity and annoyance, and even that was slight enough. One or two were making the customary laborious effort to rise when Van Effen mounted the steps.

'Please relax, gentlemen,' he said. 'Just a slight delay.' Such is the authority of even a white coat – in a street accident a crowd will make way for a man in a butcher's apron – that everybody subsided. Van Effen produced an unpleasant-looking weapon, a double-barrelled 12-bore shotgun with most of the barrel and stock removed to make for easier transport, if not accuracy. 'I am afraid this is what you might call a hold-up or hi-jack or kidnap. I don't suppose it matters very much what you call it. Just please remain where you are.'

'Good God in heaven!' The President stared at Van Effen's moonface as if he were a creature from outer space. His eyes, as if drawn magnetically, went to the King and the Prince, then he returned his outraged gaze to Van Effen. 'Are you insane? Don't you know who I am? Don't you know you're pointing a gun at the President of the United States?'

'I know. You can't help being what you are any more than I can help being what I am. As for pointing guns at presidents, it's a long if not very honourable tradition in our country. Please do not give any trouble.' Van Effen looked directly at General Cartland – he'd had him under indirect observation from the moment he had entered the coach. 'General, it is known that you always carry a gun. Please let me have it. Please do not be clever. Your .22 can be nasty enough if it is accurate enough: this whippet will blast a hole the size of your hand through your chest. You are not the man, I know, to confuse courage with suicide.'

Cartland smiled faintly, nodded, produced a small, black, narrow automatic and handed it across.

Van Effen said, 'Thank you. I'm afraid you will have to remain seated for the moment at least. You have only my word for it, but if you offer no violence you will receive none.'

A profound silence descended. The King, eyes closed and hands folded across his chest, appeared to be communing either with himself or with the All-powerful. Suddenly he opened his eyes, looked at the President and said: 'Just how safe are the vaults in Fort Knox?'

IV

'You'd better believe me, Hendrix,' Branson said. He was talking into a hand-held microphone. 'We have the President, the King and the Prince. If you will wait a minute or two I'll have the President himself confirm that to you. Meantime, please don't attempt anything so stupid or rash as to try to approach us. Let me give you a demonstration. I assume you have some patrol cars near the south entrance and that you are in radio contact with them?'

Hendrix didn't look like anyone's conception of a Chief of Police. He looked like a professorial refugee from the campus of the near-by university. He was tall, slender, dark, slightly stooped and invariably immaculately groomed and conservatively dressed. A great number of people temporarily or permanently deprived of their freedom would have freely if blasphemously attested to the fact that he was very very intelligent indeed. There was no more brilliant or brilliantly effective policeman in the country. At that moment, however, that fine intelligence was in temporary abeyance. He felt stunned and had about him the look of a man who has just seen all his nightmares come true.

He said: 'I am.'

'Very well. Wait.'

Branson turned and made a signal to the two men at the rear of the coach. There was a sudden explosive whoosh from the recoil-less missile weapon mounted at the rear. Three seconds later a cloud of dense grey smoke erupted between the pylons of the south tower. Branson spoke into the microphone. 'Well?'

'Some kind of explosion,' Hendrix said. His voice was remarkably steady. 'Lots of smoke, if it is smoke.'

'A nerve gas. Not permanently damaging, but incapacitating. Takes about ten minutes before it oxidizes. If we have to use it and a breeze comes up from the north-west, north or north-east – well, it will be your responsibility, you understand.'

'I understand.'

'Conventional gas-masks are useless against it. Do you understand that also?'

'I understand.'

'We have a similar weapon covering the northern end of the bridge. You will inform police squads and units of the armed forces of the inadvisability of attempting to move out on to the bridge. You understand that too?'

'Yes.'

'You will have been informed of the presence of two naval helicopters hovering over the bridge?'

'Yes.' The rather hunted look had left Hendrix's face and his mind was clearly back into top gear. 'I find it rather puzzling, I must say.'

'It needn't be. They are in our hands. Have an immediate alarm put through to all local army and naval air commanders. Tell them if any attempt is made to dispatch fighters to shoot down those helicopters they will have very unpleasant effects on the President and his friends. Tell them that we shall know immediately whenever any such plane does lift off. The Mount Tamalpais radar stations are in our hands.'

'Good God!' Hendrix was back to square one.

'He won't help. They are manned by competent radar operators. No attempt will be made to retake those stations whether by land or airborne assault. If such an assault is made we are aware that we have no means of preventing it. However, I do not think that the President, King or Prince would look kindly upon any individual who was responsible for depriving them of, say, their right ears. Please do not think that I am not serious. We shall deliver them, by hand, in a sealed plastic bag.'

'No such attempt will be made.' Captain Campbell, a burly, sandy-haired, red-faced and normally jovial character whom Hendrix regarded as his right-hand man, regarded Hendrix with some surprise, not because of what he had just said but because it was the first time he had ever seen Hendrix with beads of sweat on his brow. In an unconscious gesture Campbell reached up and touched his own forehead, then looked with a feeling of grave disquiet at the dampened back of his hand.

Branson said: 'I hope you mean what you say. I will contact you shortly.'

'It will be in order if I come down to the bridge? It would appear that I have to set up some kind of communications headquarters and that seems the most logical place for it to be.'

'That will be in order. But do not move out on to the bridge. And please prevent any private cars from entering the Presidio.

Violence is the very last thing we want but if some arises I do not wish innocent people to suffer.'

'You are very considerate.' Hendrix sounded, perhaps justifiably, more than a little bitter.

Branson smiled and replaced the microphone.

V

The gas inside the lead coach had vanished but the effect it had had on the occupants had not. All were still profoundly unconscious. Some two or three had fallen into the aisle without, apparently, having sustained any injuries in the process. For the most part, however, they just remained slumped in their seats or had fallen forward against the backs of the seats in front of them.

Yonnie and Bartlett moved among them but not in the capacity of ministering angels. Bartlett, at twenty-six, was the youngest of Branson's men, and looked every inch a fresh-faced college boy which every inch he was not. They were searching every person in the coach, and searching them very thoroughly indeed, those who were being subjected to this indignity being in no position to object. The lady journalists were spared this but their handbags were meticulously examined. It said much for the standards that Branson imposed that none of the several thousand dollars that passed through the hands of Yonnie and Bartlett found its way into either of their pockets. Robbery on a grand scale was big business: robbery on a small scale was petty larceny and not to be tolerated. In any event, they weren't looking for money, they were looking for guns. Branson had reasoned, and correctly as it turned out, that there would be several special agents in the journalists' coach, whose assignment would be not the direct protection of the President and his guests but the surveillance of the journalists themselves. Because of the world-wide interest aroused by the visit of the Arabian oil princes to the United States, at least ten of those journalists aboard were from abroad – four from Europe, the same from the Gulf States and one each from Nigeria and Venezuela, countries which might well be regarded as having a pressing interest in any transactions between the major oil states and the United States.

They found three such guns and pocketed them. The three owners of the guns were handcuffed and left where they were. Yonnie and Bartlett descended and joined the man who was guarding the six still largely uncomprehending policemen who were handcuffed together in single file. Another man was seated behind one of the bazooka-like missile firers that was guarding the north tower. Here, as at the southern end, everything was completely under control, everything had gone precisely as Branson had meticulously and with much labour planned over the preceding months. Branson had every reason to be feeling agreeably pleased with himself.

VI

Branson, as he stepped down from the rear coach, looked neither pleased nor displeased. Things had gone as he had expected them to and that was that. His followers had often remarked, although never in his hearing, on Branson's almost staggering self-confidence: on the other hand they had to admit that he had never, as yet, failed to justify his utter trust in himself. Of Branson's permanent nucleus of eighteen men, nine of them had spent various times in various penitentiaries up and down the country reflecting upon the vagaries of fortune. But that was before they had been recruited by Branson. Since then not one of the eighteen had even got as far as a court-room far less the prison walls: when it was taken into account that those included such semi-permanent guests of the United States Government as Parker this record could be regarded as an achievement of no little note.

Branson walked forward to the presidential coach. Van Effen was standing in the doorway. Branson said: 'I'm moving the lead coach ahead a bit. Tell your driver to follow me.'

He moved into the lead coach and with Yonnie's help dragged clear the slumped driver. He slid into the vacant seat, started the engine, engaged gear, straightened out the coach and eased it forward for a distance of about fifty yards, bringing it to a halt with the use of the hand-brake. The presidential coach followed, pulling up only feet behind them.

Branson descended and walked back in the direction of the south tower. When he came to the precise middle of the bridge – the point at which the enormous suspension cables were at their lowest – he looked behind him and again in front of him. The fifty yards of the most central section of the bridge, the sections where the helicopter rotors would be most unlikely to be fouled by the cables, even if subjected to the unseen and unforeseen vagaries of wind, was clear. Branson walked clear of the area and waved to the two machines chattering overhead. Johnson and Bradley brought their naval helicopters down easily and with the minimum of fuss. For the first time in its long and august history the Golden Gate Bridge was in use as a helipad.

Branson boarded the presidential coach. Everyone there was instinctively aware that he was the leader of their kidnappers, the man behind their present troubles, and their reception of him did not even begin to border on the cordial. The four oil men and Cartland looked at him impassively: Hansen, understandably, was more jittery and nervous than ever, his hands and eyes for ever on the rapid and almost furtive move: Muir was his usual somnolent self, his eyes half-closed as if he were on the verge of dropping off to sleep: Mayor Morrison, who had won so many medals in the Second World War that he could scarcely have found room for them even on his massive chest, was just plain furious: and so, indisputably, was the President: that expression of kindly tolerance and compassionate wisdom which had endeared him to the hearts of millions had for the moment been tucked away in the deep freeze.

Branson said without preamble but pleasantly enough: 'My name is Branson. Morning, Mr President. Your Highnesses. I would like—'

'*You* would like!' The President was icily angry but he had the expression on his face and the tone in his voice under control: you don't have two hundred million people call you President and behave like an unhinged rock star. 'I suggest we dispense with the charade, with the hypocrisy of empty politeness. Who are you, sir?'

'I told you. Branson. And I see no reason why the normal courtesies of life should not be observed. It would be pleasant if we were to begin our relationship – an enforced introduction on your side, I agree – on a calmer and more reasonable basis. It would make things so much more pleasant if we behaved in a more civilized fashion.'

'Civilized?' The President stared at him in a genuine astonishment that swiftly regressed to his former fury. 'You! A person like you. A thug! A crook! A hoodlum! A common criminal. And you dare suggest we behave in a more civilized fashion.'

'A thug? No. A crook? Yes. A hoodlum? No. A common criminal? No. I'm a most uncommon criminal. However, I'm not sorry you adopt this attitude. Having you express yourself with such hostility to me doesn't mean that it eases my conscience in what I may have to do to you. I don't have any conscience. But it makes life that much simpler for me. Not having to hold your hand – I don't speak literally, you understand – makes it all that much easier for me to achieve my ends.'

'I don't think you'll be called upon to hold any hands, Branson.' Cartland's voice was very dry. 'How are we to regard ourselves? As kidnappees? As ransom for some lost cause you hold dear?'

'The only lost cause I hold dear is standing before you.'

'Then hostages to fortune?'

'That's nearer it. Hostages to a very large fortune, I trust.' He looked again at the President. 'I genuinely do apologize for any affront or inconvenience caused by me to your foreign guests.'

'Inconvenience!' The President's shoulders sagged as he invoked his tragic Muse. 'You don't know what irreparable damage you have done this day, Branson.'

'I wasn't aware that I had done any yet. Or are you referring to their Highnesses here? I don't see what damage I can have caused there. Or are you referring to your little trip to San Rafael today – I'm afraid we'll have to postpone that for a bit – to inspect the site of what will be the biggest oil refinery in the world?' He smiled and nodded towards the oil princes. 'They really have you and Hansen over a barrel there, don't they, Mr President – an oil barrel? First they rob you blind over oil sales, accumulate so much loot that they can't find homes for all of it, conceive the bright idea of investing it in the land of the robbed, come up with the concept of building this refinery and petro-chemical complex on the West Coast and running it themselves – with your technical help, of course – on their own oil which would cost them nothing. The foreseeable profits are staggering, a large portion of which would be passed on to you in the form of vastly reduced oil prices. Bonanzas all round. I'm afraid international finance is beyond my scope – I prefer to make my money in a more direct fashion. If you think your deal is going to slip through because of the offence now being given to those Arabian gentlemen you must be an awful lot more naïve than a President of the United States has any right to be. Those are not gentlemen to be swayed by personal considerations. They have tungsten steel where their hearts should be and IBM computers for brains.' He paused. 'I'm not being very polite to your guests, am I?'

Neither the King nor Prince Achmed were quite so impassive now: their eyes, as they looked at Branson, were expressive of a distinct yearning.

Cartland said: 'You seem to be in no great hurry to get on with whatever you intend to get on with.'

'How right you are. The need for speed has now gone. Time is no longer of the essence except that the longer I spend here the more profitable it is going to be for me. That I shall explain later. In the meantime, the longer you remain here the more time it will give both you and your peoples both here and in the Gulf States to appreciate just what a pretty pickle you find yourselves in. And, believe me, you are in a pickle. Think about it.'

Branson walked to the rear of the coach and spoke to the blond young soldier who was manning the massive communication complex. 'What's your name?'

The soldier, who had heard all that had gone on and obviously didn't like any of it, hesitated, then said grudgingly: 'Boyann.'

Branson handed him a piece of paper. 'Get this number, please. It's just local.'

'Get it yourself.'

'I did say "please".'

'Go to hell.'

Branson shrugged and turned. 'Van Effen?'

'Yes?'

'Bring Chrysler here.' He turned to Boyann. 'Chrysler has forgotten a great deal more about telecommunications than you've learnt so far. You think I hadn't anticipated meeting up with young heroes?' He spoke again to Van Effen. 'And when you bring him take Boyann here out and have him thrown over the side of the bridge into the Golden Gate.'

'Right away.'

'Stop!' The President was shocked and showed it. 'You would never dare.'

'Give me sufficient provocation and I'll have you thrown over the side too. I know it seems hard but you've got to find out some way, some time, that I mean what I say.'

Muir stirred and spoke for the first time. He sounded tired. 'I think I detect a note of sincerity in this fellow's voice. He may, mark you, be a convincing bluffer. I, for one, wouldn't care to be the person responsible for taking the chance.'

The President bent an inimical eye on the Under-Secretary but Muir seemed to have gone to sleep. Cartland said in a quiet voice: 'Boyann, do what you are told.'

'Yes, sir.' Boyann seemed more than happy to have had the decision taken out of his hands. He took the paper from Branson who said: 'You can put it through to the phone by that chair opposite the President's?' Boyann nodded. 'And patch it in to the President's?' Boyann nodded again. Branson left and took his seat in the vacant armchair.

Boyann got through immediately: clearly, the call had been awaited.

'Hendrix,' the voice said.

'Branson here.'

'Yes. Branson. Peter Branson. God, I might have guessed!' There was a silence then Hendrix said quietly: 'I've always wanted to meet you, Branson.'

'And so you shall, my dear fellow, and much sooner than you think. I'd like to speak to you later. Meantime, I wouldn't be surprised if the President didn't want to have a word with you.' Branson stood up, not without difficulty, and offered both the telephone and seat to Morrison who in turn struggled to his feet and accepted the offer with alacrity.

The President ran true to the form of any President who might have been so unfortunate as to find himself in his position. He ran through the whole gamut of incredulity, outrage, disbelief and horror that not only the Chief Executive but, even more important, foreign potentates should find themselves in a situation so preposterous as to be, in his opinion, without parallel in history. He laid the blame, predictably, entirely at Hendrix's door – security cover, as the President knew all too well, was arranged by Washington and the local police forces did precisely what they were told to do, but the President's memory, logic and sense of justice had gone into a state of shock – and ended up by demanding that Hendrix's duty was to clear up the whole damnable mess and that he should do something about it immediately.

Hendrix, who had had a great deal longer time to consider the situation, remained admirably calm. He said: 'What do you suggest I do about it, sir?'

The incoherent splutterings that followed were indication enough that constructive suggestions were at that moment some light years away from the President's mind. Morrison took advantage of the momentary hiatus.

'Bernard? John here.' Morrison smiled without meaning to. 'The voters aren't going to like this, Bernard.'

'All one hundred and fifty million of them?'

Again the same smile. 'If we must think nationally, yes.'

'I'm afraid this is going to turn into a national problem, John. In fact, you know damn well it already is. And on the political side it's too big for either of us.'

'You cheer me greatly, Bernard.'

'I wish someone would cheer me. Do you think our friend would let me speak to the general?'

'I'll ask.' He asked and Branson nodded amiably enough. The other occupants of the coach eyed one another with a mounting degree of suspicion and apprehension, both directed against Branson. The man was too utterly sure of himself. And, as matters stood at that moment, there seemed to be little reason why he shouldn't be. He just didn't hold all the aces in the pack – he held a pack full of aces.

Hendrix said: 'General Cartland? Hendrix. The way I see it, sir, this is going to be as much a military operation as a police one. Much more so, if I'm any judge. I should call in the senior military officers on the coast?'

'Higher than that.'

'The Pentagon?'

'At once.'

'Local action?'

'Damn all. Wait until the situation stabilizes itself – and we find out what this madman wants.' Branson smiled politely but as usual the smile never touched his eyes. 'According to what he says himself – if you can believe a word he says – time is not of the essence. I think he wants to talk to you.'

Branson took the phone from Cartland and eased himself comfortably into the armchair. 'One or two questions and requests, Hendrix. I think I am in the position to expect answers and compliance with whatever I want. Wouldn't you agree?'

'I'm listening.'

'Has the news been broken yet?'

'What the hell do you mean broken? Half of San Francisco can see you stuck out on that damned bridge.'

'That's no way to speak of my favourite bridge. Nationwide is what I mean.'

'It'll get around fast enough.'

'See that it gets around now. The communication media, as those people term themselves nowadays, are going to be interested. I am prepared to allow, no, that's wrong, I insist that you put a helicopter, no, two helicopters at the disposal of some of the hundreds of news cameramen who will wish to record this historic event. The Bay area is thick with suitable machines, both military and civilian.'

There was a silence then Hendrix said: 'What the devil do you want those for?'

'Obviously, surely. Publicity. The maximum exposure. I want every person in America and indeed every person in the world who is within reach of a television set to see just what a predicament the President and his Arabian friends are in. And they are in a predicament, wouldn't you say?'

Another silence. 'This publicity, of course, you will use as a lever to get public opinion on your side, to help you obtain what you want, whatever that might be?'

'What else?'

Hendrix said heavily: 'You wouldn't like me to send a coach-load of reporters on to the bridge, would you?'

Branson smiled into the telephone. 'A coach-load of reporters I wouldn't mind but I don't much fancy a coach-load of FBI men armed to the teeth and disguised as reporters. No, I think we'll pass that one up. Besides, reporters we have, our own coach-load.'

'What's to prevent me from loading those helicopters up with troops, maybe paratroopers?'

Branson sighed. 'Only your own common sense. We've got hostages, or had you forgotten? A bullet can reach the President far more quickly than a paratrooper ever could.' Branson glanced at the President, whose expression indicated that he clearly didn't care to be used as a bargaining counter.

'You wouldn't dare. You'd defeat your own ends. You'd have nothing left to blackmail us with.'

'I'd still have the Arabs. Try me and see. You're whistling in the dark and you know it. Or do you want to go down in history as the man responsible for the deaths of a president, a king and a prince?' Hendrix made no reply. It was clearly not a role he envisaged for himself. 'However, it hasn't escaped me that there might be some death-or-glory hotheads who would stop at nothing in taking blind gambles, so I've got my second request to make now. This area is crammed with military stations – the Presidio itself, Fort Baker, Treasure Island, Forts Funston, Miley and Mason, Fort Barry, Cronkite – you name them, they're around and all within easy reach of here by road. I'd be very surprised if between them they can't rustle up the two mobile self-propelled rapid-fire anti-aircraft guns which I want on the bridge within the hour. Plenty of ammunition, of course – and the army will test them out first. You know how some of that hardware gets afflicted with all kinds of jinxes.'

'You're quite mad.'

'A divine sort of madness. Instructions now.'

'I refuse.'

'You refuse? General Cartland?'

Cartland heaved himself upright and walked heavily down the coach. He took the phone and said quietly: 'Do what the madman asks. Don't you recognize megalomania when you hear it?'

'That was very unkind, general.' Branson smiled and retrieved the phone. 'You have the message, Hendrix?'

'I have the message.' Hendrix sounded as if he were being strangled.

'My third request. Call up a couple of squads of army engineers. I want two sets of steel barriers built on the bridge, one under either tower. They are to be strong enough to stop a tank and high enough – barbed at the top, of course – to prevent anyone from climbing over. The north barrier is to be unbroken, the south with a hinged central section, wide enough to permit the passage of a jeep, and capable of being opened from the inside – our side – only. The barriers will be anchored to the sides of the bridge by bolting or welding and secured to the roadway by pneumatically driven spikes. But the army will know a great deal more about such things than I do. I shall supervise the operations personally.'

Hendrix seemed to be having some difficulty with his breathing. Finally he said: 'Why?'

'It's those nasty fogs that come rolling in from the Pacific all the time. More often than not they cover the bridge – in fact I can see one coming in right now.' Branson sounded almost apologetic. 'It would be too easy to rush us under fog cover.'

'And why the hinged section in the south barrier?'

'I thought I told you. To permit the passage of a jeep. For such things as negotiating committees, a doctor if need be and the transport of the best food and drink in town.'

'Jesus! You have your nerve, Branson.'

'Nerve?' Branson was hurt. 'This humanitarian consideration of the well-being of my fellow men? You call that nerve? Kings and presidents are not accustomed to going hungry. Among other things you don't want to go down in history as, Hendrix, includes, I'm sure, being the man responsible for starving kings and presidents to death. Think of the verdict of history.'

Hendrix was silent. He may or may not have been thinking about the verdict of history.

Branson went on: 'And we must not forget the delicate sensibilities of royalty. Before the barriers are in place we'd like to have a couple of mobile latrine vans in position. Equipped, of course, to the very highest standards – and that does not include being loaded to the gunwales with FBI agents. You have all that, Hendrix?'

'It's been recorded.'

'Then set the wheels in motion. Or must I call in General Cartland again?'

'It will be done.'

'Now?'

'Now.'

Branson cradled the phone on his knee and looked at it wonderingly. 'And he didn't even tell me I couldn't get off with it.' He lifted the phone again. 'Last request, Hendrix, but the most important one. The President is temporarily incapacitated. How can one talk to the leader of a leaderless nation?'

'The Vice-President is already in Chicago. He's on his way to O'Hare airfield now.'

'Splendid. Splendid. Co-operation without even asking for it. But I'm afraid I'll also have to ask for the co-operation of one or two other senior ministers of the government. I know it's asking for a lot but I feel—'

'Spare me your schoolboy humour, Branson.' There was an edge to Hendrix's voice now but it was a tired edge. 'I suppose you have some people in mind?'

'Just a couple, that's all.' Branson had a gift for sounding eminently reasonable when making the most unreasonable demands.

'And if you get them and the Vice-President together here I suppose you'll make all three of them hostages too.'

'No. You've only got my word for it, of course, but no. You're losing whatever grip you had, Hendrix. You don't kidnap negotiators. If you did you'd have to negotiate with someone else and so on down the line until we came to someone like you.' Branson waited for comment but Hendrix appeared to be beyond comment. 'I want the Secretary of State.'

'He's on his way.'

'A mind-reader, no less! From where?'

'Los Angeles.'

'How very convenient. How come he was there?'

'An IMF meeting.'

'IMF? Then that means—'

Branson replaced the receiver. 'Well, well, well. Little Peter Branson *vis-à-vis* the Secretary of the Treasury. What a *tête-à-tête* this should be. I thought the day would never come.'

'Yes,' Hendrix said wearily. 'The Secretary of the Treasury was there. He's flying up with him.'

— 4 —

PAUL REVSON surfaced slowly, almost reluctantly, to a state of consciousness. His eyelids felt leaden, his head fuzzy and he thought that he had gone slightly deaf. Otherwise he felt no after-effects from having been gassed – he knew he must have been gassed but everything had happened so quickly after the explosion under the driver's feet that he had no clear recollection of what had happened. As his eyesight cleared he looked around him. By his side a girl with a mop of blonde hair was huddled forward against the back of the seat before her, her neck twisted at an uncomfortable angle. Some people, he saw, were lying in the aisle, apparently asleep. A score of others were still in their seats, all resting at the most uncomfortable angles: some of them, like himself, were just beginning to stir. He peered through the coach window, blinked unbelievingly, then stared again. As a born and bred San Franciscan it took him nothing flat to realize that their coach was halted almost squarely in the middle of the Golden Gate Bridge. It was a circumstance, he felt, which called for some explanation.

He turned his immediate attention to the girl at his side. She was worth anyone's attention. She was possessed of a slight figure, hardly strong enough, one would have thought, to lug around the heavy ciné camera which, shoulder-slung, accompanied her everywhere. The blonde hair was so bleached – naturally, Revson thought – that it almost qualified for the description of platinum, and she was quite beautiful with a very pale skin that the sun never appeared to touch. She was, she had given him to understand, a fashion photographer for one of the major TV companies and as the official party of this presidential trip was exclusively male it was rather difficult to understand just why she was there. It didn't make sense, but then, again, neither did most presidential trips. Her name was equally preposterous. April Wednesday, she called herself, and her press card bore this out. Revson could only assume that she had been born of singularly unimaginative parents who, as christening day approached, had seized upon the birth date as the easy way out.

He put his hands on her shoulders and gently pulled her upright. The blonde head lolled against his shoulder. He had no idea how to revive people who had suffered from some form of gas poisoning. Should he shake her, slap her cheek gently or just let her sleep it off? He was spared the resolution of this problem when she stirred, shivered for some reason or other – although she was clad in only a thin and markedly abbreviated green silk dress, the temperature in the bus must have been in the eighties – then opened her eyes and gazed unblinkingly at Revson's.

In a face not noticeably lacking other commendable features, those eyes were by far the most remarkable feature. They were huge, clear, of a startling deep sea-green and were possessed of an odd quality of purity and innocence. Revson wondered idly just how devious she was: any young woman who toted a camera for a TV company must have lost her innocence quite some time ago, assuming she was possessed of any in the first place.

She said, not taking her eyes from his: 'What happened?'

'At a guess, some joker must have let off a gas bomb. The instant effect variety. How do you feel?'

'Punch-drunk. Hung-over. You know what I mean?' He nodded. 'Why would anyone want to do a thing like that?'

'Why a lot of things.' He looked at his watch. 'Why, after an hour and ten minutes, are we still stranded in the middle of the Golden Gate Bridge?'

'What!'

'Look around you.'

She looked around her, slowly acknowledging the reality of the surroundings. Suddenly she stiffened and caught hold of the hand that was still around her shoulders.

'Those two men across the aisle.' Her voice had dropped to a whisper. 'They're wearing handcuffs.'

Revson bent forward and looked. The two large and still sleeping men were undoubtedly wearing handcuffs.

'Why?' Again the whisper.

'How should I know why? I've just come to myself.'

'Well, then, why aren't *we* wearing them?'

'How should – we are among the blessed.' He looked over his shoulder and saw the presidential coach parked just behind them. 'Excuse me. As a good journalist I think the odd probing question is in order.'

'I'm coming with you.'

'Sure.' She stepped into the aisle and he followed. Instead of moving directly after her he lifted the coat lapel of the nearest of the sleeping men. An empty shoulder holster was much in evidence. He followed the girl. At the front door he noticed that the driver, still sound asleep, was propped against the right-hand front door, quite some distance from his seat: obviously, he hadn't made it there under his own steam.

He joined the girl on the bridge. A very large and extremely ugly policeman – Yonnie had the kind of face that would have given any force a bad name – was pointing a machine-pistol at them. That a policeman should be pointing a gun at them was peculiar enough. That a policeman should be armed with a machine-gun was even more peculiar. Most peculiar of all, however, was the spectacle of six scowling and clearly unhappy policemen standing in a line, each attached to the other by a pair of handcuffs.

April Wednesday stared at them in astonishment, then looked at Revson. He said: 'I agree. This would seem to call for some kind of explanation.'

'You'll have it.' Branson, walking easily, talking easily,

had just appeared round the front of the presidential bus. 'What's your name?'

'Revson.'

'Sorry about this. You too, young lady.'

'Helicopters!' she said.

'Yes, they are, aren't they? Explanations will be forthcoming but not severally. When your friends have all come to then we'll have a little talk.' Branson walked away towards the rear coach. His step was almost jaunty and he did not seem too displeased with life. He looked at the bank of cloud moving in slowly, very slowly, from the west. If it troubled him he did not show it. He reached the crashed police car and spoke to the man standing guard. 'Have our four friends recovered, Chrysler?'

'Yes, sir. I wouldn't say there're in very high spirits, though.' Chrysler was a lean, dark, intelligent-looking young man and it only required the addition of a brief case to see him as an up-and-coming attorney. He was indeed, as Branson had told Boyann, a tele-communications expert. He was also very good with combination locks and frightening people with guns.

'I dare say. Let them stay in the car. Easier than getting them out and handcuffing them. When the four FBI men – at least from the fact that they were armed I assume they were FBI men – in the lead coach have come to, take a couple of the boys and escort them, along with the six cops up front, the four here and the two inside our coach half-way towards the south tower. Sixteen in all and any one a potential menace if we keep them here. Half-way there take off whatever handcuffs there are – very useful things, handcuffs, you never know when we may need them again – then let them walk off the bridge under their own steam. Okay?'

'It's done.' He pointed to the west, to the slowly advancing bank of fog. 'Do you like that, Mr Branson?'

'Could have done without it. We'll cope when it comes. Looks as if it may well pass under the bridge anyway.'

'Mr Branson.' It was Jensen, beckoning urgently from the front door of the rear coach. 'Mount Tamalpais. Urgent.'

Branson ran into the coach, seated himself in front of the console and lifted the microphone. 'Branson.'

'Giscard. We've picked up a blip. Coming from the south

– well, a bit east of south. Light plane, looks like. Maybe eight miles out.'

'Thank you.' Branson made another switch. South and a little east. That could only be San Francisco International Airport. 'Chief of Police Hendrix. At once.'

Hendrix was on the phone in seconds. 'What now?'

'I told you to keep a clear air-space. Our radar's picked up a blip, airport direction—'

Hendrix interrupted. His voice was sour. 'You wanted to see Messrs Milton and Quarry, didn't you?' Milton was the Secretary for State, Quarry the Secretary of the Treasury. 'They came in from Los Angeles fifteen minutes ago and are flying up direct by helicopter.'

'Where are they landing?'

'In the Military Reservation in the Presidio. Two, three minutes by car.'

'Thanks.' Branson made the switch to Mount Tamalpais. Giscard acknowledged. Branson said: 'No sweat. Friends. But watch that scanner – the next one may not be a friend.'

'Will do, Mr Branson.'

Branson rose, made to leave the coach then stopped and looked at the bound man in the rear of the aisle. He said to Jensen, who had taken the place of the bound man: 'You can get back to calling yourself Harriman again. Untie Jensen here.'

'Sending him off the bridge?'

For once Branson hesitated and didn't like the feeling at all. Hesitation was not in his nature. Whether he arrived at decisions intellectually or instinctively he almost invariably did so immediately: the few mistakes he'd made in his life had invariably been associated with hesitation. He made up his mind.

'We'll keep him. He might come in useful, I don't know how yet, but he just might. And he *is* deputy director of the FBI. He's no minnow to have in our net. Tell him the score but keep him here until I give the word.'

He left and walked towards the lead coach. At least a score of people were lined up outside the coach under the watchful eyes and guns of Yonnie and his two colleagues. They had, understandably, a general air of bafflement about them.

Branson saw that included among them were four handcuffed men. He looked inside the coach, saw that it was empty, and turned to Peters.

'Take those four gentlemen with the handcuffs and the six policemen down to Chrysler. He'll know what to do with them.'

He turned to look at the oncoming fog. Close-up, it was coming in a deal faster than it had seemed at a distance. But it was a low bank: with luck it would pass under the bridge. Even if it didn't, he imagined that they could cope by using suitable threats against the President and his friends, but he wouldn't feel really happy about those intermittent fogs until the steel barriers were in position at either end of the bridge.

He turned and looked at the correspondents. There were four women among them but only one of them, the green-eyed blonde with Revson, could truthfully have claimed to have been a post-war baby – World War Two, that was.

'You can all relax,' Branson said. 'No harm is going to come to any of you. In fact, when I have finished you'll be given a free choice – to walk off the bridge in safety or stay aboard the bridge, equally in safety.' He smiled his generous empty smile. 'I somehow fancy that most of you will elect to stay. When I have finished you will realize, I hope, that a story like this does not fall into your laps every week.'

When he had finished, not one of those frantically scribbling and furiously camera-clicking journalists and photographers was under any doubt whatsoever: a story like this fell into their laps once in a lifetime, if they had the luck to have a very long life, that was. Physical violence would have been required to remove any of them from the Golden Gate Bridge. They were slap bang in the middle of an unprecedented episode in criminal history and one that bade fair to become part of the more general history of their times.

The fog had reached the bridge now, but not enveloped it. Thin wisps of it drifted over the top but the main body of the fog rolled by twenty feet below the bridge: the effect was to produce an odd feeling of weightlessness, of suspension in space, as if the bridge was afloat on the insubstantial bedrock of water vapour.

Branson said: 'You have elected to remain so you must

accept some guide rules. In the rear coach there are three telephone lines to town. Those are for my own personal and emergency use but you will be allowed to use them once – to contact your photographic services, newspapers, wire services or whatever to arrange for a representative to be stationed at the southern end of the bridge to pick up your despatches and photographs. This can be done three times a day at times yet to be arranged. Markers will be arranged in an oblong around the presidential coach and no one will cross those without permission. No one will interview any person inside the presidential coach without my permission or the consent of the party concerned: it would be more satisfactory all round and fairer to all concerned if, say, the President were to hold a press conference out here, but that I cannot and will not force anyone to do. The helicopters will be similarly cordoned off and that will also be forbidden territory. Twenty yards south of my coach and twenty yards north of yours white lines will be painted across the bridge. Those will be your demarcation limits. Five yards beyond those lines will be a guard with a machine-pistol and his orders will be not to warn but to shoot anyone who steps over those lines. Finally, you will be confined to your coach during the hours of darkness: this rule will only be relaxed if some particularly newsworthy happening occurs. I will be the judge of what is newsworthy. Anyone unwilling to abide by those ground rules may leave now.'

Nobody left.

'Any questions?' Branson watched the fog roll eastwards, obscuring Alcatraz Island, as the newsmen conferred among themselves. Two men took a step forward. Both were middle-aged, dressed in well-cut, conservative suits, one almost completely bald, the other with grizzled hair and beard, both inordinately bushy. The bald man said: 'We have.'

'Your names?'

'I'm Grafton – UP. This is Dougan – Reuters.'

Branson regarded them with an interest that was pointless to conceal. Those two could reach more newspapers worldwide than all the rest put together. 'And the question?'

'We would be right in saying, Mr Branson, that you didn't exactly get up this morning and say, "This would be a fine day for kidnapping the President of the United States"?'

'You would.'

Dougan said: 'This operation bears all the hallmarks of long and meticulous planning. Without condoning your actions one has to admit that you appear to have left nothing to chance and have foreseen every eventuality. How long did the planning take?'

'Three months.'

'That's not possible. The details of this itinerary were released only four days ago.'

'The details were known in Washington three months ago.'

Grafton said: 'On the evidence before us we have to believe you. Why do you think this was kept under wraps so long?'

'In order to obviate the possibility of people like me doing exactly what I have done.'

'How did you get the advance information?'

'I bought it.'

'How? Where?'

'In Washington, as in many other places, thirty thousand dollars buys a lot of information.'

Dougan said: 'Would you care to name names?'

'That's a stupid question. Any others?'

A dark-suited lady of indeterminate years said: 'Yes. Here we have all the signs of a highly experienced professionalism. We can assume that this is not your first foray outside the law?'

Branson smiled. 'You may assume what you like. What's past is prologue.'

She persisted. 'Do you have a criminal record, Mr Branson?'

'I have never been in court in my life. Anything else?'

'Of course.' It was Dougan. 'The thing that we all want to know. Why?'

'That you will find out in the course of a press conference I shall be holding within two hours. At the conference will be a TV camera and crew representing the three main companies. Also present will be the Secretary of State and the Secretary of the Treasury. Vice-President Richards we expect later but not in time for the conference.'

Experienced newsmen and newswomen though they were they appeared to be at a temporary loss for words. Finally Dougan said carefully: 'Would it be true to say of you that you subscribe to the belief that if a thing is worth doing it's worth doing well?'

'A pragmatic philosophy, but it works. You may now use the telephones in my coach. Three at a time.'

Branson turned away and took a step towards the presidential coach when Yonnie's voice stopped him.

'Jesus!' Yonnie, mouth inelegantly agape, was staring out to the west. 'You see what I see, Mr Branson?'

Branson saw what he saw. Not much more than half a mile away the fog-bank came to an abrupt end as if it had been sliced off by a cleaver. Less than a mile beyond that again could be seen the superstructure of a very large vessel indeed. Although the hull of the vessel was still hidden by the fog-bank there was, from what could be seen of it, very little doubt as to its identity. Branson stood still for a second or two, ran for the presidential coach, entered, hurried down the aisle oblivious to curious stares of the seated men and said quickly to Boyann: 'Hendrix. Hurry!' He indicated a phone in a recess beside the console. 'That one.'

Hendrix was on the line immediately. When Branson spoke his voice was cold, almost savage, a marked departure from the norm: even Branson had defences that could be breached.

'Hendrix. Want I should send the President's ears now?'

'What the hell do you mean?'

'What do *you* mean? Or is that little paddleboat just out there by happenstance? Call it off.'

'God's sake, call what off?'

Branson spoke his words clearly and spaced them distinctly. 'There is a very large battleship approaching the Golden Gate Bridge. I don't want it to approach. I don't know what you have in mind but I don't think I would like it. Call it off!'

'I just don't know what you're talking about. Hold on.' While the line was silent Branson beckoned to Van Effen, who approached down the aisle.

Branson said quickly: 'There's a battleship approaching the bridge. Trouble? I don't know. What I do know is I want everybody under cover at once, the press in their own coach, our men in ours. Doors to be closed. Then come back at once.'

Van Effen nodded to where a red-haired young man was

standing by the driver's seat, his hand resting on a pistol that was stuck in his belt. 'Think Bradford can manage?'

Branson pulled out his own pistol and laid it in the telephone recess. 'I'm here too. Hurry.' He was vaguely disappointed in Van Effen. Bradford could have carried out his warder duties just as effectively by going outside and standing near the door but for the creation of the properly threatening climate of menace and intimidation it was better that he remain in the full view of the captives. Then Hendrix was on the phone again.

'That is the battleship USS *New Jersey*. San Francisco is her home base for several months of the year. This is one of her regular fuel and food reprovisioning returns to base. She's coming at this particular time because she can only get under the bridge at low tide.'

That much, Branson knew, was true. The tide, he had observed, was out and it seemed highly unlikely that the authorities could whistle up a battleship at such short notice – less than two hours. And it was difficult to see what use could be made of it – certainly they were unlikely to blow up the bridge with the President on it. But Branson had a profound distrust of his fellow men, which was one of the reasons he had survived so long. He said: 'Stop it. It's not to come under the bridge. Want I should throw one of your oil boys on to its bridge as it passes beneath?'

'For God's sake, are you a nut, a complete madman?' Branson smiled to himself, the sharp edge of anxiety in Hendrix's voice was unmistakable. 'We're trying to raise him'.

II

Correspondents and guards alike were crowding the western side of the bridge fascinated by the approach of the giant battleship. Although reason said that there was no danger in the battleship's passing under the bridge there was a growing degree of tension among the spectators. The superstructure towered so high that it seemed certain that some sections of it must inevitably strike the bridge and this feeling existed in spite of the elementary reasoning which would have reassured them that the ship must have made the same passage many times in the past and the Navy was not in the habit of putting at risk some hundred million dollar battleship in a let's-try-it-and-see effort.

One person showed no apparent interest in the approach of the *New Jersey*. Revson, alone in the front coach, was intent on securing a considerable length of green cord, so slender as to be hardly more than the thickness of a stout thread, to a black cylinder about eight inches in length and one in diameter. He thrust both cylinder and cord into the capacious pocket of his bush jacket, left the bus, took a bearing on the approaching superstructure of the battleship and wandered casually round to the right-hand side of the coach. As he did so he could see Van Effen hurrying across to the far side of the bridge where the spectators were grouped. What Van Effen's purpose was he couldn't be sure but there was an urgency behind his half-trot that told Revson that the time at his own disposal might be very short.

He forced himself not to hurry but sauntered towards the east side of the bridge. No one took any notice of him because there was no one there to do so. He leant casually against the side and as casually withdrew cylinder and cord from his pocket. He glanced, seemingly aimlessly, around him, but if he were arousing cause for suspicion no one was giving any indication of this. Swiftly, without moving either hands or elbows, he let some hundred feet slide through his fingers then secured the cord to a strut. He trusted his estimate of length was reasonably accurate then dismissed the thought: what was done was done. He returned leisurely to the coach, took his seat and transferred what was left of the green cord to the bottom of April Wednesday's carry-all. If his dangling cord were discovered and a search of their personal belongings carried out he would rather that the cord be discovered elsewhere than in his possession. Even if it were found in her bag he doubted whether she would come to any harm. She'd been on the other side of the bridge since the *New Jersey* had first appeared behind the bank of cloud and there would be sufficient witnesses to attest to that: April Wednesday was the sort of person whose absence would not go lightly unremarked. Even if she were to find herself in trouble that he could bear with fortitude: he didn't care who came under suspicion as long as it was not himself.

III

'You have to believe me, Branson.' Hendrix's voice could hardly have been said to carry a note of pleading, an alien exercise to a man of his nature, but there was no questioning the earnestness, the total sincerity in the tone. 'The *New Jersey*'s captain has heard no news of what happened and he thinks it all an elaborate joke at his expense. You can't blame him. He sees the damned bridge standing safe and sound as it's stood for forty years. Why should anything be wrong?'

'Keep trying.'

Van Effen entered and closed the door of the presidential coach securely behind him. He approached Branson.

'All safely corralled. Why?'

'I wish I knew. Almost certainly Hendrix is right and this is just sheer coincidence. But on the one chance in a hundred that it isn't? What would they use? Not shells, no kind of high explosive. Gas shells.'

'No such things.'

'Wrong. There are. They wouldn't mind temporarily knocking out the President and a few oil sheikhs if they could saturate the centre of the bridge with some knock-out gas and lay us all low. Then the troops and police, like enough with gas-masks, could come and take us at their leisure. But the insulation is tight in those air-conditioned coaches.'

'It's pretty far-fetched.'

'And what *we* are doing is not? Wait.' Hendrix was on the phone again.

'We've tried, Branson, and at last he agrees with us. But he refuses to do anything. Says he has too much way on and to try to take turning or reversing action at this stage would endanger both the battleship and the bridge. And he says his money would be on the *New Jersey* if it hit a tower. A forty-five-thousand-ton battering ram takes a lot of stopping.'

'You'd better pray, Hendrix.' Branson hung up and moved towards the centre of the coach, Van Effen behind him, and peered through the right-hand windows, waiting for the battleship's superstructure to reappear from under the bridge.

The President's voice was nothing if not testy. 'Just what is happening, Branson?'

'You know. The USS *New Jersey* is passing beneath us.'

'So? Doubtless going about its lawful occasions.'

'You'd better hope so. You'd better hope the captain doesn't start throwing things at us.'

'At us?' The President paused and pondered the possibility of an awful *lèse-majesté*.

'At *me*?'

'We all know you're the Commander-in-Chief of the Armed Forces. At the moment, however, you're a bit isolated from the lower echelons. What happens if the captain considers it his duty to act upon his own initiative? Anyway, we'll soon find out. Here he comes now.'

The superstructure of the *New Jersey* had moved into view. All nine of the seated captives struggled to their feet and crowded close to the right-hand windows. One of them crowded very closely indeed on Branson who suddenly became aware of something, obviously metallic, jabbing painfully into his left kidney.

'Initiative, you said, Mr Branson.' It was Sheikh Iman, the one with the beard, and he was still beaming. 'Your own gun. Tell your men to drop theirs.'

'Good man!' There was triumph in the President's voice and an element of vindictiveness that the voters wouldn't have liked at all.

Branson said patiently: 'Put that gun away. Don't you know when you're dealing with professionals?'

He turned around slowly and Iman proved Branson's implied point that he was not a professional by letting Branson hold his gaze for all of a second. A gun boomed, Iman shrieked in pain, dropped his gun and clutched a shattered shoulder. Sheikh Kharan stooped swiftly to retrieve the gun from the floor and cried out in agony as Branson's heel crushed his hand against the metal: a peculiar crackling splintering sound left no doubt that several of Kharan's fingers had been broken. Branson picked up his gun.

Van Effen was apologetic but not unduly so.

'Had to, I'm afraid, Mr Branson. If I'd warned him – well,

I didn't want any gunfight in the OK corral with all those nasty ricochets from the bullet-proof glass. He might have done himself an injury.'

'Quite right.' Branson looked through the window again. The *New Jersey* was now almost a half mile away and its captain was obviously not in a belligerent mood. Branson turned away and spoke to Bradford.

'Go to our coach and fetch the first-aid box. Bring Peters.'

'Peters, Mr Branson?'

'Used to be field corpsman. Take your seats, gentlemen.' Unhappily, they took their seats: the President looked especially deflated. Branson wondered briefly just how hollow a man he might be then dismissed the line of thought as unprofitable. 'I don't think I have to warn you not to try anything so silly again.' He went to the communications console and picked up the phone. 'Hendrix?'

'Here. Satisfied now?'

'Yes. Warn the harbour-master or whoever the responsible official is that there is to be no more traffic under the bridge. Either way.'

'No more traffic? You'll bring the entire port to a standstill. And the fishing fleet—'

'The fishing fleet can go fish in the bay. Send an ambulance and a doctor and do it quickly. A couple of men here have gotten themselves hurt, one badly.'

'Who? How?'

'The oil ministers – Iman and Kharan. Self-inflicted injuries, you might say.' As he spoke Branson watched Peters hurry into the coach, approach Iman and start scissoring away the sleeve of his coat. 'There will be a TV van coming to the bridge soon. Let it through. I also want some chairs brought on to the bridge – forty should do.'

'Chairs?'

'You don't have to buy them,' Branson said patiently. 'Confiscate them from the nearest restaurant. Forty.'

'Chairs?'

'Things you sit on. I'm going to hold a news conference in an hour or so. You don't stand around at news conferences. You sit around.'

Hendrix said carefully: 'You're going to hold a news conference and you're going to televise it live?'

'That's it. Nationwide.'

'You're out of your mind.'

'My mental health is my concern. Milton and Quarry there yet?'

'You mean the Secretary and the Secretary of the Treasury?'

'I mean Milton and Quarry.'

'They've just arrived and are with me now.'

Hendrix looked at the two men who were with him then inside the big mobile communications van. Milton, the Secretary of State, was a tall, thin, dyspeptic character with no hair, rimless steel-legged glasses and an enviable reputation in Foreign Offices around the world: Quarry, white-haired, plump and cheerful, had a kindly avuncular air about him which many men, even some very highly intelligent ones, had taken to be a reflection of the true personality of the man: his reputation as a banker and economist stood as high as that of Milton in his field.

Milton said: 'It would be easy to say "He's quite crazy, of course." Is he?'

Hendrix spread his hands. 'You know what they say. Crazy like a fox.'

'And violent, it would seem?'

'No. Violence he uses only as a last resort and even then only when pushed into a corner. Iman and Kharan must have made the mistake of pushing him into a corner.'

Quarry said: 'You would seem to know a fair bit about him?'

Hendrix sighed. 'Every senior police officer in the States knows about him. And in Canada, Mexico and God knows how many South American countries.' Hendrix sounded bitter. 'So far he has spared Europe his attentions. It's only a matter of time, I'm sure.'

'What's his speciality?'

'Robbery. He robs trains, planes, armoured cars, banks and jewellers. Robbery, wherever possible, as I say, without violence.'

Quarry was dry. 'I gather he is quite successful?'

'Quite successful! To the best of our knowledge he has been

operating for at least a dozen years and the lowest estimate of his takings in that time is twenty million dollars.'

'Twenty million!' For the first time there was a note of respect in Quarry's voice, the banker and economist in him surfacing. 'If he's got all that money, why does he want more?'

'Why did Niarchos and Getty and Hughes want more? Maybe he's just a businessman in the way that they are businessmen and he's hooked on his job. Maybe he finds it a stimulating intellectual exercise. Maybe it's sheer greed. Maybe anything.'

Milton said: 'Has he ever been convicted?'

Hendrix looked pained. 'He's never even been arrested.'

'And that has something to do with the fact that neither of us has ever heard of him?'

Hendrix gazed through the van window at the magnificent sweep of the Golden Gate Bridge. There was a far-off look of yearning in his eyes. He said: 'Let us say, sir, that we do not care to advertise our failures.'

Milton smiled at him. 'John and I' – he nodded at the Secretary of the Treasury – 'frequently suffer from the same bashfulness and for the same reasons. Infallibility is not the lot of mankind. Anything known about this man – apart from what is known about his criminal activities?'

Hendrix said sourly: 'It wouldn't be hard to know more about him than we do about his life of crime. Pretty well documented background, really. A WASP from out east. Comes from what they call a good family. Father a banker and when I say banker I mean he owned – still does, I believe – his own bank.'

'Branson,' the Treasury Secretary said. 'Of course. Know him. Not personally, though.'

'And something else that will interest you, sir – professionally. Branson took a degree in economics and went to work in his father's bank. While he was there he took a PhD – and no coffee-grinder diploma school either – genuine Ivy League. Then for his post-graduate course he took up the subject of crime – something to do with having worked in his old man's bank, maybe.' Hendrix looked gloomy. 'I suppose we could say that he has graduated in that subject now too – *summa cum laude*.'

Milton said: 'You seem to have almost a degree of admiration for this person, Hendrix?'

'I'd give my pension to see him behind bars. Both as a man and a policeman he outrages whatever passes for my sensibilities. But one can't help respecting sheer professionalism, no matter how misused.'

'My sentiments too, I'm afraid,' Milton said. 'He's not a particularly retiring person, this Branson of yours?'

'I wish he were mine. If you mean does he suffer from our bouts of bashfulness, no, sir, he does not.'

'Arrogant?'

'To the point, perhaps, of megalomania. At least, that's what General Cartland says, and I wouldn't care to dispute what the general says.'

'Few would.' Milton spoke with some feeling. 'Speaking of self-opinionated characters, where art thou at this hour, my James?'

'Sir?'

'What other self-opinionated character is there? I refer to Mr Hagenbach, the self-opinionated head of our FBI. I would have thought he would have been the first man hot-foot to the scene.'

'Washington says they don't know where he is. They're trying every place they can think of. I'm afraid he's a very elusive man, sir.'

'Man's got a mania for secrecy.' Milton brightened. 'Well, if he's watching his TV in an hour or so he should be considerably enlightened. What a perfectly splendid thought – the head of our FBI the last man in America to know about this.' He thought for a moment. 'Branson's insistence on maximum publicity – TV, radio I'll be bound, newsmen, photographers – has he ever declared himself publicly like this before? I mean, before or during any of his criminal activities?'

'Never.'

'The man must be terribly sure of himself.'

'In his place, so would I.' Quarry appeared distracted. 'What can we do to the man? As I see it, he's in an impregnable, quite unassailable position.'

'I wouldn't give up hope, sir. We have one or two experts

looking for an answer. Admiral Newson and General Carter are in our HQ now working on this.'

'Newson. Carter. Our twin geniuses of finesse.' Quarry seemed more discouraged than ever. 'Never use one hydrogen bomb where two will suffice. Someone should send our Arabian oil friends word that they're about to become involved in a nuclear holocaust.' He gestured through his window towards the bridge. 'Just look at it. Just think of it. A totally impossible situation – if it weren't for the fact that we can see now that it's all too possible. Total, absolute isolation, completely cut off from the world – and in the full view of everybody in San Francisco – everybody in the world, for that matter, as soon as those TV cameras start turning. A figurative stone's throw away – and they might as well be on the moon.' He sighed heavily. 'One must confess to a feeling of utter helplessness.'

'Come, come, John.' Milton was severe. 'Is this the spirit that won the West?'

'The hell with the West. I'm thinking about me. I don't have to be very clever to know beyond any doubt that I am going to be the man in the middle.'

Hendrix said: 'Sir?'

'Why else do you think this ruffian summoned the Secretary of the Treasury to his royal presence?'

IV

Hands in pockets, as if deep in thought, Revson wandered along the east side of the bridge, stopping frequently to gaze at, and presumably admire the panorama stretched out before him – to his left the tip of Belvedere beyond Fort Baker, Tiburon and Angel Island, the largest in the Bay; to his right the city itself and straight ahead Alcatraz Island and beyond it Treasure Island: between the two the rapidly diminishing shape of the *New Jersey* was heading for its berth at Alameda. He made frequent stops, as if peering over the side. On one of those occasions he reached casually for the green cord he'd attached to the strut and hefted it. It was weightless.

'What are you doing?'

He turned unhurriedly. April Wednesday's big green eyes, if not exactly alive with curiosity, held a certain puzzlement.

'You do have flannel feet. I thought I was the only person within miles – well, yards.'

'What are you doing?'

'When I look at this marvellous view here and then at you I really don't know which I prefer. I think you. Have any people ever told you that you're really rather beautiful?'

'Lots.' She caught the green cord between finger and thumb and started to lift it then made a muffled sound of pain as his hand closed none too gently over hers.

'Leave that alone.'

She rubbed her hand, looked around her and said: 'Well?'

'I'm fishing.'

'Not for compliments, that's for sure.' She massaged her knuckles tenderly, then looked at him with some uncertainty. 'Fishermen tell tall tales, don't they?'

'I've done it myself.'

'Tell me one.'

'Are you as trustworthy as you're beautiful?'

'Am I beautiful? And I'm not fishing. Honest.'

'You are.'

'Then I'm trustworthy too.' They smiled at each other and he took her arm. 'A really tall one?'

'Yes, please.'

'Why ever not?' They walked slowly away together.

V

Hendrix replaced the receiver in its cradle. He looked at Milton and Quarry. 'You are ready, gentlemen?'

'Act One, Scene One, and all the world's a stage. That's wrong somehow.' Milton rose and looked critically at Quarry. 'The shirt's wrong too, John. White shows up badly on TV. Should be blue – like me – or the President. Blue shirts are all he has; you never know when a TV camera is lurking round the next corner.'

'Oh, shut up.' Quarry turned morosely towards the rear door of the van then stopped as a motor-cycle policeman drew up with a suitably dramatic screeching of tyre and smell of burning rubber, dismounted, propped his machine and hurried to the rear steps of the van. He held up his hand to Hendrix. 'For you sir.'

Hendrix took the eight-inch-long narrow cylinder. 'It's got my name on it, all right. Where did you get it from?'

'The pilot boat brought it in from the *New Jersey*. The captain – of the *New Jersey*, that is – thought it might be very urgent.'

— 5 —

THE CENTRE section of the Golden Gate Bridge was fast assuming the appearance of an embryonic town sprawling, inchoate and wholly disorganized as those burgeoning settlements tend to be, but nonetheless possessed of a vitality, a feverish restlessness that augured well for its expansive future. The fact that all the buildings were on wheels and that all the village elders, seated in solemn conclave, were immaculately dressed and had clearly never done a single day's physical toil in their collective lives, did little to detract from the curious impression that here were the pioneers pushing forwards the limits of the wild frontier.

There were three coaches and three police cars – the third had just brought Hendrix, Milton and Quarry. There were two large, glaze-windowed vehicles which bore the euphemistic legend 'Rest Room': painted in becoming red and yellow stripes they had been borrowed from an itinerant circus currently stopped-over in the city. There was an ambulance, which Branson had commandeered for purposes best known to himself, a large side-counter wagonette which had provided hot meals, a very large TV camera truck with its generator placed at a discreet hundred yards distance and, finally, a van that was unloading blankets, rugs and pillows to help ease the new settlers through the rigours of their first night.

There were, of course, the discordant, even jarring items. The helicopters, the tracked anti-aircraft guns, the patrolling armed men, the army engineers at a distance on either side busily erecting steel barricades – those did tend to project a disturbing hint of violence to come. And yet they were not entirely alien there: so bizarre were the circumstances that the normal would have tended to look sadly out of place. The unreality of it all, when matched up against the outside world, had its own strange reality in this particular point in time and place. And for those participating in the scene, the reality of their situation was all too self-evident. No one smiled.

The cameras were in position, so were the hostages, the three newly arrived men and, behind them in the second row, sat the journalists. The photographers had taken up positions best suited to themselves, none of them more than a few feet distant from an armed guard. Facing them, in solitary splendour, sat Branson. Close by him on the ground lay a peculiar object, a length of heavy canvas with cone-shaped objects embedded in it: beside it lay a heavy metal box, its lid closed.

'I will not detain you unnecessarily, gentlemen,' Branson said. Whether or not he was enjoying his moment of glory, the knowledge that he held some of the most powerful men in the world at his complete mercy, the consciousness that a hundred million people were looking at and listening to him, was quite impossible to say. He was calm, relaxed, unnervingly confident of and in himself, but displaying no other visible emotion. 'You will have guessed why we all find ourselves here and why I am here.'

'The reason why I'm here, I take it,' Quarry said.

'Exactly.'

'You will bear in mind that, unlike you, I am not a law unto myself. The final decision is not mine.'

'Appreciated.' Branson could have been conducting some urbane seminar in an Ivy college. 'That comes later. First things first, don't you think Mr Quarry?'

'Money.'

'Money.'

'How much?' Quarry's reputation for disconcerting bluntness had been easily earned.

'One moment, Mr Secretary.' The President had his weaknesses no less than the two hundred million people for whom he was the elected head of state and high on the list was an almost pathological dislike of being upstaged. 'What do you want this money for, Branson?'

'What's that got to do with it – supposing it's any of your business?'

'It is my business. I must state categorically if you want it for any subversive activities, for any evil practices whatsoever, and especially for any anti-American activities – well, I tell you here and now that you can have my body first. Who am I compared to America?'

Branson nodded approval. 'Stoutly spoken, Mr President, especially considering the fact that you have left your speech-writers behind. I hear the voice of our founding fathers, the clarion call of the conscience that lies at the grass-roots of America. The Grand Old Party are going to love you for that. It should be worth another two million votes come November. However, quite apart from the fact that you don't mean a word you say, I have to reassure you that this money is required for purely apolitical purposes. It's for a private trust, in fact. Branson Enterprises, Inc. Me.'

The President wasn't a man to be easily knocked off stride – if he were he wouldn't have been President. 'You have just mentioned the word "conscience". You have none?'

'I don't honestly know,' Branson said frankly. 'Where money is concerned, none. Most of the really wealthy men in the world are moral cripples, basically criminally-minded types who maintain a façade of spurious legality by hiring lawyers as morally crippled as they are themselves.' Branson appeared to muse. 'Multi-millionaires, politicians, lawyers – which of them lies furthest beyond the moral pale? But don't answer that – I may unintentionally be putting you in an invidious position. We're all rogues, whether under the hypocritical cover of legalism or out in the noon-day sun, like me. I just want some fast money fast and I reckon this is as good a way as any of getting it.'

Quarry said: 'We accept that you are an honest thief. Let us come to cases.'

'My reasonable demands?'

'The point, Mr Branson.'

Branson surveyed the Arabian oil barons – now without

Iman who was in hospital – and the President.

'For this lot, on the hoof, in prime condition and no haggling about pennies – three hundred million dollars. That's a three followed by eight nothings.'

To the many million viewers throughout America it was immediately obvious that there had been a sound transmission breakdown. The silence, however, was more than compensated for by the wide and interesting variety of expressions registered on the faces of those on the screen, which ranged from total outrage through total incomprehension through total incredulity to total shock: indeed, in those few imperishable moments, sound would have been an unforgiveable intrusion. Predictably, in view of the fact that he was accustomed to dealing with figures which contained large numbers of zeros, Secretary of the Treasury Quarry was the first to recover.

'You did say what I thought I heard you say?'

'Three zero zero, comma, zero zero zero, comma, zero zero zero period. If you give me a blackboard and some chalk I'll write it out for you.'

'Preposterous! Lunatic! The man's mad, mad, mad.' The President, whose now puce colour showed up rather well on colour television, clenched his fist and looked round in vain for a table to bang it on. 'You know the penalty for this, Branson – kidnapping, blackmail, extortion under threats on a scale—'

'A scale quite unprecedented in the annals of crime?'

'Yes. On a scale quite – shut up! The death penalty can be invoked for treason – and this is high treason – and if it's the last thing I do—'

'That might be any moment. Rest assured, Mr President, that you won't be around to pull the switch. You better believe me.' He produced his pistol. 'As a token of my intent, how would you like a hundred million viewers to see you being shot through the knee-cap – then you really would need that cane of yours. It's a matter of indifference to me.' And in his voice there was a chilling indifference that carried far more conviction than the words themselves. The President unclenched his fist and seemed not so much to sink into his chair as to deflate into it. The puce was assuming a greyish hue.

'You people have to learn to think big,' Branson went on. 'This is the United States of America, the richest country in the world, not a banana republic. What's three hundred million dollars? A couple of Polaris submarines? A tiny fraction of what it cost to send a man to the moon? A fraction of one per cent of the gross national product? If I take one drop from the American bucket who's going to miss it – but if I'm not allowed to take it then a lot of people are going to miss you, Mr President, and your Arabian friends.

'And to think what you are going to lose, you and America. Ten times that, a hundred times that? To start with the San Rafael refinery deal will fall through. Your hopes of becoming a most favoured nation receiving oil at rock-bottom prices are gone for ever. In fact, if their Highnesses fail to return to their homeland it is certain that a total oil embargo would be placed on the States which would send the country into a bottomless recession which would make 1929 look like a Sunday afternoon picnic.' He looked at Hansen, the energy czar. 'You would agree, Mr Hansen?'

Clearly, the last thing that Hansen wanted to do was to agree with anyone. His nervous tics were rapidly assuming the proportions of a St Vitus's Dance. Head darting, he looked around for succour in his hour of need. He swallowed, he coughed into his hands, he looked imploringly at the President and seemed almost on the point of breaking down when the Secretary of the Treasury came to his rescue.

Quarry said: 'I would read the future the same way.'

'Thank you.'

The King raised his hand. 'A word, if you will.' The King was a man of a very different calibre from the President. As one who had had to remove, permanently more often than not, quite a number of his closest relatives in order to get his crown, the rough and tumble of life was hardly a new experience for him: he had lived with violence all his life and would very probably die with or because of it.

'Of course.'

'Only the blind have their eyes closed to reality. I am not blind. The President will pay.' The President had no comment to make on this generous offer: he was staring down at the roadway like a fortune teller peering into his crystal ball and not wanting to tell his client what he sees there.

'Thank you, Your Highness.'

'You will of course be hunted down and killed afterwards no matter where you seek to hide in the world. Even if you were to kill me now your death is already as certain as tomorrow's sun.'

Branson was unconcerned. 'As long as I have you, Your Highness, I have no worries on that score. I should imagine that any of your subjects who as much as endangered your life far less being responsible for your losing it would find himself rather precipitately in paradise – if regicides go to paradise, which I don't think should be allowed. And I hardly think you're the type of man to run to the side of the bridge now and jump over in order to incite the faithful to come after me with their long knives.'

'Indeed.' The hooded eyes were unblinking. 'And what if I were not the sort of person you think I am?'

'If you were to jump – or try to?' Again the chilling indifference. 'Why do you think I have a doctor and ambulance here? Van Effen, if anyone is as misguided as to make a break for it – what are your instructions?'

Van Effen matched the indifference. 'Chop his foot off with my machine-pistol. The doctor will fix him up.'

'We might even – eventually – provide you with an artificial foot. You're worth nothing to me dead, Your Highness.' The hooded eyes had closed. 'Well, the ransom figure? Agreed? No objectors? Splendid. Well, that's for starters.'

'Starters?' It was General Cartland speaking and one could almost see the firing squad mirrored in his eyes.

'To begin with, that means. There's more. Two hundred million dollars more. That's what I want for the Golden Gate Bridge.'

This time the state of traumatic shock did not last quite so long – there is a limit to how much the human mind can take. The President raised his eyes from the depths of the bottomless pit he was scanning and said dully: 'Two hundred million dollars for the Golden Gate Bridge?'

'It's a bargain. At the price, practically a give-away. True, it cost only about forty million to build and the asking price of two hundred million just exactly represents the five-fold inflation over the past forty years. But, money apart, think of the fearful cost of replacing it. Think of the noise, the dust, the pollution, the disruption to all the city traffic as all those thousands of tons of steel have to be brought in, of the tourists who will cripple the city's economy by staying away in their tens of thousands. Beautiful though San Francisco is, without the Golden Gate it would be like Mona Lisa without her smile. Think – and this is for a period of at least one year, perhaps two – of all those Marin County motorists who couldn't get to the city – it's a long way round by the San Rafael bridge – or, come to that, the city motorists who couldn't get to Marin County. The hardship would be intolerable for everyone – except for the owners of the ferry-boat companies who would become millionaires. And who am I to grudge the entrepreneur the making of an honest dollar? Two hundred million dollars? Philanthropy, that's what it is.'

Quarry, the man accustomed to thinking in rows of noughts, said: 'If we do not accede to this monstrous request, what do you intend to do with the bridge? Take it away and pawn it somewhere?'

'I'm going to blow it up. A two-hundred-foot drop – it should be the most almighty splash the West Coast has ever seen.'

'Blow it up! Blow up the Golden Gate Bridge!' Mayor Morrison, whose normal boiling point was just above freezing, was on his feet, his face suffused with ungovernable anger and had launched himself at Branson before anyone realized what was happening, certainly before Branson had realized. In tens of millions of American homes they saw Branson being knocked backwards off his seat, his head striking heavily against the roadway as Morrison, all two hundred and twenty pounds of him, followed him down and struck at his face with berserker fury. Van Effen stepped forward and brought the butt of his machine-pistol down on Morrison's neck. He immediately swung round to cover the seated men with his gun but the precaution was superfluous, no one was showing any inclination to follow Morrison's example.

It was a full twenty seconds before Branson could sit up,

and then only groggily. He accepted a pad of medical gauze and dabbed at a smashed lip and a very bloody nose. He looked at Morrison, then at the doctor.

'How is he?'

The doctor carried out a brief examination. 'He'll be all right, he's not even concussed.' The doctor glanced at Van Effen without enthusiasm. 'Your friend seems to be able to judge those things to a nicety.'

'Practice,' Branson explained thickly. He accepted another gauze pad in place of the already blood-saturated one and rose unsteadily to his feet. 'Mayor Morrison doesn't know his own strength.'

Van Effen said: 'What shall I do with him?'

'Leave him be. It's his city, it's his bridge. My fault – I just trod on a man's dreams.' He looked at Morrison consideringly. 'On second thoughts you'd better handcuff him – behind the back. Next time he might knock my head off my shoulders.'

General Cartland came to his feet and walked towards Branson. Van Effen levelled his gun menacingly but Cartland ignored him. He said to Branson: 'You fit to talk?'

'I'm fit to listen, anyway. He didn't get round to my ears.'

'I may be Chief of Staff but to trade I'm an army engineer. That means I know explosives. You can't blow up the bridge and you should know it. You'd require a wagon-load of explosives to bring down those towers. I don't see any wagon-load of explosives.'

'We don't need them.' He pointed to the thick canvas strap with the conical mounds embedded in it. 'You're the expert.'

Cartland looked at the strap, then at Branson, then at the seated watchers, then back at the strap again. Branson said: 'Suppose you tell them. My mouth hurts, I can't imagine why.'

Cartland took a long look at the massive towers and the cables suspended from them. He said to Branson: 'You have experimented?' Branson nodded. 'Successfully – or you wouldn't be here?' Branson nodded again.

Reluctantly, almost, Cartland turned to the seated hostages and journalists. 'I was wrong. I'm afraid Branson can indeed bring the bridge down. Those cones you see embedded in the canvas strap contain some conventional explosives – TNT amatol, anyway something of the requisite power. Those cones are called "bee-hives", and because of their concave bases are designed to direct at least eighty per cent of their explosive value inwards. The idea, I should imagine, is to wrap one of those canvas straps with its hundredweight or whatever of high explosive round one of the suspension cables, probably high up near the top of a tower.' He looked at Branson again. 'I should imagine you have four of those.' Branson nodded. 'And designed to fire simultaneously.' He turned back to the others. 'I'm afraid that would be it. Down it all comes.'

There was a brief silence, which must have been very nailbiting for TV watchers, a silence caused by the fact that Branson understandably didn't feel very much like speaking and the others couldn't think of very much to say. Cartland said eventually: 'How can you be sure they all go off together?'

'Simple. Radio wave that activates an electric cell that burns the wire in a mercury fulminate detonator. Up goes the primer and up goes the bee-hive. One's enough. The others go up by sympathetic detonation.'

Quarry said heavily: 'I suppose that ends your demands for the day?'

'Not quite.' Branson turned a palm up in an apologetic gesture. 'But it's only a trifle.'

'One wonders what *you* might consider a trifle.'

'A quarter of a million dollars.'

'Astonishing. By your standards, a grain of sand. And what might that be for?'

'My expenses.'

'Your expenses.' Quarry breathed deeply, twice. 'My God Branson, you are the piker to end all pikers.'

'I'm used to people calling me names.' He shrugged. 'I don't hurt so easily any more and one learns to take the rough with the smooth. Now, as to payment – you are going to pay me, aren't you?'

No one said whether they were going to pay him or not.

'I have to make arrangements with a friend in New York who has friends in certain European banks.' He looked at his watch. 'It's noon now so it's either eight or nine o'clock in Central Europe and all good Central European bankers knock off at six precisely. So I'd be greatly obliged if you'd let me have your decision by seven o'clock in the morning.'

Quarry said cautiously: 'What decision?'

'As to the availability of the funds and the form that they will take. Not that I care very much what they are, anything from Euro-dollars to stock in suitably selected off-shore funds. You, of all people, should find little problem in handling such things with a certain amount of discretion – witness, for instance, the hundreds of millions of dollars you've funded such organizations as the CIA for subversive activities overseas without the poor taxpayer being any the wiser. A childishly simple routine for your Treasury. Not that I care whether those funds are traceable or not: just as long as they are convertible.

'When my New York friend has informed us that those funds have all arrived at their several destinations – and that shouldn't take more than another twenty-four hours, say until noon the same day – we shall take our farewells of you. Our hostages will of course, accompany us.'

'And where are you taking us?' Cartland demanded.

'You I'm not taking anywhere. The armed services may regard you as invaluable but your value to me as a bargaining counter is zero. Besides, you're the only man here who could conceivably cause me trouble. Not only are you a man of action but you're far too lean – let me have men about me that are fat and all that bit. The President and his three remaining oil friends. There's no harm in telling you that I have a friend in the Caribbean who is the President of an island that doesn't and never will have an extradition treaty with the United States. He's willing to put us up, bed and breakfast, for a million dollars a night.'

No one had anything to say to this. In terms of the sums of money that Branson had so recently been bandying about, it seemed a reasonable enough charge.

'One point,' Branson said. 'I did not mention that as from noon the following day – day after tomorrow that is – there will be a penalty clause, an escalation charge you might call it, for every hour's delay in the reported lodgment of the funds. Two million dollars an hour.'

'You do place a certain value on your time, don't you, Mr Branson,' Quarry said.

'If I don't, who will? Would there be any more questions?'

'Yes,' Cartland said. 'How do you propose to get to this island paradise of yours?'

'Fly there. How else? A ten-minute flight in our helicopters to the International Airport and we board our plane there.'

'You have all this arranged? You have a plane standing by?'

'Well, it doesn't know it's standing by but it will soon enough.'

'What plane?'

'Air Force 1, I believe you call it.'

Even Cartland was shaken out of his habitual reserve. 'You mean you're going to hi-jack the presidential Boeing?'

'Be reasonable, general. You surely can't expect your President to judder his way down to the Caribbean in a clapped-out DC3? It's the logical, the only way of transporting world leaders who are accustomed to the ultimate in luxury travel. We'll show them the latest films. Brief though their incarceration may be we'll make it as comfortable as possible for them. We might even get some more new films when we fly them back to the States again.'

'We?' Cartland said carefully.

'My friends and I. I feel it only right – no, more than that, our bounden duty – that we should see them safely back again. How any man of any sensitivity can bear to live in that monstrosity they call the White House I don't know but, after all, there's no place like home.'

Milton was equally careful. 'You mean you're going to set foot on American soil again?'

'My own, my native land. Why ever not? You disappoint me, Mr Milton.'

'I do?'

'You do. Apart from the Supreme Court and the Attorney General I would have thought that the Secretary of State would know as much about our law and constitution as any other man in the land.' There was silence. Branson looked around but there was still silence so he addressed himself to the Secretary again. 'Or don't you know that bit where it says that no man who has been granted a full and free pardon by the State for any crime, actual or alleged, can ever again be arraigned on that same charge?'

It took at least ten seconds for the full implications to dawn and it was then that the Potomac, in the person of the Chief Executive, burst its banks. It was also then that the President lost twice the number of the putative votes he might have gained from his earlier statement that he would sacrifice himself for America. He could hardly be blamed. Devious some politicians may be and others are armoured in pachydermal hides: but never had the President encountered such Machiavellian effrontery. Even Presidents may be forgiven the odd earthy turn of phrase within the privacy of their own four walls but they customarily abjure such phraseology when addressing the electorate. But, momentarily, the President had totally forgotten the fact that he was, in effect, addressing the electorate: he was appealing to a mindless heaven for justice. And it was in that direction that his anguished face was lifted as he stood there, arms rigidly outstretched and fists clenched, his face assuming a peculiarly purplish hue.

'Half a (deleted) billion dollars! *And* a (deleted) full and free pardon! God al-(deleted)-mighty!' He lowered his gaze from the cloudless sky and turned the full fury of his wrath on Branson who, disappointingly had not been struck down by a bolt from heaven.

Branson murmured to the doctor: 'You have your cardiac arrest unit handy?'

'This is not funny.'

The President warmed to his theme. 'You evil twisted (deleted) bastard! If you imagine—'

Cartland, belatedly, reached his side, touched his arm and whispered urgently: 'You're on television, sir.'

The President, cut off in mid-expletive, looked at him, screwed his eyes shut in sudden comprehension, opened them again, looked the camera squarely in the eye and addressed it in measured tones.

'I, as the elected representative and Chief Executive of the American people, will not stand for this vile blackmail, the machinations of this evil and amoral man. The American people will not stand for it. Democracy will not stand for it. Come what may we shall fight this cancer in our midst—'

'How?' Branson asked.

'How?' The President tried manfully to control his blood pressure at the thought of this, but full rationality had not yet returned to him. 'The entire resources of every investigative agency in those United States of ours, the entire weight of the armed forces, the full majesty of law and order will be brought to bear—'

'You're not up for re-election for six months yet. How?'

'When I have consulted with the senior cabinet members.'

'You're through with consulting anyone, except on my say-so. A full and free pardon. If not, your stay on this tropical island may be indefinitely extended. Most of the island, as I say, is pretty close to paradise: but there's a small stockaded section in one corner of the island that's been modelled rather closely on the Devil's Island that used to be. The Generalissimo has to have some place for his political dissidents, and as he doesn't care for them overly much the majority of them never emerge again. It's a combination of hard labour, fever and starvation. I somehow don't see the King here with a pickaxe in his hand. Nor yourself for that matter.

'And instead of waffling on about the nation's moral rectitude, you might give thought to another possible predicament of your guests here. It is no secret that both the King and Prince have trusted Government ministers and relatives who are just yearning to try their thrones for size. If your friends' stay in the Caribbean were to be unduly prolonged, one rather suspects that they would have neither kingdom nor sheikhdom to return to. You appreciate, of course, that American opinion would never let you deal with their usurpers – especially as you would be the one held to blame for it. Bang goes November. Bang goes San Rafael. Here comes either redoubled oil prices or a total embargo and, in either case, a disastrous national recession. You won't even rate a footnote in history. At best if they ever get round to compiling a list of history's most stupid and disastrous leaders, then you have a fair chance of making the *Guinness Book of Records*. But history itself? No.'

'You have quite finished?' The President's anger had seemingly evaporated and he had attained a sort of resigned dignity.

'For the moment.' Branson motioned to the TV cameramen that the performance was over.

'May I have a word with the King, Prince, my governmental colleagues and the Chief of Police?'

'Why not? Especially if it helps you to arrive at your decision more quickly.'

'In privacy?'

'Certainly. Your coach.'

'In the strictest privacy?'

'The guard will remain outside. As you know, the coach is sound-proof. The strictest privacy, I promise you.'

They moved away, leaving Branson alone. He beckoned Chrysler, his tele-communications expert.

'Is the bug in the presidential coach activated?'

'Permanently.'

'Our friends are having a top-level secret discussion in there. Wouldn't you care to have a rest in our coach? You must be tired.'

'Very tired, Mr Branson.'

Chrysler made his way to the rear coach and sat by the driver's seat in front of the console. He made a switch and lifted a single ear-phone. Apparently satisfied with what he heard he replaced the ear-phone and made another switch. A tape recorder started humming.

II

April Wednesday said to Revson: 'Well, what did you make of that?'

'I'd love to see the Nielsen ratings when they re-run that later in the day.' They were walking to and fro along the western or deserted side of the bridge. 'What a cast. Rehearsals would have ruined it.'

'You know I don't mean that.'

'I know. He's quite a boy, our Peter Branson. Highly intelligent – but we know that already – all the angles figured, every eventuality taken care of far in advance, he'd have made an excellent general. You could – at least I could – almost like and admire the guy, except for the fact that, the odd half billion apart, he plainly does this for kicks, he's a moral vacuum and the ordinary standards of right and wrong just do not hold good for him, they simply don't exist. There's something strangely empty about him.'

'His bank-book isn't going to be. But I didn't mean that either.'

'I know that too. In answer to your unspoken question, yes he has us helpless.'

'Do you intend to do anything about it?'

'Intentions are one thing, achievements another.'

'Well, you just can't walk up and down there doing nothing. After what you told me this morning—'

'I know what I told you this morning. A little respectful silence, if you please. Can't you see I'm thinking?'

After some little time he said: 'I've thought.'

'I can't wait.'

'Have you ever been sick?'

She lifted her brows which had the effect of making the huge green eyes larger than ever. With those eyes, Revson reflected, she could wreck a cardinals' council in nothing flat. To keep his mind on the work on hand, he looked away. She said: 'Of course I've been sick. Everybody's been sick some time.'

'I mean really sick. Hospital. Like that.'

'No. Not ever.'

'You're going to be very soon. In hospital. Sick. If you're still prepared to help, that is.'

'I've told you that already.'

'Asperity ill becomes a lovely lady. There's quite an element of risk. If you're caught, Branson would make you talk. Half a billion dollars is a lot of money to have at stake. You'd talk very quickly.'

'Even more quickly than that. I'm not one of your wartime resistance heroines and I don't like pain. Caught at what?'

'Delivering a letter for me. Leave me alone for a few minutes will you.'

Revson unshipped his camera and took some still shots, of the coaches, helicopters, anti-aircraft guns and guards, trying as much as possible to keep the southern tower and the San Franciscan skyline in the background, clearly a dedicated craftsman at work. He then turned his attention and lens towards the ambulance and the white-jacketed doctor leaning against it.

The doctor said: 'Instant fame for me, is it?'

'What else? Everyone wants to be immortalized.'

'Not this doctor. And an ambulance you can film anywhere.'

'You need psychiatric help.' Revson lowered his camera. 'Don't you know that it's positively anti-social in this country not to want to hog the camera lens? My name's Revson.'

'O'Hare.' O'Hare was youthful, cheerful, red-haired and his Irish ancestry lay no more than a generation behind him.

'And what do you think of this lovely little set-up?'

'For quotation?'

'I'm a cameraman.'

'Aw, hell, quote me if you want. I'd just love to belt smarty-pants' ears off.'

'It figures.'

'What?'

'The red hair.'

'I'd feel the same if I were black, blond or bald as a coot. Arrogant smoothies do something to me. And I don't like the way he needles the President and publicly humiliates him.'

'You're a President man, then?'

'Hell, he's a Californian, I'm a Californian, I voted for him last time and I'll do so next time. Okay, so he's stuffy and over-does the kindly uncle bit but he's the best we have. Not that that says a great deal – but, well, he's really a decent old stick.'

'Decent old stick?'

'Don't blame me, I was educated in England.'

'Would you like to help him?'

O'Hare looked at Revson thoughtfully. 'Funny question. Sure I would.'

'Would you help me to help him?'

'How can you help him?'

'I'll try and I'll tell you how – if you say "yes", that is.'

'And what makes you think you can help more than anyone else?'

'Special qualifications. I'm a Government employee.'

'So what's with the camera, then?'

'And I always thought it took a fair amount of intelligence

to qualify as a doctor. What do you expect me to be carrying – a foot-wide plaque on my chest saying "I am an FBI agent"?'

O'Hare smiled, but only faintly. 'Well, no. But the story is that all the FBI men were left asleep in a down-town garage. Except for a few on the press coach who were rousted out and marched off the bridge.'

'We don't put all our eggs in one basket.'

'And agents don't usually disclose their identity either.'

'Not this agent. I'd disclose my identity to anyone if I were in trouble. And I'm in trouble now.'

'As long as it's not unethical—'

'I wouldn't bring a blush to the Hippocratic cheek. That guaranteed, would you consider it unethical to help put Branson behind bars?'

'Is that guaranteed too?'

'No.'

'Count on me. What do you want done?'

'We have a lady photographer with us who is young, rather beautiful, by the unlikely name of April Wednesday.'

'Ha!' O'Hare brightened considerably. 'The green-eyed blonde'

'Indeed. I want her to take a message ashore, if that's the word, for me and bring me back an answer within a couple of hours. I propose to code this message, film it and give you the spool. It's about half the size of a cigarette and I'm sure you can easily conceal it in one of the many tubes and cartons you must carry with you. Anyway, no one questions a doctor's integrity.'

'Don't they, now?' O'Hare spoke with some feeling.

'There's no hurry. I'll have to wait till Messrs Milton, Quarry and Hendrix have been escorted off the bridge. By which time, too, I expect that the trusty Mr Hagenbach will have arrived from wherever he has been lurking.'

'Hagenbach? You mean that old twister—'

'You are referring to my respected employer. Now, this is just an ambulance. Apart from your usual medical kit, heart unit, oxygen kit to stitch together the misguided who step out of line, I don't suppose you carry anything much more sophisticated.' O'Hare shook his head.

'So you don't have any radiological gear or clinical investigative equipment and most certainly not operational facilities, even if you did have an anaesthetist, which you haven't. I suggest then that, when Miss Wednesday takes most painfully ill in about an hour or so, you diagnose something that may demand, or may not demand – doctors can't take chances – immediate hospital diagnosis and possible surgery. Something like a grumbling appendix or suspected peritonitis or suchlike. Don't ask me.'

'I wouldn't.' O'Hare looked at Revson with some disfavour. 'You seem to be unaware that even the rawest intern, no matter how damp behind the ears, can diagnose appendicitis with his hands, figuratively, in his pockets.'

'I am aware. But I'm damned if I could do it. And I'm pretty certain that no one else on this bridge could do it either.'

'You have a point. Right. But you'll have to give me fifteen to twenty minutes' notice – before I call in Branson or whoever. The odd jab or two to induce the proper symptoms. No danger.'

'Miss Wednesday has just informed me that she is allergic to pain.'

'She won't feel a thing,' O'Hare said in his best dentist's voice. 'Besides, it's for the homeland.' He looked at Revson consideringly. 'I believe you gentlemen of the press are handing your stuff over at the south barrier in two hours' time. Couldn't it wait till then?'

'And get my answer back by carrier pigeon next week? I want it this afternoon.'

'You *are* in a hurry.'

'During the war – World War Two, that is – Winston Churchill used to annotate all instructions to his military and governmental staff with just three scribbled words: "Action this day". I am a great admirer of Sir Winston.'

He left the slightly bemused O'Hare and returned to April Wednesday. He told her that O'Hare had okayed his request and her first question was: 'Want I should bring back a miniaturized transceiver radio?'

He gave her a kind look.

'Thoughtful, but no. Electronic surveillance of all kinds can hardly be your province. Such a transceiver I have, screwed into the base of my camera. But that little revolving disc above the villains' coach means only one thing – they have an automatic radio-wave scanner. They'd pick me up in five seconds. Now listen carefully and I'll tell you exactly what I want you to do and how I want you to behave.'

When he had finished she said: 'Understand. But I don't much care for the thought of the kindly healer there running amok with his hypodermic.'

'You won't feel a thing,' Revson said soothingly. 'Besides, it's for the fatherland.'

He left her and walked casually across to the press coach. The imperial conference in the presidential coach was still in full plenary session, and though the speech inside was wholly inaudible from where Revson stood it was clear from the gestures and expressions of those inside that all they had succeeded in reaching so far was a marked degree of difference in opinion. Their problem, Revson reflected, was hardly one susceptible to the ready formation of a consensus of opinion. Branson and Chrysler were up front in the rear coach, apparently dozing, which they probably weren't – though it wouldn't have mattered very much if they were, for alert guards were very much in evidence patrolling between the freshly-painted boundary lines on the bridge. Members of the various news media stood around in groups, wearing an air of almost hushed anticipation as if expecting the next momentous occasion to happen along any second now, which seemed as likely as not.

Revson entered the press coach. It was deserted. He made his way to his own seat, unshipped his camera, produced a pad and felt pen and began, quickly and without hesitation, to write what was apparently pure gibberish. There were those who were lost without their code-books but Revson was not one of them.

— 6 —

HAGENBACH the chief of the FBI, was a burly and formidable character in his middle sixties, with short-cropped grey hair, short-cropped grey moustache, slightly hooded light blue eyes which never appeared to blink and a face possessed of a total non-expression which it had taken him years of hard work to acquire. It was said that among the upper echelons of his FBI there was a sweepstake as to the day and date when Hagenbach would first be seen to smile. The sweepstake had been running for five years.

Hagenbach was a very able man and looked it. He had no friends and he looked that too. Men with a consuming passion seldom do and Hagenbach was a man with a consuming passion. As was said of one of his illustrious predecessors, he was alleged to have a file on every senator and congressman in Washington, not to mention the entire staff of the White House. He could have made a fortune in blackmail but Hagenbach was not interested in money. Nor was he interested in power, as such. Hagenbach's total dedication lay in the extirpation of corruption, whenever and wherever he might encounter it.

He looked at Admiral Newson and General Carter, the former plump and rubicund, the latter tall and lean and looking disconcertingly like his superior, General Cartland. Both men he had known, and well, for almost twenty years and had not once called either by his first name. That anyone should address Hagenbach by his Christian name was unthinkable. It would also have been extremely difficult as no one seemed to know it. He was the type of man who didn't need a first name.

Hagenbach said: 'So those are the only tentative proposals for action you have come up with so far?'

'The situation is unprecedented,' Newson said. 'Carter

and I are fundamentally men of direct action. To date, direct action seems out of the question. Let's hear your ideas.'

'I've only just arrived. Have you any *immediate* proposals for the moment?'

'Yes. Await the arrival of the Vice-President.'

'The Vice-President is a nincompoop. You know that. I know that. We all know that.'

'Be that as it may, he's the only man in the United States who can approve and authorize any course of action we may eventually decide to make. Also, I think we had first better wait and consult Mr Milton, Mr Quarry and Chief Hendrix when they're released.'

'If they're released.'

'Hendrix is certain they will be and Hendrix knows far more about Branson than we do. Besides, he has to negotiate with somebody.' He picked up the message that had arrived from Revson via the *New Jersey*. 'How much reliance do you place on this?'

Hagenbach took the note and read it aloud.

' "Please wait. No precipitate action. No violence – especially no violence. Let me evaluate the situation. Cannot use transceiver – the bandits have an automatic radio-wave scanner in constant use. Will communicate with you this afternoon." '

Hagenbach laid down the paper. 'Quite a bit, actually.'

Carter said: 'What's he like, this Revson of yours?'

'Ruthless, arrogant, independent, dislikes authority, a loner who consults superior officers only under duress and even then goes his own way.'

Newson said: 'That doesn't sound very encouraging. What's a hot-head like that doing along on a trip like this?'

'He's no hot-head. His mind is as near ice-cold as any man's can be. I also forgot to say that he's highly intelligent, very ingenious and extremely resourceful.'

'Then he's a hand-picked man?' Newson said. Hagenbach nodded. 'You hand-picked him?' Again the nod. 'So he's the best in the business?'

'I can't say. You know the size of our organization. I can't possibly know all the field agents. He's just the best I happen to know.'

'Is he good enough to cope with Branson?'

'I don't know because I don't know Branson. What's for sure, for once Revson is going to depend heavily on outside help.' There was a degree of satisfaction in Hagenbach's voice.

Carter said: 'And how in hell is he going to communicate with us this afternoon?'

'I have no idea.' Hagenbach nodded to Revson's note. 'He got that through, didn't he?' There was a brief pause as the Admiral and General respectfully contemplated the note. 'Would either of you gentlemen have thought of that?' They shook their heads. 'Me neither. Resourceful is what I said.'

II

Branson walked up and down the bridge between the rear and Presidential coaches. No nervous pacing, no signs of strain or tension, he could have been taking a pleasant saunter in the afternoon sun, and, indeed, the afternoon was extremely pleasant. The skies were cloudless, the view all around came straight from the pages of a fairy-tale book and the waters of the Golden Gate and the Bay sparkled in the warm sun. Having had his fill of the view, Branson consulted his watch, strolled unhurriedly towards the presidential coach, knocked on the door, opened it and stepped inside. He surveyed the occupants and the sound of voices stilled.

Branson said pleasantly: 'You have arrived at a decision, gentlemen?' There was no reply. 'Am I to take it, then, that you have arrived at an impasse?'

The President lowered the very large gin and martini with which he had been sustaining himself.

'We require more time for our deliberations.'

'You've had all the time you're going to have. You could sit here all day and get no further. If all your minds weren't so devious and at the same time so closed to the facts of life, you'd recognize this for the painfully simple issue it is. Pay up or else. And don't forget the escalation penalty clause.'

The President said: 'I have a proposal to make.'

'Let's hear it.'

'Permit the King, Prince and Sheikh Kharan to go. I shall remain as hostage. The situation would remain the same. You would still have the President of the United States. For that matter I can't see why you don't let *all* the hostages in this coach go.'

Branson was admiring. 'My heavens, what a perfectly splendid gesture. Noble, I should say. Why, do that, and the electorate would demand that they re-alter the constitution and let their hero run for another three terms instead of one.' He smiled and went on without a change in tone. 'No way, Mr President. Apart from the fact that I shudder at the very thought of you being in the White House for the next thirteen years I've always dreamt of holding a hand of cards with four aces in it. Here I've got four. One is not enough. And has it ever occurred to you that if you *were* to be the only hostage left on the Golden Gate Bridge the Government, in the person of your Vice-President who would just love to sit behind that table in the Oval Office, might be sorely tempted to achieve some sort of immortality by wiping out this monstrous band of criminals who have kidnapped you and your Arabian friends? Nothing drastic of course – nobody who destroyed this bridge could ever hope to be President. A single supersonic fighter-bomber from Alameda would do the job nicely. And if one of his rockets went off course slightly – well, that's just bad luck, an Act of God and pilot's error.'

The President spilt a considerable amount of his gin and martini on the carpet.

Branson looked at Quarry, Milton and Hendrix in turn, said: 'Gentlemen,' and left the coach. The three men followed. The President carefully didn't watch them go. He appeared to have found something of profound interest in the depths of what remained of his drink.

Outside, Branson spoke to Van Effen. 'Get that TV van and crew back here again. Make sure the TV companies are notified.'

Van Effen nodded. 'It would be wrong of you to let the nation suffer this agonizing suspense. Where are you going?'

'To the south end with those three gentlemen.'

'As guaranteed escort for their safety? Can't they take the word of a gentleman?'

'Not that. I just want to inspect the progress being made on the barrier. Saves the walk, that's all.'

The four men climbed into the police car and drove off.

III

Still alone in the press coach, Revson watched them go then returned his attention to the three small sheets of notepaper on his knees. Each was smaller than the average postcard and all three were covered with small, neat and incomprehensible writing. He focused his camera and photographed each three times – Revson always covered his bets. He then took each paper in turn, set fire to it and crushed the blackened remains in his ash-tray. It was a very curious paper for it gave off no smoke. He then wound off the camera spool, sealed it and wrapped it in a very thin lead foil; as he had promised O'Hare, the completed result was no larger than half a cigarette.

He reloaded his camera and went outside. The atmosphere of suspense and excitement had markedly heightened. He spoke to a near-by newspaperman – understandably, he knew none of them by name.

'Something new afoot?'

'Branson's just sent for the television van again.'

'Do you know why?'

'No idea.'

'Nothing very important, probably. Maybe he's always had a yen to appear on TV. Maybe he's just wanting to keep the pressure on the nation and the government – and the Arabian governments too, for this time the big three companies will be geared for action, the satellites will be ready and waiting and so will be all the Arabian Gulf. The executives of the big companies will be hard put to it to shed crocodile tears for the plight of their beloved President and at the same time refrain from jumping for joy. The biggest show on earth and all for free. What's the odds Branson won't be putting on a late show about two in the morning?'

Revson shot about a dozen other pictures. The chances of its being discovered that he had taken no pictures at all were remote in the extreme, but then again Revson always covered his bets. He drifted casually across to where O'Hare was leaning against his ambulance and shook a cigarette from its pack.

'Light, doctor?'

'Sure.' O'Hare produced a lighter and lit it. Revson cupped the flame in his hands to shield it from the very slight breeze and as he did so he slid the spool into O'Hare's palm.

'Thanks, doc.' He looked idly around. There was no one within earshot. 'How long to hide?'

'One minute. I have the place for it.'

'Two minutes and you'll have your patient.'

O'Hare went into the ambulance while Revson sauntered half-way across the bridge where April Wednesday was prudently standing alone, a circumstance normally very difficult for her to achieve. She looked at him, wet her lips and tried to smile at him. It wasn't a very successful effort.

Revson said: 'Who's that solid dependable-looking character standing by the engine of the ambulance?'

'Grafton. United Press. A nice man.'

'Go and collapse gracefully against him. Discretion is of the essence. We don't want any undue fuss. But first let me get to the other side of the bridge. I want to be at a safe distance when you're taken ill.'

When Revson reached the far side of the bridge he turned and looked back. April had already begun to head in the direction of the ambulance. Her gait seemed a little unsteady but not markedly so. She may be scared, he thought – and she unquestionably was – but she can act.

She was about fifteen feet distant from Grafton when he first saw her or, more precisely, when she first attracted his attention. He regarded her slightly wavering approach with curiosity, a curiosity which quickly turned to concern. He took two quick steps forward and caught her by the shoulders. She leaned gratefully against him, lips and eyes compressed as in pain.

'April Wednesday,' he said. 'What's the matter, girl?'

'I've a terrible pain. It just hit me now.' Her voice was husky and she was holding herself with both hands. 'It – it feels like a heart attack.'

'How would you know?' Grafton said reasonably, his tone reassuring. 'And wherever your heart is, it's not on the right-hand side of your tummy. Don't misinterpret me, but some people have all the luck.' He took her firmly by the arm. 'There's a doctor only five yards from here.'

From the far side of the bridge Revson watched them vanish round to the rear of the ambulance. As far as he could reasonably tell, he had been the only person to observe the brief by-play.

IV

Branson walked unhurriedly away from the half-completed southern barrier, apparently well satisfied with the progress of the work in hand. He reached the rear coach and swung up to sit beside Chrysler.

'Any more sensational revelations?'

'No, Mr Branson. It's all become a bit repetitive and boring. You can have a play-back or transcript if you like but it's not worth it.'

'I'm sure it's not. Tell me.'

'Can I switch off, Mr Branson? They're really not worth listening to.'

'They never were. Well?'

'Same old story. About the payment. Still arguing.'

'But they're going to pay.'

'No question. It's whether to pay now or stall. Latest opinion poll has four for, two undecided, two against. The King, the Prince and Kharan are all for the money being handed over now – Treasury money, of course. Mayor Morrison is of the same mind.'

'That's understandable. He'd pay a billion dollars within the hour to ensure the safety of his beloved bridge.'

'Cartland and Muir have no preference either way, the only difference being that General Cartland is willing to fight us to the death. The President and Hansen are very much against immediate payment.'

'Again understandable. Hansen's never made a decision in his life and the President would stall for ever, hoping for a miracle to happen, hoping to save the nation the loss of a half billion for which, rightly or wrongly, he would probably be blamed, hoping to save face and his presidental image. Let them stew in their own juice.' He turned as Peters appeared in the doorway. 'Something wrong?'

'Nothing that affects us, sir. Seems Dr O'Hare has some

medical problem on his hands. He'd like to see you as soon as possible.'

V

When Branson entered the ambulance he found April lying on the hinged side bed, a discreet six inches of her midriff showing, her face chalk-white. Branson did not much care for finding himself in the presence of sick people and this was obviously a sick person. He looked enquiringly at O'Hare.

O'Hare said: 'I've a very sick young lady on my hands, here, Mr Branson. I want her removed to hospital immediately.'

'What's wrong?'

'Look at her face.'

It was indeed ashen, an effect easily achieved by the application of an odourless talcum.

'And at her eyes.'

They were opaque with enormously dilated pupils, the effect of the first of the two jabs that O'Hare had given her. Not that the eyes hadn't been big enough to begin with.

'Feel her pulse.'

Reluctantly, Branson lifted the slender wrist and dropped it almost immediately.

'It's racing,' he said. And indeed it was. O'Hare had probably been a little too thorough there. The rate of the pulse when she had entered the ambulance had already been so high as to render the second injection unnecessary.

'Would you care to feel the distension on the right-hand side of the abdomen?'

'No, I would not.' Branson was emphatic.

'It could be a grumbling appendix. It could be a threatened peritonitis. The signs are there. But I have no proper diagnostic equipment, no X-ray facilities, no way of carrying out abdominal surgery and, of course, no anaesthetist. Hospital, and pretty damn quick.'

'No!' April had sat up in bed, fear in her face. 'No! Not hospital! They'll cut me up! Surgery! I've never even *been* in a hospital in my life.'

O'Hare put his hands on her shoulders, firmly and not bothering to be gentle, and pressed her back down again.

'And if I'm not that sick? If it's only a tummy-ache or something? Mr Branson wouldn't let me back. The only scoop of my life. And I'm scared!'

O'Hare said: 'It's more than a tummy-ache, lassie.'

'You can come back,' Branson said. 'But only if you do what the doctor and I say.' He nodded towards the door and stepped down. 'What do you think really is the matter with her?'

'A doctor doesn't have to discuss a patient with a layman.' O'Hare was showing every symptom of losing his patience. 'And I can tell you this, Branson. Make off with half a billion dollars and you'll probably end up as some kind of folk hero. It's happened often before, although not, admittedly, on this scale. But let this girl die because you denied her access to medical care and you'll become the most hated man in America. They'll never stop till they get you. To start with, the CIA will find you wherever you are in the world – and they won't bother to bring you to trial.'

Branson showed no signs of losing his patience. He said mildly: 'You don't have to threaten me, doctor. She'll get her medical care. I'm just asking as a favour.'

'In confidence?' Branson nodded. 'You don't have to be a doctor to see that she's a pretty sick kid. But there is more than one way of being sick. Is she threatened with appendicitis or peritonitis? I don't think so. She's an excitable, intense, highly-strung kid who lives on her nerves. Under pressure, as of now, those could produce an emotional trauma or psychosomatic disorders which are capable of causing the symptoms we've just seen. It's rare, but it exists. In medicine, there's a condition called the Malthusian syndrome where a person can actually will himself into producing – faking, if you want to call it that – symptoms of a non-existent disease. Not in this case – if it is what I think it is, it's involuntary. But you see my position – I can't take chances. She may require intensive medical diagnosis or psychiatric evaluation. The first I can do myself, but I need hospital equipment. The second I can't – I'm not a psychiatrist. Either way I must get to hospital. We're wasting time.'

'I won't keep you long. Do you mind if we search your ambulance?'

O'Hare stared at him. 'What the hell for? What do you think I'm carrying? Bodies? Narcotics – well, quite a lot, really. What do you think I would be taking off this bridge that I didn't bring on to it? I'm a doctor, not an FBI agent.'

'We'll forget it. Another question. Do you mind if we send a guard along – for observation purposes?'

'Send half a dozen. They'll get damned little observation done.'

'What's that supposed to mean?'

'It means that Harben – he's chief of surgery – cherishes his unit like a new-born baby. He wouldn't give a damn about you and your bridge. If any of your men tried to force their way into emergency reception of the emergency theatre he'd have a dozen sharp-shooters there in ten minutes. I'm not joking – I've seen him do it.'

'We'll forget that, too. It's unimportant.'

'One thing that is important. Will you phone, ask them to have the emergency operating theatre ready and Dr Huron standing by.'

'Dr Huron?'

'Senior psychiatrist.'

'Right.' Branson smiled faintly. 'Do you know that a presidential route is always laid out so that it's never more than a few minutes from the nearest hospital? Just in case. Convenient, isn't it?'

'Very.' O'Hare turned to the driver. 'Start the siren.'

As the ambulance moved towards the south tower they were passed by a TV van and generator truck coming the other way. Immediately, cameramen, photographers and reporters began moving into what they assumed would be the same TV arena as before. Some cameramen were so overcome by the occasion that they began wasting film on the forthcoming truck as if this were an unprecedented spectacle in itself.

Revson was not one of those who joined in the surge forward. He moved in the opposite direction and regained his seat in the deserted press coach. He unclipped the base of his camera, removed the miniaturized transceiver, slipped it into a side pocket, reached into his carrier bag and fed spare film into the base of his camera. He was just reclipping the base of his camera when he became aware of being watched. He looked up. Blue eyes under blond hair, a head the approximate shape of a sugar cube and a vacuous smile. Revson believed in that vacuous smile the way he believed in Santa Claus. Branson would have settled for nothing less than an exceptional man when picking his lieutenant.

'Revson, isn't it?'

'Yes. Van Effen, I believe.'

'Yes. Why aren't you out there with the others, recording this historical moment for posterity?'

'First, what is there to record yet? Second, the big eye of TV can do a damned sight better job of posterity-recording than I can do. Third, if you'll excuse the hackneyed phrase, what I'm after is the human interest angle. Fourthly, I prefer to load in the shadow.'

'That looks a most exceptional camera.'

'It is.' Revson permitted himself a small proprietary smile that almost bordered on a smirk. 'Hand-made and assembled. Swedish. A rare species. The only camera in the world that can take colour stills, black and white stills and is a ciné camera at the same time.'

'May I have a look? I'm a bit of a camera buff myself.'

'Certainly.' The battery-powered air-conditioning in the coach, Revson thought, was falling down on the job.

Van Effen examined the camera with the eye of a connoisseur. Inadvertently, as it seemed, his hand touched the spring clip at the base. A dozen cassettes and spools tumbled on the seat beside Revson.

'I *am* sorry. It would seem that I'm not all that much of a camera buff.' He inverted the camera and looked with admiration at the recessed base. 'Very very ingenious.' While Revson sat, acutely conscious of the slight bulge caused by the transceiver in his side pocket, Van Effen meticulously replaced cassettes and spools in the base, closed the flap and handed the camera back to Revson. 'Excuse my curiosity.'

'Well, you went to the right finishing school, anyway.'

'It always shows.' Van Effen gave him his vacuous smile and left.

Revson did not mop his brow for it was a gesture alien to

his nature. Had he been a brow-mopper, he would have done so. He wondered if Van Effen had noticed the two tiny spring clips in the base. He probably had. Had he realized their significance? Equally probably not. They could have been the retaining clips for any number of esoteric attachments.

Revson turned in his seat. The hostages were descending from their coach, the President manfully substituting for his black scowl a calm, resolute and statesmanlike expression. Even Van Effen, Revson saw, had his eyes on them. Revson left the coach by the door opposite the driver's so that he was on the blind side of all the spectators and participants. He leaned his elbows in brief contemplation on the outer rail, then opened his right hand, the one that held the transceiver. He had read somewhere that it took a solid object, accelerating at thirty-two feet per second, only three seconds to fall from the bridge to the Golden Gate and he gravely doubted whether the man responsible for those figures could count. Nobody had noticed anything amiss. Revson had covered his bets again.

He made his unhurried and silent entry into the coach again, closed the door quietly behind him and emerged, much less quietly, from the opposite door. Van Effen turned, smiled vaguely, then turned back his attention to the circus on hand.

As before, Branson had everything stage-managed to perfection, hostages and newsmen seated in their proper places, ciné and still cameramen strategically positioned although, this time, there was one minor but significant difference from the previous occasion. This time Branson had two TV cameras instead of one. Without further ado Branson, calm, relaxed and as assured as ever, re-embarked upon his psychological warfare. Apart from being a born general and a born stage manager, he could also have been a born anchor-man on TV. He divided his attention fairly evenly between the TV lens and those seated beside him. After a wholly unnecessary introduction of himself, the President, the King and the Prince, his first reference, not unsurprisingly, was to cameras.

'We have, this afternoon, two television cameras with us. One for the illustrious company you are now viewing, the other facing the other way towards the south or San Franciscan shore. The second one is a tracking camera with a telephoto zoom lens, that, up to half a mile, can give the clarity of resolution that one would expect at the distance of ten feet. As there is no trace of fog this afternoon it should be able to perform its function admirably. Its function is as follows.'

Branson lifted the canvas cover from a large, rectangular box then, microphone in hand, went and sat in a specially reserved vacant chair by the President. He gestured towards the object he had just unveiled.

'A courtesy gesture towards our assembled guests. A rather splendid colour TV set. No better obtainable anywhere. American, of course.'

The President had to make himself heard. After all, most of the so-called civilized eyes in the world were upon him. He said, with heavy sarcasm and a cold distaste: 'I'll wager you haven't paid for your TV set, Branson.'

'That's hardly relevant. The point is that I don't want to make you and your guests feel like second-class and deprived citizens. All the world will be able to see in close detail how we are going to attach the first of our explosive charges to one of the cables by the south tower and I feel it would be unjust to deprive you of the same privilege. After all, at a distance of over two thousand feet and an elevation of over five hundred feet, it would be difficult for even the keenest-eyed to appreciate the finer points of this operation. But the box here will show you everything you want.' Branson smiled. 'Or don't want. Now, please direct your attention to the vehicle descending the ramp from the rear coach.'

They so directed their attention. What they saw could also be seen on the TV set before them. The vehicle looked like a stripped-down, miniaturized golf-cart. It was self-propelled but silent, clearly electrically powered. The driver, Peters, stood on a tiny platform at the rear immediately over the batteries. On the flat steel platform before him was a large coil of very thin rope and, at the very front, a small, double-drummed winch.

At the foot of the ramp, Peters stopped the vehicle. Four men appeared from the rear of the coach. The first two were carrying an obviously very heavy canvas strap of explosives – similar to the one that Branson had earlier demonstrated on TV. This they deposited, very carefully indeed, on the vehicle's platform beside the rope. The other two men carried objects about eight feet in length: one was a boat-hook, the other an H-sectioned steel beam with butterfly screw clamps at one end and a built-in pulley at the other.

'The tools of our trade,' Branson said. 'You should be able to guess what they're all for but in any event this will be explained to you when they are put to use. Two things are of particular interest: the explosives and the rope. That strap of explosives is ten feet long and contains thirty bee-hives of high explosive, each five pounds in weight: the rope, which is a quarter of a mile long, looks, and is thinner than the average clothes-line, but, as it is made of steel-cored nylon, has a breaking strain of eight hundred pounds which is exactly five times as much as will be required of it.' He gestured to Peters, who nodded, eased open the circular control wheel and trundled off in the direction of the south tower. Branson looked directly at the TV lens.

He said: 'For those of you who don't know, and apart from the citizens of San Francisco there will be many who will not know, those towers are something less than solid structures.' On the TV set before him and on countless millions of sets throughout the world, the south tower came into sharp, close focus. 'These towers consist of steel framework boxes called cells. Each is about the size of a phone booth, but twice as high, riveted together and connected by manholes. Each tower consists of over five thousand such cells. They contain elevators and ladders – a rather staggering twenty-three miles of them.'

He reached under his seat and brought up a manual.

'As you will appreciate, it would be very easy for the inexperienced to get lost inside this labyrinth. Once, when they were building this bridge, two men spent the entire night inside the north tower trying to find their way out, and indeed, Joseph Strauss, the designer and builder of this bridge, was capable of getting completely lost inside the tower. It was with this in mind that Strauss produced this twenty-six page manual – well, not this one, this is a facsimile I was fortunate enough to come by – instructing inspectors how to find their way about inside the towers.

'At this moment, two of my men, each with a copy of this manual – although they hardly need them, they're using the elevator – are at, or nearing, the top of the east tower there, the one facing towards the bay. They are carrying with them nothing except a fifteen-pound weight, the purpose of which you will shortly discover. May we observe the progress of our electric truck, please?'

The telephoto TV camera obligingly descended and closed on Peters, travelling along the wrong side of the bridge. Even as they watched, it slowed and came to a halt almost directly under the lowest of the four massive cross-struts of the south tower.

Branson said: 'Elevation, please.'

Again the telephoto camera focused on the saddle – the curved steel housing over which the cable passed – on the bayside tower. Almost immediately two men came into sight by the saddle, tiny figures for those directly observing from the middle of the bridge, close-up for those looking at the TV screens.

'On cue, on time,' Branson said with some satisfaction. 'In those matters, co-ordination is of the essence. I dare say that not one in ten thousand of you would care to be where those two men are now. Quite frankly, neither would I. One misstep and it's over seven hundred and fifty feet down to the Golden Gate: only a seven-second fall but at a hundred and seventy miles an hour hitting water is no different from hitting solid concrete. But those two are as safe as you would be in a church pew. Spidermen, they're called – the workers you can see standing on girders a thousand feet above the streets of New York or Chicago when they're building a new skyscraper.'

The camera closed on Peters again. He produced a pistol, unusual as to both length of barrel and width of muzzle, took brief aim upwards and fired. Neither camera could track nor eye see the nature of the missile ejected: what the camera did show, four seconds after firing, was that Bartlett, one of the men by the saddle, had a green cord safely in his hands. He reeled this in swiftly. At the end of the cord was a leather-hung pulley, which in turn was attached to one end of the rope. Two and a half minutes elapsed before the rope was in Bartlett's hands.

He held this securely while his partner, Boyard, undid both cord and pulley. Bartlett reeled in about another dozen feet, cut this section off with a knife and handed it to Boyard, who secured one end to a strut and another to the strap of the pulley. The rope was then passed through the pulley, through a hole at its top, to a pear-shaped lead weight which the men had brought up with them. Both weight and rope were then released and sank swiftly down to bridge level again.

Peters caught the weight, undid the knot that secured the rope but did not withdraw the rope. Instead he passed it through the pulley in the steel beam and a ring at the end of the boat-hook and secured all three together. He took a few turns of the other end of the rope round one of the drums of the winch and started up the electric motor.

The winch, though small, was powerful and fast. From bridge to saddle took less than a minute and a half. There was a gentle breeze blowing from the north, apparently freshening as the altitude increased, and the rope and its burden swayed quite noticeably, striking each of the cross-struts, at times quite forcibly, on the way up. Peters seemed unconcerned, his gaze fixed on Bartlett. As the rope and its cargo neared the top Bartlett made a horizontal waving motion of his arm. Peters eased the winch drum to a crawl. Bartlett made a slow upwards beckoning motion with his arm then stretched it out horizontally. Peters unwound the rope after stopping the winch, leaving only one turn on the drum.

Bartlett and Boyard pulled in the beam and boat-hook, detached them along with the lead weight, passed the rope through the pulley and resecured the lead weight. They then eased out the H-beam for a distance of about six feet then clamped the inner end to a strut, tightening the butterfly nuts to their maximum. Bartlett signalled Peters who took the last turn off the drum. Weight and rope sank rapidly downwards.

Two minutes later the rope was on its way up again, this time with the canvas strap of explosives which dangled at its full length, fastened to the rope by two heavy metal buckles at one end of the strap. Unlike the previous occasion Peters now moved with great caution, the drum moving very slowly and occasionally stopping altogether. General Cartland commented on this to Branson.

'Your winchman is trying to eliminate all sway?'

'Yes. We don't want that strap of explosives to bang against one of the cross-struts.'

'Of course. I'd forgotten how sensitive fulminate of mercury detonators are.'

'The detonators are in Bartlett's pocket. But the primers can be temperamental too. That's why we have that extended beam up top – to give clearance. Also, it's asking a bit much for even two strong men to haul a hundred and sixty pounds – not a hundredweight as you estimated, General – over five hundred feet vertically upwards.'

They watched the explosive safely negotiate the second top cross-strut. Cartland said: 'So it's one strap there, one on the opposite cable and the other two at the north tower?'

'No. We've changed our minds on that. We suspect that the suspension cables – and don't forget that there are over twenty-seven thousand spun wires inside the steel sheath – may be considerably stronger than the mock-up we used for the test. So we're going to use all four explosive straps at the south tower, a pair on each cable. That will leave no margin for doubt. And if the south end of the bridge falls into the Golden Gate it seems reasonable to expect that the north end will follow suit. Whether the north tower – don't forget it will then be bearing most of the weight of the four-thousand-two-hundred-feet span – will be pulled down too we haven't been able to determine but it seems pretty close to a certainty.'

Van Effen took two quick steps forwards and clicked off the safety catch on his machine-pistol. Mayor Morrison, half out of his seat, slowly subsided back into it but his fists were still tightly clenched, his eyes still mad.

By now, Bartlett and Boyard had the boat-hook round the rope and were steadily, cautiously and without too much trouble, overhanding the explosives in towards themselves. Soon it disappeared out of the range of the telephoto TV camera. So, immediately afterwards, did all of Bartlett except for head and shoulders.

'Inserting the detonators?' Cartland asked. Branson nodded and Cartland gestured to the section of the cable nearest them. At that point, in the centre of the bridge, the cable dipped until it was almost within arm's length. 'Why go to all that immense labour? Wouldn't it have been easier just to fix the charges here?'

'Easier, yes, but there's no guarantee that severing the cables in mid-bridge would bring the bridge down. There's no way of knowing: what's for sure is that no one has ever carried out a control test or experiment on this sort of thing. Suspension bridges come expensive. If the cables were severed here the towers, as far as weight is concerned, would still be in a fair state of equilibrium. Bridge might sag a little or a lot, it might break but it wouldn't drop the whole span clear into the water. My way, success is guaranteed. You wouldn't expect me to charge two hundred million for a botched-up job, would you?'

General Cartland didn't say whether he would or he wouldn't.

'Besides, if things go wrong, that is, if you turn out to be stingy with the money, I intend to trigger off the explosives immediately we take off. I don't want to be within half a mile of six hundred pounds of high explosives when it goes up.'

The President said carefully: 'You mean the triggering device is aboard one of those helicopters?'

Branson gave a patient sigh. 'I've always maintained that all presidential candidates should undergo an IQ test. Of course it is. In the nearest one. What did you expect me to do? Press a button inside a coach and then go down with the coach and bridge to the bottom of the Golden Gate?'

Branson removed his disbelieving gaze from the President and returned it to the TV screen before him. Bartlett, with Boyard steadying him, had the canvas strip wrapped round the cable, hard up against the saddle and was buckling tight the second of the two straps that held the strap securely in position. That done, he moved back along with Boyard to admire their handiwork. The camera then left them and zeroed in on the section of cable wrapped in the lethal embrace of the high explosive.

Branson smiled broadly. 'Well, now, isn't that a perfectly splendid sight?'

Cartland remained poker-faced. 'It all depends upon your point of view.'

7

VICE-PRESIDENT Richards switched off the TV set. He looked thoughtful, shocked and concerned all at one and the same time. When he spoke, those emotions were reflected in his voice.

'That was a remarkably effective performance. One has to confess that our villainous friend appears to know exactly what he is about and has the total ability to carry out his numerous threats. At least, that is how I see it, but I'm just a newcomer to the scene. Do you gentlemen see it any differently?'

The Vice-President was a tall, genial, loquacious southerner, much given to slapping – one could not call it clapping – the unwary rather painfully on the back and was an internationally-known gourmet, a fact amply testified to by his ample figure. He was far from being the nincompoop Hagenbach had alleged – Hagenbach's opinion stemmed from the fact that theirs were two totally differing personalities: he was forceful, shrewd, intelligent and was remarkably well informed on a very wide range of topics: if he had one fault it was that he had, unlike Hagenbach, a consuming desire for power. Branson had hardly been exaggerating when he had suggested that a yearning look came into Richards's eyes whenever he entered the Oval Office in the White House.

Richards looked, without much hope, around the company assembled in the office of the hospital supervisor. Hagenbach, Hendrix and the two Secretaries sat around a small table. Newson and Carter, as if to demonstrate the exclusivity of the highest echelons of the military, sat at a second and smaller table. O'Hare, arms folded and leaning against a radiator, wore the wry, slightly amused, slightly condescending expression that most doctors reserve for all those who are not also doctors. April Wednesday sat, quietly and alone, in a corner chair.

From the silence that followed it was clear that none of the gentlemen present saw it any differently.

Richards's geniality yielded to a certain amount of testiness. 'You, Hagenbach, what do you propose to do?'

Hagenbach restrained himself. Even though he was the head of the FBI he had to pay his due respect, albeit lip-service respect, to the Vice-President.

'I suggest we await the transcription of Revson's message, sir.'

'Transcription! Transcription! Was it necessary for this man of yours to complicate things by sending in code?'

'On the face of it, no. Revson has a near-mania for secrecy, that must be admitted, and is extraordinarily security-conscious. The same might be said about myself. Agreed, the message came through with safety and ease. On the other hand, as Miss Wednesday here has testified, Branson did contemplate searching the ambulance. With the proverbial toothcomb, he might have come up with something. But not with this microfilm.' He looked up as a young man, dressed in the immaculate conservative grey of a Wall Street broker, came through the doorway and handed him two typed sheets of paper.

'Sorry it took so long, sir. It was a bit difficult.'

'So is Revson.' Hagenbach read quickly through the papers, totally oblivious of the impatience of the others. He looked up at the young man. 'You like and you value your position in our organization, Jacobs?'

'You don't have to say that, sir.'

Hagenbach tried to smile but, as ever, failed to crack the ice barrier. 'I apologize.' It was a measure of Hagenbach's concern over the matter in hand that he had never previously been heard to say sorry to anyone.

'You don't have to say that either, sir.' Jacobs left the room.

Hagenbach said: 'This is what Revson says. "To give you the maximum time to obtain what I require for my immediate needs, I will state those first of all." '

Admiral Newson coughed. 'Do your subordinates usually address you in such a peremptory tone?'

'Not usually. He goes on: "I want four hundred yards of blue or green thin cord, cylindrical waterfront containers for written messages and a variably hooded morse-flashlight. Then I would like an aerosol, two pens – one white, one red, – and a CAP air pistol. Please order those immediately. Without them, I cannot hope to operate." '

General Carter said: 'Goobledook. What are those terms supposed to mean?'

Hagenbach said: ' I am not sure if I should tell you. That does not refer to you personally, general. Senior officers, cabinet ministers and, of course, senior police officers, are entitled to be privy to such information. But there are – ah – civilians present.'

O'Hare said mildly: 'Doctors don't talk. What's more they don't leak secret information to the press either.'

Hagenbach favoured him with a very old-fashioned look then said to April: 'And you, Miss Wednesday?'

She said: 'I'd talk my head off if you as much as showed me a pair of thumb-screws. You wouldn't have to put them on, showing would be quite enough. Otherwise, no.'

Hagenbach said to Hendrix: 'How's Branson with thumb-screws and young ladies?'

'No way. Master criminal though he is he has a remarkable reputation for gallantry towards women. He has never carried out a robbery where a woman might be involved, far less hurt.'

'But Mr Revson told me—'

'I rather fancy,' Hagenbach said, 'that Revson wanted you to act scared. So he threw a scare into you.'

April Wednesday was indignant: 'Has he no scruples?'

'In private life, a model of integrity. On business – well, if he has scruples he has so far hidden the fact very well. As to those objects he asked for, the aerosol contains exactly the same knock-out nerve gas that Branson used with such effect on the bridge. No permanent damage whatsoever – the presence of Miss Wednesday testifies to that. The pens – they look like ordinary felt pens – fire tiny tipped needles that also knock out people.'

Admiral Newson said: 'Why two colours?'

'The red knocks you out a bit more permanently.'

'One assumes that a "bit more permanently" means

permanently.'

'Could happen. The air pistol – well, it has the advantage of almost complete silence.'

'And the CAP bit?'

Hagenbach's hesitation betrayed a degree of reluctance.

'It means the bullets are tipped.'

'Tipped with what?'

Hagenbach's reluctance turned into something close to embarrassment.

'Cyanide.'

After a brief and understandable silence Richards said heavily: 'This Revson of yours. Is he a direct descendant of Attila the Hun?'

'He is an extremely effective operative, sir.'

'Loaded down with a lethal armoury like that, I don't for a moment doubt it. He has killed?'

'So have thousands of police officers.'

'And what's his score to date?'

'I really couldn't say, sir. In his reports, Revson lists only the essentials.'

'Only the essentials.' Richards's echo had a hollow ring to it. He shook his head and said no more.

'If you will excuse me for a moment.' Hagenbach wrote quickly on a notepad, opened the door and handed the note to a man outside. 'Have those items here within the hour.' He returned and picked up the transcript again.

'To continue. "In what little time I've had I've tried to make an assessment of Branson's character. In original concept, planning, organization and execution, the man is quite brilliant. He would have made an excellent general, for his appreciation of both strategy and tactics is masterly. But nobody can be that good. He has his failings, which I hope can be used to bring him down. He has a divine belief in his own infallibility. This belief carries with it the seeds of his own destruction. No one is infallible. Second, he is possessed of a colossal vanity. He could just as easily have held those TV interviews – I've only seen one of Branson's love affairs with the public but there are bound to be more – at, say, the south tower – but, no, he had to have it smack in the middle, surrounded by his own private press corps. In his place I would have had the whole press corps off the bridge in five minutes. It seems it just has not occurred to him that the ranks of the press corps may have been infiltrated. Third, he should have searched the doctor and Miss Wednesday and then the ambulance, if necessary throwing every single item of medical equipment into the Golden Gate, before allowing it to leave the bridge: in other words, he is not security-conscious enough.

' "How to deal with them? I have no idea yet. I would like some guidance. I have suggestions but I don't think any of them is practical.

' "No one can cope with seventeen heavily armed men. But of those seventeen only two matter. Some of the other fifteen are bright but only Branson and Van Effen are natural leaders. Those two I could kill." '

'Kill!' April Wednesday's shocked green eyes stared out of her pale face. 'The man's a monster.'

Hagenbach was dry. 'At least, he's a realistic monster.' He read on. ' "It's feasible, but unwise. The others would then almost certainly over-react and I wouldn't care to be responsible for the health of the President and his friends. This is a second last resort.

' "Would it be possible to have a submarine standing by under the bridge during the hours of darkness, with only the top of the conning tower showing? I could certainly pass messages and pick up anything I wanted that way. What else, I don't know. I can't for instance, visualize the President descending two hundred feet of rope ladder. He'd fall off after ten feet.

' "When Branson's men are fixing the charges would it be possible to send a two thousand volt jolt through the cables? I know this would electrify the entire bridge but those standing on the roadway or inside the coaches should be safe enough." '

Richards said: 'Why two thousand volts?'

Hagenbach sounded almost apologetic. 'Electric chair voltage.'

'I owe an apology to the shade of Attila.'

'Yes. "One drawback to this is that someone, say the President, might be leaning his elbows on the side of the bridge or sitting on a crash barrier. That would mean a new presidential election. I need expert advice. Or could we aim a laser beam at the charges when in position? The beam would certainly cut through the canvas. If the charge were to fall on to the bridge it would certainly detonate on impact but as most of the explosive force would be dissipated in thin air, damage to the roadway would not be severe. It is sure that it wouldn't bring the bridge down. Trouble is, the laser beam might detonate the charge instead. Please advise.

' "Under suitable cover would it be possible to introduce men into the tower? Natural fog would be fine. Phoney oil fire depending on the direction of the wind? I don't know. But the thing is to get men to the top, return the lift and then cut off the power to the elevators. Any person who gets to the top after five hundred odd feet of ladders isn't going to be in much shape to do anything.

' "Is it possible to introduce some form of knock-out drugs in the food? Something that would lay them out for half an hour, maybe an hour and not too fast-acting? If anyone were to keel over with the first bite you can imagine Branson's reaction. The individual food trays would have to be marked so that seventeen of them would go to the seventeen for whom they were intended." '

Hagenbach looked at O'Hare. 'There are such drugs?'

'I'm sure of it. The concoction of Mickey Finns is not my speciality, but Dr Isaacs – he's the chief of the Drugs and Narcotics Section – knows as much about those brews as anyone in the country. Catherine de Medici could never have coped with him.'

'That's useful.' Hagenbach returned his attention to the final brief section of the transcript. ' "Please let me have your suggestions. All I myself can really do at the moment is to try to deactivate the radio trigger that sets off the charges without leaving any signs that it has been tampered with. That in itself should be simple. It's getting at the damned thing that's difficult. It has, of course, to be in one of the helicopters and those are bathed in light both night and day and are heavily guarded. I'll try." That's all.'

Newson said: 'You mentioned a second last resort. What's the last resort?'

'Your guess is as good as mine. If he has a last resort, he's keeping it to himself. Now, sooner than pass those notes around I'll have them Xeroxed. Minutes only and you'll each have a copy.' He left the room, approached Jacobs, the man who had handed him the typescript, and said quietly: 'Have this Xeroxed. Ten copies.' He pointed to the last paragraph. 'Blank this off. And for God's sake make sure that this original gets back to me and not anyone else.'

Jacobs was back in the promised few moments. He distributed six and handed the remaining copies and the original to Hagenbach, who folded the original and stuck it in an inside pocket. Then all seven carefully studied the report. And again. And again.

General Carter said, almost complainingly: 'Revson certainly doesn't leave me very much for my imagination to work on. Candidly, he doesn't leave anything. Maybe it's just not one of my days.'

'Then it's not one of mine either,' Newson said. 'Your man seems to have covered the ground pretty comprehensively, Hagenbach. Sounds like a very useful man to have on our side.'

'He is. But even Revson requires room to manoeuvre. He has none.'

Quarry said, tentatively: 'I know this is not my field but it occurs to me that the key lies in the helicopters. We have the means to destroy those?'

Carter said: 'That's no problem. Planes, guns, rockets, wire-guided anti-tank missiles. Why?'

'That's the only way Branson and his men can leave. And as long as he remains on the bridge he can't detonate his charges. So what happens then?'

Carter looked at the Secretary of the Treasury without admiration.

'I can think of three things. First, Branson would call for a mobile crane, have it dump the choppers into the Golden Gate and demand two replacements within the hour or he'd send us a neat little parcel containing the President's ears. Second, whether it's a shell, rocket or missile, it's impossible to localize or contain the blast effect and some innocent bystanders might end up in the same condition as the choppers. Third, has it occurred to you that though the blast might well destroy the radio-activating device for the explosive charge, it might equally well trigger it off? Even with only one end of one cable gone that bridge is going to sag and assume a crazy angle in nothing flat, and nothing that is not nailed down would have a hope of remaining on that bridge. If that were to happen, Mr Secretary, and the President and his guests knew you were the man responsible, I don't think that their last thoughts of you, as they sat there in their coach at the bottom of the Golden Gate, would be very charitable ones.'

Quarry sighed. 'I'd better stick to counting my pennies. I told you this wasn't my field.'

Richards said: 'I suggest we all have twenty minutes' silent meditation and see what we come up with.'

They did just that and when the twenty minutes were up Hagenbach said: 'Well?'

All, apparently, was not well. The silence was profound.

'In that case, I suggest we start considering which are the less awful of Revson's options.'

II

The return of the ambulance to the centre of the bridge at about six o'clock in the evening was greeted with warmth and interest. Even being in the spotlight of the eyes of the world loses its dramatic effect if one has nothing to do. Branson's TV broadcasts apart, the middle of the bridge offered little in the way of entertainment.

When April, pale-faced and still apparently shaken, stepped from the ambulance, Branson was the first to greet her.

'How do you feel?'

'I feel such a fool.' She rolled up a sleeve to exhibit the punctures O'Hare had inflicted upon her earlier in the day. 'Two little pricks and I'm as right as rain.'

She walked away and sat down rather heavily on one of the many chairs scattered around her. Her colleagues gathered round.

Branson said to O'Hare: 'She doesn't look as right as rain to me.'

'If you mean she's still not back to normal, I agree. Same appearance, different causes. Last time you saw her she was on a high: now it's a low. My guess was right, it seems – just an emotional trauma. She's been sound asleep for the past two hours under heavy sedation. Dopey, that's all. Dr Huron, the psychiatrist, didn't want her to return, but she made such a damned noise about not getting back and this being her last chance or whatever that he decided that it might be better for her to return. No worry. I've brought back enough of the same sedative to last us for a week out here.'

'For the sake of all of us, let's hope you won't need a quarter of it.'

Revson waited until the last of April's welcomers had left her for the TV, a show of peculiar interest to all as the programme was devoted exclusively to a re-run of Branson's early afternoon broadcast. Nobody, Revson was unsurprised to observe, was more interested than Branson himself. But then Branson had no more to occupy his time than anyone else. The only person who seemed remotely active was Chrysler, who visited the rear coach at regular intervals. He wondered why.

Revson sat beside the girl. She looked at him coldly.

He said: 'What's the matter with you?' She remained silent. 'Don't tell me. Somebody's been turning you against me.'

'Yes. You. I don't like killers. Especially I don't like killers who plan their next murders cold-bloodedly in advance.'

'Come, come. That's putting it a bit strongly.'

'Is it? Cyanide guns? Lethal pens? Shot through the back, I should imagine.'

'My, my, we are bitter. Three things. First, those weapons are used only in acute emergency and then only to save lives, to stop bad people killing good people, although perhaps you would rather have it the other way round. Second, it doesn't matter to a dead man where he has been shot. Third, you have been eavesdropping.'

'I was invited to listen.'

'People make mistakes. Clearly, they invited the wrong person. I could be flippant and say I owe a duty to the taxpayer, but I'm not in the mood.' April looked at the hard face, listened to the voice from which all trace of the normal bantering warmth had vanished and realized with apprehension that indeed he was not in the mood. 'I have a job to do, you don't know what you're talking about, so we'll dispense with your moral strictures. I assume you brought the equipment I asked for. Where is it?'

'I don't know. Dr O'Hare does. For some reason he didn't want me to know in case we were questioned and the ambulance searched.'

'For some reason! For an obvious and excellent reason. O'Hare is no fool.' A flush touched the pale cheeks but he ignored it. 'All of it?'

'So I believe.' She tried to speak stiffly.

'Never mind your wounded pride. And don't forget you're in this up to your lovely neck. Hagenbach have any instructions for me?'

'Yes. But he didn't tell me. He told Dr O'Hare.' Her voice was acid or bitter or both. 'I suppose that makes Mr Hagenbach no fool either.'

'Don't take those things so much to heart.' He patted her hand and smiled warmly. 'You've done an excellent job. Thank you.'

She tried a tentative smile. 'Maybe you are a little bit human after all, Mr Revson.'

'Paul. One never knows.' He smiled again, rose and left. At least, he thought, he was semi-human enough not to inflict further damage upon her *amour propre* by telling her that the last little bit of by-play had been purely for the benefit of Branson who had momentarily lost interest in the screen – he was not then on camera – and was casting a speculative look at them. Not that that necessarily meant anything suspicious or sinister. Branson was much given to casting speculative looks at everybody. April was beautiful and he may well have thought that she was wasting this beauty on the wrong company.

Revson sat on a seat not far from Branson and watched the last twenty minutes of the broadcast. The inter-cutting between the presidential group and the top of the south tower had been most skilfully done and the overall impact was all that Branson could ever have wished. Branson watched it intently. His face betrayed no particular sign of satisfaction, but then Branson's face registered precisely what he wanted it to and was no mirror of his inner thoughts and feelings. When the broadcast finished Branson rose and stopped briefly by Revson's chair.

'Revson, isn't it?' Revson nodded. 'And how does all this strike you?'

'Just the same as it strikes a million other people, I guess.' This was it, Revson thought, this is one part of his Achilles' heel. Branson knew he was a genius but he had no objection to people saying so. 'A feeling of total unreality. This just can't be happening.'

'But it is, isn't it? A very satisfactory beginning, don't you think?'

'I can quote?'

'Certainly. Call it an exclusive if you want. How do you see the scenario developing?'

'Just as you have programmed it. I can't see anything to stop you. You have them, most unfortunately, at your total mercy.'

'Most unfortunately?'

'What else? I don't want to overdo the American citizen bit and although you may be a master criminal, a genius in your own immoral fashion, to me you're still a crook, a crook so bent as to make a spiral staircase look like a fireman's ladder.'

'I rather like that. I may quote you in turn?' Branson seemed genuinely gratified. One could hardly have called him thin-skinned.

'There's no verbal copyright.'

'Alas, universal disapproval, not to say disapprobation, would seem to be my lot.' Branson didn't sound too unhappy about it. 'That's a most unusual camera you have there.'

'Almost, but not quite unique.'

'May I have a look at it?'

'If you wish. But if you want to examine it for the reasons I imagine you want to examine it then you're about four hours too late.'

'What is that supposed to mean?'

'It means that your very able lieutenant, Van Effen, has the same nasty suspicious mind as you have. He has already taken my camera apart.'

'No radios? No offensive weapons?'

'Look for yourself.'

'That won't be necessary now.'

'A question. I don't want to inflate your already super-expanded ego—'

'Don't you think you might be taking chances. Revson?'

'No. You have the reputation of being a non-violent criminal.' Revson waved his arm. 'Why all this? You could have made a fortune in any business you cared to enter.'

Branson sighed. 'I tried it. Business is so dull, don't you think? This at least gives me the opportunity to exercise most of my capacities.' He paused. 'You're a bit odd, yourself. A cameraman. You don't look, act or speak like one.'

'How's a cameraman supposed to look, act and speak? You look in the mirror when you shave. Do you see a criminal? I see a Wall Street Vice-President.'

'*Touché*. What's your paper or magazine?'

'Free-lance, but I'm accredited to the London *Times*.'

'But you're American?'

'News has no boundaries. Not any longer. I prefer to work the foreign beat, where the action is.' Revson smiled faintly. 'At least, until today. That used to mean South-East Asia. Not any more. Europe and the Middle East.'

'So what are you doing here?'

'Pure happenstance. Just passing through, you might say, from New York to a special assignment in China.'

'When are you due to leave for there?'

'Tomorrow.'

'Tomorrow? You'll want to get off the bridge tonight. As I've said, members of the media are free to leave whenever they choose.'

'You, Branson, must be out of your mind.'

'China can wait?'

'China can wait. Unless, of course, you're planning to kidnap Chairman Mao.'

Branson smiled the smile that never touched his eyes and walked away.

III

Revson, camera poised, stood outside the open front right door of the rear coach. He said: 'Do you mind?'

Chrysler turned round. He looked at Revson in some surprise, then smiled. 'Why me for this honour?'

'Because my camera is tired of taking photographs of Branson and the assorted big-wigs. Mind? I'm now compiling a rogues' gallery of Branson's henchmen.' Revson smiled to remove offence. 'You're Chrysler, aren't you? The telecommunications expert?'

'If that's what they call me, yes.'

Revson took two or three shots, thanked Chrysler, and moved away. For good measure and local colour, he took some more pictures of Branson's men. They all seemed to have been infected by Branson's massive self-confidence and cheerfully, in some cases almost eagerly, acceded to Revson's requests. After the last of those shots he crossed to the west side of the bridge, sat on the crash barrier and lit a ruminative cigarette.

After a few minutes O'Hare, hands thrust deep in his white coat, came strolling by. Hundreds of pictures and thousands of words of reports had already been dispatched by the south tower and there were at least twenty of the media men – and women – who now had nothing better to do who were strolling aimlessly up and down the centre of the bridge. Revson took a couple of routine shots of O'Hare, who came and sat beside him.

He said: 'I saw you talking to Miss Wednesday. Suffering from a degree of pique, is she?'

'Our April could be happier. You have it all?'

'Both weapons and instructions.'

'Everything I asked for is camouflaged?'

'I would say so. The two pens are clipped to my medical clipboard, there for anyone to see. We doctors are models of efficiency. The gun with the tipped bullets is in the cardiac arrest unit. This is wax-sealed and the seal has to be broken before the unit can be opened. The unit is sealed. Not that it would matter very much if it were opened. The gun lies in a false bottom and you have to know how to open it. I mean, it can't be done by accident. You have to know. I know.'

'You seem to be positively enjoying youself, doctor.'

'Well, yes. It makes a change from treating ingrowing toenails.'

'I hope you'll enjoy coming under the heading of "Classified" for the rest of your life. How come you carry those peculiar units in your hospital?'

'We don't. But your director appears to be on very close terms with his counterpart in the CIA. I tell you, we were completely taken over by experts.'

'That means you're double classified for life. My cord and containers?' O'Hare seemed a mile away.

'My cord and containers?' O'Hare returned to the world.

'Modesty compels me to admit that I came up with this one. Four containers. Empty. Lab. samples printed on the outside. Who's going to question that? The cord is wrapped round a square wooden framework with two hooks and two lures attached to one end.'

'You're going fishing over the side of the bridge?'

'I'm going fishing. It can get quite boring out here, you know.'

'Something tells me it's not going to be that way long. I suppose it's unnecessary to ask you about the nerve gas?'

O'Hare smiled broadly. 'I'd rather you did, actually.'

'Must you speak English English?'

'I told you. London educated. It's an aerosol can, clamped just above my note-desk. Anyone can see it. Product, ostensibly, of a nationally-known aerosol company. People called Prestige Fragrance of New York. Rather charming, really. The colour, I mean. Forest brown, I believe. A scaled-down version of their seven-ounce can. Freon pressure three times normal. Effective range ten feet.'

'Do the Prestige people know about this?'

'Heavens, no. The CIA are not overly concerned with patent rights.' O'Hare smiled, almost dreamily. 'On the back of the can it says "fragrant and piquant" and "keep away from children". On the front it says "Sandalwood". Can't you just see Branson or any of his minions who don't know what sandalwood smells like giving themselves an exploratory whiff?'

'No, I can't. I'll pick up the pens later tonight. Now, what were Hagenbach's instructions?'

'Hagenbach and company. A committee meeting and an agreed decision. The Vice-President was there, along with

Admiral Newson, General Carter, Hendrix, Quarry and Milton.'

'And yourself and April Wednesday.'

'We plebs know our place. Total silence on our part. First off, there's no possibility of electrifying the bridge. Nothing to do with the possibility of a President or King sitting where we are now and having their pants roasted. The voltage could be produced, but not the wattage. Not for umpteen thousand tons of steel. Besides, the potential victims would have to be earthed. A bird can perch in perfect safety on a high-tension wire.

'Second piece of expert advice was about laser beams. You wondered if they would slice through the canvas wrapping of the explosive belts. Certainly, say the boys in Berkeley. But the tremendous heat generated when a laser beam strikes a solid object would turn the bridge wire – I think that's what they called it – in the detonator white-hot immediately.'

'Poof?'

'As you so rightly observe, "poof". Four things they did agree on, however.

'A submarine they can provide. Apparently, it will call for some critical underwater navigation to get there and a fair bit of fancy juggling to keep the boat in position once it gets there. Apart from the tides there are lots of very nasty currents in the Golden Gate. But the admiral reckons he has just the man for the job. And in the absence of any instructions to the contrary they propose to park this boat under the front coach, your press coach, that is.'

'My omission. They're right, of course.' Revson glanced idly round but no one was paying any undue attention to them except General Cartland, a physical fitness fanatic who was counter-marching briskly to and fro along the central section of the bridge. He gave them a keen glance in passing but that signified nothing. General Cartland invariably gave everyone a keen glance in passing. Hansen, the energy czar, with the excess nervous energy to burn, was also engaged in the same exercise, but his attention was devoted exclusively to the toes of his shoes. He did not walk with Cartland. There was no antipathy between the two men: they simply had nothing in common.

O'Hare continued. 'They agreed with your suggestion that the south tower be occupied. As you didn't specify whether it was the east or west section which should be occupied, they're a bit in the dark. The meteorological forecast is rather good. Heavy fog is expected before dawn and to remain until about ten in the morning. They'd better be right. The wind tomorrow will be westerly so that any cover from the smoke of burning oil will be out of the question. But they still don't know which section of the tower to occupy.'

'One item I forgot to ask you about. It was about this hooded flashlight with the variable shutter that—'

'I have it.'

'If Branson and company came across it?'

'Medical requisite, my dear fellow. Eye examination, dilation of pupils and so forth. You know morse?'

Revson was patient. 'I just want to read books at night in the coach.'

'Sorry. One of my off-moments. From the east side of the bridge aim approximately forty-five degrees right. They'll have two men on watch in relays, all night. They can't signal you back, of course, so for "message acknowledged and understood" they'll send up a firework rocket from Chinatown. Followed by lots of others so as not to arouse any suspicions. The setting off of fireworks, bangers, crackers or whatever you call them is illegal in this city, but in Chinatown the police bend a tolerant and indulgent eye towards it. Chinese national pastime, you know. You should see the Chinese New Year. Shortly after I arrived – just a few months ago—'

Revson was even more patient. 'I am a San Franciscan.'

'Ah, well. But you still don't know which section of the south tower—'

'I'll find out.'

'You seem very sure of yourself?'

'Not at all. But I'm sure of our April Wednesday. Branson has given her more than a passing glance. I shall have her employ her feminine wiles to discover which cable is next for the explosive treatment. And when.'

'You're still very sure of yourself. Now. Your suggestion about drugged food. Unanimous approval. This evening meal. Dr Isaacs – he's our narcotics wizard in the hospital – has been busy stirring up his witch's cauldron. Seventeen unpleasant surprises.'

'Very quick work.' Revson was uneasy. 'How are the surprises to be identified?'

'No problem. The usual airline plastic food in the usual airline plastic trays. Those trays have carrying lugs. The bad trays, if I may put it that way, will have indentations on the underside of the lugs. Tiny, but enough to be detected by normally sensitive finger-tips.'

'Well, doctor, you haven't been wasting your time, that I have to say. Obviously we'll have to be very careful. If anything can be wrong it will go wrong – one of Parkinson's laws or something like that. I shall appoint myself head waiter – with Branson's prior approval. Second, you will have April Wednesday in for a routine check as the meal wagon arrives and will remain there until the meals have been distributed. In the ambulance, I mean.'

'Why?'

'Parkinson's Law. If something goes wrong, you two would be the first under suspicion – you've left the bridge and returned. Third, I can get word to the presidential coach.'

'How?'

'I'll figure a way.'

'And the press coach?'

'No guarantee. I'm no master-mind. If one or two of them get the wrong trays – well, I can take care of the one or two villains who get the right trays.'

O'Hare looked at Revson with a certain lack of admiration. 'You don't care how you use people, do you?'

'I have things to do and I do what I can. I weigh the odds but I don't know what the odds are.' Revson paused. 'I'm fighting in the dark. I'm a blind man, if you like, and my hands are tied behind me. Perhaps you'd care to think again about your last remark.'

O'Hare thought. 'I apologize. Your pens and the flashlight will be waiting whenever you care to step by. And one last thing. They approve your intention to neutralize the triggering device.'

'I appreciate that. You don't have any magic potion that will make me invisible?'

'Alas, no.' O'Hare turned and walked away.

IV

Revson lit and smoked another cigarette, tossed the butt over the side, rose and sauntered across to the rows of chairs. April was still sitting where he had left her. He took the seat beside her.

He said: 'When the evening meal wagon comes I want you to go to the ambulance. For a check-up.'

She didn't look at him. 'Yes, sir. Whatever you say, sir.'

Revson breathed deeply. 'I shall try to conceal my slow burn, what the Victorians would call my mounting exasperation. I thought we had parted friends.'

'I don't much care for being a mindless puppet.'

'We're all puppets. I, too, do what I'm told. I don't always like it, but I have a job to do. Please don't make my job more difficult than it already is. The doctor will tell you why you're there. He'll also tell you when to leave.'

'Yes, Mr Revson. As a forcibly co-opted member of your secret service, I do what I'm told.'

Revson decided against any more deep breathing. 'Before that, I'd like you to have a word with our Mr Branson. I fancy he has one, if not two, of his cold codfish eyes upon you.'

She turned her head slowly and gave him the full treatment of her luminous green eyes. 'And you, of course, don't?'

Revson held her gaze for some seconds, then considered the tarmac of the Golden Gate Bridge. 'I try to look the other way. Besides, my eyes are not those of a cod. Find out from him on which cable he intends to affix his next explosive charge – and when. Wait a few moments after I've left and then make a casual encounter.'

He looked at her again. The eyes were bigger and greener than ever and held an almost mischievous glint. She was smiling. It wasn't much of a smile, but it was there. She said: 'You'll end up by making me as devious and cunning as yourself.'

'Heaven forfend.' Revson rose and made his way back to his previous seat on the crash barrier, which was less than twenty yards from the demarcation painted line where a man in the middle of the bridge, with a Schmeisser machine-pistol, kept constant vigil. General Cartland, military stride *in excelsis*, was approaching. Revson stood, lifted his camera and snapped off three quick shots.

He said: 'May I have a word with you, sir?'

Cartland stopped. 'You may not. No interview, exclusive or otherwise. I may be a spectator in this damned circus, but I'm no performer.' He walked on.

Revson was deliberately brusque. 'You'd better speak to me, general.'

Cartland stopped again. His glacial stare drilled through Revson's eyes into the wide blue yonder.

'What did you say?' Each word was spaced out slowly and carefully. Revson was on the parade ground, a court martialled officer about to be stripped of insignia and buttons and have his sword broken over a knee.

'Don't ignore me, sir.' Deference now replaced brusqueness. 'Hagenbach wouldn't like it.'

'Hagenbach?' Cartland and Hagenbach, men possessed of almost identical casts of mind, were as intimate as two loners could ever be. 'What's Hagenbach to you?'

'I suggest you come and sit beside me, general. Please relax and act casual.'

It was entirely alien to Cartland's nature to relax and 'act casual', but he did his best. He sat and said: 'I repeat, what's Hagenbach to you?'

'Mr Hagenbach is very important to me. He pays my salary when he remembers.'

Cartland looked at him for a long moment then, as if to demonstrate that he was not totally like Hagenbach, he smiled. His smile was nowhere near as frosty as his face. 'Well, well. A friend in need is a friend indeed. Your name?'

'Paul Revson.'

'Revson? Revson! James has talked to me about you. And not only once.'

'Sir, you must be the only person in the United States who knows his first name.'

Cartland nodded his agreement. 'There aren't many around.

You know he has you slated for the hot seat in five years' time?'

'I should live that long.'

'Well, well.' Cartland seemed to be very fond of 'Well, well'. 'A very neat job of infiltration, if I may say so.'

'The chief's idea, not mine.' Revson stood up and snapped off some more photographs. He said, apologetically: 'Local colour. You will please not tell any of your colleagues on the presidential coach—'

'Colleagues? Clowns!'

'You will please not tell any of the clowns that you have met me.'

'I retract my remark. The President is a personal friend.'

'That is known, sir. The President and the clowns. I would not include the Mayor among the latter. If you want to talk to them privately, take a walk. Your coach is bugged.'

'If you say so, Revson.'

'I know so, sir. There's a tape recorder whirling away busily in the rear coach. You heard it. I didn't.'

'I heard it. I've never heard of you.'

'General Cartland, you should join our organization.'

'You think?'

'I retract in turn. A Chief of Staff can go nowhere except down.'

Cartland smiled again. 'To mint a new phrase, tell me all.'

Revson stood, walked away some paces, took more pictures, returned, sat down and told all. When he had finished, General Cartland said: 'What do you want me to do?'

'I don't want. One does not give instructions to the Chief of Staff.'

The Chief of Staff became the Chief of Staff. 'The point, Revson.'

'Take your sedentary friends for a walk. Tell them about the coach being bugged. Tell them how to identify their own safe food trays.'

'No problem. That all?'

'One last thing, General Cartland. I'm a bit hesitant about this, but as you would say, to the point. It is known – at least I know – that you habitually carry a gun.'

'Past tense. I have been relieved of it.'

'You still have your holster?'

'I have.'

'I'll give you a replacement that will fit very snugly into your .22.'

'You do your homework, Revson. It will be a pleasure.'

'The bullets are cyanide-tipped, sir.'

Cartland didn't hesitate. 'Still a pleasure.'

— 8 —

THE EVENING meal wagon arrived at seven-thirty. The occupants of the presidential coach were close to the north painted barrier, huddled in what appeared to be deep conversation. April Wednesday, under the watchful eye of a guard, made her quiet way towards the ambulance. Revson sat, apparently half-dozing, in a chair. He started as a hand touched his shoulder.

'Food, my China-bound friend.' Branson, with his smile.

Revson sat upright. 'Wine, one trusts?'

'The best vintages that money can buy.'

'Whose money?'

'Irrelevancies bore me.' Branson was regarding him with an appraising eye.

Revson stood and looked around him. 'Your honoured guests along there—'

'They are being informed.'

'You might have at least given them time to have their pre-dinner cocktail. Well, not the President's Arab friends—'

'Time for that. The food is in hot cupboards.' Branson did some more appraisal. 'You know, Revson, you interest me. You might even say you intrigue me. There's a certain – what shall I call it – intransigence about you. I still don't see you as a man behind a camera.'

'And I don't see you as the man behind the most massive hold-up of all time. Too late for you to go back to Wall

Street?'

Branson clapped Revson on the shoulder. 'On behalf of the President, let's go and sample some of the superior vintages.'

'Explain yourself.'

'Who knows what our Medici friends in the Presidio might be up to?'

'I hadn't thought of that. You trust nobody?'

'No.'

'Me? A guinea-pig?'

'Yes. You and Cartland make me uneasy.'

'A weakness. You should never confess to them. Lead on, MacDuff.'

Arrived at the meal wagon Branson said to the white and blue striped attendant: 'Your name?'

The attendant gave an odd sort of sketchy salute. 'Tony, Mr Branson.'

'What wines do you have?'

'Three reds, three white, Mr Branson.'

'Array them before us, Tony, Mr Revson here is an internationally-known *sommelier*. A judge of wine, in other words.'

'Sir.'

Six bottles and six glasses appeared on the counter. Revson said: 'Just a quarter in each glass. I don't want to fall off the bridge during the night. Have you bread and salt?'

'Yes, Mr Revson.' Tony clearly regarded himself as being in the presence of lunatics.

Interspersed with the bread and salt Revson sampled all six vintages. At the end he said: 'All uniformly excellent. I must tell the French vintners about this. The best Californian matches up with the best French.'

Branson said: 'It would appear that I owe you an apology, Revson.'

'No way. Let's do it again. Or will you join me in one of the – ah – approved wines?'

'It would seem safe to do so.' Tony clearly considered himself in the presence of a couple of head cases.

'I suggest one of your own. A Gamay Beaujolais from your Almaden vineyards.'

'Ah.' Branson pondered. 'Tony?'

'Mr Revson has excellent taste, sir.'

They consumed their wines in a leisurely fashion. Branson said: 'I agree with both of your assessments. You are ready to serve dinner, Tony?'

'Yes, sir.' He smiled. 'I have already served one. About twenty minutes ago, I'd say. Mr Hansen. He snatched a plate and said that as the energy czar he needed energy.'

'It figures.' Branson turned a lazy head. 'In the coach, I presume?'

'No, sir. He took his tray across to the east crash barrier. There.' He followed his pointing finger then softly said: 'Jesus!'

'Jesus what?'

'Look.'

They looked. Hansen, slowly toppling off the barrier, fell to the roadway and lay there, his body jerking. Branson and Revson crossed the six road lanes and reached him in as many seconds.

Hansen was vomiting violently. They spoke to him, but he seemed incapable of answering. His body went into strange and frightening convulsions.

Revson said: 'Stay here. I'll get O'Hare.'

O'Hare and April were together in the ambulance when he arrived. Understandably enough, he was welcomed with lifted eyebrows.

Revson said: 'Quickly. I think that Mr Hansen – hungry, it seems – picked up the wrong dinner tray. He looks in pretty bad shape to me.'

O'Hare was on his feet. Revson barred his way.

'I think your Dr Isaacs has stirred up a more powerful brew than he imagined. If this is the effect it has – well, I want you to go across there and diagnose some form of food poisoning. Call in some chemical analyst or whatever you call them. Nobody, but nobody, must touch that food again. I don't want wholesale murder on my hands.'

'I understand.' O'Hare picked up his emergency bag and left at speed.

April said: 'What's gone wrong, Paul?'

'I don't know. Some foul-up. Maybe I'm to blame. Stay here.'

When he arrived across the bridge Branson was standing upright and O'Hare slowly straightening. Revson looked at them both then addressed himself to O'Hare. 'Well?'

O'Hare let go the limp wrist he was holding. 'I'm afraid that Mr Hansen is dead.'

'Dead?' For once, Branson was clearly shocked. 'How can he be dead?'

'Please. For the moment, I'm in charge. This plastic centre plate is almost empty. I assume that Hansen ate it all.'

O'Hare bent over the dead man and breathed deeply. His nose wrinkled. Very slowly, he straightened again.

'Can't be salmonella. That takes time. Not even botulinus. It's quick, but not this quick.' O'Hare looked at Branson. 'I want to talk to the hospital.'

'I don't understand. Perhaps you'd like to talk to me first?'

O'Hare sounded weary. 'I suppose. The smell – it comes from the pancreas – is unmistakable. Some form of food poisoning. I don't know. Doctors have their specialities and this is not one of mine. The hospital, please.'

'You don't mind if I listen in?'

'Listen in all you want.'

II

O'Hare was on the phone in the rear end of the presidential coach. Branson held the President's side-phone. Revson sat in the next deeply upholstered chair.

O'Hare said: 'How long will it take you to contact Hansen's private physician?'

'We're in contact now.'

'I'll wait.'

They all waited. They all looked at one another, while carefully not looking at one another. The phone became activated again.

'O'Hare?'

'Sir?'

'Hansen is – was – just recovering from his second – and almost fatal – heart attack.'

'Thank you, sir. That explains everything.'

'Not quite.' Branson was his old balanced self again. 'I

want two analytical chemists out here to determine the source of this infection, if that's what you would call it. The food tray, I mean. Separate examinations. If they disagree, one of them is going to go over the side.'

O'Hare sounded even more weary. 'Such specialists we have in San Francisco. I know two of the the top people. The only thing they have in common is their total disagreement with each other.'

'In which case they will both be thrown over the side. You will accompany them. Make contact now.'

O'Hare made contact. Revson said to Branson: 'Only an American would have this gift for making friends and influencing people.'

'I'll talk to you later. O'Hare?'

'They'll come. Only if you promise immunity. Damn it all and to hell, Branson, why should their lives be put at risk?'

Branson considered. 'Their lives will not be put at risk. Leave that phone. I want it.' He made a signal through the window. After a few seconds, Van Effen entered. He was carrying his Schmeisser in a rather unsympathetic manner. Branson moved to the rear.

He said: 'Let me talk to Hendrix.'

Not more than two seconds elapsed before Hendrix was on the phone.

'Hendrix?' Branson was his usual unemotional self. 'I have promised immunity to the doctors coming out here. I want you and the Vice-President to accompany them.' There was a brief delay, then Hendrix came through again on the intercom.

'Mr Richards agrees. But you are not to hold the Vice-President as a hostage.'

'I agree in turn.'

'Your word?'

'For what it's worth. You have to believe me, don't you? You're in no position to bargain.'

'No position. I have a dream, Branson.'

'I know. But I think handcuffs are so inelegant. I will see you in a very few minutes. Send out the TV truck. Alert the networks.'

'Again?'

'I think it very important that the nation should be made aware of the establishment's *modus operandi.*' Branson rested the phone.

III

In the communications wagon just off the Presidio, Hendrix in turn, rested his phone and looked at the six men clustered around him. He addressed himself to Hagenbach.

'Well, you have it. Hansen dead. Nobody's fault, really. How was anybody to know that he had a critical heart condition? And how – and why – did nobody know about it?'

Hagenbach said heavily: 'I knew. Like nearly all senior Government officials Hansen was intensely secretive about his physical health. He was in Bethseda twice in the last nine months and the second time was touch and go. It was reported that he was receiving treatment for overwork, exhaustion. So I think if anyone is to blame it's me.'

Quarry said: 'You're talking nonsense and you know it. Who could possibly have foreseen this? It's not your fault and it's certainly not Dr Isaacs's fault. He told us the drug was perfectly safe for any normal healthy adult. You cannot question the judgement of a man of his reputation. He wasn't to know that Hansen wasn't a normal healthy adult far less anticipating that Hansen would misguidedly pick up the wrong plate. And what's going to happen now?'

Hendrix said: 'It's obvious what's going to happen now. We seven are going to be publicly indicted as murderers.'

IV

The TV crew had arrived on the centre of the bridge but were, momentarily, inactive. The two specialist doctors were analysing the food and, despite O'Hare's predictions, for once seemed to be agreeing with each other. The President was talking quietly to the Vice-President. From the expressions on their faces it seemed they didn't have very much to talk about.

Branson was alone with Hendrix in the presidential coach.

Branson said: 'Do you honestly expect me to believe that you and Hagenbach know nothing about this?'

Hendrix said wearily: 'Nothing. There's been a botulinus outbreak down-town in the past few days.' He pointed towards the TV set in the middle of the roadway. 'If you watch that at all, you must have heard of it.' He pointed again towards the evening meal wagon where the two doctors were busily at work. 'They were convinced before arrival what the trouble was.' He refrained from adding that he'd told the doctors to find not more than a dozen cases of poisoning. 'You have lives on your hands, Branson.'

'Don't we all. Get on that phone there. Some more hot meals. The first three, taken by random sample, will be by the President, the King and the Prince. You do understand, don't you?'

V

Revson was in the ambulance with O'Hare and April Wednesday. She was lying blanket-covered on the hinged-down bed.

She said, drowsily: 'Did you have to do this to me?'

'Yes. You don't like thumb-screws.'

'No. Maybe you're not the monster I thought you were. But Dr O'Hare—'

'Dr O'Hare, as he would say in his own native tongue, is a different kettle of fish. What did Branson say?'

She said sleepily: 'Same cable. Bay side.'

Her eyelids closed. O'Hare took Revson by the arm. His voice was quiet. 'Enough.'

'How long?'

'Two hours. Not less.'

'The pens.'

O'Hare withdrew the pens from his clip-board. 'You do know what you're doing?'

'I hope.' He thought briefly, then said:

'You're going to be questioned.'

'I know. You want your torch?'

'Later.'

VI

Kylenski was the senior of the two doctors examining the food trays. He said to Branson: 'My colleague and I have found twelve infected food trays.'

Branson looked at Van Effen then back at Kylenski. 'That all? Twelve? Not seventeen?'

Kylenski had a grey beard, grey moustache and aquiline aristocratic stare. 'Twelve. Spoiled meat. Some form of botulinus. You don't even have to taste it. You can smell it. Well, I can. Apparently Hansen didn't.'

'Lethal?'

'In this concentration, normally, no. This infected food didn't kill Hansen. Well, not directly. But it was almost certainly responsible for reactivating this long-standing and severe heart ailment which did kill him.'

'What would the effect of this be on the average healthy adult?'

'Incapacitating. Violent vomiting, possibility of stomach haemorrhaging, unconsciousness or something pretty close to it.'

'So a man would be pretty helpless?'

'He'd be incapable of action. Most likely of thought, too.'

'What a perfectly splendid prospect. For some.' Branson looked again at Van Effen. 'What do you think?'

'I think I want to know what you want to know.' Van Effen turned to Kylenski. 'This poison or whatever it is – could it have been deliberately introduced?'

'Who on earth would want to do a thing like that?'

Branson said: 'Answer the question.'

'Any doctor specializing in this field, any research fellow, even a reasonably competent laboratory assistant could produce the necessary toxin culture.'

'But he would have to be a doctor or in some way associated with the medical profession? I mean, this would call for trained knowledge and laboratory facilities?'

'Normally, yes.'

Branson said to the meal wagon attendant: 'Come out from behind that counter, Tony.'

Tony came. His apprehension was unmistakable.

Branson said: 'It's not all that hot, Tony. It's turning quite cool, in fact. Why are you sweating?'

'I don't like all this violence and guns.'

'No one has offered you any violence or even pointed a gun at you, although I'm not saying that both of them aren't going to happen to you in the very near future. I suggest, Tony, that you are suffering from a guilty conscience.'

'Me? Conscience?' Tony actually mopped his brow; if his conscience wasn't troubling him something else clearly was. 'God's sake, Mr Branson—'

'Fairy stories are fairy stories but they don't run to a dozen coincidences at a time. Only a fool would accept that. But there had to be some way of identifying the poisoned plates. What way, Tony?'

'Why don't you leave him alone, Branson?' Vice-President Richards's voice was at once harsh and contemptuous. 'He's only a van driver.'

Branson ignored him. 'How were the plates to be identified?'

'I don't know! I don't! I don't even know what you are talking about!'

Branson turned to Kowalski and Peters. 'Throw him into the Golden Gate.' His voice was as level and conversational as ever.

Tony made an animal-like noise but offered no resistance as Kowalski and Peters took an arm apiece and began to march him away. His face was ashen and rivulets of sweat were now pouring down his face. When he did speak his voice was a harsh unbelieving croak.

'Throw me off the bridge! That's murder! Murder! In the name of God I don't know—'

Branson said: 'You'll be telling me next that you have a wife and three kids.'

'I've got nobody.' His eyes turned up in his head and his legs sagged under him until he had to be dragged across the roadway. Both the Vice-President and Hendrix moved in to intercept the trio. They stopped as Van Effen lifted his Schmeisser.

Van Effen said to Branson: 'If there was a way of identifying those plates, that would be important and dangerous information. Would you entrust Tony with anything like that?'

'Not for a second. Enough?'

'He'll tell anything he knows. I suspect it won't be much.' He raised his voice. 'Bring him back.'

Tony was brought back and released. He sagged wearily to the roadway, struggled with difficulty to his feet and clung tremblingly to the luncheon wagonette. His voice shook as much as his frame.

'I know nothing about the plates. I swear it!'

'Tell us what you do know.'

'I thought something was far wrong when they loaded the food into my van.'

'At the hospital?'

'The hospital? I don't work at the hospital. I work for Selznick's.'

'I know them. The caterers for open-air functions. Well?'

'I was told the food was ready when I got there. I'm usually loaded and away in five minutes. This time it took three-quarters of an hour.'

'Did you see anybody from the hospital when you were waiting at Selznick's?'

'Nobody.'

'You'll live a little longer, Tony. Provided you don't eat that damned food of yours.' He turned to O'Hare. 'Well, that leaves only you and the fragile Miss Wednesday.'

'You insinuating that either of us might have been carrying secret instructions from your alleged poisoners?' There was more contempt than incredulity in O'Hare's tone.

'Yes. Let's have Miss Wednesday here.'

O'Hare said: 'Leave her alone.'

'You said – who do you think is in charge here?'

'Where a patient of mine is concerned, I am. If you want her here, you'll have to carry her. She's asleep in the ambulance, under heavy sedation. Can't you take my word?'

'No. Kowalski, go check. You know, a couple of stiff fingers in the abdomen.'

Kowalski returned within ten seconds. 'Out like a light.'

Branson looked at O'Hare. 'How very convenient. Maybe you didn't want her subjected to interrogation?'

'You're a lousy psychologist, Branson. Miss Wednesday is not, as you know, cast in the heroic mould. Can you imagine anyone entrusting her with any vital information?' Branson made no reply. 'Apart from that, the only good thing that's ever been said about you is that you never molest women.'

'How do you know that?'

'Chief of Police Hendrix told me. He seems to know a lot about you.'

'You confirm that, Hendrix?'

Hendrix was curt. 'Why shouldn't I?'

Branson said: 'So that leaves only you, doctor.'

'As a prime suspect? You're losing your grip.' He nodded at Hansen's sheet-covered form on a stretcher. 'I don't want to sound sanctimonious but as a doctor my job is to save lives, not take them away. I have no wish to be struck off the medical register. Besides, I haven't left the ambulance since before the food wagon arrived. I couldn't very well be there identifying your damned food trays and be in the ambulance at the same time.'

Branson said: 'Kowalski?'

'I can vouch for that, Mr Branson.'

'But you were talking to people after you returned and before the food wagon arrived.'

Kowalski said: 'He did. To quite a few people. So did Miss Wednesday.'

'We can forget her. The good doctor here.'

'A fair number of people.'

'Anyone in particular? I mean long earnest chats, that sort of thing?'

'Yes.' Kowalski appeared to be extremely observant or have an uncomfortably good memory or both. 'Three. Two with Miss Wednesday—'

'Forget the lady. She'd plenty of time to talk to him in the ambulance to and from hospital. Who else?'

'Revson. A long talk.'

'Overhear anything?'

'No. Thirty yards away and downwind.'

'Anything pass between them?'

'No.' Kowalski was definite.

Branson said to O'Hare: 'What did you talk about?'

'Medical privilege.'

'You mean mind my own damned business?'

O'Hare said nothing. Branson looked at Revson.

'No medical privileges,' Revson said. 'Cabbages and kings. I've talked to at least thirty people, including your own men, since we arrived. Why single this out as a special case?'

'I was hoping you could tell me.'

'There's nothing to tell.'

'You're pretty cool, aren't you?'

'A clear conscience. You should try it some time.'

'And, Mr Branson.' Kowalski again. 'Revson also had a long talk with General Cartland.'

'Oh. More cabbages and kings, general?'

'No. We were discussing the possibilities of ridding this bridge of some of its more undesirable elements.'

'Coming from you, I can well believe it. A fruitful talk?'

Cartland looked at him in icy silence.

Branson looked thoughtfully at Van Effen. 'I have a feeling, just a feeling, mind you, that we have an infiltrator in our midst.'

Van Effen gazed at him with his impassive moonface and said nothing.

Branson went on: 'I think that would rule out the doctor. Apart from the fact that we've checked out on his credentials, I have the odd instinct that there is a trained agent loose on this bridge. That again would rule out O'Hare, who's just here by happenstance anyway. You share my instinct?'

'Yes.'

'Who?'

Van Effen didn't hesitate. 'Revson.'

Branson beckoned Chrysler. 'Revson here claims to be an accredited correspondent of the *Times* of London. How long would it take you to check that out?'

'Using the presidential tele-communications?'

'Yes.'

'Minutes.'

Revson said: 'I suppose I'm supposed to show a degree of high indignation, but I won't bother. Why me? Why assume it's any of the news media members? Why not one of your own men?'

'Because I hand-picked them personally.'

'Just the same way that Napoleon did his marshals. And

look how many of them turned against him in the end. How you can expect devoted loyalty from a bunch of cut-throats like this, however hand-picked, is beyond me.'

'You'll do for the moment,' Van Effen said comfortably. He touched Branson's arm and pointed to the west. 'We may not have all that much time.'

'You're right.' Dark, heavy, ominous clouds were rolling in from the Pacific, although still some miles distant. 'The audiences wouldn't like it at all if they were to see their President and Vice-President, not to mention their oil friends, sitting here getting soaked in a thunderstorm. Ask Johnson to organize the cameras and the seating.' He waited thoughtfully until Van Effen had done this then took him across to where Revson was standing alone. He said to Van Effen: 'Revson tells me that you have already searched his camera.'

'Yes. But I didn't take it to pieces.'

'Maybe we should.'

'And maybe you shouldn't.' For once, Revson let anger show. 'Do you know that it takes a man five years' training to learn just how to assemble one of those cameras? I'd rather you kept the damned thing for the duration of our stay here than have it ruined.'

'Call his bluff and have it stripped,' Branson said.

'I agree.' Van Effen said to Revson, almost soothingly. 'We'll have Chrysler do it. He's as close to a mechanical genius as anyone I know. It will be intact.' To Branson he said: 'I've also searched his carry-all, the upholstery of his seat, below the seat and the rack above. Clean.'

'Search him.'

'Search me?' More than a trace of truculence remained in Revson's face. 'I've already been searched.'

If there had been a grain of rice on Revson's person, including inside the coat lining, Van Effen wouldn't have missed it. Apart from keys, coins and an inoffensive little knife, all he came up with were papers.

'The usual,' Van Effen said. 'Driving licence, social security, credit cards, press cards—'

'Press cards,' Branson said. 'Any of them identify him with the London *Times*?'

'There's this.' Van Effen handed the card across to Branson. 'Looks pretty kosher to me.'

'If he is who or what we think he might be, he wouldn't be likely to hire the worst forger in town.' He handed the card back, a slight frown on his face. 'Anything else?'

'Yes.' Van Effen opened a long envelope. 'Airline ticket. For Hong Kong.'

'It wouldn't be dated for tomorrow?'

'It is. How did you know?'

'He told me so himself. What do you think?'

'I don't know.' For a moment, as Van Effen idly fingered Revson's felt pens both he and Branson were only a heart's beat from death. But Van Effen, his mind on something else, reclipped them and opened Revson's passport. He flipped rapidly through the pages. 'Certainly gets around. Lots of South-East Asia passports, last about two years ago. Near East immigration stamps galore. Not many European or London stamps, but that signifies nothing. They are an idle bunch across there and British and most European – Western European – passport officers only stamp your passports if they feel in need of the exercise. How does it all sound to you?'

'Ties in with what he told me himself. You?'

'If he's a bad one, I would call this an excessive cover-up. Why not Milwaukee? Or even San Francisco?'

Branson said: 'You a San Franciscan?'

'By adoption.'

Van Effen said: 'Who'd spend a dozen years travelling the world just to establish a background, an alibi like this?'

Chrysler came up. Branson looked at him in slight surprise. 'Through already?'

'The President has a hot line to London. I hope you don't mind. Revson's clean. He's a fully accredited correspondent of the London *Times*.'

Revson said to Chrysler: 'Branson wants you to take my camera to pieces. There's a time-bomb or a radio inside it. Watch you don't blow yourself up. After that, you'd better make damn sure you put it all together again.'

Chrysler received Branson's nod, smiled, took the camera and left. Revson said: 'Will that be all? Or do you want to unscrew my false heels?'

Branson wasn't amused. 'I'm still not satisfied. How am I to know that Kylenski here is not in cahoots with the poisoners? How am I to know that he was not instructed to find only a dozen poisoned plates so as to kill our suspicions? There should have been seventeen tampered trays. There should – there must be someone on the bridge capable of identifying them. I want you, Revson, to sample one of the trays that Kylenski has declared safe.'

'You want me – you want to kill me off with botulinus on the off-chance that Kylenski has made a mistake? I'm damned if I will. I'm no human guinea-pig.'

'Then we'll try some of them out on the President and his oil friends here. Royal guinea-pigs, if you will. This should make medical history. If they resist, we'll force-feed them.'

Revson was about to make the obvious point that they could force-feed him equally well but immediately changed his mind. Cartland had not yet had the opportunity to inform those in the presidential coach as to how the infected trays could be identified: O'Hare apart, he was the only one who could. Revson turned his palms upwards. 'God knows what you're after but I trust the two doctors here. If they say there are so many uncontaminated trays, I believe them. So you can have your plebeian guinea-pig.'

Branson looked at him closely. 'Why have you changed your mind?'

Revson said conversationally: 'You know, Branson, you're endlessly over-suspicious. From the expression of your lieutenant, Van Effen there, I would say that he agrees with me.' No harm could come, Revson thought, from sowing the odd seed of dissention. 'Some people might even interpret it as a sign of weakness, of uncertainty. I'm agreeing because I don't care so much for you. A chink in everybody's armour. I'm beginning to believe that your belief in your own infallibility may rest on rather shaky ground. Besides, plebs are expendable: Presidents and Kings are not.'

Branson smiled his confident smile and turned to Tony. 'Lay out ten of the uncontaminated plates on the counter.' Tony did so. 'Now, Revson, which one would you care to sample?'

'You're slipping, Branson. You've still the lingering suspicion that I might be able to identify the poisoned trays. Suppose you choose for me?' Branson nodded and pointed at one of the trays. Revson moved forward, lifted the indicated tray and sniffed it slowly and cautiously. The surreptitious movements of his finger-tips found no traces of tiny indentations on the underside of the plastic lugs. This tray was clean. He took a spoon, dug into the centre of what looked like a browned-over cottage pie, and sampled the meat. He grimaced, chewed, swallowed, then repeated the process. He laid down the tray in disgust.

Branson said: 'Not to your liking?'

'If I were in a restaurant I'd send this back to the kitchen. Better, I'd take it there and empty it over the chef's head – not that the person who made this could ever be called a chef.'

'Contaminated, you'd think?'

'No. Just plain bloody lousy.'

'Perhaps you'd care to sample another one?'

'No, I would not. Besides, you said, just one sample.'

Branson said persuasively: 'Come on. Be co-operative.'

Revson scowled but co-operated. The next tray, too, was clean. He went through the same performance and had no sooner done so when Branson handed him a third tray.

This one had indentations on the underside of the lugs.

Revson broke the skin, sniffed suspiciously, tasted a little and at once spat it out. 'I don't know whether this is contaminated or not, but it tastes and smells even lousier than the other two. If that's possible.' He pushed the tray under Kylenski's nose, who sniffed it and passed it across to his colleague.

Branson said: 'Well?'

Kylenski was hesitant. 'Could be. A marginal, a borderline case. It would require lab. testing.' He looked thoughtfully at Revson. 'Do you smoke?'

'No.'

'Drink?'

'Birthdays and funerals only.'

Kylenski said: 'That could account for it. Some non-smokers and non-drinkers can have an extraordinarily acute sense of taste and smell. Revson is obviously one of those.'

Without consulting anyone, Revson examined another six

trays. He pushed them all away and turned to Branson. 'My opinion, for what it's worth?' Branson nodded. 'Most – not all, but most – of those trays are off. With some, you've almost got to imagine it. Others stink. I think the whole damn lot is contaminated. In varying degrees.'

Branson looked at Kylenski. 'Possible?'

Kylenski looked uncomfortable. 'It happens. Botulinus can vary widely in its degree of concentration. Only last year there was a double family outing in New England. Ten in all. Among other things, they had sandwiches. Again the botulinus bug. Five died, two were slightly ill, three unaffected. But the sandwiches were all spread with the same meat paste.'

Branson and Van Effen walked apart. Van Effen said: 'Enough?'

'You mean you see no point in going ahead with this?'

'You stand to lose credibility, Mr Branson.'

'I agree. I'm not happy about it, but I agree. Trouble is, we've really, basically, only got Revson's word for it.'

'But he's identified twenty – in all – contaminated trays: three more than was necessary.'

'Who says so? Revson?'

'After all the proofs, you still don't trust him?'

'He's too cool, too relaxed. He's obviously highly trained, highly competent – and I'm damned sure that it's not in photography.'

'He could be in that, too.'

'I wouldn't doubt it.'

'So you're still going to treat this as a case of deliberate poisoning?'

'Where our vast viewing public is concerned? Who's to gainsay me? There's only one mike and it's in my hand.'

Van Effen looked towards the south tower. 'Food wagon number two on its way.'

VII

Branson had the TV cameras, the honoured guests, the newspapermen and still cameramen in position in very short order indeed. The black thunderous clouds from the west were steadily marching in on them. Among those seated, the only difference in composition was that Hansen's seat had been taken over by the Vice-President. The cameras were turning and Branson, seated next to the President, was talking into the microphone.

He said: 'I am calling upon all viewers in America and throughout the world to be witnesses to a particularly heinous crime that has been committed upon this bridge just over an hour ago, a crime that I trust will persuade you that not all criminals are those who stand without the law. I would ask you to look at this food wagon which, as you can see, has its counter covered with food trays. Harmless, if not particularly appetizing food trays, you would think, such as any major airline would serve up to its passengers. But are they really harmless?' He turned to the man on his other side and the camera was now back on them. 'This is Dr Kylenski, a leading forensic expert on the West Coast. A specialist in poisons. Are those trays really harmless, Dr Kylenski?'

'No.'

'You'll have to speak up, doctor.'

'No. They are not harmless. Some are contaminated.'

'How many?'

'Half. Maybe more. I have no laboratory resources to hand.'

'Contaminated. That means infected. What are they infected with, doctor?'

'A virus. Botulinus. A major source of severe food poisoning.'

'How severe? Can it be deadly?'

'Yes.'

'Frequently?'

'Yes.'

'Normally it occurs naturally – spoiled food, things like that?'

'Yes.'

'But a culture of it can be manufactured synthetically or artificially in a laboratory.'

'That's putting it very loosely.'

'We're talking primarily to laymen.'

'Yes.'

'And it could be injected synthetically into already prepared but otherwise harmless food?'

'I suppose so.'

'Yes or no?'

'Yes.'

'Thank you, Dr Kylenski. That will be all.'

VIII

Revson, still without his camera, was standing by the ambulance with O'Hare. 'For a person who's never been inside a court-room, Branson seems to have mastered the prosecuting counsel bit pretty well.'

'It's all this TV.'

IX

Branson said: 'I put it to all of you who are watching that the authorities – military, police, FBI, Government or whoever – have made a deliberate attempt to murder or at least incapacitate those of us who have taken over the Presidential entourage and this bridge. There must be someone on this bridge who knew how to identify poisoned trays and see that they fell into the right hands – that is, the hands of my colleagues and myself. The attempt, fortunately, failed, but there has been one casualty whom I shall mention later.'

'Meantime, I would draw your attention to the fact that a second food wagon has arrived.' A camera obligingly drew the viewers' attention to this fact. 'It seems incredible that the authorities would be so obtuse as to try the same gambit again but, on the other hand, they have already shown that they are incredibly obtuse. So we are going to select three trays at random and offer them to the President, King and Prince. If they survive, we may reasonably assume that the food is uncontaminated. If, on the other hand, they become seriously ill – or worse – the world will know that the guilt cannot be laid at our door. We are in permanent radio-telephone contact with the police and military authorities ashore. They have one minute to tell us whether this food is contaminated or not.'

Mayor Morrison was on his feet. Van Effen lifted his Schmeisser fractionally but Morrison ignored him. He said to Branson: 'Apart from the personal indignity and affront you are heaping on the President and his royal guests couldn't you pick someone a bit lower down the scale for your experiment?'

'Such as yourself?'

'Such as myself.'

'My dear Mayor, your personal courage is beyond dispute. That is well known. Your intelligence, however, isn't. If anyone is to be put to the test it will be the three men who are probably the most important in the United States today. Their untimely disappearance from the scene would have the maximum inhibiting effect on would-be poisoners. In the olden days, the serfs tasted the food of their rulers: I find it rather amusing that the roles should be reversed. Please sit.'

X

'Megalomaniac bastard,' Revson said.

O'Hare nodded. 'He's all of that but a lot more. He knows damn well there isn't a chance in the world of the food being spiked but he's going through the charade all the same. He's not only enjoying his own showmanship, he's getting a positively sadistic kick out of it all, particularly in humiliating the President.'

'You think he's sick? In the head? Certifiably, I mean?'

'I'm no psychiatrist. He could get all he wants without those histrionics and TV spectaculars. What's for sure, he's got a grudge against society in general and the President in particular. Certainly, he's in it for the money, but he's in it for something else: as if he wanted to become a nationally – or internationally – recognized figure.'

'In that case, he's made a fair start. In fact, he's gone as far as he can go. Now it seems as if he's overcompensating for something. Lord knows what.'

They watched three trays of food being brought towards the rows of chairs. O'Hare said: 'Reckon they'll sample that?'

'They'll eat it. In the first place, they couldn't bear the indignity of being force-fed in front of hundreds of millions of viewers. The President's courage is known well enough – you will remember his record during World War Two in the Pacific. Again, as President, he has to give a lead to the nation

– if he refused to eat while his oil friends did, he'd be a dead duck at the next election. Conversely, his oil friends would lose face if the President ate and they didn't.'

They ate. After Chrysler had given a negative signal from the Presidential coach, Branson nodded towards the trays. The President – inevitably, he was not a man to be upstaged by anyone – was the first to get busy with knife and fork. It could hardly be said that he ate with unrestrained gusto but he plodded along stolidly enough and had finished more than half his meal before he laid down his eating tools.

Branson said: 'Well?'

'I wouldn't offer it to my guests in the White House but it's palatable enough.' In spite of the deep humiliation he must have been experiencing, the President was maintaining a remarkable degree of *sang-froid*. 'A little wine would have helped, though.'

'You shall have as much as you want in a few moments. I imagine a great number of people are also going to feel like a restorative pretty soon, too. Incidentally, if you people are still interested, we shall be fixing our second strap of explosives at nine o'clock tomorrow morning. Our time, of course. And now, could we have the cameras on that stretcher there.'

Two men stood at the head of the canvas-shrouded stretcher. At a word from Branson they pulled back the top section of the canvas. The cameras zoomed in on the pallid, haggard face of the dead man, held it for all of ten interminable and hushed seconds, then returned to Branson.

He said: 'John Hansen, your energy czar. Death certified as due to botulinus poisoning. For what may be the first time in history a wanted criminal accuses the legal authorities of murder. Second degree murder it may be, but I nevertheless indict them on a charge of murder.'

XI

Hagenbach was in full vitriolic flow. Some phrases like 'evil, twisted, macabre, vicious bastard' were just identifiable, but the rest was wholly unprintable. Newson, Carter, Milton and Quarry were momentarily silent but their faces showed clearly enough that they totally identified themselves with Hagenbach's expressed convictions. Hagenbach, being only human, finally ran out of breath.

'He's made us look very bad indeed.' In the circumstances, Milton's restraint was remarkable.

'Bad?' Quarry looked around for another word then gave up. 'If he pulls another one like this – if *we* pull another one like this – Branson will have half the nation on his side. What's to do next?'

Hagenbach said: 'Wait till we hear from Revson.'

'Revson?' Admiral Newson seemed unenthusiastic. 'He's hardly distinguished himself so far.'

'A hundred to one it wasn't Revson's fault,' Hagenbach said. 'And don't forget the final decision was ours. We bear a collective responsibility, gentlemen.'

They sat around the table bearing this intolerable responsibility, each one an Atlas bearing his own private world on his shoulders.

— 9 —

ON THE GOLDEN Gate Bridge that evening events happened in fairly quick but ordered fashion. A special ambulance appeared and took away the stretcher bearing the remains of Hansen. An autopsy was to be performed, which seemed to be a singular waste of time but was apparently mandatory under State law when a person had died in unusual circumstances. Dr Kylenski and his colleague, with a marked absence of reluctance, accompanied the ambulance. Newsmen, captives and captors had their evening meal, the first two with a notable but understandable lack of appetite but with a thirst, equally notable and understandable, so marked that further liquid supplies had to be commandeered. The two TV trucks left and, shortly afterwards, the two food wagons. Last to go were Vice-President Richards and Hendrix. The Vice-President had spent a long time in an earnest private discussion with the President, just as had General Cartland with Hendrix.

Both Branson had watched with a certain amused tolerance but had paid little attention. From their grim and depressed expressions it was clear that their discussions had been totally fruitless. No other result could have been expected. It may well have been that Branson was suffering from a certain degree of euphoria after the dramatic effect of his last broadcast: from his expression it was impossible to tell.

Branson approached Kowalski, just as Richards and Hendrix turned towards their waiting police car. 'Well?'

'My life on it, Mr Branson. I had my eye on Hendrix and the Vice-President every second. At no time did Revson approach within twenty yards of either man.'

Branson was aware that Kowalski, a very bright youngster indeed, was looking at him with an expression of barely restrained curiosity. Branson gave his usual faint and empty smile.

'You wondering what's bugging me about Revson?'

'Not wondering, sir. Interested. I've known you for three years now, sir. I shouldn't imagine you see many fairies at the bottom of your garden.'

'Don't you, now?' Branson turned and called to Richards. 'Wait.' To Kowalski: 'What's that supposed to mean?'

'Well. Revson. He's been searched to pieces. He's passed every test. Maybe if the boys and I knew what you are—'

'Every test. With flying colours. Perhaps his flag flies too high. Would you have sampled those charming botulinus dinners?'

'My oath and I wouldn't.' He hesitated. 'Well, if it was a direct order from you—'

'And with a gun in your back?'

Kowalski said nothing.

Branson said: 'Revson doesn't take orders from me. And he had no gun in his back.'

'Maybe he takes orders from someone else.'

'Maybe he does at that. Just a very close eye, Kowalski.'

'If I have to stay awake all night.'

'You know, I think I'd rather appreciate that.' Branson walked away towards the police car. Kowalski looked after him very thoughtfully indeed.

The Vice-President and Hendrix were standing impatiently by the opened doors of the police car. Branson came up and said: 'You will not have forgotten the deadline, gentlemen?'

'Deadline?'

Branson smiled. 'Do not be so deliberately obtuse, Mr Vice-President. The transfer of certain monies to Europe. Half a billion dollars – plus, of course, my quarter million expenses. Noon. Tomorrow.'

Richard's chilling glare should have petrified Branson on the spot. Branson remained unaffected.

'And don't forget the escalation clause. Two million dollars for every hour's delay. And, of course, the free pardon. I expect that will take some time, I suppose your Congress will be a little stuffy about that. But we – your friends and I – can rest comfortably in the Caribbean till that comes through. I bid you good evening, gentlemen.'

He walked away and stopped at the opened door of the rear coach. Revson was there, slinging over his shoulder the strap of the camera which Chrysler had just handed back to him. Chrysler smiled at Branson.

'Clean as a whistle, Mr Branson. My word, I wish I had one of those.'

'You can have a dozen very soon. You had another camera, Revson.'

'Yes.' Revson sighed. 'Do you want me to fetch it for you?'

'I'd rather not. Will you get it, Chrysler?'

'Five back, inside seat,' Revson said helpfully. 'It's on the seat.'

Chrysler returned with the camera, showed it to Branson. 'An Asahi-Pentax. I have one myself. Those things are so jammed with miniaturized electronic equipment that you couldn't hide a pea inside it.'

'Assuming, of course, that it is not just an empty shell.'

'Ah.' Chrysler looked at Revson. 'Loaded?' Revson shook his head. Chrysler opened the back just as Van Effen joined them and displayed the rear of the camera. 'The genuine article.' He snapped the back closed.

Revson took his camera back. He spoke to Branson, his

tone as cold as his face. 'Maybe you'd like to look at my watch. Could be a transistorized two-way radio. All the best investigators in the comic strips wear one.'

Branson said nothing. Chrysler took Revson's wrist, pressed a knob on either side of the watch. Illuminated red figures appeared, one set giving the date, the other the time. Chrysler dropped the wrist.

'Pulsar digital. You couldn't hide a grain of sand inside one of those things.'

Revson turned with deliberate contempt on his heel and walked away. Chrysler went inside the coach. Van Effen said: 'Still bugged, Mr Branson? So he's annoyed. Wouldn't you be if you'd been put through the hoop the way you've put him through the hoop? Besides, if he'd anything to hide he wouldn't let his animosity show so plain, he'd keep a very low profile indeed.'

'Maybe that's the way he expects us to react. Or maybe he's clear.' Branson looked thoughtful almost to the extent of being worried. 'But I can't shake off the feeling that there's something wrong, and it's a feeling that's never let me down before. I'm convinced, don't ask me how, that someone on the bridge has some means of communicating with someone on land. I want every inch of every person – and that includes our illustrious guests – searched, and to hell with the ladies' feelings. Every inch of their personal belongings, every inch of every coach.'

'Immediately, Mr Branson.' There was acquiescence in the tone but no great enthusiasm. 'And the rest rooms?'

'Those too.'

'And the ambulance?'

'Yes. I think I'll attend to that myself.'

II

O'Hare looked up in mild surprise as Branson entered the ambulance. 'Don't tell me that the botulinus has struck again?'

'No. I'm here to search this ambulance.'

O'Hare rose from his stool, his face tight. 'I don't allow civilians to touch my medical supplies.'

'You're going to allow this one. If necessary, I'll call one of my men and have you held either at pistol-point or tied up while I conduct my search.'

'And just what in the hell do you think you're looking for?'

'That's my concern.'

'So I can't stop you. I just warn you that we carry quite a lot of dangerous drugs and surgical equipment here. If you poison yourself or slice an artery, here's one doctor who's not going to help you.'

Branson nodded to April Wednesday who was sleeping peacefully on the side bunk. 'Lift her off.'

'Lift her – what do you think—'

'Do it immediately or I call a guard.'

O'Hare lifted the slight form in his arms. Branson pummelled every inch of the thin mattress, lifted it, looked under it and said: 'Put her back.'

Branson carried out a thorough search of all the medical equipment in the ambulance. He knew exactly what he was looking for and nothing he examined looked even remotely like what he hoped to find. He looked around, picked up a torch suspended from one side of the ambulance, switched it on and twisted the top, opening and then narrowing the hooded shutter. 'A peculiar flashlight, O'Hare.'

O'Hare said wearily: 'It's an ophthalmic torch. Every physician carries one. You can diagnose a dozen different diseases by the dilation of the pupils of the eyes.'

'This can be useful. Come with me.' He went down the rear steps of the ambulance, went round to the front and jerked open the driver's door. The driver, peering at a lurid magazine in the now fading light, looked round in surprise.

Branson said: 'Out!' The man descended and Branson, offering no explanation, searched him comprehensively from head to foot. He then climbed inside the driving compartment, examined the upholstery, opened various lockers and shone the torch inside. He descended and said to the driver: 'Open the engine hood.'

This was done. Again with the aid of the torch he carried out a thorough inspection of the compartment and found nothing worthy of his attention. He went round to the rear of the ambulance and re-entered. O'Hare followed, politely removed the torch from Branson's hand and replaced it.

Branson indicated a metal canister held in place by a spring clip. He said: 'What's that?'

O'Hare gave a creditable impression of a man whose patience was wearing very very thin. 'An aerosol air-freshener.' It was the fake Prestige can that contained the knock-out gas.

Branson freed the can. 'Sandalwood,' he said. 'You have an exotic taste in perfumes.' He shook the can, listened to the gurgling inside, then replaced the canister in its clip. O'Hare hoped that the dampness on his brow didn't show.

Branson finally directed his attention to the big oiled-wood box on the floor. 'And what's this?'

O'Hare didn't answer. Branson looked at him. O'Hare was leaning with a negligent elbow on top of a locker, his expression a mixture of barely concealed impatience and bored indifference.

Branson said sharply: 'You heard me.'

'I heard you. I've had just about enough of you, Branson. If you expect me to show any obedience or respect for you, then you're way out of your mind. I'm beginning to think you are illiterate. Can't you see those big red letters? They spell out "Cardiac Arrest Unit". Emergency equipment for patients who have, or may shortly be expected to have, a heart attack.'

'Why the big red seal in front?'

'There's more to it than just that red seal. The whole unit is hermetically sealed. The entire interior of that box and all the equipment it contains is completely sterilized before the box is sealed. One does not inject an unsterilized needle in or near the heart of a cardiac patient.'

'What would happen if I broke that seal?'

'To you, nothing. You'd just be committing the most cardinal sin in any hospital. You'd render the contents useless. And the way you're carrying on the President is a prime candidate for a heart attack at any moment.' O'Hare was acutely conscious that the aerosol can was only inches from his hand. If Branson broke the seal and started delving deeper he intended to use the aerosol without a second thought: Branson could hardly be expected to be the person who would fail to recognize a cyanide air pistol when he saw it.

Branson's face was without expression. 'The President—'

'I'd sooner turn in my licence than insure the President for anything. I am a doctor. Twice your needling and public humiliation have driven him into a state of near-apoplexy. You never know, third time you may be lucky. Go on and break the bloody seal. What's another death on your conscience?'

'I've never been responsible for anybody's death in my life.' Without as much as looking at O'Hare, Branson abruptly left the ambulance. O'Hare went to the rear door and looked after him thoughtfully. Revson was ambling across the roadway and Branson spared him neither a word nor a glance, behaviour uncharacteristic of Branson who was much given to directing penetrating glances at everyone, usually for no reason whatsoever. Revson looked after him in some puzzlement, then strolled off towards the ambulance.

Revson said: 'You just been put through the grinder, too?'

'That you can say again.' O'Hare spoke with some feeling. 'You, too?'

'Not me. I've been searched so often that nobody would bother. Everybody else was, though. It must have been pretty thorough. I heard more than one ladylike scream of protest.' He looked after the departing Branson. 'Our mastermind seems unusually preoccupied.'

'He was acting a bit oddly when he left.'

'He drew a blank, obviously.'

'Yes.'

'Didn't even investigate your one sealed container – the cardiac unit?'

'That's when he started behaving oddly. I'm pretty sure that he was about to break the seal when I pointed out that that would de-sterilize the equipment and render it useless. I also pointed out that I considered the President a prime candidate for a heart attack and that I regarded him as being the prime cause for this. That was when he backed off.'

'Understandable, I would have thought. He doesn't want to lose his principal hostage.'

'That wasn't the impression he gave me. He also said another funny thing when he left, that he'd never been responsible for anyone's death in his life.'

'To the best of my knowledge that's true. Maybe he just didn't want to spoil his good record.'

'Could have been, could have been.' But the puzzled expression was still on O'Hare's face.

III

Van Effen regarded Branson with a curiosity that his face didn't register. Branson, he thought, was a shade less than his old ebullient self. Van Effen said: 'Well, how did you find the ambulance and the good doctor? Clean?'

'The ambulance is. God damn it all, I quite forgot to go over O'Hare.'

Van Effen smiled. 'One tends to. Pillar of moral rectitude. I'll go look at him.'

'How did it go with you?'

'There were ten of us and we were pretty thorough – and pretty thoroughly unpopular. If there was a silver dollar on the Golden Gate Bridge we'd have found it. We didn't find any silver dollars.'

But then Branson and his men had been searching the wrong places and the wrong people. They should have searched Chief of Police Hendrix before he'd been allowed to leave the bridge.

IV

Hagenbach, Milton, Quarry, Newson and Carter were seated round the long oblong table in the communications wagon. There were bottles of liquor on a wall-mounted sideboard and, judging from the levels of the liquids in the bottles and the glasses in front of the five men, they weren't there for purely decorative purposes. The five appeared to be concentrating on two things only: not speaking to one another and not looking at one another. The bottoms of their glasses appeared to hold a singular fascination for them: comparatively, the average funeral parlour could have qualified as an amusement arcade.

A bell rang softly at the inner end of the wagon. A shirt-sleeved policeman, seated before a battery of telephones, lifted one and spoke softly into it. He turned and said: 'Mr Quarry, sir. Washington.'

Quarry rose to his feet with the alacrity of a French aristocrat going to the guillotine and made his way to the communications desk. His end of the conversation appeared to consist of a series of dispirited grunts. Finally he said, 'Yes, as planned,' returned to the table and slumped into his chair. 'The money has been arranged just in case it's needed.'

Milton said heavily: 'Can you see it not being needed?'

'The Treasury also agrees that we should stall them for up to twenty-four hours from noon tomorrow.'

Milton's lugubriousness didn't alter. 'By Branson's escalation demands that means close on another fifty million dollars.'

'Peanuts to what he's asking.' Milton made a still-born attempt to smile. 'Might give one of our brilliant minds time to come up with a brilliant idea.' He relapsed into a silence which no one seemed inclined to break. Hagenbach reached for a bottle of scotch, helped himself and passed the bottle around. They resumed their mournful inspection of the depth of their glasses.

The bottle was not long left undisturbed. Richards and Hendrix entered and, without speaking, sat down heavily in two vacant chairs. The Vice-President's hand reached the bottle just fractionally before that of Hendrix.

Richards said: 'How did we look on TV tonight?'

'God-damned awful. But no more awful than the seven of us sitting around here without a single idea in our heads.' Milton sighed. 'Seven of the allegedly best governmental and law enforcement minds in the business. The best we can do is drink scotch. Not a single idea among us.'

Hendrix said: 'I think perhaps Revson has.' He fished a piece of paper from the inside of a sock and handed it to Hagenbach. 'For you.'

Hagenbach unfolded the note, cursed and shouted to the operator.

'My decoder. Quick.' Hagenbach was back in business and, predictably, he turned to Hendrix: he wouldn't have asked Richards for the time of day. 'How are things out there? Anything we don't know? How come Hansen died?'

'To put it brutally, hunger, greed. Seemingly he snitched one of the food trays before he could be warned which were the dangerous ones and how they could be identified.'

Milton sighed. 'He always was a voracious eater. Compulsive, you might say. Something wrong with his metabolic system, I suppose. Speak no ill of the dead but I often told him that he was digging his grave with his own teeth. Looks like that's what happened.'

'No fault of Revson's?'

'None in the world. But there's worse. Your man Revson is under heavy suspicion. Branson, as we all have cause to know, is a very very clever man and he's convinced there's an infiltrator in their midst. He's also almost equally convinced that it's Revson. I think the man is working on sheer instinct. He can't pin a thing on Revson.'

'Who's also a very very clever man.' Hagenbach paused then looked sharply at Hendrix. 'If Branson is so suspicious of Revson would he let him get within a mile of you, knowing that you were going ashore?'

'Revson didn't come anywhere near me. General Cartland gave me the message. Revson gave the message to Cartland.'

'So Cartland is in on this?'

'He knows as much about it as we do. Revson is going to give him the cyanide pistol. Never thought our Chief of Staff was so positively blood-thirsty. He seems actually to be looking forward to using it.'

Carter said: 'You know Cartland's reputation as a tank commander in the Second World War. After all the comparatively decent Italians and Germans he disposed of then, do you think he's going to worry about doing away with a few really bad hats?'

'You should know. Anyway, I went into one of their awful rest rooms and shoved the note down my sock. I suspected that the Vice-President here and I might be searched before we left the bridge. We weren't. Your Revson is right. Branson is both over-confident and under-conscious of security precautions.'

V

Revson and O'Hare watched Van Effen walk away. Revson himself walked away a few steps, indicating that O'Hare should follow him. Revson said: 'Well, that was a pretty thorough going-over our friend gave you. I don't think he much appreciated your remark about your hoping that he would be a patient of yours some day.'

O'Hare looked up at the darkly threatening sky, now almost directly overhead. The wind was freshening and, two hundred feet below, the white horses were showing in the Golden Gate.

O'Hare said: 'Looks like a rough night coming up. We'd be more comfortable inside the ambulance, I think, and I've some excellent whisky and brandy in there. Used, you understand, solely for the resuscitation of the sick and ailing.'

'You're going to go far in your profession. Sick and ailing describes my symptoms precisely. But I'd rather be succoured out here.'

'Whatever for?'

Revson gave him a pitying look. 'If it weren't for your good fortune in having me here, you'd very probably be the main object of Branson's suspicions. Has it not occurred to you that, during his intensive search of your ambulance, he might have planted a tiny electronic bug which you wouldn't discover in a week of searching?'

'It occurs to me now. There's a dearth of devious minds in the medical profession.'

'Do you have any gin?'

'It's odd you should ask that. I do.'

'That's for me. I told Branson that I didn't drink and that's why I have a nose like a bloodhound. I shouldn't care for him to see me with a glass of something amber in my hand.'

'Devious, devious minds.' O'Hare disappeared inside the ambulance and reappeared shortly with two glasses, the clear one for Revson. 'Health.'

'Indeed. I shouldn't wonder if that's going to be in short supply inside the next twenty-four hours.'

'Cryptic, aren't we?'

'Psychic.' Revson looked speculatively at the nearest helicopter. 'I wonder if the pilot – Johnson, I think – intends to sleep in his machine tonight.'

O'Hare gave a mock shiver. 'You ever been in a helicopter?'

'Oddly, perhaps, no.'

'I have several times. Strictly, I assure you, in the line of medical duty. These army jobs are fitted with steel-framed canvas chairs, if that's the word for them. For me, it would be a toss-up between that and a bed of nails.'

'So much I suspected. So he'll probably bed down with his fellow-villains in the rear coach.'

'The chopper appears to interest you strangely.'

Revson glanced casually around. There was no one within possible earshot.

'The detonating mechanism for the explosives is inside there. I intend – note that I only say intend – to de-activate it tonight.'

O'Hare was silent for a long moment, then said kindly: 'I think I should give you a medical. For that space between the ears. There'll be at least one armed guard on all night patrol. You know the bridge is a blaze of light all night long. So you just dematerialize yourself—'

'The sentry I can take care of. The lights will be switched off when I want them.'

'Abracadabra!'

'I've already sent a message ashore.'

'I didn't know that secret agents doubled as magicians. You produce a carrier pigeon from your hat—'

'Hendrix took it ashore for me.'

O'Hare stared at him then said: 'Another drink?'

'No befuddled wits tonight, thank you.'

'Then I'll have one.' He took both glasses and reappeared with his own. 'Look, that guy Kowalski has the general appearance and the eyes of a hawk. I'm not exactly short-sighted myself. He never took his eyes off you all the time the Vice-President and Hendrix were out here. Branson's orders, I'm certain.'

'Me, too. Who else? I never went near Hendrix. I gave the message to Cartland who passed it on to Hendrix. Kowalski was too busy watching me to bother about Cartland and Hendrix.'

'What time will the lights go off?'

'I don't know yet. I'll send a signal.'

'This means Cartland is in on this?'

'What else? By the way, I promised the general the cyanide gun. Can you get it to him?'

'One way or another.'

'No way, I suppose, of replacing that seal on the cardiac unit once it has been broken?'

'You mean in case our suspicious Mr Branson visits the ambulance again. No.' He smiled. 'It just so happens that I am carrying *two* spare seals inside the box.'

Revson smiled in turn. 'Just goes to show. A man can't think of everything. Still on the side of law and order? Still like to see Branson wearing a nice shiny pair of bracelets?'

'It's becoming a distinct yearning.'

'It might involve bending your code of ethics a little.'

'The hell with the medical ethics.'

VI

Hagenbach positively snatched the sheet of typewritten paper from his decoder. He glanced rapidly through it, his brow corrugating by the second. He said to Hendrix: 'Revson appeared to be perfectly normal when you left him?'

'Who can tell what Revson appears to be?'

'True. I don't seem to be able to make head or tail of this.' Richards said acidly: 'You might share your little secrets with us, Hagenbach.'

'He says: "It looks as if it's going to be a lousy night, which should help. I want two fake oil fires set now. Or a mixture of oil and rubber tyres. One to my south-west, say Lincoln Park, the other to the east, say Fort Mason – a much bigger fire there. Ignite the Lincoln Park one at twenty-two hundred hours. At two-two-oh-three, infra-red sights if necessary, use a laser beam to destroy the radio scanner on top of the rear coach. Wait my flashlight signal – SOS – then ignite the other. After fifteen minutes blacken out bridge and northern part of San Francisco. It would help if you could at same time arrange a massive fireworks display in Chinatown – as if a firework factory had gone up.

' "Submarine at midnight. Please provide transistorized transceiver small enough to fit base camera. Pre-set your frequency and mine and have submarine patch in on same frequency." '

There was a lengthy silence during which Hagenbach, perhaps very understandably, again reached for the scotch. The bottle was rapidly emptied. Richards finally passed his judgement.

'The man's mad, of course. Quite, quite, mad.'

Nobody, for some time, appeared inclined to disagree with him. Richards, *pro tem.* the Chief Executive of the nation, was the man to make the decision, but, apart from his observations on mental instability, he was clearly in no mood to make any kind of decision. Hagenbach took the decision out of his hands.

'Revson is probably a good deal saner than any of us here. He's brilliant, we've had proof of that. Almost certainly, he lacked the time to go into detail. Finally, anyone here got any better idea – let me amend that, anybody here got *any* idea?'

If anyone had, he was keeping it to himself.

'Hendrix, get hold of the deputy Mayor and the Fire Chief. Have those fires set. How about the fireworks?'

Hendrix smiled. 'Fireworks are illegal in San Francisco. Nineteen hundred and six and all that. It so happens we know an illegal underground factory in Chinatown. The owner will be anxious to co-operate.'

Richards shook his head. 'Mad,' he said. 'Quite, quite mad.'

— 10 —

FROM FAR OUT at sea came the first faint flickers of lightning and the distant rumble of approaching thunder. A now-recovered if somewhat wan April Wednesday, standing with Revson by the centre of the bridge, looked up at the indigo sky and said: 'It looks like being quite a night.'

'I've a feeling that way myself.' He took her arm. 'Are you afraid of thunderstorms as you appear to be of everything else?'

'I don't much fancy being stuck out on this bridge in the middle of one.'

'It's been here for almost forty years. It's not likely to fall down tonight.' He looked upwards as the first drops of rain began to fall. 'But getting wet I object to. Come on.'

They took their seats inside the lead coach, she by the window, he by the aisle. Within minutes the coach was full and within half an hour most of the occupants were dozing if not asleep. Each seat had its own individual reading light, but without exception those were either dimmed or completely out. There was nothing to see, nothing to do. It had been a long, tiring, exciting and in many ways a nerve-racking day. Sleep was not only the sensible but inevitable recourse. And the sound of drumming rain, whether on canvas or on a metal roof, has a peculiarly soporific effect.

And that the rain was now drumming was beyond dispute. It had been increasing steadily ever since the passengers had entered the coach and could now fairly be described as torrential. The approaching thunderstorm, though still some miles distant, was steadily increasing in violence. But neither rain, thunder nor lightning were any deterrent to the prowling Kowalski: he had promised Branson that he would keep his eye on Revson all night long if he had to, and that he clearly intended to do. Regularly, every fifteen minutes, he entered the coach, peered pointedly at Revson, spoke a few brief words to Bartlett, who sat sideways on guard, in the seat next to the driver's, then left. Bartlett, Revson apart, was the only alert person in the coach and this, Revson suspected, was due more to Kowalski's recurrent visits than to anything else. On one occasion Revson had overheard Bartlett ask when he was to be relieved and been curtly told that he would have to remain where he was until one o'clock, which suited Revson well enough.

At nine o'clock, when the rain was at its heaviest, Kowalski made another of his routine checks. Revson took out and armed his white pen. Kowalski turned to go. His heel was just descending the riser of the first step when he appeared to stumble. Then he fell, heavily, face-first out of the coach on to the roadway.

Bartlett was the first to reach him, Revson the second. Revson said: 'What the hell happened to him?'

'Lost his footing, far as I could see. Coach door has been open all evening and the steps are slippery as all hell.' Both men stooped to examine the unconscious Kowalski. He was bleeding quite heavily from the forehead which had obviously taken the main brunt of his fall. Revson felt his head gently with his fingers. The needle protruded almost a quarter of an inch behind Kowalski's left ear. Revson removed and palmed it.

Revson said: 'Shall I fetch the doctor?'

'Yes. Sure looks as if he needs one.'

Revson ran to the ambulance. As he approached, the light came on inside the ambulance. Revson took the aerosol can from O'Hare and thrust it into his pocket. The two men, O'Hare carrying his medical bag, ran back to the lead coach. By this time quite a number of curious journalists from the coach – activated, almost certainly, by the inbuilt curiosity that motivates all good journalists, were crowded round the unconscious Kowalski.

'Stand back,' O'Hare ordered. The journalists made way respectfully but didn't stand all that far back. O'Hare opened his bag and began to wipe Kowalski's forehead with a piece of gauze. His opened bag was quite some distance from him, and in the dim light, the driving rain and aided by the total concentration of all on the injured man, it was no great feat for Revson to extract an oil-skinned packet from the bag and send it spinning under the coach. He, but only he, heard the gentle thump as it struck the kerb on the far side. He then pressed in among the curious onlookers.

O'Hare straightened. 'A couple of volunteers to help me get him across to the ambulance.' There was no lack of volunteers. They were about to lift him when Branson came running up.

'Your man's had a pretty nasty fall. I want him in the ambulance for a proper examination.'

'Did he fall or was he pushed?'

'How the hell should I know? You're wasting what could be valuable time, Branson.'

Bartlett said: 'He fell all right, Mr Branson. He slipped on the top step and hadn't a chance to save himself.'

'Certain?'

'Of course I'm bloody certain.' Bartlett was justifiably indignant. He spoke again, but a crashing peal of thunder drowned out his next words. He repeated himself. 'I was within two feet of him at the time – and I hadn't a chance to save him.'

O'Hare paid no more attention to him. With the help of two others he carried Kowalski across to the ambulance. Branson looked at the group of journalists still there, caught sight of Revson.

'Where was Revson at the time?'

'Revson was nowhere near him. He was in his seat, five back there. Everyone was in their seats. Christ, Mr Branson, I'm telling you. It was a pure bloody accident.'

'Must have been.' Clad only in already totally sodden shirt-sleeves and trousers, Branson shivered. 'Jesus, what a night!' He hurried across to the ambulance and as he arrived the two men who had helped O'Hare to carry Kowalski came down the ambulance steps. Branson went inside. O'Hare had already had Kowalski's leather jacket removed and his right sleeve rolled beyond the elbow, and was preparing a hypodermic injection.

Branson said: 'What's that for?'

O'Hare turned in irritation. 'What the hell are you doing here? This is doctor's work. Get out!'

The invitation passed unheeded. Branson picked up the tube from which O'Hare had filled his hypodermic. 'Anti-tetanus? The man's got a head wound.'

O'Hare withdrew the needle, covered the pin-prick with antiseptic gauze. 'I thought even the most ignorant layman knew that when a man has been injured in the open the first thing he gets is an anti-tetanus injection. You've obviously never seen tetanus.' He sounded Kowalski with his stethoscope, took his pulse and then his temperature.

'Get an ambulance from the hospital.' O'Hare pushed

Kowalski's sleeve further up and started to wind the blood-pressure-band round it.

Branson said: 'No.'

O'Hare didn't answer until after he'd taken the pressure. He then repeated: 'Get the ambulance.'

'I don't trust you and your damned ambulances.'

O'Hare didn't answer. He jumped down the steps and strode off through rain that was now rebounding six inches high off the roadway. He was back shortly with the two men who had helped him carry Kowalski across. O'Hare said: 'Mr Grafton. Mr Ferrers. Two highly respected, even eminent journalists. Their words carry a great deal of weight. So will their word.'

'What's that meant to mean?' For the first time since his arrival on the bridge Branson wore just the slightest trace of apprehension.

O'Hare ignored him, addressed himself to the two journalists. 'Kowalski here has severe concussion, possibly even a skull fracture. The latter is impossible to tell without an X-ray. He also has shallow, rapid breathing, a weak and feathery pulse, a temperature and abnormally low blood pressure. This could indicate a few things. One of them cerebral haemorrhaging. I want you gentlemen to bear witness to the fact that Branson refuses to allow an ambulance to come for him. I want you to bear witness to the fact that if Kowalski dies Branson and Branson alone will be wholly responsible for his death. I want you to bear witness to the fact that Branson is fully aware that if Kowalski dies he will be guilty of the same charge as he recently levelled against persons unknown – murder. Only, in his case, I think it would have to be an indictment of the first degree.'

Grafton said: 'I shall so solemnly bear witness.'

Ferrers said: 'And I.'

O'Hare looked at Branson with contempt. 'And you were the person who said to me that you'd never in your life been responsible for the death of a single person.'

Branson said: 'How am I to know that once they get him ashore they won't keep him there?'

'You're losing your grip, Branson.' The contempt was still in O'Hare's voice: he and Revson had deliberated long enough on how best to wear down Branson psychologically. 'As long as you have a President, a King and a Prince, who the hell is going to hold a common criminal like this as a counter-ransom?'

Branson made up his mind. It was difficult to tell whether he was motivated by threats or a genuine concern for Kowalski's life. 'One of those two will have to go tell Chrysler to call the ambulance. I'm not keeping my eyes off you until I see Kowalski safely transferred to the other ambulance.'

'Suit yourself,' O'Hare said indifferently. 'Gentlemen?'

'It will be a pleasure.' The two journalists left. O'Hare began to cover Kowalski in blankets.

Branson said with suspicion: 'What are you doing that for?'

'Heaven preserve me from ignorant laymen. Your friend here is in a state of shock. Rule number one for shock victims – keep them warm.'

Just as he finished speaking there was a massive thunderclap directly above, so close, so loud, that it was positively hurtful to the ear-drums. The reverberations took many long seconds to die away. O'Hare looked speculatively at Branson then said: 'Know something, Branson? That sounded to me just like the crack of doom.' He poured some whisky into a glass and added a little distilled water.

Branson said: 'I'll have some of that.'

'Help yourself,' O'Hare said agreeably.

II

From the comparative comfort of the lead coach – comparative, for his clothes were as soaked as if he had fallen into the Golden Gate – Revson watched another ambulance bear away Kowalski's stretchered form. For the moment Revson felt as reasonably content as was possible for a man in his slowly chilling condition. The main object of the exercise had been to get his hands on the cord, canister, torch and aerosol. All of those he had achieved. The first three were still under the bus by the kerb-side: the fourth nestled snugly in his pocket. That all this should have been done at the expense of Kowalski, the most relentlessly vigilant of all Branson's guards and by a long way the most suspicious, was just an added bonus. He bethought himself of the aerosol. He gave April Wednesday a gentle nudge and, because people were still talking in varying degrees of animation about the latest incident, he did not find it necessary to keep his voice especially low.

'Listen carefully, and don't repeat my words, no matter how stupid my question may appear. Tell me, would a young lady of – ah – delicate sensibilities – carry a miniature aerosol air-freshener around with her?'

Beyond a blink of the green eyes she showed no reaction. 'In certain circumstances I suppose so, yes.'

He placed the can between them. 'Then please put this in your carry-all. Sandalwood, but I wouldn't try sniffing it.'

'I know very well what's in it.' The can disappeared. 'I suppose it doesn't matter very much if I'm caught with it? If they bring out those old thumb-screws—'

'They won't. They already searched your carry-all, and the person who made the search almost certainly wouldn't remember the contents of one of a dozen bags he's searched. No one's keeping an eye on you: I'm way out on my own as Suspect Number One.'

III

By ten o'clock silence and sleep had returned to the coach. The rain had eased, until it could be called no more than heavy, but still the lightning crackled and the thunder boomed with unabated enthusiasm. Revson glanced over his shoulder to the south-west. There were no signs of any unusual activities in the direction of Lincoln Park. He wondered if those ashore had misinterpreted his message or deliberately ignored it. Both possibilities he thought unlikely: more likely, because of the heavy rain, they were having difficulty in igniting a fire.

At seven minutes past ten a red glow appeared to the south-west. Revson was almost certainly the first person on the bridge to notice it but he thought it impolitic to draw attention to the fact. Within half a minute the dark oily flames were at least fifty feet high.

It was Bartlett who first called attention to this phenomenon and he did so in a very emphatic fashion. He stood in the open doorway behind the driver's seat and shouted: 'Jesus, would you look at that!'

Almost everyone immediately started awake and looked. They couldn't see much. Rain still lashed the outside of the windows and the insides were pretty well steamed up. Like a bunch of lemmings hell-bent on a watery suicide they poured out through the door. The view was certainly very much better from there and well worth the seeing. The flames, already a hundred feet high and topped by billowing clouds of oily smoke, were increasing by the second. Still of the same lemming-like mind and totally oblivious of the rain, they began to run across the bridge to obtain a better view. The occupants of the presidential and rear coaches were doing exactly the same. Nothing attracts people more than the prospects of a good-going disaster.

Revson, though among the first out of the lead coach, made no attempt to join them. He walked unhurriedly round the front of the coach, walked back a few feet, stooped and recovered the oil-skin package. No one paid any attention to him, even had he been visible beyond the bulk of the coach, because they were all running in and looking towards the opposite direction. He removed the torch from the package, angled it forty-five degrees to his right and made his SOS signal, just once: he then pocketed the torch and made his more leisurely way across to the other side of the bridge, glancing occasionally over his left shoulder. Half-way across he saw a rocket, a not very spectacular one, curving up to the south-east.

He reached the far crash barrier and joined O'Hare who was standing some little way apart from the others. O'Hare said: 'You'd make quite an arsonist.'

'That's just by the way of introduction. Wait till you see the next one. Not to mention the fireworks. Sheer pyromania, that's what it is. Let's look at the front end of the rear coach.'

They looked. A full minute passed and nothing happened. O'Hare said: 'Hm. Worrisome?'

'No. Just running a little bit behind schedule, I should think. Don't even blink.'

O'Hare didn't and so he saw it – a tiny intense spark of

bluish-white that could have lasted only milli-seconds. O'Hare said: 'You saw it too?'

'Yes. Far less than I thought it would be.'

'End of radio-wave scanner?'

'No question.'

'Would anyone inside the coach have heard it?'

'That's academic. There's no one inside the rear coach. They're all across here. But there is some sign of activity at the rear of the presidential coach. A dollar gets a cent that Branson's asking some questions.'

IV

Branson was indeed asking some questions. Chrysler by his side, he was talking forcefully into a telephone.

'Then find out and find out now.'

'I'm trying to.' It was Hendrix and he sounded weary. 'I can be held responsible for a lot of things but I can't be held responsible for the forces of nature. Don't you realize this is the worst lightning storm the city has had in years? There are dozens of outbreaks of small fires and the Firemaster tells me his force is fully extended.'

'I'm waiting, Hendrix.'

'So am I. And God only knows how you imagine this fire in Lincoln Park can affect you. Sure, it's giving off clouds of oil smoke, but the wind's from the west and the smoke won't come anywhere near you. You're jumping at shadows, Branson. Wait. A report.' There was a brief silence then Hendrix went on: 'Three parked road oil tankers. One had its loading hose partly on the ground so it was earthed. Witnesses saw this tanker being struck by lightning. Two fire engines are there and the fire is under control. Satisfied?'

Branson hung up without replying.

V

The fire was indeed under control. Firemen, taking their convincing time, were now smothering the barrels of blazing oil with foam extinguishers. Fifteen minutes after the fire had first begun – or been noticed – it was extinguished. Reluctantly, almost – they were now so wet that they couldn't possibly get any wetter – the watchers by the west barrier turned and made their way back to the coaches. But their evening's entertainment had only just begun.

Another fire bloomed to the north. It spread and grew with even greater rapidity than the previous one, becoming so bright and intense that even the lights in the concrete towers of down-town San Francisco seemed pale by comparison. Branson, who had made his way back to his own coach, now ran back to the presidential coach. A bell was ringing in the communications section in the rear. Branson snatched the phone. It was Hendrix.

Hendrix said: 'Nice to forestall you for once. No, we are not responsible for this one either. Why in the hell should we set off a fire where all the smoke is being carried away from you east over the bay? The meteorological officer says that there's a lightning strike once every three or four seconds. And it's not cloud to cloud stuff, it's mainly cloud to earth. On the law of averages, he says, something combustible has to go in one in twenty. I'll keep you posted.'

For the first time, Hendrix hung the phone up on him. Branson slowly replaced his own. For the first time, lines of strain were beginning to etch themselves round the corners of his mouth.

The blue-veined flames were towering now to a height of six or seven hundred feet, as high as the highest building in the city. The smoke given off was dense and bitingly acrid, which is generally the case when several hundred used tyres are added to an oil-based fire. But half a dozen giant fire engines and as many again mobile foam wagons were in very close attendance indeed. On the bridge the more nervous of the newspapermen and cameramen were speculating as to whether the fire would spread to the city itself, a rather profitless speculation as the wind was entirely in the wrong direction. Mayor Morrison stood by the eastern crash barrier, fists clenched, tears streaming down his face, cursing with a nonstop fluid monotony.

O'Hare said to Revson: 'I wonder if the King and the Prince see the irony in all this. After all, it's probably their own oil that they're seeing going up.' Revson made no reply and O'Hare touched his arm. 'Sure you haven't overdone things a bit this time, old boy?' In moments of stress, his English education background tended to show through.

'I wasn't the one with the matches.' Revson smiled. 'No worry, they know what they're about. What I am looking forward to seeing now is the firework display.'

VI

In the presidential communications centre the phone rang again. Branson had it in a second.

'Hendrix. It's an oil storage tank in Fort Mason.' There was no oil storage tank in Fort Mason, but Branson was not a Californian far less a San Franciscan and it was highly unlikely that he was aware of that. 'I've just been on the radio to the Fire Commissioner. He says its bark is worse than its bite and that there's no danger.'

'And what the hell is that, then?' Branson's voice was a shout, his normal monolithic calm in at least temporary abeyance.

'What's what?'

Hendrix's calm served only to deepen Branson's apprehension. 'Fireworks! Dozens of them! Fireworks! Can't you see them?'

'Not from where I sit I can't. Wait.' Hendrix went to the rear door of the communications wagon. Branson hadn't been exaggerating. The sky was indeed full of fireworks, of every conceivable colour and design, at least half of them exploding in glittering falling stars. If Branson had been his usual calm and observant self, Hendrix reflected, he might have noticed that the fireworks, nearly all of a medium trajectory, were firing to the north-east which was the shortest distance between where they were coming from and the nearest stretch of water. All of them, without exception, would fizzle out in the waters of San Francisco Bay. Hendrix returned to the phone.

'They appear to be coming from the Chinatown area and sure as hell they aren't celebrating the Chinese New Year. I'll call back.

VII

Revson said to O'Hare: 'Take your white coat off. It's too conspicuous or will be when it gets dark.' He gave O'Hare his white felt pen. 'You know how to use this?'

'Depress the clip and press the button on top.'

'Yes. If anyone comes too near – well, aim for the face. You'll have to extract the needle.'

'Me and my medical ethics.'

VIII

Branson picked up the phone. 'Yes?'

'It was Chinatown. A firework factory there was struck. That damned thunder and lightning doesn't just seem to want to go away. God knows how many more outbreaks of fire we'll have tonight.'

Branson left the coach and joined Van Effen by the east barrier. Van Effen turned.

'Not often you see a sight like this, Mr Branson.'

'I'm afraid I'm not in the mood to enjoy it.'

'Why?'

'I've a feeling that this is being staged for our benefit.'

'How could this possibly affect us? Nothing's changed as far as we're concerned. Don't let's forget our presidential and royal hostages.'

'Even so—'

'Even so your antennae are tingling?'

'Tingling! They're jumping. I don't know what's going to happen next but I've the feeling that I'm not going to enjoy it.'

It was at that moment that the bridge and the whole of northern San Francisco blacked out.

For some few seconds the silence on the bridge was total. The darkness wasn't total but it came fairly close to being that way. The only illumination came from the faint lighting from the coaches – to conserve the batteries most of the individual reading lights were out, the others dimmed – and the orange-red glow from the distant oil fire. Van Effen said softly: 'Your antennae, Mr Branson. You know you could make a fortune hiring them out.'

'Start up the generator. We'll have the searchlights on the north and south towers. See that the self-propelled guns are ready, loaded, crews standing by. Three men with submachine-guns to be by each gun. I'll go south, you north and alert them. After that, you're in charge of both. I'll try to find out from that bastard Hendrix what this is all about.'

'You don't seriously expect a frontal assault, Mr Branson.'

'I frankly don't know what the hell to expect. What I do know is that we take no chances. Hurry!'

Branson ran south. As he passed the rear coach he shouted: 'Chrysler! The generator. Quick, for God's sake.'

The generator was running before either Branson or Van Effen reached the respective defensive positions. The powerful searchlights came on illuminating both towers: the reverse effect was to plunge the central portion of the bridge into even deeper gloom than before. The guns were readied, machine-gunners in close attendance. Van Effen stayed where he was. Branson ran back towards the central coach. But both Branson and Van Effen were concentrating their efforts on the wrong things and in the wrong directions. They should have been where Revson was.

IX

Revson was crouched in the nose section of the leading helicopter, the variably shuttered flashlight in his hand reduced to scarcely more than a pin-hole of light. He had had no trouble in locating the triggering device: it was between the pilot's seat and the one opposite to it.

With the screwdriver blade of his knife Revson had already removed the four screws that secured the top-plate and the top-plate itself. It was a simple enough device. On the outside of the device was a vertical lever padlocked in position in its top position. When this was depressed it brought a copper arm down between two spring-loaded interior copper arms, so completing the circuit. Twin pieces of flex led from those last two to two crocodile spring-loaded clamps, each secured to the terminals of two nickel-cadmium Nife cells connected up in series. That would produce a total of only three volts, little enough, one would have thought, to activate the radio trigger: but that Branson would have it all expertly calculated out in advance Revson did not for a moment doubt.

He didn't bother to sever or disconnect anything. He merely removed the crocodile clips from the terminals, lifted the Nife cells free, broke the connection between them and stuffed one in each jacket pocket. Had he disconnected or severed anything Branson could have carried out some sort of jury rig: but Revson would have wagered heavily that Branson carried no spare Nife cells. There was no earthly reason why he should have done. He began to replace the cover-plate.

X

Hendrix sounded angry, a man near the breaking point of exasperation. 'What do you think I am, Branson? A bloody magician? I just sit here and snap my fingers and presto! all the lights in the north half of the city go out? I've told you and I tell you again that two of the main transformers have gone out. How I don't know yet, but you don't have to be a genius to know that our old friend from the skies above has been at work again. What did you expect us to do – throw in a tank regiment against you? We knew you had those heavy guns and searchlights – and your priceless hostages. Think we're morons? I'm beginning to think that you're the moron. I'm beginning to think that you're losing your grip. I'll call back'. Hendrix hung up. Branson did the same, almost smashing the phone-rest in the process. It was the second occasion in a very brief space of time that it had been suggested to him that he was losing his grip. His lips were compressed. It was a suggestion he didn't much care for, far less care to contemplate. He remained seated where he was.

XI

Revson closed the helicopter door softly and dropped lightly to the ground. A few paces away he could see O'Hare silhouetted against the still towering but slowly diminishing flames. He called his name softly and O'Hare approached.

'Let's walk to the west side,' Revson said. 'No shooting practice?'

'Nobody as much as looked at the place, far less came near it. Even if they had looked, I doubt whether they would have seen anything. After staring so long at that fire and the fireworks, looking back to the centre of the bridge would have been like looking into total darkness. You know, no night sight.' He handed Revson the white pen. 'Have your little toy back. I remain ethically unbent.'

'And you can have your flashlight back.' Revson handed it over. 'I suggest you return it to your ambulance. At the same time I suggest we might retrieve that pistol and give it to General Cartland. I also suggest you give it to him. I don't want to be seen being too chummy with the General. Tell him not to use it till he gets the word. Ever seen one of those before?' He took a Nife cell from his pocket and handed it to O'Hare who peered at it in the near darkness.

'Some sort of battery?'

'Yes. There were two of them and I have the other. They were to be used to power the explosives' triggering device.'

'And you left no trace of your coming and going?'

'None.'

'So we walk towards the side of the bridge.'

They lobbed the cells into the Golden Gate and walked to the ambulance. O'Hare ushered Revson in first, then followed, closing the door. He said: 'I think we should use the torch. The sudden appearance of bright lights in the windows might attract suspicious attention. After all, we're supposed to be out there enjoying the sights.'

It took O'Hare less than two minutes to break the Cardiac Arrest Unit seal, lift out some equipment, open up, after a series of intricate operations, a secret compartment in the bottom of the box, retrieve the cyanide gun, replace the equipment, close and reseal the lid. O'Hare placed the gun in an inside coat pocket and said complainingly: 'I'm beginning to become ethical all over again.'

XII

Hendrix said over the phone: 'It wasn't the transformers after all. There have been so many breaks and shorts in the city's electrical equipment tonight that the generators' over-load coils just packed up.'

'How long?' Branson asked.

'A few minutes. No more.'

XIII

As was his habit, General Cartland was standing alone by the east barrier. He turned and saw O'Hare who said quietly: 'A word, sir, if you please.'

XIV

The lights of San Francisco and the Golden Gate Bridge came on five minutes later. Branson left the presidential coach and went to meet Van Effen. He said: 'Still think I could make a fortune hiring out my antennae?' He was smiling.

Van Effen wasn't. He said: 'Do me a favour. Just hang on to them a little while yet.'

'Don't tell me your antennae are at work too?'

'If they're not, they sure have good stand-ins.'

XV

The last of the fireworks fizzled to extinction, the oil fire in Fort Mason sank down into a sullen deep-red glow, the lightning and thunder eased, although not markedly so, but the rain showed no sign of abating: had fire broken out in San Francisco that night, it would surely have been rained to extinction. Now that the night's entertainment was patently over, everyone became very conscious that the rain had become very chilly indeed. There was an almost concerted movement back to the coaches.

Revson was in the window seat by the time April Wednesday came in. She hesitated, then sat down beside him. She said: 'And why do you want my seat? I thought it was customary for the lady to be offered the inside seat.'

'To keep her from falling into the aisle during the night? Don't you know this is the golden age of women's lib? However, that's not my real reason. Is it possible for me to reach the aisle without disturbing you in the process?'

'That's a silly question?'

'Is it? I mean, possible?'

'You can see it isn't.'

'Would you be prepared to swear – short of thumb-screws, that is – that I never once disturbed you in the course of the night?'

'You propose to disturb me, then?'

'Yes. Will you?'

She smiled. 'I think I've shown that I can lie with the best of them.'

'You're not only beautiful, but you're good.'

'Thank you. Where were you thinking of going?'

'Do you really want to know? I think you'd better not. Think of the thumb-screws, the rack, being broken on the wheel—'

'But Chief of Police Hendrix said that Branson never offered violence to women.'

'That was the Branson of yore. But he's become jittery now, more than a little rattled. He might find himself driven to a point where he's compelled to abandon his scruples.'

It wasn't the completely sodden thin silk dress she was wearing that made her shiver. 'I think I'd rather not know. When are you—'

'Just before midnight.'

'Then I shan't sleep a wink before then.'

'Excellent. Give me a shake at five minutes to.' Revson closed his eyes and appeared to relax comfortably in his seat.

XVI

By five minutes to midnight everyone in the coach appeared to be asleep: despite their cold and discomfort nearly all had been asleep for over an hour. Even April Wednesday was asleep, her head on Revson's shoulder, huddling close to him for warmth. She was quite unaware of this. Even the guard, Bartlett, almost certainly because Kowalski's prowling figure was no longer there to keep him on the *qui vive*, was much nearer sleep than wakefulness, his head nodding on his chest, only occasionally, and with longer intervals in between, jerking his head upright. Only Revson, his eyes closed, was as awake and alert as a cat on a midnight prowl. He nudged April and whispered in her ear. She started awake and looked at him, her eyes uncomprehending.

'Time to go,' he said softly. It was almost dark inside the coach, the only illumination coming from the dimmed light over the driver's seat and from the lights of the bridge itself. 'Give me the aerosol.'

'The what?' Suddenly she was wide awake, the white of the smudged eyes – the pupils could have been any colour – huge in the gloom. 'Of course.' She reached under her seat and brought up the aerosol can. Revson tucked it in his inside left coat pocket. She said: 'How long will you be?'

'With luck, twenty minutes. Perhaps half an hour. I'll be back.'

She kissed him lightly on the cheek. 'Please take care.'

Revson had no comment on this highly unnecessary advice. 'Move into the aisle. Quietly as you can.'

He passed by her and moved silently forwards, his white pen in his hand. Bartlett's head was on his chest. Revson pressed the button at a distance of less than a foot and the needle lodged behind Bartlett's left ear. Revson eased him back until his head dangled over the back of his seat. The drug, apart from inducing unconsciousness, had a temporarily paralysing effect so there seemed little enough likelihood that Bartlett would slip off his seat. April watched all this without any expression: the only indication of her feelings was the tip of a tongue that sought to moisten dry lips.

There had to be a patrolling guard, Revson knew – he had, in fact, seen him several times – and he had to be taken care of. He peered cautiously through the open driver's doorway. A guard was indeed approaching, coming up from the south, walking a few feet wide of the coaches and carrying a shoulder-slung machine-carbine. Revson thought he recognized him as Johnson, one of the helicopter pilots, but couldn't be sure. Revson switched off Bartlett's dimmed light and remained where he was. He had the aerosol can in his hand but at the last moment changed his mind and brought out the pen instead. A person recovering from the effects of the knock-out needles invariably awoke none the worse for his experience and usually assumed that he had just dropped off to sleep: but as Revson could tell from his own experience of that morning, a person awakening from a gas knock-out felt nauseated and thoroughly hung-over and under no illusion at all that he had been anaesthetized in one way or another. It didn't seem a good idea to have Johnson report this to Branson.

Revson pressed the button and jumped down at the same instant to catch Johnson before he keeled over on to the roadway, less for humanitarian reasons than to prevent the metallic sound of the carbine striking the roadway. He removed the needle from Johnson's forehead, hauled him as silently as possible inside the coach and jammed him in a very uncomfortable position in front of the driver's seat. Johnson was in no position to feel any discomfort and Revson didn't want to risk the possibility of any passenger awakening – highly unlikely though it seemed – and finding an unconscious stranger lying in the aisle.

April Wednesday had gone back to her lip-licking.

XVII

Revson emerged by the near-side front door. In the bright lights of the bridge he might almost as well have stepped out into daylight. He had no doubt that his activities were being carefully watched from both north and south shores through powerful night glasses, but that was of no concern. What mattered was that he was effectively shielded from the other two coaches, though he seriously doubted whether there was anyone keeping watch in either or, indeed, whether anybody at all was awake. In point of fact both Van Effen and Chrysler were talking quietly to each other in the rear coach, but it was impossible for them to see Revson.

Revson crossed the crash barrier, pulled himself to the rail and peered down. Below, all was total blackness. The submarine could or could not have been there: he just had to hope it was.

He descended and pulled the oil-skin container from under

the coach. Inside was the fishing line and a weighted lab. sample canister – weighted, because the wind was still gusting and he had to be sure that the line descended reasonably vertically.

He cut off hooks and lures at the end of the fishing line and attached the canister to the line. He eased the canister over the side and started unwinding the line from its square wooden framework. After about thirty seconds of this he stopped, held the line delicately between forefinger and thumb and waited for some sort of acknowledging tug. There was none. He lowered it another ten feet. Still no answering tug. Perhaps the submarine wasn't there, perhaps the captain was finding it impossible to maintain position because of the tides and strong currents. But then Admiral Newson had said that he knew the very man who could do just that and it was unlikely that a man of Newson's reputation would make any mistake. Revson lowered the line another ten feet then sighed aloud with relief when he felt two sharp tugs on the line.

Twenty seconds later there came another two sharp tugs. Revson overhanded the line in with all possible speed. When he estimated there were only a few feet of line left he leaned far out and pulled in at a much slower speed. He had no wish to bang the radio, however gently, against the steelwork of the bridge. Finally, he had it in his hand, a waterproof bag with the line securely fixed round its neck. He descended to the side of the bus to examine his catch. He cut the securing line with his knife and peered inside. There it was – a tiny gleaming transistorized transceiver.

'Strange hour to go fishing, Revson,' Van Effen said behind him. For a second, no more, Revson remained immobilized. He was holding the bag at chest level and his hand slid stealthily into his left inner pocket. 'I'd like to see just what kind of fish one catches at night in the Golden Gate. Turn round, Revson, slow and easy. I'm a nervous character and you know what that can do to trigger fingers.'

Revson turned round, slow and easy, in the manner of a man who knows all about nervous trigger fingers. He already had the aerosol inside the bag. He said resignedly: 'Well, I suppose it was too good to last.'

'So Branson was right all along.' Van Effen, moon-shaped

face as expressionless as ever, was between five and six feet away. He had his machine-pistol in both hands, held loosely, but with his forefinger indubitably on the trigger. Revson would have been a dead man before he'd covered half the distance between them. But Van Effen was clearly expecting no resistance. 'Let's see what you have there. Slow and easy, now. Slow and easy.'

Slowly, easily, Revson withdrew the aerosol. It was so small that it was almost hidden in his hand. He knew that the can was pressurized to three times the normal and that its effective range was ten feet. Or so O'Hare had told him and Revson had a great deal of faith in O'Hare.

Van Effen shifted the gun under his right arm and pointed the barrel straight at Revson. 'Let me see that.'

'Slow and easy?'

'Slow and easy?'

Revson stretched his arm out unhurriedly. Van Effen's face was no more than three feet away when he pressed the button. He dropped the aerosol and snatched Van Effen's machine-pistol: again he wished to obviate any metallic sounds. He looked down at the crumpled figure at his feet. He had come to form a certain regard for Van Effen, both as a man and a professional: but regrets were not in Revson's line of business. He retrieved the aerosol, took the transceiver and pressed a switch.

'Revson here.'

'Hagenbach.' Revson lowered the volume.

'This is a closed VHF line? No possibility of interception?'

'None.'

'Thank you for the radio. I have a problem here. One of disposal. Van Effen caught me but I caught him. Gas. He recognized me, of course, and can't remain on the bridge. I could throw him into the Golden Gate but I don't want to. He's done nothing to deserve anything like that. He might even turn State evidence. May I speak to the submarine captain, please.'

A new voice came through. 'Captain here. Commander Pearson.'

'My congratulations, captain, and thank you for the radio. You heard what I said to Mr Hagenbach.'

'Yes.'

'Would you be prepared to accept another passenger even although he is unconscious?'

'We aim to please.'

'Would you have a line or rope aboard easy enough for me to haul up but strong enough to take a man's weight? I'd need about five hundred feet.'

'Goodness, no. Wait till I check.' There was a brief silence, then Pearson's voice came through again. 'We have three thirty-fathom coils. Joined together that should be more than enough.'

'Splendid. I'll send my cord down again. Moment, please. I'll have to get a weight for it first.' He strap-hung the radio round his neck to leave his hands free and his eye lighted almost immediately on Van Effen's machine-pistol. He secured the cord to the trigger guard and immediately began to lower away. He spoke into the radio.

'The line's on the way down. It's weighted with Van Effen's machine-pistol and the cord is tied to the trigger-guard. I mean, I wouldn't like anyone to shoot themselves by accident.'

'The Navy is accustomed to the handling of offensive weapons, Mr Revson.'

'No offence, captain. When I get the rope up I'll pass it over a rail and secure it to Van Effen. Double bowline round the thighs, a turn round his waist and his hands tied behind his back so that the rope can't slip over his shoulders.'

'We have openings in the Service for resourceful young men like you.'

'I'm afraid the age qualification cut-off lies far behind me. When I have him ready can you have two or three of your men lower him down over the rail? Damned if I'm going to try myself. As I said, it's my age.'

'You wouldn't believe how modernized today's Navy is. We'll use a winch.'

Revson said apologetically: 'I'm just a land-lubber.'

'We have your cord and gun and nobody's shot down anybody.' There was a brief pause. 'Haul away.'

Revson brought in the rope. It looked hardly thicker than a clothes-line, but Revson didn't doubt that Pearson knew what he was about. He trussed Van Effen in the manner he'd described then dragged him to the edge. He said into the radio: 'Ready to take the strain?'

'Ready.'

Revson eased him over the edge. For a moment Van Effen dangled there, then disappeared downwards into the darkness. The rope over the rail went slack and Pearson's voice came over the radio.

'We have him.'

'Intact?'

'Intact. All for tonight?'

'Yes. Thank you for your co-operation.' Revson wondered briefly what Van Effen's reaction would be when he found himself in a submarine, then spoke again into the radio. 'Mr Hagenbach?'

'Here.'

'You heard it all?'

'Yes. Not a bad job.' Hagenbach was not much given to showering fulsome congratulations on his subordinates.

'I've been lucky. The triggering mechanism for the explosives has been deactivated. Permanently.'

'Good. Very good.' This, from Hagenbach, was the equivalent to the Roman tribute offered a highly successful general after he'd conquered his second or third country in succession. 'Mayor Morrison *will* be pleased to know this.'

'When he knows it. I suggest that in a couple of hours' time you douse the bridge lights again and effect entry into the east side south tower. You have the men, sir?'

'Hand-picked.'

'Don't forget to tell them to remove the detonators on the explosives. Just precautionary, you know.'

'Ha!' Hagenbach's deflation was like a snowflake in the river. 'Of course.'

'And another thought. Before you cut the lights you might use the laser on their south-facing searchlight.'

'We will, my boy, we will.'

'Please don't contact me at any time. I might be carrying the radio on me and might be in a very awkward position, such as talking to Branson, when the call-up buzzer goes off.'

'We'll keep a permanent listening watch for you.'

XVIII

Hagenbach looked round his colleagues. His face almost broke into a smile but he just managed to keep his record intact. He looked at each one in turn, trying to conceal his complacency, but not trying too hard, then finally directed his attention towards the Vice-President.

' "Mad" was the word you used, sir. "Quite mad".'

Richards took it very well. 'Well, perhaps a divine sort of madness. Deactivating that triggering device is a major step forward in itself. If only, as you say, Morrison knew.'

'There do appear to be no limits to his resourcefulness,' Quarry said. 'The right man, in the right place, at the right time, if ever there was. But it still doesn't solve the central problem of the plight of our hostages.'

'I wouldn't worry.' Hagenbach leaned back comfortably in his chair. 'Revson will think of something.'

— 11 —

THE ONLY THING Revson was thinking about was how very pleasant it would be to have a few hours' blissful sleep. He'd dragged an already stirring Johnson from his cramped position in front of the driver's seat and propped him on the second step of the coach entrance, head and shoulders resting more or less comfortably against the hand-rail. A minute or two, Revson thought, and he would come to. Even Bartlett was beginning to stir restlessly in his drugged sleep. Different people reacted widely in the length of time it took them to recover from the effect of the knock-out needles. Johnson and Bartlett appeared to have very similar reaction times.

Revson moved silently down the aisle. April Wednesday was wide awake. She swung out to let him pass to the inside seat then sat again. Before removing his soaking coat and dumping it on the floor, he passed her the aerosol. She stooped and thrust it in the bottom of her carry-all. She whispered: 'I didn't think I'd see you again. How did it go?'

'Well enough.'

'What happened?'

'You want to know? Really?'

She thought and shook her head. There were still visions of thumb-screws in her head. Instead, she said softly: 'What's that round your neck?'

'Good God!' From sleepiness Revson was jerked into immediate wide-awakeness. The little transceiver still dangled from his neck. What a sight for a roving Branson. He lifted the transceiver from his neck, unclipped the straps, picked up his camera and inserted the radio in its base.

She said: 'What's that?'

'Just a teeny-weeny hand camera.'

'It's not. It's a radio.'

'Call it what you like.'

'Where did you get it from? I mean, this coach – everything – has been searched from top to bottom.'

'From a passing friend. I have friends everywhere. You may well have saved my life there. I could kiss you for it.'

'Well?'

When it came to kissing she was nowhere near as fragile as she looked. Revson said: 'That was the nicest part of the whole evening. Of the whole day. Of a whole lot of days. Some day, some time, when we get off this damned bridge, we must try that again.'

'Why not now?'

'You're a brazen—' He caught her arm and nodded. Somewhere up front someone was stirring. It was Johnson. He rose to his feet with surprising quickness and looked up and down the bridge. Revson could just picture what was going on in his mind. His last recollection would have been of seeing the steps of the lead coach and his natural assumption would be that he had just sat down for a moment to rest. One thing was for sure, he would never admit to Branson that he'd slept for even a second. He stepped into the bus and prodded Bartlett with the muzzle of his machine-gun. Bartlett started awake and stared at him.

'You asleep?' Johnson demanded.

'Me? Asleep?' Bartlett was amazed, indignant. 'Can't a man rest his eyes for a moment without having accusations like that thrown at him?'

'Just see that you don't rest them for too long.' Johnson's voice was coldly self-righteous. He descended the steps and walked away.

Revson murmured to April: 'I was sleepy but I'm not now. But I not only want to appear to be asleep, I want to *be* asleep if any turmoil breaks out in the very near future, which I strongly suspect might happen. Don't happen to have any sleeping tablets on you, do you?'

'Why on earth should I? This was supposed to be a day trip, remember.'

'I remember.' He sighed. 'Well, there's nothing else for it. Give me the aerosol can.'

'Why?'

'Because I want to take just the tiniest whiff of it. Then take the can from my hand and tuck it away again.'

She hesitated.

'Remember this dinner – those lots of dinners – I'm going to take you to just as soon as we get ashore.'

'I don't remember anything of the kind.'

'Well, remember it now. But I can't very well take you if I'm at the bottom of the Golden Gate, can I?'

She shuddered and reached reluctantly into her carry-all.

In the rear coach Chrysler put his hand on Branson's shoulder and shook him gently. Branson, despite what must have been his exhaustion, was immediately awake, immediately alert.

'Trouble?'

'I don't know. I'm worried, Mr Branson. Van Effen left here just, he said, to make a normal check on things. He hasn't come back.'

'How long ago was that?'

'Half an hour, sir.'

'God, Chrysler, why didn't you wake me before now?'

'Two things. I knew you needed sleep and we all depend on you. And if ever I knew a man who could take care of himself it's Van Effen.'

'He was carrying his machine-pistol?'

'Have you ever seen him without it since we came on this bridge?'

Branson rose from his seat, picked up his own gun and said: 'Come with me. Did you see which way he went?'

'North.'

They walked to the presidential coach. Peters, the guard, was sitting sideways in the driver's seat, smoking. He turned quickly as a gentle tap came on the door, removed a key from an inner pocket and turned it in the lock. Branson opened the door from the outside and said quietly: 'Have you seen any signs of Van Effen?' He could, in fact, have raised his voice a couple of dozen decibels and it would have made no difference: when it comes to the terms of stertorous snoring, presidents, royalty, generals, mayors and assorted government ministers are no different from the common run of mankind.

'Yes, Mr Branson. Must have been about half an hour ago. I saw him walk towards the nearest rest room there.'

'Did you see him come out again?'

'No. Quite frankly, I wasn't looking outside. I don't bother much. My job is to see that none of those gentlemen makes for the communications desk or rushes me and takes away my gun and key. I don't much fancy having my own gun pointed at my own head. I keep my eyes for what goes on inside this coach not what goes on outside it.'

'And right you are. No reflections on you, Peters.' Branson closed the door and heard the key turn in the lock. They made for the nearest rest room. A very brief search indicated that it was empty. So was the other rest room. They made their way to the ambulance. Branson opened the rear door, used a small torch to locate a switch and flooded the ambulance with light. A shirt-sleeved O'Hare covered with a single blanket, was sound asleep on the side-hinged cot. Branson shook him awake. It took some shaking.

O'Hare opened the rather bleary eyes, winced at the bright overhead light, looked at the two men then at his watch.

'Quarter to one! What the hell do you want at this time of the morning?'

'Van Effen's missing. Have you seen him?'

'No, I haven't seen him.' O'Hare showed a faint stirring

of what could have been professional interest. 'Was he sick or something?'

'No.'

'Then why bother me? Perhaps,' O'Hare said hopefully, 'he's fallen over the side.'

Branson studied the doctor briefly. O'Hare's eyes were slightly puffy, but Branson was experienced enough to realize that it was the puffiness of sleepiness not of sleeplessness. He gestured Chrysler to leave, followed, switched out the light and closed the door behind him.

Johnson, machine-gun slung, was walking towards them. He came up to them, stopped and said: ''Evening, Mr Branson. 'Morning rather.'

'Have you seen Van Effen?'

'Van Effen? When?'

'Inside the past half-hour.'

Johnson shook his head positively. 'Definitely not.'

'But he was out on the bridge. You were on the bridge. If he was here, then you must have.'

'Sorry. No. It's possible he was and possible that I didn't see him. I walk to and fro all the time – it's the best way of keeping awake. I don't keep glancing over my shoulder all the time.' Johnson thought or appeared to think. 'He may have been on the bridge but he may have left it. By that I mean he may for reasons best known to himself have chosen to walk on the other side of the buses.'

'Why should he do that?'

'How should I know? Maybe he wanted to keep in concealment. Maybe anything. How should I know what goes on in Van Effen's mind?'

'True.' Branson had no particular wish to antagonize Johnson who, apart from being an ex-naval officer, was a highly experienced helicopter pilot and an essential part of his escape plans. He said mildly: 'I just suggest that you stand in the middle here and look around from time to time. You're hardly likely to go to sleep on your feet – you're due for relief in fifteen minutes.'

He and Chrysler made their way towards the lead coach. There was a half-dimmed light up front and they could see the glow of Bartlett's cigar. Branson said: 'Well, at least all the guards seem to be on the alert – which makes it all the more difficult to understand Van Effen's disappearance.'

Bartlett said briskly. "Morning, Mr Branson. Making your rounds? All's well here.'

'Have you seen Van Effen? In the past half-hour?'

'No. You can't find him?'

'Let's say he's missing.'

Bartlett thought. 'I won't ask stupid questions like "How can he be missing?" Who saw him last?'

'Peters. Not that that helps. Anybody left this coach in the past half-hour?'

'Nobody's left this coach since we came in after the fire.'

Branson walked back to Revson's seat. April Wednesday was wide awake. Revson, eyes closed, was breathing deeply, heavily. Branson shone the torch in his eyes. There was no reaction. Branson lifted an eyelid. There was no involuntary twitching or muscular resistance in the eyelid which is invariable when the eyelid of a conscious person is raised. Branson concentrated his beam on one eye. A rather glazed eye looked out unseeingly, unblinkingly. Branson dropped the eyelid.

Branson said: 'Out like a light. That's for sure.' If there was disappointment in his voice he concealed it well. 'How long have you been awake, Miss Wednesday?'

'I haven't been to sleep. Maybe I shouldn't have come back to the bridge.' She smiled tremulously. 'I'm just a cowardy-custard, Mr Branson. I hate thunderstorms.'

'I'm not going to hurt you, Miss Wednesday.' He reached out a hand and ran a finger gently across her lips while she looked at him in perplexity. Her lips were as dry as dust. Branson remembered O'Hare's summing up of her emotional and nervous stability or lack of it.

'You *are* scared.' He smiled and patted her shoulder. 'Not to worry. The storm's almost passed away.' He left.

She was scared, but not for the reasons given. She'd been terrified that Branson would try to shake or even slap Revson awake and find it impossible to arouse him.

II

Twenty minutes later Branson and Chrysler stood by the doorway of the rear coach. Chrysler said: 'There's no way he can be on the bridge, Mr Branson.'

'I agree. Let me hear you think aloud, Chrysler.'

Chrysler made a deprecating gesture. 'I'm a follower, not a leader.'

'Nevertheless.'

'I'll try. I can speak freely?' Branson nodded. 'First, Van Effen didn't jump. Not only is he the last person I'd ever associate with suicide, but he was also only days away from a seven-figure fortune. He didn't defect. You said I could speak freely. Again he stood to lose a fortune, he was totally loyal and to defect he'd have had to walk two thousand feet towards either tower and Johnson couldn't have missed that. So he's met with an accident. You're sure it couldn't have been the doctor?'

'Positive.'

'And it wasn't Revson. The only person I could think of is General Cartland. He could be dangerous. But Peters—' Chrysler broke off and thought. 'You know, Mr Branson, I don't think this would have happened if Kowalski had been on the prowl tonight.' He paused. 'I'm beginning to wonder if Kowalski's accident really *was* an accident.'

'I have wondered. Your conclusions, Chrysler?'

'Somewhere in this barrel there's another rotten apple. It could be one of us.'

'A disquieting thought but one that has to be considered. Although why anyone should throw away a fortune—'

'Maybe the Government, some way, some how, has promised someone to double their cut if—'

'This is just idle speculation.' Branson's creased brow gave the lie to his words. 'Suspecting everyone in sight only leads to hysteria and hysterics is one thing we can't afford. And your final conclusion on Van Effen?'

'The same as yours. He's at the bottom of the Golden Gate.'

III

Van Effen was, in fact, seated in the communications wagon ashore. Hagenbach and Hendrix were seated across the table from him. Two policemen with drawn guns stood by the doorway. Van Effen wasn't quite his usual expressionless self. He looked slightly dazed, whether from the shock of finding himself in the predicament he was in or because he was still suffering from the after-effects of the gassing was difficult to say.

Van Effen said: 'So I under-estimated Revson?'

'When you get up to San Quentin you'll find quite a few others who will endorse your views.' Hagenbach looked at Van Effen. 'Speaking of San Quentin, you appreciate you can't hope for less than ten years with no hope of remission.'

'There's an occupational hazard in every job.'

'There doesn't have to be.'

'I don't understand you.'

'We can do a deal.'

'No deal.'

'You've nothing to lose and a great deal to gain. Ten years of your life, to be precise.'

'No deal.'

Hagenbach sighed. 'I rather thought that might be your attitude. Admirable but misguided.' He looked at Hendrix. 'You would agree?'

Hendrix said to the policemen: 'Handcuff him and take him to the maximum security wing of the military hospital. Tell the doctors that Mr Hagenbach will be along in a few minutes. Make sure the recorders are working.'

Van Effen said: 'Hospital? Recorders? You mean drugs.'

'If you won't co-operate with us we'll just have to settle for your unwilling co-operation. Unconscious co-operation, if you wish.'

Van Effen cracked his moonface in an almost contemptuous smile. 'You know that no court will accept a confession made under duress.'

'We don't need any confession from you. We already have enough on you to put you away for as long as we wish. We just want a little helpful information from you. A judicious mixture of sodium pentothal and a few other choice herbs will make you sing like a lark.'

'That's as maybe.' The contempt was still in Van Effen's face. 'Even you have to obey the law of the land. Lawmen who extract information by illegal means are subject to automatic prosecution and automatic imprisonment.'

Hagenbach was almost genial. 'Dear me, dear me. I thought even you, Van Effen, would have heard of a presidential pardon. Or have you forgotten that you kidnapped a President?'

IV

At ten minutes to three that morning an Air Force lieutenant on the south shore twirled two knobs on a highly sophisticated piece of equipment until the cross-hairs on his ultra-violet telescopic sights were lined up dead centre on the centre of Branson's southern-facing searchlight. He jabbed a button, just once.

V

At five minutes to three, three men climbed into a strangely-shaped low-slung vehicle which was concealed from the bridge by the communications truck. A rather nondescript individual in a grey coat climbed behind the wheel while the other two sat in the back seat. They were clad in grey overalls and looked curiously alike. Their names were Carmody and Rogers. They were both in their mid-thirties and looked tough and competent in a rather gentlemanly way. Whether they were gentlemen or not was not known: whether they were tough and competent was beyond dispute. They didn't look like explosives experts but they were that too. Both carried pistols and both carried silencers for those pistols. Carmody carried a canvas bag containing a tool-kit, two aerosol gas cans, a ball of heavy cord, adhesive tape and a torch. Rogers had a similar bag with a walkie-talkie, Thermos and sandwiches. They were obviously well-equipped for whatever task they had in mind and prepared for a stay of some duration.

VI

At three o'clock all the lights on the Golden Gate Bridge and the adjacent parts of the city blacked out. The man in the grey coat started up his flat truck and the electric vehicle whirred almost silently towards the south tower.

VII

The duty policeman picked up the phone in the communications wagon. It was Branson and he wasn't in a jovial mood. 'Hendrix?'

'The Chief is not here.'

'Then get him.'

'If you could tell me what the matter—'

'The bridge lights have gone again. Get him.'

The policeman laid down his phone and walked to the rear of the wagon. Hendrix sat on a stool by the open door, a walkie-talkie in his hand, a cup of coffee in the other. The walkie-talkie crackled.

'Carmody here, chief. We're inside the tower and Hopkins is half-way back with the electric cart already.'

'Thank you.' Hendrix put down the walkie-talkie. 'Branson? A mite anxious?'

Hendrix finished off his coffee in a leisurely fashion, crossed the wagon, picked up the phone and yawned.

'I was asleep. Don't tell me. The lights are out again. We've been having black-outs all over the city tonight. Hold on.'

VIII

In the presidential coach, Branson held on. Chrysler came running down the aisle. The President looked at him blearily. The oil barons snored steadily on. Branson, phone still in hand, looked round. Chrysler said quickly: 'South searchlight is out of action.'

'It's not possible.' Branson's face was beginning to show deeper lines of strain. 'What's wrong?'

'God knows. It's black out there. Generator seems fine.'

'Then run for the north one and turn it round. No. Wait.' Hendrix was on the phone. 'One minute you say?' He turned to Chrysler. 'Forget it. The lights are coming on again.' Branson spoke into the phone again. 'Don't forget. I want Quarry on this phone at seven sharp.'

Branson replaced the phone and walked up the aisle. The President stopped him.

'When is this nightmare going to stop?'

'That's up to your Government.'

'I've no doubt the Government will accede to your requests. You interest me, Branson, you interest all of us here. Why this bitter grudge against society?'

Branson smiled his empty smile. 'Society I can take or leave.'

'Then why the grudge against me? Why the public humiliation? You've been invariably polite to everyone else. Isn't it enough to hold the nation to ransom without making a fool of me at the same time?'

Branson made no answer.

'You don't like my politics, perhaps?'

'Politics bore me.'

'I was speaking to Hendrix today. He tells me your father is an extremely wealthy banker back east. A multi-millionaire. You envy a man who's made it to the very top. You couldn't wait to inherit his bank and his millions so you took the only other course open to you. Crime. And you haven't made it. And you haven't had recognition – except that of a few top policemen. So you're a failure. So you bear a grudge. So you take it out, symbolically, on America's leading citizen.'

Branson said wearily, 'You, Mr President, are a lousy diagnostician and an even lousier psychiatrist. Okay, okay, insults again, but this is private. You may fear no more the lash of my tongue. But to think that your decisions can affect over two hundred million Americans.'

'What do you mean?'

'It's how wrong you can get. Branson, senior, that model of integrity and propriety, is a double-dyed bastard. He was also – and still is – a double-dyed crook. A renowned investment banker, you understand, but it didn't do his investors much good. They were mainly people of modest means. I at least rob wealthy institutions. I found this out when I worked in his bank. I wouldn't have taken a lousy dollar from him.

I didn't even give him the pleasure of disinheriting me. I just told him what I thought of him and his lousy bank and walked out. As for recognition – who wants it?'

'You certainly achieved more in the past eighteen hours than your father did in a lifetime.' The President was understandably sour.

'That's notoriety. Who wants that either? And for money – I already am a multi-millionaire.'

'And still you want more?'

'My motives are my business. Sorry to have interrupted your sleep, sir.' Branson left.

Muir, in the next armchair, said: 'Now, that was rather peculiar.'

'So you weren't asleep?'

'One hates to interrupt. The Branson in the still watches of the night is not the Branson of the daylight hours. Forthcoming, one might almost say. Polite. Almost as if he was seeking for some kind of self-justification. But obviously bitter as hell about something.'

'If he doesn't want recognition and doesn't need the money then what the hell are we doing stuck out on this damned bridge?'

'Ssh. Mayor Morrison might hear you. I don't know. With your permission, Mr President, I'm going back to sleep.'

IX

When Carmody and Rogers reached the top of the south tower and stepped outside the lift, Carmody reached an arm in, pressed a button and withdrew his arm as the door began to close. Both men stepped outside and gazed down silently at the darkened and barely visible bridge some five hundred feet below them. After a minute Carmody withdrew the walkie-talkie from his canvas bag, extended the aerial and said: 'You can cut the power now. The lift's been down for thirty seconds.'

He replaced the walkie-talkie and removed his overalls. Over his purposely-chosen dark shirt he wore a leather harness with a heavy steel buckle at the back. A nylon rope spliced to the buckle was wound several times round his waist. He was in the process of unwinding this when the bridge lights and the aircraft warning lights on top of the towers came on again. Carmody said: 'A chance of our being spotted, you think?'

'Thinking of the aircraft lights?' Carmody nodded. 'No chance. Not from their angle. And I understand their south searchlight isn't working too well.'

Carmody unwound the rest of the rope and passed the end to Rogers. 'A couple of turns, if you would, Charles, then hang on real good.'

'Depend on it. If you take a dive that means I'll have to disarm the damned thing myself – with no one to hold me.'

'We should get danger money for this.'

'You're a disgrace to the Army bomb disposal squad.'

Carmody sighed, moved out on to the giant cable and began to remove the detonators from the explosives.

X

It was six-thirty in the morning when Revson stirred and woke. He looked at April and saw that her green eyes were on his. There were heavy shadows under her eyes and her normally pale skin was now even more unnaturally so.

He said: 'You don't look to me as if you've rested any too well.'

'I didn't sleep all night.'

'What? With me here to look after you?'

'It's not me I'm worried about. It's you.'

He said nothing.

'Do you feel hung-over? After your – your sleeping pill?'

'No. Guess I must have slipped into a natural sleep. That all you worried about?'

'No. Branson was here just before one o'clock. He examined your eyes with a torch to see if you were still asleep.'

'No sense of privacy, that man. You'd think—'

'I think he's again cast you in the role of prime suspect.'

'Suspected of what?'

'Van Effen's missing.'

'Is he now?'

'You don't seem much concerned.'

'What's Van Effen to me or me to Van Effen? No more alarms during the night?'

'At three o'clock the bridge lights went off again.'

'Ah!'

'Nothing surprises you much, does it?'

'Why should the lights going out surprise me? Could have been a dozen reasons for it.'

'I think the reason is sitting right by me.'

'I was asleep.'

'You weren't asleep when you were out on the bridge at midnight. I'll bet your new little – ah – camera wasn't all that inactive either.' She leaned towards him, her eyes moving from one of his to the other. 'You didn't by any chance just happen to kill Van Effen last night?'

'What do you think I am? A murderer for hire?'

'I don't know what to think. You will not have forgotten that I heard the contents of the message you sent when I was taken to the hospital. I remember the exact words. "Only Branson and Van Effen are natural leaders. Those two I could kill." '

'I did say that. I didn't kill Van Effen last night. My life on it. Van Effen, in my opinion, is alive and well, if not exactly flourishing.'

'That's not what Branson thinks.'

'How should you know that?'

'After Bartlett left – was relieved—'

'Bartlett didn't mention to Branson that he might just possibly have dozed off for a moment?'

'What do you think?'

'Okay, so he was alert and watchful as all hell. And then?'

'And then this – this gorilla came on.' Revson looked at the new guard. Hirsute, incredibly beetle-browed, with a negligible clearance between brows and hairline: April's description didn't flatter gorillas any.

'Yonnie,' Revson said. 'Branson's mobile think-tank.'

'Chrysler came by, more than once. I heard him saying to that man that he and Branson knew that Van Effen was at the bottom of the Golden Gate.'

'I'm looking forward to seeing his face when he finds out, just possibly for the first time in his life, how wrong he can be.'

'You don't want to tell me?'

'No. Neither do you.'

'You seem very sure of yourself.'

'About that, yes.'

'Can you make an end to all this?'

'That, I'm afraid, is another matter.' He thought and smiled. 'If I try very hard, can I take you out for dinner tonight?'

'Tonight!'

'You heard.'

'You can take me to Timbuctoo if you want.'

'Hussies. You can always tell them.'

XI

The phone call-up in the communications centre in the presidential coach buzzed at exactly seven o'clock. Branson picked it up. 'Yes.'

'Quarry here. We have acceded to your preposterous demands and made the necessary arrangements. We're waiting to hear from your contact in New York.'

'Waiting to hear – you should have heard two hours ago.'

Quarry said wearily: 'We're waiting to hear from him again.'

'When did he call?'

'As you said, two hours ago. He's making some arrangements with what he calls "European friends".'

'He was to have given you a password.'

'He did. Hardly original, I thought. "Peter Branson."'

Branson smiled broadly and replaced the receiver. He was still smiling when he stepped out into the early morning sunlight. Chrysler was there and he wasn't smiling at all. Chrysler was exhausted, he'd temporarily taken over the roles of both Van Effen and Kowalski. But the reason for his worry lay elsewhere. Branson said: 'Money side is all fixed up.'

'That's splendid, Mr Branson.'

Branson's smile disappeared. 'You seem less than overjoyed.'

'There are a couple of things I'd like to show you.'

Chrysler led them to the south-facing searchlight. 'You probably know that a searchlight is not like an ordinary torch or flashlight. I mean it doesn't use lamps. It comes from an electric arm that jumps between two electrodes. Something like the sparking plug in a car except that there the spark is intermittent. Here the arc is continuous. Look at the electrode on the left.'

Branson looked. 'It looks as if it's been melted or bent or something like that. And one must assume that those electrodes are designed to withstand the tremendous heat generated by the arc.'

'Precisely. And something you haven't seen. This tiny hole here in the glass.'

'What are you trying to tell me, Chrysler?'

'There's something else.' Chrysler, walking slowly back with Branson, pointed to the roof of the rear coach. 'The radio-wave scanner. It's kaput, knocked out. Since we checked and double-checked that there are no transceivers – apart from ours – on the bridge, we haven't bothered using it. I just happened to check by accident this morning. I went up and had a look. There's a scorch mark on the base of the revolving spindle.'

'Could have been caused by lightning? Both cases? After all, God knows there was plenty of it around last night.'

'I would point out, Mr Branson, that neither the radio-wave scanner or the searchlight are earthed: both are mounted on rubber wheels.'

'The scanner—'

Chrysler said patiently: 'The coach's rubber wheels.'

'Then what?'

'I think they're using a laser beam on us.'

XII

Even at that early hour all seven of the decision-makers ashore were gathered round the table in the communications wagon when the phone rang. The duty policeman picked it up.

'Branson here. Get me General Carter.'

'He can't be far away. Hang on please.' The policeman covered the mouth-piece. 'It's Branson for you, general.'

'Switch on the speaker so that we can all hear what he has to say. Tell him I've just come in.'

'The general has just arrived.'

Carter took the phone. 'Branson?'

'Carter, use that laser beam on us just once again and we'll throw, say, Mr Muir over the side. For starters.'

The other six at the table looked at one another with quick apprehension and, possibly, the relieved thought in their minds that it was Carter who had to field this one.

'Explain yourself.'

'One of our searchlights and radio-wave scanner have been knocked out. All signs point to a laser beam.'

'You're a fool.'

There was a brief silence. Branson, clearly, had been taken momentarily aback. Then he said: 'Muir won't think so when he's on his way down to the Golden Gate.'

'I repeat you're a fool and if you can listen I'll tell you why. In the first place you're not an expert and wouldn't recognize the signs of laser damage if it was on your breakfast plate. In the second place, there are no such units in the Bay area – if there were I'd be the first person to know. In the third place, if we had laser beams we could have picked off every one of your villains as they walked about the bridge – or don't you know how accurate and deadly a laser beam is? With the proper telescopic sights you can puncture a football at ten thousand yards.'

'You seem to know a suspiciously great deal about lasers, general.' It was a negative remark and Branson could have been either thinking or stalling for time.

'I don't deny it. I've been trained in them, I even helped in the development of them. Every general has his own trade or speciality. General Cartland is an explosives expert. I'm an electronics engineer. Where was I? Yes. In the fourth place we could have immobilized your helicopters without your knowing anything about it until you tried to take off. You're putting ideas into my head, Branson. Lastly, the probable cause was an electrical discharge – lightning.'

'Neither the searchlight nor scanner was earthed. They're mounted on rubber wheels.'

Carter let irritation creep into his voice. 'I'd stick to robbing banks if I were you. You don't have to be earthed to be struck by lightning. It happens to planes hundreds of times a year at altitudes up to twenty-five thousand feet. Would you call those earthed? Lightning has also quite an affinity for metal.' He paused. 'Of course, you have a generator for your searchlight, almost certainly a petrol generator and as you wouldn't want to be asphyxiated by carbon monoxide fumes you wouldn't have it inside a coach. Tell me, do you also use the generator to recharge your coach batteries – through a transformer, I mean?'

There was the barest pause then Branson said: 'Yes.'

Carter sighed. 'Must I do all the thinking for you, Branson? There you have a massive great lump of metal solidly earthed to the roadway and directly connected to both searchlight and scanner. What a target for any wandering lightning flash. Would there be anything more?'

'Yes. Pass the word that I want the TV cameras in position and ready at 9 a.m.'

Carter hung up. Richards said approvingly: 'Quite a performance for the crack of dawn. Takes more than a few stars to make a general, I suppose. I have a feeling that our Branson must be feeling more than a little harried by this time. And when shall we be giving our own TV performance?'

Hagenbach said: 'Directly after Branson's, I should think. Nine-thirtyish. Moment of maximum psychological impact and all that sort of thing.'

'As our – ah – anchor-man, you have your lines ready?'

Hagenbach didn't deign to reply.

XIII

Branson said: 'Well, you go along with that?'

'Carter's no fool, that's sure.' Chrysler was uncertain. 'But if it were lightning transmitted through the generator why didn't it just jump from one electrode to the next instead of making a hole in the searchlight glass? I mean, where was it going?'

'I'm afraid it's not my field.'

'I'm beginning to think it's not mine either. But I'm damned sure there's something fishy afoot.' He hesitated. 'Maybe I wasn't so bright with that one but I've another idea, Mr Branson.'

'Ideas are what I need. Myself, I'm fresh out of them.'

Coming from Branson, Chrysler thought, that was quite a remarkable statement.

'I do my best, but I'm no Van Effen. Besides, I feel just about all in. Even you can't keep going twenty-four hours a day. You need a new lieutenant – not to say a fresh one – and with respects to my colleagues, well—'

'Out with it.'

'Now that our men are in possession of the Mount Tamalpais radar stations, I think Parker is quite capable of looking after things himself. I suggest you send a chopper to bring in Giscard. You know him even better than I do. He's tough, he's a leader, he's resourceful, he doesn't panic and in some ways he's very astute: by that I mean, all respects to you, Mr Branson, he's never seen the inside of a court-room. It would take a helluva load off your back.'

'You're quite right, of course. If I didn't need a break I should have thought of that myself. Get hold of either Johnson or Bradley – no, Bradley: Johnson had guard duty. Tell him to move right away. I'll get on the phone and tell Giscard. I'll also warn our friends ashore what's going to happen to them if they try to interfere. Not that they should need telling by now.'

Branson made his calls, winced at the clattering roar as the Sikorsky lifted cleanly off the bridge and headed north. At least Carter had been telling the truth about one thing: the helicopter hadn't been subjected to the attentions of a laser beam.

XIV

Revson said to April: 'I don't want to sound indelicate but wouldn't you like to pay a visit to the ladies' – ah – powder room?'

She stared at him. 'What on earth for? Oh, well, you'll have a reason.'

'Yes. Just repeat this after me.' She repeated it four times then said: 'Is that all?'

'Yes.'

'Once would have been enough.'

'Well, you never know what the help's like these days.'

'Why can't you do it yourself?'

'It's urgent and I want it done now. There are four ladies aboard this bridge and at least fifty men. Your chances of privacy and seclusion are all that higher.'

'And what are you going to do? You look pretty scruffy to me.'

'To re-phrase the old song, I've left my razor in San Francisco. Then breakfast. The wagon's due at seven-thirty.'

'I wish I had an appetite.' She rose and spoke briefly to Yonnie who bared his teeth in a fearful grimace that he probably regarded as being a charmingly graceful assent.

XV

The transistor in front of Hagenbach buzzed. He pulled it towards him and raised the volume. The other six men bent forward in eager expectancy. This call could be from only one source. They were wrong.

'Mr Hagenbach?' A feminine voice.

'Speaking.'

'April Wednesday.'

Hagenbach took it with remarkable aplomb. 'Carry on, my dear.'

'Mr Revson wants to know as soon as possible if it's possible to reduce the last resort to a non-lethal level. He wants you to have as much time as possible to try. That's why I'm calling now.'

'I'll try. I can't guarantee.'

'He says to lay down a pattern of smoke bombs one minute before. He says he'll radio you one minute before that.'

'And I want to talk to Revson just as urgently. Why isn't he doing this himself?'

'Because I'm in the ladies' toilets. Somebody's coming.' The voice trailed away in a whisper and the transceiver went dead.

Hagenbach called to the communications desk: 'The armoury. Emergency. General Carter. I'm going to need your help on this one.'

'The ladies' toilet,' Quarry said unbelievingly. 'Are there no depths to which this man of yours won't descend?'

'Be reasonable. You didn't expect him to be there himself. Knowing Revson, I rate that an "A" for gentlemanly conduct.'

Vice-President Richards spoke slowly and distinctly. 'Up in the hospital you told us that you didn't know what "the last resort" was.'

Hagenbach looked at him coldly. 'Vice-Presidents should know better. No one has ever become the head of the FBI without being a master of prevarication.'

XVI

Breakfast arrived on mid-bridge at seven-thirty. Branson passed it up which, in view of the shock awaiting his nervous system, was perhaps as well. At seven-forty-five Bradley made a perfect touch-down in his Sikorsky. Giscard, grim-faced and purposeful, stepped down on to the bridge not, oddly enough, looking at all incongruous in his police sergeant's uniform. He probably had more photographs taken of him in the next five minutes than he'd had in the whole of his previous existence – which would not have been difficult: Giscard, as a purely professional safeguard, made it his business never to have his photograph taken. But even the redoubtable Giscard had come too late. At eight o'clock an already troubled Branson – no hint of concern showed in his composed and confident face – received his first and far from faint intimations of mortality.

Branson was deep in conversation with a fresh and confident Giscard when Reston, duty guard on the Presidential coach, came hurrying up. 'Phone, Mr Branson.'

Giscard said: 'I'll take care of things, Mr Branson. You try to get some rest.' He touched him lightly on the shoulder. 'There's nothing to worry about.' Giscard had no means of knowing it but it was the most way-out prophecy he'd ever made or would ever be likely to make again.

It was Hagenbach on the phone. He said: 'I've bad news for you, Branson. Kyronis doesn't want to see you. Not now. Not ever.'

'Who?' Branson saw the marbled knuckles on the hand holding the phone and made a conscious effort to relax.

'K-Y-R-O-N-I-S. The president of that Caribbean island paradise of yours. I'm afraid you're not welcome.'

'I don't know what you're talking about.'

'I'm afraid you do. And I'm afraid your world-wide publicity campaign has scared the poor man out of his wits. We didn't find him, he called us. He's on the international line right now. Shall I patch him in?'

Branson didn't say whether he should patch him in or not. A high-pitched voice with a pronounced Caribbean accent came to his ear.

'You fool, Branson. You madman. You wide-mouthed boaster. You had to tell the world that you were going to the Caribbean. You had to tell the world that it had a prison stockade in one corner. You had to tell the world that it had no extradition treaty with the United States. You damn fool, how long do you think it would take American Intelligence to piece that together? I called them before they came calling on me. Their fleet has already moved out from their Guantanamo base in Cuba. Their C54s are lined up on the runways in Fort Lauderdale with God knows how many paratroopers and marines standing by. They could take our little principality over in ten minutes and your Vice-President has assured me that they would consider it a pleasure.' Kyronis stopped to take what appeared to be his first breath since he started his tirade.

Branson said nothing.

'Megalomania, Branson. Megalomania. I always warned you it was the one thing that could bring you down. Sheer, bloody megalomania.'

Branson hung up the phone.

— 12 —

GISCARD TOOK the news with remarkable aplomb. 'So Kyronis has ratted on us. It's not the end of the world and I don't see that it changes a single thing. I think this is just part of a war of nerves, attrition, you know, psychological warfare. Okay; so you've been here – what is it? – twenty-three hours and I don't know what the strains have been like. But I'm sure of this – with no other way of getting at you they're trying to pressurize you into making a mistake. It's kind of like a poker game but with no cards in their hands all they can do is bluff.' Giscard nodded to the presidential coach. 'What's bluff when you hold all the cards in your hands?'

'There speaks the voice of reason, is that it?' Branson smiled. 'You forget that I *know* Kyronis's voice.'

'Sure you do. I don't doubt it was Kyronis. I also don't doubt that the Government, through some fast checking by the CIA or the FBI, got to him first.'

'What makes you think that?'

'Because Kyronis has your VHF number. He could have radioed you direct instead of causing all this hullabaloo. But that wouldn't have suited our friends' department of psychological warfare.'

'And I've had an idea, Mr Branson.' Chrysler had shed much of his weariness since Giscard's arrival. 'Who needs Kyronis? The presidential Boeing can reach half a dozen countries anywhere in the world that have no extradition treaty with the USA. A dozen, for all I know. But there's no need to go further than the Caribbean. You've been thinking big all along, Mr Branson. Now's the time to keep on thinking big.'

Branson rubbed his forehead. 'Think big aloud. Someone has to this morning.'

'Havana. There's no extradition treaty with them. Sure, there's an agreement to repatriate hi-jackers, but no one's going to return the hi-jacker of the presidential Boeing – especially if the President has a pistol to his head. Okay, so the US is prepared to take over Kyronis's tiny islet. Cuba is a vastly different proposition. Castro has a first-class army, air force and navy. Any attempt to get the President out would lead to nothing short of full-scale war. And don't forget that Castro is Moscow's blue-eyed boy. An armed invasion of Cuba would bring a violent reaction and I don't think the US would be prepared to risk an eyeball-to-eyeball nuclear confrontation over a miserable half billion dollars.'

Branson nodded slowly. 'Curiously enough, that was where Van Effen wanted to go. And for much the same reasons.'

'And can't you see how Castro would just love it? He'd go on TV and weep and wail and wring his hands and say how much he'd love to be of help but his hands are hopelessly tied. Then when the cameras are switched off he falls about the place laughing.'

Branson said: 'Gentlemen, you have restored my faith in human nature. At least my own nature. Havana it is. Now. Our next show is at nine. All the tackle and explosives as before. Peters can drive the electric truck as before. Bartlett and Boyard fixed the last lot – let's give Reston and Harrison a go.' Branson smiled. 'They think they're better than Bartlett and Boyard and should have had the privilege of the first attempt. See they carry walkie-talkies. Which reminds me. Chrysler, I want to be in a position where I can lay hands on a telephone wherever I happen to be. I don't want to have to keep running to the President's coach. I just want a direct line to Hagenbach and company. You can fix one up in our coach?'

'I'd have to go through the local exchange.'

'So what? By all means. Tell them to keep the line permanently open. I want a lead to where I'll be sitting when the TV is on. And can you get a radio-telephone link from the lead helicopter?'

'Turn a knob, is all. What's that for, Mr Branson?'

'We're going to need it some time. Better sooner than never.'

II

It was another glorious morning of blue and gold, a cloudless sky, a fairy-tale setting which achieved the impossible of making even the grim fortress of Alcatraz into an islet of shimmering beauty. As on the previous day a low deep bank of fog was approaching from the west. Out of all three coaches there was only one person who was not savouring the delights of the morning or, in the case of Branson's men, on duty.

Revson sat in his seat, elbow on the window ledge, hand cupped to his cheeks so that no one could see his lips moving.

Hagenbach said: 'Turn the volume down, put the transceiver to your ear.'

'Impossible. My head and shoulders are above window level. I can bend down for a few seconds. But be quick.'

Revson's camera was upside down on his knees, the transceiver nestling in the opened recess. He turned down the volume and put his head low. After about fifteen seconds he straightened and looked carelessly around. Nobody was paying any attention to him. He turned up the volume.

'Well?' Hagenbach's voice was querulous. 'Aren't you surprised?'

'Not all that much. Are you going to tell him?'

'Remember, you don't give any signal to go until I'm all through at this end.'

'I'll remember. How about the CUBs?'

'The experts aren't all that happy about the prospects.'

'Then use a few of them only and make up for the rest in gas bombs. Are you in touch with the two men at the top of the tower?'

'Carmody and Rogers. Yes.'

'Tell them if they nab anyone to take them down to the pier of the tower.'

'Why?'

'Look. I'm exposed. Is the admiral there?'

Hagenbach refrained from questions though it must have cost him a considerable effort. Newson came through.

Revson said: 'Do you have any small, quiet boats, sir?'

'Electrically powered?'

'Ideally.'

'In abundance.'

'When the fog comes in, do you think you could get one alongside the pier of the south tower?'

'Consider it done.'

'With a breeches buoy pistol and suitable ropes?'

'No problem.'

'Thank you, sir. Mr Hagenbach?'

'Yes. Secretive bastard, aren't you?'

'Yes, sir. The laser unit is ready for action? Ah, good. Would you have it lined up on the drive shaft of the rotor of the lead helicopter – that's to say, the one furthest from you. Have it locked in position so that it can hit its target even through dense smoke.'

'Why on earth—'

'Somebody coming.'

Revson looked around. There was nobody coming, but he'd no desire to bandy words with Hagenbach. He clipped the base of the camera, slung it over his shoulder and left the coach.

III

'A bit of trouble, sir.' Chrysler handed a walkie-talkie to Branson.

'Reston here, Mr Branson.' Reston and Harrison had set off less than ten minutes earlier for the south pier. 'The lift is out of order.'

'Damn. Wait.' Branson looked at his watch. Eight twenty-five. His performance was due to start at nine. He crossed to the rear coach where Chrysler had already obtained a direct line to the communications centre ashore.

'Branson here.'

'Hendrix. Don't tell me what you're after. I know. I was speaking to the bridge commissioners a few moments ago. They tell me that the breaker for the tower lifts was burnt out during the night.'

'Why isn't it repaired?'

'They've been working on it for three hours.'

'And how much longer—'

'Half an hour. Perhaps an hour. They can't be certain.'

'Call me the moment it's fixed.'

He returned to his walkie-talkie. 'Sorry, you'll have to climb. The lift's being repaired.'

There was a silence then Reston said: 'Jesus. All that way?'

'All that way. It's not Everest. Should be straightforward. And you have your manual.' He laid down the walkie-talkie and said to Giscard: 'I don't envy them, myself. Another psychological pin-prick?'

'Could be. But after a night like last night, well—'

IV

Revson joined O'Hare by the west barrier. He said without preamble: 'How hermetic is the rear door of your ambulance?'

O'Hare had ceased to be surprised at anything Revson said. 'Why?'

'Say oxygen were to be abstracted from the inside. How would you get on?'

'We've oxygen bottles, of course. Not to mention the oxygen in the cardiac unit.'

'You may need it. Ever heard of CUB-55s? Short for Cluster Bomb Units.' O'Hare shook his head. 'Well, there's liable to be a few around in the next hours – this morning, I shouldn't be surprised. They are lethal asphyxiation bombs, one of the more delightful of the recent advances in weaponry. They suck the oxygen from the air and leave not a mark on the victims.'

'You should know. But – well, it's far fetched.'

'A pity you couldn't ask the hundreds who died at Xuan Loc because of them. The Cambodian Government made frequent use of them in South-East Asia. The bombs, I regret to say, were supplied then by the United States Navy.'

'This classified information?'

'No. Hanoi made plenty of noise about it at the time.'

'And you're going to use those bombs?'

'Yes. I'm trying to have them denatured, you know, their lethal potential lessened. At least, the experts are.'

'Can they do it?'

'There's a certain lack of optimism.'

'Who thought this one up? You?' Revson nodded, just once.

'You, Revson, are a cold-blooded bastard. Hasn't it occurred to you that the innocent will suffer, maybe die, as well as the guilty?'

'Not for the first time, I repeat that all doctors should be given an intelligence test before they're allowed to practise. The innocent will not suffer. The innocent will be in their coaches and, because it's going to be hot, they'll have the air-conditioning on. That means closed doors and the recirculation of cleaned used air. When you see the first smoke bomb drop, make for cover.'

Revson walked away and touched Grafton on the arm. 'May I have a word with you?' Grafton hesitated, shook his head in puzzlement, then followed. When he judged they were out of earshot of the nearest person, Revson stopped.

Grafton said: 'Do we have to take a walk to talk?'

'In this case, yes. We haven't been introduced. You're Mr Grafton of UP, doyen of the newsmen on this bridge?'

'If you want to flatter me, yes. And you're Mr Revson, food-taster to Royalty.'

'Just a sideline with me.'

'You have another business. Don't tell me.' Grafton regarded him with cool grey, judicial eyes. 'Federal Bureau of Investigation.'

'Thank you for sparing me the trouble of convincing you. I'm glad your name's not Branson.'

V

General Cartland said: 'If you can't have those CUB-55s denatured, as you call it, some local funeral parlour is in for a brisk bit of business.'

'You prepared to use that cyanide pistol?'

'*Touché*.'

VI

Several minutes before nine Branson had his usual stage set. He seemed as calm and relaxed as ever, the only change in his normal behaviour being that he had been polite, almost deferential, in his seating of the President. At nine o'clock the cameras began to turn.

At nine o'clock, too, Reston and Harrison, sweating profusely and complaining bitterly of the pain in their legs, reached the top of their last ladder. Rogers, eyeing them over his silenced pistol, said sympathetically: 'You must be *exhausted* after your long climb, gentlemen.'

VII

Giscard whispered in Branson's ear: 'You better get on with it, Mr Branson. Looks as if that fog is coming in just about bridge level.'

Branson nodded, then carried on speaking into the microphone. 'So I'm sure you will be all as delighted as I am to know that the Government has acceded to our very reasonable requests. However, until we receive final confirmation, we feel we might as well pass our time profitably and instruct and entertain you at the same time. In show-business jargon, there will be repeat performances at eleven and one o'clock. I really do urge you to watch those. You will certainly never see other performances like them in your lives.

'As before, you can see the electric truck with its explosives and equipment leaving for the south tower. Now if we can have the zoom camera we shall be seeing two of my colleagues appearing on top of the south tower.' The zoom camera obliged but the top of the tower was bereft of any sign of life. A minute later it was still bereft.

Branson said easily: 'There seems to be a slight hold-up. A temporary delay. Please don't go away.' He was smiling the confident smile of one who knew that not one of his millions of watchers would have dreamed of going away when the phone on the road beside his chair rang. Branson smiled at the unseen millions, said: 'Excuse me,' covered the microphone with his hand and picked up the phone.

'Hendrix here. Lift's fixed.'

'Now you tell me. Do you know how long it should take a man to climb up to the top?'

'Don't tell me your men have – rather are trying to climb

to the top. They must be mad. You must be mad to have sent them.'

'They have a manual.'

'What manual?'

'A copy of the original.'

'Then they can be lost for days. Because of internal changes that manual was scrapped twenty years ago. They can be lost all day in there.'

Branson replaced the phone. Still covering the microphone he said to Giscard: 'Lift's working. Get Bartlett and Boyard here at the double. Tell them not to forget the weight.' He spoke into the microphone again. 'Sorry, viewers. A slight hitch.'

The viewers spent the next ten minutes being rewarded with a variety of panoramic shots of the Golden Gate and the marvellous surrounding scenery, with Branson giving an occasional commentary. After ten minutes he said: 'Right. South tower again.'

Bartlett and Boyard were there, hands held high in salute. Then, along with Peters, they repeated their previous day's performance and had the second strap of explosives alongside the first in a remarkably short space of time. Bartlett and Boyard waved again and disappeared inside the tower. Rogers eyed them over his silenced pistol. 'You really are experts. What a pity. Now you've put us to the trouble of having to remove a second set of detonators.'

VIII

The phone by Branson rang as he was delivering a farewell speech to the camera. He picked it up.

'Hagenbach here. Sorry to have to cut in and cut you off but we have our own little show to watch. You're off the air now and your viewers are now seeing and watching us. Same channel. We've just watched your splendid production. Now, perhaps, you'd like to watch our little show.'

The screen's picture changed to a close-up of Hagenbach. To San Franciscans, at least, his background was unquestionably that of the Presidio.

Hagenbach said: 'There seems little we can do to prevent

this criminal Branson, from achieving his criminal ends. But from all this, some good might yet come. I give you Mr Richards, the Vice-President of the United States.'

Richards made an imposing figure at the microphone. A convivial and highly articulate man at the best of times, years of dominating conferences and campaigning across the nation had honed his natural abilities as a speaker until he had reached a stage where he could have recited the alphabet backwards and still held his audience spell-bound. But he put his gifts into cold storage that morning: this was a moment that was neither for conviviality nor rhetoric. As became a man at the very heart of a national crisis, he was stern, quiet and, exceptionally for him, brief and to the point.

'Unfortunately, what you have just heard is correct. No matter how distasteful and humiliating this present situation may be, there is no possibility in the world of endangering the President, his royal guests and the good name of America. We submit to blackmail. This criminal Branson would appear to have got away with the blackmailing equivalent of murder but I wish him to listen to me very carefully. On information I have received this morning, information, as I shall shortly prove, of the most reliable kind, I believe that Branson is very near the end of his road. I believe he will very soon be alone and friendless. I believe he will have no one left in the world to turn to. I believe every man's hand will be against him. And I believe that those hands that will be reaching out most eagerly to strike him down, as they most surely will, are the hands of his devoted criminal followers who misguidedly imagine their leader to be a man of honour and integrity.' Richards lapsed into momentary rhetoric. 'Those are hands that will literally cut him down just as he, figuratively, intends to stab them all in the back.'

Some of Branson's men were looking at him in a vague and baffled incomprehension. Revson and O'Hare exchanged enquiring glances. Only Branson seemed entirely at his ease, lounging back in his chair, a faintly contemptuous smile on his lips.

'I said that I had information of the most reliable kind. As your Vice-President, I have been accused more than once of not exactly being given to understatement. In this case I was.

What I have is impeccable proof. Ladies and gentlemen and, indeed, viewers, throughout the world, may I present to you the man who, until the early hours of this morning, was Branson's most devoted lieutenant. Mr Johann Van Effen.'

The camera changed to a picture of five men in medium shot sitting in adjoining chairs. The man in the centre was unquestionably Van Effen, who appeared to be his normal relaxed self and to be chatting with seeming amiability to his companions. The picture wasn't close enough to show the glazed eyes, the fact that he was still under the influence of drugs, the drugs which had made him talk his head off during three long hours of probing by a skilled police psychiatrist who, in turn, had received continual prompting from Hagenbach.

Richards went on: 'From left to right: Admiral Newson, naval commander, west coast: San Francisco Chief of Police Hendrix: Mr Van Effen: Mr Hagenbach, head of the FBI: and General Carter, officer commanding, west coast. If I may be permitted a feeble joke, I doubt whether Van Effen has ever found himself in such law-abiding company in his life.'

IX

Branson had very definitely stopped both lounging and relaxing. He was sitting far forward in his chair and for once his feelings were showing: the expression on his face could be described as nothing else other than stunned disbelief.

X

'Van Effen,' Richards said, 'defected in the very early hours of this morning. He defected for what he, and indeed I, believed to have been very compelling reasons. He departed for the excellent reason that he is still a comparatively young man and would like to live a little longer. Incidentally, as the acting Head of State, I have already guaranteed Van Effen immunity from the due processes of the law. His information has been invaluable, as has been his information of eight major robberies in the past three years in each of which – as we now know – Branson was the leader.

'But I digress. He defected because he feared for his life. He defected because Branson had suggested to him that he and Van Effen share the ransom money equally. The rest could go to hell and, presumably, prison. Apart from the fact that Van Effen does appear to be possessed of a belief in honesty between thieves, he was only too well aware that if he went along with this the next back to feel the blade of a knife – literally – would be his own. Van Effen feels strongly that his ex-comrades should be made aware of what lies in store for them. He has, he tells me, already persuaded four of Branson's men to defect along with him and we expect them shortly. When they arrive we shall show them on the screen. If you can at all, I suggest you don't stray too far from your television sets.'

XI

O'Hare said: 'Jesus! Talk about sowing seeds of dissension. How's Branson going to cope with this, recover from this? Brilliant. As the Veep says, who's going to trust him now among his own men. This your idea, Revson?'

'I wish it were. But even I am not as crafty, evil and devious as that. The unmistakable hand of Hagenbach.'

'I never thought that Van Effen—'

'Whatever you're about to say, he didn't. Hagenbach made sure that there were no close-ups of Van Effen. Had there been, even a layman would have seen that Van Effen was doped to the eyes.'

'Doped? If he defected—'

'An involuntary defection. I gassed him and lowered him down to an – ah – passing submarine.'

'Of course. What else? An – ah – passing submarine.' O'Hare favoured him with the look of a psychiatrist who finds himself with an intractable case on his hands.

'Dear, dear. You don't believe me.'

'But of course, old boy.'

'You're under stress again,' Revson said kindly. 'Talking English English.' He patted the base of his camera. 'How do you think I got hold of a brand-new radio transceiver in the middle of the night?'

O'Hare stared at him. He said with an effort: 'And the four other promised defectors. Submariners all?'

'Hell, no. Forcible abduction, all within the past half hour.'

O'Hare got back to his staring.

XII

In the Mount Tamalpais radar station, Parker, until lately Giscard's number two, looked away from the TV set and at the four men gathered around him. He said: 'Sold down the river.'

From the silence that met this observation, it was clear that the others agreed with him. But it could hardly have been called an agreeable silence.

XIII

Richards was trying hard to show that he was not actively enjoying himself. He said into his microphone: 'I can see that the fog is going to pass over the bridge so you won't be able to see me in a couple of minutes. Don't suppose it will last long, though. When it clears, we'll show you your four other faithful henchmen who have defected from you. I will leave you with one last observation. Your money's guaranteed, but watch how you go: I understand it takes exactly six minutes to block the major runways at Havana Airport.'

Branson, his face quite without expression, rose and walked to the rear coach, Giscard following. It was noticeable that his own men either looked at him with puzzlement or thoughtfulness or just averted their eyes. After entering the coach, Giscard went to the back and returned with scotch and two glasses. He poured two large drinks and said: 'I'm against drinking in the morning, too.'

Branson, most uncharacteristically, drained half his glass in one gulp. He said: 'How does your back feel, Giscard?'

'With eleven years working for you and a seven figure bank balance, my back feels okay. I suggest we cut the comedy, Mr Branson. This could be damned serious. With the exception of Van Effen, Yonnie and myself, none of your men has known you for even as long as a year. I forgot Chrysler. But the rest – did you watch their faces as we came here?'

Branson shook his head slowly. 'They just didn't know what to think. Blame them?'

'No. Blame Van Effen?'

'If I believed the sun wasn't going to set tonight, I'd believe he defected. He didn't. Notice that the camera showed no close-up, and that he wasn't invited to speak?' He broke off as Chrysler appeared at the doorway.

Branson said: 'It's all right. Come in. You look unhappy.'

'I am unhappy. I heard what Giscard just said. They let Van Effen stay in the background because he was drugged. I'll bet he told them his life story without realizing one word of what he was saying. Van Effen defect? Never. And there's another thing I'm unhappy about. Bartlett and Boyard should have been back by this time. They haven't even appeared at the south tower. What's more, they're not going to. I know who the next four so-called defectors are going to be.'

Branson said: 'Drugs. No defection. Coercion. We're all agreed on that. But – *how did Van Effen leave the bridge?*'

Giscard said: 'God knows. I wasn't here. Could it have been during one of the two black-outs you had that night?'

Branson said: 'He was with me on both occasions. Any ideas, Chrysler?'

'None. It's as I said, Mr Branson. There's a rotten apple in the barrel somewhere.' He looked out moodily at the fog drifting over the bridge. 'It's getting so that I don't like this bridge much any more.'

— 13 —

CARMODY removed the last of the detonators from the second strap of explosives and gingerly rejoined Rogers on the top of the south tower. He picked up the walkie-talkie. 'General Carter please.' There was a few seconds' delay then Carter came through. Carmody said: 'We've got them, sir.

Shall Rogers and I take a stroll across to the other side? Branson, I believe, has promised another show at eleven. It'll be the west cable, this time, and we quite like our job of being a reception committee.'

'It's a sensible precaution although I somehow don't think that Branson is going to risk any more of his men in the south tower.'

'Ah! Our four friends made it to *terra firma*, sir?'

'With me now. Pity you haven't a TV up there, you and Rogers. Some splendid shows on today.'

'There'll be repeats. We must leave, sir. Fog's thinning quickly down below.'

II

The fog, in fact, moved into the bay in less than five minutes leaving the bridge brilliant in the bright sunshine. Branson, pacing up and down a short section of the bridge, stopped as Chrysler approached.

'Hagenbach on the phone, Mr Branson. He says to switch on the television in two minutes' time.'

Branson nodded. 'We all know what this is going to be.'

This time Hagenbach was the master of ceremonies. He hadn't prepared his lines as well as the Vice-President but he made his point with considerable impact.

'It does look as if Branson's criminal empire, if not at least crumbling, is showing signs of coming apart at the seams. The Vice-President promised you that more defectors would appear. That Van Effen had talked four more into deserting the sinking ship. Well, they have just so done as you can see for yourselves.'

Another camera picked up a table with four men sitting around it, each with a glass in his hand. A bottle stood on the middle of the table. They could hardly be described as a gay and happy group but then they had no reason to be.

Hagenbach moved into camera range. 'There they are then, ladies and gentlemen. Left to right, Messrs Reston, Harrison, Bartlett and Boyard. Incidentally, one of Branson's top men is in hospital with a fractured skull. One does wonder what will happen next. Thank you for your kind attention.'

The cameras had just stopped turning when a policeman came running up to Hagenbach. 'Telephone for you, sir. It's Mount Tamalpais.'

Ten seconds later Hagenbach was inside the communications wagon, listening intently. He replaced the receiver and looked at Hendrix, Newson and Carter. 'How long would it take to provide two helicopters, one with a TV camera and crew, the other with armed police?'

Carter said: 'Ten minutes. Twelve at the most.'

III

Giscard said bitterly. 'Attrition, attrition, attrition. Pin-pricks and more pin-pricks. A steady undermining of confidence in those of us who are left. And not a thing in the world you can do about it, nothing to justify any violent retaliatory action against the hostages. They're just using the TV to play you at your own game, Mr Branson.'

'Yes, they are.' Branson didn't seem unduly disturbed: what he'd seen had come neither as shock nor surprise to him. 'One has to admit that they're quite good at it.' He looked at Giscard and Chrysler. 'Well, gentlemen, I've made up my mind. Your thoughts?'

Giscard and Chrysler looked briefly at each other. It was not in character with Branson that he should ask anyone's opinion.

'We've got our hostages trapped here,' Chrysler said. 'Now I'm the one who's beginning to feel trapped on this damned bridge. We've no freedom of movement.'

Giscard said: 'But we would have in the presidential Boeing. And it has the finest communications system in the world.'

'So we make orderly preparations for, if need be, an emergency take-off. I am in agreement. They shall pay for this. Just to show them I mean what I say, I'm still going to bring down their damned bridge. Now, I hardly think it would be wise to wrap the remaining two explosive devices round the west cable at the top of the north tower.'

'Not,' Giscard said, 'unless you want to have another couple of involuntary defectors.'

'So we wrap them round the cable just where we are here. At the lowest point, between the two helicopters. That should do satisfactorily enough, I think.'

Some half hour later, shortly after the last two of the explosive straps had been secured to the west cable, Chrysler came up to Branson. 'Hagenbach. He says there'll be an interesting programme coming on in just two minutes. Five minutes after the programme he's going to call you. He says two very important messages are coming through from the east.'

'I wonder what that conniving old devil is up to now?' Branson went and took his accustomed viewing place. Automatically, the seats beside and behind him filled up. The screen came to life.

It portrayed something that looked like an enormous white golf ball – one of the Mount Tamalpais radar scanners. Then the camera zoomed in on a group of about ten men, policemen in their shirt sleeves, all armed with submachine-guns. Slightly in front of them stood Hendrix, a microphone in his hand. The camera followed as Hendrix moved forwards towards an opening door. Five men emerged, all with their hands high. The leading man of the five stopped when he was within three feet of Hendrix.

Hendrix said: 'You're Parker?'

'Yes.'

'I'm Hendrix. Chief of Police, San Francisco. Do you men surrender voluntarily?'

'Yes.'

'Why?'

'Better than being hunted and gunned down by you – or stabbed in the back by that bastard Branson.'

'You're under arrest. Get into the van.' Hendrix watched them go then spoke again into the microphone. 'When it comes to making speeches, I'm afraid I'm not in the same league as the Vice-President or Mr Hagenbach, so I won't even try. All I can say, with due modesty on the part of all of us, is that ten defectors is not a bad morning's bag. And the morning is not over yet. Incidentally, there will be no more broadcasts from us for at least an hour.'

IV

Revson stood up and glanced round casually. In the space of only two seconds he caught the eye of both General Cartland and Grafton. Slowly, casually, the newsmen and the hostages began to drift off to their separate coaches, the former presumably to write up their despatches or refill cameras, the latter, almost certainly, in the pursuit of refreshments – the President looked particularly thirsty. Besides, the comfort of an air-conditioned coach was vastly to be preferred to the already uncomfortable heat out on the bridge.

V

Giscard said in anger: 'The fool, the fool, the bloody fool! Why did he have to let himself be duped so easily?'

There was just a trace of weary acceptance in Branson's voice. 'Because he had no Giscard there beside him, that's why.'

'He could have phoned you. He could have phoned me.'

'What might have been. No older phrase in any language. I don't really blame him.'

Chrysler said: 'Has it occurred to you, Mr Branson, that when you've received your ransom money and returned the hostages, they might want most if not all of it back if you want their prisoners freed? They're no fools and they know damned well that you wouldn't let your men down.'

'There'll be no deal. I admit it's going to make things a bit more tricky, but there'll be no deal. Well, I suppose I'd better go and see what friend Hagenbach wants.' Branson rose and walked towards the rear coach, his head bent in thought.

VI

Mack, the guard, waited until the last of his illustrious hostages had entered the presidential coach, locked the door and pocketed the key. His machine-pistol was dangling from one hand.

He turned round to see Cartland's little pistol not three feet from him.

Cartland said: 'Don't try anything, I beg you. Try to lift and fire that gun and it is the last thing you ever do.' Cartland's calm impersonal voice carried immense conviction. 'Gentlemen, I ask you to bear witness to—'

'That funny little pop-gun?' Mack was openly contemptuous. 'You couldn't even hurt me with that thing, but I'd still cut you to pieces.'

'Bear witness to the fact that I warned this man that this "pop-gun" is loaded with cyanide-tipped bullets. Just has to break the skin and you won't even feel it. You'll be a dead man before you hit the floor.'

'In my country,' the King observed, 'he'd already be dead.'

With the possible exception of Yonnie, none of Branson's men was a fool. Mack was no fool. He handed over his gun. Cartland marched him to the rear of the coach, pushed him into the washroom, extracted the inside key and locked the door from the outside.

The President said: 'Well?'

Cartland said: 'There's going to be some rather violent unpleasantness outside in a minute or two. I don't want to risk any of you at this late date. I want this door kept sealed and locked because our friends ashore are going to use a special and very lethal bomb which sucks oxygen from the atmosphere and leaves you very dead. Thirdly, Branson is going to come around very quickly with the intention of shooting up one or two of you if the nastiness doesn't stop. But if the door's locked and he can't get in he can fire all day at this bullet-proof glass and make no impression. Fourthly, although we now have two guns, we're not going to use them when we do leave here as we must eventually. I don't want a gunfight at the OK corral. We'll be loaded into a helicopter but the helicopter isn't going any place.'

The President said: 'Where did you get all this information from?'

'A well-informed source. Fellow who gave me this gun. Revson.'

'Revson. How does he tie in? Don't know the chap.'

'You will. He's stated as Hagenbach's successor in the FBI.'

The President was plaintive. 'It's like I always say: no one ever tells me anything.'

VII

Revson was much less verbose and not at all forthcoming with explanations. Ensuring that he was the last man in, he turned and chopped the unsuspecting Peters below the right ear just as Peters turned the key in the lock. Revson relieved him of both key and machine-pistol, dragged him in and propped him in the driver's seat, then brought out his radio.

'Revson here.'

'Hendrix.'

'Ready yet?'

'Hagenbach's still on the phone to Branson.'

'Let me know immediately he's through.'

VIII

'So the money's in Europe,' Branson said into the phone. 'Excellent. But there had to be a code-word.'

'There was. Very appropriate this time.' Hagenbach's voice was dry. ' "Off-shore." '

Branson permitted himself a slight smile.

IX

Hendrix's voice came through on Revson's receiver. He said: 'They're through.'

'Clear with Hagenbach.'

'Clear.'

'Now.'

Revson didn't replace the transistor in his camera case. He put it in his pocket, unslung his camera and laid it on the floor. He unlocked the door, leaving the key in the lock, opened the door a judicious crack and peered back. The first smoke bomb burst about two hundred yards away just as Branson descended from the rear coach. A second, twenty yards nearer, burst about two seconds later, Branson still remained as he was, as if momentarily paralyzed. Not so

O'Hare, Revson observed, who moved very swiftly into the back of his ambulance, closing the door hard behind him: the driver, Revson assumed, was already inside.

Branson broke from his thrall. He leapt inside the rear coach, lifted a phone and shouted: 'Hagenbach! Hendrix!' He had apparently overlooked the fact that if Hendrix had been at Mount Tamalpais some five minutes previously, he could hardly have returned by that time.

'Hagenbach speaking.'

'What the hell do you think you're up to?'

'I'm not up to anything.' Hagenbach's voice was infuriatingly unconcerned.

The dense clouds of smoke were now no more than a hundred yards away.

'I'm going inside the presidential coach.' He was still shouting. 'You know what that means.' He thrust the phone back and pulled out his pistol. 'Giscard, tell the men to prepare for an attack on the south. They must be mad.' Johnson and Bradley had advanced from the rear of the coach but he thrust them back. 'You two I can't afford to lose. Not now. Stay here. That goes for you, too, Giscard. Tell the men, get back here, and tell Hagenbach what I'm doing.' Giscard eyed him with understandable concern. An erratic, repetitive and slightly incoherent Branson he had not encountered before: but then Giscard had not spent the previous twenty-four hours on the Golden Gate Bridge.

Two more smoke bombs had fallen by the time Branson jumped down to the roadway. The pall of smoke, thick and dense now totally obscuring the south tower was no more than fifty yards away. He rushed to the door of the presidential coach, grabbed the handle and tried to wrench the door open: but the door remained immovable.

Another smoke bomb exploded. This one was just short of the rear coach. Branson battered at the window of the door with the butt of his pistol and peered inside. The driver's seat, the seat which Mack, the guard, should have been occupying, was empty. General Cartland appeared at the doorway as the next smoke bomb burst not ten yards away.

Branson shouted at him, quite forgetting that he was only mouthing words – for the coach was totally sound-proof – and pointed at the driver's seat. Cartland shrugged his shoulders. Branson loosed off four quick shots at the lock and wrenched the handle again but the presidential coach had been specifically designed to withstand assaults of this nature, which was as well for Branson: Cartland's right hand, held behind his back, had the forefinger on the trigger of the cyanide gun.

The next bomb burst directly opposite Branson and the dense, acrid evil-smelling fumes were on him in seconds. Branson fired two more shots at the lock and tried again.

Revson withdrew the key from the door of the lead coach, dropped down to the roadway, shut the door, locked it and left the key in position. A smoke bomb burst immediately opposite him.

Vile though the fumes were to both nostrils and throat, they were not incapacitating. Running his fingers along the side of the presidential coach, Branson made his way back to the rear coach, opened the now closed door and went inside, closing the door behind him. The air in the coach was clear, the lights were on, the air-conditioning unit was functioning and Giscard was on the phone.

Branson managed to control his coughing. 'I couldn't get in. Door's locked and no sign of Mack. Get anything?'

'I got Hagenbach. He says he knows nothing about this. I don't know whether to believe him or not. He's sent for the Vice-President.'

Branson snatched the phone from him and as he did Richard's voice came through. 'You this fellow Giscard?'

'Branson.'

'There is no attack. There will be no attack. Do you think we're mad – you there with guns at the heads of seven hostages? It's the Army, in the shape of Carter, who's gone mad. Heaven alone knows what he intended to achieve. He refuses to answer the phone. I've sent Admiral Newson to stop him. It's that or his career.'

In the communications wagon, Richards turned to look at Hagenbach. 'How did I sound?'

For the first time in his years of contact with Richards, Hagenbach permitted an expression of approval to appear on his face. 'You're keeping the wrong kind of company, Mr Vice-President. You're as devious as I am.'

X

Giscard said: 'Do you believe him?'

'God only knows. It's sense. It's logical. Stay here. And keep that door closed.'

Branson dropped down to the roadway. The smoke was thinning now but there was still enough of it to make his eyes water and start him coughing again. On his third step he bumped into a vaguely-seen shape in the opacity. 'Who's that?'

'Chrysler.' Chrysler was almost convulsed in his paroxysms of coughing. 'What the hell's going on, Mr Branson?'

'God knows. Nothing, according to Richards. Any signs of an attack?'

'Any signs of an – I can't see a bloody yard. No sounds, anyway.'

Just as he spoke, there came half a dozen cracks in rapid succession. Chrysler said: 'Those weren't smoke bombs.'

In a few seconds it was clear that they were indeed not smoke bombs. Both men started to gasp, searching for oxygen and unable to find it. Branson was the first to guess at what might be happening. He held his breath, grabbed Chrysler by the arm and dragged him towards the rear coach. Seconds later they were inside, the door closed behind them, Chrysler lying unconscious on the floor, Branson barely conscious on his feet.

Giscard said: 'What in God's name—'

'Air-conditioning maximum.' Branson's voice came in short painful gasps. 'They're using CUBs.'

Unlike O'Hare, Giscard knew what CUBs were. 'Asphyxiation bombs?'

'They're not playing any more.'

XI

Neither was General Cartland. Mack's machine-pistol in hand, he unlocked the washroom door. Mack gave him a baleful glare but with the machine-pistol's muzzle six inches from his stomach was unable to give any more direct expression of his feelings.

Cartland said: 'I'm the Army Chief of Staff. In an emergency such as this I am responsible to no one, including the President, for my actions. Give me the door key or I'll shoot you dead.'

Two seconds later the door key was in Cartland's hand. Cartland said: 'Turn round.'

Mack turned and almost immediately collapsed to the floor. The impact from the butt of Cartland's machine-pistol may have been too heavy, but from the indifferent expression on Cartland's face it was clear that he didn't particularly care one way or another. He locked the washroom door behind him, pocketed the key, walked forward, thrust the machine-pistol out of sight beneath the chair of a rather dazed President, and made his way to the control panel in front of the driver's seat. He touched a few buttons without effect, pulled and pushed some switches then turned sharply as the entrance window slid down. He took two paces, sniffed the air, wrinkled his nose and quickly moved back to push the last switch he'd touched in the other direction. The window closed. Again, very briefly, Cartland touched the switch. The window slid down an inch. Cartland moved across and dropped the door key outside, returned and closed the window.

XII

Two minutes later the gentle western breeze from the Pacific had blown the now dispersing fumes into the bay. The bridge was clear. Branson opened the door of the rear coach: the air was sweet and fresh and clean. He stepped down, looked at the figures lying on the ground and started running. Giscard, Johnson and Bradley followed him. A slowly recovering Chrysler sat up but remained where he was, shaking his head from side to side.

They checked the men lying on the bridge. Giscard said: 'They're all alive. Unconscious, totally knocked out, but they're still breathing.'

Branson said: 'After CUBs? I don't understand. Load them aboard your chopper, Bradley, and take off when you're ready.'

Branson ran towards the presidential coach and immediately saw the key on the ground. He picked it up and opened the bullet-scarred door. Cartland was standing by the driver's seat. Branson said: 'What happened here?'

'You tell me. All I know is that your guard locked the door from the outside and ran. He ran when the smoke reached here. I assume that the smoke wasn't really smoke, just a smoke-screen, to allow another defector to escape.'

Branson stared at him, first shook his head, then nodded. 'Stay here.'

He ran towards the lead coach. He at once saw the key in the lock, twisted it and opened the door. He looked at the slumped and clearly unconscious Peters, mounted the steps and looked down the coach. He said: 'Where's Revson?'

'Gone.' A well-rehearsed and apparently uncomprehending Grafton spoke in a weary voice. 'I can tell you only three things. He chopped your guard. He spoke on what looked like a miniature radio. Then, when the smoke came, he left, locked the door from the outside and ran. Look, Branson, we're only bystanders, civilians from your point of view. You promised us safety. What's happening out there?'

'Which way did he run?'

'Towards the north tower. He'll have reached there long ago.'

Branson remained silent for quite some time. When he spoke, it was in his accustomed measured tones. 'I am going to destroy this bridge. I do not kill innocent people. Can anybody here drive a coach?'

A young journalist stood up. 'I can.'

'Get this coach off the bridge. Immediately. Through the south barrier.'

He closed the door and ran towards the ambulance. The rear door opened as he approached. O'Hare appeared and said: 'Well, you certainly know how to lay on entertainment for your guests.'

'Get off this bridge. This moment.'

'Whatever for?'

'Stay if you like. I'm going to blow up this damned bridge.'

Branson left, not running now, just walking quickly. He saw a dazed Chrysler emerging from the rear coach. He said: 'Go stay by the President's coach.'

Giscard and Johnson were standing by the rear helicopter.

Bradley was leaning through an opened window. Branson said: 'Go now. Meet you at the airport.'

Bradley lifted his helicopter cleanly off the bridge even before Branson had reached the President's coach.

XIII

Revson lifted himself from his cramped position on the floor of the rear seat of the lead helicopter and glanced briefly through a window. The seven hostages, escorted by Branson, Giscard and Chrysler, were approaching the helicopter. Revson sank back into hiding and pulled the transceiver from his pocket. He said: 'Mr Hagenbach?'

'Speaking.'

'Can you see the rotor on this helicopter?'

'I can. We all can. We all have glasses on you.'

'First turn the rotor takes, the laser beam.'

The seven hostages were ushered in first. The President and the King sat in the two front seats on the left, the Prince and Cartland on the right. Behind them, the Mayor, Muir and the oil sheikh took up position. Giscard and Chrysler took up separate positions in the third row. Each had a gun in his hand.

XIV

The ambulance was approaching the south tower when O'Hare tapped on the driver's window. The window slid back.

O'Hare said: 'Turn back to the middle of the bridge.'

'Turn back! Jesus, Doc, he's about to blow up the damn bridge.'

'There's going to be some sort of an accident but not the kind you think. Turn back.'

XV

Johnson was the last to enter the helicopter. When he was seated Branson said: 'Right. Lift off.'

There came the usual ear-numbing clattering roar, a roar

which rapidly developed into a screaming sound, the sound of an engine running far above its rated revolutions, but even so not loud enough to drown a fearsomely clattering sound outside. Johnson leaned forward and all the noise suddenly ceased.

Branson said: 'What's wrong? What happened?'

Johnson stared ahead, then said quietly: 'I'm afraid you were right about the laser beam, Mr Branson. The rotor's just fallen into the Golden Gate.'

Branson reacted very quickly. He lifted a phone and pressed a button. 'Bradley?'

'Mr Branson?'

'We've had some trouble. Come back to the bridge and pick us up.'

'I'm afraid I can't do that. I've had some trouble myself – a couple of Phantom jets riding herd on me. I'm to land at the International Airport. I'm told there will be a welcoming committee.'

Revson was silently on his feet, white pen in hand. He pressed the button twice and, almost in unison, both men slumped forward then, quite unexpectedly and to Revson's shocked dismay, toppled far from silently into the aisle, their guns clattering on the metallic floor.

Branson twisted round and there was a pistol in his hand: Revson was too far away for his tipped needles to carry. Branson took careful aim, squeezed slowly and steadily, then cried out in pain as the President's cane slashed across his cheek. Revson threw himself to the floor of the aisle, his right hand clamping on the butt of Giscard's gun. By the time Branson had wrenched away the President's cane and swung round again, Revson was ready. All he could see of Branson was his head: but he was ready.

XVI

They stood in a group, isolated but not twenty yards from the ambulance, the President, the Vice-President, the seven decision-makers and Revson. Revson had a firm grip on April Wednesday's arm. They stood and watched in silence as the shrouded stretcher was lowered from the helicopter and carried through the dozens of armed police and soldiers to the waiting ambulance. Nobody had anything to say: there was nothing to say.

The President said: 'Our royal friends?'

Richards said: 'Can't wait to get to San Rafael tomorrow. They're more than philosophic about the entire episode. They're downright pleased. Not only has it all given America a great big black eye but it will make them national heroes at home.'

The President said: 'We'd better go talk to them.'

He and Richards made to turn away when Revson said: 'Thank you, sir.'

The President looked at him in incredulity. '*Me? You* thank *me?* I've already thanked *you* a hundred times.'

'Yes, sir. As a rule I don't like owing favours but I rather care for having my life saved.'

The President smiled and, along with Richards, turned and walked away.

Hagenbach said to Revson: 'Well, let's go to the office and have your full report.'

'Ah, that. What's the penalty for disobeying an order by the head of the FBI?'

'You get fired.'

'Pity. I quite liked my job. My proposal is that I shower, shave, change, take Miss Wednesday for lunch and *then* file my report in the afternoon. I guess you owe me at least that.'

Hagenbach pondered, then nodded.

'I guess I do.'

Two thousand miles away, among the higher echelons in the FBI headquarters, someone just came into a minor sweep-stake fortune.

Hagenbach smiled.

CARAVAN TO VACCARÈS

PROLOGUE

THEY HAD COME a long way, those gypsies encamped for their evening meal on the dusty greensward by the winding mountain road in Provence. From Transylvania they had come, from the *pustas* of Hungary, from the High Tatra of Czechoslovakia, from the Iron Gate, even from as far away as the gleaming Rumanian beaches by the waters of the Black Sea. A long journey, hot and stifling and endlessly, monotonously repetitive across the already baking plains of Central Europe or slow and difficult and exasperating and occasionally dangerous in the traversing of the great ranges of mountains that had lain in their way. Above all, one would have thought, even for those nomadic travellers, a tiring journey.

No traces of any such tiredness could be seen in the faces of the gypsies, men, women and children all dressed in their traditional finery, who sat or squatted in a rough semi-circle round two glowing coke braziers, listening in quietly absorbed melancholy to the hauntingly soft and nostalgic *tsigane* music of the Hungarian steppes. For this apparent lack of any trace of exhaustion there could have been a number of reasons: as the very large, modern, immaculately finished and luxuriously equipped caravans indicated, the gypsies of today travel in a degree of comfort unknown to their forebears who roamed Europe in the horse-drawn, garishly-painted and fiendishly uncomfortable covered-wagon caravans of yesteryear: they were looking forward that night to the certainty of replenishing coffers sadly depleted by their long haul across Europe – in anticipation of this they had already changed from their customary drab travelling clothes: only three days remained until the end of their pilgrimage, for pilgrimage this was: or perhaps they just had remarkable powers of recuperation. Whatever the reason, their faces reflected no signs of weariness, only gentle pleasure and bitter-sweet memories of faraway homes and days gone by.

But one man there was among them whose expression – or lack of it – would have indicated to even the most obtusely unobservant that, for the moment at least, his lack of musical appreciation was total and his thoughts and intentions strictly confined to the present. His name was Czerda and he was sitting on the top of the steps of his caravan, apart from and behind the others, a half-seen shadow on the edge of darkness. Leader of the gypsies and hailing from some unpronounceable village in the delta of the Danube, Czerda was of middle years, lean, tall and powerfully built, with about him that curiously relaxed but instantly identifiable stillness of one who can immediately transform apparent inertia into explosive action. He was dressed all in black and had black hair, black eyes, black moustache and the face of a hawk. One hand, resting limply on his knee, held a long thin smouldering black cigar, the smoke wisping up to his eyes, but Czerda did not seem to notice or care.

His eyes were never still. Occasionally he glanced at his fellow-gypsies, but only briefly, casually, dismissively. Now and again he looked at the range of the Alpilles, their gaunt forbidding limestone crags sleeping palely in the brilliant moonlight under a star-dusted sky, but for the most part he glanced alternately left and right along the line of parked caravans. Then his eyes stopped roving, although no expression came to replace the habitual stillness of that face. Without haste he rose, descended the steps, ground his cigar into the earth and walked soundlessly to the end of the row of caravans.

The man who stood waiting in the shadows was a youthful scaled-down replica of Czerda himself. Not quite so broad, not quite so tall, his swarthily aquiline features were cast in a mould so unmistakably similar to that of the older man that it was unthinkable that he could be anything other than his son. Czerda, clearly a man not much given to superfluous motion or speech, raised a questioning eyebrow: his son nodded, led him out on to the dusty roadway, pointed and made a downward slicing, chopping motion with his hand.

From where they stood and less than fifty yards away soared an almost vertical massive outcrop of white limestone rock, but an outcrop which has no parallel anywhere in the world, for its base was honeycombed with enormous rectangular entrances, cut by the hand of man – no feat of nature could possibly have reproduced the sharply geometrical linearity of those apertures in the cliff face: one of those entrances was quite huge, being at least forty feet in height and no less in width.

Czerda nodded, just once, turned and looked down the road to his right. A vague shape detached itself from shadow and lifted an arm. Czerda returned the salute and pointed towards the limestone bluff. There was no acknowledgment and clearly none was necessary, for the man at once disappeared, apparently into the rock face. Czerda turned to his left, located yet another man in the shadows, made a similar gesture, accepted a torch handed him by his son and began to walk quickly and quietly towards the giant entrance in the cliff face. As they went, moonlight glinted on the knives both men held in their hands, very slender knives, long-bladed and curved slightly at the ends. As they passed through the entrance of the cave they could still distinctly hear the violinists change both mood and tempo and break into the lilting cadences of a gypsy dance.

Just beyond the entrance the interior widened out and heightened until it was like the inside of a great cathedral or a giant tomb of antiquity. Both Czerda and his son switched on their torches, the powerful beams of which failed to penetrate the farthest reaches of this awesome man-made cave, and man-made it unquestionably was, for clearly visible on the towering side-walls were the thousands of vertical and horizontal scores where long-dead generations of Provençals had sawn away huge blocks of the limestone for building purposes.

The floor of this entrance cavern – for, vast though it was, it was no more than that – was pitted with rectangular holes, some of them large enough to hold a motor car, others wide and deep enough to bury a house. Scattered in a few odd corners were mounds of rounded limestone rock but, for the most part, the floor looked as if it had been swept only that day. To the right and left of the entrance cavern led off two other huge openings, the darkness lying beyond them total, impenetrable. A doom-laden place, implacable in its hostility, foreboding, menacing, redolent of death. But Czerda and his son seemed unaware of any of this, quite unmoved: they turned and walked confidently towards the entrance to the right-hand chamber.

II

Deep inside the heart of this vast warren, a slight figure, a barely distinguishable blur in the pale wash of moonlight filtering down through a crack in the cavern roof, stood with his back to a limestone wall, fingers splayed and pressed hard against the clammy rock behind him in the classically frozen position of the fugitive at bay. A youth, no more than twenty, he was clad in dark trousers and a white shirt. Around his neck he wore a silver crucifix on a slender silver chain. The crucifix rose and fell, rose and fell with metronomic regularity as the air rasped in and out of his throat and his heaving lungs tried vainly to satisfy the demands of a body that couldn't obtain oxygen quickly enough. White teeth showed in what could have been a smile but was no smile, although frozen lips drawn back in the rictus of terror can look like one. The nostrils were distended, the dark eyes wide and staring, his face as masked in sweat as if it had been smeared with glycerine. It was the face of a boy with two demons riding on his shoulders: almost at the end of his physical resources, the knowledge of the inevitability of death had triggered off the unreasoning and irrecoverable panic that pushes a man over the edge of the abyss into the mindless depths of madness.

Momentarily, the fugitive's breathing stopped entirely as he caught sight of two dancing pools of light on the floor of the cavern. The wavering beams, steadily strengthening, came from the left-hand entrance. For a moment the young gypsy stood as one petrified, but if reason had deserted him the instinct for survival was still operating independently, for with a harsh sobbing sound he pushed himself off the wall and ran towards the right-hand entrance to the cavern, canvas-soled shoes silent on the rocky floor. He rounded the corner, then slowed down suddenly, reached out groping hands in front of him as he waited for his eyes to become accustomed to the deeper darkness, then moved on slowly into the next cavern, his painfully gasping breathing echoing back in eerie whispers from the unseen walls around him.

Czerda and his son, their torch beams, as they advanced, ceaselessly probing through an arc of 180°, strode confidently through the archway linking the entrance cavern to the one just vacated by the fugitive. At a gesture from Czerda, both men stopped and deliberately searched out the furthermost recesses of the cavern: it was quite empty. Czerda nodded, almost as if in satisfaction, and gave a peculiar, low-pitched two-tone whistle.

In his hiding-place, which was no hiding-place at all, the gypsy appeared to shrink. His terrified eyes stared in the direction of his imagined source of the whistle. Almost at once, he heard an identical whistle, but one which emanated from another part of this subterranean labyrinth. Automatically, his eyes lined up to search out the source of this fresh menace, then he twisted his head to the right as he heard a third whistle, exactly the same in timbre and volume as the previous two. His staring eyes tried desperately to locate this third danger, but there was nothing to be seen but the all-encompassing darkness and no sound at all to break the brooding silence except the far-off keening of the gypsy violins, a far-off reminder of another safer and saner world that served only to intensify the sinister stillness inside that vaulted place of horror.

For a few moments he stood, fear-crazed now and wholly irresolute, then, within the space of as many seconds, the three double whistles came again, but this time they were all closer, much closer, and when he again saw the faint wash of light emanating from the two torches he had seen earlier, he turned and ran blindly in the only direction which seemed to afford a momentary respite, careless or oblivious of the fact that he might run into a limestone wall at any moment. Reason should have told him this but he was now bereft of reason: it was but instinct again, the age-old one that told him that a man does not die before he has to.

He had taken no more than half-a-dozen steps when a powerful torch snapped on less than ten yards ahead of him. The fugitive stopped abruptly, staggering but not falling, lowered the forearm that he had flung up in automatic reflex to protect his eyes and stared for the first time, with narrowed eyes, in a barely conscious attempt to identify the extent and immediacy of this fresh danger confronting him, but all his shrinking eyes could make out was the vaguely discernible bulk of the shapeless figure of the man behind the torch. Then slowly, very slowly, the man's other hand came forward until it was brightly lit by the beam of the torch: the hand held an evilly curved knife that glittered brilliantly in the torch-light. Knife and torch began to move slowly forward.

The fugitive whirled around, took two steps, then stopped as abruptly as he had before. Two other torches, knives again showing in their powerful beams, were scarcely further away than the man behind him. What was so terrifying, so nerve-destroying, about the measured advances of all three was the unhurriedly remorseless certainty.

'Come now, Alexandre,' Czerda said pleasantly. 'We're all old friends, aren't we? Don't you want to see us any more?'

Alexandre sobbed and flung himself to his right in the direction where the light from the three torches showed the entrance to yet another cavern. Panting as a deer does just before the hounds drag it down, he half-stumbled, half-ran through the entrance. None of his three pursuers made any attempt to cut him off or run after him: they merely followed, again walking with that same purposeful lack of haste.

Inside this third cavern, Alexandre stopped and looked wildly around. A small cavern this time, small enough to let him see that all the walls here were solid, hostilely and uncompromisingly solid, without as much as the tiniest aperture to offer any hope of further flight. The only exit was by the way he had come in and this was the end of the road.

Then the realization gradually penetrated his mind, numbed though it was, that there was something different about this particular cavern. His pursuers with their torches were not yet in sight, so how was it that he could see so well? Not clearly, there wasn't enough light for that, but well enough in contrast with the Stygian darkness of the cavern he had just left behind.

Almost at his feet there lay a huge pile of rock and rubble, clearly the result of some massive fall or cave-in in the past. Instinctively, Alexandre glanced upwards. The rubble, piled at an angle of about forty degrees from the horizontal, didn't seem to have a summit. It just stretched on and on and

Alexandre's gradually lifting eyes could see that it stretched upwards for a vertical height of at least sixty feet before it ended. And where it ended it had to end – for there, at the very top, was a circular patch of star-studded sky. That was where the light came from, he dimly realized, from some roof collapse of long ago.

His body was already beyond exhaustion but now some primeval drive had taken over and the body was no longer its own master, in much the same way as his mind had lost control of it. Without a glance to see whether his pursuers were in sight or not, Alexandre flung himself at the great rock pile and began to claw his way upwards.

The rock pile was unstable and dangerous to a degree, a secure footing impossible to obtain, he slid a foot backwards for every eighteen inches of upward progress made, but for all that the momentum induced by his frenzied desperation overcame the laws of gravity and friction co-efficients and he made steady if erratic progress up that impossibly crumbling slope that no man in his normal senses would ever have attempted.

About one third of the way up, conscious of an increase in the amount of illumination beneath him, he paused briefly and looked downwards. There were three men standing at the foot of the rubble now, lit torches still in their hands. They were gazing up towards him but making no attempt to follow. Oddly enough, their torch beams were not pointing up towards him but were directed towards the floor at their feet. Even had his confused mind been able to register this oddity Alexandre had no time to consider it, for he felt his precarious hand- and foot-holds giving way beneath him and started scrabbling his way upwards again.

His knees ached abominably, his shins were flayed, his fingernails broken, the palms of his bleeding hands open almost to the bone. But still Alexandre climbed on.

About two-thirds of the way up he was forced to pause a second time not because he chose to but because, for the moment, his bleeding limbs and spent muscles could take him no farther. He glanced downwards and the three men at the foot of the rockfall were as they had been before, immobile, their torches still pointed at their feet, all three gazing upwards.

There was an intensity in their stillness, a curious aura of expectancy. Vaguely, somewhere deep in the deep befogged recesses of what little was left of his mind, Alexandre wondered why. He turned his head and looked up to the starry sky above and then he understood.

A man, highlit under the bright moon, was seated on the rim of the rockfall. His face was partly in shadow but Alexandre had little difficulty in making out the bushy moustache, the gleam of white teeth. He looked as if he was smiling. Maybe he was smiling. The knife in his left hand was as easily visible as the torch in his right. The man pressed the button of his torch as he came sliding over the rim.

Alexandre's face showed no reaction for he had nothing left to react with. For a few moments he remained immobile as the man with the moustache came sliding down towards him, triggering off a small avalanche of boulders as he came, then tried to fling himself despairingly to one side to avoid the impact and the knife of his pursuer, but because of his frantic haste and the fact that he was now being severely buffeted about the body by the bounding limestone rocks he lost his footing and began to slide helplessly downwards, rolling over and over quite uncontrollably with no hope in the world of stopping himself. So treacherously loose had the surface of the rockfall become that even his pursuer was able to preserve his balance only by taking huge bounding leaps down the rockfall and the volume of the torrent of stones now crashing on to the floor of the cavern was indicated clearly enough by the alacrity with which the three men at the foot of the rockfall moved back at least ten paces. As they did so they were joined by a fourth man who had just come through the cavern entrance, then immediately afterwards by Alexandre's pursuer, whose great leaping steps had taken him past the still tumbling boy.

Alexandre landed heavily on the floor, arms instinctively clutched over his head to protect it from the cascading stones that continued to strike his body for a period of several seconds until the rain of rocks ceased. For as long again he remained dazed, uncomprehending, then he propped himself to his hands and knees before rising shakily to his feet. He looked at the semi-circle of five men, each with a knife in hand, closing in inexorably on him and now his mind was no longer uncomprehending. But he no longer had the look of a hunted animal, for he had already been through all the terrors of death and he was now beyond that. Now, unafraid, for there was nothing left of which to be afraid, he could look into the face of death. He stood there quietly and waited for it to come to him.

III

Czerda stooped, laid a final limestone rock on top of the mound that had now grown at the foot of the rockfall, straightened, looked at the handiwork of his men and himself, nodded in apparent satisfaction and gestured towards the others to leave the cavern. They left. Czerda took one last look at the oblong mound of stones, nodded again, and followed.

Once outside the entrance cave and into what now appeared to be the intolerably harsh glare of bright moonlight that bathed the Alpilles, Czerda beckoned to his son who slowed his pace and let the others precede them.

Czerda asked quietly: 'Any more would-be informers amongst us, do you think, Ferenc?'

'I don't know.' Ferenc shrugged his doubt. 'Josef and Pauli I do not trust. But who can be sure?'

'But you will watch them, Ferenc, won't you? As you watched poor Alexandre.' Czerda crossed himself. 'God rest his soul.'

'I will watch them, Father.' Ferenc dismissed the answer to the question as being too obvious for further elaboration. 'We'll be at the hotel inside the hour. Do you think we shall make much money tonight?'

'Who cares what pennies the idle and foolish rich throw our way? Our paymaster is not in that damned hotel, but that damned hotel we have visited for a generation and must keep on visiting.' Czerda sighed heavily. 'Appearances are all, Ferenc, my son, appearances are all. That you must never forget.'

'Yes, Father,' Ferenc said dutifully. He hastily stuck his knife out of sight.

Unobtrusively, unseen, the five gypsies made their way back

to the encampment and sat down, at a discreet distance from one another, just outside the perimeter of an audience still lost in the sadly-happy rapture of nostalgia as the volume and pace of the violin music mounted to a crescendo. The braziers were burning low now, a faint red glow barely visible in the bright moonlight. Then, abruptly and with a splendid flourish, the music ceased, the violinists bowed low and the audience called out their appreciation and clapped enthusiastically, none more so than Czerda who buffeted his palms together as if he had just heard Hiefetz giving of his best in the Carnegie Hall. But even as he clapped, his eyes wandered, away from the violinists, away from the audience and the gypsy camp, until he was gazing again at the honeycombed face of the limestone cliffs where a cave had so lately become a tomb.

— 1 —

'THE CLIFF battlements of Les Baux, cleft and rent as by a giant axe, and the shattered, gaunt and terrible remnants of the ancient fortress itself are the most awesomely desolate of all ruins in Europe.' Or so the local guide-book said. It went on: 'Centuries after its death Les Baux is still an open tomb, a dreadful and dreadfully fitting memorial to a medieval city that lived most violently and perished in agony: to look upon Les Baux is to look upon the face of death imperishably carved in stone.'

Well, it was pitching it a bit high, perhaps, guide-books do tend towards the hyperbolic, but the average uncertified reader of the guide would take the point and turn no somersaults if some wealthy uncle had left him the place in his will. It was indisputably the most inhospitable, barren and altogether uninviting collection of fractured and misshapen masonry in western Europe, a total and awesome destruction that was the work of seventeenth-century demolition squads who had taken a month and heaven alone knew how many tons of gunpowder to reduce Les Baux to its present state of utter devastation: one would have been equally prepared to believe that the same effect had been achieved in a couple of seconds that afternoon with the aid of an atom bomb: the annihilation of the old fortress was as total as that. But people still lived up there, lived and worked and died.

At the foot of the western vertical cliff face of Les Baux lay a very fittingly complementary feature of the landscape which was sombrely and justifiably called the Valley of Hell, partly because of the barren desolation of its setting between the battlements of Les Baux to the east and a spur of the Alpilles to the west, partly because in summer time this deeply-sunk gorge, which opened only to the south, could become almost unbearably hot.

But there was one area, right at the northern extremity of this grim cul-de-sac, that was in complete and unbelievably startling contrast to the bleakly forlorn wastes that surrounded it, a green and lovely and luxurious oasis that, in the context, could have been taken straight out of the pages of a fairy-tale book.

It was, in brief, an hotel, an hotel with gratefully tree-lined precincts, exotically designed gardens and a gleamingly blue swimming pool. The gardens lay to the south, the immaculate pool was in the centre, beyond that a large tree-shaded patio and finally the hotel itself with its architectural ancestry apparently stemming from a cross between a Trappist monastery and a Spanish *hacienda.* It was, in point of fact, one of the best and – almost by definition – one of the most exclusive and expensive hotel-restaurants in Southern Europe: the Hotel Baumanière.

To the right of the patio, approached by a flight of steps, was a very large forecourt and leading off from this to the south, through an archway in a magnificently sculptured hedge, was a large and rectangular parking area, all the parking places being more than adequately shaded from the hot summer sun by closely interwoven wicker-work roofing.

The patio was discreetly illuminated by all but invisible lights hung in the two large trees which dominated most of the area, overhanging the fifteen tables scattered in expensively sophisticated separation across the stone flags. Even the tables were something to behold. The cutlery gleamed. The crockery shone. The crystal glittered. And one did not have to be told that the food was superb, that the Châteauneuf had ambrosia whacked to the wide: the absorbed silence that had fallen upon the entranced diners could be matched only by the reverential hush one finds in the great cathedrals of the world. But even in this gastronomical paradise there existed a discordant note.

This discordant note weighed about 220 pounds and he talked all the time, whether his mouth was full or not. Clearly, he was distracting all the other guests; he'd have distracted them even if they had been falling en masse down the north face of the Eiger. To begin with, his voice was uncommonly loud, but not in the artificial fashion of the *nouveau riche* or the more impoverished members of the lesser aristocracy who feel it incumbent upon them to call to the attention of the lesser orders the existence of another and superior strain of *homo sapiens*. Here was the genuine article: he didn't give a damn whether people heard him or not. He was a big man, tall, broad and heavily built: the buttons anchoring the straining folds of his double-breasted dinner-jacket must have been sewn on with piano wire. He had black hair, a black moustache, a neatly-trimmed goatee beard and a black-beribboned monocle through which he was peering closely at the large menu card in his hand. His table companion was a girl in her mid-twenties, clad in a blue mini-dress and quite extravagantly beautiful in a rather languorous fashion. At that moment she was gazing in mild astonishment at her bearded escort who was clapping his hands imperiously, an action which resulted in the almost instantaneous appearance of a dark-jacketed restaurant manager, a white-tied head waiter and a black-tied assistant waiter.

'*Encore*,' said the man with the beard. In retrospect, his gesture of summoning the waiting staff seemed quite superfluous: they could have heard him in the kitchen without any trouble.

'Of course.' The restaurant manager bowed. 'Another entrecôte for the Duc de Croytor. Immediately.' The head waiter and his assistant bowed in unison, turned and broke into a discreet trot while still less than twelve feet distant.

The blonde girl stared at the Duc de Croytor with a bemused expression on her face.

'But, Monsieur le Duc—'

'Charles to you,' the Duc de Croytor interrupted firmly. 'Titles do not impress me even although hereabouts I'm referred to as Le Grand Duc, no doubt because of my impressive girth, my impressive appetite and my vice-regal manner of dealing with the lower orders. But Charles to you, Lila, my dear.'

The girl, clearly embarrassed, said something in a low voice which apparently her companion couldn't hear for he lost no time in letting his ducal impatience show through.

'Speak up, speak up! Bit deaf in this ear, you know.'

She spoke up. 'I mean – you've just *had* an *enormous* entrecôte steak.'

'One never knows when the years of famine will strike,' Le Grand Duc said gravely. 'Think of Egypt. Ah!'

An impressively escorted head waiter placed a huge steak before him with all the ritual solemnity of the presentation of crown jewels except that, quite clearly, both the waiter and Le Grand Duc obviously regarded the entrecôte as having the edge on such empty baubles any time. An assistant waiter set down a large ashet of creamed potatoes and another of vegetables while yet another waiter reverently placed an ice bucket containing two bottles of rosé on a serving table close by.

'Bread for Monsieur le Duc?' the restaurant manager enquired.

'You know very well I'm on a diet.' He spoke as if he meant it, too, then, clearly as an after-thought, turned to the blonde girl. 'Perhaps Mademoiselle Delafont—'

'I couldn't possibly.' As the waiters left she gazed in fascination at his plate. 'In twenty seconds—'

'They know my little ways,' Le Grand Duc mumbled. It is difficult to speak clearly when one's mouth is full of entrecôte steak.

'And I don't.' Lila Delafont looked at him speculatively. 'I don't know, for instance, why you should invite me—'

'Apart from the fact that no one ever denies Le Grand Duc anything, four reasons.' When you're a duke you can interrupt without apology. He drained about half a pint of wine and his enunciation improved noticeably. 'As I say, one never knows when the years of famine will strike.' He eyed her appreciatively so that she shouldn't miss his point. 'I knew – I know – your father, the Count Delafont well – my credentials are impeccable. You are the most beautiful girl in sight. And you are alone.'

Lila, clearly embarrassed, lowered her voice, but it was no good. By this time the other diners clearly regarded it as *lèse-majesté* to indulge in any conversation themselves while the Duc de Croytor was holding the floor, and the silence was pretty impressive.

'I'm not alone. Nor the most beautiful girl in sight. Neither.' She smiled apologetically, as if afraid she had been overheard, and nodded in the direction of a near-by table. 'Not while my friend Cecile Dubois is here.'

'The girl you were with earlier this evening?'

'Yes.'

'My ancestors and I have always preferred blondes.' His tone left little room for doubt that brunettes were for the plebs only. Reluctantly, he laid down his knife and fork and peered sideways. 'Passable, passable, I must say.' He lowered his voice to a conspiratorial whisper that couldn't have been heard more than twenty feet away. 'Your friend, you say. Then who's that dissipated-looking layabout with her?'

Seated at a table about ten feet away and clearly well within earshot of Le Grand Duc, a man removed his horn-rimmed glasses and folded them with an air of finality: he was conservatively and expensively dressed in grey gaberdine, was tall, broad-shouldered, black-haired and just escaped being handsome because of the slightly battered irregularity of his deeply-tanned face. The girl opposite him, tall, dark, smiling and with amusement in her green eyes, put a restraining hand on his wrist.

'Please, Mr Bowman. It's not worth it, is it? Really?'

Bowman looked into the smiling face and subsided. 'I am strongly tempted, Miss Dubois, strongly tempted.' He reached for his wine but his hand stopped half-way. He heard Lila's voice, disapproving, defensive.

'He looks more like a heavy-weight boxer to me.'

Bowman smiled at Cecile Dubois and raised his glass.

'Indeed.' Le Grand Duc quaffed another half goblet of rosé. 'One about twenty years past his prime.'

Wine spilled on the table as Bowman set down his glass with a force that should have shattered the delicate crystal. He rose abruptly to his feet, only to find that Cecile, in addition to all her other obviously fine points, was possessed of a set of excellent reflexes. She was on her feet as quickly as he was, had insinuated herself between Bowman and Le Grand Duc's table, took his arm and urged him gently but firmly in the direction of the swimming pool: they looked for all the world like a couple who had just finished dinner and decided to go for a stroll for the digestion's sake. Bowman, though with obvious reluctance, went along with this. He had about him the air of a man for whom the creation of a disturbance with Le Grand Duc would have been a positive pleasure but who drew the line at having street brawls with young ladies.

'I'm sorry.' She squeezed his arm. 'But Lila *is* my friend. I didn't want her embarrassed.'

'Ha! You didn't want *her* embarrassed. Doesn't matter, I suppose, how embarrassed *I* am?'

'Oh, come on. Just sticks and stones, you know. You really don't look the least little bit dissipated to me.' Bowman stared at her suspiciously, but there was no malicious amusement in her eyes: she was pursing her lips in mock but friendly seriousness. 'Mind you, I can see that not everyone would like to be called a layabout. By the way, what *do* you do? Just in case I have to defend you to the duke – verbally, that is.'

'Hell with the duke.'

'That's not an answer to my question.'

'And a very good question it is too.' Bowman paused reflectively, took off his glasses and polished them. 'Fact is, I don't do anything.'

They were now at the farther end of the pool. Cecile took her hand away from his arm and looked at him without any marked enthusiasm.

'Do you mean to tell me, Mr Bowman—'

'Call me Neil. All my friends do.'

'You make friends very easily, don't you?' she asked with inconsequential illogic.

'I'm like that,' Bowman said simply.

She wasn't listening or, if she was, she ignored him. 'Do you mean to tell me you never work? You never do anything?'

'Never.'

'You've no job? You've been trained for nothing? You can't do *anything*?'

'Why should I spin and toil?' Bowman said reasonably. 'My old man's made millions. Still making them, come to that. Every other generation should take it easy, don't you think – a sort of re-charging of the family batteries. Besides, I don't *need* a job. Far be it from me,' he finished piously, 'to deprive some poor fellow who really needs it.'

'Of all the specious arguments ... How could I have misjudged a man like that?'

'People are always misjudging me,' Bowman said sadly.

'Not you. The duke. His perception.' She shook her head, but in a way that looked curiously more like an exasperated affection than cold condemnation. 'You really are an idle layabout, Mr Bowman.'

'Neil.'

'Oh, you're incorrigible.' For the first time, irritation.

'And envious.' Bowman took her arm as they approached the patio again and because he wasn't smiling she made no attempt to remove it. 'Envious of you. Your spirit, I mean. Your year-long economy and thrift. For you two English girls to be able to struggle by here at £200 a week each on your typists' salaries or whatever—'

'Lila Delafont and I are down here to gather material for a book.' She tried to be stiff but it didn't become her.

'On what?' Bowman asked politely. 'Provençal cookery? Publishers don't pay that kind of speculative advance money. So who picks up the tab? UNESCO? The British Council?' Bowman peered at her closely through his horn-rimmed glasses but clearly she wasn't the lip-biting kind. 'Let's all pay a silent truce to good old Daddy, shall we? A truce, my dear. This is too good to spoil. Beautiful night, beautiful food, beautiful girl.' Bowman adjusted his spectacles and surveyed the patio. 'Your girl-friend's not bad either. Who's the Slim Jim with her?'

She didn't answer at once, probably because she was momentarily hypnotized by the spectacle of Le Grand Duc holding an enormous balloon glass of rosé in one hand while with the other he directed the activities of a waiter who appeared to be transferring the contents of the dessert trolley on to the plate before him. Lila Delafont's mouth had fallen slightly open.

'I don't know. He says he's a friend of her father.' She looked away with some difficulty, saw and beckoned the passing restaurant manager. 'Who's the gentleman with my friend?'

'The Duc de Croytor, madam. A very famous wine-grower.'

'A very famous wine-drinker, more like.' Bowman ignored Cecile's disapproving look. 'Does he come here often?'

'For the past three years at this time.'

'The food is especially good at this time?'

'The food, sir, is superb here at any time.' The Baumanière's manager wasn't amused. 'Monsieur le Duc comes for the annual gypsy festival at Saintes-Maries.'

Bowman peered at the Duc de Croytor again. He was spooning down his dessert with a relish matched only by his speed of operation.

'You can see why he has to have an ice-bucket,' Bowman observed. 'To cool down his cutlery. Don't see any signs of gypsy blood there.'

'Monsieur le Duc is one of the foremost folklorists in Europe,' the manager said severely, adding with a suave side-swipe: 'The study of ancient customs, Mr Bowman. For centuries, now, the gypsies have come from all over Europe, at the end of May, to worship and venerate the relics of Sara, their patron saint. Monsieur le Duc is writing a book about it.'

'This place,' Bowman said, 'is hotching with the most unlikely authors you ever saw.'

'I do not understand, sir.'

'I understand all right.' The green eyes, Bowman observed, could also be very cool. 'There's no need – what on earth is that?'

The at first faint then gradually swelling sound of many engines in low gear sounded like a tank regiment on the move. They glanced down towards the forecourt as the first of many gypsy caravans came grinding up the steeply winding slope towards the hotel. Once in the forecourt the leading caravans began arranging themselves in neat rows round the perimeter while others passed through the archway in the hedge towards the parking lot beyond. The racket, and the stench of diesel and petrol fumes, while not exactly indescribable or unsupportable, were in marked contrast to the peaceful luxury of the hotel and disconcerting to a degree, this borne out by the fact that Le Grand Duc had momentarily stopped eating. Bowman looked at the restaurant manager, who was gazing up at the stars and obviously communing with himself.

'Monsieur le Duc's raw material?' Bowman asked.

'Indeed, sir.'

'And now? Entertainment? Gypsy violin music? Street roulette? Shooting galleries? Candy stalls? Palm reading?'

'I'm afraid so, sir.'

'My God!'

Cecile said distinctly: 'Snob!'

'I fear, madam,' the restaurant manager said distantly, 'that my sympathies lie with Mr Bowman. But it is an ancient custom and we have no wish to offend either the gypsies or the local people.' He looked down at the forecourt again and frowned. 'Excuse me, please.'

He hurried down the steps and made his way across the forecourt to where a group of gypsies appeared to be arguing heatedly. The main protagonists appeared to be a powerfully built hawk-faced gypsy in his middle forties and a clearly distraught and very voluble gypsy woman of the same age who seemed to be very close to tears.

'Coming?' Bowman asked Cecile.

'What? Down there?'

'Snob!'

'But you said—'

'Idle layabout I may be but I'm a profound student of human nature.'

'You mean you're nosey?'

'Yes.'

Bowman took her reluctant arm and made to move off, then stepped courteously to one side to permit the passage of a bustling Le Grand Duc, if a man of his build could be said to bustle, followed by a plainly reluctant Lila. He carried a notebook and had what looked to be a folklorist's gleam in his eye. But bent though he was on the pursuit of knowledge he hadn't forgotten to fortify himself with a large red apple at which he was munching away steadily. Le Grand Duc looked like the sort of man who would always get his priorities right.

Bowman, a hesitant Cecile beside him, followed rather more leisurely. When they were half-way down the steps a jeep was detached from the leading caravan, three men piled aboard and the jeep took off down the hill at speed. As Bowman and the girl approached the knot of people where the gypsy was vainly trying to calm the now sobbing woman, the restaurant manager broke away from them and hurried towards the steps. Bowman barred his way.

'What's up?'

'Woman says her son has disappeared. They've sent a search party back along the road.'

'Oh?' Bowman removed his glasses. 'But people don't disappear just like that.'

'That's what I say. That's why I'm calling the police.'

He hurried on his way. Cecile, who had followed Bowman without any great show of enthusiasm, said: 'What's all the fuss? Why is that woman crying?'

'Her son's disappeared.'

'And?'

'That's all.'

'You mean that nothing's happened to him?'

'Not that anyone seems to know.'

'There could be a dozen reasons. Surely she doesn't have to carry on like that.'

'Gypsies,' Bowman said by way of explanation. 'Very emotional. Very attached to their offspring. Do you have any children?'

She wasn't as calmly composed as she looked. Even in the lamplight it wasn't difficult to see the red touching her cheeks. She said: 'That wasn't fair.'

Bowman blinked, looked at her and said: 'No, it wasn't.

Forgive me. I didn't mean it that way. If you had kids and one was missing, would you react like that?'

'I don't know.'

'I said I was sorry.'

'I'd be worried, of course.' She wasn't a person who could maintain anger or resentment for more than a fleeting moment of time. 'Maybe I'd be worried stiff. But I wouldn't be so – so violently grief-stricken, so hysterical, well not unless—'

'Unless what?'

'Oh, I don't know. I mean, if I'd reason to believe that – that—'

'Yes?'

'You know perfectly well what I mean.'

'I'll never know what women mean,' Bowman said sadly, 'but this time I can guess.'

They moved on and literally bumped into Le Grand Duc and Lila. The girls spoke and introductions, Bowman saw, were inevitable and in order. Le Grand Duc shook his hand and said, 'Charmed, charmed,' but it was plain to see that he wasn't in the least bit charmed, it was just that the aristocracy knew how to behave. He hadn't, Bowman noted, the soft flabby hand one might have expected: the hand was hard and the grip that of a strong man carefully not exerting too much pressure.

'Fascinating,' he announced. He addressed himself exclusively to the two girls. 'Do you know that *all* those gypsies have come from the far side of the Iron Curtain? Hungarian or Rumanian, most of them. Their leader, fellow called Czerda – met him last year, that's him with that woman there – has come all the way from the Black Sea.'

'But how about frontiers?' Bowman asked. 'Especially between East and West.'

'Eh? What? Ah?' He finally became aware of Bowman's presence. 'They travel without let or hindrance, most of all when people know that they are on their annual pilgrimage. Everyone fears them, thinks that they have the evil eye, that they put spells and curses on those who offend them: the Communists believe it as much as anyone, more, for all I know. Nonsense, of course, sheer balderdash. But it's what people believe that matters. Come, Lila, come. I have the feeling that they are going to prove in a most co-operative mood tonight.'

They moved off. After a few paces the duke stopped and glanced round. He looked in their direction for some time, then turned away, shaking his head. 'A pity,' he said to Lila in what he probably imagined to be *sotto voce*, 'about the colour of her hair.' They moved on.

'Never mind,' Bowman said kindly. 'I like you as you are.' She compressed her lips, then laughed. Grudges were not for Cecile Dubois.

'He's right, you know.' She took his arm, all was forgiven, and when Bowman was about to point out that the duke's convictions about the intrinsic superiority of blonde hair did not carry with it the stamp of divine infallibility, she went on, gesturing around her: 'It really is quite fascinating.'

'If you like the atmosphere of circuses and fairgrounds,' Bowman said fastidiously, 'both of which I will go a long way to avoid, I suppose it is. But I admire experts.'

And that the gypsies were unquestionably experts at the particular task on hand was undeniable. The speed and co-ordinated skill with which they assembled their various stalls and other media of entertainment were remarkable. Within minutes and ready for operation they had assembled roulette stands, a shooting gallery, no fewer than four fortune-tellers' booths, a food stall, a candy stall, two clothing stalls selling brilliantly-hued gypsy clothes and, oddly enough, a large cage of mynah birds clearly possessed of that species' usual homicidal outlook on life. A group of four gypsies, perched on the steps of a caravan, began to play soulful mid-European music on their violins. Already the areas of the forecourt and car-park were almost uncomfortably full of scores of people circulating slowly around, guests from the hotel, guests, one supposed, from other hotels, villagers from Les Baux, a good number of gypsies themselves. As variegated a cross-section of humanity as one could hope to find, they shared, for the moment, what appeared to be a marked unanimity of outlook – all, from Le Grand Duc downwards, were clearly enjoying themselves with the notable exception of the restaurant manager who stood on the top of the forecourt steps surveying the scene with the broken-hearted despair and martyred resignation of a Bing watching the Metropolitan being taken over by a hippie festival.

A policeman appeared at the entrance to the forecourt. He was large and red and perspiring freely, and clearly regarded the pushing of ancient bicycles up precipitous roads as a poor way of spending a peacefully warm May evening. He propped his bicycle against a wall just as the sobbing gypsy woman put her hands to her face, turned and ran towards a green-and-white-painted caravan.

Bowman nudged Cecile. 'Let's just saunter over there and join them, shall we?'

'I will not. It's rude. Besides, gypsies don't like people who pry.'

'Prying? Since when is concern about a missing man prying? But suit yourself.'

As Bowman moved off the jeep returned, skidding to an unnecessary if highly dramatic stop on the gravel of the court. The young gypsy at the wheel jumped out and ran towards Czerda and the policeman. Bowman wasn't far behind, halting a discreet number of feet away.

'No luck, Ferenc?' Czerda asked.

'No sign anywhere, Father. We searched all the area.'

The policeman had a black notebook out. 'Where was he last seen?'

'Less than a kilometre back, according to his mother,' Czerda said. 'We stopped for our evening meal not far from the caves.'

The policeman asked Ferenc: 'You searched in there?'

Ferenc crossed himself and remained silent. Czerda said: 'That's no question to ask and you know it. No gypsy would ever enter those caves. They have an evil reputation. Alexandre – that's the name of the missing boy – would never have gone in there.'

The policeman put his book away. 'I wouldn't go in there myself. Not at this time of night. The local people believe it's cursed and haunted and – well – I was born here. Tomorrow, when it's daylight—'

'He'll have turned up long before then,' Czerda said confidently. 'Just a lot of fuss about nothing.'

'Then that woman who just left – she is his mother—'

'Yes.'

'Then why is she so upset?'

'He's only a boy and you know what mothers are.' Czerda half-shrugged in resignation. 'I suppose I'd better go and tell her.'

He left. So did the policeman. So did Ferenc. Bowman didn't hesitate. He could see where Czerda was going, he could guess where the policeman was heading for – the nearest *estaminet* – so was momentarily interested in the movements of neither. But in Ferenc he was interested, for there was something in the alacrity and purposefulness with which he walked quickly through the archway into the parking lot that bespoke some fixed intent. Bowman followed more leisurely and stopped in the archway.

On the right-hand side of the lot was a row of four fortune-tellers' booths, got up in the usual garishly-coloured canvas. The first in the row was occupied, a notice said, by a certain Madame Marie-Antoinette who offered a money back if not satisfied guarantee. Bowman went inside immediately, not because of any particular predilection for royalty or parsimony or both, but because just as Ferenc was entering the most distant booth he paused and looked round directly at Bowman and Ferenc's face was stamped with the unmistakably unpleasant characteristics of one whose suspicions could be instantly aroused. Bowman passed inside.

Marie-Antoinette was a white-haired old crone with eyes of polished mahogany and a gin-trap for a mouth. She gazed into a cloudy crystal ball that was cloudy principally because it hadn't been cleaned for months, spoke to Bowman encouragingly about the longevity, health, fame and happiness that could not fail to be his, took four francs from him and appeared to go into a coma, a sign Bowman took to indicate that the interview was over. He left. Cecile was standing just outside, swinging her handbag in what could have been regarded as an unnecessarily provocative fashion and looking at him with a degree of speculative amusement perhaps uncalled for in the circumstances.

'Still studying human nature?' she asked sweetly.

'I should never have gone in there.' Bowman took off his glasses and peered myopically around. The character running the shooting gallery across the parking lot, a short thick-set lad with the face of a boxer who had had a highly unspectacular career brought to an abrupt end, was regarding him with a degree of interest that verged on the impolite. Bowman put his spectacles back on and looked at Cecile.

'Your fortune?' she enquired solicitously. 'Bad news?'

'The worst. Marie-Antoinette says I will be married in two months. She must be wrong.'

'And you not the marrying kind,' she said sympathetically. She nodded at the next booth, which bore a legend above the entrance. 'I think you should ask Madame What's-her-name for a second opinion.'

Bowman studied Madame Zetterling's come-on, then looked again across the car-park. The gallery attendant appeared to be finding him as fascinating as ever. Bowman followed Cecile's advice and went inside.

Madame Zetterling looked like Marie-Antoinette's elder sister. Her technique was different inasmuch as the tools of her trade consisted of a pack of very greasy playing cards which she shuffled and dealt with a speed and dexterity that would have had her automatically blackballed in any casino in Europe, but the forecast for his future was exactly the same. So was the price.

Cecile was still waiting outside, still smiling. Ferenc was standing now by the archway in the hedge and had clearly taken over the eye-riveting stint from the shooting-stall attendant. Bowman polished his glasses some more.

'God help us,' Bowman said. 'This is nothing but a matrimonial agency. Extraordinary. Uncanny.' He replaced his glasses. Lot's wife had nothing on Ferenc. 'Quite incredible in fact.'

'What is?'

'Your resemblance,' Bowman said solemnly, 'to the person I'm supposed to marry.'

'My, my!' She laughed, pleasantly and with genuine amusement. 'You *do* have an original mind, Mr Bowman.'

'Neil,' Bowman said, and without waiting for further advice

entered the next booth. In the comparative obscurity of the entrance he looked round in time to see Ferenc shrug his shoulders and move off into the forecourt.

The third fortune-teller made up the cast for the three witches of *Macbeth*. She used tarot cards and ended up by telling Bowman that he would shortly be journeying across the seas where he would meet and marry a raven-haired beauty and when he said he was getting married to a blonde the following month she just smiled sadly and took his money.

Cecile, who now clearly regarded him as the best source of light entertainment around, had a look of frankly malicious amusement on her face.

'What shattering revelation this time?'

Bowman took his glasses off again and shook his head in perplexity: as far as he could see he was no longer the object of anyone's attention. 'I don't understand. She said: "Her father was a great seaman, as was his, as was his." Doesn't make any kind of sense to me.'

It did to Cecile. She touched a switch somewhere and the smile went out. She stared at Bowman, green eyes full of perplexed uncertainty.

'My father is an admiral,' she said slowly. 'So was my grandfather. And great-grandfather. You – you could have found this out.'

'Sure, sure. I carry a complete dossier on every girl I'm about to meet for the first time. Come up to my room and I'll show you my filing cabinets – I carry them about in a pantechnicon. And wait, there's more. I quote again: "She has a rose-shaped strawberry birthmark in a place where it can't be seen." '

'Good God!'

'I couldn't have put it better myself. Hang on. There may be worse yet to come.' Bowman made no excuse and gave no reason for entering the fourth booth, the only one that held any interest for him, nor was it necessary: the girl was so shaken by what she'd just been told that the oddity of Bowman's behaviour must have suddenly become of very secondary importance.

The booth was dimly lit, the illumination coming from an

Anglepoise lamp with a very low wattage bulb that cast a pool of light on a green baize table and a pair of hands that lay lightly clasped on the table. Little of the person to whom the hands belonged could be seen as she sat in shadow with her head bent but enough to realize that she would never make it as one of the three witches of *Macbeth* or even as Lady Macbeth herself. This one was young, with flowing titian hair reaching below her shoulders and gave the vague impression, although her features were almost indistinguishable, that she must be quite beautiful: her hands certainly were.

Bowman sat on the chair opposite her and looked at the card on the table which bore the legend: 'Countess Marie le Hobenaut.'

'You really a countess, ma'am?' Bowman asked politely.

'You wish to have your hand read?' Her voice was low, gentle and soft. No Lady Macbeth: here was Cordelia.

'Of course.'

She took his hand in both of hers and bent over it, her head so low that the titian hair brushed the table. Bowman kept still – it wasn't easy but he kept still – as two warm tears fell on his hands. With his left hand he twisted the Anglepoise and she put a forearm up to protect her eyes but not before he had time to see that her face *was* beautiful and that the big brown eyes were sheened with tears.

'Why is Countess Marie crying?'

'You have a long lifeline—'

'Why are you crying?'

'Please.'

'All right. Why are you crying, please?'

'I'm sorry. I – I'm upset.'

'You mean I've only got to walk into a place—'

'My young brother is missing.'

'Your brother? I know someone's missing. Everyone knows. Alexandre. But your brother. They haven't found him?'

She shook her head, the titian hair brushing across the table.

'And that's your mother in the big green-and-white caravan?'

A nod this time. She didn't look up.

'But why all the tears? He's only been missing for a little while. He'll turn up, you'll see.'

Again she said nothing. She put her forearms on the table and her head on her forearms and cried silently, her shoulders shaking uncontrollably. Bowman, his face bitter, touched the young gypsy's shoulder, rose and left the booth. But when he emerged the expression on his face was one of dazed bewilderment. Cecile glanced at him in some trepidation.

'Four kids,' Bowman said quietly. He took her unresisting arm and led her through the archway towards the forecourt. Le Grand Duc, the blonde girl still with him, was talking to an impressively scar-faced and heavily built gypsy dressed in dark trousers and frilled off-white shirt. Bowman ignored Cecile's disapproving frown and halted a few convenient feet away.

'A thousand thanks, Mr Koscis, a thousand thanks,' Le Grand Duc was saying in his most gracious lord of the manor voice. 'Immensely interesting, immensely. Come, Lila, my dear, enough is enough. I think we have earned ourselves a drink and a little bite to eat.' Bowman watched them make their way towards the steps leading to the patio, then turned and looked consideringly at the green-and-white caravan.

Cecile said: 'Don't.'

Bowman looked at her in surprise.

'And what's wrong with wanting to help a sorrowing mother? Maybe I can comfort her, help in some way, perhaps even go looking for her missing boy. If more people would be more forthcoming in times of trouble, be more willing to risk a snub—'

'You really are a fearful hypocrite,' she said admiringly.

'Besides, there's a technique to this sort of thing. If Le Grand Duc can do it, I can. Still your apprehensions.'

Bowman left her there nibbling the tip of a thumb in what did appear to be a very apprehensive manner indeed and mounted the caravan steps.

At first sight the interior appeared to be deserted, then his eyes became accustomed to the gloom and he realized he was standing in an unlighted vestibule leading to the main living quarters beyond, identifiable by a crack of light from an imperfectly constructed doorway and the sound of voices, women's voices.

Bowman took a step through the outer doorway. A shadow detached itself from a wall, a shadow possessed of the most astonishing powers of acceleration and the most painful solidity. It struck Bowman on the breastbone with the top of a head that had the unforgiving consistency of a cement bollard: Bowman made it all the way to the ground without the benefit of even one of the caravan steps. Out of the corner of an eye he was dimly aware of Cecile stepping hurriedly and advisedly to one side then he landed on his back with a momentarily numbing impact that took care of any little air that the bullet-head had left in his lungs in the first place. His glasses went flying off into the middle distance and as he lay there whooping and gasping for the oxygen that wouldn't come the shadow came marching purposefully down the steps. He was short, thick-set, unfriendly, had a speech to make and was clearly determined on making it. He stooped, grabbed Bowman by the lapels and hauled him to his feet with an ease that boded ill for things to come.

'You will remember me, my friend.' His voice had the pleasant timbre of gravel being decanted from a metal hopper. 'You will remember that Hoval does not like trespassers. You will remember that next time Hoval will not use his fists.'

From this Bowman gathered that on this occasion Hoval did intend to use his fists and he did. Only one, but it was more than enough. Hoval hit him in the same place and, as far as Bowman could judge from the symptoms transmitted by a now nearly paralysed midriff, with approximately the same amount of force. He took half-a-dozen involuntary backward steps and then came heavily to earth again, this time in a seated position with his hands splayed out behind him. Hoval dusted off his hands in an unpleasant fashion and marched back up into the caravan again. Cecile looked around till she located Bowman's glasses, then came and offered him a helping hand which he wasn't too proud to accept.

'I think Le Grand Duc must use a different technique,' she said gravely.

'There's a lot of ingratitude in this world,' Bowman wheezed.

'Isn't there just? Through with studying human nature for the night?' Bowman nodded, it was easier than speaking. 'Then for goodness' sake let's get out of here. After that, I need a drink.'

'What do you think *I* require?' Bowman croaked.

She looked at him consideringly. 'Frankly, I think a nanny would be in order.' She took his arm and led him up the steps to the patio. Le Grand Duc, with a large bowl of fruit before him and Lila by his side, stopped munching a banana and regarded Bowman with a smile so studiously impersonal as to be positively insulting.

'That was a rousing set-to you had down there,' he observed.

'He hit me when I wasn't looking,' Bowman explained.

'Ah!' Le Grand Duc said non-committally, then added in a penetrating whisper when they'd moved on less than half-a-dozen feet: 'As I said, long past his prime.' Cecile squeezed Bowman's arm warningly but unnecessarily: he gave her the wan smile of one whose cup is overfull and led her to their table. A waiter brought drinks.

Bowman fortified himself and said: 'Well, now. Where shall we live? England or France?'

'What?'

'You heard what the fortune-teller said.'

'Oh, my God!'

Bowman lifted his glass. 'To David.'

'David?'

'Our eldest. I've just chosen his name.'

The green eyes regarding Bowman so steadily over the rim of a glass were neither amused nor exasperated, just very thoughtful. Bowman became very thoughtful himself. It could be that Cecile Dubois was, in that well-turned phrase, rather more than just a pretty face.

— 2 —

CERTAINLY, two hours later, no one could have referred to Bowman's as a pretty face. It could be said in fairness that, owing to various troubles it had encountered from time to time, it didn't have very much going for it in the first place but the black stocking mask he'd pulled up almost to the level of his eyes gave it an even more discouraging look than it normally possessed.

He'd changed his grey gaberdine suit for a dark one and his white shirt for a navy roll-neck pullover. Now he put the spectacles he had worn for disguise away in his suitcase, switched off the overhead light and stepped out on to the terrace.

All the bedrooms on that floor opened on to the same terrace. Lights came from two of them. In the first, the curtains were drawn. Bowman moved to the door and its handle gave fractionally under his hand. Cecile's room, he knew: a trusting soul. He moved on to the next lit window, this one uncurtained, and peered stealthily round the edge. A commendable precaution, but superfluous: had he done an Apache war dance outside that window it was doubtful whether either of the two occupants would have noticed or, if they had, would have cared very much. Le Grand Duc and Lila, his black and her blonde head very close together, were seated side by side in front of a narrow table: Le Grand Duc, a tray of canapés beside him, appeared to be teaching the girl the rudiments of chess. One would have thought that the customary vis-à-vis position would have been more conducive to rapid learning: but then, Le Grand Duc had about him the look of a man who would always adopt his own strongly original attitude to all that he approached. Bowman moved on.

The moon still rode high but a heavy bar of black cloud was approaching from the far battlements of Les Baux. Bowman descended to the main terrace by the swimming pool but did not cross. The management, it seemed, kept the patio lights burning all night and anyone trying to cross the patio and descend the steps to the forecourt would have been bound to be seen by any gypsy still awake: and that there were gypsies who were just that Bowman did not doubt for a moment.

He took a sidepath to the left, circled the hotel to the rear and approached the forecourt uphill from the west. He moved very slowly and very quietly on rubber soles and kept to deep shadow. There was, of course, no positive reason why the gypsies should have any watcher posted: but as far as this particular lot were concerned, Bowman felt, there was no positive reason why they shouldn't. He waited till a cloud drifted over the moon and moved into the forecourt.

All but three of the caravans were in darkness. The nearest and biggest of the lit caravans was Czerda's: bright light came from both the half-opened door and a closed but uncurtained side window. Bowman went up to that window like a cat stalking a bird across a sunlit lawn and hitched an eye over the sill.

There were three gypsies seated round a table and Bowman recognized all three: Czerda, his son Ferenc and Koscis, the man whom Le Grand Duc had so effusively thanked for information received. They had a map spread on the table and Czerda, pencil in hand, was indicating something on it and clearly making an explanation of some kind. But the map was on so small a scale that Bowman was unable to make out what it was intended to represent, far less what Czerda was pointing out on it nor, because of the muffling effect of the closed window, could he distinguish what Czerda was saying. The only reasonable assumption he could make from the scene before him was that whatever it was Czerda was planning it wouldn't be for the benefit of his fellow men. Bowman moved away as soundlessly as he had arrived.

The side window of the second illuminated caravan was open and the curtains only partially drawn. Closing in on this window Bowman could at first see no one in the central portion of the caravan. He moved close, bent forward and risked a quick glance to his right and there, at a small table near the door, two men were sitting playing cards. One of the men was unknown to Bowman but the other he immediately and feelingly recognized as Hoval, the gypsy who had so unceremoniously ejected him from the green-and-white caravan earlier in the night. Bowman wondered briefly why Hoval had transferred himself to the present one and what purpose he had been serving in the green-and-white caravan. From the ache Bowman could still feel in his midriff the answer to that one seemed fairly clear. But why?

Bowman glanced to his left. A small compartment lay beyond an open doorway in a transverse partition. From Bowman's angle of sight nothing was visible in the compartment. He moved along to the next window. The curtains on this one were drawn, but the window itself partly open from the top, no doubt for ventilation. Bowman moved the curtains very very gently and applied his eye to the crack he had made. The level of illumination inside was very low, the only light coming from the rear of the caravan. But there was enough light to see, at the very front of the compartment, a three-tiered bunk and here lay three men, apparently asleep. Two of them were lying with their faces turned towards Bowman but it was impossible to distinguish their features: their faces were no more than pale blurs in the gloom. Bowman eased the curtains again and headed for the caravan that really intrigued him – the green-and-white one.

The rear door at the top of the caravan steps was open but it was dark inside. By this time Bowman had developed a thing about the unlit vestibules of caravans and gave this one a wide berth. In any event it was the illuminated window half-way down the side of the caravan that held the more interest for him. The window was half-open, the curtains half-drawn. It seemed ideal for some more peeking.

The caravan's interior was brightly lit and comfortably furnished. There were four women there, two on a settee and two on chairs by a table. Bowman recognized the titian-haired Countess Marie with, beside her, the grey-haired woman who had been involved in the altercation with Czerda – Marie's mother and the mother of the missing Alexandre. The two other young women at the table, one auburn-haired and about thirty, the other a slight dark girl with most ungypsy-like cropped hair and scarcely out of her teens, Bowman had not seen before. Although it must have been long past their normal bed-times, they showed no signs of making any preparations for retiring. All four looked sad and forlorn to a degree: the mother and the dark young girl were in tears. The dark girl buried her face in her hands.

II

'Oh, God!' She sobbed so bitterly it was difficult to make the words out. 'When is it all going to end? *Where* is it all going to end?'

'We must hope, Tina,' Countess Marie said. Her voice was dull, totally devoid of hope. 'There is nothing else we can do.'

'There *is* no hope.' The dark girl shook her head despairingly. 'You know there's no hope. Oh, God, why did Alexandre have to do it?' She turned to the auburn-haired girl. 'Oh, Sara, Sara, your husband warned him only today—'

'He did, he did.' This was from the girl called Sara and she sounded no happier than the others. She put her arm round Tina. 'I'm so terribly sorry, my dear, so terribly sorry.' She paused. 'But Marie's right, you know. Where there's life there's hope.'

There was silence in the caravan. Bowman hoped, and fervently, that they would break it and break it soon. He had come for information but had so far come across nothing other than the mildly astonishing fact of four gypsies talking in German and not in Romany. But he wanted to learn more and learn it quickly for the prospect of hanging around that brightly illuminated window indefinitely lacked appeal of any kind: there was something in the brooding atmosphere of tragedy inside that caravan and menace outside calculated to instil a degree of something less than confidence in the bystander.

'There is no hope,' the grey-haired woman said heavily. She dabbed at her eyes with a handkerchief. 'A mother knows.'

Marie said: 'But, Mother—'

'There's no hope because there's no life,' her mother interrupted wearily. 'You'll never see your brother again, nor you your fiancé, Tina. I know my son is dead.'

There was silence again, which was just as well for Bowman

for it was then that he heard the all but imperceptible sound of a fractionally disturbed piece of gravel, a sound which probably saved his life.

Bowman whirled round. He'd been right about one thing, anyway: there was menace abroad that night. Koscis and Hoval were frozen in a crouched position less than five feet away. Both men were smiling. Both held long curving knives in their hands and the lamplight gleamed dully off them in a very unpleasant fashion.

They'd been waiting for him, Bowman realized, or someone like him; they'd been keeping tabs on him ever since he'd entered the forecourt or maybe even long before that, they'd just wanted to give him enough rope to hang himself, to prove that he was up to what they would regard as no good – no good for themselves – and, when satisfied, eliminate the source of irritation: their actions, in turn, certainly proved to him that there was something sadly amiss with this caravan heading for Saintes-Maries.

The realization of what had happened was instantaneous and Bowman wasted no time on self-recriminations. There would be a time for those but the time was assuredly not when Koscis and Hoval were standing there taking very little trouble to conceal the immediacy of their homicidal intentions. Bowman lunged swiftly and completely unexpectedly – for a man with a knife does not usually anticipate that one without a knife will indulge in such suicidal practices – towards Koscis, who instinctively drew back, lifting his knife high in self-defence. Prudently enough, Bowman didn't complete his movement, but threw himself to his right and ran across the few intervening yards of forecourt leading to the patio steps.

He heard Koscis and Hoval pounding across the gravel in pursuit. They were saying things, to Bowman unintelligible things, but even in Romany the burden of their remarks was clear. Bowman reached the fourth step on his first bound, checked so abruptly that he almost but didn't quite lose his balance, wheeled round and swung his right foot all in one movement. Koscis it was who had the misfortune to be in the lead: he grunted in agony, the knife flying back from his hand, as he fell backwards on to the forecourt.

Hoval came up the steps as Koscis went down them, his

right arm, knife pointing upwards, hooking viciously. Bowman felt the tip of the knife burning along his left forearm and then he'd hit Hoval with a great deal more force than Hoval had earlier hit him, which was understandable enough, for when Hoval had hit him he'd been concerned only with his personal satisfaction: Bowman was concerned with his life. Hoval, too, fell backwards, but he was luckier than Koscis: he fell on top of him.

Bowman pushed up his left sleeve. The wound on the forearm was about eight inches long but, although bleeding quite heavily, was little more than a superficial cut and would close up soon. In the meantime, he hoped it wouldn't incapacitate him too much.

He forgot about that trouble when he saw a new one approaching. Ferenc was running across the forecourt in the direction of the patio steps. Bowman turned, hurried across the patio to the steps leading to the upper terrace and stopped briefly to look back. Ferenc had both Koscis and Hoval on their feet and it was clear that it was only a matter of seconds before all three were on their way.

Three to one and the three with knives. Bowman carried no weapon of any kind and the immediate prospect was uninviting. Three determined men with knives will always hunt down an unarmed man, especially three men who appeared to regard the use of knives as second nature. A light still showed from Le Grand Duc's room. Bowman pulled down his black face mask and burst through the doorway: he felt he didn't have time to knock. Le Grand Duc and Lila were still playing chess but Bowman again felt that he didn't have time to worry about mildly surprising matters of that nature.

'For God's sake, help me, hide me!' The gasping, he thought, might have been slightly overdone but in the circumstances it came easily. 'They're after me!'

Le Grand Duc looked in no way perturbed, far less startled. He merely frowned in ducal annoyance and completed a move.

'Can't you see we're busy?' He turned to Lila who was staring at Bowman with parted lips and very large rounded eyes. 'Careful, my dear, careful. Your bishop is in great danger.' He spared Bowman a cursory glance, viewing him with distaste. 'Who are after you?'

'The gypsies, that's who. Look!' Bowman rolled up his left sleeves. 'They've knifed me!'

The expression of distaste deepened.

'You must have given them some cause for offence.'

'Well, I was down there—'

'Enough!' He held up a magisterial hand. 'Peeping Toms can expect no sympathy from me. Leave at once.'

'Leave at once? But they'll get me—'

'My dear.' Bowman didn't think Le Grand Duc was addressing him and he wasn't. He patted Lila's knee in a proprietorial fashion. 'Excuse me while I call the management. No cause for alarm, I assure you.'

Bowman ran out through the doorway, checked briefly to see if the terrace was still deserted. Le Grand Duc called: 'You might close that door after you.'

'But, Charles—' That was Lila.

'Checkmate,' said Le Grand Duc firmly, 'in two moves.'

There was the sound of footsteps, running footsteps, coming across the patio to the base of the terrace steps. Bowman moved quickly to the nearest port in the storm.

Cecile wasn't asleep either. She was sitting up in bed holding a magazine and attired in some fetching negligée that, in happier circumstances, might well have occasioned admiring comment. She opened her mouth, whether in astonishment or the beginning of a shout for help, then closed it again and listened with surprising calmness as Bowman stood there with his back to the closed door and told her his story.

'You're making all this up,' she said.

Bowman hoisted his left sleeve again, an action which by now he didn't much like doing as the coagulating blood was beginning to stick wound and material together.

'Including this?' Bowman asked.

She made a face. 'It *is* nasty. But why should they—'

'Ssh!' Bowman had caught the sound of voices outside, voices which rapidly became very loud. An altercation was taking place and Bowman had little doubt that it concerned him. He turned the handle of the door and peered out through a crack not much more than an inch in width.

Le Grand Duc, with Lila watching from the open doorway, was standing there with arms outspread like an overweight traffic policeman, barring the way of Ferenc, Koscis and Hoval. That they weren't immediately recognizable as those three was due to the fact that they'd obviously considered it prudent to take time out to wrap some dirty handkerchiefs or other pieces of cloth about their faces in primitive but effective forms of masks, which explained why Bowman had been given the very brief breathing space he had been.

'This is private property for guests only,' Le Grand Duc said sternly.

'Stand aside!' Ferenc ordered.

'Stand aside? I am the Duc de Croytor—'

'You'll be the dead Duc de—'

'How dare you, sir!' Le Grand Duc stepped forward with a speed and co-ordination surprising in a man of his bulk and caught the astonished and completely unprepared Ferenc with a round-house right to the chin. Ferenc staggered back into the arms of his companions who had momentarily to support him to prevent his collapse. There was some moments' hesitation, then they turned and ran from the terrace, Koscis and Hoval still having to support a very wobbly Ferenc.

'Charles.' Lila had her hands clasped in what is alleged to be the classic feminine gesture of admiration. 'How brave of you!'

'A *bagatelle*. Aristocracy versus ruffians – class always tells.' He gestured towards his doorway. 'Come, we have yet to finish both the chess and the canapés.'

'But – but how can you be so calm? I mean, aren't you going to phone? The management? Or the police?'

'What point? They were masked and will be far away by this time. After you.'

They went inside and closed their door. Bowman closed his.

'You heard?' She nodded. 'Good old duke. That's taken the heat off for the moment.' He reached for the door handle. 'Well, thanks for the sanctuary.'

'Where are you going?' She seemed troubled or disappointed or both.

'Over the hills and far away.'

'In your car?'

'I haven't got one.'

'You can take mine. Ours, I mean.'

'You mean that?'

'Of course, silly.'

'You're going to make me a very happy man one day. But for the car, some other time. Goodnight.'

Bowman closed her door behind him and was almost at his own room when he stopped. Three figures had emerged from the shadows.

'First you, my friend.' Ferenc's voice was no more than a whisper, maybe the idea of disturbing the duke again didn't appeal to him. 'Then we attend to the little lady.'

Bowman was three paces from his own door and he had taken the first even before Ferenc had stopped talking – people generally assume that you will courteously hear them out – and had taken the third before they had moved, probably because the other two were waiting for the lead from Ferenc and Ferenc's reactions were temporarily out of kilter since his brief encounter with Le Grand Duc. In any event, Bowman had the door shut behind him before Ferenc's shoulder hit it and had the key turned before Ferenc could twist the door handle from his grip.

He spent no time on brow-mopping and self-congratulation but ran to the back of the apartment, opened the window and looked out. The branches of a sufficiently stout tree were less than six feet away. Bowman withdrew his head and listened. Someone was giving the door handle a good going over, then abruptly the sound ceased to be replaced by that of running footsteps. Bowman waited no longer: if there was one thing that had been learnt from dealing with those men it was that procrastination was uninsurable.

As a piece of arboreal trapeze work there was little enough to it. He just stood on the sill, half-leaned and half-fell outwards, caught a thick branch, swung into the bole of the tree and slid to the ground. He scrambled up the steep bank leading to the road that encircled the hotel from the rear. At the top he heard a low and excited call behind him and twisted round. The moon was out again and he could clearly see the three of them starting to climb up the bank: it was equally clear that the knives they held in their hands weren't impeding their progress at all.

Before Bowman lay the choice of running downhill or up. Downhill from the Baumanière lay open country, uphill lay Les Baux with its winding streets and back-alleys and labyrinth of shattered ruins. Bowman didn't hesitate. As one famous heavy-weight boxer said of his opponents – this was after he had lured the unfortunates into the ring – 'They can run but they can't hide.' In Les Baux Bowman could both run and hide. He turned uphill.

He ran up the winding road towards the old village as quickly as the steepness, his wind and the state of his legs would permit. He hadn't indulged in this sort of thing in years. He spared a glance over his shoulder. Neither, apparently, had the three gypsies. They hadn't gained any that Bowman could see: but they hadn't lost any either. Maybe they were just pacing themselves for what they might consider to be a long run that lay ahead: if that were the case, Bowman thought, he might as well stop running now.

The straight stretch of road leading to the entrance to the village was lined with car-parks on both sides but there were no cars there and so no place to hide. He passed on through the entrance.

After about another hundred yards of what had already become this gasping lung-heaving run Bowman came to a fork in the road. The fork on the right curved down to the battlemented walls of the village and had every appearance of leading to a cul-de-sac. The one to the left, narrow and winding and very steep, curved upwards out of sight and while he dreaded the prospect of any more of that uphill marathon it seemed to offer the better chance of safety so he took it. He looked behind again and saw that his momentary indecision had enabled his pursuers to make up quite a bit of ground on him. Still running in this same unnerving silence, the knives in their hands glinting rhythmically as their arms pumped to and fro, they were now less than thirty yards distant.

At the best speed he could, Bowman continued up this narrow winding road. He slowed down occasionally to peer briefly and rather desperately into various attractive dark openings on both sides, but mainly to the right, but he knew it was his labouring lungs and leaden legs that told him that those entrances were inviting, his reason told him that those attractions were almost certainly fatal illusions, leading to culs-de-sac or some other form of trap from which there could be no escape.

And now, for the first time, Bowman could hear behind him the hoarse and rasping breathing of the gypsies. They were clearly in as bad shape as he was himself but when he glanced over his shoulder he realized this was hardly cause for any wild rejoicing, he was hearing them now simply because they were that much closer than they had been: their mouths were open in gasping exertion, their faces contorted by effort and sheened in sweat and they stumbled occasionally as their weakening legs betrayed them on the unsure footing of the cobblestones. But now they were only fifteen yards away, the price Bowman had paid for his frequent examinations of possible places of refuge. But at least their nearness made one decision inevitable for him: there was no point in wasting any further time in searching for hiding-places on either side for wherever he went they were bound to see him go and follow. For him now the only hope of life lay among the shattered ruins of the ancient fortress of Les Baux itself.

Still pounding uphill he came to a set of iron railings that apparently completely blocked what had now turned from a narrow road into no more than a winding metalled path. I'll have to turn and fight, he thought, I'll have to turn and then it will be all over in five seconds, but he didn't have to turn for there was a narrow gap between the right-hand side of the railing and a desk in an inlet recess in the wall which was clearly the pay-box where you handed over your money to inspect the ruins. Even in that moment of overwhelming relief at spotting this gap, two thoughts occurred to Bowman: the first the incongruous one that that was a bloody stupid set-up for a pay-box where the more parsimoniously minded could slip through at will, the second that this was the place to stand and fight, for they could only squeeze through that narrow entrance one at a time and would have to turn sideways to do so, a circumstance which might well place a swinging foot on a par with a constricted knife arm: or it did seem like a good idea to him until it fortunately occurred that while he was busy trying to kick the knife from the hand of one man the other two would be busy throwing their knives at him through or over the bars of the railing and at a distance of two or three feet it didn't seem very likely that they would miss. And so he ran on, if the plodding, lumbering, stumbling progress that was now all he could raise could be called running.

A small cemetery lay to his right. Bowman thought of the macabre prospect of playing a lethal hide-and-seek among the tombstones and hastily put all thought of the cemetery out of his mind. He ran on another fifty yards, saw before him the open plateau of the Les Baux massif, where there was no place to hide and from which escape could be obtained only by jumping down the vertical precipices which completely enclosed the massif, turned sharply to his left, ran up a narrow path alongside what looked like a crumbling chapel and was soon among the craggy ruins of the Les Baux fortress itself. He looked downhill and saw that his pursuers had fallen back to a distance of about forty yards which was hardly surprising as his life was at stake and their lives weren't. He looked up, saw the moon riding high and serene in a new cloudless sky and swore bitterly to himself in a fashion that would have given great offence to uncounted poets both alive and dead. On a moonless night he could have eluded his pursuers with ease amidst that great pile of awesome ruins.

And that they were awesome was beyond dispute. The contemplation of large masses of collapsed masonry did not rank among Bowman's favourite pastimes but as he climbed, fell, scrambled and twisted among that particular mass of masonry and in circumstances markedly unconducive to any form of aesthetic appreciation there was inexorably borne in upon him a sense of the awful grandeur of the place. It was inconceivable that any ruins anywhere could match those in their wild, rugged yet somehow terrifyingly beautiful desolation. There were mounds of shattered building stones fifty feet high: there were great ruined pillars reaching a hundred feet into the night sky, pillars overlooking vertical cliff faces of which the pillars appeared to be a natural continuation and in some cases were: there were natural stairways in the shattered rock face, natural chimneys in the remnants of those man-made cliffs, there were hundreds of apertures, in the rock, some just large enough for a man to squeeze through, others large enough to accommodate a double-decker. There were strange paths let into the natural rock, some man-made, some not, some precipitous, some almost horizontal, some wide enough to bowl along in a coach and four, others narrow and winding enough to have daunted the most mentally retarded of mountain goats. And there were broken, ruined blocks of masonry everywhere, some big as a child's hand, others as large as a suburban house. And it was all white, eerie and dead and white: in that brilliantly cold pale moonlight it was the most chillingly awe-inspiring sight Bowman had ever encountered and not, he reflected, a place he would willingly have called home. But, here, tonight, he had to live or die.

Or they had to live or die, Ferenc and Koscis and Hoval. When it came to the consideration of this alternative there was no doubt at all in Bowman's mind as to what the proper choice must be and the choice was not based primarily on the instinct of self-preservation, although Bowman would have been the last to deny that it was an important factor: those were evil men and they had but one immediate and all-consuming ambition in life and that was to kill him; but that was not what ultimately mattered. There was no question of morality or legality involved, just the simple factor of logic. If they killed him now they would, he knew, go on to commit more and more heinous crimes: if he killed them, then they wouldn't. It was as simple as that. Some men deserve to die and the law cannot deal with them until it is too late and the law is not an ass in this respect, it's just because of inbuilt safeguards in every legal constitution designed to protect the rights of the individual that it is unable to cope in advance with those whose ultimate evil or murderous intent is beyond rational dispute but beyond legal proof. It was the old, old story of the greatest good of the greatest number and it was merely fortuitous, Bowman reflected wryly, that he happened to be one of the greatest number. If he had been scared he was no longer scared now, his mind was quite cold and detached. He had to get high. If he got to a certain height where they couldn't reach him it would be stalemate: if he went higher and they still tried to follow him the danger to the greatest good of the greatest number was going to be effectively reduced. He looked up at the towering shattered crags bathed in the white moonlight and started to climb.

Bowman had never had any pretensions towards being a climber but he climbed well that night. With the devil himself behind him he would normally have made good speed: with three of them he made excellent time. Looking back from time to time, he could see that he was steadily outdistancing them but not to the extent that they ever lost sight of him for more than a few seconds at a time. And now they were clearly recognizable for whom they were for now they had completely removed their home-made masks. They had probably arrived, and rightly, at the safe conclusion that up in the wild desolation of those ruins in the middle of the night they no longer required them and even if they were seen on the way back it wouldn't matter, for the *corpus delicti* would have vanished for ever and no charge could be laid against them other than that of entering the fortress without paying the required admission fee of a franc per head, which they would probably have regarded as a reasonable exchange for a night's work well done.

Bowman stopped climbing. Through no fault of his own, because he was totally unfamiliar with the terrain, he had made a mistake. He had been aware that the walls of the narrow gully up which he was scrambling had been rapidly steepening on both sides, which hadn't worried him unduly because it had happened twice before, but now as he rounded a corner he found himself faced with a vertical wall of solid rock. It was a perfect cul-de-sac from which there was no escape except by climbing, and the vertical walls were wholly unclimbable. The blank wall facing Bowman was riddled by cracks and apertures but a quick glance at the only three or four that were accessible to him showed no moonlight at the far end, only uncompromising darkness.

He ran back to the corner, convinced he was wasting his time. He was. The three men had been in no doubt as to the direction in which he had disappeared. They were forty yards away, no more. They saw Bowman, stopped and came on again. But not so hurriedly now. The very fact that Bowman had turned back to check on their whereabouts would be indication enough that he was in serious trouble.

A man does not die before he has to. He ran back into the cul-de-sac and looked desperately at the apertures in the rock. Only two were large enough to allow a man to enter. If he could get inside one and turn around the darkness behind him would at least counter-balance the advantages of a man with a knife – and, of course, only one man could come at a time. For no reason at all he chose the right-hand aperture, scrambled up and wriggled inside.

The limestone tunnel started narrowing almost immediately. But he had to go on, he was not yet in total concealment. By the time he estimated that he was hidden the tunnel was no more than two feet wide and scarcely as high. It would be impossible for him to turn, all hc could do was lie there and be hacked piecemeal at someone's leisure. And even that, he realized now, would not be necessary: all they would have to do would be to wall up the entrance and go home for a good night's sleep. Bowman inched ahead on hands and knees.

He saw a pale glow of light ahead. He was imagining it, he thought, he knew he must be imagining it, but when he suddenly realized that what lay ahead was a corner in the tunnel, he knew he wasn't. He reached the corner and wriggled round with difficulty. Before him he saw a patch of star-studded sky.

The tunnel had suddenly become a cave. A small cave, to be sure, a good deal less than head-high and its lip ending in nothingness less than six feet away: but a cave. He crawled to the lip and looked down. He at once wished he hadn't: the plain lay hundreds of sheerly vertical feet below, the rows of dusty olive trees so impossibly distant that they couldn't even be fairly described as toy bushes.

He leaned out another few vertiginous inches and twisted his head to look upwards. The top of the cliff lay no more than twenty feet above – twenty smoothly vertical feet with neither finger- nor toe-hold in sight.

He looked to the right and that was it. That was the path that even the moronic mountain goat would have balked at, a narrow broken ledge extending down at not too acute an angle to a point that passed, as he now saw, some four feet below the lip of the cave. The path, for want of a better word, went right to the top.

But even the moronic goat, which Bowman was not, will refuse suicidal chances acceptable to the sacrificial goat, which Bowman undoubtedly was, for death and suicide come to the same thing anyway. He didn't hesitate, for he knew with certainty that if he did he would elect to remain and fight it out in that tiny cave sooner than face that dreadful path. He swung out gingerly over the rim, lowered himself till he had located the ledge with his feet and started to edge his way upwards.

He shuffled along with his face to the wall, arms wide outstretched, palms in constant contact with the rock-face, not because of any purchase that could be gained, for there was none, but because he was no mountaineer, had no particular head for heights and knew very well that if he looked down he'd inevitably just lean out and go tumbling head over heels to the olive groves far below. A crack Alpinist, it was possible, would have regarded the climb as just a light Sunday afternoon workout but for Bowman it was the most terrifying experience of his life. Twice his foot slipped on loose stone, twice chunks of limestone disappeared into the abyss, but after a life-time that was all of two minutes long he made it and hauled himself over the brink and into safety, sweating like a man in a Turkish bath and trembling like a withered leaf in the last gale of autumn. He'd thought he wouldn't be scared again and he had been wrong: but now he was back on terra firma and it was on terra firma that he operated best.

He ventured a quick glance over the edge. There was no one in sight. He wondered briefly what had delayed them, maybe they'd thought he was lurking in the shadow in the cul-de-sac, maybe they'd picked the wrong aperture to start with, maybe anything. He'd no time to waste wondering, he had to find out, and immediately, whether there was any escape from the pinnacle he was perched on. He had to find out for three very good and urgent reasons. If there was no other escape route he knew in his heart that no power on earth would ever make him face that descent to the cave and that he'd just have to stay there till the buzzards bleached his bones – he doubted whether there were any buzzards in those parts but the principle of the thing was pretty well fixed in his mind. If there was an escape route, then he'd have to guard against the possibility of being cut off by the gypsies. Thirdly, if there was such a route and they regarded it as unassailable, they might just elect to leave him there and go off to deal with Cecile Dubois whom they clearly, if erroneously, suspected of being a party to his irritatingly interfering behaviour.

He crossed the no more than ten yards of the flat limestone summit, lowered himself flat and peered over the edge. His circumspection was needless. There *was* an escape route, a very steep scree-laden slope that debouched gradually into an area of massive limestone boulders which in turn gave on to Les Baux plateau massif itself. Uninviting but feasible.

He made his way back to the cliff-side and heard voices, at first indistinctly, then clearly.

'This is madness!' It was Hoval speaking and for the first time Bowman shared a point of view with him.

'For you, Hoval, for a mountaineer from the High Tatra?' Ferenc's voice. 'If he went this way, we can too. You know that if we do not kill this man everything will be lost.'

Bowman looked down. He could see Hoval quite clearly and the heads of Ferenc and Koscis.

Koscis, apparently trying to postpone a decision, said: 'I do not like killing, Ferenc.'

Ferenc said: 'Too late to be queasy now. My father's orders are that we do not return until this man lies dead.'

Hoval nodded reluctantly, reached down his feet, found the ledge and started to edge his way along. Bowman rose, looked around, located a limestone boulder that must have weighed at least fifty pounds, lifted it chest high and returned to the brink of the precipice.

Hoval was obviously a great deal more experienced than Bowman for he was making about twice the best speed that Bowman had been able to manage. Ferenc and Koscis, heads and shoulders clearly visible now, were glancing anxiously sideways, watching Hoval's progress and almost certainly far from relishing the prospect of having to emulate him. Bowman waited till Hoval was directly beneath him. Hoval had once already tried to murder and now was coming to try to murder again. Bowman felt no pity and opened his hands.

The boulder, with a curious absence of sound, struck head and shoulders: the whole brief sequence, indeed, was characterized by an eerie silence. Hoval made no sound at all on the long way down and may well have been dead before he started to fall: and no sound of what must have been an appalling impact came from either Hoval or the boulder that had killed him as they plunged into the olive groves so far away. They just disappeared soundlessly from sight, vanished in the darkness below.

Bowman looked at Ferenc and Koscis. For several seconds they crouched there, their faces stunned, for catastrophe rarely registers instantaneously, then Ferenc's face became savagely transformed. He reached inside his jacket, snatched out a gun, pointed it upwards and fired. He knew Bowman was up there but he could have had no idea where he was. It was no more than the uncontrollable expression of an access of blind fury but Bowman took a couple of rapid backward steps all the same.

The gun introduced a new dimension. Clearly, because of their predilection for knives, they had intended to dispose of Bowman as quietly and unobtrusively as possible, but Ferenc, Bowman felt sure, did not carry a gun unless he intended to use it in the last resort and that was plainly at hand: they were going to get him at no matter what risk to themselves. Bowman reflected briefly that whatever he had so nearly stumbled across must literally be a matter of life and death, then he turned and ran. Ferenc and Koscis would already be heading back through the tunnel on the assumption that there might be an escape route open to Bowman: in any event it would be pointless for them to remain where they were as any action they might try to take there would result only in their untimely end. Untimely, that is, from their point of view.

He ran down the steep slope of scree because he had no alternative but to run, taking increasingly huge bounding steps to maintain what was left of his balance. Three-quarters of the way down to the waiting jumble of limestone boulders his loss of balance passed the point of no return and he fell, rolling diagonally downhill, trying frantically and with a total lack of success to brake himself. The braking was done for him, violently and painfully, by the first of the boulders with which he came into contact and it was his right knee that took the major brunt of the impact.

He was sure he had smashed the knee-cap for when he tried to rise his leg just gave under him and he sat down again. A second time he tried it and this time with a little more success, the third time he made it and he knew the knee-cap had just been momentarily paralysed. Now it felt merely numb although he knew it must hurt badly later and would be severely bruised. He hobbled on his way through the thinning scattering of boulders at about half the best speed he could normally have made for the knee kept collapsing under him as if it had a will of its own.

A puff of white smoke flew off from a boulder just in front of him and the sound of the shot was almost simultaneous. Ferenc had anticipated too well. Bowman didn't try to take cover because Ferenc could see where he was and had Bowman tried to hide Ferenc would just have walked down to the place of concealment and put the pistol to his head to make quite sure that he didn't miss. Bowman made off down the slope, twisting and doubling among the rocks to throw Ferenc off aim, not even trying to locate where his pursuers were for the knowledge would have been useless to him anyway. Several shots came close, one kicking up a small cloud of soil at his right foot, but the combination of his swerving run and the fact that Ferenc had himself to dodge in and out among the rocks must have made him an almost impossible target. Besides, to shoot accurately downhill is notoriously difficult at the best of times. In between the shots Bowman could hear the sound of their pounding footsteps and he knew they were gaining on him: but still he didn't look round for if he were going to be shot through the back of the head he felt he'd just as soon not know about it in advance.

He was clear of the rocks now and running straight over the hard-packed earth towards the railed entrance to the village. Ferenc, closing up and also running straight, should have had his chance then but the firing had stopped and Bowman could only assume that he had run out of ammunition. He might well, Bowman realized, carry a spare magazine but if he did he would have been hard put to it to reload on the dead run.

Bowman's knee was hurting now but, contradictorily, it was bearing up much better. He glanced behind. His pursuers were still gaining, but more slowly. Bowman passed through the railed upper entrance to the village and ran down to the fork where he had hesitated on the way up. The two gypsies were not yet in sight but the sound of their running feet was clear. They would expect him, Bowman hoped, to continue out through the lower entrance to the village, so he turned left down the short road that led to the old battlements of the town. The road debouched into a small square, a cul-de-sac, but he was past caring about that. He registered the fact, without knowing why, that an ancient wrought-iron cross stood in the centre of the square. To the left was an equally ancient church, facing it was a low wall with apparently nothing beyond it and, between church and wall, a high face of vertical rocks with deep man-made apertures cut into it, for reasons that couldn't be guessed at.

He ran across to the low rock and peered over it. It was certainly no low rock on the other side: it dropped almost two hundred vertical feet to what looked like scrub trees at the foot.

Ferenc had been cleverer than Bowman thought he would have been. He was still peering over the wall when he heard the sound of running feet approaching the square, one set of feet: they'd split up to investigate both avenues of escape. Bowman straightened and hurried soundlessly across the square and hid in the shadows of one of the deep recesses cut in the natural rock.

Koscis it was. He slowed down on entering the square, his stertorous breathing carrying clearly in the night air, walked past the iron cross, glanced at the open doorway of the church, then, as if guided by some natural instinct, came heading straight towards the particular niche where Bowman stood as deeply pressed back in the shadow as he possibly could. There was a peculiar inevitability about the unhesitating manner of his approach. He held his knife, thumb on top of the handle, at what appeared to be his favourite waist-high level.

Bowman waited until the gypsy was fractionally away from the point which would make discovery certain, then hurled himself from the dark niche, managing to grab his knife wrist more by good luck than good judgement. Both men fell heavily to the ground, fighting for possession of the knife. Bowman tried to twist Koscis's right wrist but it seemed to be made of overlaid strands of wire hawser and Bowman could feel the wrist slowly breaking free from his grasp. He anticipated the inevitable by suddenly letting go and rolling over twice, rising to his feet at the same instant as Koscis did. For a moment they looked at each other, immobile, then Bowman backed away slowly until his hands touched the low wall behind him. He had no place to run to any more and no place to hide.

Koscis advanced. His face, at first implacable, broke into a smile that was notably lacking in warmth. Koscis, the expert with a knife, was savouring the passing moment.

Bowman threw himself forward, then to the right, but Koscis had seen this one before. He flung himself forward to intercept the second stage of the movement, his knife arcing up from knee level, but what Koscis had forgotten was that Bowman knew he had seen this one before. Bowman checked with all the strength of his right leg, dropped to his left knee and as the knife hooked by inches over his head, his right shoulder and upper arm hit the gypsy's thighs. Bowman straightened up with a convulsive jerk and this, combined with the speed and accelerating momentum of Koscis's onrush lifted the gypsy high into the air and sent him, useless knife still in hand, sailing helplessly over the low wall into the darkness below. Bowman twisted round and watched him as he fell, a diminishing manikin tumbling over and over in almost incredibly slow motion, his passing marked only by a fading scream in the night. And then Bowman couldn't see him any more and the screaming stopped.

For a few seconds Bowman stood there, a man held in thrall, but only for a few seconds. If Ferenc hadn't been afflicted with a sudden and total deafness he was bound to have heard that eldritch fear-crazed scream and come to investigate and immediately.

Bowman ran from the square towards the main street: halfway up the narrow connecting lane he slid into a darkened alleyway for he'd heard Ferenc coming and for a brief moment saw him as he passed the end of the alleyway, pistol in one hand, knife in the other. Whether the pistol had been reloaded or not or whether Ferenc had balked at firing it so near the village was impossible to say. Even in what must have been that moment of intolerable stress Ferenc was still possessed of a sufficient instinct of self-preservation to keep exactly to the middle of the road where he couldn't be ambushed by an unarmed man. His lips were drawn back in an unconscious snarl compounded of rage and hate and fear and his face was the face of a madman.

— 3 —

IT ISN'T EVERY woman who, wakened in the middle of the night, can sit bolt upright in bed, sheets hauled up to the neck, hair dishevelled and eyes blurred with sleep and still look as attractive as if she were setting out for a ball, but Cecile Dubois must have been one of the few. She blinked, perhaps, rather more than a would-be dancer would have done, then gave Bowman what appeared to be a rather penetrating and critical look, possibly because as a result of all that climbing in the ruins and falling down scree-covered slopes Bowman's dark broadcloth had lost some of its show-room sheen: in fact, now that he could clearly see it for the first time, it was filthily dirty, stained and ripped beyond repair. He waited for her reaction, sarcastic, cynical or perhaps just plain annoyed, but she wasn't an obvious sort of girl.

She said: 'I thought you'd be in the next country by this time.'

'I was almost in another land altogether.' He took his hand from the light switch and eased the door until it was almost but not quite closed. 'But I came back. For the car. And for you.'

'For me?'

'Especially for you. Hurry up and get dressed. Your life's not worth a tinker's cuss if you stay here.'

'My life? But why should I—'

'Up, dress and pack. Now.' He crossed to the bed and

looked at her, and although his appearance wasn't very encouraging it must have been convincing for she compressed her lips slightly, then nodded. Bowman returned to the door and looked out through the crack he had left. Very fetching though the dark-haired Miss Dubois might be, he reflected, it did not mean that she had to conform to the beautiful brunette pattern: she made decisions, quickly accepted what she regarded as being inevitable and the 'if you think I'm going to get dressed while you're standing there' routine apparently hadn't even crossed her mind. Not that he would have seriously objected but, for the moment, the imminent return of Ferenc held prior claim to his attentions. He wondered briefly what was holding Ferenc up; he should have posted hotfoot by that time to report to his old man that they had encountered some unexpected difficulties in the execution of their assignment. It could have been, of course, that even then Ferenc was prowling hopefully and stealthily through the back alleys of Les Baux with a gun in one hand, a knife in the other and murder in his heart.

'I'm ready,' Cecile said.

Bowman looked round in mild astonishment. She was, too, even to the extent of having combed her hair. A strapped suitcase lay on her bed. 'And packed?' Bowman asked.

'Last night.' She hesitated. 'Look, I can't just walk off without—'

'Lila? Leave her a note. Say you'll contact her Poste Restante, Saintes-Maries. Hurry. Back in a minute – I have to collect my stuff.'

He left her there, went quickly to his own room and paused briefly at the door. The south wind sighed through the trees and he could hear the splash of the fountain in the swimming pool but that was all he could hear. He went into his room, crammed clothes anyhow into a suitcase and was back in Cecile's room within the promised minute. She was still scribbling away industriously.

'Poste Restante, Saintes-Maries, that's all you've got to write,' Bowman said hastily. 'Your life story she probably knows about.'

She glanced up at him, briefly and expressionlessly over the rims of a pair of glasses that he was only mildly surprised to see that she was wearing, reduced him to the status of an insect on the wall, then got back to her writing. After another twenty seconds she signed her name with what seemed to Bowman to be a wholly unnecessary flourish considering the urgency of the moment, snapped the spectacles in the case and nodded to indicate that she was ready. He picked up her suitcase and they left, switching off the light and closing the door behind them. Bowman picked up his own suitcase, waited until the girl had slid the folded note under Lila's door, then both walked quickly and quietly along the terrace, then up the path to the road that skirted the back of the hotel. The girl followed closely and in silence behind Bowman and he was just beginning to congratulate himself on how quickly and well she was responding to his training methods when she caught his left arm firmly and hauled him to a stop. Bowman looked at her and frowned but it didn't seem to have any effect. Short-sighted, he thought charitably.

'We're safe here?' she asked.

'For the moment, yes.'

'Put those cases down.'

He put the cases down. He'd have to revise his training methods.

'So far and no farther,' she said matter-of-factly. 'I've been a good little girl and I've done what you asked because I thought there was possibly one chance in a hundred that you weren't mad. The other ninety-nine per cent of my way of thinking makes me want an explanation. Now.'

Her mother hadn't done much about training her either, Bowman thought. Not, at least, in the niceties of drawing-room conversation. But someone had done a very good job in other directions, for if she were upset or scared in any way it certainly didn't show.

'You're in trouble,' Bowman said. 'I got you into it. Now it's my responsibility to get you out of it.'

'*I'm* in trouble?'

'Both of us. Three characters from the gypsy caravan down there told me that they were going to do me in. Then you. But first me. So they chased me up to Les Baux and then through the village and the ruins.'

She looked at him speculatively, not at all worried or

concerned as she ought to have been. 'But if they chased you—'

'I shook them off. The gypsy leader's son, a lovable little lad by the name of Ferenc, is possibly still up there looking for me. He has a gun in one hand, a knife in the other. When he doesn't find me he'll come back and tell Dad and then a few of them will troop up to our rooms. Yours and mine.'

'What on earth have *I* done?' she demanded.

'You've been seen with me all evening and you've been seen to give refuge, that's what you've done.'

'But – but this is ridiculous. I mean, taking to our heels like this.' She shook her head. 'I was wrong about that possible one per cent. You *are* mad.'

'Probably.' It was, Bowman thought, a justifiable point of view.

'I mean, you've only got to pick up the phone.'

'And?'

'The police, silly.'

'No police – because I'm not silly, Cecile. I'd be arrested for murder.'

She looked at him and slowly shook her head in disbelief or incomprehension or both.

'It wasn't so easy to shake them off tonight,' Bowman went on. 'There was an accident. Two accidents.'

'Fantasy.' She shook her head as she whispered the word again. 'Fantasy.'

'Of course.' He reached out and took her hand. 'Come, I'll show you the bodies.' He knew he could never locate Hoval in the darkness but Koscis's whereabouts would present no problem and as far as proving his case was concerned one corpse would be as good as two any time. And then he knew he didn't have to prove anything, not any more. In her face, very pale now but quite composed, something had changed. He didn't know what it was, he just registered the change. And then she came close to him and took his free hand in hers. She didn't start having the shakes, she didn't shrink away in horrified revulsion from a self-confessed killer, she just came close and took his other hand.

'Where do you want to go?' Her voice was low but there were no shakes in it either. 'Riviera? Switzerland?'

He could have hugged her but decided to wait for a more propitious moment. He said: 'Saintes-Maries.'

'Saintes-Maries!'

'That's whcre all the gypsies are going. So that's where I want to go.'

There was a silence, then she said without any particular inflection in her voice: 'To die in Saintes-Maries.'

'To live in Saintes-Maries, Cecile. To justify living, if you like. We idle layabouts have to, you know.' She looked at him steadily, but kept silent: he would have expected this by now; she was a person who would always know when to be silent. In the pale wash of moonlight the lovely face was grave to the point of sadness. 'I want to find out why a young gypsy is missing,' Bowman went on. 'I want to find out why a gypsy mother and three gypsy girls are terrified out of their lives. I want to find out why three other gypsies tried their damnedest to kill me tonight. And I want to find out why they're even prepared to go to the extraordinary lengths of killing you. Wouldn't you like to find those things out too, Cecile?'

She nodded and took her hands away. He picked up the suitcases and they walked down circumspectly past the main entrance to the hotel. There was no one around, no sound of any person moving around, no hue and cry, nothing but the soft quiet and peacefulness of the Elysian Fields or, perhaps, of any well-run cemetery or morgue. They carried on down the steeply winding road to where it joined the transverse road running north and south through the Valley of Hell and there they turned sharply right – a ninety-degree turn. Another thirty yards and Bowman gratefully set the cases down on the grassy verge.

'Where's your car parked?' he asked.

'At the inner end of the parking area.'

'That *is* handy. Means it has to be driven out through the parking lot and the forecourt. What make?'

'Peugeot 504. Blue.'

He held out his hand. 'The keys.'

'Why? Think I'm not capable of driving my own car out of—'

'Not out of, *chérie*. Over. Over anyone who tries to get in your way. Because they will.'

'But they'll be asleep—'

'Innocence, innocence. They'll be sitting around drinking slivovitz and waiting happily for the good news of my death. The keys.'

She gave him a very old-fashioned look, one compounded of an odd mixture of irritation and speculative amusement, dug in her handbag and brought out the keys. He took them and, as he moved off, she made to follow. He shook his head.

'Next time,' he said.

'I see.' She made a face. 'I don't think you and I are going to get along too well.'

'We'd better,' he said. 'For your sake, for my sake, we'd better. And it would be nice to get you to that altar unscarred. Stay here.'

Two minutes later, pressed deeply into shadow, he stood at the side of the entrance to the forecourt. Three caravans, the three he had examined earlier, still had their lights burning, but only one of them – Czerda's – showed any sign of human activity. It came as no surprise to him to discover that his guess as to what Czerda and his headmen would be doing had proved to be so remarkably accurate, except that he had no means of checking whether the alcohol they were putting away in such copious quantities was slivovitz or not. It was certainly alcohol. The two men sitting with Czerda on the caravan steps were cast in the same mould as Czerda himself, swarthy, lean, powerfully built, unmistakably Central European and unprepossessing to a degree. Bowman had never seen either before nor, looking at them, did he care very much whether he ever saw either of them again. From the desultory conversation, he gathered they were called Maca and Masaine: whatever their names it was clear that fate had not cast them on the side of the angels.

Almost directly between them and Bowman's place of concealment stood Czerda's jeep, parked so that it faced the entrance of the forecourt – the only vehicle there so positioned: in an emergency, clearly, it would be the first vehicle that would be pressed into service and it seemed to Bowman prudent to do something about that. Crouched low, moving slowly and silently across the forecourt and at all times keeping the jeep directly between him and the caravan steps, he arrived at the front end of the jeep, edged cautiously towards the near front tyre, unscrewed the valve cap and inserted the end of a match into the valve using a balled-up handkerchief to muffle the hiss of the escaping air. By and by the rim of the wheel settled down until it was biting into the inner carcass of the tread. Bowman hoped, fervently if belatedly, that Czerda and his friends weren't regarding the front near wing in any way closely for they could not have failed to be more than mildly astonished by the fact that it had sunk a clear three inches closer to the ground. But Czerda and his friends had, providentially, other and more immediate concerns to occupy their attention.

'Something is wrong,' Czerda said positively. 'Very far wrong. You know that I can always tell about those things.'

'Ferenc and Koscis and Hoval can look after themselves.' It was the man whose name Bowman thought to be Maca and he spoke confidently. 'If this Bowman ran, he could have run a very long way.'

'No.' Bowman risked a quick glance round the wing of the jeep and Czerda was now on his feet. 'They've been gone too long, far too long. Come. We must look for them.'

The other two gypsies rose reluctantly to their feet but remained there, as Czerda did, their heads cocked and slowly turning. Bowman had heard the sound as soon as they had, the sound of pounding feet from the patio by the pool. Ferenc appeared at the top of the steps, came down three at a time and ran across the forecourt to Czerda's caravan. It was the lurching stumbling run of a man very close to exhaustion and from his distressed breathing, sweating face and the fact that he made no attempt to conceal the gun in his hand it was clear that Ferenc was in a state of considerable agitation.

'They're dead, Father!' Ferenc's voice was a hoarse gasping wheeze. 'Hoval and Koscis. They're dead!'

'God's name, what are you saying?' Czerda demanded.

'Dead! Dead, I tell you! I found Koscis. His neck is broken, I think every bone in his body is broken. God knows where Hoval is.'

Czerda seized his son by the lapels and shook him violently. 'Talk sense! Killed?' His voice was almost a shout.

'This man Bowman. He killed them.'

'He killed – he killed – and Bowman?'

'Escaped.'

'Escaped! Escaped! You young fool, if this man escapes Gaiuse Strome will kill us all. Quickly! Bowman's room!'

'And the girl's.' Ferenc's wheezing had eased fractionally. 'And the girl's.'

'The girl?' Czerda asked. 'The dark one?'

Ferenc nodded violently. 'She gave him shelter.'

'And the girl's,' Czerda agreed viciously. 'Hurry.'

The four men ran off towards the patio steps. Bowman moved to the offside front tyre and because this time he didn't have to bother about muffling the escaping hiss of air he merely unscrewed the valve and threw it away. He rose and, still stooping, ran across the forecourt and through the sculptured arch in the hedge to the parking space beyond.

Here he ran into an unexpected difficulty. A blue Peugeot, Cecile had said. Fine. A blue Peugeot he could recognize any time – in broad daylight. But this wasn't day-time, it was night-time, and even although the moon was shining the thickly-woven wickerwork roofing cast an almost impenetrable shadow on the cars parked beneath it. Just as by night all cats are grey so by night all cars look infuriatingly the same. Easy enough, perhaps, to differentiate between a Rolls and a Mini, but in this age of mindless conformity the vast majority of cars are disturbingly alike in size and profile. Or so, dismayingly, Bowman found that night. He moved quickly from one car to the next, having to peer closely in each case for an infuriating length of time, only to discover that it was not the car he was seeking.

He heard the sound of low voices, but voices angry and anxious, and moved quickly to the archway. Close by Czerda's caravan, the four gypsies, who had clearly discovered that their birds had flown, were gesticulating and arguing heatedly, holding their council of war and obviously wondering what in hell to do next, a decision Bowman didn't envy their having to make for in their position he wouldn't have had the faintest idea himself.

Abruptly, the centre of his attention altered. Out of the corner of an eye he had caught sight of something which, even in that pale moonlight, definitely constituted a splash of colour.

This brightly-hued apparition, located on the upper terrace, consisted of a pair of garishly-striped heliotrope pyjamas and inside the pyjamas was no other than Le Grand Duc, leaning on the balustrade and gazing down towards the forecourt with an expression of what might have been mild interest or benign indifference or, indeed, quite a variety of other expressions as it is difficult to be positive about those things when a large part of what can be seen of the subject's face consists of jaws champing regularly up and down while most of the remainder is concealed by a large red apple. But, clearly, however, he wasn't in the grip of any violent emotion.

Bowman left Le Grand Duc to his munching and resumed his search. The inner end of the parking lot, she had said. But her damned Peugeot wasn't at the inner end. He'd checked twice. He turned to the west side and the fourth one along was it. Or he thought it was. A Peugeot, anyway. He climbed inside and the key fitted the ignition. Women, he thought bitterly, but didn't pursue the subject with himself, there were things to be done.

The door he closed as softly as he could: it seemed unlikely that the faint click would have been heard in the forecourt even if the gypsies hadn't been conducting their heated council of war. He released the hand-brake, engaged first gear and kept the clutch depressed, reached for and turned on the ignition and headlamp switches simultaneously. Both engine and lamps came on precisely together and the Peugeot, throwing gravel from its rear wheels, jumped forward, Bowman spinning the wheel to the left to head for the archway in the hedge. At once he saw the four gypsies detach themselves from the rear of Czerda's caravan and run to cover what they accurately assumed would be the route he would take between the archway and the exit from the forecourt. Czerda appeared to be shouting and although his voice couldn't be heard above the accelerating roar of the engine his violent gesticulations clearly indicated that he was telling his men to stop the Peugeot although how he proposed to do this Bowman couldn't imagine. As he passed through the archway he could see in the blaze of the headlamps that Ferenc was the only one carrying a firearm and as he was pointing it directly at Bowman he didn't leave Bowman with very much option other than to point the car directly at him. The panic registering suddenly on Ferenc's face showed that he had lost all interest in using the gun and was now primarily concerned with saving himself. He dived frantically to his left and almost got clear but almost wasn't enough. The nearside wing of the Peugeot caught him in the thigh and suddenly he wasn't there any more, all Bowman could see was the metallic glint of his gun spinning in the air. On the left, Czerda and the two other gypsies had managed to fling themselves clear. Bowman twisted the wheel again, drove out of the forecourt and down towards the valley road. He wondered what Le Grand Duc had made of all that: probably, he thought, he hadn't missed as much as a munch.

The tyres squealed as the Peugeot rounded the right-angle turn at the foot of the road. Bowman drew up beside Cecile, stopped, got out but left the engine running. She ran to him and thrust out a suitcase.

'Hurry! Quickly!' Angrily, almost, she thrust the case at him. 'Can't you hear them coming?'

'I can hear them,' Bowman said pacifically. 'I think we have time.'

They had time. They heard the whine of an engine in low gear, a whine diminishing in intensity as the jeep braked heavily for the corner. Abruptly it came into sight and clearly it was making a very poor job indeed of negotiating the right-hand bend. Czerda was hauling madly on the steering-wheel but the front wheels – or tyres, at least – appeared to have a mind of their own. Bowman watched with interest as the jeep carried straight on, careered across the opposite bank of the road, cut down a sapling and landed with a resounding crash.

'Tsk! Tsk!' Bowman said to Cecile. 'Did ever you see such careless driving?' He crossed over the road and looked into the field. The jeep, its wheels still spinning, lay on its side while the three gypsies, who had clearly parted company with their vehicle before it had come to rest, lay in a sprawled heap about fifteen feet away. As he watched they disentangled themselves and scrambled painfully to their feet. Ferenc, understandably, was not one of the three. Bowman became aware that he had been joined by Cecile.

'You did this,' she said accusingly. 'You sabotaged their jeep.'

'It was nothing,' he said deprecatingly. 'I just let a little air out of the tyres.'

'But – but you could have killed those men! The jeep could have landed on top of them and crushed them to death.'

'It's not always possible to arrange everything as one would wish it,' Bowman said regretfully. She gave him the kind of look Dr Crippen must have got used to after he'd been hauled into court, so Bowman changed his tone. 'You don't look like a fool, Cecile, nor do you talk like one, so don't go and spoil the whole effect by behaving like one. If you think our three friends down there were just out to savour the delights of the night-time Provençal air, why don't you go and ask them how they are?'

She turned and walked back to the car without a word. He followed and they drove off in a one-sidedly huffy silence. Within a minute he slowed and pulled the car into a small cleared area on the right-hand side of the road. Through the windscreen they could see the vertical limestone bluffs with enormous man-made rectangular openings giving on the impenetrable darkness of the unseen caverns beyond.

'You're not stopping here?' Incredulity in her voice.

He switched off the engine and set the parking brake. 'I've stopped.'

'But they'll find us here!' She sounded a little desperate. 'They're bound to. Any moment now.'

'No. If they're capable of thinking at all after that little tumble they had, they'll be thinking that we're half-way to Avignon by this time. Besides, I think it's going to take them some time to recover their first fine enthusiasm for moonlight driving.'

They got out of the car and looked at the entrance to the caverns. Foreboding wasn't the word for it, nor was sinister: something stronger, much stronger. It was, quite literally, an appalling place and Bowman had no difficulty in understanding and sympathizing with the viewpoint of the policeman back at the hotel. But he didn't for a moment believe that you had to be born in Les Baux and grow up hand-in-hand with all the ancient superstitions in order to develop a night phobia about those caves: quite simply it was a place into which no man in his right mind would venture after the sun had gone down. He was, he hoped, in his right mind, and he didn't want to go in. But he had to.

He took a torch from his suitcase and said to Cecile: 'Wait here.'

'No! You're not going to leave me alone here.' She sounded pretty vehement about it.

'It'll probably be an awful lot worse inside.'

'I don't care.'

'Suit yourself.'

They set off together and passed through the largest of the openings to the left: if you could have put a three-storey house on wheels you could have trundled it through that opening without any trouble. Bowman traversed the walls with his torch, walls covered with the graffiti of countless generations, then opted for an archway to the right that led to an even larger cavern. Cecile, he noticed, even although wearing flat-heeled sandals, stumbled quite a bit, more than the occasional slight undulations in the limestone floor warranted: he was pretty well sure now that her vision was a good deal less than twenty-twenty which, he reflected, was maybe why she had consented to come with him in the first place.

The next cavern held nothing of interest for Bowman. True, its vaulted heights were lost in darkness, but as only a bat could have got up there anyway that was of no moment. Another archway loomed ahead.

'This is a dreadful place.' Cecile whispered.

'Well, I wouldn't like to live here all the time.'

Another few paces and she said: 'Mr Bowman.'

'Neil.'

'May I take your arm?' In these days he didn't think they asked.

'Help yourself,' he said agreeably. 'You're not the only person in need of reassurance round here.'

'It's not that. I'm not scared, really. It's just that you keep flashing that torch everywhere and I can't see and I keep tripping.'

'Ah!'

So she took his arm and she didn't trip any more, just

shivered violently as if she were coming down with some form of malaria. By and by she said: 'What are you looking for?'

'You know damned well what I'm looking for.'

'Perhaps – well, they could have hidden him.'

'They could have hidden him. They couldn't have buried him, not unless they had brought along some dynamite with them, but they could have hidden him. Under a mound of limestone rock and stones. There's plenty around.'

'But we've passed by dozens of piles of limestone rocks. You didn't bother about them.'

'When we come to a freshly made mound you'll know the difference,' he said matter-of-factly. She shivered again, violently, and he went on: 'Why did you have to come in, Cecile? You were telling the truth when you said you weren't scared: you're just plain terrified.'

'I'd rather be plain terrified in here with you than plain terrified alone out there.' Any moment now and her teeth would start chattering.

'You may have a point there,' he admitted. They passed, slightly uphill this time, through another archway, into another immense cavern: after a few steps Bowman stopped abruptly.

'What is it?' she whispered. 'What's wrong?'

'I don't know.' He paused. 'Yes, I do know.' For the first time he shivered himself.

'You, too?' Again that whisper.

'Me, too. But it's not that. Some clod-hopping character has just walked over my grave.'

'Please?'

'This is it. This is the place. When you're old and sinful like me, you can smell it.'

'Death?' And now her voice was shaking. 'People can't smell death.'

'I can.'

He switched off the torch.

'Put it on, put it on!' Her voice was high-pitched, close to hysteria. 'For God's sake, put it on. *Please*.'

He detached her hand, put his arm round her and held her close. With a bit of luck, he thought, they might get some synchronization into their shivering, not as much perhaps as the ballroom champions on TV got in their dancing, but enough to be comfortable. When the vibrations had died down a little he said: 'Notice anything different about this cavern?'

'There's light! There's light coming from somewhere.'

'There is indeed.' They walked slowly forward till they came to a huge pile of rubble on the floor. The jumble of rocks stretched up and up until at the top they could see a large squarish patch of star-dusted sky. Down the centre of this rockfall, all the way from top to bottom, was a narrow patch of disturbed rubble, a pathway that seemed to have been newly made. Bowman switched on his torch and there was no doubt about it: it was newly made. He traversed the base of the rockfall with the beam of the torch and then the beam, almost of its own volition, stopped and looked on a mound of limestone rocks, perhaps eight feet in length by three high.

'With a freshly made mound of limestone,' Bowman said, 'you can see the difference.'

'You can see the difference,' she repeated mechanically.

'Please. Walk away a little.'

'No. It's funny, but I'm all right now.'

He believed her and he didn't think if was funny. Mankind is still close enough to the primeval jungles to find the greatest fear of all in the unknown: but here, now, they knew.

Bowman stooped over the mound and began to throw stones to one side. They hadn't bothered to cover the unfortunate Alexandre to any great depth for inside a moment Bowman came to the slashed remnants of a once white shirt, now saturated in blood. Lying in the encrusted blood and attached to a chain was a silver crucifix. He unclipped the chain and lifted both it and the crucifix away.

II

Bowman parked the Peugeot at the spot in the valley road where he had picked up Cecile and the cases. He got out.

'Stay here,' he said to Cecile. 'This time I mean it.' She didn't exactly nod her head obediently but she didn't argue either: maybe his training methods were beginning to improve. The jeep, he observed without any surprise, was where he'd last seen it: it was going to require a mobile crane to get it out of there.

The entrance to the Baumanière's forecourt seemed deserted but he'd developed the same sort of affectionate trust for Czerda and his merry band of followers as he would have for a colony of cobras or black widow spiders so he pressed deep into the shadows and advanced slowly into the forecourt. His foot struck something solid and there was a faint metallic clink. He became very still but he'd provoked no reaction that he could see or hear. He stooped and picked up the pistol that he'd inadvertently kicked against the base of a petrol pump. Young Ferenc's pistol, without a doubt. From what last Bowman had seen of Ferenc he didn't think he'd have missed it yet or would be wanting to use if for some time: but Bowman decided to return it to him all the same. He knew he wouldn't be disturbing anyone for lights from inside Czerda's caravan still shone through the windows and the half-open door. Every other caravan in the forecourt was in darkness. He crossed to Czerda's caravan, climbed the steps soundlessly and looked in through the doorway.

Czerda, with a bandaged left hand, bruised cheek and large strip of sticking-plaster on his forehead, wasn't looking quite his old self but he was in mint condition compared to Ferenc to whose injuries he was attending. Ferenc lay on a bunk, moaning and barely half-conscious, exclaiming in pain from time to time as his father removed a blood-soaked bandage from his forehead. When the bandage was at last jerked free to the accompaniment of a final yelp of pain, a pain that had the effect of restoring Ferenc to something pretty close to complete consciousness, Bowman could see that he had a very nasty cut indeed across his forehead, but a cut that faded into insignificance compared to the massive bruising of forehead and face: if he had sustained other bodily bruises of a comparable magnitude Ferenc had to be suffering very considerably and feeling in a very low state indeed. It was not a consideration that moved Bowman: if Ferenc had had his way he, Bowman, would be in a state in which he'd never feel anything again.

Ferenc sat shakily up on the bunk while his father secured

a fresh bandage, then sat forward, put his elbows on his knees, his face in his hands and moaned.

'In God's name, what happened? My head—'

'You'll be all right,' Czerda said soothingly. 'A cut and a bruise. That's all.'

'But what *happened*? Why is my head—'

'The car. Remember?'

'The car. Of course. That devil Bowman!' Coming from Ferenc, Bowman thought, that was rather good. 'Did he – did he—'

'Damn his soul, yes. He got clear away – and he wrecked our jeep. See this?' Czerda pointed to his hand and forehead. Ferenc looked without interest and looked away. He had other things on his mind.

'My gun, Father! Where's my gun?'

'Here,' Bowman said. He pointed his gun at Ferenc and walked into the caravan: the blood-stained chain and crucifix dangled from his left hand. Ferenc stared at him: he looked as a man might look with his head on the block and the executioner starting the back swing on his axe, for executioner Ferenc would have been in Bowman's position. Czerda, whose back had been to the door, swung round and remained as immobile as his son. He didn't seem any more pleased to see Bowman than Ferenc did. Bowman walked forward, two paces, and placed the bloody crucifix on a small table.

'His mother might like to have that,' he said. 'I should wipe the blood off first, though.' He waited for some reaction but there was none so he went on: 'I'm going to kill you, Czerda. I'll have to, won't I, for no one can ever prove you killed young Alexandre. But I don't require proof, all I need is certainty. But not yet. I can't do it yet, can I? I mustn't cause innocent people to die, must I? But later. Later I kill you. Then I kill Gaiuse Strome. Tell him I said so, will you?'

'What do you know of Gaiuse Strome?' he whispered.

'Enough to hang him. And you.'

Czerda suddenly smiled but when he spoke it was still in the same whisper.

'You've just said you can't kill me yet.' He took a step forward.

Bowman said nothing. He altered the pistol fractionally

until it was lined up on a spot between Ferenc's eyes. Czerda made no move to take a second step. Bowman looked at him and pointed to a stool close to the small table.

'Sit down,' he said, 'and face your son.'

Czerda did as he was told. Bowman took one step forward and it was apparent that Ferenc's reactions weren't yet back in working order for his suddenly horrified expression in what little was left of his face that was still capable of registering expressions and his mouth opening to shout a warning came far too late to be of any aid to Czerda who crashed heavily to the floor as the barrel of Bowman's gun caught him behind the ear.

Ferenc bared his teeth and swore viciously at him. At least that was what Bowman assumed he was doing for Ferenc had reverted to his native Romany but he hadn't even started in on descriptions when Bowman stepped forward wordlessly, his gun swinging again. Ferenc's reactions were even slower than Bowman had imagined: he toppled head-long across his father and lay still.

'What on earth—' The voice came from behind Bowman. He threw himself to one side, dropping to the floor, whirled round and brought the gun up: then, more slowly, he rose. Cecile stood in the doorway, her green eyes wide, her face stilled in shock.

'You fool,' Bowman said, savagely. 'You almost died there. Don't you know that?' She nodded, the shock still in her face. 'Come inside. Shut the door. You *are* a fool. Why the hell didn't you do what I asked and stay where you were?'

Almost as if in a trance she stepped inside and closed the door. She stared down at the two fallen men, then back at Bowman again.

'For God's sake, why did you knock those two men senseless? Two injured men?'

'Because it was inconvenient to kill them at present,' Bowman said coldly. He turned his back on her and began to search the place methodically and exhaustively. When one searches any place, be it gypsy caravan or baronial mansion, methodically and exhaustively, one has to wreck it completely in the process. So, in an orderly and systematic fashion, Bowman set about reducing Czerda's caravan to a total ruin.

He ripped the beds to pieces, sliced open the mattresses with the aid of a knife he'd borrowed from the recumbent Czerda, scattering the flock stuffing far and wide to ensure that there was nothing hidden inside, and wrenched open cupboards, all locked, again with the aid of Czerda's knife. He moved into the kitchen recess, smashed all the items of crockery that were capable of holding anything, emptied the contents of a dozen food tins into the sink, smashed open preserving jars and a variety of wine bottles by the simple expedient of knocking them together two at a time and ended up by spilling the contents of the cutlery drawers on the floor to ensure that there was nothing hidden beneath the lining paper. There wasn't.

Cecile, who had been watching this performance still in the same kind of hypnotic trance, said: 'Who's Gaiuse Strome?'

'How long were you listening?'

'All the time. Who's Gaiuse Strome?'

'I don't know,' Bowman said frankly. 'Never heard of him until tonight.'

He turned his attention to the larger clothing drawers. He emptied the contents of each in turn on the floor and kicked them apart. There was nothing there for him, just clothes.

'Other people's property doesn't mean all that much to you, does it?' By this time Cecile's state of trance had altered to the dazed incomprehension of one trying to come to grips with reality.

'He'll have it insured,' Bowman said comfortingly. He began an assault on the last piece of furniture still intact, a beautifully carved mahogany bureau worth a small fortune in anybody's money, splintering open the locked drawers with the now invaluable aid of the point of Czerda's knife. He dumped the contents of the first two drawers on the floor and was about to open a third when something caught his eye. He stooped and retrieved a pair of heavy rolled-up woollen socks. Inside them was an elastic-bound package of brand-new crackling banknotes with consecutive serial numbers. It took him over half a minute to count them.

'Eighty thousand Swiss francs in one-thousand-franc notes,' Bowman observed. 'I wonder where friend Czerda got eighty thousand Swiss francs in one-thousand-franc notes? Ah, well.' He stuffed the notes into a hip pocket and resumed the search.

'But – but that's stealing!' It would be too much, perhaps, to say that Cecile looked horrified but there wasn't much in the way of admiration in those big green eyes: but Bowman was in no mood for moral disapprobation.

'Oh, shut up!' he said.

'But you've *got* money.'

'Maybe this is how I get it.'

He broke open another drawer, sifted through the contents with the toe of his shoe, then turned as he heard a sound to his left. Ferenc was struggling shakily to his feet, so Bowman took his arm, helped him to stand upright, hit him very hard indeed on the side of the jaw and lowered him to the floor again. The shock was back in Cecile's face, a shock mingled with the beginnings of revulsion, she was probably a gently nurtured girl who had been brought up to believe that the opera or the ballet or the theatre constituted the ideal of an evening's entertainment. Bowman started in on the next drawer.

'Don't tell me,' he said. 'Just an idle layabout laying about. Not funny?'

'No.' She had her lips compressed in a very school-marmish way.

'I'm pressed for time. Ah!'

'What is it?' In even the most puritanical of females repugnance doesn't stand a chance against curiosity.

'This.' He showed her a delicately fashioned rosewood lacquered box inlaid with ebony and mother-of-pearl. It was locked and so exquisitely made that it was quite impossible to insert the point of even Czerda's razor-sharp knife into the microscopic line between lid and box. Cecile seemed to derive a certain malicious satisfaction from this momentary problem for she waved a hand to indicate the indescribable wreckage that now littered almost every square inch of the caravan floor.

'Shall I look for the key?' she asked sweetly.

'No need.' He laid the rosewood box on the floor and jumped on it with both heels, reducing it at once to splintered matchwood. He removed a sealed envelope from the ruins, opened it and extracted a sheet of paper.

On it was a typewritten – in capitals – jumble of apparently meaningless letters and figures. There were a few words in plain language but their meaning in the context was completely obscure. Cecile peered over his shoulder. Her eyes were screwed up and he knew she was having difficulty in seeing.

'What is it?' she asked.

'Code, looks like. One or two words straight. There's "Monday", a date – 24 May – and a place-name – Grau du Roi.'

'Grau du Roi?'

'A fishing port and holiday resort down on the coast. Now, why should a gypsy be carrying a message in code?' He thought about this for a bit but it didn't do him any good: he was still awake and on his feet but his mind had turned in for the night. 'Stupid question. Up, up and away.'

'What? Still two lovely drawers left unsmashed?'

'Leave those for the vandals.' He took her arm so that she wouldn't trip too often on the way to the door and she peered questioningly at him.

'Meaning you can break codes?'

Bowman looked around him. 'Furniture, yes. Crockery, yes. Codes, no. Come, to our hotel.'

They left. Before closing the door Bowman had a last look at the two still unconscious and injured men lying amidst the irretrievably ruined shambles of what had once been a beautifully appointed caravan interior. He felt almost sorry for the caravan.

— 4 —

WHEN BOWMAN woke up the birds were singing, the sky was a cloudless translucent blue and the rays of the morning sun were streaming through the window. Not the window of an hotel but the window of the blue Peugeot which he'd pulled off the road in the early hours of the morning into the shelter of a thick clump of trees that had seemed, in the darkness, to offer almost total concealment from the road. Now, in daylight, he could see that it offered nothing of the kind and that they were quite visible to any passer-by who cared to cast a casual sideways glance in their direction and, as there were those not all that far distant whose casual sideways glances he'd much rather not be the object of, he deemed it time to move on.

He was reluctant to wake Cecile. She appeared to have passed a relatively comfortable night – or what had been left of the night – with her dark head on his shoulder, a fact that he dimly resented because he had passed a most uncomfortable night, partly because he'd been loath to move for fear of disturbing her but chiefly because his unaccustomedly violent exercise of the previous night had left him with numerous aches in a wide variety of muscles that hadn't been subjected to such inconsiderate treatment for a long time. He wound down the driver's window, sniffed the fresh cool morning air and lit a cigarette. The rasp of the cigarette lighter was enough to make her stir, straighten and peer rather blearily about her until she realized where she was.

She looked at him and said: 'Well, as hotels go, it was cheap enough.'

'That's what I like,' Bowman said. 'The pioneering spirit.'

'Do I *look* like a pioneer?'

'Frankly, no.'

'I want a bath.'

'And that you shall have and very soon. In the best hotel in Arles. Cross my heart.'

'You *are* an optimist. Every hotel room will have been taken weeks ago for the gypsy festival.'

'Indeed. Including the one *I* took. I booked my room two months ago.'

'I see.' She moved pointedly across to her own side of the seat which Bowman privately considered pretty ungrateful of her considering that she hadn't disdained the use of his shoulder as a pillow for the most of the night. 'You booked your room two months ago, Mr Bowman—'

'Neil.'

'I have been very patient, haven't I, Mr Bowman? I haven't asked questions?'

'That you haven't.' He looked at her admiringly. 'What a wife you're going to make. When I come home late from the office—'

'Please. What *is* it all about? Who are you?'

'A layabout on the run.'

'On the run? Following the gypsies that—'

'I'm a vengeful layabout.'

'I've helped you—'

'Yes, you have.'

'I've let you have my car. You've put me in danger—'

'I know. I'm sorry about that and I'd no right to do it. I'll put you in a taxi for Martignane airport and the first plane for England. You'll be safe there. Or take this car. I'll get a lift to Arles.'

'Blackmail!'

'Blackmail? I don't understand. I'm offering you a place of safety. Do you mean that you're prepared to come with me?'

She nodded. He looked at her consideringly.

'Such implicit trust in a man with so much and so very recently spilled blood on his hands?'

She nodded again.

'I still don't understand.' He gazed forward through the windscreen. 'Could it be that the fair Miss Dubois is in the process of falling in love?'

'Rest easy,' she said calmly. 'The fair Miss Dubois has no such romantic stirrings in mind.'

'Then why come along with me? Who knows, they may be all lying in wait – the mugger up the dark alleyway, the waiter with the poison phial, the smiler with the knife beneath the cloak – any of Czerda's pals, in fact. So why?'

'I honestly don't know.'

He started up the Peugeot. 'I'm sure I don't know either.' But he did know. And she knew. But what she didn't know was that he knew that she knew. It was, Bowman thought, all very confusing at eight o'clock in the morning.

They'd just regained the main road when she said: 'Mr Bowman, you may be cleverer than you look.'

'That would be difficult?'

'I asked you a question a minute or two ago. Somehow or other you didn't get around to answering it.'

'Question? What question?'

'Never mind,' she said resignedly. 'I've forgotten what it was myself.'

II

Le Grand Duc, his heliotrope-striped pyjamas largely and mercifully obscured by a napkin, was having breakfast in bed. His breakfast tray was about the same width as the bed and had to be to accommodate the vast meal it held. He had just speared a particularly succulent piece of fish when the door opened and Lila entered without the benefit of knocking. Her blonde hair was uncombed. With one hand she held a wrap clutched round her while with the other she waved a piece of paper. Clearly, she was upset.

'Cecile's gone!' She waved the paper some more. 'She left this.'

'Gone?' Le Grand Duc transferred the forkful of fish to his mouth and savoured the passing moment. 'By heavens, this red mullet is superb. Gone where?'

'I don't know. She's taken all her clothes with her.'

'Let me see.' He stretched out his hand and took the note from Lila. ' "Contact me Poste Restante Saintes-Maries." Rather less than informative, one might say. That ruffianly fellow who was with her last night—'

'Bowman? Neil Bowman?'

'That's the ruffianly fellow I meant. Check if he's still here. And your car.'

'I hadn't thought of that.'

'One has to have the mind for it,' Le Grand Duc said kindly. He picked up his knife and fork again, waited until Lila had made her hurried exit from the room, laid down knife and fork, opened a bedside drawer and picked up the notebook which Lila had used the previous night while she was acting as his unpaid secretary when he had been interviewing the gypsies. He compared the handwriting in the notebook with that on the sheet of paper Lila had just handed him: it was indisputably the same handwriting. Le Grand

Duc sighed, replaced the notebook, let the scrap of paper fall carelessly to the floor and resumed his attack on the red mullet. He had finished it and was just appreciatively lifting the cover of a dish of kidneys and bacon when Lila returned. She had exchanged her wrap for the blue mini-dress she had been wearing the previous evening and had combed her hair: but her state of agitation remained unchanged.

'He's gone, too. And the car. Oh, Charles, I *am* worried.'

'With Le Grand Duc by your side, worry is a wasted emotion. Saintes-Maries is the place, obviously.'

'I suppose so.' She was doubtful, hesitant. 'But how do I get there? My car – our car—'

'You will accompany me, *chérie*. Le Grand Duc always has some sort of transport or other.' He paused and listened briefly to a sudden babble of voices. 'Tsk! Tsk! Those gypsies can be a noisy lot. Take my tray, my dear.'

Not without some difficulty, Lila removed the tray. Le Grand Duc swung from the bed, enveloped himself in a violently-coloured Chinese dressing-gown and headed for the door. As it was clear that the source of the disturbance came from the direction of the forecourt the Duke marched across to the terrace balustrade and looked down. A large number of gypsies were gathered round the rear of Czerda's caravan, the one part of the caravan that was invisible from where Le Grand Duc was standing. Some of the gypsies were gesticulating, others shouting: all were clearly very angry about something.

'Ah!' Le Grand Duc clapped his hands together. 'This is fortunate indeed. It is rare that one is actually on the spot. This is the stuff that folklore is made of. Come.'

He turned and walked purposefully towards the steps leading down to the terrace. Lila caught his arm.

'But you can't go down there in your pyjamas!'

'Don't be ridiculous.' Le Grand Duc swept on his way, descended the steps to the patio, ignored – or, more probably, was oblivious of – the stares of the early breakfasters on the patio and paused at the head of the forecourt steps to survey the scene. Already, he could see, the parking lot beyond the hedge was empty of caravans and two or three of those that had been in the forecourt had also disappeared while others were obviously making preparations for departure. But at least two dozen gypsies were still gathered round Czerda's caravan.

Like a psychedelic Caligula, with an apprehensive and highly embarrassed Lila following, Le Grand Duc made his imperious way down the steps and through the gypsies crowding round the caravan. He halted and looked at the spectacle in front of him. Battered, bruised, cut and heavily bandaged, Czerda and his son sat on their caravan's steps, both of them with their heads in their hands: both physically and mentally, their condition appeared to be very low. Behind them several gypsy women could be seen embarking on the gargantuan task of cleaning up the interior of the caravan which, in the daytime, looked to be an even more appalling mess than it had been by lamplight. An anarchist with an accurate line in bomb-throwing would have been proud to acknowledge that handiwork as his own.

'Tsk! Tsk! Tsk!' Le Grand Duc shook his head in a mixture of disappointment and disgust. 'A family squabble. Very quarrelsome, some of those Romany families, you know. Nothing here for the true folklorist. Come, my dear, I see that most of the gypsies are already on their way. It behoves us to do the same.' He led her up the steps and beckoned a passing porter. 'My car, and at once.'

'Your car's not here?' Lila asked.

'Of course it's not here. Good God, girl, you don't expect my employees to sleep in the same hotel as I do? Be here in ten minutes.'

'Ten minutes! I have to bath, breakfast, pack, pay my bill—'

'Ten minutes.'

She was ready in ten minutes. So was Le Grand Duc. He was wearing a grey double-breasted flannel suit over a maroon shirt and a panama straw hat with a maroon band, but for once Lila's attention was centred elsewhere. She was gazing rather dazedly down at the forecourt.

'Le Grand Duc,' she repeated mechanically, 'always has some sort of transport or other.'

The transport in this case was a magnificent and enormous handmade cabriolet Rolls-Royce in lime and dark green.

Beside it, holding the rear door open, stood a chauffeuse dressed in a uniform of lime green, exactly the same shade as that of the car, piped in dark green, again exactly the same shade as the car. She was young, petite, auburn-haired and very pretty. She smiled as she ushered Le Grand Duc and Lila into the back seat, got behind the wheel and drove the car away in what, from inside the car, was a totally hushed silence.

Lila looked at Le Grand Duc who was lighting a large Havana with a lighter taken from a most impressively button-bestrewed console to his right.

'Do you mean to tell me,' she demanded, 'that you wouldn't let so deliciously pretty a creature stay in the same hotel as yourself?'

'Certainly not. Not that I lack concern for my employees.' He selected a button in the console and the dividing window slid silently down into the back of the driver's seat. 'And where did you spend the night, Carita, my dear?'

'Well, Monsieur le Duc, the hotels were full and—'

'Where did you spend the night?'

'In the car.'

'Tsk! Tsk!' The window slid up and he turned to Lila. 'But it is, as you can see a very comfortable car.'

III

By the time the blue Peugeot arrived in Arles a coolness had developed between Bowman and Cecile. They had been having a discussion about matters sartorial and weren't quite seeing eye to eye. Bowman pulled up in a relatively quiet side-street opposite a large if somewhat dingy clothing emporium, stopped the engine and looked at the girl. She didn't look at him.

Well?' he said.

'I'm sorry.' She was examining some point in the far distance. 'It's not on. I think you're quite mad.'

'Like enough,' he nodded. He kissed her on the cheek, got out, took his case from the rear seat and walked across the pavement, where he stopped to examine some exotic costumes in the drapery window. He could clearly see the reflection of the car and, almost equally clearly, that of Cecile. Her lips were compressed and she was distinctly angry. She appeared to hesitate, then left the car and crossed to where he was standing.

'I could hit you,' she announced.

'I wouldn't like that,' he said. 'You look a big strong girl to me.'

'Oh, for heaven's sake, shut up and put that case back in the car.'

So he shut up and put the case back in the car, took her arm and led her reluctantly into the faded emporium.

Twenty minutes later he looked at himself in a full-length mirror and shuddered. He was clad now in a black, high-buttoned and very tightly fitting suit which gave him some idea how the overweight and heroically corseted operatic diva must feel when she was reaching for a high C, a floppy white shirt, black string tie and wide-brimmed black hat. It was a relief when Cecile appeared from a dressing-room, accompanied by a plump, pleasant middle-aged woman dressed in black whom Bowman assumed to be the manageress. But he observed her only by courtesy of peripheral vision, any man who didn't beam his entire ocular voltage directly at Cecile was either a psychiatric case or possessed of the visual acuity of a particularly myopic barnyard owl.

He had never thought of her as an eyesore but now he realized, for the first time but for keeps, that she was a stunningly lovely person. It wasn't because of the exquisite dress she wore, a beautiful, beautifully fitting, exotic and clearly very expensive gypsy costume that hadn't missed out on many of the colours of the rainbow, nor because of her white ruched mantilla head-dress affair, though he had heard tell that the awareness of wearing beautiful things gives women an inner glow that shows through. All he knew was that his heart did a couple of handsprings and it wasn't until he saw her sweet and ever so slightly amused smile that he called his heart to order and resumed what he hoped was his normally inscrutable expression. The manageress put his very thoughts in words.

'Madame,' she breathed, 'looks beautiful.'

'Madame,' he said, '*is* beautiful,' then reverted to his old self again. 'How much? In Swiss francs. You take Swiss francs?'

'Of course.' The manageress summoned an assistant who started adding figures while the manageress packed clothes.

'She's packing up *my* clothes.' Cecile sounded dismayed. 'I can't go out in the street like this.'

'Of course you can.' Bowman had meant to be heartily reassuring but the words sounded mechanical, he still couldn't take his eyes off her. 'This is fiesta time.'

'Monsieur is quite correct,' the manageress said. 'Hundreds of young Arlésiennes dress like this at this time of year. A pleasant change and very good for them it is, too.'

'And it's not bad for business either.' Bowman looked at the bill the assistant had just handed him. 'Two thousand, four hundred Swiss francs.' He peeled three thousand-franc notes from Czerda's roll and handed them to the manageress. 'Keep the change.'

'But monsieur is too kind.' From her flabbergasted expression he took it that the citizens of Arles were not notably open-handed when it came to the question of gratuities.

'Easy come, easy go,' he said philosophically and led Cecile from the shop. They got into the Peugeot and he drove for a minute or two before pulling up in an almost deserted car-park. Cecile looked at him enquiringly.

'My cosmetic case,' he explained. He reached into his case in the back seat and brought out a small black zipped leather bag. 'Never travel without it.'

She looked at him rather peculiarly. 'A man doesn't carry a cosmetic case.'

'This one does. You'll see why.'

Twenty minutes later, when they stood before the reception desk of the grandest hotel in Arles, she understood why. They were clad as they had been when they had left the clothing emporium but were otherwise barely recognizable as the same people. Cecile's complexion was several shades darker, as was the colour of her neck, hands and wrists, she wore bright scarlet lipstick and far too much rouge, mascara and eye-shadow: Bowman's face was now the colour of well-seasoned mahogany, his newly acquired moustache dashing to a degree. The receptionist handed him back his passport.

'Your room is ready, Mr Parker,' he said. 'This is Mrs Parker?'

'Don't be silly,' Bowman said, took Cecile's suddenly stiff arm and followed the bell-boy to the lift. When the bedroom door closed behind them, she looked at Bowman with a noticeable lack of enthusiasm.

'Did you *have* to say that to the receptionist?'

'Look at your hands.'

'What's wrong with my hands – apart from the fact that that stuff of yours has made them filthy?'

'No rings.'

'Oh!'

'Well might you "Oh!" The experienced receptionist notices those things automatically – that's why he asked. And *he* may be asked questions – any suspicious couples checked in today, that sort of thing. As far as the criminal stakes are concerned a man with his lady-love in tow is automatically above suspicion – it is assumed that he has other things in mind.'

'There's no need to talk—'

'I'll tell you about the birds and bees later. Meantime, what matters is that the man trusts me. I'm going out for a bit. Have your bath. Don't wash that stuff off your arms, face and neck. There's little enough left.'

She looked into a mirror, lifted up her hands and studied both them and her face. 'But how in heaven's name am I going to have a bath without—'

'I'll give you a hand, if you like,' Bowman volunteered. She walked to the bathroom, closed and locked the door. Bowman went downstairs and paused for a moment outside a telephone kiosk in the lobby, rubbing his chin, a man deep in thought. The telephone had no dialling face which meant that outgoing calls were routed through the hotel switchboard. He walked out into the bright sunshine.

Even at that early hour the Boulevard des Lices was crowded with people. Not sightseers, not tourists, but local tradesmen setting up literally hundreds of stalls on the broad pavements of the boulevard. The street itself was as crowded as the pavements with scores of vehicles ranging from heavy trucks to handcarts unloading a variety of goods that ran the gamut from heavy agricultural machinery, through every type of food, furniture and clothes imaginable, down to the gaudiest of souvenir trinkets and endless bunches of flowers.

Bowman turned into a post office, located an empty telephone booth, raised the exchange and asked for a Whitehall number in London. While he was waiting for the call to come through he fished out the garbled message he had found in Czerda's caravan and smoothed it out before him.

IV

At least a hundred gypsies knelt on the ground in the grassy clearing while the black-robed priest delivered a benediction. When he lowered his arm, turned, and walked towards a small black tent pitched near by, the gypsies rose and began to disperse, some wandering aimlessly around, others drifting back to their caravans which were parked just off the road a few miles north-east of Arles: behind the caravans loomed the majestic outline of the ancient Abbey de Montmajour.

Among the parked vehicles, three were instantly identifiable: the green-and-white caravan where Alexandre's mother and the three young gypsy girls lived, Czerda's caravan which was now being towed by a garishly yellow-painted breakdown truck and Le Grand Duc's imposing green Rolls. The cabriolet hood of the Rolls was down for the sky was cloudless and the morning already hot. The chauffeuse, her auburn hair uncovered to show that she was temporarily off-duty, stood with Lila by the side of the car: Le Grand Duc, reclining in the rear seat, refreshed himself with some indeterminate liquid from the open cocktail cabinet before him and surveyed the scene with interest.

Lila said: 'I never associated *this* with gypsies.'

'Understandable, understandable,' Le Grand Duc conceded graciously. 'But then, of course, you do not know your gypsies, my dear, while I am a European authority on them.' He paused, considered and corrected himself. '*The* European authority. Which means, of course, the world. The religious element can be very strong, and their sincerity and devotion never more apparent than when they travel to worship the relics of Sara, their patron saint. Every day, in the last period of their travel, a priest accompanies them to bless Sara and their – but enough? I must not bore you with my erudition.'

'Boring, Charles? It's all quite fascinating. What on earth is that black tent for?'

'A mobile confessional – little used, I fear. The gypsies have their own codes of right and wrong. Good God! There's Czerda going inside.' He glanced at his watch. 'Nine-fifteen. He should be out by lunch-time.'

'You don't like him?' Lila asked curiously. 'You think that he—'

'I know nothing about the fellow,' Le Grand Duc said. 'I would merely observe that a face such as his has not been fashioned by a lifetime of good works and pious thoughts.'

There was certainly little enough indicative of either as Czerda, his bruised face at once apprehensive and grim, closed and secured the tent flap behind him. The tent itself was small and circular, not more than ten feet in diameter. Its sole furnishing consisted of a cloth-screen cubicle which served as a confessional booth.

'You are welcome, my son.' The voice from the booth was deep and measured and authoritative.

'Open up, Searl,' Czerda said savagely. There was a fumbling motion and a dark linen curtain dropped to reveal a seated priest, with rimless eye-glasses and a thin ascetic face, the epitome of the man of God whose devotion is tinged with fanaticism. He regarded Czerda's battered face briefly, impassively.

'People may hear,' the priest said coldly. 'I'm Monsieur le Curé, or "Father".'

'You're "Searl" to me and always will be,' Czerda said contemptuously. 'Simon Searl, the unfrocked priest. Sounds like a nursery rhyme.'

'I'm not here on nursery business,' Searl said sombrely. 'I come from Gaiuse Strome.'

The belligerence slowly drained from Czerda's face: only the apprehension remained, deepening by the moment as he looked at the expressionless face of the priest.

'I think,' Searl said quietly, 'that an explanation of your unbelievably incompetent bungling is in order. I hope it's a very good explanation.'

V

'I must get out! I must get out!' Tina, the dark crop-haired young gypsy girl stared through the caravan window at the confessional tent, then swung round to face the other three gypsy women. Her eyes were red and swollen, her face very pale. 'I must walk! I must breathe the air! I – I can't stand it here any more.'

Marie le Hobenaut, her mother and Sara looked at one another. None of them looked very much happier than Tina. Their faces were still as sad and bitter as they had been when Bowman had watched them during the night, defeat and despair still hung as heavily in the air.

'You will be careful, Tina?' Marie's mother said anxiously. 'Your father – you must think of your father.'

'It's all right, Mother,' Marie said. 'Tina knows. She knows now.' She nodded to the dark girl who hurried through the doorway, and went on softly: 'She was so very much in love with Alexandre. You know.'

'I know,' her mother said heavily. 'It's a pity that Alexandre hadn't been more in love with her.'

Tina passed through the rear portion of the caravan. Seated on the steps there was a gypsy in his late thirties. Unlike most gypsies, Pierre Lacabro was squat to the point of deformity and extremely broad, and also unlike most gypsies who, in their aquiline fashion, are as aristocratically handsome as any people in Europe, he had a very broad, brutalized face with a thin cruel mouth, porcine eyes and a scar, which had obviously never been stitched, running from right eyebrow to right chin. He was, clearly, an extremely powerful person. He looked up as Tina approached and gave her a broken-toothed grin.

'And where are *you* going, my pretty maid?' He had a deep, rasping, gravelly and wholly unpleasant voice.

'For a walk.' She made no attempt to keep the revulsion from her face. 'I need air.'

'We have guards posted – and Maca and Masaine are on the watch. You know that?'

'Do you think I'd run away?'

He grinned again. 'You're too frightened to run away.'

With a momentary flash of spirit she said: 'I'm not frightened of Pierre Lacabro.'

'And why on earth should you be?' He lifted his hands, palms upwards. 'Beautiful young girls like you – why, I'm like a father to them.'

Tina shuddered and walked down the caravan steps.

VI

Czerda's explanation to Simon Searl had not gone down well at all. Searl was at no pains to conceal his contempt and displeasure: Czerda had gone very much on the defensive.

'And what about me?' he demanded. '*I'm* the person who has suffered, not you, not Gaiuse Strome. I tell you, he destroyed everything in my caravan – and stole my eighty thousand francs.'

'Which you hadn't even earned yet. That was Gaiuse Strome's money, Czerda. He'll want it back: if he doesn't get it he'll have your life in place of it.'

'In God's name, Bowman's vanished! I don't know—'

'You will find him and then you will use this on him.' Searl reached into the folds of his robe and brought out a pistol with a screwed-on silencer. 'If you fail, I suggest you save us trouble and just use it on yourself.'

Czerda looked at him for a long moment. 'Who *is* this Gaiuse Strome?'

'I do not know.'

'We were friends once, Simon Searl—'

'Before God, I have never met him. His instructions come either by letter or telephone and even then through an intermediary.'

'Then do you know who this man is?' Czerda took Searl's arm and almost dragged him to the flap of the tent, a corner of which he eased back. Plainly in view was Le Grand Duc who had obviously replenished his glass. He was gazing directly at them and the expression on his face was very thoughtful. Czerda hastily lowered the flap. 'Well?'

'That man I have seen before,' Searl said. 'A wealthy nobleman, I believe.'

'A wealthy nobleman by the name of Gaiuse Strome?'

'I do not know. I do not wish to know.'

'This is the third time I have seen this man on the pilgrimage. It is also the third year I have been working for Gaiuse Strome. He asked questions last night. This morning he was down looking at the damage that had been done to our caravan. And now he's staring straight at us. I think—'

'Keep your thinking for Bowman,' Searl advised. 'That apart, keep your own counsel. Our patron wishes to remain anonymous. He does not care to have his privacy invaded. You understand?'

Czerda nodded reluctantly, thrust the silenced pistol inside his shirt and left. As he did, Le Grand Duc peered thoughtfully at him over the rim of his glass.

'Good God!' he said mildly. 'Shriven already.'

Lila said politely: 'I beg your pardon, Charles.'

'Nothing, my dear, nothing.' He shifted his gaze and caught sight of Tina who was wandering disconsolately and apparently aimlessly across the grass. 'My word, there's a remarkably fine-looking filly. Downcast, perhaps, yes, definitely downcast. But beautiful.'

Lila said: 'Charles, I'm beginning to think that you're a connoisseur of pretty girls.'

'The aristocracy always have been. Carita, my dear, Arles and with all speed. I feel faint.'

'Charles!' Lila was instant concern. 'Are you unwell? The sun? If we put the hood up—'

'I'm hungry,' Le Grand Duc said simply.

Tina watched the whispering departure of the Rolls then looked casually around her. Lacabro had disappeared from the steps of the green-and-white caravan. Of Maca and Masaine there was no sign. Quite fortuitously, as it seemed, she found herself outside the entrance to the black confessional tent. Not daring to look round to make a final check to see whether she was under observation, she pushed the flap to one side and went in. She took a couple of hesitating steps towards the booth.

'Father! Father!' Her voice was a tremulous whisper. 'I must talk to you.'

Searl's deep grave voice came from inside the booth: 'That's what I'm here for, my child.'

'No, no!' Still the whisper. 'You don't understand. I have terrible things to tell you.'

'Nothing is too terrible for a man of God to hear. Your secrets are safe with me, my child.'

'But I don't *want* them to be safe with you! I want you to go to the police.'

The curtain dropped and Searl appeared. His lean ascetic face was filled with compassion and concern. He put his arm round her shoulders.

'Whatever ails you, daughter, your troubles are over. What is your name, my dear?'

'Tina. Tina Daymel.'

'Put your trust in God, Tina, and tell me everything.'

VII

In the green-and-white caravan Marie, her mother and Sara sat in gloomy silence. Now and again the mother gave a half sob and dabbed at her eyes with a handkerchief.

'Where *is* Tina?' she said at length. 'Where can she be? She takes so long.'

'Don't worry, Madame Zigair,' Sara said reassuringly. 'Tina's a sensible girl. She'll do nothing silly.'

'Sara's right, Mother,' Marie said. 'After last night—'

'I know. I know I'm being foolish. But Alexandre—'

'Please, Mother.'

Madame Zigair nodded and fell silent. Suddenly the caravan door was thrown open and Tina was thrown bodily into the room to fall heavily and face downwards on the caravan floor. Lacabro and Czerda stood framed in the entrance, the former grinning, the latter savage with a barely controlled anger. Tina lay where she had fallen, very still, clearly unconscious. Her clothes had been ripped from her back which was blood-stained and almost entirely covered with a mass of wicked-looking red and purplish weals: she had been viciously, mercilessly whipped.

'Now,' Czerda said softly. 'Now will you all learn?'

The door closed. The three women stared in horror at the cruelly mutilated girl, then fell to their knees to help her.

— 5 —

BOWMAN'S CALL to England came through quickly and he returned to his hotel within fifteen minutes of having left it. The corridor leading to his bedroom was thickly carpeted and his footfalls soundless. He was reaching for the handle of the door when he heard voices coming from inside the room. Not voices, he realized, just one – Cecile's – and it came only intermittently: the tone of her voice was readily recognizable but the muffling effect of the intervening door was too great to allow him to distinguish the words. He was about to lean his ear against the woodwork when a chambermaid carrying an armful of sheets came round a corner of the corridor. Bowman walked unconcernedly on his way and a couple of minutes later walked as unconcernedly back. There was only silence in the room. He knocked and went inside.

Cecile was standing by the window and she turned and smiled at him as he closed the door. Her gleaming dark hair had been combed or brushed or whatever she'd done with it and she looked more fetching than ever.

'Ravishing,' he said. 'How did you manage without me? My word, if our children only look—'

'Another thing,' she interrupted. The smile, he now noticed, lacked warmth. 'This Mr Parker business when you registered. You did show your passport, didn't you – Mr Bowman?'

'A friend lent it to me.'

'Of course. What else? Is your friend very important?'

'How's that?'

'What is your *job*, Mr Bowman?'

'I've told you—'

'Of course. I'd forgotten. A professional idler.' She sighed. 'And now – breakfast?'

'First, for me, a shave. It'll spoil my complexion but I can fix that. Then breakfast.'

He took the shaving kit from his case, went into the

bathroom, closed the door and set about shaving. He looked around him. She'd come in here, divested herself of all her cumbersome finery, had a very careful bath to ensure that she didn't touch the stain, dressed again, reapplied to the palms of her hands some of the stain he'd left her and all this inside fifteen minutes. Not to mention the hair brushing or combing or whatever. He didn't believe it, she had about her the fastidious look of a person who'd have used up most of that fifteen minutes just in brushing her teeth. He looked into the bath and it was indubitably still wet so she had at least turned on the tap. He picked up the crumpled bath-towel and it was as dry as the sands of the Sinai desert. She'd brushed her hair and that was all. Apart from making a phone call.

He shaved, re-applied some war-paint and took Cecile down to a table in a corner of the hotel's rather ornate and statuary-crowded patio. Despite the comparatively early hour it was already well patronized with late breakfasters and early coffee-takers. For the most part the patrons were clearly tourists, but there was a fair sprinkling of the more well-to-do Arlésiens among them, some dressed in the traditional fiesta costume of that part, some as gypsies.

As they took their seats their attention was caught and held by an enormous lime and dark green Rolls-Royce parked by the kerb: beside it stood the chauffeuse, her uniform matching the colours of the car. Cecile looked at the gleaming car in frank admiration.

'Gorgeous,' she said. 'Absolutely gorgeous.'

'Yes indeed,' Bowman agreed. 'You'd hardly think she could drive a great big car like that.' He ignored Cecile's old-fashioned look and leisurely surveyed the patio. 'Three guesses as to the underprivileged owner.'

Cecile followed his line of sight. The third table from where they sat was occupied by Le Grand Duc and Lila. A waiter appeared with a very heavy tray which he set before Le Grand Duc who picked up and drained a beaker of orange juice almost before the waiter had time to straighten what must have been his aching back.

'I thought that fellow would never come.' Le Grand Duc was loud and testy.

'Charles.' Lila shook her head. 'You've just *had* an *enormous* breakfast.'

'And now I'm having another one. Pass the rolls, *ma chérie*.'

'Good God!' At their table, Cecile laid a hand on Bowman's arm. 'The duke – *and* Lila.'

'What's all the surprise about?' Bowman watched Le Grand Duc industriously ladling marmalade from a large jar while Lila poured him coffee. 'Naturally he'd be here – where the gypsies are, there the famous gypsy folklorist will be. And, of course, in the best hotel. There's the beginning of a beautiful friendship across there. Can she cook?'

'Can she – funnily enough, she can. A very good one, too. Cordon Bleu.'

'Good Lord! He'll kidnap her.'

'But what is she still doing with him?'

'Easy. You told her about Saintes-Maries. She'll want to go there. And she hasn't a car, not since we borrowed it. He'll definitely want to be going there. And he has a car – a pound to a penny that's his Rolls. And they seem on pretty good terms, though heaven knows what she sees in our large friend. Look at his hands – they work like a conveyor belt. Heaven grant I'm never aboard a lifeboat with him when they're sharing out the last of the rations.'

'I think he's good-looking. In his own way.'

'So's an orang-utan.'

'You don't like him, do you?' She seemed amused. 'Just because he said you were—'

'I don't trust him. He's a phoney. I'll bet he's not a gypsy folklorist, has never written a thing about them and never will. If he's so famous and important a man why has neither of us ever heard of him? And why does he come to this part three years running to study their customs? Once would be enough for even a folklore ignoramus like me.'

'Maybe he likes gypsies.'

'Maybe. And maybe he likes them for all the wrong reasons.'

Cecile looked at him, paused and said in a lowered voice: 'You think he's this Gaiuse Strome?'

'I didn't say anything of the kind. And don't mention that name in here – you still want to live, don't you?'

'I don't see—'

'How do you know there's not a real gypsy among all the ones wearing fancy dress on this patio?'

'I'm sorry. That was silly of me.'

'Yes.' He was looking at Le Grand Duc's table. Lila had risen and was speaking. Le Grand Duc waved a lordly hand and she walked towards the hotel entrance. His face thoughtful, Bowman's gaze followed her as she crossed the patio, mounted the steps, crossed the foyer and disappeared.

'She *is* beautiful, isn't she?' Cecile murmured.

'How's that?' Bowman looked at her. 'Yes, yes of course. Unfortunately I can't marry you both – there's a law against it.' Still thoughtful, he looked across at Le Grand Duc, then back at Cecile. 'Go talk to our well-built friend. Read his palm. Tell his fortune.'

'What?'

'The duke there. Go—'

'I don't think that's funny.'

'Neither do I. Never occurred to me when your friend was there – she'd have recognized you. But the duke won't – he hardly knows you. And certainly wouldn't in that disguise. Not that there's the slightest chance of him lifting his eyes from his plate anyway.'

'No!'

'Please, Cecile.'

'No!'

'Remember the caverns. I haven't a lead.'

'Oh, God, don't!'

'Well, then.'

'But *what* can I do?'

'Start off with the old mumbo-jumbo. Then say you see he has very important plans in the near future and if he is successful – then stop there. Refuse to read any more and come away. Give him the impression that he has no future. Observe his reactions.'

'Then you really do suspect—'

'I suspect nothing.'

Reluctantly she pushed back her chair and rose. 'Pray to Sara for me.'

'Sara?'

'She's the patron saint of the gypsies, isn't she?'

Bowman watched her as she moved away. She side-stepped politely to avoid bumping into another customer who had just entered, an ascetic and other-worldly looking priest: it was impossible to imagine Simon Searl as anything other than a selfless and dedicated man of God in whose hands one would willingly place one's life. They murmured apologies and Cecile carried on and stopped at the table of Le Grand Duc, who lowered his coffee cup and glanced up in properly ducal irritation.

'Well, what is it?'

'Good morning, sir.'

'Yes, yes, yes, good morning.' He picked up his coffee cup again. 'What is it?'

'Tell your fortune, sir?'

'Can't you see I'm busy? Go away.'

'Only ten francs, sir.'

'I haven't got ten francs.' He lowered his cup again and looked at her closely for the first time. 'But by Jove, though, if only you'd blonde hair—'

Cecile smiled, took advantage of the temporary moment of admiration and picked up his left hand.

'You have a long lifeline,' she announced.

'I'm as fit as a fiddle.'

'And you come of noble blood.'

'Any fool can see that.'

'You have a very kind disposition—'

'Not when I'm starving.' He snatched away his hand, used it to pick up a roll, then glanced upwards as Lila came back to the table. He pointed his roll at Cecile. 'Remove this young pest. She's upsetting me.'

'You don't *look* upset, Charles.'

'How can you see what's happening to my digestion?'

Lila turned to Cecile with a smile that was half-friendly, half-apologetic, a smile that momentarily faded as she realized who it was. Lila put her smile back in place and said: 'Perhaps you would like to read my hand?' The tone was perfectly done, conciliatory without being patronizing, a gently implied rebuke to Le Grand Duc's boorishness. Le Grand Duc remained wholly unaffected.

'At a distance, if you please,' he said firmly. 'At a distance.'

They moved off and Le Grand Duc watched them go with an expression as thoughtful as possible for one whose jaws are moving with metronomic regularity. He looked away from the girls and across the table where Lila had been sitting. Bowman was looking directly at him but almost immediately looked away. Le Grand Duc tried to follow Bowman's altered line of sight and it seemed to him that Bowman was looking fixedly at a tall thin priest who sat with a cup of coffee before him, the same priest, Le Grand Duc realized, as he'd seen blessing the gypsies by the Abbey de Montmajour. And there was no dispute as to where the object of Simon Searl's interest lay: he was taking an inordinate interest in Le Grand Duc himself. Bowman watched as Lila and Cecile spoke together some little way off: at the moment Cecile was holding Lila's hand and appearing to speak persuasively while Lila smiled in some embarrassment. He saw Lila press something into Cecile's hand, then abruptly lost interest in both. From the corner of his eye he had caught sight of something of much more immediate importance: or he thought he had.

Beyond the patio was the gay and bustling fiesta scene in the Boulevard des Lices. Tradesmen were still setting up last-minute stalls but by this time they were far out-numbered by sightseers and shoppers. Together they made up a colourful and exotic spectacle. The rare person dressed in a sober business suit was strikingly out of place. Camera-behung tourists were there in their scores, for the most part dressed with that excruciatingly careless abandon that appears to afflict most tourists the moment they leave their own borders, but even they formed a relatively drab back-cloth for the three widely differing types of people who caught and held the eye in the splendid finery of their clothes – the Arlésienne girls so exquisitely gowned in their traditional fiesta costumes, the hundreds of gypsies from a dozen different countries and the *guardians*, the cowboys of the Camargue.

Bowman leaned forward in his seat, his eyes intent. Again he saw what had attracted his attention in the first place – a flash of titian hair, but unmistakable. It was Marie le Hobenaut and she was walking very quickly. Bowman looked away as Cecile rejoined him and sat down.

'Sorry. Up again. A job. Left on the street—'

'But don't you want to hear – and my breakfast—'

'Those can wait. Gypsy girl, titian hair, green and black costume. Follow her. See where she's going – and she's going some place. She's in a tearing hurry. Now!'

'Yes, sir.' She looked at him quizzically, rose and left. He did not watch her go. Instead, he looked casually around the patio. Simon Searl, the priest, was the first to go and he did so almost immediately, leaving some coins by his coffee cup. Seconds later, Bowman was on his feet and following the priest out into the street. Le Grand Duc, with his face largely obscured by a huge coffee cup, watched the departure of both.

Among the colourful crowds, the very drabness of Searl's black robes made him an easy figure to follow. What made him ever easier to follow was the fact that, as befitted a man of God, he appeared to have no suspicions of his fellow-men for he did not once look back over his shoulder. Bowman closed up till he was within ten feet of him. Now he could clearly see Cecile not much more than the same distance ahead of Searl and, occasionally, there was a brief glimpse of Marie le Hobenaut's titian hair. Bowman closed up even more on Searl and waited his opportunity.

It came almost at once. Hard by a group of fish-stalls half-a-dozen rather unprepossessing gypsies were trying to sell some horses that had seen better days. As Bowman, no more than five feet behind Searl now, approached the horses he bumped into a dark, swarthy young man with a handsome face and hairline moustache: he sported a black sombrero and rather flashy, tight-fitting dark clothes. Both men murmured apologies, side-stepped and passed on. The dark young man took only two steps, turned and looked after Bowman, who was now almost lost to sight, edging his way through the group of horses.

Ahead of him, Searl stopped as a restive horse whinnied, tossed its head and moved to block his progress. The horse reared, Searl stepped prudently backwards and as he did so Bowman kicked him behind the knee. Searl grunted in agony and fell to his sound knee. Bowman, concealed by horses on both sides of him, stooped solicitously over Searl and chopped the knuckles of his right hand into the base of the man's neck. Searl collapsed.

'Watch those damned horses!' Bowman shouted. At once several gypsies quieted the restive horses and pulled them apart to make a clear space round the fallen priest.

'What happened?' one of them demanded. 'What happened?'

'Selling that vicious brute?' Bowman asked. 'He ought to be destroyed. Kicked him right in the stomach. Don't just stand there. Get a doctor.'

One of the gypsies at once hurried away. The others stooped low over the prostrate man and while they did so Bowman made a discreet withdrawal. But it wasn't so discreet as to go unobserved by the same dark young man who had earlier bumped into Bowman: he was busy studying his fingernails.

II

Bowman was finishing off his breakfast when Cecile returned.

'I'm hot,' she announced. She looked it. '*And* I'm hungry.'

Bowman crooked a finger at a passing waiter.

'Well?'

'She went into a chemist's shop. She bought bandages – yards and yards – and a whole lot of cream and ointment and then she went back to the caravans – in a square not far from here—'

'The green-and-white caravan?'

'Yes. There were two women waiting for her at the caravan door and then all three went inside.'

'Two women?'

'One middle-aged, the other young with auburn hair.'

'Marie's mother and Sara. Poor Tina.'

'What do you mean?'

'Just rambling.' He glanced across the courtyard. 'The love-birds across there.'

Cecile followed his gaze to where Le Grand Duc, who was now sitting back with the relieved air of a man who has narrowly escaped death from starvation, smiled indulgently at Lila as she put her hand on his and talked animatedly.

Bowman said: 'Is your girl-friend simple-minded or anything like that?'

She gave him a long cool look. 'Not any more than I am.'

'Um. She knew you, of course. What did you tell her?'

'Nothing – except that you had to run for your life.'

'Didn't she wonder why *you* came?'

'Because I wanted to, I said.'

'Tell her I was suspicious of the duke?'

'Well—'

'It doesn't matter. She have anything to tell you?'

'Not much. Just that they stopped by to watch a gypsy service this morning.'

'Service?'

'You know – religious.'

'Regular priest?'

'So Lila said.'

'Finish your breakfast.' He pushed back his chair. 'I won't be long.'

'But I thought – I thought you would want to know what the duke said, his reactions. After all, that's why you sent me.'

'Was it?' Bowman seemed abstracted. 'Later.' He rose and entered the hotel: the girl watched him go with a puzzled expression on her face.

III

'Tall, you say, El Brocador. Thickset. Very fast.' Czerda rubbed his own battered and bandaged face in painfully tender recollection, and looked at the four men seated at the table in his caravan – El Brocador, the swarthy young man Bowman had bumped into in the street, Ferenc, Pierre Lacabro and a still shaken and pale Simon Searl who was trying to rub the back of his neck and the back of his thigh simultaneously.

'His face was darker than you say,' El Brocador said. 'And a moustache.'

'Dark faces and a moustache you can buy in shops. He can't hide his stock in trade – violence.'

'I hope I meet this man soon,' Pierre Lacabro said. His tone was almost wistful.

'I wouldn't be in too much of a hurry,' Czerda said drily. 'You didn't see him at all, Searl?'

'I saw nothing. I just felt those two blows in the back – no, I didn't even feel the second blow.'

'Why in God's name did you have to go to that hotel patio anyway?'

'I wanted to get a close-up of this Duc de Croytor. It was *you*, Czerda, who made me curious about him. I wanted to hear his voice. Who he spoke to, see if he has any contacts, who—'

'He's with this English girl. He's harmless.'

'Clever men do things like that,' Searl said.

'Clever men don't do the things you do,' Czerda said grimly. 'Now Bowman knows who you are. He almost certainly knows now that someone in Madame Zigair's caravan has been badly hurt. If the Duc de Croytor is who you think he is then he must know now that you suspect him of being Gaiuse Strome – and, if he is, he's not going to like any of those three things at all.' The expression on Searl's face left no doubt but that he himself was of the same opinion. Czerda went on: 'Bowman. He's the only solution. This man must be silenced. Today. But carefully. Quietly. By accident. Who knows what friends this man may not have?'

'I have told you how this can be done,' El Brocador said.

'And a good way. We move on this afternoon. Lacabro, you're the only one of us he does not know. Go to his hotel. Keep watch. Follow him. We dare not lose him now.'

'That will be a pleasure.'

'No violence,' Czerda warned.

'Of course not.' He looked suddenly crestfallen. 'But I don't know what he looks like. Dark and thickset – there are hundreds of dark and thickset—'

'If he's the man El Brocador described and the man I remember seeing on the hotel patio,' Searl said, 'he'll be with a girl dressed as a gypsy. Young, dark, pretty, dressed mainly green and gold, four gold bangles on her left wrist.'

IV

Cecile looked up from the remains of her breakfast as Bowman joined her at her table.

'You took your time,' she observed.

'I have not been idle. I've been out. Shopping.'

'I didn't see you go.'

'They have a back entrance.'

'And now?'

'Now I have urgent business to attend to.'

'Like this? Just sitting here?'

'Before I attend to the urgent thing I have to attend to I've something else urgent to attend to first. And that involves sitting here. Do you know they have some very nosey Chinese in the city of Arles?'

'What on earth are you talking about?'

'Couple sitting over by Romeo and Juliet there. Don't look. Man's big for a Chinese, forty, although it's always hard to say with them. Woman with him is younger, Eurasian, very good-looking. Both wearing lightly-tinted sun-glasses with those built-in reflectors so that you can't see through them from the outside.'

Cecile lifted a cup of coffee and looked idly round the patio. She said: 'I see them now.'

'Never trust people with reflecting sun-glasses. He seems to be displaying a very keen interest in Le Grand Duc.'

'It's his size.'

'Like enough.' Bowman looked thoughtfully at the Chinese couple, then at Le Grand Duc and Lila, then back at the Chinese again. Then he said: 'We can go now.'

She said: 'This urgent business – this first urgent business you had to attend to—'

'Attended to. I'll bring the car round to the front.'

Le Grand Duc watched his departure and announced to Lila: 'In about an hour we mingle with our subjects.'

'Subjects, Charles?'

'Gypsies, dear child. But first, I must compose another chapter of my book.'

'Shall I bring you pen and paper?'

'No need, my dear.'

'You mean – you mean you do it all in your head? It's not possible, Charles.'

He patted her hand and smiled indulgently.

'What you can get me is a litre of beer. It's becoming uncommonly warm. Find a waiter, will you?'

Lila moved obediently away and Le Grand Duc looked after her. There was nothing indulgent about the expression on his face when he saw her talk briefly and smilingly to the gypsy girl who had so recently read her fortune: there was nothing indulgent about it when he examined the Chinese couple at an adjacent table: even less so when he saw Cecile join Bowman in a white car in the street: and least of all when he observed another car move off within seconds of Bowman's.

Cecile gazed in perplexity round the interior of the white Simca. She said: 'What's all this about, then?'

'Such things as phones,' he explained. 'Fixed it while you were having breakfast. Fixed two of them in fact.'

'Two what?'

'Two hired cars. Never know when you're going to run short.'

'But – but in so short a time.'

'Garage is just down the street – they sent a man to check.' He took out Czerda's barely depleted wad of Swiss notes, crackled it briefly and returned it. 'Depends upon the deposit.'

'You really are quite amoral, aren't you?' She sounded almost admiring.

'How's that again?'

'The way you throw other people's money around.'

'Life is for the living, money for the spending,' Bowman said pontifically. 'No pockets in a shroud.'

'You're hopeless,' she said. 'Quite, quite hopeless. And why this car, anyway?'

'Why that get-up you're wearing?'

'Why – oh, I see. Of course the Peugeot's known. I hadn't thought of that.' She looked at him curiously as he turned the Simca in the direction of a sign-post saying 'Nimes'. 'Where do you think you're going?'

'I'm not quite sure. I'm looking for a place where I can talk undisturbed.'

'To me?'

'Still your apprehensions. I'll have all the rest of my life to talk to you. When we were on the patio a battered-looking gypsy in a battered-looking Renault sat and watched us for ten minutes. Both of them are about a hundred yards behind us now. I want to talk to the battered-looking gypsy.'

'Oh!'

'Well might you say "Oh!" How, one wonders, is it that Gaiuse Strome's henchmen are on to us so soon?' He gave her a sidelong glance. 'You're looking at me in a very peculiar manner, if I may say so.'

'I'm thinking.'

'Well?'

'If they're on to you, why did you bother switching cars?'

Bowman said patiently: 'When I hired the Simca I didn't know they were on to me.'

'And now you're taking me into danger again? Or what might be danger?'

'I hope not. If I am, I'm sorry. But if they're on to me, they're on to the charming gypsy girl who has been sitting by my side – don't forget that it was you that the priest was tailing when he met up with his unfortunate accident. Would you rather I'd left you behind to cope with them alone?'

'You don't offer very much in the way of choices,' she complained.

'I've got very little to offer.' Bowman looked in the mirror. The battered Renault was less than a hundred yards behind. Cecile looked over her shoulder.

'Why don't you stop here and talk to him? He'd never dare do anything here. There are far too many people around.'

'Far too many,' Bowman agreed. 'When I talk to him I don't want anyone within half a mile.'

She glanced at him, shivered and said nothing. Bowman took the Simca over the Rhône to Trinquetaille, turned left on to the Albaron road and then left again on to the road that ran south down the right bank of the river. Here he slowed and gently brought the car to a stop. The driver of the Renault, he observed, did the same thing at a discreet distance to the rear. Bowman drove the Simca on its way again: the Renault followed.

A mile farther on into the flat and featureless plains of the Camargue Bowman stopped again. So did the Renault. Bowman got out, went to the rear of the car, glanced briefly at the Renault parked about a hundred yards away, opened the boot, extracted an implement from the tool-kit, thrust it inside his jacket, closed the boot and returned to his seat. The implement he laid on the floor beside him.

'What's that?' Cecile looked and sounded apprehensive.

'A wheel-brace.'

'Something wrong with the wheels?'

'Wheel-braces can have other uses.'

He drove off. After a few minutes the road began to climb slightly, rounded an unexpectedly sharp left-hand corner and there suddenly, almost directly beneath them and less than twenty feet away, lay the murkily gleaming waters of the Grand Rhône. Bowman braked heavily, was out of the car even as it stopped and walked quickly back the way he had come. The Renault rounded the corner and its driver, caught completely unawares, slewed the car to a skidding stop less than ten yards from Bowman.

Bowman, one hand behind his back, approached the Renault and jerked the driver's door open. Pierre Lacabro glared out at him, his broad brutalized face set and savage.

'I'm beginning to think you're following me around,' Bowman said mildly.

Lacabro didn't reply. Instead, with one hand on the wheel and the other on the door frame to afford him maximum leverage he launched himself from the car with a speed surprising for a man of his bulk. Bowman had been prepared for nothing else. He stepped quickly to one side and as the driving Lacabro hurtled past him he brought the wheel-brace swinging down on Lacabro's left arm. The sound of the blow, the surprisingly loud crack of a breaking bone and Lacabro's shriek of pain were almost instantaneous.

'Who sent you?' Bowman asked.

Lacabro, writhing on the ground and clutching his damaged left forearm, snarled something incomprehensible in Romany.

'Please, please listen,' Bowman said. 'I'm dealing with murderers. I know I'm dealing with murderers. More important, I know how to deal with murderers. I've already broken one bone – I should think it's your forearm. I'm prepared to go right on breaking as many bones as I have to – assuming you stay conscious – until I find out why those four women in that green-and-white-painted caravan are terrified out of their lives. If you do become unconscious, I'll just sit around and smoke and wait till you're conscious again and break a few more bones.'

Cecile had left the Simca and was now only feet away. Her face was very pale. She stared at Bowman in horror.

'Mr Bowman, do you mean—'

'Shut up!' He returned his attention to Lacabro. 'Come now, tell me about those ladies.'

Lacabro mouthed what was almost certainly another obscenity, rolled over quickly and as he propped himself up on his right elbow Cecile screamed. Lacabro had a gun in his hand but shock or pain or both had slowed his reactions. He screamed again and his gun went flying in one direction while the wheel-brace went in another. He clutched the middle of his face with both hands: blood seeped through his fingers.

'And now your nose is gone, isn't it?' Bowman said. 'That dark girl, Tina, she's been hurt, hasn't she? How badly has she been hurt? Why was she hurt? Who hurt her?'

Lacabro took his hands away from his bleeding face. His nose wasn't broken, but it still wasn't a very pretty sight and wouldn't be for some time to come. He spat blood and a broken tooth, snarled again in Romany and stared at Bowman like a wild animal.

'*You* did it,' Bowman said with certainty. 'Yes, you did it. One of Czerda's hatchet-men, aren't you? Perhaps *the* hatchet-man. I wonder, my friend. I wonder. Was it *you* who killed Alexandre in the caverns?'

Lacabro, his face the face of a madman, pushed himself drunkenly to his feet and stood there, swaying just as drunkenly. He appeared to be on the verge of total collapse, his eyes turning up in his head. Bowman approached and, as he did so Lacabro, showing an incredible immunity to pain, an animal-like cunning and an equally animal-like power of recuperation, suddenly stepped forward and brought his right fist up in a tremendous blow which, probably due more to good fortune than calculation, struck Bowman on the side of the chin. Bowman staggered backwards, lost his balance and fell heavily on the short turf only a few feet away from the vertical drop into the Rhône. Lacabro had his priorities right. He turned and ran for the gun which had landed only a foot or two from where Cecile was standing, the shock in her face reflected in the immobility in her body.

Bowman pushed himself rather dizzily up on one arm. He

could see it all happening in slow motion, the girl with the gun at her feet, Lacabro lurching towards it, the girl still stock-still. Maybe she couldn't even see the damn thing, he thought despairingly, but her eyes couldn't be all that bad, if she couldn't see a gun two feet away she'd no right to be out without a white stick. But her eyes weren't quite so bad as that. Suddenly she stooped, picked up the gun, threw it into the Rhône, then, with commendable foresight, dropped flat to the ground as Lacabro, his battered bleeding face masked in blood and hate, advanced to strike her down. But even in that moment of what must have been infuriating frustration and where his overriding instinct must have been savagely to maim the girl who had deprived him of his gun, Lacabro still had his priorities right. He ignored the girl, turned and headed for Bowman in a low crouching run.

But Cecile had bought Bowman all the time he needed. By the time Lacabro reached him he was on his feet again, still rather dazed and shaken but a going concern nonetheless. He avoided Lacabro's first bull-rush and wickedly swinging boot and caught the gypsy as he passed: it so chanced that he caught him by the left arm. Lacabro shouted in agony, dragged his arm free at whatever unknown cost to himself and came again. This time Bowman made no attempt to avoid him but advanced himself at equal speed. His clubbing right hand had no difficulty in reaching Lacabro's chin, for now Lacabro had no left guard left. He staggered backwards several involuntary paces, tottered briefly on the edge of the bluff, then toppled backwards into the Rhône. The splash caused by his impact on the muddied waters seemed quite extraordinarily loud.

Bowman looked gingerly over the crumbling edge of the bluff: there was no sign of Lacabro. If he'd been unconscious when he'd struck the water he'd have gone to the bottom and that was that: there could be no possibility of locating him in those dark waters. Not that Bowman relished the prospect of trying to rescue the gypsy: if he were not unconscious he would certainly express his gratitude by doing his best to drown his rescuer. Bowman did not feel sufficiently attached to Lacabro to take the risk.

He went to the Renault, searched it briefly, found what he expected to find – nothing – started up the engine, let in first gear, aimed it for the bank of the river and jumped out. The little car trundled to the edge of the bluff, cartwheeled over the edge and fell into the river with a resounding crash that sent water rising to a height of thirty feet.

Much of this water rained down on Lacabro. He was half-sitting, half lying on a narrow ledge of pebble and sand under the overhang of the bluff. His clothes were soaked, his right hand clutched his left wrist. On his dazed and uncomprehending face was a mixture of pain and bewilderment and disbelief. It was, by any reckoning, the face of a man who has had enough for one day.

Cecile was still sitting on the ground when Bowman approached her. He said: 'You're ruining that lovely gypsy costume sitting there.'

'Yes, I suppose I am.' Her voice was matter-of-fact, remarkably calm. She accepted his hand, got to her feet and looked around her. 'He's gone?'

'Let's say I can't find him.'

'That wasn't – that wasn't fair fighting.'

'That was the whole idea behind it, pet. Ideally, of course, he would have riddled me with bullets.'

'But – but can he swim?'

'How the hell should I know?' He led her back to the Simca and after they'd gone a mile in silence he looked at her curiously. Her hands were trembling, her face had gone white and when she spoke her voice was a muted whisper with a shake in it: clearly some sort of delayed shock had set in.

She said: 'Who *are* you?'

'Never mind.'

'I – I saved your life today.'

'Well, yes, thanks. But you should have used that gun to shoot him or hold him up.'

There was a long pause, then she sniffed loudly and said in almost a wail: 'I've never fired a gun in my life. I can't *see* to fire a gun.'

'I know. I'm sorry about that. I'm sorry about everything, Cecile. But I'm sorriest of all that I ever got you into this damnably ugly mess. God, I should have known better.'

'Why blame yourself?' Still the near-sob in her voice. 'You had to run some place last night and my room—' She broke off, peered at him and whispered: 'You're thinking of something else, aren't you?'

'Let's get back to Arles,' he said. She peered at him some more, looked away and tried to light a cigarette but her hand shook so much he did it for her. Her hand was still shaking when they got back to the hotel.

— 6 —

BOWMAN DREW UP outside the hotel entrance. Not five yards away Lila sat alone by a table just inside the patio entrance. It was difficult to say whether she looked primarily angry or disconsolate: she certainly did not look happy.

'Boy-friend's ditched her,' Bowman announced. 'Meet me in fifteen minutes. Alleyway at the back entrance of the hotel. Stay out of sight till you see a blue Citroën. I'll be inside. Stay off the patio. You'll be safe in the foyer.'

Cecile nodded to Lila. 'Can I talk to her?'

'Sure. Inside.'

'But if we're seen—'

'It won't matter. Going to tell her what a dreadful person I am?'

'No.' A shaky smile.

'Ah! Then you're going to announce our forthcoming nuptials.'

'Not that either.' Again the smile.

'You want to make your mind up.'

She put a hand on his arm. 'I think you might even be rather a kind person.'

'I doubt whether the lad in the Rhône would share your sentiments,' Bowman said drily.

The smile vanished. She got out, Bowman drove off, she watched him disappear with a small frown creasing her forehead, then went on to the patio. She looked at Lila, nodded towards the hotel foyer: they went in together, talking.

'You're sure?' Cecile asked. 'Charles recognizes Neil Bowman?'

Lila nodded.

'How? Why?'

'I don't know. He's very, very shrewd, you know.'

'Something more than a famous wine-grower or folklorist, you would say?'

'I would say.'

'And he doesn't trust Bowman?'

'That puts it very mildly indeed.'

'Stalemate. You know what Bowman thinks of the duke. I'm afraid my money's on my man, Lila. He disposed of another of the bad men today—'

'He did *what*?'

'Threw him into the Rhône. I saw him do it. He says—'

'So that's why you looked like a ghost when I saw you just now.'

'I felt a bit like one, too. He says he's killed two others. I believe him. And I saw him lay out two more. Local colour is local colour but that would be ridiculous, you can't fake a dead man. He's on the side of the angels, Lila. Not, mind you, that I can see the angels liking it very much.'

'I'm no angel and I don't like any part of it,' Lila said. 'I'm out of my depth and I don't know how to cope. What *are* we to do?'

'You're no more lost than I am. Do? Do what we were told to do I suppose?'

'I suppose so.' Lila sighed and resumed her earlier woe-begone expression. Cecile peered at her.

'Where is Charles?'

'He's gone.' Her gloom deepened. 'He's just gone off with that little chauffeuse – that's what *he* calls her – and told me to wait here.'

'Lila!' Cecile stared at her friend. 'It's not possible—'

'Why? Why is it not? What's wrong with Charles?'

'Nothing, of course. Nothing at all.' Cecile rose. 'Two minutes for an appointment. Our Mr Bowman does not like to be kept waiting.'

'When I think of him with that little minx—'

'She looked a perfectly charming young girl to me.'

'That's what I thought, too,' Lila admitted. 'But that was an hour ago.'

II

Le Grand Duc was not, in fact, with the little minx, nor was he anywhere near her. In the square where the Rumanian and Hungarian caravans were pulled up, there were no signs of either Carita or the huge green Rolls and neither could have been said to be normally inconspicuous. Le Grand Duc, on the contrary, was very much in evidence: not far from the green-and-white caravan and with note-book in hand, he was talking with considerable animation to Simon Searl. Czerda, as befitted the leader of the gypsies and an already established acquaintance of Le Grand Duc, was close by but taking no part in the conversation: Searl, from what few signs of emotion that occasionally registered in his thin ascetic face, looked as if he wished he were taking no part in it either.

'Vastly obliged, Monsieur le Curé, vastly obliged.' Le Grand Duc was at his regally gracious best. 'I can't tell you how impressed I was by the service you held in the fields by the Abbey, this morning. Moving, most moving. By Jove, I'm adding to my store of knowledge every minute.' He peered more closely at Searl. 'Have you hurt your leg, my dear fellow?'

'A slight strain, no more.' The only obvious strain was in his face and voice.

'Ah, but you must look after those slight strains – can develop very serious complications, you know. Yes, indeed, very serious.' He removed his monocle, swinging it on the end of its thick black ribbon, the better to observe Searl. 'Haven't I seen you somewhere before – I don't mean at the Abbey. Yes, yes, of course – outside the hotel this morning. Odd, I don't recall you limping then. But then, I'm afraid my eye-sight—' He replaced his monocle. 'My thanks again. And watch that strain. Do exercise the greatest care, Monsieur le Curé. For your own sake.'

Le Grand Duc tucked the notebook in an inner pocket and marched majestically away. Czerda looked at Searl, the unbandaged parts of his face registering no expression. Searl, for his part, licked dry lips, said nothing, turned and walked away.

III

To even a close observer who knew him, the man behind the wheel of the gleamingly blue Citroën parked in the alleyway behind the hotel must have been almost totally unrecognizable as Bowman. He was dressed in a white sombrero, dark glasses, an excruciating blue-and-white polka-dotted shirt, an unbuttoned, embroidered black waistcoat, a pair of moleskin trousers and high boots. The complexion was paler, the moustache larger. Beside him on the seat lay a small purse-stringed bag. The offside front door opened and Cecile peered in, blinking uncertainly.

'I don't bite,' Bowman said encouragingly.

'Good God!' She slid into her seat. 'What – what's this?'

'I'm a *guardian*, a cowboy in his Sunday best, one of many around. Told you I'd been shopping. Your turn, now.'

'What's in that bag?'

'My poncho, of course.'

She eyed him with the speculative look that had now become almost habitual with her as he drove her to the clothing emporium they'd visited earlier that morning. After a suitable lapse of time the same manageress fluttered around Cecile, making gushing, admiring remarks, talking with her arms as much as with her voice. Cecile was now attired in the fiesta costume of an Arlésienne, with a long sweeping darkly embroidered dress, a ruched lace white bodice and a wimpled hat of the same material. The hat was perched on a dark red wig.

'Madame looks – fantastic!' the manageress said ecstatically.

'Madame matches the price,' Bowman said resignedly. He peeled off some more banknotes and led Cecile to the Citroën where she sat and smoothed the rich material of her dress approvingly.

'Very nice, I must say. You like dressing girls up?'

'Only when I'm being bank-rolled by criminals. That's hardly the point. A certain dark gypsy girl has been seen with me. There's not an insurance company in Europe would look at that dark gypsy girl.'

'I see.' She smiled wanly. 'All this solicitude for your future wife?'

'Of course. What else?'

'The fact that, quite frankly, you can't afford to lose your assistant at the moment?'

'Never occurred to me.'

He drove the Citroën close to the point where the Hungarian and Rumanian caravans were parked in the square. He stopped the Citroën, lifted his purse-stringed bag, got out, straightened and turned. As he did so, he bumped into a large pedestrian who was sauntering slowly by. The pedestrian stopped and glared at him through a black-beribboned monocle: Le Grand Duc was not accustomed to being bumped into by anyone.

'Your pardon, m'sieur,' Bowman said.

Le Grand Duc favoured Bowman with a look of considerable distaste. 'Granted.'

Bowman smiled apologetically, took Cecile's arm and moved off. She said to him, *sotto voce* and accusingly: 'You did that on purpose.'

'So? If he doesn't recognize us, who will?' He took another couple of steps and halted. 'Well, now, what could this be?'

There was a sudden stir of interest as a plain black van turned into the square. The driver got out, made what was evidently an enquiry of the nearest gypsy who pointed across the square, entered the van again and drove it across to the vicinity of Czerda's caravan. Czerda himself was by the steps, talking to Ferenc: neither appeared to have made much progress in the recovery from their injuries.

The driver and an assistant jumped down, went to the rear of the van, opened the doors and, with considerable difficulty and not without willing help, they slid out a stretcher on which, left arm in sling and face heavily bandaged, lay the recumbent form of Pierre Lacabro. The malevolent gleam in the right eye – the left one was completely shut – showed clearly that Lacabro was very much alive. Czerda and Ferenc, consternation in their faces, moved quickly to help the stretcher-bearers. Inevitably, Le Grand Duc was one of the first on the immediate scene. He bent briefly over the battered Lacabro, then straightened.

'Tsk! Tsk! Tsk!' He shook his head sadly. 'Nobody's safe on the roads these days.' He turned to Czerda. 'Isn't this my poor friend Mr Koscis?'

'No.' Czerda spoke with considerable restraint.

'Ah! I'm glad to hear it. Sorry for this poor fellow of course. By the way, I wonder if you'd tell Mr Koscis that I'd like to have another word with him when he's here? At his convenience, of course.'

'I'll see if I can find him.' Czerda helped move the stretcher towards the steps of his own caravan and Le Grand Duc turned away, narrowly avoiding coming into collision with the Chinese couple who had earlier been on the patio of the hotel. He doffed his hat in gallant apology to the Eurasian woman.

Bowman had missed none of the by-play. He looked first at Czerda, whose face was registering a marked degree of mixed anger and apprehension, then at Le Grand Duc, then at the Chinese couple: he turned to Cecile.

'There now,' he whispered. 'I knew he could swim. Let's not show too keen a degree of interest in what's going on.' He led her away a few paces. 'You know what I want to do – it'll be safe, I promise.'

He watched her as she wandered casually past Czerda's caravan and stopped to adjust a shoe in the vicinity of the green-and-white caravan. The window at the side was curtained but the window itself slightly ajar.

Satisfied, Bowman moved off across the square to where a group of horses were tethered by some trees close by several other caravans. He looked aimlessly around to check that he was unobserved, saw Czerda's caravan door close as the stretcher was brought inside, dug into his bag and fetched out a fistful of coiled, brown-paper sheathed objects, each one fitted with an inch of blue touch-paper: they were, quite simply, old-fashioned fire-crackers . . .

In Czerda's caravan, Czerda himself, Ferenc, Simon Searl and El Brocador were gathered round Pierre Lacabro's still recumbent form. The expression on what little could be seen of Lacabro's face registered a degree of unhappiness that was not entirely attributable to his physical sufferings: he had about him the wounded appearance of one whose injuries are not being accorded their due meed of loving care and concerned sympathy.

'You fool, Lacabro!' Czerda's voice was almost a shout. 'You crazy idiot! No violence, I told you. *No* violence.'

'Maybe you should have told Bowman instead,' El Brocador suggested. 'Bowman knew. Bowman was watching. Bowman was waiting. Who is going to tell Gaiuse Strome?'

'Who but our unfrocked friend here,' Czerda said savagely. 'I do not envy you, Searl.'

From the look on Searl's face it was clear that he didn't envy himself either. He said unhappily: 'That may not be necessary. If Gaiuse Strome is who we now all think he is, then he knows already.'

'Knows?' Czerda demanded. 'What can he know? He doesn't know that Lacabro is one of my men and so one of his. He doesn't know that Lacabro didn't have a road accident. He doesn't know that Bowman is responsible. He doesn't know that once again we've managed to lose track of Bowman – while at the same time Bowman appears to know all our movements. If you think you have nothing to explain, Searl, you're out of your mind.' He turned to Ferenc. 'Round up the caravans. Now. We leave inside the half-hour. Tell them that tonight we camp by Vaccarès. What was that?'

There had come clearly and sharply the sound of a series of sharp reports. Men shouted, horses whinnied in fear, a policeman's whistle blew and still the series of flat staccato explosions continued. Czerda, followed by the three others, rushed to the door of his caravan and threw it open.

They were not alone in their anxiety and curiosity to discover the source of the disturbance. It would hardly be exaggeration to claim that within thirty seconds every pair of eyes in the square was trained on the north-eastern part of it where a group of gypsies and *guardians*, Bowman prominently active among them, were fighting to restrain a rearing, milling, whinnying and now thoroughly fear-crazed group of horses.

One pair of eyes was otherwise engaged and those belonged to Cecile. She was pressed close in to the side of the green-and-white-painted caravan, standing on tiptoe and peering through a gap she had just made in the curtain.

It was dark inside the curtained caravan but the darkness was far from total and even Cecile's eyes quickly became accustomed to the gloom: when they did it was impossible for her to restrain her involuntary shocked gasp of horror. A girl with dark cropped hair was lying face down on a bunk – obviously the only way she could possibly lie. Her bare and savagely mutilated back had not been bandaged but had been liberally covered with salves of some kind. From her continuous restive movements and occasional moans it was clear that she was not sleeping.

Cecile lowered the curtain and moved off. Madame Zigair, Sara and Marie le Hobenaut were on the steps of the caravan, peering across the square, and Cecile walked by them as unconcernedly as she could, which was not easy when her legs felt shaky and she was sick inside. She crossed the square and rejoined Bowman who had just succeeded in calming down one of the panic-stricken horses. He released the horse, took her arm and led her towards where they'd left the Citroën parked. He looked at her, but didn't have to look closely.

'You didn't like what you saw, did you?' he said.

'Teach me how to use a gun and I'll use it. Even although I can't see. I'll get close enough.'

'As bad as that?'

'As bad as that. She's hardly more than a child, a little thin creature, and they've practically flayed the skin from her back. It was horrible. The poor child must be in agony.'

'So you don't feel so sorry for the man I threw in the Rhône?'

'I would. If I met him. With a gun in my hand.'

'No guns. I don't carry one myself. But I take your point.'

'And you seem to take my news very calmly.'

'I'm as mad as you are, Cecile, only I've been mad about it for a long time and I can't keep showing it all the time. As for the beating the girl got, it had to be something like that. Like Alexandre, the poor kid got desperate and tried to pass on a message, some information, so they taught her what they thought would be a permanent lesson to herself and the other women, and it probably will.'

'What information?'

'If I knew that I'd have those four women out of that caravan and in safety in ten minutes.'

'If you don't want to tell, don't tell.'

'Look, Cecile—'

'It's all right. It doesn't matter.' She paused. 'You know that I wanted to run away this morning? Coming back from the Rhône?'

'I wouldn't have been surprised.'

'Not now. Not any more. You're stuck with me now.'

'I wouldn't want to be stuck with anyone else.'

She looked at him almost in surprise. 'You said that without smiling.'

'I said it without smiling,' he said.

They reached the Citroën, turned and looked back towards the square. The gypsies were milling around in a state of great activity. Ferenc, they could see, was going from one caravan to the next, speaking urgently to the owners, and as soon as he left them they began making preparations to hitch their towing units on to the caravans.

'Pulling out?' Cecile looked at Bowman in surprise. 'Why? Because of a few firecrackers?'

'Because of our friend who's been in the Rhône. And because of me.'

'You?'

'They know now, since our friend returned from his bathe, that I'm on to them. They don't know how much I know. They don't know what I look like now but they know that I'll be looking different. They do know that they can't get me here in Arles because they can't have any idea where I am or where I might be staying. They know that to get me they'll have to isolate me and to do that they'll have to draw me out into the open. Tonight they'll camp in the middle of nowhere, somewhere deep in the Camargue. And there they'll hope to get me. For they know now that wherever their caravans are, there I'll be too.'

'You are good at making speeches, aren't you?' There was no malice in the green eyes.

'It's just practice.'

'And you haven't exactly a low opinion of yourself, have you?'

'No.' He regarded her speculatively. 'Do you think they have?'

'I'm sorry.' She touched the back of his hand in a gesture of contrition. 'I talk that way when I'm scared.'

'Me too. That's most of the time. We'll leave after you've picked your things up from the hotel and, in the best Pinkerton fashion, tail them from in front. Because if we follow them, they'll string out watchers at regular intervals to check every car that follows. And there won't be all that many cars moving south – tonight's the big fiesta night in Arles and most people won't be moving down to Saintes-Maries for another forty-eight hours.'

'They would recognize us? In these rigouts? Surely they can't—'

'They can't recognize us. They can't possibly be on to us yet. Not this time. I'm positive. They don't have to be. They'll be looking for a car with a couple in it. They'll be looking for a car with Arles number-plates, because it'll have to be a rented car. They'll be looking for a couple in disguise, because they'll have to be in disguise, and in those parts that means only gypsy or *guardian* fiesta costumes. They'll be looking for a couple with by now certain well-known characteristics such as that you are slender, have high cheekbones and green eyes, while I'm far from slender and have certain scars on my face that only a dye can conceal. How many cars with how many couples going south to Vaccarès this afternoon will match up with all those qualifications?'

'One.' She shivered. 'You don't miss much, do you?'

'Neither will they. So we go ahead of them. If they don't catch up with us we can always turn back to find out where they've stopped. They won't suspect cars coming from the south. At least, I hope to God they don't. But keep those dark glasses on all the time: those green eyes are a dead giveaway.'

Bowman drove back to the hotel and stopped about fifty yards from the patio, the nearest parking place he could get. He said to Cecile: 'Get packed. Fifteen minutes. I'll join you in the hotel inside ten.'

'You, of course, have some little matter to attend to first?'

'I have.'

'Care to tell me what it is?'

'No.'

'That's funny. I thought you trusted me now.'

'Naturally. Any girl who is going to marry me—'

'I don't deserve that.'

'You don't. I trust you, Cecile. Implicitly.'

'Yes.' She nodded as if satisfied.

'I can see you mean that. What you don't trust is my ability not to talk under pressure.'

Bowman looked at her for several moments.

'Did I suggest, sometime during the middle watches of the night, that you weren't – ah – quite as bright as you might be?'

'You called me a fool several times, if that's what you mean.'

'You can get around to forgiving me?'

'I'll work on it.' She smiled, got out of the car and walked away. Bowman waited till she had turned into the patio, left the car, walked back to the post office, picked up a telegram that was awaiting him in the Poste Restante, took it back to the car and opened it. The message was in English and uncoded. It read: MEANING UNCLEAR STOP QUOTE IT IS ESSENTIAL THAT CONTENTS BE DELIVERED AIGUES-MORTES OR GRAU DU ROI BY MONDAY 24 MAY INTACT AND REPEAT AND INCOGNITO STOP IF ONLY ONE POSSIBLE DO NOT DELIVER CONTENTS STOP IF POSSIBLE RELATIVE EXPENDITURE IMMATERIAL STOP NO SIGNATURE.

Bowman re-read the message twice and nodded to himself. The meaning was far from unclear to him: nothing, he thought, was unclear any more. He produced matches and burnt the telegram, piece by piece, in the front ashtray, grinding the charred paper into tiny fragments. He glanced around frequently to see if anyone was taking an unusual interest in his unusual occupation but no one was. In his rear mirror he could see Le Grand Duc's Rolls stopped at traffic lights some three hundred yards away. Even a Rolls, he reflected, had to stop at a red light: Le Grand Duc must find such annoying trifles a constant source of ducal irritation. He looked through the windscreen and could see the Chinese and his Eurasian lady leisurely sauntering towards the patio, approaching from the west.

Bowman wound down his window, tore his telegram envelope into tiny shreds and dropped them to the gutter: he hoped the citizens of Arles would forgive him his wanton litter-bugging. He left the car and passed into the hotel patio, meeting the Chinese couple on the way. They looked at Bowman impassively from behind their reflector glasses but Bowman did not as much as glance their way.

IV

Le Grand Duc, stalled at the traffic lights, was, surprisingly enough displaying no signs of irritation at all. He was absorbed in making notes in a book which, curiously, was not the one he habitually used when adding to his increasing store of gypsy folklore. Satisfied, apparently, with what he had written, he put the book away, lit a large Havana and pressed the button which controlled the dividing window. Carita looked at him enquiringly in the rear-view mirror.

'I need hardly ask you, my dear,' Le Grand Duc said, 'if you have carried out my instructions.'

'To the letter, Monsieur le Duc.'

'And the reply?'

'Ninety minutes, with luck. Without it, two and a half hours.'

'Where?'

'Replies in quadruplicate, Monsieur le Duc. Poste Restante, Arles, Saintes-Maries, Aigues-Mortes and Grau du Roi. That is satisfactory, I hope?'

'Eminently.' Le Grand Duc smiled in satisfaction. 'There are times, my dear Carita, when I hardly know what I'd do without you.' The window slid silently up, the Rolls whispered away on the green light and Le Grand Duc, cigar in hand, leaned back and surveyed the world with his customary patriarchal air. Abruptly, after a rather puzzled glance through the windscreen of the car, he bent forward all of two inches, an action which, in Le Grand Duc, indicated an extraordinarily high degree of interest. He pressed the dividing window button.

'There's a parking space behind that blue Citroën. Pull in there.'

The Rolls slowed to a stop and the duke performed the

almost unheard-of feat of opening the door and getting out all by himself. He strolled leisurely forward, halted and looked at the pieces of yellow telegram paper lying in the gutter, then at the Chinese who was slowly straightening with some of the pieces in his hand.

'You seem to have lost something,' Le Grand Duc said courteously. 'Can I be of help?'

'You are too kind.' The man's English was immaculate, Oxbridge at its most flawless. 'It is nothing. My wife has just lost one of her ear-rings. But it is not here.'

'I am sorry to hear it.' Le Grand Duc carried on, sauntered through the patio entrance, passed by the seated wife of the Chinese and nodded fractionally in gracious acknowledgement of her presence. She was, Le Grand Duc noted, unmistakably Eurasian and quite beautiful. Not blonde, of course, but beautiful. She was also wearing two ear-rings. Le Grand Duc paced with measured stride across the patio and joined Lila, who was just seating herself at a table. Le Grand Duc regarded her gravely.

'You are unhappy, my dear.'

'No, no.'

'Oh, yes, you are. I have an infallible instinct for such things. For some extraordinary reasons you have some reservations about me. Me! Me, if I may say so, the Duc de Croytor!' He took her hand. 'Phone your father, my friend the Count Delafont, and phone him now. He will reassure you, you've my word for that. Me! The Duc de Croytor!'

'Please, Charles. Please.'

'That's better. Prepare to leave at once. A matter of urgency. The gypsies are leaving – at least the ones we're interested in are leaving – and where they go we must follow.' Lila made to rise but he put out a restraining hand. ' "Urgency" is a relative term. In about, say, an hour's time – we must have a quick snack before departing for the inhospitable wastes of the Camargue.'

— 7 —

TO THE NEWCOMER the Camargue does indeed appear to be an inhospitable wasteland, an empty wasteland, a desolation of enormous skies and limitless horizons, a flat and arid nothingness, a land long abandoned by life and left to linger and wither and die all summer long under a pitiless sun suspended in the washed-out steel-blue dome above. But if the newcomer remains long enough, he will find that first impressions, as they almost invariably do, give a false and misleading impression. It is, it is true, a harsh land and a bleak land, but one that is neither hostile nor dead, a land that is possessed of none of the uniformly dreadful lifelessness of a tropical desert or a Siberian tundra. There is water here, and no land is dead where water is: there are large lakes and small lakes and lakes that are no lakes at all but marshes sometimes no more than fetlock deep to a horse, others deep enough to drown a house. There are colours here, the ever-changing blues and greys of the wind-rippled waters, the faded yellows of the beds of marshes that line the *étangs*, the near-blackness of smooth-crowned cypresses, the dark green of windbreak pines, the startlingly bright green of occasional lush grazing pastures, strikingly vivid against the brown and harsh aridity of the tough sparse vegetation and salt-flats hard-baked under the sun that occupy so much the larger part of the land area. And, above all, there is life here: birds in great number, very occasional small groups of black cattle and, even more rarely, white horses: there are farms, too, and ranches, but these are set so far back from roads or so well-concealed by windbreaks that the traveller rarely sees them. But one indisputable fact about the Camargue remains, one first impression that never changes, one that wholly justifies its time-and-again description as being an endless plain: the Camargue is as featurelessly smooth and flat as a sun-warmed summer sea.

For Cecile, as the blue Citroën moved south between Arles and Saintes-Maries, the Camargue was nothing but an increasingly featureless desolation: her spirits became correspondingly increasingly depressed. Occasionally she glanced at Bowman but found no help there: he seemed relaxed, almost cheerful, and if the consideration of the recently spilled blood he had on his hands bore heavily on him he was concealing his feelings remarkably well. Probably, Cecile thought, he had forgotten all about it: the thought made her feel more depressed than ever. She surveyed the bleak landscape again and turned to Bowman.

'People *live* here?'

'They live here, they love here, they die here. Let's hope we don't today. Die here, I mean.'

'Oh, do be quiet. Where are all the cowboys I've heard of – the *guardians* as you call them?'

'In the pubs, I should imagine. This is fiesta day, remember – a holiday.' He smiled at her. 'I wish it was for us too.'

'But your life is one long holiday. You said so.'

'For us, I said.'

'A pretty compliment.' She looked at him consideringly. 'Can you tell me, offhand, when you last had a holiday?'

'Offhand, no.'

Cecile nodded, looked ahead again. Half a mile away, on the left-hand side of the road, was a fairly large group of buildings, some of them quite substantial.

'Life at last,' she said. 'What's that?'

'A *mas*. A farm, more of a ranch. Also a bit of a dude ranch – living accommodation, restaurant, riding school. Mas de Lavignolle, they call it.'

'You've been here before, then?'

'All those holidays,' Bowman said apologetically.

'What else?' She turned her attention to the scene ahead again, then suddenly leaned forward. Just beyond the farm was a windbreak of pines and just beyond that again there was coming into view a scene that showed that there could, indeed, be plenty of life in the Camargue. At least a score of caravans and perhaps a hundred cars were parked haphazardly on the hard-packed earth on the right-hand side of the road. On the left, in a field which was more dust than grass, there were lines of what appeared to be brightly coloured tents. Some of the tents were no more than striped awnings with, below them, trestle tables which, dependent on what was piled on them, acted as either bars or snackbars. Other and smaller canvas-topped stalls were selling souvenirs or clothes or candy, while still others had been converted into shooting galleries, roulette stands and other games of chance. There were several hundred people milling around among the stalls, obviously enjoying and making the most of the amenities offered. Cecile turned to Bowman as he slowed to let people cross the road.

'What's all this, then?'

'Obvious, isn't it? A country fair. Arles isn't the only place in the Camargue – some of the people hereabouts don't even consider it as being part of the Camargue and act accordingly. Some communities prefer to provide their own diversions and amusements at fiesta time – the Mas de Lavignolle is one of them.'

'My, my, we are well-informed, aren't we?' She looked ahead again and pointed to a large oval-shaped arena with its sides made, apparently, of mud and wattles.

'What's that? A corral?'

'That,' Bowman said, 'is a genuine old-fashioned bull-ring where the main attraction of the afternoon will take place.'

She made a face. 'Drive on.'

He drove on. After less than fifteen minutes, at the end of a long straight stretch of dusty road he pulled the blue Citroën off the road and got out. Cecile looked at him enquiringly.

'Two straight miles of road,' he explained. 'Gypsy caravans travel at thirty miles an hour. So, four minutes' warning.'

'And a panic-stricken Bowman can be on his way in less than fifteen seconds?'

'Less. If I haven't finished off the champagne, longer. But enough. Come. Lunch.'

II

Ten miles to the north, on the same road, a long convoy of gypsy caravans was heading south, raising an immense cloud of dust in its passing. The caravans, normally far from inhibited in the brightness and diversity of their colours, seemed now, in their striking contrast to the bleakness of the landscape around them, more gay and exotic than ever.

The leading vehicle in the convoy, the yellow breakdown truck that had been pressed into the service of hauling Czerda's caravan, was the only one that was completely dust-free. Czerda himself was driving, with Searl and El Brocador seated beside him. Czerda was looking at El Brocador with an expression on his face that came as close to admiration as his presently rather battered features were capable of expressing.

He said: 'By heavens, El Brocador, I'd rather have you by my side than a dozen incompetent unfrocked priests.'

'I am not a man of action,' Searl protested. 'I never have claimed to be.'

'You're supposed to have brains,' Czerda said contemptuously. 'What happened to them?'

'We mustn't be too hard on Searl,' El Brocador said soothingly. 'We all know he's under great pressure, he's not, as he says, a man of action and he doesn't know Arles. I was born there, it is the back of my hand to me. I know every shop in Arles that sells gypsy costumes, fiesta costumes and *guardian* clothes. There are not so many as you might think. The men I picked to help me were all natives too. But I was the lucky one. First time, first shop – just the kind of shop Bowman would choose, a seedy old draper's in a side-street.'

'I hope, El Brocador, that you didn't have to use too much – ah – persuasion?' Czerda was almost arch about it and it didn't become him at all.

'If you mean violence, no. Those aren't my methods, you know that, and besides I'm far too well known in Arles to try anything of the sort. Anyway, I didn't have to, nobody would have had to. I know Madame Bouvier, everyone knows her, she'd throw her own mother in the Rhône for ten francs. I gave her fifty.' El Brocador grinned. 'She couldn't tell me enough fast enough.'

'A blue and white polka-dotted shirt, white sombrero and black embroidered waistcoat.' Czerda smiled in anticipation. 'It'll be easier than identifying a circus clown at a funeral.'

'True, true. But first we must catch our hare.'

'He'll be there,' Czerda said confidently. He jerked a thumb in the direction of the following caravans. 'As long as they are here, he'll be here. We all know that by this time. You just worry about your part, El Brocador.'

'No worry there.' El Brocador's confidence matched Czerda's own. 'Everyone knows what mad Englishmen are like. Just another crazy idiot who tried to show off before the crowd. And dozens of witnesses will have seen him tear free from us in spite of all we could do to stop him.'

'The bull will have specially sharpened horns? As we arranged?'

'I have seen to it myself.' El Brocador glanced at his watch. 'Can we not make better time? You know I have an appointment in twenty minutes.'

'Never fear,' Czerda said. 'We shall be in Mas de Lavignolle in ten minutes.'

III

At a discreet distance behind the settling dust the lime-green Rolls swept along in its customary majestic silence. The cabriolet hood was down, with Le Grand Duc sitting regally under the shade of a parasol which Lila held over him.

'You slept well?' she asked solicitously.

'Sleep? I never sleep in the afternoons. I merely had my eyes closed. I have many things, far too many things, on my mind and I think better that way.'

'Ah! I didn't understand.' The first quality one required in dealing with Le Grand Duc, she had learned, was diplomacy. She changed the subject rapidly. 'Why are we following so few caravans when we've left so many behind in Arles?'

'I told you, those are the ones I am interested in.'

'But why—'

'Hungarian and Rumanian gypsies are my special field.' There was a finality about the way he spoke that effectively sealed off that particular line of discussion.

'And Cecile. I'm worried about—'

'Your friend Miss Dubois has already left and unless I am much mistaken—' his tone left no room to doubt the impiety of any such thought – 'she is also on this road and considerably ahead of us. She was, I must concede,' he added reflectively, 'attired in a very fetching Arlésienne fiesta dress.'

'A gypsy dress, Charles.'

'Arlésienne fiesta,' Le Grand Duc said firmly. 'I miss very little, my dear. Gypsy costume when you saw her, perhaps. But Arlésienne when she left.'

'But why should she—'

'How should I know?'

'You saw her go?'

'No.'

'Then how—'

'Our Carita here also misses very little. She left with, it seems, a shady-looking individual in *guardian* clothes. One wonders what happened to that other ruffian – Bowman, wasn't it? Your friend appears to possess a unique talent for picking up undesirables.'

'And me?' Lila was suddenly tight-lipped.

'*Touché!* I deserved that. Sorry, I did not intend to slight your friend.' He gestured with a hand ahead and to the left where a long narrow line of water gleamed like burnished steel under the early afternoon sun. 'And what is that, my dear?'

Lila glanced at it briefly. 'I don't know,' she said huffily.

'Le Grand Duc never apologizes twice.'

'The sea?'

'Journey's end, my dear. Journey's end for all the gypsies who have come hundreds, even thousands of miles from all over Europe. The Etang de Vaccarès.'

'Etang?'

'Lake. Lake Vaccarès. The most famous wildlife sanctuary in Western Europe.'

'You *do* know a lot, Charles.'

'Yes, I do,' Le Grand Duc conceded.

IV

Bowman packed up the remains of lunch in a wicker basket, disposed of what was left of a bottle of champagne and closed the boot of the car.

'That was delightful,' Cecile said. 'And how thoughtful of you.'

'Don't thank me, thank Czerda. He paid for it.' Bowman

looked north along the two-mile stretch of road. It was quite empty of traffic. 'Well, back to Mas de Lavignolle. The caravans must have stopped at the fair. Heigh-ho for the bull-fight.'

'But I hate bull-fights.'

'You won't hate this one.'

He reversed the Citroën and drove back to Mas de Lavignolle. There seemed to be many fewer people there than there had been when they had passed through even although the number of cars and caravans had almost doubled, a discrepancy easily and immediately accounted for as soon as the Citroën had stopped by the sound of laughter and shouting and cheering coming from the nearby bull-ring. For the moment Bowman ignored the bull-ring: remaining seated in the car, he looked carefully around him. He did not have to look for long.

'To nobody's surprise,' he announced, 'Czerda and his missionary pals have turned up in force. At least, their caravans have, so one assumes that Czerda and company have also.' He drummed his fingers thoughtfully on the steering wheel. 'To nobody's surprise, that is, except mine. Curious, curious. One wonders why?'

'Why what?' Cecile asked.

'Why they're here.'

'What do you mean? You expected to find them here. That's why you turned back, wasn't it?'

'I turned back because the time-factor, their delay in overtaking us, convinced me that they must have stopped somewhere and this seemed as likely a place as any. The point is that I would not have expected them to stop at all until they reached some of the lonely encampments on one of the *étangs* to the south where they could have the whole wide Camargue all to themselves. But instead they choose to stop here.'

He sat in silence and she said: 'So?'

'Remember I explained in some detail back in Arles just why I thought the gypsies were pulling out so quickly?'

'I remember some of it. It was a bit confusing.'

'Maybe I was confusing myself. Somewhere a flaw in the reasoning. My reasoning. But where?'

'I'm sorry. I don't understand.'

'I don't think I'm exaggerating my own importance,' Bowman said slowly. 'Not, at least, as far as they are concerned. I'm convinced they're under pressure, under very heavy pressure, to kill me as quickly as humanly possible. When you're engaged on a job of great urgency you don't stop off and spend a peaceful summer's afternoon watching a bull-fight. You press on and with all speed. You entice Bowman to a lonely camp-site at the back of beyond where, because he's the only person who's not a member of your group, he can be detected and isolated with ease and disposed of at leisure. You do not stop at a fair-cum-bull-fight where he would be but one among a thousand people, thereby making isolation impossible.' Bowman paused. 'Not, that is, unless you knew something that he didn't know, and *knew* that you could isolate him even among that thousand. Do I make myself clear?'

'This time I'm not confused.' Her voice had dropped almost to a whisper. 'You make yourself very clear. You're as certain as can be that they'll get you here. There's only one thing you can do.'

'Only one thing,' Bowman agreed. He reached for the door handle. 'I've got to go and find out for sure.'

'Neil.' She gripped his right wrist with surprising strength.

'Well, at last. Couldn't keep on calling me Mr Bowman in front of the kids, could you? Victorian.'

'Neil.' There was pleading in the green eyes, something close to desperation, and he felt suddenly ashamed of his flippancy. 'Don't go. Please, please, don't go. Something dreadful is going to happen here. I know it.' She ran the tip of her tongue over dry lips. 'Drive away from here. Now. This moment. Please.'

'I'm sorry.' He forced himself to look away, her beseeching face would have weakened the resolution of an angel and he had no reason to regard himself as such. 'I have to stay and it may as well be here. It may as well be here for a showdown there has to be, it's inevitable, and I still think I stand a better chance here than I would on the shores of some lonely *étang* in the south.'

'You said, "I *have* to stay"?'

'Yes.' He continued to look ahead. 'There are four good reasons and they're all in that green-and-white caravan.' She made no reply and he went on: 'Or just Tina alone, Tina and her flayed back. If anyone did that to you I'd kill him. I wouldn't think about it, I'd just naturally kill him. Do you believe that?'

'I think so.' Her voice was very low. 'No, I know you would.'

'It could just as easily have been you.' He altered his tone slightly and said: 'Tell me, now, would you marry a man who ran away and left Tina?'

'No, I would not.' She spoke very matter-of-factly.

'Ha!' He altered his tone some more. 'Am I to take it from that that if I *don't* run away and leave Tina—' He broke off and looked at her. She was smiling at him but the green eyes were dim, she didn't know whether to laugh or cry and when she spoke it could have been a catch in her voice or the beginning of laughter.

'You're quite, quite hopeless,' she said.

'You're repeating yourself.' He opened the door. 'I won't be long.'

She opened her own door. '*We* won't be long,' she corrected him.

'You're not—'

'I am. Protecting the little woman is all very nice but not when carried to extremes. What's going to happen in the middle of a thousand people? Besides, you said yourself they can't possibly recognize us.'

'If they catch you with me—'

'If they catch you, I won't be there, because if they can't recognize you then their only way of getting you is when you are doing something you shouldn't be doing, like breaking into a caravan.'

'In broad daylight? You think I'm insane?'

'I'm not sure.' She took his arm firmly. 'One thing I *am* sure about. Remember what I said back in Arles? You're stuck with me, mate.'

'For life?'

'We'll see about that.'

Bowman blinked in surprise and peered at her closely. 'You make me a very happy man,' he said. 'When I was a little boy and I wanted something and my mother said "We'll see about that" I knew I'd always get it. All feminine minds work the same way, don't they?'

She smiled at him serenely, quite unperturbed. 'At the risk of repeating myself again, Neil Bowman, you're a lot cleverer than you look.'

'My mother used to say that too.'

The paid their admission money, climbed steps to the top of the arena. The terraces were comfortably full, colourfully crowded with hundreds of people, very few of whom could be accused of being drably dressed: *guardians* and gypsies were there in about equal proportions, there was a sprinkling of Arlésiens in their fiesta best but most of the spectators were either tourists or local people.

Between the spectators and the sanded ring itself was an area four feet wide, running the entire circumference of the ring and separated from it by a wooden barrier four feet high: it was into this area, the *callajon*, that the *razateur* leapt for safety when things were going too badly for him.

In the centre of the ring a small but uncommonly vicious-looking black Camargue bull appeared bent upon the imminent destruction of a white-costumed figure who pirouetted and swerved and twisted and closely but easily avoided the rushes of the increasingly maddened bull. The crowd clapped and shouted their approval.

'Well!' Cecile, wide-eyed and fascinated, her fears in temporary abeyance, was almost enjoying herself. 'This is more like a bull-fight!'

'You'd rather see the colour of the man's blood than the bull's?'

'Certainly. Well, I don't know. He hasn't even got a sword.'

'Swords are for the Spanish *corridas* where the bull gets killed. This is the Provençal *cours libre* where nobody gets killed although the occasional *razateur* – the bull-fighter – does get bent a bit. See that red button tied between the horns? He's got to pull that off first. Then the two bits of string. Then the two white tassels tied near the tips of the horns.'

'Isn't it dangerous?'

'It's not a way of life I'd choose myself,' Bowman admitted. He lifted his eyes from the programme note he held in his hand and looked thoughtfully at the ring.

'Anything wrong?' Cecile asked.

Bowman didn't reply immediately. He was still looking at the ring where the white-clad *razateur*, moving in a tight circle with remarkable speed but with all the controlled grace of a ballet dancer, swerved to avoid the charging bull, leaned over at what appeared to be an impossible angle and deftly plucked away the red button secured between the bull's horns, one of which appeared almost to brush the *razateur*'s chest.

'Well, well,' Bowman murmured. 'So that's El Brocador.'

'El who?'

'Brocador. The lad in the ring there.'

'You know him?'

'We haven't been introduced. Good, isn't he?'

El Brocador was more than good, he was brilliant. Timing his evasive movements with ice-cold judgement and executing them with an almost contemptuous ease, he continued to avoid the bull's furious rushes with consummate skill: in four consecutive charges he plucked away the two strings that had supported the red button and the two white tassels that had been secured to the tips of the horns. After removing the last tassel and apparently unaware of the bull's existence, he bowed deeply and gravely to the crowd, ran lightly to the barrier and vaulted gracefully into the safety of the *callajon* as the bull, now only scant feet behind, charged full tilt into the barrier, splintering the top plank. The crowd clapped and roared its approval.

But not all of them. There were four men who were not only refraining from enthusiastic applause, they weren't even looking at the bull-ring. Bowman, who had himself spent very little time in watching the spectacle, had picked them out within two minutes of arriving on the terraces – Czerda, Ferenc, Searl and Masaine. They weren't watching the bull-ring because they were too busy watching the crowd. Bowman turned to Cecile.

'Disappointed?'

'What?'

'Very slow bull.'

'Don't be horrid. What on earth is this?'

Three clowns, dressed in their traditional baggy and garishly-coloured garments, with painted faces, large false noses and ridiculous pill-boxes perched on their heads, had appeared in the *callajon*. One carried an accordion which he started to play. His two companions, both managing to trip and fall flat on their faces in the process, climbed over the barrier into the ring and, when they had picked themselves up, proceeded to do a sailor's hornpipe.

As they danced, the *toril* gate opened and a fresh bull appeared. Like its predecessor, it was a small black Camargue bull but what it lacked in inches it more than made up for in sheer bad temper for it had no sooner caught sight of the two dancing clowns than it lowered its head and charged. It went for each clown in turn but they, without in any way breaking step or losing the rhythm of the dance, glided and pirouetted to safety as if unaware of the bull's existence: they were, obviously *razateurs* of the highest order of experience.

Temporarily, the music stopped, but the bull didn't: it charged one of the clowns who turned and ran for his life, screaming for help. The crowd shouted with laughter. The clown, momentarily incensed, stopped abruptly, shook his fist at them, looked over his shoulder, screamed again, ran, mistimed his leap for the barrier and brought up heavily against it, the bull only feet away. It seemed inevitable that he must be either impaled or crushed. Neither happened, but he did not escape entirely unscathed for when he miraculously broke clear it could be seen that his baggy trousers were hooked on to one of the bull's horns. The clown, clad in white ankle-length underpants, continued his flight, still screaming for help, pursued by a now thoroughly infuriated bull who trailed the trousers along behind him. The crowd was convulsed.

The four gypsies weren't. As before, they ignored the action in the bull-ring. But now they were no longer still. They had begun to move slowly through the crowd, all moving in a clockwise fashion, closely scanning the faces of all whom they passed by. And as closely as they observed others, Bowman observed them.

Down in the *callajon* the accordionist began to play 'Tales from the Vienna Woods'. The two clowns came together and waltzed gravely in the centre of the ring. Inevitably, the bull charged the dancing couple. He was almost upon them when they waltzed apart from each other, each completing a single turn before joining up again immediately the bull's headlong rush had carried him beyond them.

The crowd went wild. Cecile laughed to the extent that she had to use a handkerchief to dab tears from her eyes. There was no trace of a smile on Bowman's face: with Czerda not twenty feet away and heading straight for him, he didn't feel like smiling.

'Isn't it marvellous?' Cecile said.

'Marvellous. Wait here.'

She was instantly serious, apprehensive. 'Where are you—'

'Trust me?'

'Trust you.'

'A white wedding. I won't be long.'

Bowman moved leisurely away. He had to pass within a few feet of Czerda who was still scrutinizing everyone he went by with a thoroughness that lifted eyebrows and brought frowns. A few feet further on, close to the exit, he passed behind the politely clapping Chinese couple that he'd seen before in Arles. They were, he thought, a remarkably distinguished looking couple. As it was extremely unlikely that they had come all the way from China, they obviously must be European residents. He wondered idly what manner of occupation such a man would pursue in Europe, then dismissed the thought from his mind: there were other and more urgent matters to occupy his attention.

He circled the arena at the back, walked about two hundred yards south down the road, crossed it and made his way back north coming up at the back of Czerda's caravans which were parked in two tight rows well back from the side of the road. The caravans appeared to be completely deserted. Certainly there was no apparent guard on Czerda's caravan or on the green-and-white caravan, but on that afternoon he was interested in neither. The caravan he *was* interested in, as he was now certain it would be, did have a guard. On a stool on the top of the steps the gypsy Maca was sitting, beer-bottle in hand.

Bowman sauntered leisurely towards the caravan: as he approached Maca lowered his beer-bottle, looked down at him and scowled warningly. Bowman ignored the scowl, approached even more closely, stopped and inspected both

Maca and the caravan, taking his time about it. Maca made a contemptuous jerking movement with his thumb, unmistakably indicating that Bowman should be on his way. Bowman remained where he was.

'Clear off!' Maca ordered.

'Gypsy swine,' Bowman said pleasantly.

Maca, obviously doubting that he had heard aright, stared for a brief moment of incredulity, then his face contorted in rage as he shifted his grip to the neck of the bottle, rose and jumped down. But Bowman had moved even more quickly and he struck Maca very hard indeed even before the gypsy's feet had reached the ground. The combined effect of the blow and his own momentum had a devastating effect on Maca: eyes unfocused, he staggered back dazedly. Bowman struck him again with equal force, caught the now unconscious man before he could fall, dragged him round to one side of the caravan, dropped him and pushed him out of sight of any casual passer-by.

Bowman glanced quickly around him. If anyone had seen the brief fracas he was taking care not to publicize the fact. Twice Bowman circled the caravan but there was no lurking watcher in the shadows, no hint of danger to be seen. He climbed the steps and entered the caravan. The rear, smaller portion of the caravan was empty. The door leading to the forward compartment was secured by two heavy bolts. Bowman slid back the bolts and passed inside.

For a moment his eyes were unable to penetrate the gloom. The curtains were drawn and very heavy curtains they were, too. Bowman drew them back.

At the front of the caravan was the three-tiered bunk he had observed when he had peered in late the previous night: as before, three men lay on those bunks. Previously, that had been a matter of no significance: bunks are for sleeping in and one would have expected to find them occupied in the night-time: one would not have expected to find them occupied in the early afternoon. But Bowman had known that he would find them occupied.

All three men were awake. They propped themselves up on their elbows, eyes, accustomed to deep gloom, blinking in the harsh light of the Camargue. Bowman advanced wordlessly, reached over the man in the lowermost bunk and picked up his right hand. The wrist belonging to that hand was manacled to a ring-bolt let into the front wall of the caravan. Bowman let his wrist fall and examined the man in the middle bunk: he was similarly secured. Bowman didn't trouble to look at the wrist of the man on top. He stepped back and looked at them thoughtfully.

He said: 'Count le Hobenaut, husband of Marie le Hobenaut, Mr Tangevec, husband of Sara Tangevec and the third name I do not know. Who are you, sir?' This to the man in the bottom bunk, a middle-aged, greying and very distinguished looking person.

'Daymel.'

'You are Tina's father?'

'I am.' The expression on his face was that of a man receiving his executioner and not his saviour. 'Who in the name of God are you?'

'Bowman. Neil Bowman. I've come to take you three gentlemen away.'

'I don't know who you are.' This from the man in the middle bunk who didn't seem any happier to see Bowman than Daymel had been. 'I don't care who you are. For God's sake go away or you'll be the death of us all.'

'You are the Count le Hobenaut?' The man nodded. 'You heard about your brother-in-law? Alexandre?'

Le Hobenaut looked at him with an odd speculative desperation on his face, then said: 'What about my brother-in-law?'

'He's dead. Czerda murdered him.'

'What crazy talk is this? Alexandre? Dead? How can he be dead? Czerda promised us—'

'You believed him?'

'Of course. Czerda has everything to lose—'

'You two believe him?' Bowman asked. They nodded. 'A man who trusts a killer is a fool. You are fools – all three of you. Alexandre *is* dead. I found his body. If you think he's alive why not ask Czerda if you can see him? Or you, Daymel. Why don't you ask Czerda if you can see your daughter?'

'She's not – she's—'

'She's not dead. Just half dead. They flayed her back. Why

did they kill Alexandre? Because they were both trying to tell someone something. What was it that they were trying to tell, gentlemen?'

'I beg you, Bowman.' Le Hobenaut's distress was but one step removed from terror. 'Leave us!'

'Why are you so terrified for them? Why are they so terrified for you? And don't tell me again to go for I'm not going until I know the answers.'

'You'll never know the answers now,' Czerda said.

— 8 —

BOWMAN TURNED round slowly for there was nothing to be gained by haste now. Of the shock, of the inevitably profound chagrin, there was no sign in his face. But Czerda, standing in the doorway with a silenced gun in his hand and Masaine, beside him, with a knife in his, made no attempt to disguise their feelings. Both men were smiling and smiling broadly, although their smiles were noticeably lacking in warmth. At a nod from Czerda, Masaine advanced and tested the shackles securing the three men. He said: 'They have not been touched.'

'He was probably too busy explaining to them just how clever he was.' Czerda did not trouble to conceal the immense amount of satisfaction he was deriving from the moment. 'It was all too simple, Bowman. You really are a fool. Shopkeepers in Arles who receive a gratuity of six hundred Swiss francs are hardly likely to forget the person who gave it to them. I tell you, I could hardly keep a straight face when I was moving through the crowd there pretending to look for you. But we had to pretend, didn't we, to convince you that we hadn't recognized you or you'd never have come out into the open, would you? You fool, we had you identified before you entered the arena.'

'You might have told Maca,' Bowman murmured.

'We might, but Maca is no actor, I'm afraid,' Czerda said

regretfully. 'He wouldn't have known how to make a fake fight look real. And if we'd left no guard at all you'd have been doubly suspicious.' He stretched out his left hand. 'Eighty thousand francs, Bowman.'

'I don't carry that sort of loose change with me.'

'*My* eighty thousand francs.'

Bowman looked at him with contempt. 'Where would a person like you get eighty thousand francs?'

Czerda smiled, stepped forward unexpectedly and drove the silenced barrel of his gun into Bowman's solar plexus. Bowman doubled up, gasping in agony.

'I would have liked to strike you across the face, as you struck me.' He had removed his smile. 'But for the moment I prefer that you remain unmarked. The money, Bowman?'

Bowman straightened slowly. When he spoke, his voice came as a harsh croak.

'I lost it.'

'You *lost* it?'

'I had a hole in my pocket.'

Czerda's face twisted in anger, he lifted his gun to club Bowman, then smiled. 'You'll find it within the minute, you'll see.'

II

The green Rolls-Royce slowed as it approached the Mas de Lavignolle. Le Grand Duc, still with a parasol being held above his head, surveyed the scene thoughtfully.

'Czerda's caravans,' he observed. 'Surprising. One would not have expected the Mas de Lavignolle to be of any particular interest to our friend Czerda. But a man like that will always have a good reason for what he is doing. However, he will doubtless consider it a privilege to inform me of his reasons . . . What is it, my dear?'

'Look ahead.' Lila pointed. 'Just there.'

Le Grand Duc followed the direction of her arm. Cecile, flanked by El Brocador and Searl, the first all in white, the second all in black, mounted the steps of a caravan and disappeared inside. The door closed behind them.

Le Grand Duc pressed the dividing window button. 'Stop

the car, if you please.' To Lila he said: 'You think that's your friend? Same dress, I admit, but all those Arlésienne fiesta dresses look the same to me, especially from the back.'

'That's Cecilc.' Lila was positive.

'A *razateur* and a priest,' Le Grand Duc mused. 'You really must admit that your friend does have a marked propensity for striking up the most unusual acquaintanceships. You have your notebook?'

'I have what?'

'We must investigate this.'

'You're going to investigate—'

'Please. No Greek chorus. Everything is of interest to the true folklorist.'

'But you can't just barge in—'

'Nonsense. I am the Duc de Croytor. Besides, I never barge. I always make an entrance.'

III

The ache in his midriff, Bowman guessed, was as nothing compared to some of the aches that he was going to come by very shortly – if, that was, he would then be in a position to feel anything. There was a gleam in Czerda's eye, a barely-contained anticipation in the face that bespoke ill, Bowman thought, for the immediate future.

He looked round the caravan. The three shackled men had in their faces the uncomprehending and lacklustre despair of those to whom defeat is already an accepted reality. Czerda and Masaine had pleasantly anticipatory smiles on their faces, El Brocador was serious and thoughtful and watchful, Simon Searl had a peculiar look in his eyes which made his unfrocking a readily comprehensible matter, while Cecile just looked slightly dazed, a little frightened, a little angry but as far removed from hysteria as could be.

'You understand now,' Czerda said, 'why I said you'd find the money within the minute.'

'I understand now. You'll find it—'

'What money?' Cecile asked. 'What does that – that monster want?'

'His eighty thousand francs back again – minus certain

small outlays I've been compelled to make – and who can blame him?'

'Don't tell him anything!'

'And don't you understand the kind of men you're dealing with? Ten seconds from now they'll have your arm twisted up behind your back till it's touching your ear, you'll be screaming in agony and if they happen to break your shoulder or tear a few ligaments, well, that's just too bad.'

'But – but I'll just faint—'

'Please.' Bowman looked at Czerda, carefully avoiding Cecile's gaze. 'It's in Arles. Safe-deposit in the station.'

'The key?'

'On a ring. In the car. Hidden. I'll show you.'

'Excellent,' Czerda said. 'A disappointment to friend Searl, I'm afraid, but inflicting pain on young ladies gives me no pleasure though I wouldn't hesitate if I had to. As you shall see.'

'I don't understand.'

'You will. You are a danger, you have been a great danger and you have to go, that's all. You will die this afternoon and within the hour so that no suspicion will ever attach to us.'

It was, Bowman thought, as laconic a death sentence as he'd ever heard of. There was something chilling in the man's casual certainty.

Czerda went on: 'You will understand now why I didn't injure your face, why I wanted you to go into that bull-ring unmarked.'

'Bull-ring?'

'Bull-ring, my friend.'

'You're mad. You can't make me go into a bull-ring.'

Czerda said nothing and there was no signal. Searl, eagerly assisted by a grinning Masaine, caught hold of Cecile, forced her face downwards on to a bunk and, while Masaine pinned her down, Searl gripped the collar of the Arlésienne costume and ripped it down to the waist. He turned and smiled at Bowman, reached into the folds of his clerical garb and brought out what appeared to be a version of a hunting stock, with a fifteen-inch interwoven leather handle attached to three long thin black thongs. Bowman looked at Czerda and Czerda wasn't watching anything of what was going on: he was watching Bowman and the gun pointing at Bowman was motionless.

Czerda said: 'I think perhaps you will go into that bull-ring?'

'Yes.' Bowman nodded. 'I think perhaps I will.'

Searl put his stock away. His face was twisted in the bitter disappointment of a spoilt child who has been deprived of a new toy. Masaine took his hands away from Cecile's shoulders. She pushed herself groggily to a sitting position and looked at Bowman. Her face was very pale but her eyes were mad. It had just occurred to Bowman that she was, as she'd said, quite capable of using a gun if shown how to use one when there came from outside the sound of a solid measured tread: the door opened and Le Grand Duc entered with a plainly apprehensive Lila trailing uncertainly behind him. Le Grand Duc pushed the monocle more firmly into his eye.

'Ah, Czerda, my dear fellow. It's you.' He looked at the gun in the gypsy's hand and said sharply: 'Don't point that damned thing at me!' He indicated Bowman. 'Point it at that fellow there. Don't you know he's your man, you fool?'

Czerda uncertainly trained his gun back on Bowman and just as uncertainly looked at Le Grand Duc.

'What do you want?' Czerda tried to imbue his voice with sharp authority but Le Grand Duc wasn't the properly receptive type and it didn't come off. 'Why are you—'

'Be quiet!' Le Grand Duc was at his most intimidating, which was very intimidating indeed. '*I* am speaking. You are a bunch of incompetent and witless nincompoops. You have forced me to destroy the basic rule of my existence – to bring myself into the open. I have seen more intelligence exhibited in a cageful of retarded chimpanzees. You have lost me much time and cost me vast trouble and anxiety. I am seriously tempted to dispose of the services of you all – permanently. And that means you as well as your services. What are you doing here?'

'What are we doing here?' Czerda stared at him. 'But – but – but Searl here said that you—'

'I will deal with Searl later.' Le Grand Duc's promise was imbued with such menacing overtones that Searl at once looked acutely unhappy. Czerda looked nervous to a degree that was almost unthinkable for him, El Brocador looked puzzled and Masaine had clearly given up thinking of any kind. Lila simply looked stunned. Le Grand Duc went on: 'I did not mean, you cretin, what you are doing in Mas de Lavignolle. I meant what are you doing here, as of this present moment, in this caravan.'

'Bowman here stole the money you gave me,' Czerda said sullenly. 'We were—'

'He what?' Le Grand Duc's face was thunderous.

'He stole your money,' Czerda said unhappily. 'All of it.'

'All of it!'

'Eighty thousand francs. That's what we've been doing – finding out where it is. He's about to show me the key to where the money is.'

'I trust for your sake that you find it.' He paused and turned as Maca came staggering into the caravan, both hands holding what was clearly a very painful face.

'Is this man drunk?' Le Grand Duc demanded. '*Are* you drunk, sir? Stand straight when you talk to me.'

'He did it!' Maca spoke to Czerda, he didn't appear to have noticed Le Grand Duc, for his eyes were for Bowman only. 'He came along—'

'Silence!' Le Grand Duc's voice would have intimidated a Bengal tiger. 'My God, Czerda, you surround yourself with the most useless and ineffectual bunch of lieutenants it's ever been my misfortune to encounter.' He looked round the caravan, ignoring the three manacled men, took two steps towards where Cecile was sitting and looked down at her. 'Ha! Bowman's accomplice, of course. Why is she here?'

Czerda shrugged. 'Bowman wouldn't co-operate—'

'A hostage? Very well. Here's another.' He caught Lila by the arm and shoved her roughly across the caravan. She stumbled, almost fell, then sat down heavily on the bunk beside Cecile. Her face, already horror-stricken, now looked stupefied.

'Charles!'

'Be quiet!'

'But Charles! My father – you said—'

'You are a feather-brained young idiot,' Le Grand Duc said with contempt. 'The real Duc de Croytor, to whom I fortunately bear a strong resemblance, is at present in the upper Amazon, probably being devoured by the savages in the Matto Grosso. I am *not* the Duc de Croytor.'

'We know that, Mr Strome.' Simon Searl was at his most obsequious.

Again displaying his quite remarkable speed, Le Grand Duc stepped forward and struck Searl heavily across the face. Searl cried out in pain and staggered heavily, to bring up against the wall of the caravan. There was silence for several seconds.

'I have no name,' Le Grand Duc said softly. 'There is no such person as you mentioned.'

'I'm sorry, sir.' Searl fingered his cheek. 'I—'

'Silence!' Le Grand Duc turned to Czerda. 'Bowman has something to show you? Give you?'

'Yes, sir. And there's another little matter I have to attend to.'

'Yes, yes, yes. Be quick about it.'

'Yes, sir.'

'I shall wait here. We must talk on your return, mustn't we, Czerda.'

Czerda nodded unhappily, told Masaine to watch the girls, put his jacket over his gun and left accompanied by Searl and El Brocador. Masaine, his knife still drawn, seated himself comfortably. Maca, tenderly rubbing his bruised face, muttered something and left, probably to attend to his injuries. Lila, her face woebegone, looked up at Le Grand Duc.

'Oh, Charles, how could you—'

'Ninny!'

She stared at him brokenly. Tears began to roll down her cheeks. Cecile put an arm round her and glared at Le Grand Duc. Le Grand Duc looked through her and remained totally unaffected.

IV

'Stop here,' Czerda said.

They stopped, Bowman ahead of Czerda with a silencer prodding his back, El Brocador and Searl on either side of him, the Citroën ten feet away.

'Where's the key?' Czerda demanded.

'I'll get it.'

'You will not. You are perfectly capable of switching keys or even finding a hidden gun. Where is it?'

'On a key ring. It's taped under the driver's seat, back, left.'

'Searl?' Searl nodded, went to the car, Czerda said sourly: 'You don't trust many people, do you?'

'I should, you think?'

'What's the number of this deposit box?'

'Sixty-five.'

Searl returned. 'These are ignition keys.'

'The brass one's not,' Bowman said.

Czerda took the keys. 'The brass one's not.' He removed it from the ring. 'Sixty-five. For once, the truth. How's the money wrapped?'

'Oilskin, brown paper, sealing-wax. My name's on it.'

'Good.' He looked round. Maca was sitting on the top of some caravan steps. Czerda beckoned him and he came to where they were, rubbing his chin and looked malevolently at Bowman. Czerda said: 'Young José has a motor-scooter, hasn't he?'

'You want a message done. I'll get him. He's in the arena.'

'No need.' Czerda gave him the key. 'That's for safe deposit sixty-five Arles station. Tell him to open it and bring back the brown paper parcel inside. Tell him to be as careful with it as he would be with his own life. It's a very, very valuable parcel. Tell him to come back here as soon as possible and give it to me and if I'm not here someone will know where I've gone and he's to come after me. Is that clear?'

Maca nodded and left. Czerda said: 'I think it's time we paid a visit to the bull-ring ourselves.'

They crossed the road but went not directly to the arena but to one of several adjacent huts which were evidently used as changing rooms, for the one they entered was behung with *matadors*' and *razateurs*' uniforms and several outfits of clowns' attire. Czerda pointed to one of the last. 'Get into that.'

'That?' Bowman eyed the garish rigout. 'Why the hell should I?'

'Because my friend here asks you to.' Czerda waved his gun. 'Don't make my friend angry.'

Bowman did as he was told. When he was finished he was far from surprised to see El Brocador exchange his conspicuous white uniform for his dark suit, to see Searl pull on a long blue smock, then to see all three men put on paper masks and comic hats. They appeared to have a craving for anonymity, a not unusual predilection on the part of would-be murderers. Czerda draped a red flag over his gun and they left for the arena.

When they arrived at the entrance to the *callajon* Bowman was mildly astonished to discover that the comic act that had been in process when he'd left was still not finished: so much seemed to have happened since he'd left the arena that it was difficult to realize that so few minutes had elapsed. They arrived to find that one of the clowns, incredibly, was doing a handstand on the back of the bull, which just stood there in baffled fury, its head swinging from side to side. The crowd clapped ecstatically: had the circumstances been different, Bowman thought, he might even have clapped himself.

For their final brief act the clowns waltzed towards the side of the arena to the accompaniment of their companion's accordion. They stopped, faced the crowd side by side and bowed deeply, apparently unaware that their backs were towards the charging bull. The crowd screamed a warning: the clowns, still bent, pushed each other apart at the last moment and the bull hurtled wildly over the spot where they had been standing only a second previously and crashed into the barrier with an impact that momentarily stunned it. As the clowns vaulted into the *callajon* the crowd continued to whistle and shout their applause. It occurred to Bowman to wonder whether they would still be in such a happily carefree mood in a few minutes' time: it seemed unlikely.

The ring was empty now and Bowman and his three escorts had moved out into the *callajon*. The crowd stared with interest and in considerable amusement at Bowman's attire and he was, unquestionably, worth a second glance. He was clad in a most outlandish fashion. His right leg was enclosed in red, his left in white and the doublet was composed of red and white squares. The flexible green canvas shoes he wore were so ludicrously long that the toes were tied back to the shins. He wore a white conical pierrot's hat with a red pompom on top: for defence he was armed with a slender three-foot cane with a small tricolor at the end of it.

'I have the gun, I have the girl,' Czerda said softly. 'You will remember?'

'I'll try.'

'If you try to escape, the girl will not live. You believe me?'

Bowman believed him. He said: 'And if I die, the girl will not live either.'

'No. Without you, the girl is nothing, and Czerda does not make war on women. I know who you are now, or think I do. It is no matter. I have discovered that you never met her until last night and it is unthinkable that a man like you would tell her anything of importance: professionals never explain more than they have to, do they, Mr Bowman? And young girls can be made to talk, Mr Bowman. She can do us no harm. When we've done what we intend to do, and that will be in two days, she is free to go.'

'She knows where Alexandre is buried.'

'Ah, so. Alexandre? Who is Alexandre?'

'Of course. Free to go?'

'You have my word.' Bowman didn't doubt him. 'In exchange, you will now put on a convincing struggle.' Bowman nodded. The three men grabbed him or tried to grab him and all four staggered about the *callajon*. The colourful crowd were by now in excellent humour, gay, chattering, relaxed: all evidently felt that they were having a splendid afternoon's entertainment and that this mock-fight that was taking place in the *callajon* – for mock-fight it surely was, there were no upraised arms, no blows being struck in anger – was but the prelude to another hilariously comic turn, it had to be, with the man trying to struggle free dressed in that ridiculous pierrot's costume. Eventually, to the accompaniment of considerable whistling, laughter and shouts of encouragement, Bowman broke free, ran a little way along the *callajon* and vaulted into the ring. Czerda ran after him, made to clamber over the barrier but was caught and restrained by Searl and El Brocador, who pointed excitedly to the north end of the ring. Czerda followed their direction.

They were not the only ones looking in that direction. The crowd had suddenly fallen silent, their laughter had ceased and the smiles vanished: puzzlement had replaced their humour, a puzzlement that rapidly shaded into anxiety and apprehension. Bowman's eyes followed the direction of those of the crowd: he could not only understand the apprehension of the crowd, he reflected, but shared it to the fullest extent.

The northern *toril* gate had been drawn and a bull stood at the entrance. But this was not the small light black bull of the Camargue that was used in the *cours libre* – the bloodless bull-fight of Provence: this was a huge Spanish fighting bull, one of the Andalusian monsters that fight to the death in the great *corridas* of Spain. It had enormous shoulders, an enormous head and a terrifying spread of horn. Its head was low but not as low as it would be when it launched itself into its charge: it pawed the ground, alternately dragging each front hoof backwards, gouging deep channels in the dark sand.

Members of the crowd were by this time looking at one another in uneasy and rather fearful wonder. For the most part they were *aficionados* of the sport and they knew that what they were seeing was quite unprecedented and this could be no better than sending a man, no matter how brave and skilful a *razateur* he might be, to his certain death.

The giant bull was now advancing slowly into the ring, at the same time still contriving to make those deep backwards scores in the sand. Its great head was lower than before.

Bowman stood stock-still. His lips were compressed, his eyes narrow and still and watchful. Some twelve hours previously, when inching up the ledge on the cliff-face in the ruined battlements of the ancient fortress he had known fear, and now he knew it again and admitted it to himself. It was no bad thing, he thought wryly. Fear it was that sent the adrenalin pumping, and adrenalin was the catalyst that triggered off the capacity for violent action and abnormally swift reaction: as matters stood now he was going to need all the adrenalin he could lay hands on. But he was coldly aware that if he survived at all it could only be for the briefest of periods: all the adrenalin in the world couldn't save him now.

From the safety of the *callajon* Czerda licked his lips, half in unconscious empathy with the man in the ring, half in anticipation of things to come. Suddenly he tensed and the whole crowd tensed with him. An eerie silence as of death enveloped the arena. The great bull was charging.

With unbelievable acceleration for a creature of its size it came at Bowman like an express train. Bowman, unblinking, his racing mind figuring out the correlation between the speed of the bull and the rapidly narrowing distance between them, stood as a man would who is frozen with fear. Trance-like, fearful, the spectators stared in horror, convinced in their minds that this mad pierrot's destruction was only a couple of heart-beats away. Bowman waited for one of those heart-beats to tick away and then, when the bull was less than twenty feet and a second away, he flung himself to his right. But the bull knew all about such tactics, for with remarkable speed in so massive an animal it veered instantly to its left to intercept: but Bowman had only feinted. He checked violently and threw himself to the left and the bull thundered harmlessly by, the huge right horn missing Bowman by a clear foot. The crowd, unbelieving, heaved a long collective sigh of relief, shook their heads at one another and murmured their relief. But the apprehension, the tension, still lay heavily in the air.

The Andalusian bull could brake as swiftly as it could accelerate. It pulled up in a shower of sand, whirled round and came at Bowman again without pause. Again Bowman judged his moment to a fraction of a second, again he repeated the same manoeuvre, but this time in the reverse order. Again the bull missed, but this time only by inches. There came another murmur of admiration from the crowd, this time to the accompaniment of some sporadic hand-clapping: the tension in the air was beginning to ease, not much, but enough to be perceptible.

Again the bull turned but this time it stood still, less than thirty feet away. Quite without moving, it watched Bowman, just as Bowman, quite without moving, watched it. Bowman stared at the great horns: there could be no doubt about it, their tips had been filed to sharp points. It occurred to Bowman, with a curious sense of detachment, that he had rarely encountered a more superfluous refinement: whether the horns had been sharpened or filed to the diameter of a penny it wouldn't have made a ha'porth of difference: a swinging hook of one of those giant horns with all the power of those massive shoulder and neck muscles behind it would go straight through his body irrespective of the condition of the tip. Indeed, being gored by the sharpened horn might prove the easier and less agonizing way to die but it was a matter of academic importance anyway, the end result would be inevitable and the same.

The bull's red eyes never wavered. Did it think, Bowman wondered, was it thinking? Was it thinking what he was thinking, that this was but a game of Russian roulette insofar as the terms of probabilities went? Would he expect Bowman to execute the same manoeuvre next time, refuse to be drawn, carry straight on and get him while Bowman had checked to fling himself the other way? Or would he think that Bowman's next evasive action might not be a feint but the real thing, swerve accordingly and still get him? Bluff and double-bluff, Bowman thought, and it was pointless to speculate: the laws of blind chance were at work here and sooner or later, sooner rather than later, for on every occasion he had only a fifty-fifty chance, one of those horns would tear the life out of him.

The thought of that fifty-fifty chance prompted Bowman to risk a quick glance at the barrier. It was only ten feet away. He turned and sprinted for it, three steps, aware that behind him the bull had broken into its charge, aware ahead of him, in the *callajon*, of the figure of Czerda with the red flag over his arm, but the gun beneath clearly hanging downwards. He knew, as Bowman knew he knew, that Bowman had no intention of leaving the ring.

Bowman spun, back to the barrier, to face the bull. Pirouetting like a spinning top, he moved swiftly away along the barrier as the onrushing enraged bull hooked viciously with his right horn, the sharpened point brushing Bowman's sleeve but not even tearing the material. The bull crashed into the barrier with tremendous force, splintered the top two planks, then reared up with his forefeet on top of the planks as he tried furiously to climb over. Some time elapsed before the bull realized that Bowman was still in the same ring though by this time a prudent distance away.

By now the crowd was clapping and shouting its approval. Smiles were reappearing and some were even beginning to enjoy what had originally appeared to be a ludicrously one-sided and suicidal contest.

The bull stood still for a full half minute, shaking its great head slowly from side to side as if dazed by the power of its head-on collision with the barrier, which it very probably was. When it moved this time, it had changed its tactics. It didn't charge Bowman, it stalked him. It walked forward as Bowman walked backward, slowly gaining on him, and when it abruptly lowered its head and charged it was so close that Bowman had no room left for manoeuvre. He did the only thing open to him and leapt high in the air as the bull tried to toss him. He landed on the bull's shoulders, somersaulted and came to the ground on his feet: although hurt and badly winded he miraculously succeeded in retaining his balance.

The crowd roared and whistled its admiration. Laughing in delight, they clapped one another on the back. Here, below that pierrot's disguise, must be one of the great *razateurs* of the day. *The* great *razateur* of the day. Some of the spectators looked almost sheepish at having worried about the capacity for survival of so great a master as this.

V

The three manacled prisoners on their bunks, the two girls and Masaine watched in some trepidation as Le Grand Duc paced restlessly up and down the length of the caravan, glancing in mounting irritation at his watch.

'What in the devil's name is taking Czerda so long?' he demanded. He turned to Masaine. 'You, there. Where have they taken Bowman?'

'Why, I thought you knew.'

'Answer, you cretin!'

'For the key. For the money. You heard. And then to the bull-ring, of course.'

'The bull-ring? Why?'

'Why?' Masaine was genuinely puzzled. 'You wanted it done, didn't you?'

'Wanted what done?' Le Grand Duc was exercising massive restraint.

'Bowman. To get him out of the way.'

Le Grand Duc laid hands on Masaine's shoulders and shook him in a no longer to be contained exasperation.

'Why the bull-ring?'

'To fight a bull, of course. A huge black Spanish killer. Bare hands.' Masaine nodded at Cecile. 'If he doesn't, we're going to kill her. This way, Czerda says, no suspicion can fall on us. Bowman should be dead by now.' Masaine shook his head in admiration. 'Czerda's clever.'

'He's a raving maniac!' Le Grand Duc shouted. 'Kill Bowman? Now? Before we've made him talk? Before I know his contacts, how he broke our ring? Not to mention the eighty thousand francs we haven't got yet. At once, fellow! Stop Czerda! Get Bowman out of there before it's too late.'

Masaine shook his head stubbornly. 'My orders are to stay here and guard those women.'

'I shall attend to you later,' Le Grand Duc said chillingly, 'I cannot, must not be seen in public with Czerda again. Miss Dubois, run at once—'

Cecile jumped to her feet. Her Arlésienne costume was not the thing of beauty that it had been but Lila had effected running repairs sufficient to preserve the decencies. She made to move forward, but Masaine barred her way.

'She stays here,' he declared. 'My orders—'

'Great God in heaven!' Le Grand Duc thundered. 'Are you defying me?'

He advanced ponderously upon a plainly apprehensive Masaine. Before the gypsy could even begin to realize what was about to happen Le Grand Duc smashed down his heel, with all his massive weight behind it, on Masaine's instep. Masaine howled in agony, hobbled on one leg and stooped to clutch his injured foot with both hands. As he did so Le Grand Duc brought down his locked hands on the base of Masaine's neck, who collapsed heavily on the floor, unconscious before he struck it.

'Swiftly, Miss Dubois, swiftly!' Le Grand Duc said urgently. 'If not already gone, your friend may well be *in extremis.*'

And *in extremis* Bowman undoubtedly was. He was still on his feet – but it was only an exceptional will-power and instinct, though fast fading, for survival that kept him there.

His face was streaked with sand and blood, twisted in pain and drawn in exhaustion. From time to time he held his left ribs which appeared to be the prime source of the pain he was suffering. His earlier pierrot finery was now bedraggled and dirtied and torn, two long rips on the right-hand side of his tunic were evidences of two extremely narrow escapes from the scything left horn of the bull. He had forgotten how many times now he'd been on the sanded floor of the arena but he hadn't forgotten the three occasions when his visits there had been entirely involuntary: twice the shoulder of the bull had hurled him to the ground, once the back-sweep of the left horn had caught him high on the left arm and sent him somersaulting. And now the bull was coming at him again.

Bowman side-stepped but his reactions had slowed, and slowed badly. Providentially, the bull guessed wrongly and hooked away from Bowman but his left shoulder struck him a glancing blow, though from something weighing about a ton and travelling at thirty miles an hour the word 'glancing' is a purely relative term. It sent Bowman tumbling head over heels to the ground. The bull pursued him, viciously trying to gore, but Bowman had still enough awareness and physical resources left to keep rolling over and over, desperately trying to avoid those lethal horns.

The crowd had suddenly become very quiet. This, they knew, was a great *razateur*, a master mime and actor, but surely no one would carry the interests of his art to the suicidal lengths where, every second now as he rolled over the sand, he escaped death by inches and sometimes less, for twice in as many seconds the bull's horns tore through the back of the doublet.

Both times Bowman felt the horn scoring across his back and it was this that galvanized him to what he knew must be his final effort. Half a dozen times he rolled away from the bull as quickly as he could, seized what was only half a chance and scrambled upright. He could do no more than just stand there, swaying drunkenly and staggering from side to side. Again, that eerie silence fell across the arena as the bull, infuriated beyond measure and too mad to be cunning any more, came charging in again, but just as it seemed inevitable that the bull must surely this time impale him, an uncontrollable drunken lurch by Bowman took him a bare inch clear of the scything horn: so incensed was the bull that he ran on for another twenty yards before realizing that Bowman was no longer in his way and coming to a halt.

The crowd appeared to go mad. In their relief, in their unbounded admiration for this demigod, they cheered, they clapped, they shouted, they wept tears of laughter. What an actor, what a performer, what a magnificent *razateur*! Such an exhibition, surely, had never been seen before.

Bowman leaned in total exhaustion against the barrier, a smiling Czerda only feet away from where he stood. Bowman was finished and the desperation in his face showed it. He was finished not only physically, he had come to the end of his mental tether. He just wasn't prepared to run any more. The bull lowered its head in preparation for another charge: again, silence fell over the arena. What fresh wonder was this miracle man going to demonstrate now?

But the miracle man was through with demonstrations for the day. Even as the silence fell he heard something that made him spin round and stare at the crowd, incredulity in his face. Standing high at the back of the crowd and waving frantically at him was Cecile, oblivious of the fact that scores of people had turned to stare at her.

'Neil!' Her voice was close to a scream. 'Neil Bowman! Come on!'

Bowman came. The bull had started on its charge but the sight of Cecile and the realization that escape was at hand had given Bowman a fresh influx of strength, however brief it might prove to be. He scrambled into the safety of the *callajon* at least two seconds before the bull thundered into the barrier. Bowman removed the pierrot's hat which had been hanging by its elastic band down the back of his neck, impaled it on one of the sharpened horns, brushed unceremoniously by the flabbergasted Czerda and ran up the terraces as quickly as his leaden legs would permit, waving to the crowd who parted to make way for him: the crowd, nonplussed though it was by this remarkable turn of events, nevertheless gave him a tumultuous reception: so unprecedented had the entire act been that they no doubt considered that this was also part of it. Bowman neither knew nor cared what their reactions were: just so long as they opened up before him and closed again after he had passed it would give him what might prove to be vital extra seconds over the inevitable pursuers. He reached the top, caught Cecile by the arm.

'I just love your sense of timing,' he said. His voice, like his breathing, was hoarse and gasping and distressed. He turned and looked behind him. Czerda was ploughing his way up through the crowd and not leaving any newly made friends behind him: El Brocador was moving on a converging course: of Searl he could see no sign. Together they hurried down the broad steps outside the arena, skirting the bull pens, stables and changing rooms. Bowman slid a hand through one of the many rips in his tunic, located his car keys and brought them out. He tightened his grip on Cecile's arm as they reached the last of the changing rooms and peered cautiously round the corner. A second later he withdrew, his face bitter with chagrin.

'It's just not our day, Cecile. That gypsy I clobbered – Maca – is sitting on the bonnet of the Citroën. Worse, he's cleaning his nails with a knife. One of those knives.' He opened a door behind them, thrust Cecile into the changing room where he himself had robed before his performance, and handed her the car keys. 'Wait till the crowd comes out. Mingle with them. Take the car, meet me at the southern end – the seaward end – of the church at Saintes-Maries. For God's sake, don't leave the Citroën anywhere near by – drive it out to the caravan park east of the town and leave it there.'

'I see.' She was, Bowman thought, remarkably calm. 'And meantime you have things to attend to?'

'As always.' He peered through a crack in the door: for the moment there was no one in sight. 'Four bridesmaids,' he said, slipped out and closed the door behind him.

VI

The three manacled men were lying in their bunks, quietly and seemingly uncaring, Lila was sniffing disconsolately and Le Grand Duc scowling thunderously when Searl came running up the steps. The apprehensive look was back on his face again and he was noticeably short of breath.

'I trust,' Le Grand Duc said ominously, 'that you are not the bearer of ill tidings.'

'I saw the girl,' Searl gasped. 'How did she—'

'By God, Searl, you and your nincompoop friend Czerda will pay for this. If Bowman is dead—' He broke off and stared over Searl's shoulder, then pushed him roughly to one side. 'Who in heaven's name is that?'

Searl turned to follow Le Grand Duc's pointing finger. A red-and-white-clad pierrot was making his way at a lurching, stumbling run across the improvised car park: it was evident that he was near total exhaustion.

'That's him,' Searl shouted. 'That's him.' As they watched, three gypsies appeared from behind some huts, Czerda unmistakably one of them, running in pursuit of Bowman and covering the ground a great deal faster than he was. Bowman looked over his shoulder, located his pursuers, swerved to seek cover among several caravans, checked again as he saw his way blocked by El Brocador and two other gypsies, turned at right-angles and headed for a group of horses tethered near by, white Camargue horses fitted with the heavy-pommelled and high-backed Camargue saddles which look more like ribbed and leather-upholstered armchairs than anything else. He ran for the nearest, unhitched it, got a foot into the peculiarly fenced stirrup and managed, not without considerable effort, to haul himself up.

'Quickly!' Le Grand Duc ordered. 'Get Czerda. Tell him if Bowman escapes neither he nor you shall. But I want him alive. If he dies, you die. I want him delivered to me within the hour at the Miramar Hotel in Saintes-Maries. I myself cannot afford to remain here another moment. Don't forget to catch that damned girl and bring her along also. Hurry, man, hurry!'

Searl hurried. As he made to cross the road he had to step quickly and advisedly to one side to avoid being run down by Bowman's horse. Bowman, Le Grand Duc could see, was swaying in the saddle to the extent that even although he had the reins in his hands he had to hold on to the pommel to remain in his seat. Beneath the artificial tan the face was pale, drawn in pain and exhaustion. Le Grand Duc became aware that Lila was standing by his side, that she too was watching Bowman.

'I've heard of it,' the girl said quietly. No tears now, just a quietness and a sadness and disbelief. 'And now I see it. Hounding a man to death.'

Le Grand Duc put a hand on her arm. 'I assure you, my dear girl—'

She struck his hand from her arm and said nothing. She didn't have to, the contempt and the loathing in her face said it all for her. Le Grand Duc nodded, turned away and watched the diminishing figure of Bowman disappearing round a bend in the road to the south.

Le Grand Duc was not the only one to take so keen an interest in Bowman's departure. Her face pressed against a small square window in the side of the changing room Cecile watched the galloping white horse and its rider till it vanished from sight. Sure knowledge of what would happen next kept her there nor did she have long to wait. Within thirty seconds five other horsemen came galloping by – Czerda, Ferenc, El Brocador, Searl and a fifth man whom she did not recognize. Dry-lipped, near tears and sick at heart, she turned away and started searching among the racks of clothes.

Almost at once she found what she wanted – a clown's outfit consisting of the usual very wide trousers, red, with wide yellow braces as support, a red-and-yellow-striped football jersey and a voluminous dark jacket. She pulled on the trousers, stuffing in the long fiesta dress as best she could – the trousers were cut on so generous a scale that the additional bagginess was scarcely noticeable – pulled the red-and-yellow jersey over her head, shrugged into the big jacket, removed her red wig and stuck a flat green cap on her head. There was no mirror in the changing room: that, she thought dolefully, was probably as well.

She went back to the window. The afternoon show was clearly over and people were streaming down the steps and across the road to their cars. She moved towards the door. Dressed as she was in a dress so shriekingly conspicuous that it conferred a degree of anonymity on the wearer, with the men she most feared in pursuit of Bowman and with plenty of people outside with whom to mingle, this, she realized, would be the best opportunity she would be likely to have to make her way undetected to the Citroën.

And, as far as she could tell, no one remarked her presence as she crossed the road towards the car or, if they did, they made no song and dance about it which, as far as Cecile was then concerned, amounted to the same thing. She opened the car, glanced forwards and back to make sure she was unobserved, slid into the driver's seat, put the key in the ignition and cried out more in fright than in pain as a large and vice-like hand closed around her neck.

The grip eased and she turned slowly round. Maca was kneeling on the floor at the back. He was smiling in a not very encouraging fashion and he had a large knife in his right hand.

— 9 —

THE HOT AFTERNOON sun beat down mercilessly on the baking plains beneath, on the *étangs*, on the marshes, on the saltflats and the occasional contrasting patches of bright green vegetation. A shimmering haze characteristic of the Camargue rose off the plains and gave a curiously ethereal quality, a strange lack of definition to all the features of the landscape, an illusion enhanced by the fact that none of those features was possessed of any vertical element. All plains are flat, but none as flat as the Camargue.

Half-a-dozen horsemen on steaming horses galloped furiously across the plain. From the air, their method of progress must have seemed peculiar and puzzling in the extreme as the horses seldom galloped more than twenty yards in a straight line and were continously swerving off course. But seen at ground level the mystery disappeared: the area was so covered with numerous marshes, ranging from tiny little patches to areas larger than a football field, that it made continuous progress in a direct line impossible.

Bowman was at a disadvantage and knew it. He was at a

disadvantage on three counts: he was, as his strained face showed and the blood-stains and dirt-streaks could not conceal, as exhausted as ever – this full-stretch gallop, involving continuous twisting and turning, offered no possibility of recuperating any strength – and his mind was as far below its decision-making best as his body was of executing those decisions: his pursuers knew the terrain intimately whereas he was a complete stranger to it: and, fairly accomplished horseman though he considered himself to be, he knew he could not even begin to compare with the expertise his pursuers had developed and refined almost from the cradle.

Constantly he urged his now flagging horse on but made little or no attempt to guide it as the sure-footed animal, abetted by experience and generations of inborn instinct, knew far better than he did where the ground was firm and where it was not. Occasionally he lost precious seconds in trying to force his horse to go in certain directions when his horse balked and insisted on choosing his own path.

Bowman looked over his shoulder. It was hopeless, in his heart he knew it was hopeless. When he had left Mas de Lavignolle he had had a lead of several hundred yards over his pursuers: now it was down to just over fifty. The five men behind him were spread out in a shallow fan shape. In the middle was El Brocador who was clearly as superb a horseman as he was a *razateur*. It was equally clear that he had an intimate knowledge of the terrain as from time to time he shouted orders and gestured with an outflung arm to indicate the direction a certain rider should go. On El Brocador's left rode Czerda and Ferenc, still heroically bandaged: on his right rode Simon Searl, an incongruous sight indeed in his clerical garb, and a gypsy whom Bowman could not identify.

Bowman looked ahead again. He could see no sign of succour, no house, no farm, no lonely horseman, nothing: and by this time he had been driven, not, he was grimly aware, without good reason, so far to the west that the cars passing on the main Arles–Saintes-Maries road were no more than little black beetles crawling along the line of the horizon.

He looked over his shoulder again. Thirty yards now, not more. They were no longer riding in a fan shape but were almost in line ahead, bearing down on his left, forcing him now to alter his own line of flight to the right. He was aware that this was being done with some good purpose in mind but, looking ahead, he could see nothing to justify this move. The land ahead appeared as normally variegated as the terrain he had just crossed: there was, directly ahead, an unusually large patch of almost dazzlingly green turf, perhaps a hundred yards long by thirty wide, but, size apart, it was in no way different from scores of others he had passed in the last two or three miles.

His horse, Bowman realized, had run its heart out and was near the end. Sweat-stained, foam-flecked and breathing heavily, it was as exhausted as Bowman himself. Two hundred yards ahead lay that invitingly green stretch of turf and the incongruous thought occurred to Bowman of how pleasant it would be to lie there, shaded, on a peaceful summer's day. He wondered why he didn't give up, the end of this pursuit was as certain as death itself: he would have given up, only he did not know how to set about it.

He looked back again. The five horsemen behind had now adopted a deep crescent shape, the outriders not much more than ten yards behind him. He looked ahead again, saw the greensward not more than twenty yards away, then the thought occurred that Czerda was now within accurate shooting range and Bowman was certain that when the five men returned to the caravans he would not be returning with them. Again he looked backwards and was astonished to see all five men reining in their horses and reining them in strongly at that. He knew something was wrong, terribly wrong, but before he could even start to think about it his own horse stopped abruptly and in an unbelievably short distance, forelegs splayed and sliding on its haunches, at the very edge of the patch of greensward. The horse stopped but Bowman did not. Still looking over his shoulder, he had been taken totally unprepared. He left the saddle, sailed helplessly over the horse's head and landed on the stretch of green grass.

He should have been knocked out, at the worst broken his neck, at the best landed heavily and bruised badly, but none of those things happened because it was at once apparent that the greensward was not what it appeared to be. He did not fall heavily or bounce or roll: instead he landed with a soggy squelching splash on a soft, cushioning and impact-absorbing material. Into this he slowly started to sink.

The five horsemen walked their horses forward, stopped, leaned on their pommels and gazed impassively downwards. Bowman had assumed a vertical position now, although leaning slightly forward. Already, he was hip-deep in the deadly quicksand with the safety of firm land no more than four feet away. Desperately he flailed his arms in an endeavour to reach it but made no progress whatsoever. The watchers remained motionless on their horses: the impassiveness on their faces was frightening in its suggestion of a total implacability.

Bowman sank to the waist. He tried a gentle swimming motion for he realized that frantic struggling was only having the opposite effect to what was intended. It slowed up the sinking but did not stop it: the sucking effect of the quicksand was terrifying in its remorselessness.

He looked at the five men. The total impassivity had disappeared. Czerda was smiling the pleased smile he reserved for occasions like this, Searl was slowly, obscenely licking his lips. All eyes were fixed on Bowman's face, but if he had any thoughts of shouting for help or begging for mercy no sign of it showed in his expressionless face. Nor were there any thoughts of it in his mind. Fear he had known on the battlements of Les Baux and in the bull-ring at Mas de Lavignolle: but here, now, there was no fear. On the other occasions there had been a chance, however slender, of survival, dependent upon his own resourcefulness, his coordination of hand and eye: but here all his hardly won knowledge and experiences and skill, his exceptional reflexes and physical attributes were useless: from a quicksand there can be no escape. It was the end, it was inevitable and he accepted it.

El Brocador looked at Bowman. The quicksand was now almost up to his armpits, only his shoulders, arms and head were now in view. El Brocador studied the impassive face, nodded to himself, turned and looked at Czerda and Searl in turn, distaste and contempt in his face. He unhooked a rope from his pommel.

'One does not do this to a man like this,' he said. 'I am ashamed for us all.' With a skilful flick of his wrist he sent the rope snaking out: it landed precisely midway between Bowman's out-stretched hands.

II

Even the most ardent publicist of the attractions of Saintes-Maries – if any such exists – would find it difficult to rhapsodize over the beauties of the main street of the town which runs from east to west along a sea-front totally invisible behind a high rock wall. It is, like the rest of the town, singularly devoid of scenic, artistic or architectural merit, although on that particular afternoon its drabness was perhaps slightly relieved by the crowds of outlandishly dressed tourists, gypsies, *guardians* and the inevitable fairground booths, shooting galleries, fortune-tellers' stands and souvenir shops that had been haphazardly set up for their benefit and edification.

It was not, one would have thought, a spectacle that would have brought a great deal of gratification to Le Grand Duc's aristocratic soul, yet, as he sat in the sidewalk café outside the Miramar hotel, surveying the scene before him, the expression on his face was mellow to the point of benevolence. Even more oddly in the light of his notoriously undemocratic principles, Carita, his chauffeuse, was seated beside him. Le Grand Duc picked up a litre carafe of red wine, poured a large amount in a large glass he had before him, a thimbleful into a small glass she had before her and smiled benevolently again, not at the passing scene but at a telegram form that he held in his hand. It was clear that Le Grand Duc's exceptional good humour was not because of Saintes-Maries and its inhabitants, but in spite of them. The source of his satisfaction lay in the paper he held in his hand.

'Excellent, my dear Carita, excellent. Exactly what we wished to know. By Jove, they have moved fast.' He contemplated the paper again and sighed. 'It's gratifying, most gratifying, when one's guesses turn out to be one hundred per cent accurate.'

'Yours always are, Monsieur le Duc.'

'Eh? What was that? Yes, yes, of course. Help yourself to some more wine.' Le Grand Duc had temporarily lost interest in both the telegram and Carita, and was gazing thoughtfully at a large black Mercedes that had just pulled up a few feet away. The Chinese couple whom Le Grand Duc had last seen on the hotel patio in Arles emerged and made for the hotel entrance. They passed by within a few feet of Le Grand Duc's table. The man nodded, his wife smiled faintly and Le Grand Duc, not to be outdone, bowed gravely. He watched them as they went inside, then turned to Carita.

'Czerda should be here soon with Bowman. I have decided that this is an inadvisable place for a rendez-vous. Too public, too public by far. There's a big lay-by about one mile north of the town. Have Czerda stop there and wait for me while you come back here for me.'

She smiled and rose to leave but Le Grand Duc raised a hand.

'One last thing before you go. I have a very urgent phone call to make and I wish it made in complete privacy. Tell the manager I wish to see him. At once.'

III

Le Hobenaut, Tangevac and Daymel were still in their bunks, still manacled to the caravan wall. Bowman, his pierrot suit now removed and his *guardian* clothes saturated and still dripping, lay on the floor with his hands bound behind his back. Cecile and Lila were seated on a bench under the watchful eyes of Ferenc and Masaine. Czerda, El Brocador and Searl were seated at a table: they weren't talking and they looked very unhappy. Their expression of unhappiness deepened as they listened to the measured tread of footsteps mounting the steps of the caravan. Le Grand Duc made his customary impressive entry. He surveyed the three seated men coldly.

'We have to move quickly.' His voice was brusque, authoritative and as cold as his face. 'I have received cabled information that the police are becoming suspicious and may well by this time be certain of us – thanks to you, Czerda, and that bungling fool Searl there. Are you mad, Czerda?'

'I do not understand, sir.'

'That's precisely it. You understand nothing. You were going to kill Bowman before he'd told us how he broke our ring, who his contacts are, where my eighty thousand francs are. Worst of all, you cretins, you were going to kill him publicly. Can't you see the enormous publicity that would have received? Secrecy, stealth, those are my watch-words.'

'We know where the eighty thousand francs are, sir.' Czerda tried to salvage something from the wreck.

'Do we? *Do* we? I suspect you have been fooled again, Czerda. But that can wait. Do you know what will happen to you all if the French police get you?' Silence. 'Do you know the rigorous penalties French courts impose on kidnappers?' Still silence. 'Not one of you here can hope to escape with less than ten years in prison. And if they can trace Alexandre's murder to you . . .'

Le Grand Duc looked at El Brocador and the four gypsies in turn. From the expressions on their faces it was quite clear that they knew what would happen if the murder could be traced to them.

'Very well, then. From this moment on your futures and your lives depend entirely on doing exactly what I order – it is not beyond my powers to rescue you from the consequences of your own folly. Exactly. Is that understood?'

All five men nodded. No one said anything.

'Very well. Unchain those men. Untie Bowman. If the police find them like that – well, it's all over. We use guns and knives to guard them from now on. Bring all their womenfolk in here – I want all our eggs in one basket. Go over our proposed plans, Searl. Go over them briefly and clearly so that even the most incompetent nincompoop, and that includes you, can understand what we have in mind. Bring me some beer, someone.'

Searl cleared his throat self-consciously and looked distinctly unhappy. The arrogance, the quietly cold competence with which he'd confronted Czerda in the confessional booth that morning had vanished as if it had never existed.

'Rendez-vous any time between last night and Monday night. Fast motor-boat waiting—'

Le Grand Duc sighed in despair and held up a hand.

'Briefly and *clearly*, Searl. Clearly. Rendez-vous where, you fool? With whom?'

'Sorry, sir.' The Adam's apple in the thin scraggy neck

bobbed up and down as Searl swallowed nervously. 'Off Palavas in the Gulf of Aigues-Mortes. Freighter *Canton*.'

'Bound for?'

'Canton.'

'Precisely.'

'Recognition signals—'

'Never mind that. The motor-boat?'

'At Aigues-Mortes on the Canal du Rhône à Sète. I was going to have it moved down to Le Grau du Roi tomorrow – I didn't think – I—'

'You never have done,' Le Grand Duc said wearily. 'Why aren't those damned women here? And those manacles still fixed? Hurry.' For the first time he relaxed and smiled slightly. 'I'll wager our friend Bowman still doesn't know who our three other friends are. Eh, Searl?'

'I can tell him?' Searl asked eagerly. The prospect of climbing out of the hot seat and transferring the spotlight elsewhere was clearly an attractive one.

'Suit yourself.' Le Grand Duc drank deeply of his beer. 'Can it matter now?'

'Of course not.' Searl smiled widely. 'Let me introduce Count le Hobenaut, Henri Tangevec and Serge Daymel. The three leading rocket fuel experts on the other side of the Iron Curtain. The Chinese wanted them badly, they have been so far unable to develop a vehicle to carry their nuclear warheads. Those men could do it. But there wasn't a single land border between China and Russia that could be used, not a single neutral country that was friendly to both the great powers and wouldn't have looked too closely at irregular happenings. So Czerda brought them out. To the West. No one would ever dream that such men would defect to the West – the West has its own fuel experts. And, at the frontiers, no one ever asks questions of gypsies. Of course, if the three men had clever ideas, their wives would have been killed. If the women got clever ideas, the men would have been killed.'

'Or so the women were told,' Le Grand Duc said contemptuously. 'The last thing that we wanted was that any harm should come to those men. But women – they'll believe anything.' He permitted himself a small smile of satisfaction. 'The simplicity – if I may say so myself, the staggering simplicity of true genius. Ah, the women. Aigues-Mortes, and with speed. Tell your other caravans, Czerda, that you will rendez-vous with them in the morning in Saintes-Maries. Come, Lila, my dear.'

'With you?' She stared at him in revulsion. 'You must be mad. Go with *you*?'

'Appearances must be maintained, now more than ever. What suspicion is going to attach to a man with so beautiful a young lady by his side? Besides, it's very hot and I require someone to hold my parasol.'

Just over an hour later, still fuming and tight-lipped, she lowered the parasol as the green Rolls-Royce drew up outside the frowning walls of Aigues-Mortes, the most perfectly preserved Crusader walled city in Europe. Le Grand Duc descended from the car and waited till Czerda had brought the breakdown truck towing the caravan to a halt.

'Wait here,' he ordered. 'I shall not be long.' He nodded to the Rolls. 'Keep a sharp eye on Miss Delafont there. You apart, no others are on any account to show themselves.'

He glanced up the road towards Saintes-Maries. Momentarily, it was deserted. He marched quickly away and entered the bleak and forbidding town by the north gate, turned right into the car-park and took up position in the concealment of a barrel organ. The operator, a decrepit ancient who, in spite of the heat of the day, was wearing two overcoats and a felt hat, looked up from the stool where he had been drowsing and scowled. Le Grand Duc gave him ten francs. The operator stopped scowling, adjusted a switch and began to crank a handle: the screeching cacophonous result was an atonal travesty of a waltz that no composer alive or dead would ever have acknowledged as his. Le Grand Duc winced, but remained where he was.

Within two minutes a black Mercedes passed in through the archway, turned right and stopped. The Chinese couple got out, looked neither to left nor right, and walked hurriedly down the main street – indeed, Aigues-Mortes's only street – towards the tiny café-lined square near the centre of the town. More leisurely and at a discreet distance Le Grand Duc followed.

The Chinese couple reached the square and halted uncertainly on a corner by a souvenir shop, not far from the statue of St Louis. No sooner had they done so than four large men in plain dark clothes emerged from the shop, two from each door, and closed in on them. One of the men showed the Chinese man something cupped in the palm of his hand. The Chinese man gesticulated and appeared to protest violently but the four large men just shook their heads firmly and led the couple away to a pair of waiting black Citroëns.

Le Grand Duc nodded his head in what could not easily have been mistaken for anything other than satisfaction, turned and retraced his steps to the waiting car and caravan.

Less than sixty seconds' drive took them to a small jetty on the Canal du Rhône à Sète, a canal that links the Rhône to the Mediterranean at Le Grau du Roi and runs parallel to the western wall of Aigues-Mortes. At the end of the jetty was moored a thirty-five-foot power-boat with a large glassed-in cabin and an only slightly smaller cockpit aft. From the lines of the broad flaring bows it appeared to be a vessel capable of something unusual in terms of speed.

The Rolls and the caravan pulled clear off the road and halted so that the rear of the caravan was less than six feet from the head of the jetty. The transfer of the prisoners from the caravan to the boat was performed smoothly, expeditiously and in such a fashion that it could have aroused no suspicion in even the most inquisitive of bystanders: in point of fact the nearest person was a rod fisherman a hundred yards away and his entire attention was obviously concentrated on what was happening at the end of his line some feet below the surface of the canal. Ferenc and Searl, each with a barely concealed pistol, stood on the jetty near the top of a short gangway while Le Grand Duc and Czerda, similarly unostentatiously armed, stood on the poop of the boat while first the three scientists, then their womenfolk, then Bowman, Cecile and Lila filed aboard. Under the threat of the guns they took up position on the settees lining the side of the cabin.

Ferenc and Searl entered the cabin, Searl advancing to the helmsman's position. For a moment Le Grand Duc and Masaine remained in the cockpit, checking that they were quite unobserved then Le Grand Duc entered the cabin, pocketed his gun and rubbed his hands in satisfaction.

'Excellent, excellent, excellent.' He sounded positively cheerful. 'Everything, as always, under control. Start the engines, Searl!' He turned and poked his head through the cabin doorway. 'Cast off, Masaine!'

Searl pressed buttons and the twin engines started up with a deep powerful throb of sound, but a sound by no means loud enough to muffle a short sharp exclamation of pain: the sound emanated from Le Grand Duc, who was still looking aft through the doorway.

'Your own gun in your own kidney,' Bowman said. 'No one to move or you die.' He looked at Ferenc and Czerda and Searl and El Brocador. At least three of them, he knew, were armed. He said: 'Tell Searl to stop the engines.'

Searl stopped the engines without having to have the message relayed through Le Grand Duc.

'Tell Masaine to come here,' Bowman said. 'Tell him I've got a gun in your kidney.' He looked round the cabin; no one had moved. 'Tell him to come at once or I'll pull the trigger.'

'You wouldn't dare!'

'You'll be all right,' Bowman said soothingly. 'Most people can get by on one kidney.'

He jabbed the gun again and Le Grand Duc gasped in pain. He said hoarsely: 'Masaine! Come here at once. Put your gun away. Bowman has his gun on me.'

There was a few seconds' silence, then Masaine appeared in the doorway. No profound thinker at the best of times, he was obviously uncertain as to what to do: the sight of Czerda, Ferenc, Searl and El Brocador busy doing nothing convinced him that nothing was, for the moment, the wise and prudent course of action. He moved into the cabin.

'Now we come up against the question of the delicate balances of power,' Bowman said conversationally. He was still pale and haggard, he felt unutterably tired and stiff and sore all over: but he felt a prince compared to the condition he'd been in two hours previously. 'A question of checks and balances. How much influence and authority can I exert on you standing here with this gun in my hand? How much of my will can I impose? So much – but only so much.'

He pulled Le Grand Duc back by the shoulder, stepped to one side and watched Le Grand Duc collapse heavily on a settee, a well-made settee which didn't break. Le Grand Duc glared at Bowman, the aristocratic voltage in the blue eyes turned up to maximum power: Bowman remained unshrivelled.

'It's difficult to believe just looking at you,' Bowman went on to Le Grand Duc, 'but you're almost certainly the most intelligent of your band of ruffians. Not, of course, that that would call for any great intelligence. I have a gun here and it is in my hand. There are four others here who also have guns and although they're not in their hands at the present moment it wouldn't take very long for the guns to get there. If it came to a fight, I think it extremely unlikely that I could get all four before one of you – more probably two – got me. I am not a Wild Bill Hickock. Moreover, there are eight innocent people here – nine, if you count me – and a gun-fight in this enclosed space would almost certainly result in some of them being hurt, even killed. I wouldn't like that any more than I would like being shot myself.'

'Get to the point,' Le Grand Duc growled.

'It's obvious, surely. What demands can I make upon you that wouldn't be too great to precipitate this gun-fight that I'm sure we all want to avoid? If I told you to hand over your guns, would you, quietly and tamely, with the knowledge that long prison sentences and probably indictments for murder awaited you all? I doubt it. If I said I'll let you go but take the scientists and their women, would you go along with that? Again, I doubt it, for they would be living evidence of your crimes, with the result that if you set foot anywhere in Western Europe you'd finish in prison and if you set foot in Eastern Europe you'd be lucky to end up in a Siberian prison camp as the Communists aren't too keen on people who kidnap their top scientists. In fact, there'd be no place left for you in any part of Europe. You'd just have to go on the *Canton* and sail all the way home with her and I don't think you'd find life in China all it's cracked up to be – by the Chinese, of course.

'On the other hand, I doubt whether you'd be prepared to fight to the death to prevent the departure of the two young ladies and myself. They're only ciphers, a couple of romantically minded and rather empty-headed young holidaymakers who thought it rather fun to get mixed up in these dark goings on.' Bowman carefully avoided looking at the two girls. 'I admit that it is possible for me to start trouble, but I don't see I would get very far: it would be only my word against yours, there wouldn't be a shred of evidence I could offer and there's no way I can think of how you could be tied up with the murder in the cave. The only evidence lies in the scientists and their wives and they would be half-way to China before I could do anything. Well?'

'I accept your reasoning,' Le Grand Duc said heavily. 'Try to make us give ourselves or the scientists up – or their wives – and you'd never leave this boat alive. You and those two young fools there are, as you say, another matter. You can arouse suspicion, but that's all you can do: better that than have two or three of my men die uselessly.'

'It might even be you,' Bowman said.

'The possibility had not escaped me.'

'You're my number one choice of hostage and safe conduct,' Bowman said.

'I rather thought I might be.' Le Grand Duc rose with obvious reluctance to his feet.

'I don't like this,' Czerda said. 'What if—'

'You want to be the first to die?' Le Grand Duc asked wearily. 'Leave the thinking to me, Czerda.'

Czerda, obviously ill at ease, said no more. At a gesture from Bowman the two girls left the cabin and climbed the gangway. Bowman, walking backwards with his gun a few inches from Le Grand Duc's midriff, followed. At the top of the gangway Bowman said to the girls: 'Get back and out of sight.'

He waited ten seconds then said to Le Grand Duc: 'Turn round.' Le Grand Duc turned. Bowman gave him a hefty shove that set him stumbling, almost falling, down the gangway. Bowman threw himself flat: there was always the off-chance of someone or ones down there changing their minds. But no shots were fired, there was no sound of footsteps on the gangway. Bowman raised a cautious head. The engines had started up again.

The power-boat was already twenty yards away and accelerating. Bowman rose quickly and, followed by Cecile and Lila, ran to the Rolls. Carita gazed at him in astonishment.

'Out!' Bowman said.

Carita opened her mouth to protest but Bowman was in no mood for protests. He jerked open the door and practically lifted her on to the road. Immediately afterwards he was behind the wheel himself.

'Wait!' Cecile said. 'Wait! We're coming with—'

'Not this time.' He leaned down and plucked Cecile's handbag from her. She stared at him, slightly open-mouthed, but said nothing. He went on: 'Go into the town. Phone the police in Saintes-Maries, tell them there's a sick girl in a green-and-white caravan in a lay-by a kilometre and a half north of the town and that they're to get her to a hospital at once. Don't tell them who you are, don't tell them a single thing more than that. Just hang up.' He nodded at Lila and Carita. 'Those two will do for a start.'

'Do for what?' She was, understandably, bemused.

'Bridesmaids.'

The road between Aigues-Mortes and Le Grau du Roi is only a few kilometres long and, for the most part, it parallels the canal at a distance of a few feet: the only boundary line between them, if such it can be called, is a thin line of tall reeds. It was through those reeds, less than a minute after starting up the Rolls, that Bowman caught his first glimpse of the power-boat, fewer than a hundred yards ahead. It was already travelling at an illegally high speed, its stern dug deep into the water, spray flying high and wide from the deflectors on the bows: the wash set up by the wake of its passing was sending waves high up both sides of the canal banks.

Searl was at the wheel, Masaine, El Brocador and Ferenc were seated but keeping a watchful eye on the passengers, while Le Grand Duc and Czerda were conversing near the after door of the cabin. Czerda still looked most unhappy.

He said: 'But how can you be *sure* that he can bring no harm to us?'

'I'm sure.' The passage of time had restored Le Grand Duc to his old confident self.

'But he'll go to the police. He's bound to.'

'So? You heard what he said himself. His solitary word against all of ours? With all his evidence half-way to China?

They'll think he's mad. Even if they don't, there's nothing in the world they can prove.'

'I still don't like it,' Czerda said stubbornly. 'I think—'

'Leave the thinking to me,' Le Grand Duc said curtly. 'Good God!'.

There was a splintering of glass, the sound of a shot and a harsh cry of pain from Searl, who abandoned the wheel in favour of clutching his left shoulder. The boat swerved violently and headed straight for the left bank: it would unquestionably have struck it had not Czerda, although older than any of his companions and the farthest from the wheel, reacted with astonishing speed, hurled himself forward and spun the wheel hard to starboard. He succeeded in preventing the power-boat from burying – and probably crushing – its bows in the bank, but wasn't in time to prevent the wildly slewing boat from crashing its port side heavily against the bank with an impact that threw all who were standing, except Czerda, and quite a few who were seated, to the deck. It was at that instant that Czerda glanced through a side window and saw Bowman, at the wheel of the Rolls-Royce and less than five yards distant on the paralleling road, taking careful aim with Le Grand Duc's pistol through an opened window.

'Down!' shouted Czerda. He was the first down himself. 'Flat on the floor.'

Again there came the sound of smashing glass, again the simultaneous report from the pistol, but no one was hurt. Czerda rose to a crouch, eased the throttle, handed the wheel over to Masaine, and joined Le Grand Duc and Ferenc who had already edged out, on all fours, to the poop-deck. All three men peered cautiously over the gun-wale, then stood upright, thoughtfully holding their guns behind their backs.

The Rolls had dropped thirty yards back. Bowman was being blocked by a farm tractor towing a large four-wheeled trailer, and balked from overtaking by several cars approaching from the south.

'Faster,' Czerda said to Masaine. 'Not too fast – keep just ahead of that tractor. That's it. That's it.' He watched the last of the north-bound cars go by on the other side of the road. 'Here he comes now.'

The long green nose of the Rolls appeared in sight beyond

the tractor. The three men in the cockpit levelled their guns and the tractor-driver, seeing them, braked and swerved so violently that he came to a rest with the right front wheel of his tractor overhanging the bank of the canal. Its abrupt braking and swerve brought the entire length of the car completely and suddenly in sight. Bowman, gun cocked in hand and ready to use, saw what was about to happen, dropped the gun and threw himself below the level of the door sills. He winced as bullet after bullet thudded into the bodywork of the Rolls. The windscreen suddenly starred and became completely opaque. Bowman thrust his fist through the bottom of the glass, kicked the accelerator down beyond the detente and accelerated swiftly away. It was obvious that, with the element of surprise gone, he stood no chance whatsoever against the three armed men in the poop. He wondered vaguely how Le Grand Duc felt about the sudden drop in the resale market value of his Rolls.

He drove at high speed past the arena on his left into the town of Grau du Roi, skidding the car to a halt at the approaches to the swing bridge that crossed the canal and connected the two sides of the town. He opened Cecile's bag, peeled money from the roll of Swiss francs he had taken from Czerda's caravan, put the roll back in the bag, thrust the bag into a cubby-hole, hoped to heaven the citizens of Grau du Roi were honest, left the car and ran down the quayside.

He slowed down to a walk as he approached the craft moored along the left bank, just below the bridge. It was a wide-beamed, high-prowed fishing boat, of wooden and clearly very solid construction, that had seen its best days some years ago. Bowman approached a grey-jerseyed fisherman of middle age who was sitting on a bollard and lethargically mending a net.

'That's a fine boat you've got there,' Bowman said in his best admiring tourist fashion. 'Is it for rent?'

The fisherman was taken aback by the directness of the approach. Matters involving finance were customarily approached with a great deal more finesse.

'Fourteen knots and built like a tank,' the owner said proudly. 'The finest wooden-hulled fishing boat in the south of France. Twin Perkins diesels. Like lightning! And so strong.

But only for charter, m'sieur. And even then only when the fishing is bad.'

'Too bad, too bad.' Bowman took out some Swiss francs and fingered them. 'Not even for an hour? I have urgent reasons, believe me.' He had, too. In the distance he could hear the rising note of Le Grand Duc's power-boat.

The fisherman screwed up his eyes as if in thought: it is not easy to ascertain the denomination of foreign banknotes at a distance of four feet. But sailors' eyes are traditionally keen. He stood and slapped his thigh.

'I will make an exception,' he announced, then added cunningly: 'But I will have to come with you, of course.'

'Of course. I would have expected nothing else.' Bowman handed over two one-thousand Swiss franc notes. There was a legerdemain flick of the wrist and the notes disappeared from sight.

'When does m'sieur wish to leave?'

'Now.' He could have had the boat anyway, Bowman knew, but he preferred Czerda's banknotes to the waving of a gun as a means of persuasion: that he would eventually have to wave his gun around he did not doubt.

They cast off, went aboard and the fisherman started the engines while Bowman peered casually aft. The sound of the power-boat's engines was very close now. Bowman turned and watched the fisherman push the throttles forward as he gave the wheel a turn to starboard. The fishing boat began to move slowly away from the quayside.

'It doesn't seem too difficult,' Bowman observed. 'To handle it, I mean.'

'To you, no. But it takes a lifetime of knowledge to handle such a vessel.'

'Could I try now?'

'No, no. Impossible. Perhaps when we get to the sea—'

'I'm afraid it will have to be now. Please.'

'In five minutes—'

'I'm sorry. I really am.' Bowman produced his pistol, pointed with it to the starboard for'ard corner of the wheelhouse. 'Please sit down there.'

The fisherman stared at him, relinquished the wheel and moved across to the corner of the wheelhouse. He said quietly, as Bowman took over the wheel: 'I knew I was a fool. I like money too much, I think.'

'Don't we all.' Bowman glanced over his shoulder. The power-boat was less than a hundred yards from the bridge. He opened the throttles wide and the fishing boat began to surge forward. Bowman dug into his pocket, came up with the last three thousand francs of Czerda's money that he had on him and threw it across to the man. 'This will make you even more foolish.'

The fisherman stared at the notes, made no attempt to pick them up. He whispered: 'When I am dead, you will take it away. Pierre des Jardins is not a fool.'

'When you are dead?'

'When you kill me. With that pistol.' He smiled sadly. 'It is a wonderful thing to have a pistol, no?'

'Yes.' Bowman reversed hold on his pistol, caught it by the barrel and threw it gently across to the fisherman. 'Do you feel wonderful too, now?'

The man stared at the pistol, picked it up, pointed it experimentally at Bowman, laid it down, picked up and pocketed the money, picked up the pistol a second time, rose, crossed to the wheel and replaced the pistol in Bowman's pocket. He said: 'I'm afraid I am not very good at firing those things, m'sieur.'

'Neither am I. Look behind you. Do you see a power-boat coming up?'

Pierre looked. The power-boat was no more than a hundred yards behind. He said: 'I see it. I know it. My friend Jean—'

'Sorry. Later about your friend.' Bowman pointed ahead to where a freighter was riding out in the gulf. 'That's the freighter *Canton*. A communist vessel bound for China. Behind us, in the power-boat, are evil men who wish to put aboard that vessel people who do not wish to go there. It is my wish to stop them.'

'Why?'

'If you have to ask why I'll take this pistol from my pocket and make you sit down again.' Bowman looked quickly behind him: the power-boat was barely more than fifty yards behind.

'You are British, of course?'

'Yes.'

'You are an agent of your government?'

'Yes.'

'What we call your Secret Service?'

'Yes.'

'You are known to our government?'

'I am to your Deuxième Bureau. Their boss is my boss.'

'Boss?'

'Chief. *Chef*.'

Pierre sighed. 'It has to be true. And you wish to stop this boat coming up?' Bowman nodded. 'Then please move over. This is a job for an expert.'

Bowman nodded again, took the gun from his pocket, moved to the starboard side of the wheelhouse and wound down the window. The power-boat was less than ten feet astern, not more than twenty feet away on a parallel course and coming up fast. Czerda was at the wheel now, with Le Grand Duc by his side. Bowman raised his pistol, then lowered it again as the fishing boat leaned over sharply and arrowed in on the power-boat. Three seconds later the heavy oaken bows of the fishing-boat smashed heavily into the port quarter of the other vessel.

'That was, perhaps, more or less what you had in mind, m'sieur,' Pierre asked.

'More or less,' Bowman admitted. 'Now please listen. There is something you should know.'

The two boats moved apart on parallel courses. The power-boat, being the faster, pulled ahead. Inside its cabin there was considerable confusion.

'Who was that madman?' Le Grand Duc demanded.

'Bowman!' Czerda spoke with certainty.

'Guns out!' Le Grand Duc shouted. 'Guns out! Get him!'

'No.'

'No? No? You dare countermand—'

'I smell petrol. In the air. One shot – poof. Ferenc, go and check the port tank.' Ferenc departed and returned within ten seconds.

'Well?'

'The tank is ruptured. At the bottom. The fuel is nearly gone.' Even as he spoke the port engine faltered, spluttered and stopped. Czerda and Le Grand Duc looked at each other: nothing was said.

Both boats had by now cleared the harbour and were out in the open sea of the Gulf of Aigues-Mortes. The power-boat, on one engine now, had dropped back until it was almost parallel with the fishing boat. Bowman nodded to Pierre, who nodded in turn. He spun the wheel rapidly, their vessel angled in sharply, they made violent contact again in exactly the same place as previously, then sheered off.

'God damn it all!' Aboard the power-boat Le Grand Duc was almost livid with fury and making no attempt to conceal it. 'He's holed us! He's holed us! Can't you avoid him?'

'With one engine, it is very difficult to steer.' Under the circumstances, Czerda's restraint was commendable. He was in no way exaggerating. The combination of a dead port engine and a holed port quarter made the maintenance of a straight course virtually impossible: Czerda was no seaman and even with his best efforts the power-boat was now pursuing a very erratic course indeed.

'Look!' Le Grand Duc said sharply. 'What's that?'

About three miles away, not more than half-way towards Palavas, a large and very old-fashioned freighter, almost stopped in the water, was sending a message by signalling lamp.

'It's the *Canton*!' Searl said excitedly. He so far forgot himself as to stop rubbing the now padded flesh wound on top of his shoulder. 'The *Canton*! We must send a recognition signal. Three long, three short.'

'No!' Le Grand Duc was emphatic. 'Are you mad? We mustn't get them involved in this. The international repercussions – look out!'

The fishing boat was veering again. Le Grand Duc and Ferenc rushed to the cockpit and loosed off several shots. The windows in the wheel-house of the fishing boat starred and broke, but Bowman and Pierre had already dropped to the deck which Le Grand Duc and Ferenc had to do at almost exactly the same moment as the heavy oaken stem of the fishing boat crashed into the port quarter at precisely the spot where they were standing.

Five times inside the next two minutes the manoeuvre was

repeated, five times the power-boat shuddered under the crushing assaults. By now, at Le Grand Duc's orders, all firing had ceased: ammunition was almost exhausted.

'We must keep the last bullets for when and where they will do the most good.' Le Grand Duc had become very calm. 'Next time—'

'The *Canton* is leaving!' Searl shouted. 'Look, she has turned away.'

They looked. The *Canton* was indeed turning away, beginning to move with increasing speed through the water.

'What else did you expect?' Le Grand Duc asked. 'Never fear, we shall see her again.'

'What do you mean?' Czerda demanded.

'Later. As I was saying—'

'We're sinking!' Searl's voice was almost a scream. 'We're sinking!' He was in no way exaggerating: the power-boat was now deep in the water, the sea pouring in through gaps torn in the hull by the bows of the fishing boat.

'I am aware of that,' Le Grand Duc said. He turned to Czerda. 'They're coming again. Hard a starboard – to your right, quickly. Ferenc, Searl, El Brocador, come with me.'

'My shoulder,' Searl wailed.

'Never mind your shoulder. Come with me.'

The four men stood just inside the doorway of the cabin as the fishing boat came at them again. But this time the power-boat, though sluggish and far from responsive because of its depth in the water, had succeeded in turning away enough to reduce the impact to the extent that the two boats merely grazed each other. As the wheelhouse of the fishing boat passed by the cabin of the power-boat, Le Grand Duc and his three men rushed out into the cockpit. Le Grand Duc waited his moment then, with that speed and agility so surprising in a man of his bulk, stood on the gunwale and flung himself on to the poop of the fishing boat. Within two seconds the others had followed.

Ten seconds after that Bowman turned round sharply as the port door of the wheelhouse opened abruptly and Ferenc and Searl stood framed there, both with guns in their hands.

'No.' Bowman spun again to locate the voice behind him. He hadn't far to look. The guns of Le Grand Duc and El

Brocador were less than a foot from his face. Le Grand Duc said: 'Enough is enough?'

Bowman nodded. 'Enough is enough.'

— 10 —

FIFTEEN MINUTES later, with the first shades of evening beginning to fall, the fishing boat, a curiously unperturbed Pierre des Jardins at the wheel, moved placidly up the Canal du Rhône à Sète. The three scientists and their womenfolk, the last of whom had been hauled aboard only seconds before the power-boat had sunk, were seated on the foredeck under the concealed guns of the gypsies, for all the world like vacation trippers enjoying a leisurely cruise in the warm summer evening. All the glass had been knocked out from the broken windows and the few bullet holes in the woodwork of the wheelhouse were discreetly camouflaged by El Brocador and Masaine, who were leaning negligently against the starboard side of the structure. Pierre apart, the only two other occupants of the wheelhouse were Bowman and Le Grand Duc, the latter with a gun in his hand.

A few kilometres up the canal they passed by the tractor and trailer that had so abruptly left the road when the shooting contest between the Rolls and the power-boat had begun. The tractor was as it had been, a front wheel still over-hanging the canal: clearly and understandably, the driver had deemed it wiser to wait for assistance rather than risk a watery grave for his tractor by trying to extricate it under its own power. The driver, oddly enough, was still there, pacing up and down with a legitimately thunderous look on his face.

Czerda joined the three men in the wheelhouse. He said worriedly: 'I do not like it, I do not like it at all. It is much too quiet. Perhaps we are going to some kind of trap. Surely some person—'

'Does that make you feel happier?' Le Grand Duc pointed in the direction of Aigues-Mortes: two black police cars, sirens wailing and blue lights flashing, were approaching at high speed. 'Something tells me that our friend the tractor driver has been complaining to someone.'

Le Grand Duc's guess proved to be correct. The police cars swept by and almost at once started slowing as the tractor driver stood in the middle of the road and frantically waved his arms. They stopped and uniformed figures jumped out of the car and surrounded the gesticulating tractor driver who was obviously retelling his story with a great deal of verve and gusto.

'Well, if the police are bothering somebody else, they can't very well be bothering us at the same time,' Le Grand Duc observed philosophically. 'Happier now, Czerda?'

'No,' Czerda said and looked as if he meant it. 'Two things. Dozens of people, hundreds for all I know, must have seen what was happening out in the gulf. Why did no one stop us on the way in? Why did no one report what was happening to the police?'

'Quite frankly, I don't know,' Le Grand Duc said thoughtfully. 'I can guess, though. Same thing happens time and again – when large numbers of people see something happening they invariably leave it to someone else to do something about it. Why, there have been cases of pedestrians watching a man being beaten to death in the street and not lifting a hand to help. Mankind is curiously apathetic about that sort of thing. Maybe it's a natural reluctance to step into the limelight. I do not profess to know. All that matters is that we came up the harbour without causing an eyebrow to be lifted. Your other question? You had two?'

'Yes.' Czerda was grim. 'What in God's name are we going to do now?'

'That is no problem.' Le Grand Duc smiled. 'Did I not tell you that we would see the good ship *Canton* again?'

'Yes, but how—'

'How long will it take us to drive to Port le Bouc?'

'Port le Bouc?' Czerda furrowed his brow. 'With the caravan and truck?'

'How else?'

'Two and a half hours. Not more than three. Why?'

'Because that's where the *Canton* has instructions to await us if any difficulty arose at the Palavas rendez-vous. It will remain there until noon tomorrow – and we will be there tonight. Don't you know by now, Czerda, that I always have another string to my bow? Many strings, in fact. And there, tonight, the scientists and their women will be taken aboard. So will Bowman. And so, to eliminate any possibility of risk whatsoever, will the two young ladies and, I'm afraid, this unfortunate fisherman here.' Pierre des Jardins glanced at Le Grand Duc, lifted an eyebrow, then concentrated on his task again: it was a minuscule reaction for a man listening to what was virtually a death sentence. 'And then, Czerda, you and your men will be as free as the air for when Bowman and his three friends arrive in China they will simply disappear and never be heard of again. The only witnesses against you will be gone for ever and no breath of suspicion will ever attach itself to you or your men on either side of the Iron Curtain.'

'If I have ever questioned you in the past, I apologize.' Czerda spoke slowly, almost reverently. 'This is genius.' He looked as a man might look after the Forth Bridge had been lifted off his back.

'Elementary, elementary.' Le Grand Duc waved a disparaging hand. 'Now, then. We shall be in sight of the jetty shortly and we don't want to give the young ladies any shocks to their delicate nervous systems, the kind of shock, for instance, that might prompt them to drive away at speed with the truck and caravan before we even reach the jetty. Everybody into the fish-hold now and keep out of sight till the word is given. You and I will remain here – seated, of course – while Bowman takes the vessel alongside. Understood?'

'Understood.' Czerda looked at him admiringly. 'You think of everything!'

'I try,' Le Grand Duc said modestly. 'I try.'

The three girls with a youngster seated on a scooter were at the head of the jetty as Bowman, apparently alone, brought the boat alongside. They ran down, secured the ropes he threw them and jumped aboard. Cecile and Lila were half-smiling, half-apprehensive, wondering what news he bore: Carita remained in the background, aloof and rather remote.

'Well?' Cecile demanded. 'Well, tell us. What happened?'

'I'm sorry,' Bowman said. 'Things have gone wrong.'

'Not for us,' Le Grand Duc said jovially. He stood up, gun in hand, accompanied by Czerda, similarly equipped, and beamed at the girls. 'Not really, I must say. How nice to see you again, my dear Carita. Had a pleasant time with the two young ladies?'

'No,' Carita said shortly. 'They wouldn't speak to me.'

'Prejudice, sheer prejudice. Right, Czerda, everyone on deck and in the caravan inside a minute.' He looked towards the head of the jetty. 'And who is that youth with the scooter?'

'That's José!' Czerda was as near a mood of excited anticipation as it would ever be possible for him to achieve. 'The boy I sent to get the money that Bowman stole from me – from us, I mean.' He stepped out on deck and waved an arm. 'José! José!'

José swung his leg over the scooter, came down the jetty and jumped aboard. He was a tall thin youth with an enormous shock of black hair, beady eyes and a prematurely knowing expression.

'The money?' Czerda asked. 'You have the money?'

'What money?'

'Of course, of course. To you, only a brown paper parcel.' Czerda smiled indulgently. 'But it was the right key?'

'I don't know.' José's mental processes quite evidently knew nothing about the intelligent expression on his face.

'What do you mean, you don't know?'

'I don't know whether it was the right key or the wrong key,' José explained patiently. 'All I know is that there are no safe-deposit boxes in the railway station in Arles.'

There was a fairly lengthy silence during which a number of thoughts, none of them particularly pleasant, passed through the minds of several of those present, then Bowman cleared his throat and said apologetically: 'I'm afraid this is all rather my fault. That was the key to my suitcase.'

There was another silence, more or less of the same length, then Le Grand Duc said with immense restraint: 'The key to your suitcase. I would have expected nothing else. Where are the eighty thousand francs, Mr Bowman?'

'Seventy thousand. I'm afraid I had to deduct a little of it. Current expenses, you know.' He nodded to Cecile. 'That dress alone cost me—'

'Where are they?' Le Grand Duc shouted. He was through with restraint for the day. 'The seventy thousand francs?'

'Ah yes. Well, now.' Bowman shook his head. 'There's so much happened since last night—'

'Czerda!' Le Grand Duc was back on balance again but it was a close thing. 'Put your pistol to Miss Dubois's head. I shall count three.'

'Don't bother,' Bowman said. 'I left it in the Les Baux caves. By Alexandre.'

'*By* Alexandre?'

'I'm not an idiot,' Bowman said tiredly. 'I knew the police might be there this morning. Rather, would be there and might find Alexandre. But it's close by.'

Le Grand Duc gave him a long, thoughtful stare then turned to Czerda. 'This would be only a minor detour on our way to Port le Bouc?'

'Another twenty minutes. No more.' He nodded towards Bowman. 'The canal here is deep. Do we need him along, sir?'

'Only,' Le Grand Duc said ominously, 'until we discover whether he's telling the truth or not.'

II

Night had fallen when Czerda pulled up in the lay-by at the head of the Valley of Hell. Le Grand Duc, who, along with El Brocador, had been Czerda's passenger in the front of the towing truck, got out, stretched himself and said: 'The ladies we will leave here. Masaine will stay behind to guard them. All the others will come with us.'

Czerda looked his puzzlement. 'We require so many?'

'I have my purpose.' Le Grand Duc was at his most enigmatic. 'Do you question my judgement?'

'Now? Never!'

'Very well, then.'

Moments later a large group of people were moving through the terrifying vastness of the tomb-like caverns. There were eleven of them in all – Czerda, Ferenc, Searl, El Brocador, the three scientists, the two girls, Bowman and Le Grand Duc. Several carried torches, their beams reflecting weirdly, whitely, off the great limestone walls. Czerda led the way, briskly, confidently, until he came to a cavern where a broken landfall led up to the vague outline of a starlit sky above. He advanced to the jumbled base of the landfall and stopped.

'This is the place,' he said.

Le Grand Duc probed with his torch. 'You are sure?'

'I am certain.' Czerda directed his torch towards a mound of stones and rubble. 'Incredible, is it not? Those idiots of police haven't even found him yet!'

Le Grand Duc directed his own torch at the mound. 'You mean—'

'Alexandre. This is where we buried him.'

'Alexandre is of no concern any more.' Le Grand Duc turned to Bowman. 'The money, if you please.'

'Ah, yes. The money.' Bowman shrugged and smiled. 'This is the end of the road, I'm afraid. There is no money.'

'What!' Le Grand Duc advanced and thrust the barrel of his gun into Bowman's ribs. 'No money?'

'It's there, all right. In a bank. In Arles.'

'You fooled us?' Czerda said incredulously. 'You brought us all this way—'

'Yes.'

'You bought your life for two hours?'

'For a man under sentence of death two hours can be a very long time.' Bowman smiled, looked at Cecile, then turned back to Czerda. 'But also a very short time.'

'You bought your life for two hours!' Czerda seemed more astonished at this fact than he was concerned by the loss of the money.

'Put it that way.'

Czerda brought up his gun. Le Grand Duc stepped forward, seized Czerda's wrist and pressed his gun-hand down. He said in a low, harsh, bitter voice: 'My privilege.'

'Sir.'

Le Grand Duc pointed his gun at Bowman, then jerked it to the right. For a moment Bowman seemed to hesitate, then shrugged. They moved away together, Le Grand Duc's gun close to Bowman's back, round a right-angled corner into another cavern. After a few moments the sound of a shot reverberated through the caverns, its echoes followed by the thud as of a falling body. The scientists looked stunned, a complete and final despair written in their faces. Czerda and his three companions looked at one another in grim satisfaction. Cecile and Lila clung to each other, both, in the reflected wash of torchlight, ashen-faced and in tears. Then all heard the measured tread of returning footsteps and stared at the right-angled corner where the two men had disappeared.

Le Grand Duc and Bowman came into view at the same instant. Both of them carried guns, rock-steady in their hands.

'Don't,' Bowman said.

Le Grand Duc nodded. 'As my friend observes, please, please, don't.'

But after a moment of total disbelief, Ferenc and Searl did. There were two sharp reports, two screams and the sound, sharply metallic, of two guns striking the limestone floor. Ferenc and Searl stood in stupefied agony, clutching shattered shoulders. The second time, Bowman reflected, that Searl had been wounded in that shoulder but he could bring himself to feel no pity for he knew now that it had been Searl who had used the whip to flay the skin from Tina's back.

Bowman said: 'Some people take a long time to learn.'

'Incorrect, Neil. Some people never learn.' Le Grand Duc looked at Czerda, the expression on his face indicating that he would have preferred to be looking elsewhere. 'We had nothing against you, from a judicial point of view, that is. Not a shred of proof, not a shred of evidence. Not until you, personally and alone, led us to Alexandre's grave and admitted to the fact that you had buried him. In front of all those witnesses. Now you know why Mr Bowman bought his life for two hours.' He turned to Bowman. 'Incidentally, where is the money, Neil?'

'In Cecile's handbag. I just kind of put it there.'

The two girls advanced, slowly, uncertainly. There were no longer any signs of tears but they were totally uncomprehending. Bowman pocketed his gun, went to them and put his arms round the shoulders of both.

'It's all right, now,' he said. 'It's all over, it really is.' He lifted his hand from Lila's shoulders, pressed her cheek with his fingertips till she turned to look at him in dazed enquiry.

He smiled. 'The Duc de Croytor is indeed the Duc de Croytor. My boss, these many years.'

EPILOGUE

BENEATH THE frowning cliffs of Les Baux, the Baumanière slept peacefully in the light of a yellow moon. Bowman, sitting on a chair and sipping a drink, lifted an eyebrow as Cecile emerged from a room, tripped and almost fell over an extension cord. She recovered herself and sat beside him.

'Twenty-four hours,' she said. 'Only twenty-four hours. I just can't believe it.'

'You want to get yourself a pair of spectacles,' Bowman observed.

'I have a pair of spectacles, thank you.'

'Then you want to wear them.' Bowman put a kindly hand on hers. 'After all, you've got your man now.'

'Oh, do be quiet.' She made no attempt to remove her hand. 'How's that young girl?'

'Tina's in hospital, in Arles. She'll be around in a couple of days. Her father and Madame Zigair are there with her now. The Hobenauts and Tangevecs are having dinner inside. Not a very festive occasion, I should imagine, but I would say they must be experiencing a certain sense of relief, wouldn't you? And Pierre des Jardins, by this time, must be home in Le Grau du Roi.'

'I can't believe it.' Bowman peered at her, then realized that she had been only half listening to him and was now on another topic altogether. 'He – he's your boss?'

'Charles? He is indeed. Nobody believes anything about Charles. I'm ex-Army Intelligence, ex-military attaché in Paris. I've got another job now.'

'I'll bet you have,' she said feelingly.

'The only other person who knows anything about this is

Pierre, the fishing-boat skipper. That's why he maintained such a marvellous sang-froid. He's sworn to secrecy. So are you.'

'I don't know if I like that.'

'You'll do what you're told. Charles, I can assure you, is much higher up the pecking order than I am. We've been together for eight years. For the last two years we've known that Iron Curtain gypsies have been smuggling things across the frontier. What, we didn't know. This time, of all people, the Russians tipped us off – but even they didn't know what was really happening.'

'But this Gaiuse Strome—'

'Our Chinese pal in Arles and elsewhere? Temporarily held by the French police. He was getting too close to things and Charles had him copped on a technicality. They'll have to let him go. Diplomatic immunity. He arranged it all – he's the Chinese military attaché in Tirhana.'

'Tirhana?'

'Albania.'

She reached into her handbag, brought out her glasses, looked at him closely and said: 'But we were told—'

'We?'

'Lila and myself, we're secretaries in the Admiralty. To keep an eye on you. We were told that one of you was under suspicion—'

'I'm sorry. Charles and I arranged that. There we were, a goodie and a baddie. We could never be seen together. We had to have a channel of communication. Girl-friends chatter. Girls get on the phone to their bosses back home. We had the channel.'

'You fixed all this?' She withdrew her hand. 'You knew—'

'I'm sorry. We had to do it.'

'You mean—'

'Yes.'

'Strawberry birthmark—'

'Sorry again.' Bowman shook his head admiringly. 'But I must say it was the most complete dossier I've ever seen.'

'I despise you! I detest you! You're the most utterly contemptible—'

'Yes, I know, and I'm not worried. What does worry me

is that so far we've only managed to fix up two bridesmaids and I said—'

'Two,' she said firmly, 'will be quite enough.'

Bowman smiled, rose, offered her his hand and together they walked arm in arm to the balustrade and looked down. Almost directly beneath them were the Duc de Croytor and Lila, seated at, inevitably, a loaded table. It was apparent that Le Grand Duc was under a very considerable emotional strain for despite the fact that he held a paper-sheathed leg of lamb in his hand he was not eating.

'Good God!' he was saying. 'Good God!' He peered at his blonde companion's lovely face from a distance of about six inches. 'I turn pale at the very thought. I might have lost you for ever. I never knew!'

'Charles!'

'You *are* a Cordon Bleu cook?'

'Yes, Charles.'

'Brochettes de queues de langoustines au beurre blanc?'

'Yes, Charles.'

'Poulet de la ferme au champagne?'

'Yes, Charles.'

'Filets de sole Retival?'

'But of course.'

'Pintadeau aux morilles?'

'My speciality.'

'Lila. I love you. Marry me!'

'Oh, Charles!'

They embraced in front of the astonished eyes of the other guests. Symbolically, perhaps, Le Grand Duc's leg of lamb fell to the floor.

Still arm in arm, Bowman led Cecile down to the patio. Bowman said: 'Don't be fooled by Romeo down there. He doesn't give a damn about the cuisine. Not where your friend is concerned.'

'The big bold baron is a little shy boy inside?'

Bowman nodded. 'The making of old-fashioned proposals is not exactly his forte.'

'Whereas it is yours?'

Bowman ushered her to a table and ordered drinks. 'I don't quite understand.'

'A girl likes to be asked to marry,' she said.

'Ah! Cecile Dubois, will you marry me?'

'I may as well, I suppose.'

'Touché!' He lifted his glass. 'To Cecile.'

'Thank you, kind sir.'

'Not you. Our second-born.'

They smiled at each other, then turned to look at the couple at the next table. Le Grand Duc and Lila were still gazing rapturously into each other's eyes, but Le Grand Duc, nevertheless, was back on balance again. Imperiously, he clapped his hands together.

'Encore!' said Le Grand Duc.

CIRCUS

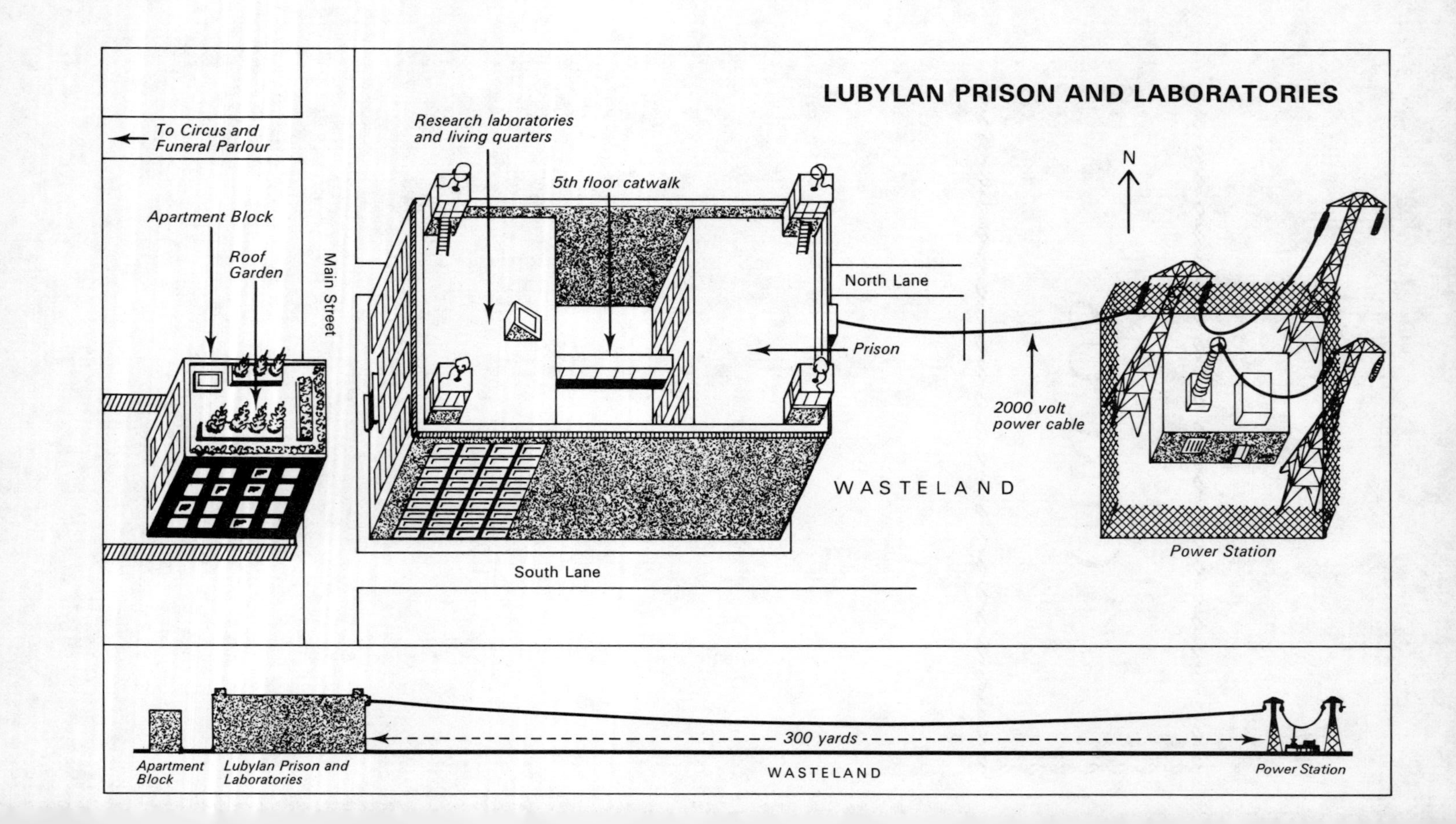
LUBYLAN PRISON AND LABORATORIES
To Circus and Funeral Parlour
Research laboratories and living quarters
5th floor catwalk
N
Apartment Block
Roof Garden
Main Street
North Lane
Prison
2000 volt power cable
WASTELAND
South Lane
Power Station
300 yards
Apartment Block
Lubylan Prison and Laboratories
WASTELAND
Power Station

— 1 —

'IF YOU WERE a genuine army colonel,' Pilgrim said, 'instead of one of the most bogus and unconvincing frauds I've ever seen, you'd rate three stars for this. Excellently done, my dear Fawcett, excellently done.'

Pilgrim was the great-grandson of an English peer of the realm and it showed. Both in dress and in speech he was slightly foppish and distinctly Edwardian: subconsciously, almost, one looked for the missing monocle, the old Etonian tie. His exquisitely cut suits came from Savile Row, his shirts from Turnbull and Asser and his pair of matched shotguns, which at 4000 dollars he regarded as being cheap at the price, came, inevitably, from Purdeys of the West End. The shoes, regrettably, were hand-made in Rome. To have him auditioned for the screen part of Sherlock Holmes would have been superfluous.

Fawcett did not react to the criticism, the praise or the understated sartorial splendour. His facial muscles seldom reacted to anything – which may have been due to the fact that his unlined face was so plump it was almost moon-shaped. His bucolic expression verged upon the bemused: large numbers of people languishing behind federal bars had been heard to testify, frequently and with understandable bitterness, that the impression Fawcett conveyed was deceptive to the point of downright immorality.

Half-hooded eyes deep-sunk in the puffy flesh, Fawcett's gaze traversed the leather-lined library and came to rest on the sparking pine fire. His voice wistful, he said, 'One would wish that promotion were so spectacular and rapid in the CIA.'

'Dead men's shoes, my boy.' Pilgrim was at least five years younger than Fawcett. 'Dead men's shoes.' He regarded his own Roman foot briefly and with some satisfaction, then transferred his attention to the splendid collection of ribbons on Fawcett's chest. 'I see you have awarded yourself the Congressional Medal of Honour.'

'I felt it was in keeping with my character.'

'Quite. This paragon you have unearthed. Bruno. How did you come across him?'

'I didn't. Smithers did, when I was in Europe. Smithers is a great circus fan.'

'Quite.' Pilgrim seemed fond of the word. 'Bruno. One would assume that he has another name.'

'Wildermann. But he never uses it – professionally or privately.'

'Why?'

'I don't know. I've never met him. Presumably Smithers never asked him either. Would you ask Pele or Callas or Liberace what their other names are?'

'You class his name with those?'

'It's my understanding that the circus world would hesitate to class those names with his.'

Pilgrim picked up some sheets of paper. 'Speaks the language like a native.'

'He is a native.'

'Billed as the world's greatest aerialist.' Pilgrim was a hard man to knock off his stride. 'Daring young man on the flying trapeze? That sort of thing?'

'That, too. But he's primarily a high-wire specialist.'

'The best in the world?'

'His fellow professionals are in no doubt about it.'

'If our information about Crau is correct, he'd better be. I see he claims to be an expert in Karate and judo.'

'He has never claimed anything of the kind. I claim it for him – rather, Smithers does, and as you know Smithers is very much an expert in those matters. He watched Bruno having a work-out down-town this morning in the Samurai Club. The instructor there is a black-belt – they don't come any higher in judo. By the time Bruno had finished with him – well, I understand the instructor disappeared with the general air of a man about to write out his resignation on the spot. Smithers said he hadn't seen Bruno chopping people around in karate: he has the feeling he wouldn't like to, either.'

'And this dossier claims that he is a mentalist.' Pilgrim

steepled his fingers in the best Holmes fashion. 'Well, good for Bruno. What the devil is a mentalist?'

'Chap that does mental things.'

Pilgrim exercised a massive restraint. 'You have to be an intellectual to be an aerialist?'

'I don't even know whether you have to be an intellectual – or even intelligent – in order to be an aerialist. It's beside the point. Practically every circus performer doubles up and does one, sometimes even two jobs in addition to his speciality in the actual arena. Some act as labourers – they have mountains of equipment to move around. Some are entertainers. Bruno doubles as an entertainer. Just outside the circus proper they have a showground, fairground, call it what you will, which is used to separate the arriving customers from their spare cash. Bruno performs in a small theatre, just a collapsible plywood job. He reads minds, tells you the first name of your great-grandfather, the numbers of the dollar bills in your pockets, what's written or drawn inside any sealed envelope. Things like that.'

'It's been done. Audience plants and the hocus-pocus of any skilled stage magician.'

'Possibly, although the word is that he can do things for which there is no rational accounting and which professional conjurers have failed to reproduce. But what interests us most is that he has a totally photographic memory. Give him an opened double-spread of, say, *Time* magazine. He'll look at it for a couple of seconds, hand it back, then offer to identify the word in any location you select. You say to him that you'd like to know what the third word in the third line in the third column on the right-hand page is and if he says it's, say "Congress", then you can lay your life it is "Congress". And he can do this in any language – he doesn't have to understand it.'

'This I have to see. *A propos*, if he's such a genius, why doesn't he concentrate exclusively on stage work? Surely he could make a fortune out of that, much more than by risking his life turning somersaults up there in the low cloud?'

'Perhaps. I don't know. According to Smithers, he's not exactly paid in pennies. He's the outstanding star in the outstanding circus on earth. But that wouldn't be his real reason. He's the lead member of a trio of aerialists called "The Blind Eagles", and without him they'd be lost. I gather they are not mentalists.'

'I wonder. We can't afford excessive sentiment and loyalty in our business.'

'Sentiment, no. Loyalty – to us – yes. To others, yes also. If they are your two younger brothers.'

'A family trio?'

'I thought you knew.'

Pilgrim shook his head. 'You called them the Blind Eagles?'

'No undue hyperbole, Smithers tell me. Not when you've seen their act. They may not quite be up in the wild blue yonder or hanging about, as you suggest, in the low cloud, but they're not exactly earth-bound either. On the up-swing of the trapeze they're eighty feet above *terra firma*. Whether you fall from eighty feet or eight hundred, the chances of breaking your neck – not to mention most of the two hundred-odd bones in your body – are roughly the same. Especially if you're blindfolded and can't tell up from down, while your body can't tell you exactly where up is and most certainly can't locate down.'

'You're trying to tell me—'

'They wear those black silk-cotton gloves when they take off from one trapeze to another. People think there may be some advanced electronic quirk in those gloves, like negative poles attracting positive poles, but there isn't. Just for better adhesion, that's all. They have no guidance system at all. Their hoods are entirely opaque but they never miss – well, obviously they never miss or they would be one Blind Eagle short by this time. Some form of extra-sensory perception, I suppose – whatever that may mean. Only Bruno has it, which is why he is the catcher.'

'This I have to see. And the great mentalist at work.'

'No problem. On the way in.' Fawcett consulted his watch. 'We could leave now. Mr Wrinfield is expecting us?' Pilgrim nodded in silence. A corner of Fawcett's mouth twitched: he could have been smiling. He said: 'Come now, John, all circus-goers are happy children at heart. You don't look very happy to me.'

'I'm not. There are twenty-five different nationalities working for this circus, at least eight of them mid- or eastern-European. How am I to know that someone out there might not love me, might be carrying a picture of me in his back pocket? Or half a dozen of them carrying pictures of me?'

'The price of fame. You want to try disguising yourself.' Fawcett surveyed his own colonel's uniform complacently. 'As a lieutenant-colonel, perhaps?'

II

They travelled to down-town Washington in an official but unidentifiable car, Pilgrim and Fawcett in the back, the driver and a fourth man in the front. The fourth man was a grey, balding anonymity of a person, rain-coated, with a totally forgettable face. Pilgrim spoke to him.

'Now, don't forget, Masters, you better be sure that you're the first man on that stage.'

'I'll be the first man, sir.'

'Picked your word?'

'Yes, sir. "Canada".'

Dusk had already fallen and ahead, through a slight drizzle of rain, loomed an oval, high-domed building festooned with hundreds of coloured lights that had been programmed to flicker on and off in a pre-set pattern. Fawcett spoke to the driver, the car stopped and, wordlessly and carrying a magazine rolled up in one hand, Masters got out and seemed to melt into the gathering crowd. He had been born to melt into crowds. The car moved on and stopped again only when it had reached as close to the building entrance as possible. Pilgrim and Fawcett got out and passed inside.

The broad passageway led directly to the main audience entrance of the big top itself – a misnomer, as the days of the great canvas structures, at least as far as the big circuses were concerned, had gone. Instead they relied exclusively on exhibition halls and auditoriums, few of which seated less than ten thousand people, and many considerably more: a circus such as this had to have at least seven thousand spectators just to break even.

To the right of the passageway glimpses could be caught of the true back-stage of the circus itself, the snarling big cats in their cages, the restlessly hobbled elephants, the horses and ponies and chimpanzees, a scattering of jugglers engaged in honing up their performances – a top-flight juggler requires as much and as constant practice as a concert pianist – and, above all, the unmistakable and unforgettable smell. To the rear of the area were prefabricated offices and, beyond those, the rows of changing booths for the performers. Opposite those, in the far corner and discreetly curved so as to minimize the audience's view of what was taking place backstage, was the wide entrance to the arena itself.

From the left of the passageway came the sound of music, and it wasn't the New York Philharmonic that was giving forth. The music – if it could be called that – was raucous, tinny, blaring, atonal, and in any other circumstances could have been fairly described as an assault on the eardrums: but in that fairground *milieu* any other kind of music, whether because of habituation or because it went so inevitably with its background, would have been unthinkable. Pilgrim and Fawcett passed through one of the several doors leading to the concourse that housed the side-show itself. It covered only a modest area but what it lacked in size it clearly compensated for in volume of trade. It differed little from a hundred other fairgrounds apart from the presence of a sixty-by-twenty, garishly-painted and obviously plywood-constructed structure in one corner. It was towards this, ignoring all the other dubious attractions, that Pilgrim and Fawcett headed.

Above the doorway was the intriguing legend: 'The Great Mentalist'. The two men paid their dollar apiece, went inside and took up discreet standing positions at the back. Discretion apart, there were no seats left – the Great Mentalist's fame had clearly travelled before him.

Bruno Wildermann was on the tiny stage. Of little more than average height, and of little more than average width across the shoulders, he did not look a particularly impressive figure, which could have been due to the fact that he was swathed from neck to ankle in a voluminous and highly-coloured Chinese mandarin's gown, with huge, billowing sleeves. His aquiline, slightly swarthy face, crowned by long black hair, looked intelligent enough, but it was a face that was more pleasant than remarkable: if he passed you in the street you would not have turned to look after him.

Pilgrim said, *sotto voce*: 'Look at those sleeves. You could hide a hutchful of rabbits up them.'

But Bruno was not bent on performing any conjuring tricks. He was confining himself strictly to his advertised role as a mentalist. He had a deep, carrying voice, not loud, with a trace of a foreign accent so slight as to make its source of origin unidentifiable.

He asked a woman in the audience to think of some object then whisper it to her neighbour: without hesitation Bruno announced what the object was and this was confirmed.

'Plant,' said Pilgrim.

Bruno called for three volunteers to come to the stage. After some hesitation three women did so. Bruno sat all three at a table, provided them with foot-square pieces of paper and envelopes to match and asked them to write or draw some simple symbol and enclose them in the envelopes. This they did while Bruno stood facing the audience, his back to them. When they had finished he turned and examined the three envelopes lying on the table, his hands clasped behind his back. After only a few seconds he said: 'The first shows a swastika, the second a question mark, the third a square with two diagonals. Will you show them to the audience please?'

The three women extracted the cards and held them up. They were undeniably a swastika, a question mark and a square with two diagonals.

Fawcett leaned towards Pilgrim: 'Three plants?' Pilgrim looked thoughtful and said nothing.

Bruno said: 'It may have occurred to some of you that I have accomplices among the audience. Well, you can't *all* be accomplices because then you wouldn't bother to come and see me, even if I could afford to pay you all, which I can't. But this should remove all doubt.' He picked up a paper plane and said: 'I'm going to throw this among you and although I can do lots of things I can't control the flight of a paper plane. Nobody ever could. Perhaps the person it touches would be good enough to come to the stage.'

He threw the paper plane over the audience. It swooped and darted in the unpredictable fashion of all paper planes then, again in the fashion of all paper planes, ended its brief flight in an ignominious nose dive, striking the shoulder of a youth in his late teens. Somewhat diffidently he left his seat and mounted the stage. Bruno gave him an encouraging smile and a sheet of paper and envelope similar to those he'd given the women.

'What I want you to do is simple. Just write down three figures and put the sheet inside the envelope.' This the youth did, while Bruno stood with his back to him. When the paper was inside the envelope Bruno turned, but did not even look at the paper far less touch it. He said: 'Add the three numbers and tell me what the total is.'

'Twenty.'

'The numbers you wrote down were seven, seven and six.'

The youth extracted the paper and held it up for the audience to see. Seven, seven and six it was.

Fawcett looked at Pilgrim, who had now adopted a very thoughtful expression indeed. Clearly, if Bruno were not genuine then he was either a consummate magician or an extraordinarily devious character.

Then Bruno announced his most difficult feat of all – that of displaying that he was possessed of a photographic memory, that of identifying, given the location, of any word in a double-spread of any magazine, irrespective of language. Masters left nothing to chance or the impetuousness of any eager-beaver who might care to forestall him, for he was on stage even before Bruno had finished his explanation. Bruno, slightly lifting amused eyebrows, took the opened magazine from him, glanced at it briefly, handed it back and looked interrogatively at Masters.

Masters said: 'Left page, second column, let me see now, seven lines down, middle word.' He looked at Bruno with a half-smile of triumphant expectation.

Bruno said: 'Canada.'

The half-smile vanished. Masters's nondescript features seemed to fall apart then he shrugged his shoulders in genuine disbelief and turned away.

Outside, Fawcett said: 'I hardly think that Bruno is likely to have the inside track on the CIA. Convinced?'

'Convinced. When does the performance start?'

'Half an hour.'

'Let's go and watch him on the high wire or whatever. If he's half as good out there – well, he's our man.'

The exhibition hall that housed the three-ring circus was completely full. The air was alive with music (this time more than tolerable music from a very competent orchestra) an air that was charged with tension and excitement and anticipation, with thousands of young children transported into an enchanted fairyland – almost, indeed, to the extent their grandparents were. Everything glittered; it was no cheap tinsel glitter, but a background that seemed the integral and inevitable part of everything a circus should be. Apart from the dun-coloured sand in the three rings, a dazzling rainbow of colours caught the eye even more than the music the ear. Circling the ring were beautiful and beautifully dressed girls on the most outrageously caparisoned elephants and if there was any colour in the spectrum that the designer had omitted it wasn't apparent to the eye. In the rings themselves clowns and pierrots vied with each other in the ludicrousness of their antics and the ridiculousness of their costumes, while both of them vied with the tumblers and the stately procession of stilt-walkers. The audience watched it all in fascination – albeit with an element of impatience, for this spectacle, magnificent as it was, was only the warm-up, the prelude to the action to come. There is no atmosphere in the world quite like that in the charged atmosphere of the big top just before the performance begins.

Fawcett and Pilgrim sat together in excellent viewing seats, almost opposite the entrance of the main ring. Fawcett said: 'Which is Wrinfield?'

Without appearing to do so, Pilgrim indicated a man sitting only two seats away in the same row. Immaculately clad in a dark blue suit, matching tie and white shirt, he had a lean, thoughtful, almost scholarly face, with neatly parted grey hair and pebble glasses.

'*That's* Wrinfield?' Pilgrim nodded. 'Looks more like a college professor to me.'

'I believe he was once. Economics. But bossing a modern circus is no longer a seat of the pants job. It's big business and running it requires corresponding intelligence. Tesco Wrinfield is a highly intelligent man.'

'Maybe too intelligent. With a name like that and on a job like this it's going to be—'

'He's a fifth generation American.'

The last of the elephants left the arena and then, to the accompaniment of a blare of trumpets and the suddenly amplified effects of the orchestra, a golden chariot, drawn by two magnificently adorned black stallions, erupted into the arena at full gallop, followed by a dozen horsemen. From time to time these horsemen retained some form of contact with their horses, but for the most part performed a series of acrobatic feats as spectacular as clearly suicidal. The crowd yelled and cheered and applauded. The circus had begun.

The performance that followed more than bore out the circus's claim that it had no peer in the world. It was superbly arranged and superbly presented and, as was to be expected, it numbered among its acts some of the best in the world: Heinrich Neubauer, an all but incomparable trainer with an uncanny power over a dozen very unpleasant Nubian lions; his only equal, Malthius, who treated the same number of even more unpleasant Bengal tigers as if they were kittens; Carraciola, who had no trouble at all in making his chimpanzees look a great deal more intelligent than he was; Kan Dahn, billed as the strongest man in the world which, on the basis of his extraordinary one-handed feats on the high wire and trapeze while seemingly unencumbered by the presence of several attractive young ladies who clung to him with a touching degree of devotion, he might well have been; Lennie Loran, a high-wire-walking comedian, who would have made any insurance agent in the country jump on his pen; Ron Roebuck, who could perform feats with a lasso that a rodeo cowboy wouldn't even dare dream about; Manuelo, a knife-thrower who could extinguish a lit cigarette at twenty feet – with his eyes bandaged; the Duryans, a Bulgarian teeterboard team who made people shake their heads in wonder; and a dozen other acts, ranging from aerial balletists to a group who climbed up tall ladders and balanced there entirely unsupported while they threw Indian clubs at each other.

After an hour or so of this Pilgrim said graciously: 'Not bad. Not bad at all. And here, I take it, is our star turn.'

The lights dimmed, the orchestra played suitably dramatic if somewhat funereal music, then the lights came on again. High up on the trapeze platform, with half a dozen coloured spotlights trained on them, stood three men clad in sparkling sequinned leotards. In the middle was Bruno. Without his mandarin's gown he now looked singularly impressive, broad-shouldered and hard and heavy muscled, every inch the phenomenal athlete he was reputed to be. The other two men were fractionally slighter than he. All three were blindfolded. The music died away, and the crowd watched in eerie silence as the three men pulled hoods over their blindfolds.

Pilgrim said: 'On balance, I think I would prefer to be down here.'

'That's two of us. I don't think I want to look.'

But look they did as the Blind Eagles went through their clearly impossible aerial routine – impossible because, apart from the occasional roll of a solitary drum in the orchestra, they had no means of knowing where each other was, of synchronizing their sightless movements. But not once did a pair of hands fail to smack safely and securely into another and waiting pair, not once did an outstretched pair of hands appear even remotely liable to miss a silently swinging trapeze. The performance lasted for all of an interminable four minutes and at the end there was another hushed silence, the lights dimmed a second time and almost the entire audience was on its feet, clapping and shouting and whistling.

Pilgrim said: 'Know anything about his two brothers?'

'Vladimir and Yoffe, I believe they're called. Nothing. I thought this was going to be a one-man job.'

'It is. And Bruno has the motivation? The incentive?'

'If any man ever had. I was making enquiries when I was in eastern Europe time before last. I couldn't find out much from our man there, but enough, I think. There were seven of the family in the circus act – dad or mum more or less retired – but only those three made it over the border when the secret police closed in. I don't even know *why* they closed in. That was six, maybe seven years ago. Bruno's wife is dead, that's for sure, there are witnesses who will testify to that –

well, they would, if they didn't live in the part of the world they do. He'd been married two weeks. What happened to his youngest brother, his father and his mother, nobody knows. They just disappeared.'

'Along with a million others. He's our man, all right. Mr Wrinfield is willing to play. Will Bruno?'

'He'll play.' Fawcett was confident, then looked thoughtful. 'He'd better. After all those weeks of trouble you've been to.'

The lights brightened. The Blind Eagles were now on a wire platform some twenty feet above ground, the wire itself stretching to another platform on the far side of the centre ring. Both other rings were empty and there was no other performer in sight except one – and he was on the ground. There was no music and among the crowd the silence was absolute.

Bruno straddled a bicycle. Across his shoulders was strapped a wooden yoke while one of his brothers held a twelve foot steel pole. Bruno edged the bicycle forward until the front wheel was well clear of the platform and waited until his brother had placed the pole in slots across the yoke. It was totally insecure. As Bruno moved off, bringing both feet on to the pedals, the brothers caught hold of the pole, leaned forward in perfect unison and swung themselves clear of the platform until, again in perfect unison, they hung suspended at the full length of their arms. The wire sagged noticeably, but Bruno didn't: slowly and steadily he pedalled away.

For the next few minutes, balanced partly by himself but mainly by the perfect timing of Vladimir and Yoffe, Bruno cycled backwards and forwards across the wire while the brothers went through a series of controlled but intricate acrobatics. On one occasion, while Bruno remained perfectly steady for seconds at a time, the brothers, necessarily moving with the same immaculate synchronization, gradually increased their pendulum swing until they were doing hand-stands on the pole. The same extraordinary hush remained with the audience, a tribute that wasn't entirely due to the performance they were witnessing: directly below them as they performed were Neubauer and his twelve Nubian lions, the head of every one of which was turned yearningly upwards.

At the end of the performance the silence in the audience

was replaced by a long and far from silent collective sigh of relief, then once again came the same standing ovation, as heartfelt and prolonged as the one that had gone before.

Pilgrim said: 'I've had enough – besides, my nerves can't take any more. Wrinfield will follow me. If he brushes by you on the way back to his seat that means that Bruno is willing to talk and that you're to follow him at a discreet distance at the end of the show. Wrinfield, I mean.'

Without making any sign or looking in any particular direction, Pilgrim rose leisurely and left. Almost at once Wrinfield did the same.

III

A few minutes later the two men were closeted in one of Wrinfield's offices, a superbly equipped secretary's dream, albeit somewhat compact. Wrinfield had a much larger if ramshackle office where most of his work was normally carried out just outside the arena itself; but that did not possess a cocktail bar as this one did. On the principle that he forbade anyone to have liquor on the circus site proper, Wrinfield accordingly denied himself the privilege also.

The office was but a tiny part of a complex and beautifully organized whole that constituted the mobile home of the circus. Every person in the circus, from Wrinfield downwards, slept aboard this train except for some independent diehards who insisted on dragging their caravans across the vast spaces of the United States and Canada. On tour the train also accommodated every single performing animal in the circus: at the end, just before the brake-van, were four massive flat-cars that accommodated all the bulky equipment, ranging from tractors to cranes that were essential for the smooth operation of the circus. In all, it was a minor miracle in ingenuity, meticulous planning and the maximum utilization of available space. The train itself was a monster, over half a mile in length.

Pilgrim accepted a drink and said: 'Bruno's the man I want. You think he will accept? If not we may well cancel your European tour.'

'He'll come, and for three reasons.' Wrinfield's speech was like the man himself, neat, precise, the words chosen with care. 'As you've seen, the man doesn't know what fear is. Like all newly naturalized Americans – all right, all right, he's been naturalized for over five years but that rates as yesterday – his patriotism towards his adopted country makes yours and mine look just that little shabby. Thirdly, he's got a very big score to settle with his former homeland.'

'Now?'

'Now. And then we speak to you?'

'I'm the last person you speak to. For both our sakes you want to be seen with me as little as possible. And don't come within a mile of my office – we have a whole battalion of foreign agents who do nothing but sit in the sun and watch our front door all the time. Colonel Fawcett – he's the uniformed person who was sitting beside me and the chief of our East European Field Operations – knows a great deal more about it than I do.'

'I didn't know that you carried uniformed personnel in your organization, Mr Pilgrim.'

'We don't. That's his disguise. He wears it so often that he's more readily recognizable in it than in civilian clothes, which is why nearly everyone calls him "the colonel". But never underestimate him.'

IV

Fawcett waited until the end of the show, dutifully applauded, turned and left without glancing at Wrinfield: Wrinfield had already given him the signal. Fawcett left the circus and made his way through the darkness and the steadily increasing rain moving slowly so that Wrinfield might not lose him. Eventually he came to the large, dark limousine in which he and Pilgrim had arrived and climbed into the back seat. A dark figure was pushed up against the far corner, his face as deeply in shadow as possible.

Fawcett said: 'Hello. My name's Fawcett. I hope that no one saw you arrive?'

The driver answered: 'No one, sir. I was keeping a pretty close look-out.' He looked out through the rain-spattered windows. 'It's not much of a night for other people to be minding other people's business.'

'It isn't.' He turned to the shadowy figure. 'A pleasure to meet you.' He sighed. 'I have to apologize for all this comic-opera cloak and dagger business, but I'm afraid it's too late now. Gets in your blood, you know. We're just waiting for a friend of yours – ah, here he comes now.' He opened the door and Wrinfield got in beside them. What little could be seen of his face didn't display a great deal in the way of carefree rapture.

'Poynton Street, Barker,' Fawcett said.

Barker nodded in silence, and drove off. Nobody spoke. Wrinfield, more than a little unhappy, kept turning restlessly in his seat and finally said: 'I think we're being followed.'

Fawcett said: 'We'd better be. If not the driver of that car would be out of a job tomorrow. That car's following us to make sure that no other car follows us. If you follow me, that is.'

'I see.' From the tone of his voice it was questionable whether Wrinfield did. He became increasingly unhappy as the car moved into what was very close to a slum area and unhappier still when it drew up in an ill-lit street outside a sleazy walk-up apartment block. He said, complainingly: 'This isn't a very nice part of town. And *this* – this looks like a house of ill-fame.'

'And a house of ill-fame it is. We own it. Very handy places, these bordellos. Who, for instance, could ever imagine that Tesco Wrinfield would enter one of those places? Come inside.'

— 2 —

FOR SUCH AN insalubrious place in such an insalubrious area the sitting-room was surprisingly comfortable, although the person who had furnished it would appear to have had a fixation about the colour russet, for the sofa, armchairs, carpet and heavily discreet curtains were all of the same colour or very close to it. A smokeless coal fire – for this was a smokeless area – did its best to burn cheerfully in the hearth. Wrinfield and Bruno occupied an armchair apiece: Fawcett was presiding over a cocktail cabinet, one of the portable kind.

Bruno said carefully: 'Tell me again, please. About this anti-matter or whatever you call it.'

Fawcett sighed. 'I was afraid you might ask me that. I know I got it right first time, because I'd memorized what I had to say and just repeated it parrot fashion. I had to because I don't really know what it's all about myself.' Fawcett handed round drinks – a soda for Bruno – and rubbed his chin. 'I'll try and simplify it this time round. Then maybe I'll be able to get some inklings of understanding myself.

'Matter, we know, is made up of atoms. There are lots of things that go to make up those atoms – scientists, it seems, are becoming increasingly baffled about the ever-increasing complexity of the atom – but all that concerns our simple minds are the two basic constituents of the atom, electrons and protons. On our earth – in the universe, for that matter – electrons are invariably negatively charged and protons positively charged. Unfortunately, life is becoming increasingly difficult for our scientists and astronomers – for instance, it has been discovered only this year that there are particles, made of God knows what, that travel at many times the speed of light, which is a very upsetting and distressing concept for all those of the scientist community – and that was one hundred per cent – who believe that *nothing* could travel faster than the speed of light. However, that's by the way.

'Some time ago a couple of astronomers – Dicke and Anderson were their names – made the inconvenient discovery, based on theoretical calculations, that there must exist positively charged electrons. Their existence is now universally accepted, and they are referred to today as positrons. Then, to complicate things still further, the existence of anti-protons was discovered – this was in Berkeley – again electrically opposite to our protons. A combination of positrons and anti-protons would give rise to what is now termed "anti-matter". That anti-matter does exist no serious scientists seriously dispute.

'Nor do they dispute that if an electron or positron or proton and anti-proton collided or both sets collided the results would be disastrous. They would annihilate each other, giving off lethal gamma rays and creating, in the process, a considerable local uproar and a blast of such intense heat that all life within ten or perhaps hundreds of square miles would be instantaneously wiped out. On this scientists are agreed. It is estimated that if only two grams of anti-matter struck our planet on the side out-facing the sun the result would be to send the earth, with all life immediately extinct, spinning into the gravitational orbit of the sun. Provided, of course, it didn't disintegrate immediately on contact.'

'A delightful prospect,' Wrinfield said. He did not have the look of a convert about him. 'No offence, but it sounds like the most idle science-fiction speculation to me.'

'Me, too. But I have to accept what I'm told. Anyway, I'm beginning to believe it.'

'Look. We don't have any of this anti-matter stuff on earth?'

'Because of anti-matter's unpleasant propensity for annihilating all matter with which it comes into contact, that should be fairly obvious.'

'Then where does the stuff come from?'

'How the hell should I know?' Fawcett hadn't intended to be irritable, he just disliked treading the murky waters of the unknown. 'We think ours is the only universe. How do we know? Maybe there lies another universe beyond ours, maybe many. It seems, according to latest scientific thinking, that if there are such universes, there is no reason why one or more should not be made of anti-matter.' Fawcett paused gloomily. 'I suppose if any intelligent beings existed there they would consider our universe as being composed of anti-matter. Of course, it could have been some rogue material thrown off at the moment of creation of our own universe. Who's to say?'

Bruno said: 'So the whole matter is speculation. It's just a hypothesis. Theoretical calculations, that's all. There is no proof, Colonel Fawcett.'

'We think there is.' He smiled. 'Forgive the use of the "we". What could have been, in the terms of human lives, a disaster of the first magnitude occurred in a happily unpopulated area of northern Siberia in 1908. When Russian scientists got around to investigating this – almost twenty years later – they discovered an area of over a hundred square miles where trees had been destroyed by heat: not fire but by instantaneous incineration which, in many cases, led to the petrification of trees in the upright position. Had this extraordinary phenomenon occurred over, say, New York or London, they would have become blackened cities of the dead.'

'Proof,' Bruno said. 'We were speaking of proof, colonel.'

'Proof. Every other known damage caused to the earth by the impact of bodies from outer space has, without exception, been caused by meteors. There was no trace of the meteor that might have caused this Siberian holocaust and no signs of any mark upon the ground where the meteor might have crashed into it; when meteors crashed into Arizona and South Africa they left enormous craters in the ground. The now accepted and indeed inevitable conclusion is that Siberia was struck by a particle of anti-matter with a mass of something of the order of one hundredth of a million of a gram.'

There was a considerable silence, then Wrinfield said: 'Well, we have already covered this. Second time round it's a bit clearer, but not much. So?'

'Some dozen years ago there was scientific speculation as to whether the Russians had discovered the secret of anti-matter but this was dismissed out of hand because – well, because of anti-matter's unpleasant propensity of annihilating all matter with which it comes into contact, the creation, harnessing and storage of it was impossible.'

'*Was* impossible. What if it were possible or about to become possible? The nation that held this secret could hold the world to ransom. Comparatively, nuclear weapons are inoffensive toys for the amusement of little toddlers.'

For a long minute no one spoke, then Wrinfield said: 'You would not be talking in this fashion unless you had reason to believe that such a weapon exists or could exist.'

'I have reason so to believe. This possibility has obsessed the intelligence agencies of all the modern world for some years now.'

'Obviously this secret is not in our hands, or you wouldn't be telling us all this.'

'Obviously.'

'And it wouldn't be in the hands of a country such as Britain?'

'That would give us no cause for anxiety.'

'Because when the chips are down they would be allies with responsible hands?'

'I couldn't have put it better myself.'

'Then this secret resides – if it does reside anywhere – in the hands of a country which, when the chips were down, would be neither friendly nor responsible?'

'Precisely.' Pilgrim, Fawcett reflected, had warned him not to underrate Wrinfield's intelligence.

Wrinfield said slowly: 'Pilgrim and I have already made some tentative arrangements, come to preliminary agreements. You will know that. But he never told me any of this.'

'The time wasn't right.'

'So now it is?'

'Now or not at all.'

'Of course, you want this secret or formula or whatever?'

Fawcett began to revise his opinion of Wrinfield's intelligence. 'What do you think?'

'What makes you think our hands are more responsible than those of a score of other nations?'

'I'm a paid employee of the United States government. Mine is not to reason why.'

'It will not have escaped you that that was precisely the reasoning adopted by the Gestapo and the SS in Germany during the Second World War or by Russia's KGB since?'

'It has not escaped me. But I don't think the analogy is very exact. The United States doesn't really want more power – we have already overkill capacity. Can you imagine what would happen if this secret fell into the hands of, say, the certifiable leaders of a couple of the new Central African republics? We simply think we have more responsible hands than most.'

'We have to hope we have.'

Fawcett tried to conceal his long slow exhalation of relief. 'That means you'll go along.'

'I'll go. A moment ago you said the time was now right to tell me. Why?'

'I hope I was right in saying I was right.'

Bruno stirred. 'What do you want of me, colonel?'

There were times, Fawcett was aware, when there was little point in beating about the bush. He said: 'Get it for us.'

Bruno rose and poured himself another soda. He drank it all down then said: 'You mean, steal it?'

'Get it. Would you call taking a gun away from a maniac stealing?'

'But why me?'

'Because you have unique gifts. I can't discuss what type of use we would propose making of those gifts until I have some sort of answer. All I know is that we are pretty certain that there is only one formula in existence, only one man who has the formula and is capable of reproducing it. We know where both man and formula are.'

'Where?'

Fawcett didn't hesitate. 'Crau.'

Bruno didn't react in at all the way Fawcett had expected. His voice, when he spoke, was as bereft of expression as his face. Tonelessly, he repeated the word: 'Crau.'

'Crau. Your old home country and your old home town.'

Bruno didn't reply immediately. He returned to his chair, sat in it for a full minute, then said: 'If I do agree, how do I get there? Illegal frontier crossing? Parachutes?'

Fawcett made a heroic – and successful – effort to conceal his sense of exultation. Wrinfield and Bruno – he'd got them both in a matter of minutes. He said matter-of-factly: 'Nothing so dramatic. You just go along with the circus.'

This time Bruno seemed to be beyond words, so Wrinfield said: 'It's quite true, Bruno. We – that is, I – have agreed to co-operate with the government on this issue. Not that I had any more idea, until this moment, what the precise issue involved was. We are going to make a short tour of Europe, mainly eastern Europe. Negotiations are already well advanced. It's quite natural. They send circus acts, dancers, singers to us: we're just reciprocating.'

'The *whole* circus?'

'No, naturally not. That would be impossible. Just the cream of the cream, shall we say.' Wrinfield smiled faintly. 'One would have imagined that to include you.'

'And if I refuse?'

'We simply cancel the tour.'

Bruno looked at Fawcett. 'Mr Wrinfield's lost profits. This could cost your government a million dollars.'

'Our government. We'd pay a billion to get hold of this.'

Bruno looked from Fawcett to Wrinfield then back to Fawcett again. He said abruptly: 'I'll go.'

'Splendid. My thanks. Your country's thanks. The details—'

'I do not need my country's thanks.' The words were cryptical but without offence.

Fawcett was slightly taken aback, sought for the meaning behind the words then decided he'd better not. He said: 'As you will. The details, as I was about to say, can wait until later. Mr Wrinfield, did Mr Pilgrim tell you that we'd be grateful if you would take along two additional people when you go abroad?'

'He did not.' Wrinfield seemed somewhat miffed. 'It would appear that there are quite a number of things that Mr Pilgrim did not tell me.'

'Mr Pilgrim knows what he is doing.' Now that he had them both Fawcett took off the velvet gloves but still remained urbane and polite. 'There was no point in burdening you with unnecessary details until we had secured the co-operation of both you gentlemen. The two people in question are a Dr Harper and an equestrienne, Maria. Our people. Very important to our purpose. That, too, I'll explain later. There are some things I must first discuss urgently with Mr Pilgrim. Tell me, Bruno, why have you agreed to do this? I must warn you that it might be extremely dangerous for you and if you're caught we'll have no option but to disown you. Why?'

Bruno shrugged. 'Who's to say why? There can be many reasons that a man can't explain even to himself. Could be gratitude – America took me in when my own country threw me out. There are people there to whom I would like to perform as great a disservice as they did to me. I know there are dangerous and irresponsible men in my old country who would not hesitate to employ this weapon, if it exists. And then you say I am uniquely equipped for this task. In what ways I don't yet know, but if it is the case how could I let another go in my place? Not only might he fail in getting what you want but he could well be killed in the process. I wouldn't like to have either of those things on my conscience.' He smiled faintly. 'Just say it's a bit of a challenge.'

'And your real reason?'

Bruno said simply: 'Because I hate war.'

'Mmm. Not the answer I expected, but fair enough.' He stood up. 'Thank you, gentlemen, for your time, your patience and above all your co-operation. I'll have the cars take you back.'

Wrinfield said: 'And yourself? How do you get to Mr Pilgrim's office?'

'The madame here and I have an understanding of sorts. I'm sure she'll provide me with some form of transport.'

II

Fawcett had keys in his hand when he approached Pilgrim's apartment – Pilgrim both worked and slept in the same premises – but he put them away. Pilgrim, most uncharacteristically, had not even locked his door, he hadn't even closed it properly. Fawcett pushed the door and went inside. The first partly irrational thought that occurred to him was that he could have been just that little bit optimistic when he had assured Wrinfield that Pilgrim knew what he was doing.

Pilgrim was lying on the carpet. Whoever had left him lying there had clearly a sufficiency of ice-picks at home, for he hadn't even bothered to remove the one he'd left buried to the hilt in the back of Pilgrim's neck. Death must have been instantaneous, for there wasn't even a drop of blood to stain his Turnbull and Asser shirt. Fawcett knelt and looked at the face. It was as calmly expressionless as it had habitually been in life. Pilgrim had not only not known what hit him, he hadn't even known he'd been hit.

Fawcett straightened, crossed to the phone and lifted it.

'Dr Harper please. Ask him to come here immediately.'

Dr Harper wasn't exactly a caricature or a conceptualized prototype of the kindly healer, but it would have been difficult to visualize him in any other role. There was a certain medical inevitability about him. He was tall, lean, distinguished in appearance, becomingly grey at the temples and wore a pair of pebbled horn-rimmed glasses which lent his gaze a certain piercing quality which might have been illusory, intentional or just habitual. Horn-rimmed pebble glasses are a great help to doctors; the patient can never tell whether he is in robust health or has only weeks to live. His dress was as immaculate as that of the dead man he was thoughtfully examining. He had his black medical bag with him but he wasn't bothering to use it. He said: 'So that's all you know about tonight?'

'That's all.'

'Wrinfield? After all, he was the only one who knew. Before tonight, I mean.'

'He knew no details before tonight. No way. And he'd no opportunity. He was with me.'

'There's such a thing as an accomplice?'

'No chance. Wait until you see him. His record's immaculate – don't you think Pilgrim spent days checking? His patriotism is beyond question; it wouldn't surprise me if he's got a "God Bless America" label sewn to his undershirt. Besides, do you think he would have gone to the time and trouble of arranging to take his whole damn circus – well, most of it – to Europe if he had intended to do this? I know there's such a thing as erecting a façade, laying down a smokescreen, dragging red herrings – you name it – but, well, I ask you.'

'It's not likely.'

'But I think we should have him and Bruno up here. Just to let them see what they're up against. And we'll have to notify the admiral immediately. Will you do that while I get hold of Barker and Masters?'

'That's the scrambler there?'

'That's the scrambler.'

Dr Harper was still on the phone when Barker and Masters arrived, Barker the driver and Masters the grey man who had confronted Bruno on the stage. Fawcett said: 'Get Wrinfield and Bruno up here. Tell them it's desperately urgent but don't tell them anything about this. Bring them in by the rear tunnel. Be quick!'

Fawcett closed but did not lock the door behind them as Dr Harper hung up. Harper said: 'We're to keep it under wraps. According to the admiral, who is the one man who would know, he had no close relatives so he died of a heart attack. Me and my Hippocratic oath. He'll be right round.'

Fawcett was gloomy. 'I thought he might be. He's going to be very happy about this. Pilgrim was the apple of his eye, and it's no secret that he was next in line for the admiral's chair. Well, let's have a couple of the boys with their little cans of dusting powder and let them have a look around. Not, of course, that they'll find anything.'

'You're so sure?'

'I'm sure. Anyone cool enough to walk away leaving the murder weapon *in situ*, as it were, is pretty confident in himself. And you notice the way he's lying, feet to the door, head pointing away?'

'So?'

'The fact that he's so close to the door is almost sure proof that Pilgrim opened it himself. Would he have turned his back on a murderer? Whoever the killer was, he was a man Pilgrim not only knew but trusted.'

III

Fawcett had been right. The two experts who had come up with their little box of tricks had turned up nothing. The only places where fingerprints might conceivably have been, on the ice-pick handle and door-knobs, were predictably clean. They were just leaving when a man entered without benefit of either permission or knocking.

The admiral looked like everybody's favourite uncle or a successful farmer or, indeed, what he was, a fleet admiral, albeit retired. Burly, red-faced, with pepper-and-salt hair and radiating an oddly kind authority, he looked about ten years younger than his acknowledged if frequently questioned fifty-five. He gazed down at the dead man on the floor, and the more kindly aspect of his character vanished. He turned to Dr Harper.

'Made out the death certificate yet? Coronary, of course.' Dr Harper shook his head. 'Then do so at once and have Pilgrim removed to our private mortuary.'

Fawcett said: 'If we could leave that for a moment, sir. The mortuary bit, I mean. I have two people coming up here very shortly, the owner of the circus and our latest – ah – recruit. I'm convinced neither of them has anything to do with this

– but it would be interesting to see their reactions. Also, to find out if they still want to go through with this.'

'What guarantee can you offer that they won't leave here and head for the nearest telephone? There isn't a newspaper in the country that wouldn't give their assistant editor for this story.'

'You think that had not occurred to me, sir?' A slightly less than cordial note had crept into Fawcett's tone. 'There is no guarantee. There's only my judgement.'

'There's that,' the admiral said pacifically. It was the nearest he could ever bring himself to an apology. 'Very well.' He paused and to recover his position said: 'They are not, I trust, knocking and entering by the front door?'

'Barker and Masters are bringing them. By the rear tunnel.'

As if on cue, Barker and Masters appeared in the doorway, then stepped aside to let Wrinfield and Bruno in. The admiral and Dr Harper, Fawcett knew, were watching their faces as intently as he was. Understandably, neither Wrinfield nor Bruno was watching them: when you find a murdered man lying at your feet your ocular attention does not tend to stray. Predictably, Bruno's reactions were minimal, the narrowing of the eyes, the tightening of the mouth could have been as much imagined as real, but Wrinfield's reactions were all that anyone could have wished for: the colour drained from his face, leaving it a dirty grey, he put out a trembling hand against the lintel to steady himself and for a moment he looked as if he might even sway and fall.

Three minutes later, three minutes during which Fawcett had told him what little he knew, a seated Wrinfield, brandy glass in hand, was still shaking. Bruno declined the offer of a restorative. The admiral had taken the floor.

He said to Wrinfield: 'Do you have any enemies in the circus?'

'Enemies? In the circus?' Wrinfield was clearly taken aback. 'Good God, no. I know it must sound corny to you but we really are one big happy family.'

'Any enemies anywhere?'

'Every successful man has. Of a kind, that is. Well, there's rivalry, competition, envy. But enemies? He looked almost fearfully at Pilgrim and shuddered. 'But not in this way.' He was silent for a moment, then looked at the admiral with an expression that approximated pretty closely to resentment and when he spoke again the tremor had gone from his voice. 'And why do you ask me those questions? They didn't kill me. They killed Mr Pilgrim.'

'There's a connection. Fawcett?'

'There's a connection. I may speak freely, sir?'

'I beg your pardon?'

'Well, there are telephone boxes and sacrificial assistant editors—'

'Don't be a fool. I've already apologized for that.'

'Yes, sir.' Fawcett briefly searched his memory and found no apology there. It seemed pointless to mention this. 'As you say, sir, there's a connection. There's also been a leak and it can only have come from within our own organization. As I said, sir, and as I have explained to these gentlemen, it's clear that Pilgrim was killed by someone well known to him. There can't have been any special leak – only you, Pilgrim, Dr Harper and myself really knew what the intentions were. But any of up to a dozen people or more – researchers, telephone operators, drivers – within the organization knew that we had been in regular touch with Mr Wrinfield. It would be unusual, if not unique, to find any intelligence or counter-intelligence agency in the world whose ranks have not been infiltrated by an enemy agent, one who eventually becomes so securely entrenched as to become above suspicion. It would be naïve of us to assume that we are the sole exception.

'It was hardly top secret that Mr Wrinfield had been in the formative stages of planning a European tour – a primarily eastern European tour – and it would have been comparatively simple to discover that Crau was on the list of towns to be visited. As far as the gentlemen in Crau are concerned – more precisely, the gentlemen responsible for the research taking place in Crau – coincidence could be coincidence but the obvious tie-up with the CIA would be that little bit too much.'

'So why kill Pilgrim? As a warning?'

'In a way, sir yes.'

'You would care to be more specific, Mr Fawcett?'

'Yes, sir. No question but that it was a warning. But to make Pilgrim's death both understandable and justifiable from their point of view – for we have to remember that though we are dealing with unreasonable men we are also dealing with reasoning men – it had to be something more than just a warning. His murder was also an amalgam of invitation and provocation. It is a warning they wished to be ignored. If they believe Mr Wrinfield's forthcoming tour is sponsored by us, and if, in spite of Pilgrim's death – which they won't for a moment doubt that we'll be convinced has been engineered by them – we still go ahead and proceed with the tour, then we must have extraordinarily pressing needs to make it. Conclusive proof they would expect to find in Crau.

'And then we would be discredited internationally. Imagine, if you can, the sensational impact of the news of the internment of an entire circus. Imagine the tremendously powerful bargaining weapon it would give the East in any future negotiations. We'd become an international laughing stock, all credibility throughout the world gone, an object of ridicule in both East and West. The Gary Powers U-plane episode would be a bagatelle compared to this.'

'Indeed. Tell me, what's your opinion of locating this cuckoo in the CIA nest?'

'As of this moment?'

'Zero.'

'Dr Harper?'

'I agree totally. No chance. It would mean putting a watcher on every one of your several hundred employees in this building, sir.'

'And who's going to watch the watchers? Is that what you mean?'

'With respect, sir, you know very well what I mean.'

'Alas.' The admiral reached into an inside pocket, brought out two cards, handed one to Wrinfield, the other to Bruno. 'If you need me, call that number and ask for Charles. Any guesses you may have as to my identity – and you must be almost as stupid as we are if you haven't made some – you will please keep to yourselves.' He sighed. 'Alas again, I fear, Fawcett, that your reading of the matter is entirely correct. There is no alternative explanation, not, at least, a remotely viable one. Nevertheless, getting our hands on this document overrides all other considerations. We may have to think up some other means.'

Fawcett said: 'There are no other means.'

Harper said: 'There are no other means.'

The admiral nodded. 'There are no other means. It's Bruno or nothing.'

Fawcett shook his head. 'It's Bruno *and* the circus or nothing.'

'Looks like.' The admiral gazed consideringly at Wrinfield. 'Tell me, do you fancy the idea of being expendable?'

Wrinfield drained his glass. His hand was steady again and he was back on balance. 'Frankly, I don't.'

'Not even being interned?'

'No.'

'I see your point. It could be a bad business. Am I to take it from that that you have changed your mind?'

'I don't know, I just don't know.' Wrinfield shifted his gaze, at once both thoughtful and troubled. 'Bruno?'

'I'll go.' Bruno's voice was flat and without colour, certainly with no traces of drama or histrionics in it. 'If I have to go, I'll go alone. I don't know – yet – how I'll get there and I don't know – yet – what I have to do when I arrive. But I'll go.'

Wrinfield sighed. 'That's it, then.' He smiled faintly. 'A man can only stand so much. No immigrant American is going to put a fifth generation American to shame.'

'Thank you, Mr Wrinfield.' The admiral looked at Bruno with what might have been an expression of either curiosity or assessment on his face. 'And thank you, too. Tell me, what makes you so determined to go?'

'I told Mr Fawcett. I hate war.'

IV

The admiral had gone. Dr Harper had gone. Wrinfield and Bruno had gone and Pilgrim had been carried away: in three days' time he would be buried with all due solemnity and the cause of his death would never be known, a not unusual circumstance amongst those who plied the trades of espionage and counter-espionage and whose careers had come to an abrupt and unexpected end. Fawcett, his face as bleak and hard as the plumpness of his face would permit, was pacing up and down the dead man's apartment when the telephone rang. Fawcett picked it up immediately.

The voice in the receiver was hoarse and shaking. It said: 'Fawcett? Fawcett? Is that you, Fawcett?'

'Yes. Who's that?'

'I can't tell you over the phone. You know damn well who it is. You got me into this.' The voice was trembling so much as to be virtually unrecognizable. 'For God's sake get down here, something terrible has happened.'

'What?'

'Get down here.' The voice was imploring. 'And for God's sake come alone. I'll be in my office. The circus office.'

The line went dead. Fawcett jiggled the receiver bar but dead the line remained. Fawcett hung up, left the room, locked the door behind him, took the lift to the underground garage and drove down to the circus through the darkness and the rain.

The external circus lights were out except for some scattered weak illumination – it was already late enough for all the circus members to have sought their night accommodation aboard the train. Fawcett left the car and hurried into the animals' quarters, where Wrinfield had his shabby little portable office. The lighting here was fairly good. Signs of human life there were none, which Fawcett, on first reaction, found rather surprising, for Wrinfield had a four-footed fortune in there: the second and almost immediate reaction was that it wasn't surprising at all for nobody in his right mind was going to make off with an Indian elephant or Nubian lion. Not only were they difficult animals to control, but disposal might have presented a problem. Most of the animals were lying down, asleep, but the elephants, asleep or not and chained by one foreleg, were upright and constantly swaying from side to side and in one large cage twelve Bengal tigers were prowling restlessly around, snarling occasionally for no apparent reason.

Fawcett made for Wrinfield's office then halted in puzzlement when he saw no light coming from its solitary window. He advanced and tested the door. It wasn't locked. He opened it and peered inside and then all the world went black for him.

— 3 —

WRINFIELD hardly slept that night which, considering the recent events and the worries they had brought in their wake, was hardly a matter for surprise. He finally rose about five o'clock, showered, shaved and dressed, left his luxurious quarters aboard the train and headed for the animal quarters, an instinctive practice of his whenever he was deeply troubled, for Wrinfield was in love with his circus and felt more at home there than anywhere in the world: the degree of rapport that existed between him and his animals certainly exceeded that which had existed between him and the reluctant economics students whom – as he now regarded it – he had wasted the best years of his life teaching. Besides, he could always pass the time with Johnny the night watchman who, despite the vast gulf in status that lay between them, was an old crony and confidant of his. Not that Wrinfield had any intention of confiding in anyone that night.

But Johnny wasn't there and Johnny wasn't the man ever to fall asleep on the job, undemanding though it was – his job was to report to the trainer concerned or the veterinary surgeon any animal that might appear off-colour. No more than slightly puzzled at first, then with increasing anxiety, Wrinfield carried out a systematic search and finally located him in a dark corner. Johnny, elderly, wizened and crippled – he'd taken one fall too many from the low wire – was securely bound and gagged but otherwise alive, apparently unharmed and furiously angry. Wrinfield loosened the gag, undid the bonds and helped the old man to his shaking legs. A lifetime in the circus had left Johnny with an extraordinary command of the unprintable and he didn't miss out a single epithet as he freely unburdened his feelings to Wrinfield.

Wrinfield said: 'Who did this to you?'

'I don't know, boss. Mystery to me. I didn't see anything. Didn't hear nothing.' Tenderly, Johnny rubbed the back of his neck. 'Sandbagged, it feels like.'

Wrinfield examined the back of his scrawny neck. It was bruised and discoloured but the skin unbroken. Wrinfield put an arm round the frail shoulders. 'Sandbagged you were. Come on. A seat in the office. I've got a little something there that'll set you up. Then we get the police.'

They were half-way towards the office when Johnny's shoulders stiffened under the supporting arm and he said in an oddly harsh and strained voice: 'I reckon we've got something a bit more important than a sandbagging to report to the cops, boss.'

Wrinfield looked at him questioningly, then followed the direction of his staring eyes. In the cage of the Bengal tigers lay the savagely mauled remains of what had once been a man. Only by the few shreds of clothing left him and the pathetically heroic row of medal ribbons did Wrinfield recognize that he was looking at all that remained of Colonel Fawcett.

II

Wrinfield gazed in horrified fascination at the still pre-dawn scene – circus workers, artistes, policemen in uniform and plainclothes detectives all milling around the animal quarters, all of them busily engaged in eradicating forever any putative clues there may have been. Ambulance men were wrapping up the unidentifiable remains of Fawcett and placing it on a stretcher. In a small group remote from the others were Malthius, the tiger trainer, Neubauer the lion tamer and Bruno, the three men who had gone into the cage and taken Fawcett out. Wrinfield turned to the admiral, whom he had first called and who, since his arrival, hadn't bothered to explain his presence or identity to anyone and it was markedly noticeable that no policeman had approached him to ask him to justify his presence there; clearly, some senior police officer had said: 'Do not approach that man!'

Wrinfield said: 'Who in God's name could have done this terrible thing, sir?'

'I'm sorry, Mr Wrinfield.' It was completely out of character for the admiral to say that he was sorry about anything. 'Sorry all round. Sorry for Fawcett, one of my ablest and most trusted deputies and a damned fine human being at that. And sorry for you, that I should have been responsible for involving you in this ghastly mess. This is the kind of publicity that any circus could do without.'

'The hell with publicity. Who, sir, who?'

'And I suppose I feel a bit sorry for myself, too.' The admiral shrugged his shoulders heavily. 'Who? Obviously the same person or persons who killed Pilgrim. Your guess as to who they are is as good as mine. The one thing for sure is that they – whoever *they* are – knew he was coming down here or they wouldn't have silenced the guard in advance – he can count himself lucky that he wasn't found inside that cage with Fawcett. There was almost certainly a false phone call. We'll soon know. I have them checking on it.'

'Checking on what?'

'Every call to our office, incoming or outgoing, except, of course, on the scrambler phones, is recorded. With luck, we'll have that recording within minutes. Meantime, I'd like to talk to those three men who took Fawcett out of the cage. Individually. I understand that one of those men is your tiger trainer. What's his name?'

'Malthius. But – but he's above suspicion.'

'I don't doubt it.' The admiral was trying to be patient. 'Do you think any murder mystery would ever be solved if we questioned only the suspects? Please have him brought.'

Malthius, a dark-eyed Bulgarian with an open face, was plainly deeply upset. The admiral said, kindly for him: 'You've no need to be so distressed.'

'*My* tigers did this, sir.'

'They would probably do it to anyone in the country except you. Or would they?'

'I don't know, sir. If a person were lying quietly, I really don't think so.' He hesitated. 'But, well in certain circumstances they might.' The admiral waited patiently and Malthius went on: 'If they were provoked. Or—'

'Yes?'

'If they smelled blood.'

'You're sure of that?'

'Of course he's sure.' The admiral, who was quite unaware of Wrinfield's intense loyalty to his men, was surprised at the asperity in his voice. 'What do you think, sir? We feed them on horse meat or beef and those are raw and smell of blood. The tigers can't wait to get at the meat and tear it to pieces with teeth and claws. Have you ever seen tigers at feeding-time?'

The admiral had a mental vision of how Fawcett must have died and shuddered involuntarily. 'No, and I don't think I'll ever want to either.' He turned back to Malthius. 'So he could have been alive, conscious or not – blood doesn't flow when you're dead – stabbed and thrown into the cage?'

'That is possible, sir. But you won't find a trace of a stab wound now.'

'I realize that. You found the door locked on the outside. Is it possible to do that from the inside?'

'No. You can bolt it from the inside. It wasn't bolted.'

'Isn't that a rather curious arrangement?'

Malthius smiled for the first time, albeit faintly. 'Not for a tiger trainer, sir. When I go into the cage I turn the key on the outside and leave it in position. Once I get inside I bolt the door – can't risk having the door swing open or being pulled open by one of the tigers and letting them loose among the crowd.' He smiled a second time, again without mirth. 'It could come in useful for me, too. If things get unpleasant for me, I just slide the bolt, get away from there and turn the key on the outside.'

'Thank you. Would you ask that friend of yours—'

'Heinrich Neubauer, sir. The lion trainer.'

'I'd like to see him.' Malthius walked dejectedly away and the admiral said: 'He seems *very* unhappy to me.'

'Wouldn't you be?' Again the unexpected asperity in Wrinfield's voice. 'He not only feels personally responsible but his tigers have for the first time acquired a taste for human flesh. Malthius is human flesh, too, you know.'

'I hadn't thought of that.'

The admiral asked Neubauer a few desultory and inconsequential questions then asked for Bruno. When he arrived the admiral said: 'You're the only one I really wanted to talk to. The other two were only a cover – we're being watched both by circus people and the police. Some of the police, by the way, think I'm a very senior police officer, others that I'm from the FBI, although why they should imagine that I can't imagine. A dreadful thing, Bruno, a quite dreadful thing. Well it looks as if poor Fawcett was correct, we're being pushed to the limit to find out how really desperate we are to go to Crau. Well, I've been pushed far enough. Who knows who's going to be next? I have no right, no one has any right, to ask you to be involved in this ghastly business any more. There's a limit to patriotism – being patriotic did Pilgrim and Fawcett a great deal of good, didn't it? You are now released from any obligations, real or imagined, that you may have had.'

'Speak for yourself.' Wrinfield's tone had remained unchanged. Whatever touched Wrinfield's beloved circus touched his rawest nerve: this had become a personal matter. 'Two good men have died. You want them to have died in vain? I'm going to Europe.'

The admiral blinked and turned to Bruno. 'And you?'

Bruno looked at him in a silence that verged on the contemptuous.

'Well.' The admiral was momentarily nonplussed. 'Off again, on again. If you're prepared to accept the risks, I'm prepared to accept your sacrifices. Utterly selfish, I know, but we desperately want those papers. I won't try to thank you, I honestly wouldn't know how to, but the least I can do is to arrange protection. I'll assign five of my best men to you – as a press corps, shall we say? – then once you are aboard the boat—'

Bruno spoke in a very quiet voice. 'If you assign any of your men to us, then nobody's going anywhere, and that includes me. And from what I'm told, although I don't understand it yet, if I don't go then there's no point in anyone else going anyway. The exception, of course, is Dr Harper; a dead man vouched for him and you can't get any better recommendation than that. As for the rest of your men – who do you think killed Pilgrim and Fawcett? Without their protection, we might have a chance.' Bruno turned abruptly and walked away. The admiral looked after him, with a slightly pained expression on his face, at a momentary but highly unusual loss for words, but was saved the necessity of making comment by the arrival of a police sergeant carrying a small black box. That the uniform was not the property of the man inside it Wrinfield was quite certain. When it came to local colour Charles – it was the only way Wrinfield could think of him – was not a man who missed much.

The admiral said: 'The recording—' and when the sergeant nodded: 'May we use your office, please, Mr Wrinfield?'

'Of course.' Wrinfield looked around him. 'Not here. In the train. Too many people.'

The office door closed behind them, the sergeant took the recorder from its casing and Wrinfield said: 'What do you expect to hear?'

'You.' Wrinfield looked his astonishment. 'Or a very close approximation of your voice. Or Bruno's. Yours were the only two voices in the circus that Fawcett knew: he wouldn't have come for anyone else.'

They heard the recording through. At the end Wrinfield said calmly: 'That's meant to be me. Shall we hear it again?'

They heard it through a second time then Wrinfield said positively: 'That's not my voice. You know it isn't.'

'My dear Wrinfield, I never dreamed it would be. I know it isn't. *Now* I know it isn't. But I had to hear it a second time to make sure. When a man speaks in that hurried and distressed fashion, his voice takes on abnormal overtones. A piece of silk stretched across the mouthpiece is a great help. I don't blame poor Fawcett for being fooled, especially when he had only the one thing on his mind at the time. But it's a damned good imitation all the same.' The admiral paused, ruminated, then looked at Wrinfield consideringly. 'To the best of my knowledge and belief, and to yours, you don't know and never have talked to any of my men. Right?' Wrinfield nodded. 'So I put it to you that this call was made by someone who knew your voice intimately and had studied it.'

'That's preposterous. If you're suggesting—'

'Precisely what I *am* suggesting, I'm afraid. Look, man, if our organization can be infiltrated don't you think your damned circus can't be too? After all, you've got twenty-five nationalities working for you: I've got only one.'

'You're the CIA. *Everyone* would want to infiltrate the CIA. Who'd want to infiltrate a harmless circus?'

'Nobody. But in the eyes of the ungodly you're not a harmless circus, you're an affiliate of the CIA and therefore ripe for infiltration. Don't let blind loyalty blind your intelligence. Let's hear that recording again. Only this time don't listen for your own voice, listen for someone else's. I should imagine you know the voice of every man in your employment. And to narrow the field, remember that most of your men speak with fairly heavy foreign accents. This is an Anglo-Saxon voice, probably American, although I can't be sure.'

They played the recording through four more times and at the end Wrinfield shook his head. 'It's no good. The distortion is far too heavy.'

'Thank you, officer, you may leave.' The sergeant snapped the case shut and left. Briefly the admiral paced up and down the full length of the office – three steps in either direction – then shook his head in the reluctant acceptance of the inevitable. 'What a charming thought. A link up between my lot and yours.'

'You're terribly certain.'

'I'm terribly certain of one thing and that's this. There isn't one man in my lot who wouldn't give up his pension rather than open the door of a tiger's cage.'

Wrinfield nodded with an equally reluctant acceptance. 'I suppose it's my turn to say that I should have thought of that.'

'That's unimportant. Point is, what are we going to do? You're under hostile surveillance, my career's on that.' He paused in momentary gloom. 'Whatever my career's going to be worth when all this is over.'

'I thought we'd settled all that.' The now accustomed touch of asperity was back in Wrinfield's voice. 'You heard what I said back in the circus. You heard what Bruno said. We go.' The admiral regarded him thoughtfully. 'A marked change of attitude since last night. Or, more properly, a marked hardening in attitude.'

'I don't think you quite understand, sir.' Wrinfield was being patient. 'This is my life, my whole life. Touch me, touch my circus. Or vice versa. We have one major card in the hole.'

'I've missed it.'

'Bruno's still in the clear.'

'I hadn't missed it and it's because I want him to stay that way that I'd like you to take this girl of ours into your employ. Her name is Maria Hopkins and although I don't know her all that well Dr Harper assures me she is a very bright operative and that her loyalty is beyond question. She's to fall in love with Bruno and he with her. Nothing more natural.' The admiral put on his sad smile. 'If I were twenty years younger I'd say there was nothing easier. She's really rather beautiful. That way she can liaise with Bruno, yourself, Dr Harper – and, up to the time of your departure, with myself – without raising any eyebrows. As an equestrienne, perhaps? That was Fawcett's idea.'

'No perhaps. She may think she's good, she may actually be good, but there's no place for amateurs in the circus. Besides there's not a man or woman on my performing staff who wouldn't spot immediately that she's not a trained circus equestrienne: you couldn't devise a surer way of calling attention to her.'

'Suggestions?'

'Yes. Fawcett mentioned this possibility in this dreadful bordello place he took us to and I've given the matter some thought. Didn't require much, really. My secretary is getting married in a few weeks to a very strange fellow who doesn't like circuses: so she's leaving. This is common knowledge. Let Maria be my new secretary. Every reason for her to be in constant contact with me, and through me your doctor and Bruno without any questions being asked.'

'Couldn't be better. Now, I'd like you to put a large box advert in the papers tomorrow for a doctor to accompany the circus to Europe. I know this isn't the way one normally recruits a medical man but we've no time to wait to use the more professional channels. This must be made clear in the advert. Besides it will make it perfectly clear that you are seeking a doctor with no one in mind and that your choice will essentially be a random one. You may have quite a few replies – it would make a nice holiday for someone who has just, say, finished his internship – but you will, of course, choose Dr Harper.

'He hasn't practised medicine for years, although I dare

say he'd find an aspirin if you twisted his arm. That's irrelevant. What matters is that he is an outstanding intelligence agent.'

'So, I was led to believe, was Pilgrim. And Fawcett.'

The admiral made a quick gesture of irritation. 'Things don't always happen in threes. Fortunes turn. Those two men knew the risks. So does Harper. Anyway, no suspicion attaches to him. There's no connection between him and the circus.'

'Has it occurred to you that "they" may check on his background?'

'Has it occurred to *you* that I might make a better owner and managing director of a circus than you are?'

'*Touché*. I asked for that.'

'Yes, you did. Two things. There's no more reason why they should check on him than any of your hundreds of employees. His background is impeccable: he's a consultant at the Belvedere and this is his way of spending part of his sabbatical at someone else's expense. Much higher qualifications and much more experienced than any of the other applicants you'll have. A natural choice. You're lucky to have him.'

'But he hasn't practised—'

'He has consulting rooms in the hospital. One of our branch offices.'

'Is nothing sacred to you people?'

'Not much. How soon are you prepared to leave?'

'Leave?'

'For Europe.'

'I have a number of alternative dates and places pencilled in for there. That's not the problem. Three more days here then we have three more engagements on the east coast.'

'Cancel them.'

'Cancel them? We never cancel – I mean, we have all arrangements made, theatres booked, saturation advertising, thousands of tickets sold in advance—'

'Compensation, Mr Wrinfield, will be on a princely scale. Think of a suitable figure and it will be lodged in your bank tomorrow.'

Wrinfield was not much given to wringing his hands but he looked as if he would have liked to indulge in just a little right then. 'We are an annual institution in those places. We have a tremendous amount of goodwill—'

'Double the figure you first thought of. Cancel. Your sea transport will be ready in New York in one week. When you sign up Dr Harper, he'll organize vaccinations and inoculations. If you have any visa problems, we'll do a little leaning. Not that I expect any trouble from the east European embassies or consulates – their countries are just dying to have you. I will be around tonight for the evening performance. So will the ravishing Miss Hopkins – but not with me. Have someone show her around, but not you.'

'I have a very bright nephew—'

'Fine. Tell him nothing. Have him give her a thorough guided tour, the new secretary getting acquainted with the physical background of her new job. Have her introduced to some of your top performers. Especially, of course, to Bruno. Let Bruno know the score in advance.'

III

Henry Wrinfield looked a great deal more like Tesco Wrinfield's son than a nephew had any right to look, although he undoubtedly was his nephew. He had the same dark eyes, the same lean studious face, the same quick intelligence; and if he wasn't quite in the same cerebral league as his uncle he was, as his uncle had said, a very bright young fellow indeed, or at least bright enough to find no hardship in the chore of escorting Maria Hopkins round the back-stage of the circus. For an hour or so he completely forgot the blue-stockinged Ivy Leaguer to whom he was engaged and was slightly surprised that, when he remembered her about an hour later – he rarely spent ten minutes without thinking about her – he experienced no twinges of conscience.

Few men would have found cause for complaint in the performance of such a task as had been entrusted to Henry, and those only misogynists in an irretrievably advanced state. She was a petite figure, although clearly not suffering from malnutrition, with long dark hair, rather splendid liquid dark eyes and an extraordinarily infectious smile and laugh. Her resemblance to the popular concept of an intelligence agent was non-existent, which may have been one of the reasons why Dr Harper reportedly held her in such high regard.

Henry, quite unnecessarily guiding her by the upper arm, showed her round the tethered and caged animals and introduced her to Malthius and Neubauer, who were putting the big cats through their last minute paces. Malthius was charming and graceful and wished her a very pleasant stay: Neubauer, though civil enough, didn't know how to be charming and wished her nothing.

Henry then led her through to the raucous blare of the fairground. Kan Dahn was there, toying with an enormous bar-bell and looking more impressively powerful than ever: he took her small hand carefully in his own gigantic one, smiled widely, announced that she was the best recruit to arrive at the circus since he himself had joined it years ago and altogether gave her a welcome so courteous it bordered on the effusive. Kan Dahn was always in high humour, although nobody was quite sure whether it stemmed from an innate good nature or because he had discovered quite some time ago that it was unnecessary for him to be unpleasant to anyone. Manuelo, the Mexican genius with the knife, was standing behind the counter of a booth, benevolently watching considerable numbers of the young and not so young throwing rubber-tipped knives at moving targets. Occasionally he would come round to the front of his booth and, throwing double-handed, would knock down six targets in half that number of seconds, just to show his customers that there was really nothing to it. He welcomed Maria with a great deal of Latin enthusiasm, putting himself entirely at her service during her stay in the circus. A little farther on, Ron Roebuck, the lasso specialist, gave her a grave but friendly welcome: as she walked away from him she was astonished and then delighted to see a shimmering whirling circle of rope drop down over her, barely touch the ground, then effortlessly rise and disappear without once touching her clothes. She turned and gave Roebuck a wide smile and he no longer looked grave.

Bruno emerged from his little performing hall as Henry and Maria approached it. He was clad in the same Mandarin robe as previously and, also as before, looked anything but impressive. Henry made the introductions and Bruno looked at her with a kind of inoffensive appraisal. As usual, it was almost impossible to tell what he was thinking, and then he smiled, a rare gesture for Bruno but one that transformed his face.

He said: 'Welcome to the circus. I hope your stay is a long and happy one.'

'Thank you.' She smiled in turn. 'This is an honour. You – you are the star of the circus?'

Bruno pointed skywards. 'All the stars are up there, Miss Hopkins. Down here there are only performers. We all do what we can. Some of us are lucky in that we have acts more spectacular than others, that's all. Excuse me. I must hurry.'

Maria, thoughtful, watched him go. Henry said in amusement: 'Not quite what you expected?'

'Well, no.'

'Disappointed?'

'A little, I suppose.'

'You won't be tonight. Nobody ever is, not when they watch the impossible.'

'Is it true that he and his brothers are completely blindfolded up there? They can't see at all?'

'No faking. They are in total darkness. But you'll notice that it's Bruno that conducts the orchestra. He's the co-ordinator and catcher. Maybe the three brothers share some telepathic gift, I don't know. Nobody else seems to know either. And if Bruno and his brothers know they're not saying.'

'Maybe it's something else.' She indicated the legend 'The Great Mentalist'. 'A photographic memory, they say, and can read people's minds.'

'I hope he didn't read yours tonight.'

'Please. And he can read the contents of sealed envelopes. If he can see through paper why can't he see through a blindfold?'

He looked at her in genuine surprise. He said: 'Miss Hopkins, you're not just a pretty face. Do you know, I'd never thought of that.' He pondered for a moment, then gave up. 'Let's go take our seats for the show. Like it, so far?'

'Very much.'

'Anything special?'

'Yes. Everybody's so terribly nice and polite.'

Henry smiled. 'We're not all just down from the trees.' He took her arm and guided her towards the arena. His blue-stocking fiancée wasn't even a cloud on his rose-coloured horizon.

IV

There was someone in the circus at that moment who was not being terribly nice and polite, but then the admiral was not a member of the circus and he certainly was not accustomed to having his will thwarted. Further, he'd had a long, tiring and very frustrating day and his normal amiability had deserted him.

'I don't think you heard me properly,' the admiral said with ominous restraint.

'You heard me, all right.' Because the back-stage entrance to the circus was ill-lit, because it was very dark and still raining outside and because his faded eyes no longer saw too well, Johnny, the nightwatchman, had failed to identify the admiral. 'The entrance for the public is farther along there. Get going!'

'You're under arrest,' the admiral said without preamble. He turned to a shadowy figure behind him. 'Take this fellow to the nearest station. Have him charged with obstructing the course of justice.'

'Easy, now, easy.' Johnny's tone had undergone a marked change. 'There's no need—' He leaned forward and peered up at the admiral. 'Aren't you the gentleman who was here when we had that bit of bother this morning?'

'If by a bit of bother you mean murder, yes. Take me to Mr Wrinfield!'

'Sorry, sir. I'm on duty here.'

'Johnny, isn't it? You still want to be on duty tomorrow, Johnny?'

Johnny took the admiral to Mr Wrinfield.

The admiral's interview with Wrinfield was brief. He said: 'You're clear for Europe. There'll be no trouble with visas.'

'Twenty-five different nationalities? In one day?'

'I have a staff of four hundred, amongst some of whom the eagle-eyed may detect some glimmering of intelligence. Dr Harper will be here at ten in the morning. Be here please. He will begin immediately. Our personal investigations and police enquiries into the murders of Pilgrim and Fawcett have turned up nothing. I don't expect they will. Future events may.'

'What kind of events?'

'I don't know. Fairly drastic in nature, I should imagine. Next, I've just put a scare into Johnny, your night watchman. That was to ensure his co-operation. He's truculent and a bit dim but I suppose reliable.'

'I'd trust him with my life.'

'We put different values on our lives. I'm putting six men on to patrol the sleeping quarters of the train at night. They're not from our organization, so you need have no worries on that score. They will be here nightly until you leave – which, incidentally, will be in five days' time.'

'Why the patrol? I'm not sure I like that.'

'Frankly, it doesn't matter whether you like it or not.' The admiral smiled, albeit tiredly, to rob the words of offence. 'From the moment you accepted this assignment, you're under government orders. It's for security. I want Johnny to act as a guide-dog.'

'Whose security?'

'Bruno's, Maria's, Harper's – and yours.'

'Mine? *I'm* in danger?'

'Quite candidly, I'm sure you're not, if for no other reason than if anything happened to you the trip would be cancelled – which wouldn't suit our friends at all. But I'm not taking the ghost of a chance.'

'And you think this patrol will help?'

'Yes. In a closed community like this their presence will be common knowledge within the hour. Put it about that the police have received threats against unspecified members of your staff. If you have any bogey-men among your crew members, this news will make them lie very low indeed.'

'As you say, you don't take many chances, do you?'

The admiral said drily: 'I think the shadows of Pilgrim and

Fawcett would entirely approve. Have Bruno and Maria met yet?' Wrinfield nodded. 'Reactions?'

'Bruno hasn't got any. If he has, he never shows them. As for Maria, well, Henry said she didn't exactly fall about.'

'Unimpressed, one might say?'

'One might.'

'She's watching the show?'

'Yes. With Henry.'

'I wonder if she's still unimpressed.'

V

'Still unimpressed?' Henry asked. He clearly wasn't, but then he couldn't keep his eyes off her.

Maria didn't answer immediately. She was staring, as if hypnotized – as ten thousand other people were doing – as the Blind Eagles went through their unbelievable and seemingly suicidal aerial routine. At the end of the performance she released her breath in a long soundless sigh.

'I don't believe it.' Her voice was almost a whisper. 'I just don't believe what I've seen.'

'I can hardly believe it myself – and I've seen it a hundred times. First impressions can be wrong, no?'

'Just how wrong.'

Half an hour later she was with Henry just outside the dressing-room area when Bruno emerged, dressed in street clothes. He was back to his old, relatively unimpressive self. He stopped, smiled at her, and said: 'I saw you at the show.'

'Blindfolded?'

'On the low wire. On the bicycle.'

She looked at him in astonishment. 'Doing that impossible act? You have time to look round the audience?'

'I have to have something to occupy my attention,' he said with mock bravado. 'Enjoy it all?' She nodded and he smiled again. 'Even the Blind Eagles? I'm only searching for compliments, of course.'

Maria looked at him without smiling, pointed upwards and said: 'A star has fallen from the sky.' She turned and walked away. From the slight corrugation of Bruno's brow it was impossible to tell whether he was puzzled or amused.

VI

Dr Harper, looking every inch the high-powered consultant that he wasn't, arrived precisely at ten o'clock the following morning, but had to wait over half an hour while Wrinfield went through the motions of interviewing several other would-be circus doctors who had turned up quite some time before ten o'clock.

Wrinfield was alone in his office when Harper knocked and entered. Harper said: 'Good morning. I'm Dr Harper.'

Wrinfield looked at him in considerable astonishment and had just opened his mouth to speak, doubtless to inform Harper that he was not likely to have forgotten him due to the fact that they had made their first acquaintance over the dead body of Pilgrim, when Harper handed him a hand-written note. It read: 'This office may be bugged. Interview me as you would any other candidate.'

'Good morning.' Wrinfield hadn't even blinked. 'I'm Wrinfield, the owner.' He launched smoothly into the interview: Harper, both while listening and answering, sat down and scribbed another note. He handed it across. It read: 'End the interview and give me the job. Ask me my immediate plans then invite me outside for a look around.'

Wrinfield said: 'Well, that's it. I'm too busy a man to spend a lifetime on making decisions. The job's yours. Frankly, when I have the choice between an experienced consultant and the young interns I've been seeing – well, I don't have much of a choice. I'm not so naïve as to imagine that you're making this a full-time career. A sabbatical – or part of it?'

'Twelve years in the Belvedere is a long time.'

'How soon could you be free, doctor?'

'Now.'

'Splendid. And what would your immediate plans be?'

'Depends on how soon you want to leave on this foreign tour.'

'Let's work towards four or five days from now.'

'Little enough time. First, Mr Wrinfield, I'd like your authorization for medical supplies, then a collection of all the passports until I see what's required in the way of vaccinations and inoculations – I understand your circus has never toured abroad before. I'm afraid that some of your high-wire and trapeze artistes will have to curtail their acts quite a bit in the next few days.'

'All that I can arrange immediately. First of all, though, I suggest you have a look around. When you see what you've taken on you might want to change your mind.'

The two men left the office and Wrinfield led the way to the centre ring of the circus itself, a spot which, in so far as potential eavesdroppers were concerned, was probably more secluded than any place for a mile around. Nonetheless, Wrinfield scuffed the sand with the toe of his shoe and looked casually around before speaking.

He said: 'And what was all that for?'

'Sorry about all that cloak and dagger stuff. We don't usually go in for it – spoils our image. Incidentally, congratulations – you'd make a splendid recruit to our organizations. Anyway, I was speaking to Charles just before I came here and we both came up with the same very nasty suspicion at the same time.'

'That my office was bugged?'

'If it were, it could explain a great deal.'

'But why all the paper notes you handed me? Why didn't you just phone and warn me?' Harper half-smiled at him and Wrinfield tapped his own head. 'That wasn't very bright. The phone could have been bugged, too.'

'Indeed. In a few minutes' time you can expect another applicant for my job. His name is Dr Morley and he will be carrying the regulation black medical bag. But he's no doctor, he's an electronics expert and his bag is packed with extremely advanced equipment for locating bugging devices. Ten minutes alone in your office and he'll find out whether it's clean or not.'

Fifteen minutes later, as Wrinfield and Harper approached the office, a tall dark man with a black bag descended the steps from it. For the benefit of watchers or listeners Wrinfield introduced them and suggested a cup of coffee in the canteen. They sat at a remote corner table.

Morley said: 'Two bugs, Miniaturized radio transmitters. One in the ceiling light, the other in the phone.'

'So I can breathe again,' Wrinfield said. Neither of the other two made any immediate reply so he went on rather uncertainly: 'I mean, those devices have been removed or deactivated?'

'Most certainly not,' Harper said. 'The bugs are still there and there they will remain, probably until we return from Europe. Do you think we want the ungodly to know that we know? Think of all the amount of false and confusing and misleading information we can feed them.' One could see that, mentally, Harper was positively rubbing his hands. 'From now on you will conduct only routine circus business in that office.' He smiled almost dreamily. 'Unless, of course, I give instructions to the contrary.'

VII

In the days that followed, four subjects increasingly and exclusively dominated conversation in the circus.

The first of those, inevitably, emanated from the mounting excitement over the forthcoming trip to Europe, a euphoric state that was not, understandably, shared by the unfortunates who were not making the foreign tour but would be returning to the winter headquarters in Florida: for purely logistical reasons, only two-thirds of the personnel would be able to make it. But for the two-thirds who were going the European visit, especially as it included a two-way ocean voyage, was regarded as nothing less than a holiday. An extremely arduous holiday it promised to be from the moment of disembarkation, but nonetheless a holiday. About half the crew were American, few of whom had ever been abroad before, partly from financial considerations, partly because the circus season was so long that they had only three weeks free in the year and this at the wrong time of the year– in the dead of winter: for them, this could be a once in a life-time experience. The remainder were predominantly European, mainly from the other side of the Iron Curtain, and this was, possibly, also a once in a lifetime experience – that of seeing their native countries and families again.

The second subject concerned the much-maligned activities of Dr Harper and his two temporarily employed trained nurses. Their degree of unpopularity was high. Harper was rigorous to the point of ruthlessness, and when it came to vaccinations and inoculations no one passed through the meshes of the wide net he cast and when any to-be-or-not-to-be questions arose he never gave anyone the benefit of the doubt. Circus people are undoubtedly tougher and fitter than the average run of mankind, but when it came to a profound aversion to injections, scratches and consequent sore arms they were no different from anyone else. But nobody could possibly doubt that they had a genuine and dedicated doctor in their midst.

The third concerned two sets of mysterious activities. The first was the patrol that so closely guarded the sleeping quarters on the train during the night. No one seriously believed that threats to lives had been made by parties unknown but then, they didn't know what else to believe. Then there was the baffling incident of two alleged electrical engineers who had come to examine the wiring of the train. They had almost finished their task before their authenticity had been questioned and the police called. Unknown to anyone in the circus except Harper, they had been detained in custody for precisely five minutes, which was all the time it took for one of them to phone the admiral and reassure him that none of the sleeping quarters on the train had been bugged.

The last, but unquestionably the most engrossing topic of the lot, concerned Bruno and Maria. To the vexation of Henry, who was not engaged in a battle with his conscience, they were not only seen increasingly in each other's company, but were also seen actively and with no attempt at concealment to seek out each other's company. The reactions to this particular development were predictably mixed. Some were amused to see Bruno's hitherto inviolate defences being breached. Others were envious – the men because Bruno had undoubtedly and apparently without effort attached the affections of a girl who politely and pointedly ignored any other approaches made to her, the women because Bruno, by far the most eligible bachelor in the circus, politely but pointedly ignored any approaches made to him. Many more were happy for Bruno, and this despite the fact that apart from Kan Dahn, Manuelo and Roebuck he had no real friends in the circus, because it was common knowledge that since the death of his wife he had been a sad, lonely and withdrawn man who never looked at women. But the majority regarded it as only natural and inevitable that the undisputed star of the circus should come together with a girl who was arguably the most lovely young lady among a plethora of lovely young ladies.

It was not until the last performance of their last night in town that Bruno rather diffidently asked her along to see his quarters aboard the train. Maria showed no diffidence in accepting his offer. He guided her stumbling footsteps along the rutted sliding track then helped her up the steep steps at the end of a coach.

Bruno had rather splendid and completely enclosed quarters, consisting of a sitting-room, kitchen-cum-dinette, bathroom – with, of all things, a sunken bath – and bedroom. Maria looked almost dazed as he led her back to the sitting-room.

He said: 'I'm told I mix what the Americans call a rather mean Martini. Only time I ever drink is after I've finished a series in a town. Alcohol and the trapeze don't mix. Will you join me?'

'Please. I must say you do live in style. You should have a wife to share all this.'

Bruno fetched ice. 'Is that a proposal?'

'No, it's not. But all this – just for one man.'

'Mr Wrinfield is very kind to me.'

She said drily: 'I don't think Mr Wrinfield is losing out on the deal. Does anyone else have accommodation like this?'

'I haven't gone around examining—'

'Bruno!'

'No.'

'Certainly not me. I have a place like a horizontal telephone box. Ah, well, I suppose there's a vast gap in status between a trainee secretary and you.'

'That's so.'

'Men! Modesty! I just don't know!'

'Come with me on the high trapeze. Blindfolded. Then you'll know.'

She shuddered, not altogether affectedly. 'I can't even stand on a chair without getting vertigo. Truly. You're welcome to your palace. Well, I suppose I can always come along and visit the palace.'

He handed her a drink. 'I'll have a special welcome mat made out for you.'

'Thank you.' She lifted her glass. 'To our first time alone. We're supposed to be falling in love. Any idea how the others think we are doing?'

'I can't speak for the others. I think I'm doing very well.' He glanced at the compressing lips and said hastily: 'I think *we're* doing very well. I suppose, as of this moment, that must be the general idea. By this time at least a hundred people must know that you're here with me. Aren't you supposed to blush or something?'

'No.'

'It's a lost art. Well, I don't suppose you came along just for my dark eyes. You have something to tell me?'

'Not really. You asked me, remember?' She smiled. 'Why?'

'Just polishing up our act.' She stopped smiling and put down her glass. He reached forward quickly and touched the back of her hand. 'Don't be a silly goose, Maria.' She looked at him uncertainly, smiled a token smile, and picked up her glass again. 'Tell me. What am I supposed to do when we get to Crau – and how am I supposed to do it?'

'Only Dr Harper knows, and he's not ready to talk yet. I should imagine that he'll tell you – us – either on the way across or when we get to Europe. But two things he did tell me this morning—'

'I knew you had something to tell me.'

'Yes. I was just trying to be a tease. It didn't work, did it? Remember those two so-called electrical engineers that the police escorted to the train? They were our people, electronic experts searching for listening devices – bugs. They concentrated on your apartment.'

'Bugs! In my apartment. Come on, Maria, that *is* a bit melodramatic.'

'Is it? The second item of news is that a few days ago they found two bugs in Mr Wrinfield's office – one for the room, one for the telephone. I suppose that's melodramatic, too?' When Bruno made no reply she went on: 'They haven't removed the bugs. Mr Wrinfield, on Dr Harper's suggestion, is on the phone to Charles several times a day, dropping vague hints and making veiled suggestions about certain members of the circus who might be of interest to him. Nothing about us, of course. In fact he's made so many suggestions that if they – whoever "they" may be – are keeping tabs on the suggested suspects they won't have time to look at far less think about anyone else. Which, of course, includes us.'

'I think they're nuts,' Bruno said candidly. 'And by "they", this time, I don't mean "they", I mean Wrinfield and Harper. Playing little kiddies' games.'

'The murders of Pilgrim and Fawcett. That was a game?'

'Preserve me from feminine logic. I wasn't talking about them.'

'Dr Harper has twenty years' experience behind him.'

'Or one year's twenty times over. OK, so I leave myself in the safe arms of the experts. Meantime, I suppose there's nothing for the sacrificial calf to do?'

'No. Well, yes. You can tell me how to get in touch with you.'

'Knock twice and ask for Bruno.'

'You have a sealed-off suite here. I won't be able to see you when the train is in motion.'

'Well, well.' Bruno smiled widely, a rare thing for him: it was the first time she had seen his smile touch his eyes. 'I make progress. You think you'll be wanting to see me?'

'Don't be silly. I may *have* to see you.'

Bruno nodded forwards. 'It's illegal to seal off any part of a coach in motion. There's a door in the corner of my bedroom that leads to the passage beyond. But it's only got one handle and that's on my side.'

'If I knock tat-tat, tat-tat, you'll know it's me.'

'Tat-tat, tat-tat,' he said solemnly. 'I love those kiddies' games.'

He escorted her back to her compartment. At the foot of the steps he said: 'Well, goodnight. Thanks for the visit.' He bent forward and kissed her lightly.

She didn't object, just said mildly: 'Isn't that carrying realism a bit too far?'

'Not at all. Orders are orders. We are supposed to be

creating a certain impression, and the chance was too good to pass up. There are at least a dozen people watching us.'

She made a face, turned and went up the steps.

— 4 —

MOST OF THE following day was given up to dismantling the bewildering variety and daunting amount of equipment inside the arena, the backstage and the fairground and loading up the half-mile-long train. To transfer this, the animal cages, the prefabricated offices, the fairground booths and Bruno's ramshackle mentalist theatre, not to mention the animals and circus members to the coaches and flat-cars, was a massive undertaking that to the layman would have appeared well-nigh impossible: the circus, with its generations of experience behind it, performed the task with an almost ludicrous ease, a smooth efficiency that reduced a seemingly hopeless confusion to a near-miracle of precision and order. Even the loading up of provisions for the hundreds of animals and humans would have seemed a most formidable task: in the event the last of the provision trucks departed less than an hour after the first had arrived. The whole operation could have been likened to an exercise in military logistics with the sole proviso that any unbiased and expert observer would have conceded that the circus had unquestionably the edge in efficiency.

II

The circus train was due to pull out at ten o'clock that night. At nine o'clock, Dr Harper was still closeted with the admiral, studying two very complicated diagrams.

The admiral had a pipe in one hand, a brandy in the other. He looked relaxed, calm and unconcerned. It was possible that he might just have been relaxed and calm but, as the sole instigator of the forthcoming operation, the man who had conceived and planned it all down to the last and most intimate details possible, it was impossible that he should not be concerned. He said: 'You have it all? Guards, entry, interior layout, exit and escape route to the Baltic?'

'I have it all. I just hope that damned ship is there for rendez-vous.' Harper folded the diagrams and pushed them deeply into the inside pocket of his coat.

'You break in on a Tuesday night. They'll be cruising offshore from the Friday to the following Friday. A whole week's grace.'

'Won't the East Germans or the Poles or the Russians be suspicious, sir?'

'Inevitably. Wouldn't you?'

'Won't they object?'

'How can they? Since when has the Baltic been anyone's private pond? Of course they're going to tie up the presence of the ship – or ships – with the presence of the circus in Crau. Inevitable, and nothing we can do about it. The circus, the circus.' The admiral sighed. 'You'd better deliver the goods, Harper, or I'm going to be on welfare before the year is out.'

Harper smiled. 'I wouldn't like that, sir. And you know better than anyone that the ultimate responsibility for the delivery of the goods doesn't lie in my hands.'

'I know. Have you formed any personal impression of our latest recruit yet?'

'Nothing more than is obvious to anyone else, sir. He's intelligent, tough, strong and appears to have been born without a nervous system. He's a very close person. Maria Hopkins says that it's impossible to get next to him.'

'What?' The admiral quirked a bushy eyebrow. 'That delightful young child? I'm sure if she really tried—'

'I didn't quite mean it that way, sir.'

'Peace, Harper, peace. I do not endeavour to be facetious. There are times that are sent to try men's souls. Although I know we have no option it is not easy to have to rely in the final analysis on an unknown. Apart from the fact that if he fails – well, there's only one way he can fail and then he'll be on my conscience for the remainder of my days. And don't you add to that burden.'

'Sir?'

'Mind your back is what I mean. Those papers you've just stuck – securely, I trust – in your inside pocket. You are aware, of course, what will happen if you are caught with those in your possession?'

Harper sighed. 'I am aware. I'll have my throat cut and end up, suitably weighted, in some canal or river. Doubtless you can always find a replacement.'

'Doubtless. But the way things are going I'm going to be running out of replacements quite soon, so I'd rather not be put to the trouble. You are quite sure you have the times of transmission and the code totally memorized?'

Harper said gloomily: 'You don't have much faith in your subordinates, sir.'

'The way things have been going recently, I don't have much faith in myself, either.'

Harper touched the bottom of his medical bag. 'This postage stamp receiver. You sure you can pick me up?'

'We're using NASA equipment. We could pick you up on the moon.'

'I somehow wish I was going there.'

III

Some six hours after departure the circus train drew into a shunting yard. Arc-lamps apart, the darkness was total and the rain very heavy. There, after an interminable period of advancing, reversing, bumping, clanking and screeching of wheels on points – the combination of all of which effectively succeeded in waking up everybody aboard – a considerable number of pre-selected coaches were detached, subsequently to be hauled south to their winter quarters in Florida. The main body of the train continued on its way to New York.

Nothing untoward happened en route. Bruno, who invariably cooked for himself, had not left his quarters once. He had been visited twice by his brothers, once by Wrinfield and once by Harper but by no one else: known to everybody as a loner, he was invariably treated as such.

Not until the train had arrived on the quay alongside the container-passenger ship that was to take them to Genoa – selected not so much for its strategic geographical position as the fact that it was one of the few Mediterranean ports with the facilities to off-load the crane-breaking coaches and flat-cars – did Bruno leave his quarters. It was still raining. One of the first persons he encountered was Maria. She was dressed in navy slacks, a voluminous yellow oilskin, and looked thoroughly miserable. She gave him the nearest she would ever be able to come to a scowl and came to the point with what he had now come to regard as her customary straightforwardness.

'Not very sociable, are you?'

'I'm sorry. But you did know where I was.'

'I had nothing to tell you.' Then, inconsequentially: 'You knew where *I* was.'

'I find telephone boxes cramping.'

'You could have invited me. While I know we're supposed to be striking up some special relationship I don't go openly chasing after men.'

'You don't have to.' He smiled to rob the next words of offence. 'Or do you prefer to do it discreetly?'

'Very amusing. Very clever. You have no shame?'

'For what?'

'Your shameful neglect.'

'Lots.'

'Then take me to dinner tonight.'

'Telepathy, Maria. Sheer telepathy.'

She gave him a look of disbelief and left to change.

IV

They switched taxis three times on the way to the pleasant Italian restaurant Maria had chosen. When they were seated Bruno said: 'Was all that necessary? The taxis, I mean?'

'I don't know. I follow orders.'

'Why are we here. You miss me so much?'

'I have instructions for you.'

'Not my dark eyes?' She smiled and shook her head and he sighed. 'You can't win them all. What instructions?'

'I suppose you're going to say that I could easily have whispered them to you in some dark corner on the quayside?'

'A prospect not without its attractions. But not tonight.'

'Why?'

'It's raining.'

'What is it like to be a romantic at heart?'

'And I like it here. Very pleasant restaurant.' He looked at her consideringly, at the blue velvet dress, the fur cape that was far too expensive for a secretary, the sheen of rain on her shining dark hair. 'Besides, in the dark I wouldn't be able to see you. Here I can. You're really very beautiful. What instructions?'

'What?' She was momentarily flustered, unbalanced by the sudden switch, then compressed her lips in mock ferociousness. 'We sail at eleven o'clock tomorrow morning. Please be in your cabin at eleven o'clock in the evening. At that hour the purser will arrive to discuss seating arrangements, or some such, with you. He's a genuine purser but he's also something else. He will make absolutely certain that there are no listening devices in your cabin.' Bruno remained silent. 'I notice you're not talking about melodrama this time.'

Bruno said with some weariness: 'Because it hardly seems worth talking about. Why on earth should anyone plant bugs in my cabin? I'm not under suspicion. But I will be if you and Harper keep on behaving in this idiotic cloak-and-dagger fashion. Why the bugging of Wrinfield's office? Why were two men sent to look for bugs in my place aboard the train? Why this character now? Too many people seeing that I'm debugged, too many people knowing that I can't possibly be all that I claim to be or that the circus claims that I am. Too many people having their attention called to me. I don't like it one little bit.'

'Please. There's no need to be like that—'

'Isn't there? Your opinion. And don't be soothing to me.'

'Look, Bruno, I'm just a messenger. Directly, there's no reason on earth why you should be under suspicion. But we are – or we're going to be up against an extremely efficient and suspicious secret police, who certainly won't overlook the slightest possibility. After all, the information we want is in Crau. We're going to Crau. You were born in Crau. And they will know that you have the strongest possible motivation – revenge. They killed your wife—'

'Be quiet!' Maria recoiled, appalled by the quiet ferocity

in his voice. 'Nobody has spoken of her to me in six and a half years. Mention my dead wife again and I'll pull out, wreck the whole operation and leave you to explain to your precious chief why it was your gaucherie, your ill manners, your total lack of feeling, your incredible insensitivity that ruined everything. You understand?'

'I understand.' She was very pale, shocked almost, tried to understand the enormity of her blunder and failed. She ran a slow tongue across her lips. 'I'm sorry, I'm terribly sorry. That was a bad mistake.' She still wasn't sure what the mistake was about. 'But never again, I promise.'

He said nothing.

'Dr Harper says please be outside your cabin at 6.30 p.m., sitting on the floor – sorry, deck – at the foot of the companionway. You have fallen down and damaged your ankle. You will be found and helped to your cabin. Dr Harper will, of course, be there almost immediately. He wishes to give you a full briefing on the nature of the operation.'

'Has he told you?' There was still a singular lack of warmth in Bruno's voice.

'He told me nothing. If I know Dr Harper he'll probably tell you to tell me nothing either.'

'I will do what you ask. Now that you've completed your business, we may as well get back. Three taxis for you, of course, rules are rules. I'll take one straight back to the ship. It's quicker and cheaper and the hell with the CIA.'

She reached out a tentative hand and touched his arm.

'I have apologized. Sincerely. How long must I keep on doing it?' When he made no answer she smiled at him and the smile was as her hand had been, tentative and uncertain. 'You'd think a person who earns as much money as you do could afford to buy a meal for a working girl like myself. Or do we go Dutch? Please don't leave. I don't want to go back. Not yet.'

'Why?'

'I don't know. It's – it's just one of those obscure – I don't know. I just want to make things right.'

'*I* was right. First time out. You *are* a goose.' He sighed, reached out for a menu and handed it to her. He gave her an odd look. 'Funny. I thought your eyes were dark. They've gone all brown. Dark, flecked brown, mind you, but still brown. How do you do it? Have you a switch or something?'

She looked at him solemnly. 'No switch.'

'Must be my eyes then. Tell me, why couldn't Dr Harper have come and told me all this himself?'

'It would have created a very odd impression if you two were seen leaving together. You never speak to each other. What's he to you or you to him?'

'Ah!'

'With us it's different. Or had you forgotten? The most natural thing in the world. I'm in love with you and you're in love with me.'

V

'He's still in love with his dead wife.' Maria's voice was flat, neutral. Elbows on the guard-rail, she was standing on the passenger deck of the M.C. *Carpentaria*, apparently oblivious to the chill night wind, watching in apparent fascination but without really registering what she was seeing as the giant dock-side cranes, with their blazing attached arc-lamps, swung the coaches inboard.

She started as a hand laid itself on her arm and a teasing voice said: 'Who's in love with who's wife, then?'

She turned and looked at Henry Wrinfield. The thin intelligent face, chalk-white in the glare of the arc-lamps, was smiling.

'You might have coughed or something,' she said reproachfully. 'You did give me a fright, you know.'

'Sorry. But I could have been wearing hob-nailed boots and you wouldn't have heard me above the racket of those damned cranes. Well, come out with it, who's in love with who?'

'What *are* you talking about?'

'Love,' Henry said patiently. 'You were declaiming something about it when I came up.'

'Was I?' Her voice was vague. 'I wouldn't be surprised. My sister says I talk non-stop in my sleep. Maybe I was asleep on my feet. Did you hear any other Freudian slips or whatever?'

'Alas, no. My loss, I'm sure. What on earth are you doing

out here? It's cold and starting to rain.' He had lost interest in the remark he'd overheard.

She shivered. 'Day-dreaming. I must have been. It's cold.'

'Come inside. They have a beautiful old-fashioned bar aboard. And warm. A brandy will make you warmer.'

'Bed would make me warmer still. Time I was there.'

'You spurn a night-cap with the last of the Wrinfields?'

'Never!' She laughed and took his arm. 'Show me the way.'

The lounge – it could hardly have been called a bar – had deep green leather armchairs, brass tables, a very attentive steward and excellent brandy. Maria had one of those, Henry had three and at the end of the third Henry, who clearly had no head for alcohol, had developed a distinct, if gentlemanly, yearning look about the eyes. He took one of her hands in his and yearned some more. Maria looked at his hand.

'It's unfair,' she said. 'Custom dictates that a lady wears an engagement ring when she is engaged, a wedding ring when she is married. No such duty devolves upon a man. I think it's wrong.'

'So do I.' If she'd said he ought to wear a cowbell around his neck he'd have agreed to that, too.

'Then where's yours?'

'My what?'

'Your engagement ring. Cecily wears one. Your fiancée. Remember? The green-eyed one at Bryn Mawr. Surely you can't have forgotten?'

The fumes evaporated from Henry's head. 'You've been asking questions about me?'

'Never a one and no need to ask either. You forgot I spend a couple of hours a day with your uncle. No children of his own so his nieces and nephews have become his pride and joy.' She gathered her handbag and rose. 'Thank you for the night-cap. Good night and sweet dreams. Be sure to dream about the right person.'

Henry watched her go with a moody eye.

VI

Maria had been in bed no more than five minutes when a knock came at her cabin door. She called: 'Come in. It's not locked.'

Bruno entered and closed the door behind him.

'It should be locked. What with characters like myself and Henry prowling around—'

'Henry?'

'Last seen calling for a double brandy. Looks like a Romeo who's just found out that he's been serenading the wrong balcony. Nice chain.'

'You've come to discuss décor at this time of night?'

'You allocated this room?'

'Funny question. As a matter of fact, no. There were seven or eight cabins to choose from, the steward, a very nice old boy, offered me my pick. I took this one.'

'Like the décor, eh?'

'Why did you come, Bruno?'

'To say goodnight, I guess.' He sat beside her, put an arm around her shoulders and held her close. 'And to apologize for snapping at you in the restaurant. I'll explain to you later – when we're on our way home.' He rose as abruptly as he had sat down, opened the door, said: 'Lock it!' and closed the door behind him. Maria stared at the door in total astonishment.

VII

The *Carpentaria* was big – close on thirty thousand tons – and had been built primarily as a bulk ore ship capable of immediate conversion into a container vessel. She was also capable of carrying nearly two hundred passengers, though hardly in trans-Atlantic passenger line style. Her two front holds were at the moment taken up by twenty circus train coaches, animal and crew member coaches mainly, while the contents of a dozen others had been unloaded on the quay and carefully stowed away in the holds. The flat-cars were securely clamped on the reinforced foredeck. In Italy they were to be met by a sufficiency of empty coaches and a locomotive powerful enough to haul them across the mountains of central Europe.

At six o'clock on the following evening the *Carpentaria*, in driving rain and heavy swell – she was stabilized to reduce roll to a minimum – was seven hours out from New York. Bruno was stretched out on a settee in his cabin – one of the very few rather sumptuous staterooms available on the vessel – when a knock came on the door and a uniformed purser entered. To Bruno's total lack of surprise he was carrying a thick black brief-case.

He said: 'Good evening, sir. Were you expecting me?'

'I was expecting someone. I suppose that's you.'

'Thank you, sir. May I?' He locked the door behind him, turned to Bruno and tapped his case. 'The paperwork for a modern purser,' he said sadly, 'is endless.'

He opened the brief-case, extracted a flat, rectangular metal box, liberally covered with dials and controls, extended an antenna from it, clamped on a pair of earphones and began, slowly, to traverse first the stateroom and then the bathroom, assiduously twirling his controls as he went. He looked like a cross between a mine detector and a water diviner. After about ten minutes he divested himself of his equipment and stowed it away in his brief-case.

'Clear,' he said. 'No guarantee, mind you – but as sure as I can be.'

Bruno indicated the brief-case. 'I know nothing about those things but I thought they were foolproof.'

'So they are. On dry land. But on a ship you have so much iron, the hull being used as a conductor, magnetic fields from all the heavy power cables – well, anyone can be fooled. I can. So can my electronic friend here.' He put out a hand to a bulkhead to steady himself as the *Carpentaria*, apparently forgetting all about its stabilizers, gave an unexpected lurch. 'Looks like a nasty night coming up. Shouldn't be surprised if we have a few sprains and bruises this evening. First night out, you know – people haven't had time to find their sea-legs.' Bruno wondered if he had seen a wink or not, it could have been imagination and he had no means of knowing how much the purser was in Harper's confidence. He made a noncommittal remark to the purser, who thanked him politely, unlocked the door and left.

Precisely at six-thirty Bruno stepped out into the passageway. It was, fortunately, quite deserted. The foot of the companionway was only six feet away. Half-seated, half-lying, he seated himself as comfortably as possible in the most suitably uncomfortable-looking position on the deck and awaited developments. Five minutes passed, and he was beginning to develop an acute cramp in his right knee, when a couple of stewards appeared and rescued him from his misery. To the accompaniment of much tongue-clacking they assisted him sympathetically to his stateroom and lowered him tenderly to his settee.

'Just you hang on a minute, guv'nor,' one of them said. He had a powerful Cockney accent. 'I'll have Dr Berenson here in a jiffy.'

It hadn't occurred to Bruno – as it apparently hadn't occurred to Harper – that the *Carpentaria* would be carrying its own doctor, which was an elementary oversight on both their parts: over and above a certain passenger capacity international law made the carrying of a ship's doctor mandatory. He said quickly: 'Could I have our own doctor, please – the circus doctor? His name is Dr Harper.'

'I know his cabin, next deck down. At once, sir.'

Harper must have been waiting in his cabin, medical bag in hand, for he arrived in Bruno's cabin, tongue-clucking and looking suitably concerned, inside thirty seconds. He locked the stateroom door after the stewards' departure, then set to work on Bruno's ankle with some extremely pungent salve and about a yard of elasticized bandage.

He said: 'Mr Carter was on schedule?'

'If Mr Carter is the purser – he didn't introduce himself – yes.'

Harper paused in his ministrations and looked around. 'Clean?'

'Did you expect anything else?'

'Not really.' Harper inspected his completed handiwork: both the visual and olfactory aspects were suitably impressive.

Harper brought over a low table, reached into an inside pocket, brought out and smoothed two detailed plans and set some photographs down beside them. He tapped one of the plans.

'This one first. The plan outline of the Lubylan Advanced Research Centre. Know it?'

Bruno eyed Harper without enthusiasm. 'I hope that's the last stupidly unnecessary question you ask this evening.' Harper assumed the look of a man trying not to look hurt. 'Before the CIA recruited me for this job—'

'How do you know it's the CIA?'

Bruno rolled his eyes upwards then clearly opted for restraint. 'Before the Boy Scouts recruited me for this job they'd have checked every step I've taken from the cradle. To your certain knowledge you know I spent the first twenty-four years of my life in Crau. How should I not know Lubylan?'

'Yes. Well. Oddly enough, they do carry out advanced research in Lubylan, most of it regrettably, associated with chemical warfare, nerve gas and the like.'

'Regrettably? The United States doesn't engage in similar research?'

Harper looked pained. 'That's not my province.'

Bruno said patiently: 'Look, doctor, if you can't trust me how can you expect me to repose implicit trust in you? It is your province and you damned well know it. Remember the Armed Forces courier service at Orly Airport. All the top-secret classified communications between the Pentagon and the American Army in Europe were channelled through there. Remember.'

'I remember.'

'Remember a certain Sergeant Johnson? Fellow with the splendidly patriotic Christian names of Robert Lee? Russia's most successfully planted spy in a generation, passed every US-Europe top military secret to the KGB for God knows how long. Remember?'

Harper nodded unhappily. 'I remember.' Bruno's briefing was not going exactly as he'd planned it.

'Then you won't have forgotten that the Russians published photo-copies of one of the top-secret directives that Johnson had stolen. It was the ultimate US contingency plan if the Soviet Union should ever overrun western Europe. It suggested that in that event the United States intended to devastate the Continent by waging bacteriological, chemical and nuclear warfare: the fact that the entire civilian population would be virtually wiped out was taken for granted. This caused a tremendous furore in Europe at the time and cost the Americans the odd European friend, about two hundred million of them: I doubt whether it even made the back page of the *Washington Post*.'

'You're very well informed.'

'Not being a member of the CIA doesn't mean you have to be illiterate. I can read. German is my second language – my mother was a Berliner. Two German magazines carried the story at the same time.'

Harper was resigned. '*Der Spiegel* and *Stern*, September 1969. Does it give you any particular pleasure in putting me on a hook and watching me wriggle?'

'That wasn't my intention. I just want to point up two things. If you don't level with me all the time and on every subject you can expect no co-operation from me. Then I want you to know why I've really gone along with this. I have no idea whether the Americans really would go ahead with this holocaust. I can't believe it but what I believe doesn't matter: it's what the East believes and if they believe that America would not hesitate to implement this threat then they might be sorely tempted to carry out a pre-emptive strike. From what I understood from Colonel Fawcett a millionth of a gram of this anti-matter would settle America's hash once and for all. I don't think anyone should have this weapon, but, for me, it's the lesser of two evils: I'm European by birth but American by adoption. I'll stick by my adopted parents. And now, could we get on with it? Lay it all on the line. Let's say I've never heard of or seen Crau and go on from there.'

Harper looked at him without enthusiasm. He said sourly: 'If it was your intention to introduce a subtle change in our relationship you have succeeded beyond any expectation you might have had. Only, I wouldn't call it very subtle. Well. Lubylan. Conveniently enough, it's situated only a quarter of a mile from the auditorium where the circus will be held: both buildings, though in the town, are, as one would expect, on the outskirts. Lubylan, as you can see, faces on to a main street.'

'There are two buildings shown on that diagram.'

'I'm coming to that. Those two buildings, incidentally, are connected by two high walls which are not shown in the plan.' Harper quickly sketched them in. 'At the back of Lubylan is only wasteland. The nearest building in that direction is an oil-fired electric power station.

'This building that abuts on the main street – let's call it the west building – is where the actual research is carried out. In the east building, the one abutting the wasteland at the back, research is also carried out, but research of a different kind and almost certainly much nastier than that carried out in the west building. In the east building they carry out a series of highly unpleasant experiments – on human beings. It's run entirely by the secret police and is the maximum security detention centre for the enemies of the State who may range from a would-be assassin of the Premier to a weak-minded dissident poet. The mortality rate, I understand, is rather higher than normal.'

'I suppose it's my turn to say that you are very well informed.'

'We don't send a man in blindfolded and with his hands tied behind his back. This, crossing the courtyard here, is an elevated fifth-floor corridor connecting the two buildings. It is glass-sided and glass-topped and kept brightly illuminated from dusk to dawn. It is impossible for anyone to use it without being seen.

'Every window in both buildings is heavily barred. All are nevertheless fitted with burglar alarms. There are only two entrances, one for each building, both time-locked and heavily guarded. The buildings are both nine storeys high and the connecting walls are the same height. The whole upper perimeter of the walls is lined with closely spaced, outward curving metal spikes, the whole with two thousand volts running through them. There's a watch-tower at every corner. The guards there have machine-guns, searchlights and klaxons. The courtyard between the two buildings, like the elevated glass corridor, is brightly lit at night – not that that matters so much: killer Dobermann Pinschers roam the place all the time.'

Bruno said: 'You have a great gift for encouraging people.'

'You'd rather not know these things? There are only two ways of escaping from this place – death by torture or death by suicide. No one has ever escaped.' Dr Harper indicated the other diagram. 'This is the plan layout of the ninth floor of the west building. This is why the government is mounting a multi-million dollar operation – to get you in here. This is where Van Diemen works, eats, sleeps and has his being.'

'Should I know the name?'

'Most unlikely. He's almost totally unknown to the public. In the western world fellow-scientists speak of him with awe. An acknowledged genius – *the* only indisputable genius – in particle research. The discoverer of anti-matter – the only man in the world who has the secret of making, storing and harnessing this fearful weapon.'

'He's Dutch?'

'Despite his name, no. He's a renegade West German, a defector. God only knows why he defected. Here you can see his laboratories and office. Here is the guards' room – the place, understandably, is guarded like Fort Knox twenty-four hours a day. And this is his living quarters – just a small bedroom, an even smaller bathroom and a tiny kitchenette.'

'You mean he hasn't got a home? It would make things a damn sight easier if he had.'

'He's got a home, all right, a splendid lake-forest mansion given him by the government. He's never even been there. He lives for nothing but his work and he never leaves here. One suspects the government is just as happy that he continues to do so: it makes their security problem comparatively simple.'

'Yes. To come back to another simple problem. You say that no one has ever escaped from Lubylan. Then how the hell do you expect me to get in there?'

'Well now.' Harper cleared his throat; he was putting his first foot on very delicate ground. 'We'd given the matter some thought, of course, before we approached you. Which is why we approached you and only you. The place, as I've said is ringed with a two thousand volt fence of steel. The power has to come from some place: it comes from the electric power station at the back of the east building. Like most high-power transmissions it comes by an overhead cable. It comes in a single loop, three hundred yards long, from a pylon in the power station to the top of the east building.'

'You're way out of your mind. You must be. If you're so crazy as to suggest—'

Harper prepared to be diplomatic, persuasive and reasonable all at once. 'Let's look at it this way. Let's think of it as just another high wire. As long as you are in contact with this cable with either hands or feet, and don't earth yourself to anything such as the anchor wire for a pylon insulator, then—'

'Let's think of it as just another high wire,' Bruno mimicked. 'Two thousand volts – that's what they use, or used to use, in the electric chair, isn't it?'

Harper nodded unhappily.

'In the circus you step from a platform on to the wire, and step off on to another platform at the other end. If I step off from the pylon on to the wire or from the wire on to the prison wall, I'll have one foot on the cable and the other to earth. I'll be frizzled in a second flat. And three hundred yards long – have you *any* kind of idea what kind of sag that entails? Can you imagine what the effects of that sag combined with whatever wind may be blowing would be like? Has it occurred to you that, at this time of year, there might be both ice and snow on that wire? God's sake, Dr Harper, don't you know that our lives depend on the friction coefficient between the soles of our feet and the wire – the cable, in this case. Believe me, doctor, you may know a lot about counter-espionage but you know damn all about the high wire.'

Harper looked even more unhappy.

'And should I ever live to cross that cable, how do I ever live to cross that courtyard – that *illuminated* courtyard patrolled by Dobermanns – or cross over that transparent aerial corridor, assuming I could ever get to it in the first place? And if I do get to the west building, how am I going to get past the guards?'

Harper was now looking acutely unhappy.

'And if I do manage that – I'm not a gambler but I'll lay a thousand to one I never make it – how am I going to locate the place where those papers are kept? I mean, I don't suppose they'd just be lying around on a table. They'll be locked away – Van Diemen may just even sleep with them under his pillow.'

Harper studiously avoided Bruno's eye. He was distinctly and understandably uncomfortable. He said: 'Locked filing cabinets or safes are no problems – I can give you keys that should open any commercial office lock.'

'And if it's a combination?'

'Looks as if you're going to need a little luck all the way.'

Bruno gazed at the deckhead, considered the enormity of this understatement, pushed the papers away and relapsed into speechlessness. After quite some time he stirred, looked at Harper, sighed and said: 'I'm afraid I'm going to need a gun. A silenced gun. With plenty of ammunition.'

Harper went through his own speechless act then said: 'You mean you're going to try?' If he were experiencing any feelings of hope or relief he didn't show them: there was only a dull disbelief in his voice.

'Once a nut, always a nut. Not a gun that fires bullets. A gas gun or one that fires anaesthetic darts. Possible?'

'That's what diplomatic bags are for,' Harper said, almost absently. 'Look, I don't think I'd properly appreciated the difficulties myself. If you think it's outright impossible—'

'You're mad. I'm mad. We're all mad. But you've got the whole damned circus at sea now – as far as I'm concerned we're at sea in more ways than one – and if nothing else we owe it to your murdered colleagues. The gun.'

Harper, clearly, was searching for suitable words and failed. He said: 'You will keep those diagrams and pictures in a place of absolute safety?'

'Yes.' Bruno rose, picked up papers and photographs, tore them into little pieces, took them to the bathroom and flushed them down the toilet. He returned and said: 'They're safe now.'

'It would be difficult for anyone to get their hands on them now. A remarkable gift. I'd be grateful if you didn't fall down the stairs – genuinely, this time – land on your head and give yourself amnesia. Any idea how you're going to set about this?

'Look, I'm a mentalist, not Merlin the wizard. How long have you known about this?'

'Not long. A few weeks.'

'Not long. A few weeks.' Bruno made it sound like a few years. 'And have *you* worked out any solution yet?'

'No.'

'And you expect me to do it in a few minutes?'

Harper shook his head and rose. 'I suppose Wrinfield will be along to see you in a short time – he's bound to hear of your accident any moment and he doesn't know it was rigged, although you can tell him that. How much do you propose telling him?'

'Nothing. If I told him this suicidal scheme you have in mind for me he'd have this ship turned round in less time than it could take him to wash his hands of you.'

— 5 —

THE DAYS PASSED uneventfully enough, if somewhat unsteadily: the *Carpentaria's* stabilizers didn't seem quite to understand what was expected of them. For the circus crew there was little enough to do other than feed the animals and keep their quarters clean. Those performers who could practise their esoteric arts practised them: those who couldn't possessed their souls in patience.

Bruno spent sufficient time with Maria to lend credence to the now almost universal belief among the circus people that here indeed was a romance that was steadily blossoming: what was even more intriguing was that there seemed to be a distinct possibility that there might be two romances getting under way, for whenever Bruno was not with her Henry Wrinfield was solicitously unsparing in the attentions he paid her. And, as Bruno spent most of his time with Kan Dahn, Roebuck and Manuelo, Henry lacked neither the time nor the opportunity; he made the most of both.

The lounge bar, a large room that seated well over a

hundred people, was invariably well patronized before dinner. On the third night out Henry sat at a remote corner table, talking earnestly to Maria. On the far side of the lounge Bruno sat playing cards with his three friends. Before the game, Roebuck and Manuelo spent their ritual ten minutes bemoaning the fact that they had no opportunity to practise their arts with lasso and knife respectively. Kan Dahn was in no way concerned about himself: clearly he was of the belief that his massive strength wasn't going to drain away from him in a matter of days: it was a belief that was widely shared.

Poker was their game. They played for low stakes and Bruno almost invariably won. The others claimed that this was because he could see through their cards, a claim that Bruno stoutly denied, although the fact that on the previous night, wearing a blindfold, he had won four consecutive hands put a query mark to his assertion. Not that he was ever in pocket at the end of a game: the winner paid for the drinks and although he, Roebuck and Manuelo consumed very little, the capacity of Kan Dahn's three hundred pound frame for beer was awesome.

Kan Dahn drained another uncounted pint, glanced across the room and tapped Bruno on the arm. 'You'd best look to your defences, my lad. Your lady-love is under siege.'

Bruno glanced across and said mildly: 'She's not my lady-love. Even if she were I don't think Henry is the type to snatch her and run. Not that he could run very far in the middle of the Atlantic.'

'Far enough,' Roebuck said darkly.

'His fair-haired dear one is back in the States,' Manuelo said severely. 'Our little Maria is here. It makes a difference.'

'Somebody,' Roebuck said, 'should tell her about Cecily.'

'Our little Maria knows all about Cecily. She told me so herself. Even knows the kind of engagement ring she wears.' Bruno glanced at the couple again, then returned to his cards. 'I do not think that they are discussing affairs of the heart.'

II

Maria and Henry were not, indeed, discussing affairs of the heart. Henry was being very very earnest, very intense and very genuinely concerned. He suddenly broke off, looked across to the bar, then back to Maria again.

'That proves it!' Henry's voice held a mixture of triumph and apprehension.

Maria said patiently: 'What proves what, Henry?'

'The fellow I told you about. The fellow who's been following you. That steward that just entered and went behind the bar. The chap with the weasel face. He's no right to be here. He doesn't work here.'

'Oh, come on now, Henry. He hasn't got a weasel face, just thin, that's all.'

'He's English,' Henry said inconsequentially.

'I've met some Englishmen who weren't criminals. And you haven't overlooked the fact that this is a British ship?'

Henry was persistent. 'I've seen him follow you half a dozen times. I know, because I've followed the two of you.' She looked at him in surprise, but this time without smiling. 'He also follows my uncle.'

'Ah!' She looked thoughtful. 'His name's Wherry. He's a cabin steward.'

'I told you he shouldn't be here. Keeping tabs on you, that's what.' He checked himself. 'A cabin steward. How do you know? Your cabin steward?'

'Your uncle's. That's where I saw him first. In your uncle's cabin.' Her thoughtful expression deepened. 'Now that you mention it, I have seen him around rather a lot. *And*, two or three times when I've been walking about, I turned around and found him close behind.'

'You bet you did.'

'And what's that meant to mean, Henry?''

'I don't know,' he admitted. 'But I'm making no mistake.'

'Why should anyone follow me? Do you think he's a detective in disguise and I'm a wanted criminal? Or do I look like a counter-spy or a secret agent or Mata Hari fifty years on?'

Henry considered. 'No, you don't look the part. Besides, Mata Hari was ugly. You're beautiful.' He adjusted his glasses the better to confirm his judgement. 'Really beautiful.'

'Henry! Remember this morning? We had agreed to confine our discussions to intellectual matters.'

'The hell with intellectual matters.' Henry thought and weighed his words with care. 'I really believe I'm falling in love with you.' He thought some more. 'Fallen.'

'I don't think Cecily would—'

'The hell with her, too – no, I didn't mean that. Sorry. Although I did mean what I said about you.' He half-turned in his seat. 'Look, Wherry's leaving.'

They watched him go, a small thin dark man with a small thin dark moustache. At his nearest approach to their table, which was about ten feet away, he flickered a glance at them then as quickly looked away again. Henry leaned back in his seat and gave her his 'I-told-you-so' look.

'A criminal. Written all over him. You saw that?'

'Yes.' She was troubled. 'But why, Henry, why?'

He shrugged. 'Do you have any valuables? Any jewellery?'

'I don't wear jewellery.'

Henry nodded his approval. 'Jewellery is for women who need it. But when a person is as lovely as you are—'

'Henry, it's getting so I just can't talk to you. This morning I said it was a lovely day and you put on your soulful expression and made disparaging remarks about the day. When I commend my peach melba you say it's not half as sweet as I am. And when we looked at the beautiful colourings of the sunset tonight—'

'I have a poetic soul. Ask Cecily. No, on second thoughts, don't ask Cecily. I can see that I'm going to have to keep a very, very close eye on you.'

'I should say that you are making a pretty good start already.'

'Ah.' An unrepentant Henry, eyes slightly glazed but not from alcohol, made no attempt to switch his adoring gaze to pastures less green. He said wistfully: 'You know, I've always wanted to be someone's Sir Galahad.'

'I wouldn't, if I were you, Henry. There's no place in the world today for Sir Galahads. Chivalry is dead, Henry. The lances and the bright swords and the days of knightly combat are gone: this is the era of the knife in the back.'

Alas for Henry, all his senses, except that of sight, were temporarily in abeyance. Her words fell on deaf ears.

III

On the fourth night out Dr Harper joined Bruno in his stateroom. He was accompanied by Carter, the purser, who had been so busy with the debugging equipment on the first night out. Carter extended his customary courteous good evening, wordlessly repeated the search performance, shook his head and left.

Harper nodded to the cocktail cabinet, poured himself a drink, savoured it and said with some satisfaction: 'We will pick up your guns in Vienna.'

'Guns?'

'Indeed.'

'You have been in touch with the States? Doesn't the radio operator raise an eyebrow?'

It was Harper's night to indulge himself to a moderate degree. He smiled. He said: 'I am my own radio operator. I have a very high frequency radio transceiver, no bigger than the average book, which can't possibly interfere with normal ship's frequencies. As Charles says, it could reach the moon. Anyway, I transmit in code. Show you the thing some time – in fact, I'll have to show it to you and explain its operation in case you have to use it. In case something should go wrong with me.'

'What should go wrong with you?'

'What should have gone wrong with Pilgrim and Fawcett? Now, we'll be picking up two guns for you, not one, and that for a reason. The anaesthetic dart gun – the missiles are more like needles, actually – is the more effective, but the word is that Van Diemen has a long-standing heart condition. So, if you should have to quieten him, the use of a dart gun is, as they say, contra-indicated. For him, the gas gun. Have you figured out a way to get inside yet?'

'A battery-powered helicopter would be splendid only there are no such things. No, I haven't figured out a way into the damned place yet.'

'Early days and fingers crossed. You know you're slated to dine with me at the captain's table tonight?'

'No.'

'Passengers are rotated for the privilege. A normal courtesy. See you then.'

IV

They had just seated themselves at the table when a steward approached, bent and whispered something discreetly into the captain's ear. The captain rose, excused himself and followed the steward from the dining saloon. He was back inside two or three minutes, looking more than vaguely perturbed.

'Odd,' he said. 'Very odd. Carter – you've met him, he's chief purser – claims that he has just been assaulted by some thug. "Mugged", I believe, is the American term for it. You know, caught round the neck from behind and choked. No marks on him, but he does seem a trifle upset.'

Harper said: 'Couldn't he just have taken a turn?'

'If he did, then his wallet left his inside pocket of its own volition.'

'In which case he's been attacked and his wallet – minus the contents, of course – is now probably at the bottom of the Atlantic. Shall I have a look at him?'

'It might be wise. Berenson is holding hands with some silly old trout who thinks she's having a heart attack. Thank you, doctor. I'll get a steward to take you.'

Harper left, Bruno said: 'That pleasant, courteous man. Who would rob a person like that?'

'I don't think Carter's character would come into it. Just someone who was short of money and reasoned that if any person would be liable to be carrying money it would be the ship's purser. An unpleasant thing to have happen on one's ship – in fact I've never known or heard of an instance before. I'll have my chief officer and some men investigate.'

Bruno smiled. 'I hope we circus people don't automatically come under suspicion. Among some otherwise reasonable citizens our reputation is not what it could be. But I don't know more honest people.'

'I don't know who is responsible, and the question, I'm afraid, is of academic importance anyway. I don't think my chief has a hope in hell of finding him.'

V

Bruno leaned over the taffrail of the *Carpentaria*, gazing contemplatively at the slight phosphorescence of the ship's wake. He stirred and turned as someone came up beside him. He said: 'Anyone in the vicinity?'

'No one,' Manuelo said.

'No bother?'

'No bother.' The startlingly white teeth gleamed in the darkness. 'You were quite right. The unfortunate Mr Carter does indeed take a regular – what do you call it—?'

'Constitutional.'

'Right. Takes his constitutional at that time of evening on the boat deck. Lots of shadows on the boat deck. Kan Dahn kind of leaned on him a little bit, Roebuck took the purser's cabin keys, brought them down to me and kept watch in the passageway while I went inside. I didn't take long. There was a funny electrical gadget inside a brief-case—'

'I think I know about that. Looked like a small radio except there were no wave-bands on it?'

'Yes. What is it?'

'A device for locating listening devices. They're a very suspicious lot aboard this boat.'

'With us around you're surprised?'

'What else?'

'There was fifteen hundred dollars, in tens, at the bottom of a trunk—'

'I didn't know about *that*. Used?'

'No. New. And in sequence.'

'How careless.'

'Looks like.' He handed a piece of paper to Bruno. 'I wrote down the serial numbers of the first and last numbers.'

'Good, good. You're quite sure they were genuine notes?'

'My life on it. I wasn't in all that hurry and I passed one out to Roebuck. He agrees.'

'That was all?'

'There were some letters addressed to him. Not to any particular address but to Poste Restante in a few cities, mostly London and New York.'

'What language? English?'

'No. I didn't recognize it. The postmark said Gdynia. That would make it Polish, wouldn't it?'

'It would indeed. Then everything was left as found, door locked and the keys returned to the sleeping Mr Carter.'

Manuelo nodded. Bruno thanked him, left, returned to his stateroom, glanced briefly at the serial numbers on the piece of paper that Manuelo had given him then flushed it down the toilet.

To no one's surprise, Carter's assailant was never found.

VI

On the evening before their arrival in Genoa Dr Harper came to Bruno's stateroom. He helped himself to a Scotch from Bruno's virtually untouched liquor cabinet.

He said: 'How goes the thinking on this entry business? Mine, I'm afraid, has bogged down to a halt.'

Bruno said gloomily: 'Maybe it would have been better, especially for the sake of my health, if mine had bogged down, too.'

Harper sat up in his armchair and pursed his lips. 'You have an idea?'

'I don't know. A glimmering, perhaps. I was wondering – have you any further information for me? Anything at all? About the interior layout of the west building and how to gain access to the ninth floor. Take the roof. Is there any access by way of ventilator shafts, trapdoors or suchlike?'

'I honestly don't know.'

'I think we can forget the ventilator shafts. In a maximum security place like this the air circulation probably vents through the side walls and would have impossibly narrow exit apertures. Trapdoors, I would have thought, they must have. How else could the guards get up to their towers or the electricians service the electric fence when the need arises. I can hardly see them climbing up ninety feet high vertical steel ladders bolted to an inside wall. Do you know whether the Lubylan runs to lifts?'

'That I do know. There's a stairs shaft runs from top to

bottom in each building with two lifts on either side of the shafts.'

'Presumably it services the ninth floor as well as the rest. That means that the lift-head – you know, where they have the pulley mechanism for the cables – must protrude above the roof. That could provide a way in.'

'It would also provide an excellent way of having yourself crushed to death if you were descending the shaft as the lift came up. It's happened before, you know, and not seldom either, with service men working on top of a lift.'

'That's a risk. Walking a frozen two thousand volt cable in a high wind – we have to assume the worst – isn't a risk? What's on the eighth floor? More laboratories?'

'Oddly, no. That belongs to the east building – the detention centre. The senior prison officers and prison staff sleep there – maybe they can't stand the sound of the screams, maybe they don't want to be around in the detention centre if the enemies of the State manage to break loose – I don't know. All the prison offices and records offices are kept there. Apart from the guards' sleeping quarters and dining quarters, all of the detention centre is given over to cells. Apart, that is, from a few charming places in the basement which are euphemistically referred to as interrogation centres.'

Bruno looked at him consideringly. 'Would it be out of order for me to enquire where you get all this detailed information from? I thought that no stranger would ever be allowed inside and that no guard would ever dare talk.'

'Not at all. We have, as they say, our man in Crau. Not an American, a native. He was imprisoned some fifteen years ago for some trifling political offence, became what we would call a trusty after a few years and had the complete run of the building. His privileged position did not affect in the slightest the complete and total hatred he nourishes for the regime in general and Lubylan and all those who work inside it in particular. He still drinks with the guards and warders from the Lubylan and one way or another manages to keep us reasonably up to date with what's going on. It's over four years since he's been discharged but the guards still regard him as a trusty and talk freely, especially when he plies them with vodka. We provide the money for the vodka.'

'It's a messy business.'

'All espionage and counter-espionage is. The glamour quotient is zero.'

'The problem still remains. There may just be a solution. I don't know. Have you mentioned any of this to Maria yet?'

'No. Plenty of time. The fewer people who know—'

'I'd like to talk to her tonight. May I?'

Harper smiled. 'Three minds are better than two? That's hardly a compliment to me.'

'If only you knew it, it is. I can't afford to have you too closely involved with anything I'm doing. You're the co-ordinator and the only person who really knows what is going on – I still don't believe that you have told me everything I might know, but it doesn't seem all that important any more. Besides, I have courted the young lady assiduously – although it was under instructions I haven't found the task too disagreeable – and people are accustomed to seeing us together now.'

Harper smiled without malice. 'They're also accustomed to seeing young Henry squiring her around, too.'

'I shall challenge him to a duel when we get some suitably central European background – the atmosphere has to be right. I don't need Maria's ideas. All I want from her is her co-operation. No point in discussing it with you until I have it.'

'No harm. When?'

'After dinner.'

'Where? Here?'

'Not here. It's perfectly proper for my doctor to come and see me – anxiously caring for one of the circus's prime properties. But, as you say – or as you infer from Carter's antics with his bug-detector – it's just possible that someone might be keeping a wary eye on me. I don't want them keeping a wary eye on her, too.'

'Then I suggest her cabin.'

Bruno thought. 'I'll do that.'

VII

Before dinner, Bruno went into the lounge bar, located Maria sitting by herself at a small corner table, sat beside her and ordered a soft drink. He said: 'This is intolerable. Incredible. Maria Hopkins sitting alone.'

She said with some asperity: 'And whose fault is that?'

'Never mine, surely?'

'I'm treated like a pariah, an outcast. There are lots of very nice men here who would love to buy me a drink and talk to me. But no, I'm the plague. The great Bruno might come in at any moment.' She brooded a bit. 'Or Henry. He's as bad. Not only is he the light and the joy of his uncle's heart – and it would be well to remember that his uncle is the big white chief – he's also developing a very intimidating line in scowls. The only person who doesn't give a damn is that enormous friend of yours. Do you know that he calls me your lady-love?'

'And are you? That's what's usually referred to as a keen, probing question.'

She treated his remark with silent disdain.

'Ah, well. And where is the rival for my lady-love's hand tonight? I've just been talking about it with Dr Harper. Henry and I are going to fight a duel when we get to the Carpathians. You should come and watch. After all, it's over you.'

'Oh, do be quiet.' She looked at him for a long moment, smiled widely in spite of herself and put her hand on his. 'What's the masculine equivalent of "lady-love"?'

'There isn't one or if there is I don't think I'd like to hear it. Where is Henry?'

'He's gone sleuthing.' Subconsciously, she lowered her voice. 'I think he's watching someone or shadowing someone. Henry has spent a great deal of time these past two days following someone he swears is following me.'

Surprisingly, Bruno was not amused. He said: 'Why didn't you tell me before?'

'I didn't think it important. I didn't take it seriously.'

'Didn't? And now?'

'I'm not sure.'

'Why should anyone be following you?'

'If I knew I'd tell you, wouldn't I?'

'Would you?'

'Please.'

'Have you told Dr Harper?'

'No. That's the point. There's nothing to tell. I don't like being laughed at. I think Dr Harper's got his reservations about me, anyway. I don't want him to think that I'm a bigger ninny than he already probably thinks I am.'

'This mystery shadower. He has a name?'

'Yes. Wherry. A cabin steward. Small man, narrow face, very pale, narrow eyes, small black moustache.'

'I've seen him. Your steward?'

'Mr Wrinfield's.'

Bruno was momentarily thoughtful, then appeared to lose interest. He raised his glass. 'I'd like to see you after dinner. Your cabin, if you please.'

She raised her glass and smiled. 'And your good health, too.'

Dinner over, Bruno and Maria made no secret of the fact that they were leaving together. This was commonplace, now, and no longer called for the raised eyebrow. Some twenty seconds after the departure Henry rose and sauntered from the dining saloon, leaving by the opposite door. Once outside he quickened his pace, crossed over to the other side, moved aft, descended a companionway and reached the passenger accommodation. Bruno and Maria were about fifty feet ahead of him. Henry moved in behind the companionway and stood in shadow.

Almost at once a figure emerged, or partially emerged from a side passage about twenty feet away on the left. He peered along the main passageway, saw Bruno and Maria and quickly withdrew into cover again but not so quickly that Henry couldn't recognize him. It was, unmistakably, Wherry. Henry experienced a very considerable degree of self-satisfaction.

Wherry ventured another look. Bruno and Maria were just disappearing round a corner to their left. Wherry moved out and followed them. Henry waited until he, too, had disappeared from sight, then moved out in stealthy pursuit. He reached the left-hand corner on soundless tip-toes, glanced round with one eye then immediately moved back into cover again. Wherry was less than six paces away, looking down a right-hand corridor. Henry didn't have to be told what Wherry was looking at – Maria's cabin was the fourth door down. When he looked again. Wherry had vanished. Henry moved, took up the position Wherry had so recently occupied and did some more head-poking. Wherry was engaged in the undignified occupation of pressing his right ear hard against a cabin door. Maria's cabin. Henry drew back and waited. He was in no hurry.

Henry let thirty seconds pass then risked another look. The passageway was empty. Without haste Henry walked along the corridor, passed Maria's cabin – he could hear the soft murmur of voices – reached the end and dropped down another companionway. He hadn't spent two days so zealously – and, as he imagined, so unobtrusively – trailing Wherry without discovering where Wherry's quarters were. That that was where he had gone Henry did not for a moment doubt.

Henry was right. Wherry had indeed gone to his cabin and was apparently so confident of himself that he had even left the door ajar. That there may have been some other reason for this apparent carelessness did not occur to Henry. Wherry was sitting with his back three-quarters turned to him, a pair of earphones, the lead of which led to a radio, clamped over his head. There was nothing unusual in this; Wherry, as did all stewards, doubled up with one of his mates, and as they were frequently on different shifts and slept at different times, the earphones insured that one could listen to the radio without disturbing the other's sleep: it was standard practice on this and most passenger ships.

VIII

Maria sat on her cabin bed and stared at Bruno in shocked disbelief. Her face was drained of colour, leaving the eyes preternaturally huge. She said in a voice that was barely more than a whisper: 'This is mad! It's crazy! It's suicidal!'

'It's all of that and a good deal else besides. But you have to appreciate that Dr Harper is in an impossible spot. As ideas go, it was an ingenious one, a desperate ingenuity, mind you, but there were no other options open to him, at least none that he could see.'

'Bruno!' She'd slipped off the bed and was on her knees beside his armchair, his left hand in both of hers; there was fear in her face and Bruno was uncomfortably aware that it wasn't fear for herself. 'You'll be killed, you know you'll be killed. Don't. Please, don't! No, Bruno. Nothing's worth your life, nothing! Oh, God, there isn't even a chance.'

He looked at her in mild surprise. 'And all the time I thought you were a tough young CIA agent.'

'Well, I'm not. Tough I mean.' There was a sheen of tears in her eyes.

Almost absently, he stroked her hair. Her face was averted. 'There might be another way, Maria.'

'There can't be another way.'

'Look.' With his free hand he swiftly sketched a diagram. 'Let's forget entrance via the power cable. The fact that those windows are barred may yet be the saving of us – well, me, anyway. I propose to get to this lane to the south of the research building. I'll take with me a length of rope with a padded hook at one end. A couple of casts and I should catch a bar on a first floor window. I haul myself up to the first floor, unhook the rope, repeat the process and reach the second floor. And so on until I get to the top.'

'Yes?' The scepticism now in her face hadn't replaced the fear, merely redoubled it. 'And then?'

'I'll find some way of silencing the guard or guards in the corner tower.'

'What is it, Bruno? What drives you? You are a driven man, don't you know that? You don't work for the CIA and this damnable anti-matter can't mean all the world to you. Yet I know – I don't think – I *know* you're willing to die to get inside that damnable prison. Why, Bruno, why?'

'I don't know.' She couldn't see his face but for a moment it was disturbed, almost wary. 'Perhaps you'd best go and ask the shades of Pilgrim and Fawcett.'

'What are they to you? You hardly knew them.' He made no reply. She went on wearily: 'So you're going to silence the guards. How are you going to find a way of silencing two thousand volts of steel fencing?'

'I'll find a way, not by putting it out of action – that's impossible – but by by-passing it. But I'm going to need your co-operation and you might end up in prison.'

'What kind of co-operation?' Her voice was toneless. 'And what's prison if you're dead?'

IX

Henry heard those words. Wherry had taken off his earphones to find some cigarettes and the conversation from Maria's cabin, faint and tinny and distorted though it was, was understandable and unmistakable. Henry craned his head a bit more and saw that the radio was not the only piece of electrical equipment in the cabin. There was a small tape recorder on the deck with both spools slowly turning.

Wherry found his cigarettes, lit one, resumed his seat, picked up the phones and was about to replace them on his head when Henry pushed the door wide and stepped inside. Wherry swung round, his eyes wide.

Henry said: 'I'd like to have that recorder if you don't mind, Wherry.'

'Mr Wrinfield!'

'Yes, Mr Wrinfield. Surprised? The recorder, Wherry.' Involuntarily, as it seemed, Wherry switched his glance to a spot above Henry's left shoulder and Henry laughed. 'Sorry, Wherry, but that's been done before.'

Henry heard the last sound he was ever to hear, an almost soundless swish in the air behind him. His ears registered it for the fleeting fraction of a second but his body had no time to react. His legs crumpled and Wherry caught him just as he struck the deck.

X

'Didn't you hear me?' Maria's voice was still colourless, without expression. 'What's prison, what's anything, if you're dead? Can't you think of me? All right, all right, so I'm being selfish, but can't you think of me?'

'Stop it! Stop it! Stop it!' He'd intended his voice to be harsh or at least cold but it sounded neither harsh nor cold to him. 'We arrive in Crau on a Thursday and leave on the following Wednesday – it's the longest stop-over on the tour. We have shows Friday, Saturday, Monday and Tuesday. Sunday is free. So on Sunday we hire a car and have ourselves a little excursion into the country. I don't know how far we'll be allowed to go, I believe restrictions have been relaxed, but it doesn't matter. We can always travel around in ever narrowing circles. What does matter – and this will have to be after dusk – is that on the way back we reconnoitre Lubylan and see if they have guards patrolling outside. If there are, I'll need your help.'

'*Please* give up this crazy idea, Bruno. Please.'

'When I'm climbing up the south side of the research building you'll be standing at the corner of the south lane and the main west street. This, I didn't mention, will be after the last show on Tuesday night. The hired car, which I trust will be comprehensively insured, will be parked a few feet away in the main street. The windows will be open and you'll have a small can of gasoline ready on the front seat. If you see a guard approaching, reach for the can, pour some fuel, not too much, on the front and rear upholstery, throw in a lighted match and stand smartly back. This will not only distract all attention but also the blaze will cast such a heavy shadow round the corner that I should be able to climb in almost complete darkness. I'm afraid you could be caught and questioned but the combination of Mr Wrinfield and Dr Harper should secure your release.' He considered this for a moment. 'On the other hand it may not.'

'You're quite mad. Quite.'

'Too late to change my spots.' He stood up and she with him. 'Must get in touch with Dr Harper now.'

She reached up and locked her fingers round the back of his neck. Her voice reflected the misery in her face.

'Please. Please, Bruno. Just for me. Please.'

He put his hands on her forearms but not to pull the fingers apart. He said: 'Look, my lady-love, we're only *supposed* to be falling in love.' His voice was gentle. 'This way there's a chance.'

She said dully: 'Either way you're a dead man.'

XI

Half-way to his stateroom Bruno found a phone and called Dr Harper. Harper was eventually located in the dining saloon. Bruno said: 'My ankle's acting up again.'

'Ten minutes and I'll be across.'

And in ten minutes' time Harper was in the stateroom as promised. He made free of Bruno's liquor cabinet, made himself at armchair ease and heard out Bruno's account of his conversation with Maria. At the end, and after due thought, he said: 'I'd say it gives you at least a fighting chance. Better than mine, I must admit. When do you propose to carry this into effect?'

'The final decision is, of course, yours. I'd thought of making the reconnaissance on Sunday and making the entry on Tuesday night. Late Tuesday night. That seems like the best plan, the best time, for we will be leaving the following day and that will give the police less time for questioning if questioning there will be.'

'Agreed.'

'If we have to make a break for it – you have escape plans?'

'We have. But they're not finalized yet. I'll let you know when they are.'

'Coming via your little transceiver? Remember you promised to show me that some time.'

'I shall. I've got to – I told you. I'll do three things at one time, show you the transceiver, give you the guns and give you the escape plans. I'll let you know when. What does Maria think of your idea?'

'A marked lack of enthusiasm. But then she was hardly over the moon about yours either. But, however unwillingly, she'll co-operate.' Bruno stopped and looked around him in some puzzlement.

Harper said: 'Something's wrong?'

'Not necessarily wrong. But the ship's slowing down. Can't you hear it? Can't you feel it? The engine revolutions have dropped right away. Why should a ship stop – well, anyway, slow down – in the middle of the Mediterranean? Well, I suppose we'll find out in good enough time.'

They found out immediately. The door was unceremoniously thrown open, with a force sufficient to send it juddering on its hinges. Tesco Wrinfield almost ran into the room.

His face was grey, his breathing heavy and short at the

same time. He said: 'Henry's missing. He's missing! We can't find him anywhere.'

Bruno said: 'Is that why the *Carpentaria* is slowing down?'

'We've been searching everywhere.' He gulped down the glass of brandy which Harper had handed to him. 'The crew has searched, is still searching everywhere. There's just no trace of him. Vanished, just vanished.'

Harper was soothing. He glanced at his watch. 'Come on, now, Mr Wrinfield, that couldn't have been more than fifteen minutes ago. And this is a very big ship.'

'With a very big crew,' Bruno said. 'They have a standardized routine for this sort of thing – searching for a missing passenger, that is. From the lifeboats to the hold they can cover every conceivable area in less time than you would believe possible.' He turned to the distraught Wrinfield. 'Sorry I can't offer you any comfort, sir – but is the captain slowing down so as not to get too far away from the place where your nephew *may* have fallen overboard?'

'I think so.' Wrinfield listened. 'We're picking up speed, aren't we?'

'And turning,' Bruno said. 'I'm afraid that means, sir, that the captain is pretty sure that Henry is not aboard. He'll be taking the *Carpentaria* through a hundred and eighty degrees and tracking back the way we came. If Henry *is* overboard he may well be swimming or afloat. This sort of thing has happened before: there's always a chance, Mr Wrinfield.'

Wrinfield looked at him with distraught disbelief on his face and Bruno did not blame him: he didn't believe it himself either.

They went on deck. The *Carpentaria*, retracing the course it had come, was making perhaps ten knots, no more. A motorized lifeboat, already manned, was swung out on its davits. Two powerful searchlights, one on either wing of the bridge, shone straight ahead. In the bows two seamen directed the beams of their portable searchlights almost vertically downwards. A little farther aft two seamen on either side waited with rope-attached and illuminated lifebelts. Beyond them still, rope-ladders, picked out in the beams of torches, hung over the side.

Twenty minutes of steadily mounting tension and dwindling

hope passed. Wrinfield abruptly left his two companions and made his way to the bridge. He found the master on the starboard wing, binoculars to his eyes. He lowered them as Wrinfield came by his side and shook his head slowly.

He said: 'Your nephew is not on the ship, Mr Wrinfield. That is for certain.' The captain looked at his watch. 'It is now thirty-eight minutes since your nephew was last seen. We are now at the precise spot where we were thirty-eight minutes ago. If he is alive – I'm sorry to be so blunt, sir – he cannot be beyond this point.'

'We could have missed him?'

'Most unlikely. Calm sea, windless night, no currents hereabouts worth speaking of and the Mediterranean, as you know, is virtually tideless. He would have been on the line we have taken.' He spoke to an officer by his side: the man disappeared inside the bridge.

Wrinfield said: 'And what now?'

'We'll take her round in a tight circle. Then in widening concentric circles, three, maybe four. Then, if we turn up nothing, we go back at the same speed to the spot where we turned.'

'And that will be it?'

'That, I'm afraid, will be it.'

'You are not very hopeful, Captain.'

'I am not very hopeful.'

XII

It took the *Carpentaria* forty minutes to complete the search pattern and return to the position where she had turned round. Maria, standing with Bruno in the shadow of a lifeboat, shivered as the throb of the engines deepened and the *Carpentaria* began to pick up speed.

She said: 'That's it, then, isn't it?'

'The searchlights have gone out.'

'And it's my fault. It's my fault.' Her voice was husky.

'Don't be silly.' He put his arm round her. 'There's no way this could have been prevented.'

'It could! It could! I didn't take him seriously enough. I – well, I didn't quite laugh at him – but, well, I didn't listen to him either. I should have told you two days ago.' She was openly weeping now. 'Or Dr Harper. He was *such* a nice person.'

Bruno heard the word 'was' and knew she had finally accepted what he himself had accepted an hour ago. He said gently: 'It would be nice if you spoke to Mr Wrinfield.'

'Yes. Yes, of course. But – well, I don't want to see people. Couldn't we – I don't like asking, but if he could come here – if you could bring him and—'

'Not on your sweet life, Maria. You're not staying here alone.'

He sensed her staring at him in the darkness. She whispered: 'Do you think that someone—'

'I don't know what to think because I don't know how or why Henry died. All I'm certain of is it was no accident: he died because he found out that someone was too interested in you and because he must have made the mistake of finding out too much. I've been asking one or two questions. Apparently he left the dining saloon just after we did. He left by another door but I suppose he wanted to avoid any obvious connection. I'm sure he wasn't directly following us – he may have taken a dim view of my association with you, but he was straight, honest and the last peeping Tom one could imagine. I think he was acting in his self-appointed guardian role. I think he was checking to see if anyone was following or watching us – Henry had a romantic streak and this sort of thing would have appealed to him. I can only assume that he did indeed find some such person, and that that person – or another person, God only knows how many unpleasant characters there may be aboard – found Henry in a highly compromising situation. Compromising to the villains, I mean. But that doesn't alter the fact that the primary object of attention was you. Just bear in mind that you can't swim very far if the back of your head has been knocked in in advance.' He produced a handkerchief and carried out running repairs to the tear-stained face. 'You come along with me.'

As they walked along the boat-deck they passed and greeted Roebuck. Bruno made an unobtrusive follow-me gesture with his hand. Roebuck stopped, turned and sauntered along about ten paces behind them.

Wrinfield was finally located in the radio office, arranging for the dispatch of cablegrams to Henry's parents and relatives. Now that the initial shock was over Wrinfield was calm and self-composed and in the event had to spend considerably more time in comforting Maria than she him. They left him there and found Roebuck waiting outside.

Bruno said: 'Where's Kan Dahn?'

'In the lounge. You'd think there's a seven-year famine of beer just round the corner.'

'Would you take this young lady down to her cabin, please?'

'Why?' Maria wasn't annoyed, just puzzled. 'Am I not capable—'

Roebuck took a firm grip on her arm. 'Mutineers walk the plank, young lady.'

Bruno said: 'And you lock your door. How long will it take you to get to bed?'

'Ten minutes.'

'I'll be along in fifteen.'

XIII

Maria unlocked the door at the sound of Bruno's voice. He entered, followed by Kan Dahn, who was carrying a couple of blankets under his arm. Kan Dahn, smiled genially at her, then wedged his massive bulk into the armchair and carefully arranged the blankets over his knees.

Bruno said: 'Kan Dahn finds his own quarters a bit cramped. He thought he'd take a rest down here.'

Maria looked at them, first in protest, then in perplexity, then shook her head helplessly, smiled and said nothing. Bruno said his good-night and left.

Kan Dahn reached out, turned down the rheostat on the flexible bedside light and angled the remaining dim glow so that it was away from the girl's face and leaving him in deep shadow. He took her hand in his massive paw.

'Sleep well, my little one. I don't want to make a thing out of this but Kan Dahn is here.'

'You can't sleep in that awful chair?'

'Not can't. Won't. I'll sleep tomorrow.'

'You haven't locked the door.'

'No,' he said happily. 'I haven't, have I?'

She was asleep in minutes and no one, most fortunately for the state of his continued good health, came calling on her that night.

— 6 —

THE ARRIVAL, unloading and disembarkation at Genoa was smooth and uneventful and took place in a remarkably short space of time. Wrinfield was his usual calm, efficient and all overseeing self and to look at him as he went about his business it would have been impossible to guess that his favourite nephew, who had been much more like a son to him, had died the previous night. Wrinfield was a showman first, last and all the way between: in the hackneyed parlance the show had to go on, and as long as Wrinfield was there that it would most certainly do.

The train, with the help of a small shunting engine, was assembled and hauled to a shunting yard about a mile away where some empty coaches and provisions for animals and humans were already waiting. By late afternoon the last of the preparations were complete, the small diesel shunter disengaged itself and was replaced by the giant Italian freight locomotive that was to haul them over the many mountains that lay in their way. In the gathering dusk they pulled out for Milan.

II

The swing through Europe, which was to cover ten countries – three in western Europe, seven in eastern Europe – turned out to be something more than a resounding success. It resembled a triumphant progress and as the circus's fame travelled before it the welcome, the enthusiasm, the adulation became positively embarrassing until the stage was reached that there were half a dozen applications for each seat available for any performance – and some of the auditoriums were huge, some bigger than any in the United States. At dingy sidings in big cities they were greeted and seen off by crowds bigger than those paying homage to the latest fabulous group of singers – or cup-winning football teams – at international airports.

Tesco Wrinfield, determinedly and with a conscious effort of will, had put the past behind him. Here he was in his element. He revelled in solution of the complexities of the vast logistical problems involved. He knew Europe, especially eastern Europe, where he had recruited most of his outstanding acts, as well as any European on the train and certainly far better than any of his executives or American-born artistes and workers. He knew that those audiences were more sophisticated about and more appreciative of the finer arts of the circus than American and Canadian audiences, and when those people's papers increasingly referred to his pride and joy as the greatest circus of all time it was undiluted balm to his showman's heart: even more heady, were that possible, were the increasing references to himself as the greatest showman on earth. Nor was he displeased with the pragmatic side of it all: and packed houses and the very high profits made ledger books a positive pleasure to peruse: one cannot be a great showman without being a great businessman as well. It came to the stage that he began calculating that, even without the United States government backing, he could still, America to America, have made a handsome profit on the tour. Not, of course, that the United States government would be apprised of this.

At least as happy were those of his artistes – over half of them – who came from eastern Europe. For them, especially for the Hungarians, Bulgarians and Romanians, whose circus training schools were the best in Europe and probably in the world, this was the long-promised home-coming. In front of their own people they excelled themselves, reaching heights of professional brilliance never attained before. The morale in a top circus is always high: even so, Wrinfield had never seen those people so happy and contented.

They swung through northern Italy, Yugoslavia, Bulgaria, Romania and Hungary then across the Curtain back into

Austria. It was after the final show of their first day in Vienna, the finale of which had been greeted with the now standard rapturous ovation, that Harper – who had kept their contacts on the Continent to the barest minimum – approached Bruno. He said: 'Come to my compartment when you are ready.'

When Bruno arrived, Harper said without preamble: 'I promised you I'd show you three things in one night. Here they are.' He unclipped the bottom of his medical bag and drew out a metal container smaller even than a box of Kleenex tissues. 'A little transistorized beauty. Earphones and mike. This switch is for power. This button is for a combination of pre-selected wave-lengths and call-up – the receiver in Washington is manned twenty-four hours a day. This spring-loaded lever is for speak-transmit. Simple.'

'You said something about a code.'

'I won't burden you with that. I know if I wrote it out you could commit it to memory in nothing flat but the CIA has a thing about committing codes to paper, however temporarily. Anyway, if you do have to use this machine – which would mean, unfortunately for me, that I would no longer be around – you wouldn't want to bother with code anyway. You just shout "Help!" in plain English.

'It's on this machine that I received confirmation of our escape route instructions today – this evening, in fact. There's a NATO exercise taking place in the Baltic in about ten days' time. An unspecified naval vessel – they're a very cagey lot in Washington; I assume it's American but I don't even know what type of craft it is – will be standing by or cruising off the coast from the Friday night until the following Friday. It carries an Air-Sea Rescue helicopter. It will land at a place I'll show you when we get there – I don't consider it wise to carry maps on me and, besides, I can't properly locate it until we get there. The ship is tuned to the same wavelength as Washington. We press this top button on the transceiver here – just as simple as that – and the helicopter comes arunning.'

'All seems perfectly straightforward. You do seem to have this organized. You know, I'm beginning to think that the Government regard Van Diemen's pieces of paper as very valuable indeed.'

'One gathers that impression. By the way, I'm curious. How long does your memory span last?'

'As long as I want.'

'So you'll be able to memorize the contents of those papers and reproduce them, say, a year later?'

'I should think so.'

'Let's hope that's the way it's going to be – that you're going to be given the chance to reproduce them, I mean. Let's hope nobody ever finds out that you got in there, did your mentalist bit and left unseen. Let's hope, in other words, that you don't have to use those.' From the breast pocket of his jacket Harper unclipped a couple of pens, one black, one red. They were of the heavy felt-Biro type with the release button at the top. 'I picked these up in town today. I don't have to tell you where I picked them up.'

Bruno looked at the pens, then at Harper. 'What on earth would I want to use those things for?'

'Whatever the faults of our science and research department, it's not lack of imagination. They positively dote on dreaming up these little toys. You don't think I'm going to let you cross two eastern frontiers with a couple of Peacemaker Colts strapped to your waist? These are guns. Yes, guns. The red one is the nasty one, the one with the anaesthetic tipped needles which are not so healthy for those with heart conditions: the other one is the gas gun.'

'So small?'

'With the micro-miniaturization techniques available today, those are positively bulky. The needle gun has an effective range of forty feet, the gas gun of not more than four. Operation is simplicity itself. Depress the button at the top and the gun is armed: press the pocket clip and the gun is fired. Stick them in your outside pocket. Let people get used to the sight of them. Now listen carefully while I outline the plans for Crau.'

'But I thought you had already agreed to the plan – my plan.'

'I did and I do. This is merely a refinement of the original part of that plan. You may have wondered why the CIA elected to send you with a medical person. When I have finished you will understand.'

III

Some four hundred and fifty miles to the north, three uniformed men sat in a brightly lit, windowless and very austere room, the furniture of which consisted mainly of metal filing cabinets, a metal table and some metal-framed chairs. All three were dressed in uniform. From the insignia they wore, one was a colonel, the second a captain, the third a sergeant. The first was Colonel Serge Sergius, a thin, hawk-faced man with seemingly lidless eyes and a gash where his mouth should have been: his looks perfectly befitted his occupation, which was that of a very important functionary in the secret police. The second, Captain Kodes, was his assistant, a well-built athletic man in his early thirties, with a smiling face and cold blue eyes. The third, Sergeant Angelo, was remarkable for one thing only, but that one thing was remarkable enough. At six feet three, Angelo was considerably too broad for his height, a massively muscular man who could not have weighed less than two hundred and fifty pounds. Angelo had one function and one only in life – he was Sergius's personal bodyguard. No one could have accused Sergius of choosing without due care and attention.

On the table a tape recorder was running. A voice said: 'and that is all we have for the moment.' Kodes leaned forward and switched off the recorder.

Sergius said: 'And quite enough. All the information we want. Four different voices. I assume, my dear Kodes, that if you were to meet the owners of those four voices you could identify them immediately?'

'Without a shadow of a doubt, sir.'

'And you, Angelo?'

'No question, sir.' Angelo's gravelly booming voice appeared to originate from the soles of his enormous boots.

'Then please go ahead, captain, for the reservation of our usual rooms in the capital – the three of us and the cameraman. Have you chosen him yet, Kodes?'

'I thought young Nicolas, sir. Extraordinarily able.'

'Your choice.' Colonel Sergius's lipless mouth parted about a quarter of an inch, which meant that he was smiling.

'Haven't been to the circus for thirty years – circuses had ceased to exist during the war – but I must say I'm looking forward with almost childish enthusiasm to this one. Especially one which is as highly spoken of as this one is. Incidentally, Angelo, there is a performer in this circus whom I'm sure you will be most interested to see, if not meet.'

'I do not care to see or meet anyone from an American circus, sir.'

'Come, come, Angelo, one must not be so chauvinistic.'

'Chauvinistic, colonel?'

Sergius made to explain then decided against the effort. Angelo was possessed of many attributes but a razor-sharp intelligence was not among them.

'There are no nationalities in a circus, Angelo, only artistes, performers: the audience does not care whether the man on the trapeze comes from Russia or the Sudan. The man I refer to is called Kan Dahn and they say that he is even bigger than you. He is billed as the strongest man in the world.'

Angelo made no reply, merely inflated his enormous chest to its maximum fifty-two inches and contented himself with a smile of wolfish disbelief.

IV

The three-day stay in Austria was by now the inevitable enormous success. From there the circus moved north and, after only one stop-over, arrived in the city where Sergius and his subordinates had moved to meet them.

At the evening performance, those four had taken the best seats about six rows back facing the centre of the centre ring. All four were in civilian clothes and all four were unmistakably soldiers in civilian clothes. One of them, immediately after the beginning of the performance, produced a very expensive-looking camera with a telephoto lens, and the sight of this produced a senior uniformed police officer in very short order indeed. The taking of photographs was officially discouraged, while with westerners the illegal possession of an undeclared camera, if discovered, was a guarantee of arrest and trial: every camera aboard the circus train had been impounded on entering the country and would not be returned until the exit frontier had been crossed.

The policeman said: 'The camera please: and your papers.'

'Officer.' The policeman turned towards Sergius and gave him the benefit of his cold insolent policeman's stare, a stare that lasted for almost a full second before he swallowed what was obviously a painful lump in his throat. He moved in front of Sergius and spoke softly: 'Your pardon, colonel. I was not notified.'

'Your headquarters were informed. Find the incompetent and punish him.'

'Sir. My apologies for—'

'You're blocking my view.'

And, indeed, the view was something not to be blocked. No doubt inspired by the fact that they were being watched by connoisseurs, and wildly enthusiastic connoisseurs at that, the company had in recent weeks gone from strength to strength, honing and refining and polishing their acts, continually inventing more difficult and daring feats until they had arrived at a now almost impossible level of perfection. Even Sergius, who was normally possessed of a mind like a refrigerated computer, gave himself up entirely to the fairyland that was the circus. Only Nicolas, the young – and very presentable – photographer, had his mind on other things, taking an almost non-stop series of photographs of all the main artistes in the circus. But even he forgot his camera and his assignment as he stared – as did his companions – in total disbelief as the Blind Eagles went through their suicidal aerial routine.

It was shortly after their performance that a nondescript individual approached Sergius and murmured: 'Two rows back, sir, ten seats to your left.' A brief nod was Sergius's only acknowledgement.

Towards the very end of the performance Kan Dahn, who appeared to grow fitter with the passing of every day, went through his paces. Kan Dahn spurned the use of props such as iron bars and bar-bells: a five-year-old could tie an iron bar in knots and lift a massive 400-pound bar-bell, provided they were made of the right material, which could be anything except iron. He invariably worked with human beings: creatures who ran, jumped and turned cartwheels could not very well be made of featherweight plastic.

As a finale, Kan Dahn paraded around the centre ring, with a heavy wooden pole resting in a yoke on his shoulders. On either side of the yoke sat five circus girls. If Kan Dahn was aware of the presence of their weight he showed no signs of it. Occasionally, he stopped to scratch the back of his left calf with his right instep. Sergius leaned across Kodes and spoke to Angelo, who was watching the spectacle with an air of determined indifference.

'Big, isn't he, Angelo?'

'All show muscle. Puffy. I once saw an old man in Athens, seventy-five if he was a day, and not a kilo, I swear, over fifty, carrying a grand piano the length of a street. Friends must have put it on his back – he could never have straightened his legs under the load – and if he didn't keep them straight he would have collapsed.'

Even as he spoke, Kan Dahn started climbing a massive step-ladder in the centre of the ring. The platform on top was about three feet square. Kan Dahn reached this without any apparent difficulty, stepped on to an inset turntable, and by a progressive twisting of his tree-trunk legs set the turntable in circular motion, slowly speeding up until the girls on the outer ends of the pole were no more than coloured kaleidoscopic blurs. Gradually he slowed, came to a stop, descended the ladder, knelt, then bowed his shoulders until the feet of the circus girls touched the sawdust. Sergius leaned across again.

'Could your old friend in Athens have done that with his piano?' Angelo made no reply. 'Do you know that they say that he can do that with fourteen girls but the management won't allow him because they say nobody will believe it?' Angelo remained silent.

The performance ended and the rapturous applause, a standing ovation, lasted several minutes. When the audience started filing out, Sergius looked for and located Wrinfield, and by judging his pace contrived to meet him at the exit gangway. He said: 'Mr Wrinfield?'

'Yes, I'm sorry, should I know you?'

'We haven't met.' Sergius pointed to the picture on the front of the souvenir programme he carried. 'The likeness, you will agree, is unmistakable. My name is Colonel Sergius.' They shook hands formally. 'Stupendous, Mr Wrinfield. Impossible. Had anyone told me that such a show existed I would have called him a liar to his face.' Wrinfield beamed, Beethoven's Ninth left him cold – this was the music that reached his heart. 'I've been a devotee of the circus ever since I was a young boy' – Sergius was as fluent a liar as the next man and a great deal more so than most – 'but never in my life have I seen anything like this.'

Wrinfield beamed some more. 'You are too kind, colonel.'

Sergius shook his head sadly. 'I wish I had the gift with words the way you have with those marvellous performers of yours. But that is not the sole reason for introducing myself. Your next stop, I know, is Crau.' He produced a card. 'I am the Chief of Police there.' Sergius carried a considerable variety of cards with him. 'Whatever I can do, I am at your service. Ask and it's done and I shall consider it a privilege. Not that I shall ever be very far from your side. It is my intention to attend every single performance, for I know I shall never see the like again. For the duration of your stay, crime in Crau can reign unchecked.'

'Again, you are too kind. Colonel Sergius, you shall be my personal – and, I hope – permanent guest at the circus. I would be honoured—' He broke off and looked at the three men, who showed no intention of moving on. 'They are with you, colonel?'

'How thoughtless of me. I'm afraid I quite got carried away.' Sergius performed the introductions while Wrinfield introduced Harper, who had been seated next to him.

Wrinfield went on: 'As I was about to say, colonel, I would be honoured if you and your men would join us in my office for a glass of your national drink.' Sergius said that the honour would be entirely theirs. It was all very cordial.

In the office, one glass became two and then three. Nicolas, permission given, clicked his camera constantly, not forgetting to take at least a dozen of a smilingly protesting Maria, who had been seated behind her desk, when they had entered.

Wrinfield said: 'I wonder, colonel, if you would like to meet some of our performers?'

'You're a mind-reader, Mr Wrinfield! I must confess that

I did have that very thought in mind but I didn't dare presume – I mean, I have sufficiently trespassed on your hospitality—'

'Maria.' Wrinfield rattled off a list of names. 'Go to the dressing-rooms and ask them if they would be kind enough to come and visit our distinguished guest.' Wrinfield, in recent weeks, had fallen victim to a certain mid-European floweriness of speech.

And so they came to see the distinguished guest, Bruno and his brothers, Neubauer, Kan Dahn, Ron Roebuck, Manuelo, Malthius and half a dozen others. Apart from a certain reserve in Angelo's attitude when he greeted Kan Dahn, everything was very pleasant indeed, fulsome congratulations offered and as modestly received. Sergius did not overstay his welcome and left almost immediately after the last handshake, he and Wrinfield exchanging mutual expressions of goodwill and cordial anticipation of their next meeting.

Sergius had a large black limousine waiting outside, with a uniformed police chauffeur and a dark man in dark clothes beside him. After about a quarter of a mile, Sergius stopped the car and issued certain instructions to the plain-clothes man, whom he addressed as Alex. Alex nodded and left the car.

Back in his hotel suite, Sergius said to Kodes and Angelo: 'You had no trouble in matching the voices with the tapes?' Both men shook their heads. 'Good. Nicolas, how long will it take you to develop those photographs?'

'To develop? Within the hour, sir. Printing will take considerably longer.'

'Just print those of Mr Wrinfield, Dr Harper, the girl – Maria, isn't it? – and the leading circus performers.' Nicolas left and Sergius said: 'You may leave, too, Angelo. I'll call you.'

Kodes said: 'Is one permitted to ask the object of this exercise?'

'One is permitted. I was about to tell you, which is why I asked Angelo to leave. A loyal soul, but one does not wish to overburden his mind with complexities.'

V

Bruno and Maria, for the first time walking arm in arm, made their way along the ill-lit street, talking with apparent animation. Some thirty yards behind them Alex followed with the unobtrusive casualness of one who has had long practice in following people without calling attention to himself. He slowed his pace as the couple ahead turned through a doorway with an incomprehensible neon sign above.

The café was ill-lit and smoke-filled from an evil-smelling brown coal-fire – the outside temperature hovered near the freezing point – but cosy and comfortable enough if one had a gas-mask ready to hand. It was half full. Seated in a wall booth were Manuelo and Kan Dahn, the former with a coffee, Kan Dahn with two litres of beer. Kan Dahn's legendary consumption of beer was excused – by Kan Dahn – on the grounds that he required it to keep his strength up: it certainly never affected his performance. Bruno spoke briefly to them and asked to be excused for not joining them. Kan Dahn smirked and said that that was perfectly all right by them: Bruno led Maria to a corner table. Only a few seconds later Roebuck sauntered in, acknowledged their presence with a wave of his hand and sat down with his two companions. The three of them talked desultorily, then started, casually at first, then with increasing urgency, to search through their pockets: from where Bruno sat it would appear that a certain degree of acrimony, not to say downright recrimination, had crept into their conversation. Finally Roebuck scowled, made a dismissive gesture, rose and crossed to Bruno's table.

He said sadly: 'Roebuck, begging for alms. Not one of us bothered to check if the others were carrying money. As it turns out, we don't have a cent. Rather, we do have thousands of cents, but we doubt whether they'll accept dollars here and Kan Dahn appears to be against washing up in the kitchen. Now, if I had comrades in distress—'

Bruno smiled, brought out a wallet, handed some notes to Roebuck, who thanked him and left. Bruno and Maria ordered an omelette apiece.

Alex, shivering in the cold on the pavement, waited until

the food had been served, crossed the street and went into a phone booth. He fed in money, dialled a number and said: 'Alex.'

'Yes?'

'I followed the man and the girl to the Black Swan. They're beginning to eat so it looks as if they'll be there for some time yet. They spoke to two other people, at another table, after their arrival, before going to their own place.'

'You sure you have the right ones?'

'I have their photographs, colonel. A third man came in shortly after the man and girl had sat down at their own table. He sat with the other two men for some time then went across to this man Bruno. He seemed to be borrowing money, at least I saw notes changing hands.'

Sergius said: 'Do you know any of those three men?'

'No, sir. But one of them I'd recognize if I didn't see him again for twenty years. A giant, the biggest man I've ever seen, bigger even than Angelo.'

'I won't award myself any prizes for guessing who that is. Come back here. No, wait. Stay out of sight so that no one inside the café can see you. I'll send Vladimir and Josef down to relieve you. I'll give them their instructions. You just have to point those people out to them. A car will be there in a few minutes.'

Inside the café, Maria said: 'What's wrong, Bruno?'

'What should be wrong?'

'You look troubled.'

'I am troubled. D-day approaches with uncommon haste. Just about a week now. Wouldn't you be troubled if you had to get inside that damned Lubylan?'

'It's not just that. You've become remote from me. Cool. Distant. I've done something you don't like? Said something wrong?'

'Don't be silly.'

She put a hand on his arm. 'Please.'

'Is this affection? Or something more? Or something else?'

'Why do you hurt me so?'

'I don't want to.' His voice lacked the ring of conviction. 'Have you ever been an actress?'

She took her hand away. There was bafflement in her face,

and pain. She said: 'I can't think what I've done wrong, I can't think what I've said wrong – and you *do* want to hurt me. Suddenly you want to hurt me. Why don't you slap me, then? Right here in public? That way you can hurt both me and my pride. I don't understand you, I just don't understand you.' She pushed back her chair. 'I can find the way.'

It was Bruno's turn to take her hand. Whether this was affection, appeal or just an attempt to restrain her it was difficult to say. He said: 'I wish I could.'

'Could what?'

'Find the way.' He looked at her, his brow slightly corrugated. 'You've been how long with the CIA?'

'Nearly four years.' The bafflement was back in her face.

'Who appointed you to this particular job?'

'Dr Harper. Why?'

'I thought it was a man called Charles.'

'He appointed me. Dr Harper made the suggestion. He was very insistent that I should be the one who should come along on this trip.'

'I'll bet he was.'

'What's that supposed to mean?'

'Merely congratulations. To Dr Harper. On his impeccable good taste. Who's Charles?'

'Just Charles.'

'He's not Charles. He has another name.'

'Why didn't you ask him?'

'He wouldn't have told me. I'd hoped you might.'

'You know that we can't divulge things such as that.'

'Well, I like that. I'm going to risk my damned life for the CIA and they can't even trust me with a straightforward piece of information like that. I thought that at least by this time I could trust you or you could trust me. It seems I was wrong – on the second count, anyway. You're willing that I should die but you're not even willing to tell me that. Trust and faith and loyalty – those are great things, aren't they? Or used to be. There doesn't seem to be too much of it around nowadays.'

'His name is Admiral George C. Jamieson.'

Bruno looked at her for a long moment, then his face slowly broke into a wide smile that transformed his whole expression. She snatched her hand away and looked at him furiously. At their table Kan Dahn nudged Roebuck and Manuelo in turn: all three watched the scene with interest.

'You horrid man! You deceitful, devious, conniving human being – if I can call you that! And you had the audacity to ask me if I had ever been an actress. I never have been but even if I had I could never hold a candle to you as an actor. Why did you do it? I don't deserve that.'

Roebuck said: 'She's getting madder by the minute.'

'How little you know of human nature,' Kan Dahn said, 'She'll be proposing to him inside thirty seconds.'

Bruno said: 'I apologize. But I had to.'

'Had to find out if I would trust you?'

'It's terribly important to me. Please forgive me.' He took her unresisting hand again and examined its ringless state with care. He said: 'It looks pretty bare to me.'

'What does?'

'You know that we're only supposed to be in love?'

'Yes.' It was Maria's turn to be silent. 'Or do you think we should stop supposing?' Her voice was hesitant, unsure.

'I don't think. I know. Do you love me, Maria?'

The voice was a whisper but the answer immediate. 'Yes.' She looked at her left hand and smiled. 'It does look a little bare, doesn't it?'

Kan Dahn leant back against the booth in an expansive fashion. 'What did your Uncle Kan Dahn tell you? Somebody buy me a drink.'

Bruno said: 'Sure?'

'Even the most intelligent man can ask the most stupid questions. Can't you see it?'

'I think I can. At least, I hope I can.'

'I've been in love with you for weeks.' She had stopped smiling now. 'In the early days I used to watch you blindfolded on that trapeze. Then after a while I had to leave the auditorium and go outside and be sick. Now I don't dare go inside at all and I'm still sick. A fraction of a second too early or too late . . .' She broke off and her eyes were wet. 'But I can still hear the music, *your* music, and when it begins I die inside.'

'Will you marry me?'

'Of course I will, you lunkhead.' She was crying openly now.

'There's no need for such language. And I'd like to point out that Kan Dahn, Manuelo and Ron are taking the greatest interest in the proceedings. I have a feeling they're taking bets on us. I've also got the feeling that I'm going to suffer when they get me alone.'

'I can't see them.' Bruno passed his handkerchief and she mopped her eyes. 'Yes, they are looking a bit this way, aren't they?' Unconsciously crumpling the handkerchief in her hand, she turned her gaze back to Bruno. 'I love you, I want to marry you – isn't that old-fashioned – I'd marry you tomorrow – but I can't love and marry the greatest aerialist in the world. I know I can't. I think you know that I can't. Do you want me to be sick all my life?'

'That wouldn't be nice for either of us. Well, it's all living and learning – I thought blackmail normally started *after* one married.'

'You live in a strange world, Bruno, if you think honesty and blackmail are the same thing.'

Bruno appeared to ponder. 'You could aways marry the greatest ex-aerialist.'

'Ex?'

'No problem.' Bruno made a throwaway gesture with his right hand. 'I'll burn my trapeze or whatever the phrase is.'

She stared at him. 'Just like – just like that? But it's your life. Bruno.'

'I have other interests.'

'What?'

'When your name is Mrs Wildermann, I'll let you know.'

'This year, next year, some time, never.' Matrimony was obviously closer to her heart than alternative occupations for a future husband.

'Could be the day after tomorrow.'

She got back to staring at him. 'Do you mean here? In this country?'

'Heaven forbid. No. In the States. Special licence. We could get the first plane out tomorrow. Nobody's going to stop us. I've plenty of money.'

She took some time to assimilate this, then said with conviction: 'You don't know what you're saying.'

Bruno said agreeably: 'Lots of times that's true. This time, no. I know what I'm saying because – and it's no exaggeration – I know we're in deadly danger. I know they're on to me. I'm pretty sure they're on to you. We were followed here tonight. I don't want—'

'Followed? How do you know?'

'I know. Later. Meantime, I don't want you to die.' For a moment Bruno rubbed his chin with a pensive hand. 'Come to that, I don't particularly want to die myself.'

'You'd let your brothers down? You'd let Mr Wrinfield and the circus down? You'd abandon this entire mission?'

'I'd abandon anything in the world for you.'

'You're running scared, Bruno?'

'Possibly. Let's go to the American embassy now and get things fixed up. It's hardly office hours, but they wouldn't turn away a couple of nationals in distress.'

She looked at him in total disbelief. Then the disbelief faded to be replaced with something very close to contempt. Then that look faded in turn to be replaced by a very thoughtful expression indeed. A faint smile touched her face, widened, and then suddenly she began to laugh. Bruno looked at her speculatively, the three men at the adjacent table in perplexity. She said: 'You're impossible. It's not enough for you to test me once, you have to do it all over again.'

It was as if she hadn't spoken. He said: 'You heard me? I'd give up the world for you. Can't you do the same for me?'

'Willingly. The whole world. But not the whole world and Bruno. If we went to the embassy, do you know what would happen? I'd be on that plane tomorrow. But you wouldn't. Oh, no, you'd stay here. Don't deny it. It's in your face. You think you're the inscrutable Bruno Wildermann. Everyone thinks so. Well, almost everyone. Three months and you won't have a secret left from me.'

Bruno said: 'I'm afraid of that. Okay, okay, so I tried and failed. Nothing new for me. Please don't tell Dr Harper any of this. He'll not only think me a fool but he'll take a dim view of my mingling, shall we say, business and pleasure.' He put money on the table. 'Let's leave. When we get to the door

I'm going to turn back on some pretext and have a word with Roebuck. While I do that, have a look around, see if there is any person who might be taking – or about to take – an interest in us.'

At the doorway, Bruno, as if recalling something, turned back. He approached Roebuck and said: 'What was he like?'

'Medium height. Black hair. Black moustache. Black coat. He followed you all the way from the circus.'

'Your compartments may be bugged. I doubt it, but no chances. See you.'

Arm in arm he walked along the street with Maria. She said curiously: 'What are those three to you?'

'Very old friends. No more. You don't put friends' heads on the chopping block. Fellow all in black, black hair, black coat. See him?'

'Saw two, but none like that. One had that horrible marcelled blond hair, the other was as bald as a coot.'

'Which means that Junior has returned to hand in his report to his boss.'

'His boss?'

'Colonel Sergius.'

'The Crau police chief?'

'He is not the Crau police chief. He's the head of the national secret police.'

She stopped and looked at him. 'How do you know? How *can* you know?'

'I know. I know him although he doesn't know me. You forget this is my country. But I know Sergius and I'll never forget him. Would you forget the man who killed your wife?'

'The man who – oh, Bruno!' She paused. 'But he must know now.'

'He knows.'

'But then he must know why you're here!'

'I imagine so.'

'I'll go with you tomorrow. I swear it.' There was a note of hysteria in her voice. 'That plane, Bruno, that plane. Don't you know you'll never leave this country alive?'

'I have things to do. And kindly modulate your voice. There's a character with horrible marcelled blond hair close behind.'

'I'm scared. I'm scared.'

'It's catching. Come along and I'll give you some real coffee.'

'Where?'

'In this accommodation of mine you envy so much.'

They walked some way in silence then she said: 'Have you thought that if they're on to you they may have bugged your place?'

'Who says we've got to discuss affairs of state?'

VI

Sergius was deeply engaged in discussing affairs of state. He said to Alex: 'That's all that happened? Bruno and the girl went into this café, spoke briefly to the two men already seated, took the girl to a separate table and ordered a meal. Then a third man appeared, joined the other two men, went to Bruno's table, borrowed some money from him and returned to his seat.' Alex nodded. 'And you said you didn't know the names of any of those men, had never seen them before, but that one of them was a giant, as big as Angelo here?'

Alex looked at Angelo. 'Bigger,' he said with some satisfaction. Angelo was sadly lacking in Kan Dahn's genial good nature and did not make the most lovable of characters.

Angelo scowled blackly but no one paid him any attention, possibly because it was difficult to differentiate between his black scowl and his normal expression.

Sergius said: 'Well, we know who that is. Would you recognize the three men from their photographs?'

'Of course.' Alex looked hurt.

'Angelo. Go tell Nicolas to bring whatever prints he has ready.'

Angelo returned with Nicolas and about twenty prints. Silently, Sergius handed them to Alex, who leafed rapidly through them. He put one on the table. 'That's the girl,' he announced.

Sergius said with restraint, 'We know that's the girl.'

'Your pardon, colonel.' Alex selected three more. 'Those.'

Sergius took them and handed them to Kodes, who glanced

at them briefly and said: 'Kan Dahn, Manuelo the knife-thrower and Roebuck, the expert with the cowboy rope.'

'Precisely.' Sergius smiled his mordant smile. 'Have them shadowed at all times.'

Kodes showed his surprise. 'The presence of those three men could have been just coincidence. After all, they are among the outstanding artistes in the circus and it is natural that they should be friends. Besides, the Black Swan is, after all, the nearest café to the circus.'

Sergius sighed. 'Alas, it was ever thus. I am left to fight on virtually alone. All the decisions have to be made, all the thinking has to be done by a senior officer, which is no doubt why I am a senior officer.' A false modesty was not one of Sergius's besetting sins. 'Our Bruno Wildermann is clever, he may also be dangerous. He suspected, only he knows how, that he was under surveillance and put his suspicions to the test. He had this man Roebuck standing by to follow whoever might follow him. This would make Roebuck – and, by implication, the other two – something just a little bit more than friends. Roebuck followed Alex. He didn't go to borrow money, he went to inform Bruno that he, Bruno, had been followed by a man with a black coat, black moustache, very stupid.' He bestowed a pitying glance on the crestfallen shadower. 'I don't suppose it ever occurred to you, Alex, to look over your shoulder? Just once?'

'I'm sorry, colonel.'

Sergius gave him a look more commonly associated with a starving crocodile which has just spotted lunch.

— 7 —

THE CIRCUS left for Crau on the Wednesday night. Before its departure Bruno had gone to Dr Harper's rail compartment. For a man with so much on his mind, facing up to what was unquestionably the crucial moment of his professional career, Harper was remarkably calm and relaxed. It was more than could be said of Wrinfield, who sat there with a drink in his hand and a most dispirited expression on his face. Wrinfield had screwed his courage to the sticking point but now that the moment was at hand he had about him the air of a man who suspects that something is about to become unstuck. Crau was a huge black cloud on his horizon.

'Evening, Bruno. A seat. What will you drink?'

'Thank you. Nothing. I've only one a week and I'm reserving that for later.'

'With the fair Miss Hopkins, one would suppose?'

'One would suppose correctly.'

'Why don't you marry the girl?' Wrinfield said sourly. 'She's getting so she's almost useless to me now, either moping or dreaming the whole day long.'

'I'm going to. Maybe she's worried and nervous. Like yourself, Mr Wrinfield.'

'Going to what?' Harper said.

'Marry her.'

'Good God!'

Bruno took no offence. 'Marriage is a common enough institution.'

Wrinfield said suspiciously: 'Does she know about this?' Wrinfield had become genuinely fond of her and had come to treat her as the daughter he'd never had, more especially since Henry's death.

'Yes.' Bruno smiled. 'So would you, if you kept your eyes open, sir. She sat next to you at table tonight.'

Wrinfield clapped his palm against his forehead. 'She was wearing a ring tonight. She's never worn a ring before. Fourth finger, left hand.' He paused and came up with a triumphant solution. 'An engagement ring.'

'You've had a lot on your mind, sir. Like Maria. I bought it this afternoon.'

'Well, congratulations. When we move off, we must come and toast the happy couple.' Bruno winced but said nothing. 'Eh, Dr Harper?'

'Indeed. I couldn't be more pleased.'

'Thank you. I didn't come to talk about the ring, though, just the company I had when I bought it. I'm afraid someone is on to me. A couple of nights ago I went with Maria to a café. It so happened Roebuck came along very soon after. He said he'd been intrigued by the behaviour of a character who emerged from the shadows of an alley near the circus when we'd passed by. Apparently he followed us all the way to the café, stopped when we stopped then took up a position across the road where he could watch us. It could have been coincidence or Roebuck's lively imagination. Last night I was pretty certain that Maria and I were being followed again but I wasn't sure. Today I was because it was in daylight. Not one shadow but two, taking the job in turns, one with artificially waved blond hair, the other completely bald. We wandered aimlessly, like a couple of tourists, wherever the fancy took us: they followed everywhere.'

'I don't like this,' Harper said.

'Thank you for not questioning my word. I don't much like it either. And I don't understand it. I've done nothing, absolutely nothing to attract any attention to myself. Maybe it's just because my name is Wildermann and Crau's my home town. It's anybody's guess. Maybe a dozen other circus people are under surveillance, too. Who's to say?'

'Most disturbing,' Wrinfield said. 'Most disturbing. What are you going to do, Bruno?'

'What can I do? Just keep going, that's all. Play it as it comes. One thing's for sure, they won't be shadowing me on the night.'

'The night?'

'Hasn't Dr Harper told you?'

'Ah. Tuesday. I wonder where we'll all be then.' With much clanking and shuddering the train began slowly to get under way.

'I know where I'll be. See you shortly.' Bruno turned to go, then stopped short at the sight of the miniature transceiver on Harper's desk. 'Tell me. I've often wondered. How is it that the customs in various countries remove just about the fillings from our teeth while you manage to sail through with that transceiver?'

'Transceiver? What transceiver?' Harper clamped the earphones to his head, touched the microphone to Bruno's chest, switched on the power and pulled the transmit switch backwards instead of forwards. The machine hummed and a narrow strip of paper emerged from an all but invisible slit at the side. After about ten seconds Harper switched off, tore the protruding few inches of paper away and showed it to Bruno. It had a long wavy line along the middle. 'A cardiograph machine, my dear Bruno. Every travelling doctor needs one. You can't imagine the fun I've had taking the cardiographs of customs official after customs official.'

'Whatever will they think of next?' Bruno left, walked along the corridors of the now-swaying train, picked up Maria from her compartment, took her along to his own, unlocked the handleless door and ushered her inside.

Bruno said: 'Shall we have some music? Romantic, to fit the occasion? Then one of my incomparable dry martinis to celebrate – if that is the word – my descent into human bondage. And – it is just a thought – a few sweet nothings in your ear.'

She smiled. 'That all sounds very pleasant. Especially the sweet nothings.'

He turned on the record player, keeping the volume low, mixed the Martinis, set them on the table, sat on the settee beside her and pressed his face against the dark hair in the approximate area of where her ear could be presumed to be. From the expressions on Maria's face, first of startlement then of sheer incredulity, it was clear that Bruno had a line in sweet nothings that she had not previously encountered.

II

Crau lay just under two hundred miles distant, so that even for a necessarily slow freight train it was no more than a brief overnight haul there, with two intermediate stops. They left in darkness, they arrived in darkness, and it was still dark when they disembarked. It was also extremely cold. The first overwhelming impression of Crau was one of bleak inhospitability, but then railway sidings, especially in cold and darkness, are not the most welcoming of places anywhere. The siding in which they had just drawn up was an inconvenient three-quarters of a mile from the circus auditorium, but the organizational genius of Wrinfield and his executive staff had been functioning with its usual smooth efficiency and a fleet of trucks, buses and private cars was already waiting alongside.

Bruno walked beside the track towards a group of circus performers and hands who stood huddled under the harsh glare of an overhead arc-lamp. After exchanging the routine good mornings he looked around for his two brothers, but failed to see them. He spoke to the man nearest him, Malthius, the tiger trainer.

'Seen my wandering brothers around? They're a very hungry couple who never fail to join me for breakfast but I haven't had the pleasure this morning.'

'No.' Malthius called out: 'Anyone seen Vladimir and Yoffe this morning?' When it soon became apparent that no one had, Malthius turned to one of his assistant trainers. 'Go and give them a shake, will you?'

The man left. Dr Harper and Wrinfield, both with fur hats and collars upturned against the gently falling snow, came up and said their good mornings. Wrinfield said to Bruno: 'Like to come with me and see what kind of exhibition hall they have for us here? For some odd reason it's called the Winter Palace, although I can't see it having any possible resemblance to that palace in Leningrad.' He shivered violently. 'Even more important, however, is the fact that I'm told that the central heating is superb.'

'I'd like to. If you could just wait a moment. Two thirds of the Blind Eagles seem to have slept in this morning. Ah! Here's Johann.'

Urgency in his voice, Malthius's assistant said: 'I think you'd better come, Bruno. Quickly!' Bruno said nothing, just jumped quickly aboard the train. Dr Harper and Wrinfield, after an uncomprehending glance at each other, followed closely behind him.

Vladimir and Yoffe had shared a double-bedded compartment, nothing like the princely quarters of their elder brother but comfortable enough for all that. They had become renowned and teased for their almost compulsive tidiness: unquestionably, they would have been distressed to see its present state.

It was a shambles and looked as if a small but determined tornado had recently passed through it. Bedding lay scattered over the floor, two chairs were broken, glasses were smashed, a small hand-basin had been splintered and even a window – of heavy plate – had been cracked and starred without however, shattering. Most ominously of all, there were bloodstains on the torn sheets and on the cream-panelled walls.

Bruno went to move inside but Harper put a restraining hand on his shoulder. 'Don't. The police wouldn't like it.'

The police, when they arrived, didn't like it at all. They were shocked that such a monstrous thing, the kidnapping of two famous American artistes – if they knew that Vladimir and Yoffe had been born less than half a mile from where they stood they were keeping the information to themselves – should happen upon their soil. The most immediate, the most rigorously thorough investigation would be held immediately. To begin with, said the inspector who had arrived to take charge, the area had to be completely cleared and cordoned off by his men, which was a lot less impressive than it sounded, for the cordoning off consisted merely of stationing two of them in the corridor. The occupants of the coach in which the brothers had slept were to remain available for questioning. Wrinfield suggested the dining-room – the temperature outside was below freezing point – and the inspector agreed. As they moved off, plain-clothes detectives and finger-print experts arrived at the scene. Wrinfield elected to join them in the dining car, after directing his immediate deputies to proceed with the unloading of the train and the setting up of the circus and the cages in the arena immediately outside it.

The air in the dining wagon was almost unbearably warm – the giant locomotive was still hooked up and would remain so throughout the day to provide the necessary heat for the animals, who would remain there until they were moved up to the circus in the evening.

Bruno stood apart with Wrinfield and Harper. Briefly, they discussed what could possibly have happened to the brothers and why; but as there was clearly no answer to either question they soon fell silent and remained that way until no less a person than Colonel Sergius himself made his entrance. His face was set in hard, bitter lines and he gave the impression that his anger was barely under control.

'Dastardly!' he said. 'Unbelievable! Humiliating! That this

should happen to guests in my country. I promise you, you shall have the full criminal investigating weight of our country behind this. What a welcome and what a black day for Crau!'

Harper said mildly: 'This can hardly be laid at the door of any citizen of Crau. They were missing when we arrived here. We had two intermediate stops on the way up. It must have happened at one of those.'

'True, true, Crau is exonerated. Does that make it any easier for us to bear, do you think? What hurts our country hurts us all.' He paused and then his voice took on a deeper timbre. 'It needn't have happened at either of those two stops.' He looked at Bruno. 'I'm sorry to have to suggest this but they might have been *thrown* off the train while in motion.'

Bruno didn't stare at him, his feelings and emotions were always too tightly under control for that, but he came close to it. 'Why should anyone do that? Why should anyone even lay hands on them? I know my brothers better than anyone in the world – they never did anyone any harm.'

Sergius looked at him pityingly. 'Don't you know that it is always the innocent who suffer? If you want to commit a burglary you don't go to the home of a notorious gangster to do it.' He turned to an aide. 'Get the radio telephone in here and get the Minister of Transport on the line for me. No, do it yourself. If he complains about still being in bed tell him I'll come and talk to him personally. Tell him I want every inch of track between the capital and here searched for two missing people. Tell him it's urgent. Tell him they may be badly hurt and that the temperature is below freezing. Tell him I want a report within two hours. Then call the Air Force. Tell them the same thing but only to use helicopters. I want their report within the hour.' The aide left.

Wrinfield said: 'You think there's a serious possibility—'

'I think nothing. A policeman's job is to overlook nothing. We'll know inside the hour. I have no faith in that old fuddy-duddy transport minister, but the Air Force is a different matter altogether. Pilots flying at ten metres, a trained observer for either side.' He looked at Bruno with what he probably intended to be a sympathetic expression. 'I commiserate with you, Mr Wildermann. I also commiserate with you, Mr Wrinfield.'

Wrinfield said: 'With me? Admittedly, two of my very best artistes are gone. True, I held them in the highest regard. But so did a score of others. So, for that matter, did everyone else in the circus.'

'The others won't have to pay the ransom. I merely advance a possibility. If such a possibility existed you would pay a great deal of money to get them back, would you not?'

'What are you talking about?'

'Alas, even in our glorious country, we have our villains. We even have kidnappers – and their favourite method of seizing a victim is from a train. And they are very desperate men – kidnapping is a capital offence in our country. This is but supposition, but a fairly strong one.' He looked again at Bruno and the gash that substituted for his mouth parted fractionally. Sergius was smiling. 'And we commiserate with ourselves. It looks as if we shall not be seeing the Blind Eagles in Crau.'

'You'll be seeing one of them.'

Sergius looked at him. A score of people looked at him. Maria slowly passed a tongue across her lips. Sergius said: 'Am I to understand—'

'I used to be a solo act before my brothers were old enough to join me. A few hours' practice and I can do it again.'

Sergius looked at him for a considering moment. 'We all know you are a man totally without nerves. Are you also a man totally without feelings?'

Bruno turned away without reply.

Sergius looked after him thoughtfully, then turned away also. He said: 'All the occupants of that coach here?'

'All present, colonel,' Wrinfield said. 'But you voiced the opinion that kidnappers were—'

'Might. And you heard what I said – a policeman's job is to overlook nothing. Anybody here heard any noise, any unusual sound during the night?' From the loud silence it was apparent that no one had heard anything. 'Very well. The brothers slept in the end compartment in the coach. Who slept next to them?'

Kan Dahn moved his massive bulk forward. 'I did.'

'Surely you heard something?'

'I already haven't answered your question. That means no. I'm a very heavy sleeper.'

Sergius looked thoughtful. 'You're big enough to do it single-handed.'

Kan Dahn's tone was mild. 'Are you accusing me?'

'I'm making an observation.'

'Vladimir and Yoffe were good friends of mine, very good friends. Everyone knows this for years. Why should I wait until now and then do something crazy like this? Besides, if I did it there would have been no signs of a struggle. An arm round each and I would have just carried them away.'

Sergius was sceptical. 'Indeed?'

'Perhaps the colonel would like a demonstration?'

'It should be interesting.'

Kan Dahn indicated the two burly uniformed policemen standing together. He said: 'They are bigger, much bigger, and stronger than the two brothers?'

'I should have thought so.'

For the giant he was Kan Dahn moved with the speed of a cat. Before the two policemen had time to assume defensive postures Kan Dahn was upon them, a gorilla arm round each of them, pinning their own arms to their sides. A moment later both men were off their feet, struggling furiously to free themselves from what, judging by the expressions on their faces, was a far from affectionate embrace.

Kan Dahn, his voice still mild, said: 'Stop struggling or I shall have to squeeze.'

Doubtless under the impression that Kan Dahn could squeeze no more, the men intensified their efforts to escape. Kan Dahn squeezed some more. One man cried out, the other grunted, both expressions of agony. Kan Dahn tightened the inexorable pressure. Both men stopped struggling. Carefully, gently, Kan Dahn set them on their feet and stood back and watched sorrowfully as the two men collapsed to the floor.

Sergius regarded the tableau thoughtfully. 'Angelo should be here this morning. You, Kan Dahn, are exonerated.' The tone was totally humourless. He turned as Captain Kodes hurried in. 'Well?'

'All we have is fingerprints, colonel. There are many sets

of two different fingerprints. Those must belong to the brothers. But we also found two other sets in rather unusual positions – against the walls, on the window, on the inside of the door – places where men might have braced themselves in the course of a violent fight.'

'So.' Sergius thought briefly, absently watching the painful efforts of the two policemen to struggle to their feet. Their sufferings obviously left him completely unmoved. He turned to Wrinfield. 'Every man in this circus will have to be fingerprinted this morning. In the Exhibition Hall, where your circus is being held.'

'Is it really necessary—'

Sergius affected weariness. 'I have a job to do. And, for the third time, a policeman's job is to overlook nothing.'

Although Crau lay roughly to the north of the capital, the main railway station did not, as one might have expected, lie to the south of the town: because of unfavourable terrain the railway line curved round the city and entered from the north. Consequently, when the black limousine of uncertain vintage set out for the Winter Palace, it drove due south along what, downtown, developed into the main thoroughfare of the city. This north-south street was, confusingly enough, called West Street.

Bruno sat in the back seat and beside him was Dr Harper. Wrinfield, whose gloomy expression was indication enough that his dark forebodings about Crau were in the process of being confirmed, sat silently beside the driver. The weather was hardly calculated to lend a certain buoyancy to the spirits: it was just after dawn, a bleak and bitter dawn with snow swirling down from the darkly lowering clouds.

Some hundred yards from the siding Harper, who was sitting in the right-hand corner, rubbed the steamy window, peered out and up, then touched Bruno on the arm.

'Never seen anything like it. What on earth is that?'

'I can't see from here.'

'On top of those buildings. Bushes, shrubs – good heavens, they've even got trees growing up there.'

'Roof gardens. Very common in central Europe. Living in a flat doesn't have to mean that you can't have your own little plot of land. Lots of them even have lawns.' Bruno rubbed his own window. The building to his left was as grim, bleak and forbidding as any he had ever seen. He counted the storeys: there were nine of them. He saw the windows, each one heavily barred. He observed the curving menace of the steel spikes that surrounded the roof, the watch-towers at the north and south corners: from that angle it was impossible to see what might be on the roofs of those towers but Bruno knew there would be searchlights and klaxons mounted there. He looked at Harper and lifted an eyebrow: the driver had smilingly shrugged when addressed in English, but the chances were high that he was one of Sergius's men and Sergius would not have picked a non-English speaker for the job. Harper caught his glance and nodded, although the confirmation was really superfluous: the reality of Lubylan all too dismayingly matched Harper's description of it. The prospect of trying to effect an entry into the fortress was as chilling as the dawn.

Some quarter of a mile farther on they passed by a row of stationary black cars lining the right-hand pavement. At the front was a wreath-covered hearse: the hour was not early but the day was: the cortège, Bruno reflected, must have quite some way to go. Across the pavement from the hearse was an establishment with draped black velvet curtains in the windows, those being the framing for what the proprietor obviously regarded as being his choicest selection of wreaths, artificial bouquets under glass domes and unengraved marble tombstones, all in black. The adjacent door was also of the same cheerful colour, relieved only by a white cross. Bruno caught a glimpse of the door opening and the foot of a coffin on the shoulders of the two leading bearers.

'How very convenient,' Bruno murmured.

Dr Harper appeared not to have heard him.

III

The Winter Palace was the pride of Crau, and deservedly so. Deliberately baroque in construction, both inside and out, it was in fact only three years old. It was a reinforced steel and concrete structure, cladded both inside and out with white marble veneer from which, presumably, the name of the building arose. The building itself consisted of a very large, elliptical covered forecourt, which gave on to the much greater elliptical stadium beyond it. The interior could not have been in greater contrast to the spires, minarets and gargoyles which so liberally be-festooned the exterior: here all the latest ideas in spectacle presentation had been incorporated, so that everything was modern, almost excruciatingly so, functional and above all adaptable. The permutations of staging and seating, always to the best advantage of performers and audience, were practically limitless. It could be and was used for opera, theatre, cinema and music-hall: it was also used for the presentation of sporting spectacles ranging from ice-hockey to covered court tennis: for the setting for a circus amphitheatre it was nothing short of superb. In the last capacity, the sharply tiered seats, each one upholstered and with its own armrests, could accommodate no fewer than eighteen thousand spectators. It was, Wrinfield declared, the finest auditorium he had ever seen, no mean compliment coming from a man who had seen the best in North America and Europe, especially when it was borne in mind that the population of Crau totalled just under a quarter million.

IV

The mass fingerprinting of the entire circus staff took place during the course of the forenoon in one of the many restaurants and bars – empty at that time of day – that lined the inner side of the forecourt. Resentment and indignation at what was pretty well regarded as cavalier and unnecessary treatment ran high, and it required much of Wrinfield's considerable tact and powers of persuasion to ensure co-operation. Sergius, supervising by remote control from the comparative comfort of Wrinfield's prefabricated office and armoured in his seemingly pachydermatous hide, remained totally unmoved by the sullenness of the circus employees, the numerous far-from-affectionate glances that were cast in his direction. Towards the end of the fingerprinting he received a telephone message, but as he spoke in his own language neither Wrinfield nor Maria, who were present with him, could understand the burden of the conversation.

Sergius drained his glass of vodka – he had the same osmotic affinity for his national drink as parched sand has for water – and said: 'Where is Bruno Wildermann?'

'He's in the stadium. But – but you're not seriously thinking of fingerprinting him? His own brothers—'

'Please. I look so foolish? Come. It concerns you, too.'

As the two men approached, Bruno turned away from the supervision of the rigging of a low wire across the centre ring. He looked without expression at Sergius and said: 'You have word, colonel?'

'Yes. Both from the railways and the Air Force. But I'm afraid both reports are negative. No trace of any person lying alongside the railway tracks.'

'So that has to make it kidnapping?'

'There would appear to be no other obvious solution.'

V

Late that afternoon, when Bruno was rehearsing his solo act on the newly slung high trapeze, he was summoned to Wrinfield's office. He slid to the ground, put on his mentalist's mandarin cloak and went to the office, which, as seemed inevitable, was only feet from the as yet empty tigers' cage. Wrinfield was at his desk, Maria at hers. Sergius and Kodes were standing. The atmosphere was half-way between the tense and the funereal.

Sergius took a piece of paper that Wrinfield was studying and handed it to Bruno. It held a printed message, in English, which said: 'The Wildermann brothers will be returned alive on the receipt of 50,000 dollars. Used bills. Any denomination. Instructions for transfer on Sunday, delivery Monday. Failure to deliver will result in delivery of two left little fingers Monday. Same fingers delivered if notes received but found to be treated for identification by infra-red, ultra-violet or X-ray. Two fingers on Tuesday. On Thursday, two one-handed trapeze artistes.'

Bruno handed the note back to Sergius.

'Your suspicions were correct.'

'I was right. No nerves. No feelings. Yes, it would appear so.'

'They seem ruthless.'

'They are.'

'And professionals?'

'Yes.'

'Do they keep their promises?'

Sergius sighed. 'Are you so naïve as to try to trap me into something? You are about to say that I seem to know a lot about them. If they are who I think they are – and this has all the hallmarks of previous ransom demands – then they are an extremely able and efficient gang of kidnappers who have carried out a number of such kidnappings in the past few years.'

'You know the members of this gang?'

'We think we know one or two.'

'Then why are they still at large?'

'Suspicion, my dear Wildermann, is not proof. One cannot ask for the death penalty on suspicion.'

'I did ask an earlier question. About their promises. Will they carry out their mutilation threats? If the ransom is paid, will they return my brothers alive?'

'I can offer no guarantee. But, judging by past experiences, the chances are high. It's only logical and good business for them, as specialists in kidnapping operations, to do so. Sounds ridiculous in this context, but it builds up good faith and good will. If a kidnapee is returned promptly and unharmed after the payment of the ransom, then the parents and relatives of the next victim will meet the demands at once, knowing the chances are good that the victim will be returned. But if the kidnappers were to accept the ransom and then kill the victim, then the relatives of the next victim might conclude that the paying of a ransom was a waste of time.'

'What are the chances of tracing them before Monday?'

'Four days? Very little, I'm afraid.'

'Then we'd better have the money ready, hadn't we?' Sergius nodded and Bruno turned to Wrinfield. 'It would take me a year to pay you back, sir.'

Wrinfield smiled, a not very happy smile. 'I'd do it for the boys themselves without any hope of return. And – I'm being purely selfish, of course – there is not and never will be another group like the Blind Eagles.'

VI

Walking casually, aimlessly, they turned right down a street opposite the undertaker's on West Street. Dr Harper said: 'Are we being followed, do you think?'

Bruno said: 'Watched, I don't know. Shadowed, no.'

Inside two or three hundred yards the street deteriorated into a winding country lane. Soon afterwards it came to a stout wooden bridge which spanned a slow-flowing and obviously very deep river, some thirty feet in width with ice already forming at both edges. Bruno examined the bridge with some deliberation, then hurried to catch up with an impatient Harper, whose circulation was clearly not geared to cope with the sub-freezing temperature.

Immediately beyond the bridge the road was swallowed up by what appeared to be virgin pine forest. Less than a quarter of a mile farther on the two men came to a large semi-circular glade lying to the right of the road.

'The helicopter,' Dr Harper said, 'will land here.'

VII

Dusk was falling when Bruno, clad in his best street clothes, returned to Wrinfield's office. Only the owner and Maria were there.

Bruno said: 'Okay if I take my fiancée for a coffee, sir?'

Wrinfield smiled, nodded, then got back to looking worried and preoccupied again. Bruno helped the girl on with her heavy Astrakhan coat and they walked out into the thinly falling snow.

Maria said crossly: 'We could have had coffee in the canteen or in your living-room. It's very cold and damp out here.'

'Nagging and not even married yet. Two hundred yards is all. You will find that Bruno Wildermann always has his reasons.'

'Such as?'

'Remember our friends of the other night, who followed us so faithfully?'

'Yes.' She looked at him, startled. 'You mean—'

'No. They've been given a rest – snow has an adverse effect upon both marcelled hair and bald heads. The lad behind us is about three inches shorter than you, with a cloth cap, torn coat, baggy trousers and scuffed shoes. Looks like a skid row graduate but he's not.'

They turned into a café that had obviously abandoned hope a generation ago. In a country where the cafés seemed to specialize in smoke and minimal lighting, this one had really touched rock bottom. Eyes immediately started to smart: a couple of guttering candles would have provided an equal level of illumination. Bruno guided Maria to a corner seat. She looked around her in distaste.

'Is this what married life is going to be like?'

'You may look back on this as one of your happiest days.' He turned round. The Chaplin-esque figure had slumped wearily into a chair close to the door, produced a ragged paper from somewhere, and sat there dispiritedly with his elbow on the table and a grimy hand to his head. Bruno turned back to Maria.

'Besides, you must admit there is a certain wild Bohemian charm to the place.' He put his finger to his lips, leaned forward and pulled up the collar of her Astrakhan coat. Nestling deep in the fold of her collar was a small shining metal device no bigger than a hazelnut. He showed it to her and she stared at him wide-eyed: 'Order up for us, will you?'

He rose, crossed to where their shadow was sitting, seized him unceremoniously by the right wrist, pulled it away from his head and twisted sharply, an action that gave rise to a sudden yelp of pain from the man but no reaction from the few other customers, who were presumably accustomed to such diversions to the point of boredom. Nestled in the man's hand was a tiny metal earphone attached to a wire. Bruno followed the wire to a small metal box, hardly larger than the average cigarette lighter, which was tucked away in a breast pocket. Bruno put those items in his own pocket and said: 'Tell your boss that the next person who follows me will be in no condition to report back again. Leave!'

The man left. Bruno went back to his table and showed the trophies. He said: 'Let's try it.' He lifted the tiny meshed metal oval to his ear. Maria turned her mouth towards the collar of her coat.

She murmured: 'I love you. Truly. Always.'

Bruno removed the earphone. 'It works just fine, although it doesn't seem to know what it's saying.' He put the equipment away. 'A persistent lot, aren't they? But so very, very obvious.'

'Not to me. I think you should be doing my job. But did you have to let him know we were on to him?'

'They know anyway. Maybe now they'll stop shadowing me and let me move around in peace. Anyway, how could I talk to you with that character invading my privacy.'

'What is there to talk about?'

'My brothers.'

'I'm sorry. I didn't mean – *why* were they taken, Bruno?'

'Well, for one thing, it's given that hypocritical, twisting, sadistic liar—'

'Sergius?'

'Are there any other hypocritical, twisted, sadistic liars around? He had the perfect excuse to fingerprint every man in the circus.'

'How will that help him?'

'Apart from giving him a feeling of power and making him feel very clever, I don't know. It doesn't matter. They're my hostages to fate. If I step too far out of line things will happen to them.'

'Have you talked to Dr Harper about this? You can't risk their lives, Bruno. You just can't. Oh, Bruno, if I lose you and they're lost and all the others in your family gone—'

'Well, really, you are the biggest crybaby I've ever met. Who on earth picked you for the CIA?'

'So you don't believe this story about the kidnapping?'

'Love me?' She nodded. 'Trust me?' She nodded again. 'Then don't discuss anything I discuss with you with any other person at all.'

She nodded a third time. Then she said: 'Including Dr Harper?'

'Including Dr Harper. He has a brilliant mind, but he's orthodox and doesn't have the central European mentality. I'm not brilliant, but I'm unorthodox and I was born right here. He might not care for some improvisations *I* might care to make.'

'What kind of improvisations?'

'There you are. The perfect wife. How come that red stain on your handkerchief? How should I know what improvisations? I don't even know myself yet.'

'The kidnapping?'

'Rubbish. He had to have a story to explain their disappearance. You heard him say he knew who a couple of the gang were but could prove nothing? If Sergius knew them he'd have them in Lubylan in nothing flat and he'd have the entire truth out of them in five minutes before they died in screaming agony. Where do you think you are – back home in New England?'

She shivered. 'But why the threats? Why say they'd cut off your brothers' fingers? Why ask for that money?'

'Background colour. Besides, liberally rewarded though Sergius may be for his nefarious activities, fifty thousand bucks in the hip pocket gives a man a very comfortable feeling of support.' He looked at his untouched coffee in distaste, put some money on the table and rose. 'Like some real coffee?'

They returned to the exhibition hall looking for transport to the train, which was almost immediately arranged. As they moved out again into the darkness and the cold they met Roebuck coming in. He was pinched-looking, bluish and shivering. He stopped and said: 'Hi. Going back to the train?' Bruno nodded. 'A lift for your tired and suffering friend.'

'What are you suffering from? Been swimming in the Baltic?'

'Come winter, all the cab-drivers in this town go into hibernation.' Bruno sat silently in front on the way to the station. When they alighted at the siding opposite the passenger coaches Bruno sensed as much as felt something being slipped into his jacket pocket.

After the coffee, sweet music and sweet nothings in Bruno's living-room, Maria left. Bruno fished out a tiny scrap of paper from his pocket. On it Roebuck had written: '4.30. West entrance. No question. My life on it.' Bruno burnt the note and washed the ashes down the hand-basin.

— 8 —

IT WAS DURING the last performance on the following night – it was officially billed as the opening night, although, in fact, there had already been two performances, a free matinée for school children and a somewhat shortened version of the full show in the afternoon – that the accident happened. Such was the rapturous enthusiasm among the huge audience that the effect was all the more shocking when it came.

The Winter Palace had not one empty seat left, and over ten thousand applications for tickets, made in advance over the previous two weeks, had had to be regretfully refused. The atmosphere at the beginning was gay, festive, electric in anticipation. The women, who gave the lie to the western concept of Iron Curtain women being habitually dressed in belted potato sacks, were dressed as exquisitely as if the Bolshoi were visiting town – which indeed it had done, though not to so tumultuous a welcome – and the men were resplendent in either their best suits or in bemedalled uniforms. Sergius, seated next to Wrinfield, looked positively resplendent. Behind the two of them sat Kodes and Angelo, the latter tending slightly to lower the whole tone of the atmosphere. Dr Harper, as ever, sat in the front row, the everpresent black bag unobtrusively under his seat.

The audience, suitably primed by all the wildly enthusiastic reports that had preceded the circus, were prepared for magnificence and that night they got it. As if to make up for the absence of the Blind Eagles – a broadcast announcement before the start of the performance had regretted that two members were indisposed (what Sergius didn't want to get into the papers didn't get into the papers) – the performers reached new heights that even astonished Wrinfield. The crowd – there were eighteen thousand there – were entranced, enthralled. Act merged into act with the smooth and flawless precision for which the circus was justly famed and each act seemed better than the one that had preceded it. But Bruno that evening surpassed them all. That night he was not only blindfolded but hooded as well and his repertoire on the high trapeze, helped only by two girls on the platforms, who handled the two free trapezes in timing with the strict metronomic music from the orchestra, had an almost unearthly magic about it, a sheer impossibility that even had the most experienced circus artistes riveted in a stage half-way between awe and outright disbelief. He climaxed his act with a double somersault between two trapezes – and his outstretched hands missed the approaching trapeze. The heart-stopping shock throughout the audience was a palpable thing – unlike the crowds at many sports ranging from auto-racing to boxing, circus audiences are always willing the performers to safety – and equally palpable was the sigh of incredulous relief when Bruno caught the trapeze with his arched heels. Just to show that there was no fluke about it, he did it all over again – twice.

The crowd went hysterical. Children and teenagers screamed, men shouted, women cried in relief, a cacophony of noise that even Wrinfield had never heard before. It took the ringmaster three full minutes and repeated broadcast appeals to restore a semblance of order to the crowd.

Sergius delicately mopped his brow with a silk handkerchief. 'No matter what you pay our young friend up there, it must always be only a fraction of what he is worth.'

'I pay him a fortune and I agree with you. Have you ever seen anything like that?'

'Never. And I know I never will again.'

'Why?'

Sergius cast about for an answer. He said: 'We have an old saying in our country: "Only once in a lifetime is a man permitted to leave himself and walk with the gods." Tonight was such a night.'

'You may be right, you may be right.' Wrinfield was hardly listening to him, he turned to talk to an equally excited neighbour as the lights dimmed. A millimetric parting appeared between the upper and lower parts of Sergius's mouth – one could not call them lips. Sergius was permitting himself another of his rare smiles.

II

The lights came on again. As usual, in the second part of his act, Bruno used the low wire – if twenty feet could be called low – strung across the cage, open at the top, where Neubauer was, as he liked to put it, conducting his choir – putting his dozen Nubian lions, an unquestionably savage lot who would permit nobody except Neubauer near them, through their paces.

For his first trip across the back of the cage on his bicycle and with his balancing pole, Bruno – without the normal burden of having to carry his two brothers – obviously found it almost ridiculously easy to perform the acrobatic balancing feats which in fact few other artistes in the circus world could emulate. The crowd seemed to sense this ease, and while appreciating the skill, daring and expertise, waited expectantly for something more. They got it.

On his next sally across the ring he had a different machine, this one with a seat four feet high, pedals clamped below the seat and a vertical driving chain four feet in length. Again he crossed and recrossed the ring, again he performed his acrobatic feats, although this time with considerably more caution. When he crossed for the third time he had the audience distinctly worried, for this time his seat was no less than eight feet in height, with a vertical drive chain of corresponding length. The concern of the audience turned to a lip-biting apprehension when, reaching the sag in the middle, both bicycle – if the strange contraption could any longer be called that – and man began to sway in a most alarming fashion and Bruno had virtually to abandon any but the most elementary acrobatics in order to maintain his balance. He made it safely there and back, but not before he had wrought considerable changes in the adrenalin, breathing and pulse rates of the majority of the audience.

For his fourth and final excursion both seat and chain were raised to a height of twelve feet. This left him with his head some sixteen feet above the low wire, thirty-six above the ground.

Sergius glanced at Wrinfield, who, eyes intent, was rubbing

his hand nervously across his mouth. Sergius said: 'This Bruno of yours. Is he in league with the chemists who sell sedatives or the doctors who specialize in heart attacks?'

'This has never been done before, colonel. No performer has ever attempted this.'

Bruno started to sway and wobble amost immediately after leaving the top platform but his uncanny sense of balance and incredible reactions corrected the swaying and brought it within tolerable limits. This time there was no attempt to perform anything even remotely resembling acrobatics. His eyes, sinews, muscles, nerves were concentrating on one thing alone – maintaining his balance.

Exactly half-way across Bruno stopped pedalling. Even the least informed among the audience knew that this was an impossible, a suicidal thing to do: when the factor of balance has reached critical dimensions – and here it already appeared to have passed that critical limit – only movement backwards or forwards could help to regain equilibrium.

'Never again,' Wrinfield said. His voice was low, strained. 'Look at them! Just look at them!'

Sergius glanced at the audience but not for longer than a fraction of a second. It was not difficult to take Wrinfield's point. Where audience participation is concerned a certain degree of vicarious danger can be tolerable, even pleasurable: but when the degree of danger becomes intolerable – and prolonged, as in this case – the pleasure turns to fear, a corroding anxiety. The clenched hands, the clenched teeth, in many cases the averted gazes, the waves of empathy washing across the exhibition hall – none of this was calculated to bring the crowds flocking back to the circus.

For ten interminable seconds the unbearable tension lasted, the wheels of the bicycle neither advancing nor going backwards as much as an inch, while its angle of sway perceptibly increased. Then Bruno pushed strongly on the pedals.

The chain snapped.

No two people afterwards gave precisely the same account of what followed. The bicycle immediately tipped over to the right, the side on which Bruno had been pressing. Bruno threw himself forward – there were no handlebars to impede his progress. Hands outstretched to cushion his fall, he landed awkwardly, sideways, on the wire, which appeared to catch him on the inner thigh and the throat, for his head bent backwards at an unnatural angle. Then his body slid off the wire, he seemed to be suspended by his right hand and chin alone, then his head slid off the wire, the grip of his right hand loosened and he fell into the ring below, landed feet first on the sawdust and immediately crumpled like a broken doll.

Neubauer, who at that moment had ten Nubian lions squatting on a semi-circle of tubs, reacted very quickly. Both Bruno and the bicycle had landed in the centre of the ring, well clear of the lions, but lions are nervous and sensitive creatures and react badly to unexpected disturbances and interruptions – and this was a very unexpected disturbance indeed. The three lions in the centre of the half-circle had already risen to all four feet when Neubauer stooped and threw handfuls of sand in their faces. They didn't sit, but they were temporarily blinded and remained where they were, two of them rubbing their eyes with massive forepaws. The cage door opened and an assistant trainer and clown entered, not running, lifted Bruno, carried him outside the cage and closed the door.

Dr Harper was with him immediately. He stooped and examined him briefly, straightened, made a signal with his hand, but it was unnecessary. Kan Dahn was already there with a stretcher.

III

Three minutes later the announcement was made from the centre ring that the famous Blind Eagle was only concussed and with any luck would be performing again the next day. The crowd, unpredictable as all crowds, rose to its collective feet and applauded for a whole minute: better a concussed Blind Eagle than a dead one. The show went on.

IV

The atmosphere inside the first-aid room was distinctly less cheerful: it was funereal. Present were Harper, Wrinfield, two of his associate directors, Sergius and a splendidly white-maned, white-moustached gentleman of about seventy. He and Harper were at one end of the room where Bruno, still on the stretcher, lay on a trestle table.

Harper said: 'Dr Hachid, if you would care to carry out your own personal examination—'

Dr Hachid smiled sadly. 'I hardly think that will be necessary.' He looked at one of the associate directors, a man by the name of Armstrong. 'You have seen death before?' Armstrong nodded. 'Touch his forehead.' Armstrong hesitated, advanced, laid his hand on Bruno's forehead. He almost snatched it away.

'It's cold.' He shivered. 'Already it's gone all cold.'

Dr Hachid pulled the white sheet over Bruno's head, stepped back and pulled a curtain which obscured the stretcher. Hachid said: 'As you say in America, a doctor is a doctor is a doctor, and I would not insult a colleague. But the law of our land—'

'The law of every land,' Harper said. 'A foreign doctor cannot sign a death certificate.'

Pen in hand, Hachid bent over a printed form. 'Fracture of spine. Second and third vertebrae, you said? Severance of spinal cord.' He straightened. 'If you wish me to make arrangements—'

'I have already arranged for an ambulance. The hospital morgue—'

Sergius said: 'That will not be necessary. There is a funeral parlour not a hundred metres from here.'

'There is? That would save much trouble. But at this time of night—'

'Dr Harper.'

'My apologies, colonel. Mr Wrinfield, can I borrow one of your men, a trusted man who will not talk?'

'Johnny, the night watchman.'

'Have him go down to the train. There's a black case under my bunk. Please have him bring it here.'

V

The back parlour of the undertaker's emporium was harshly lit with neon strip lighting which pointed up the coldly antiseptic hygiene of the surroundings, tiled walls, marble floor, stainless steel sinks. Upended coffins lined one wall. In the centre of the room were three more coffins on steel-legged marble tables. Two of those were empty. Dr Harper was pulling a sheet over the third. Beside him, the plump undertaker, a man with gleaming shoes and gleaming bald pate, virtually hopped from foot to foot, his professional feeling visibly outraged.

He said, 'But you cannot do this. Straight into the coffin, I mean. There are things to be done—'

'I will do those things. I have sent for my own equipment.'

'But he has to be laid out.'

'He was my friend. I shall do it.'

'But the shroud—'

'You will be excused for not knowing that a circus performer is always buried in his circus clothes.'

'It is all wrong. We have ethics. In our profession—'

'Colonel Sergius.' Harper's voice was weary. Sergius nodded, took the undertaker by the arm, led him some way apart and spoke quietly. He was back in twenty seconds with an undertaker three shades paler and with a key, which he handed to Harper.

'The parlour is all yours, Dr Harper.' He turned to the undertaker. 'You may leave.' He left.

'I think we should leave, too,' Wrinfield said. 'I have some excellent vodka in my office.'

VI

Maria was in the office, forehead resting on crossed arms on the desk, when the men came in. She lifted her head slowly, peering through half-closed eyes as if not seeing too well. A concerned and troubled Dr Harper was standing before her, an equally concerned Wrinfield and an impassive Sergius beside him: Sergius's facial muscles for conveying sympathy had atrophied over the years. Maria's eyes were red and puffy and glazed and her cheeks glistened. Wrinfield looked at the grief-stricken face and touched her arm awkwardly.

'Do forgive me, Maria. I had forgotten – I didn't know – we shall go at once.'

'Please, it's all right.' She dabbed at her face with some tissues. 'Please come in.'

As the other three men rather reluctantly entered and Wrinfield brought out his bottle of vodka, Harper said to her: 'How did you know? I'm so terribly sorry, Maria.' He looked at her engagement ring and looked away again. 'But how did you know?'

'I don't know. I just knew.' She dabbed at her eyes again. 'Yes, I do know. I heard the announcement about his fall. I didn't come to see – well, because I was scared to come. I was sure that if he was badly hurt he'd ask for me or you would have sent for me. But nobody came.'

In an understandably strained silence and with considerable haste the men disposed of their vodkas and filed out. Harper, the last to leave, said to Maria: 'I have to see to some equipment. I'll be back in two minutes.'

He closed the door behind him. Maria waited for some moments, rose, glanced through the window, opened the door and peered cautiously out. There was no one in the immediate vicinity. She closed the door, locked it, returned to her desk, took a tube from a drawer, removed the cap, squeezed and rubbed some more glycerine into her eyes and face. She then unlocked the door.

VII

Dr Harper returned shortly with a suitcase. He poured himself another vodka, looked everywhere except at the girl as if uncertain how to begin. Then he cleared his throat and said apologetically: 'I know you're never going to forgive me for this but I had to do it. You see, I didn't know how good an actress you might be. Not so good, I'm afraid. Your feelings do tend to show through.'

'My feelings tend – you know that Bruno and I—' She broke off, then said slowly: 'What on earth do you mean?'

He smiled at her, broadly although albeit somewhat apprehensively. 'Dry your tears and come and see.'

The first beginnings of understanding touched her face. 'Do you mean—'

'I mean come and see.'

VIII

Bruno pushed back the two covering sheets and sat up in his coffin. He looked at Harper without much enthusiasm and said reproachfully: 'Weren't in too much of a hurry, were you? How would you like to lie in a coffin wondering when some enthusiastic apprentice is going to come along and start battening down the lid?'

Maria saved Harper the necessity of a reply. When Bruno had finally disentangled himself, he climbed stiffly down to the floor, reached inside the coffin, held up a limp, dripping linen bag and said: 'And I'm soaking wet, too.'

Maria said: 'What *is* that?'

'A slight subterfuge, my dear.' Harper gave a deprecatory smile. 'An ice bag. It was necessary to give Bruno the cold clammy forehead of the deceased. Ice, unfortunately, melts.' Harper placed the case on the coffin and opened the lid. 'And, alas, we now have to cause Bruno some more suffering: we have to transform him into a thing of beauty and a joy for ever.'

The transformation took all of twenty minutes. Harper had not necessarily mistaken his profession but clearly he would have been perfectly at home in the make-up department of any film studio. He worked swiftly and skilfully and obviously derived some satisfaction from his creative handiwork. When he was finished, Bruno looked at himself in a full-length mirror and winced. The light brown wig was just that too much long and straggly, the light brown moustache a *soupçon* too luxuriant: the vivid semi-circular scar that ran from his forehead round the corner of his right eye almost to his nose was the result, clearly, of an encounter with a broken bottle: for clothes he wore a blue and white striped shirt, red tie, light brown suit with red vertical stripes, mustard socks and shoes of the same appalling colour. The rings on his fingers would appear to have had their source of origin either in a fairground stall or Christmas crackers.

Bruno said: 'A thing of beauty, the man says. I could always hire myself out as a scarecrow.' He bent a discouraging look on Maria, whose hand, discreetly covering her mouth, could not disguise the crinkling in her eyes. He looked back to Harper. 'This makes me inconspicuous?'

'The point precisely. It makes you so conspicuous that no one will bother to take a second look at you – except for those who will do a double-take to convince themselves that their eyes weren't deceiving them in the first place. It's the anonymous, furtive, grey man slinking down alleyways that attracts suspicion. You are Jon Neuhaus, a machine-tool salesman from East Germany. The passport and papers are in your inside pocket.'

Bruno dug out his passport, a venerable-looking document that attested to the fact that his salesman's duties had taken him to virtually every Iron Curtain country, some of them many times. He looked at his picture and then again at himself in the mirror. The resemblance was quite remarkable.

He said: 'This must have taken quite a time to prepare. Where was it made?'

'In the States.'

'You've had it all that time?' Harper nodded. 'You might have shown it to me earlier on. Given me time to get accustomed to the awfulness of it all.'

'You would probably have refused to come.' Harper checked his watch. 'The last train in tonight arrives in fifteen minutes. A car is waiting for you about a hundred yards down the street from here which will take you discreetly to the station, where you will make sure you are seen – you have just come off the train. The suitcase contains all the clothes and toilet gear you will require. The same car will then drive you up to a hotel where you made a reservation two weeks ago.'

'You fixed all this?'

'Yes. Rather, one of our agents did. Our man, as you might say, in Crau. Invaluable. He can fix anything in this city – he ought to, he's a big wheel in the city council. One of *his* men will be driving your car tonight.'

Bruno looked at him consideringly. 'You certainly believe in playing a tight game, Dr Harper.'

'And I survive.' Harper permitted himself a patient sigh. 'When you've spent most of your adult life in a racket like this you will discover that, at any given time, the fewer people who know anything about anything, the greater the safety factor. Maria will hire a car in the morning. Two blocks west of here is an inn called the Hunter's Horn. Be there at dusk. Maria will be there shortly afterwards. She'll look in the doorway then walk away. You will follow her. You have a singular gift for sensing when you will be shadowed so I have no worries on that score. Any change of plan or further instructions will be given you by Maria.'

'You said your man in Crau could fix anything?'

'I did say that.'

'Have him fix a few sticks of dynamite. Any explosive will do as long as it has an approximately ten-second fuse. He can fix that?'

Harper hesitated. 'I suppose. Why do you want it?'

'I'll tell you in a couple of days and that's *not* because I'm doing a Dr Harper and being all mysterious. I'm not quite sure myself but I'm developing an idea that it might help me to leave the Lubylan.'

'Bruno.' The dark anxiety was back in the girl's face again, but Bruno didn't look at her.

'I think there's a chance I might get in undetected. I don't think there's a chance in hell that I'll be able to get out undetected. I may have to leave in a very great hurry indeed and once the alarm is raised I'm sure the exits will be automatically sealed. So my best line of exit may well be to blast my way out.'

'I seem to recall you saying that you had no wish to kill anyone. A dynamite blast could kill quite a few.'

'I'll be as careful as I can. It may have to come to the inevitable choice – them or me. One hopes not. Do I get the bangers or not?'

'You'll have to give me time to think about that one.'

'Look, Dr Harper. I know you're in charge, but here and now you're not the person who matters. I am. I'm the person who's got to put his life on the line to get inside Lubylan – and out again. Not you. You're safe and sound in base camp and will disclaim all knowledge of anything if I get chopped. I'm not asking, not now, I'm demanding. I want that explosive.' He glanced down in distaste at his clothes. 'If I don't get it you can try on this suit for size.'

'I repeat, I need time.'

'I can wait.' Bruno hitched his elbows on the coffin. 'I can wait all of five seconds. I'll count them. Then I'm taking this damned suit off and going back to the circus. I wish you luck in your break-in to Lubylan. I also wish you luck when you come to explaining to the police just how you made the trifling error of certifying me as being dead. One. Two. Three.'

'This is blackmail.'

'What else? Four.'

'All right, all right, you can have your damned fireworks.' Harper pondered, then went on complainingly: 'I must say this is a side of your nature I've never seen before.'

'I'd never examined that damned Lubylan before. I've seen it now. I know my chances. Please have Maria take the explosives in her car tomorrow night. Does Wrinfield know that this was a charade tonight?'

'Of course.'

'You took a chance bringing Sergius with you here.'

'Apart from the fact that he insisted, I'd have taken a damned bigger chance if I hadn't. That would have been the one thing calculated to rouse his suspicions.'

'And he's not? Suspicious, I mean?'

'The last thing that would occur to Colonel Sergius is that anyone would ever be misguided enough to pick his parish as a place to commit suicide.'

'Money?'

'In your other inside pocket.'

'It's freezing outside.'

'There's a nice warm coat in the car.' Harper smiled. 'You're going to love it.'

Bruno nodded to the open coffin. 'That?'

'Will be weighted and the lid screwed down during the night. We will bury you on Monday morning.'

'Can I send me a wreath?'

'That would not be advisable.' Harper smiled thinly. 'You can always, of course, mingle discreetly with your mourners.'

IX

Forty minutes later Bruno was in his hotel room, unpacking, his eyes straying occasionally towards the nice warm coat that

Harper had so thoughtfully provided. It was made of thick brushed nylon, in black and white wavy vertical stripes, and looked for all the world like a four thousand guinea chinchilla. Indisputably, it was the only one of its kind in Crau and, likely enough, for some hundreds of miles around, and the stir he had caused strolling through the lobby to the reception desk had been more than considerable: when the effect of his coat was added to the fact that he had it carelessly flung open to reveal the sartorial rainbow of his suiting beneath it was understandable that hardly anyone had bothered to give his face a first glance, far less a second one.

Bruno put out the light, eased the curtains, opened the window and leaned out. His room was at the back of the hotel, overlooking a narrow warehouse-lined lane. It wasn't quite in total darkness but it wasn't far from it either. Less than four feet away were the steps of a fire-escape, the easy and, in combination with the darkened lane, the perfect way to leave the hotel. Too easy, too perfect.

In line with Harper's advocated policy of non-concealment, Bruno went down to the hotel dining-room for dinner, carrying under his arm an East Berlin newspaper, dated that day, which he had found in his case. Harper was a man to whom the most insignificant detail could be of importance. Where he had obtained it Bruno had no means of knowing. His entrance did not cause any notable sensation – the citizens of Crau or visiting firemen were too well-mannered for that. But the raised eyebrows, the smiles, the whispers were evidence that his presence had not gone un-noted. Bruno looked casually around. There was nobody in sight who looked remotely like a secret police agent, although there was little comfort in that: the best agents never did. Bruno ordered his meal, then buried himself in his newspaper.

X

At eight o'clock the following morning Bruno was once more in the dining-room, again reading a paper but this time a local news-sheet. The first thing that caught his attention was a large black-bordered box – the borders were half an inch thick – in the centre of the front page. From this he learnt that he had died during the night. The grief was profound for circus lovers the world over but nowhere, of course, as keenly felt as in Crau. There was much sentimentalizing and philosophical sorrowing over the machinations of a strange fate that had brought Bruno Wildermann home to die. He was to be buried at 11 a.m. on Monday. It was hoped that large numbers of the citizens of Crau would turn out to pay their last respects to their city's most illustrious son, the greatest aerialist of all time. Bruno took the parcel back up to his room after breakfast, found scissors and cut out the black-bordered article, which he carefully folded and placed in an inside pocket.

XI

Late that afternoon Bruno went shopping. It was a cold and sunny day and he had left his fur coat in his room. This he had done neither because of the weather nor because of any innate bashfulness. It was just too bulky to be carried inconspicuously, however well it might have been wrapped up.

This was the town that Bruno knew better than any in the world and he could have shaken off any shadower without even half thinking about it: it took him less than five minutes to know that he was not being followed. He turned down a side street, then into an even meaner street, little more than a lane, and entered the shop of a haberdasher for whom Savile Row must have lain on the far side of Paradise: even the best clothes it had for sale could not have qualified for the description of second-hand. The proprietor, an elderly stooped man, whose watery eyes swam behind thickly pebbled glasses – although it seemed an extremely remote possibility that the oldster would ever be called upon to identify him, Bruno doubted whether he could have identified members of his own family, if any – had a unique but eminently practical way of displaying the wares he had for sale. The articles of clothing were piled in untidy heaps on the floor, jackets in one pile, trousers in another, coats in another, shirts in another, and so on. Ties were conspicuous by their absence.

When Bruno emerged it was with a bulky and exceedingly grimy brown paper parcel roughly tied with some frayed twine. He made his way to the nearest public conveniences and when he emerged his transformation was complete. He was clad in ill-fitting, patched and ancient clothes, wholly disreputable, not the sort of person the average citizen would approach within yards of, far less associate with: the grimy crumpled beret was two sizes too large and fell over his ears: the dark raincoat was irreparably stained, the trousers baggy beyond belief, the creased, once-navy shirt tieless and the heels of the scuffed shoes so worn down at the back that they lent him a peculiar rolling gait. To complete matters he was surrounded by a powerful aura that afflicted people at a distance of several yards: to keep lice, fleas and other forms of wild life at bay the haberdasher was a great believer in drenching every article of apparel with a disinfectant that was as vile-smelling as it was powerful.

Clutching his brown parcel under his arm, Bruno made his leisurely way across town. Dusk was beginning to fall. He took a short cut through a large park, a section of which was given over for use as one of the city's cemeteries. Passing by an opened iron gate in the high wall that surrounded the cemetery, he was intrigued to see two men busily digging by the light of a pair of storm lanterns. Intrigued, he approached the spot and as he did two men, standing in an as yet shallow grave, straightened up and rubbed clearly aching backs.

'You work late, comrades,' Bruno said sympathetically.

'The dead wait for no man,' the elder grave-digger said in a sepulchral voice, then peering more closely, added: 'Some of us have to work for a living. Do you mind standing to the other side of the grave?'

The light wind, Bruno realized, was wafting his presence across the grave. He moved round and said: 'And whose last resting place is this?'

'A famous American, though he was born and brought up in this town. I knew his grandfather well. A Wildermann, he is. He was with a circus – the circus – in the Winter Palace. Killed in an accident. It'll be a big day here on Monday, with Johann and myself in our best suits.'

'An accident?' Bruno shook his head. 'One of those damnable buses, I'll be bound. Many's the time—'

The younger man said: 'No, you old fool. He fell off a wire

in the circus and broke his neck.' He jammed his shovel into the sandy soil. 'Do you mind? We have work to do.'

Bruno mumbled his apologies and shambled away. Five minutes later he was in the Hunter's Horn, where he had to show his money to a nose-wrinkling waiter before being served coffee. After about fifteen minutes Maria appeared in the doorway, looked around, clearly failed to recognize anybody, hesitated and moved off again. Bruno rose leisurely and rolled his way towards the door. Once in the street he lengthened his stride without increasing his pace and within a minute he was only a few feet behind her.

He said: 'Where's the car?'

She wheeled round. 'Where on earth – you weren't – yes, you were!'

'You'll feel better shortly. Where's the car?'

'Round the next corner.'

'Any car follow you?'

'No.'

The car was a nondescript battered old Volkswagen, one of hundreds similar in the town: it was parked under a street lamp. Bruno got in behind the wheel, Maria in the passenger seat. She sniffed in disgust.

'What on earth is that dreadful smell?'

'Me.'

'I appreciate that. But—'

'Just disinfectant. A very powerful one, but still a disinfectant. You'll get used to it. Quite bracing really.'

'It's awful! Why on earth—'

'Disguise,' Bruno said patiently. 'You don't actually think this is my preferred mode of dress? I think that Dr Harper underestimates Colonel Sergius. I may be Jon Neuhaus, a citizen in good standing from a friendly satellite country, but I'm still an East German. I'm an outsider – and you can bet Sergius has every outsider tabbed from the moment he's within twenty miles of Crau. He will know – if he wishes – within ten minutes of any stranger checking in to any hotel in Crau. He'll have a complete description of me. I have the documentation so he won't give me a second thought. But he'll give a second thought if a respectable sales representative for a major firm is found in a sleazy dump like the Hunter's Horn or parked indefinitely in the shadow of the Lubylan. Don't you think?'

'Agreed. In that case there is only one thing to do.' She opened her handbag, extracted a small eau-de-cologne aerosol, sprayed herself liberally, then squirted the contents over Bruno. When she had finished Bruno sniffed.

'The disinfectant wins,' he announced and, indeed, instead of the cologne having a neutralizing effect it had a compounding effect. Bruno lowered the windows and hastily moved off, his eye as much on the rear-view mirror as on the road. He twisted and turned through the darkened street and alleyways until any tail car there might have been must have been irretrievably lost. As they drove, they briefly rehearsed the plans for the Lubylan break in on the Tuesday night. Then Bruno said: 'Got the stuff I asked for?'

'In the boot. Not what you asked for – Dr Harper's contact couldn't get that. He says you're to be very careful with this stuff – it seems you've only to look at it and it will explode.'

'Good God! Don't tell me he's got me nitro-glycerine?'

'No. It's called amatol.'

'That's all right, then. It's the detonator he'll be worried about. Fulminate of mercury, isn't it?'

'Yes, he said that.'

'Seventy-seven grains. Very temperamental stuff. It will have a length of RDX fuse and a chemical igniter.'

'Yes. He did say that.' She looked at him curiously. 'How come you're an expert on explosives?'

'I'm not. I read about it some years ago and just sort of filed the information away.'

'Must be quite a filing cabinet you've got in there. This instant and total recall bit – how's it done?'

'If I knew that I'd be making a fortune out of it instead of fooling my life away on a trapeze. Now, there's something else I want. First a large, eight by eight – preferably – sheet of rubber matting or hide leather.'

She took his hand and said: 'What do you want that for?' Her eyes told him that she knew.

'What do you think? To throw over that damned electrified fence, of course. A tumbler's mat would do fine. Also I require a rope with a padded hook. I want to see them both as soon as possible. Ask Dr Harper to arrange for those things and have them put in the boot of the car. Would you like to have lunch with me tomorrow?'

'What?'

'I want to see that stuff.'

'Oh. I'd love to.' She inhaled deeply. 'No, I wouldn't. Not if you're wearing those clothes. Anyway, no half-decent restaurant would let you through the front door.'

'I'll change.'

'But if we're seen together – in daylight, I mean—'

'There's a charming little inn in a charming little village about ten miles from here. Nobody will know us there and nobody will be looking anyway: I'm dead. Which reminds me. It's less than an hour since I was talking to a couple of grave-diggers.'

'We are being humorous again, are we?'

'Fact. Very interesting.'

'In the Hunter's Horn?'

'In the cemetery. I asked them who it was for and they said it was for me. Well, the American who fell off the wire. It's not everyone who's privileged enough to watch his own grave being dug. They were making a very neat job of it, I must say.'

'Please.' She shivered. 'Must you?'

'Sorry. That wasn't funny. I just thought it was. Now, you'll go to this village – it's called Kolszuki – by car and I'll go by train. We'll meet at the station there. We might as well go now and check the train time-tables at the Crau station. You'll have to get clearance from Dr Harper, of course.'

XII

On a very spartan metal table in a very spartan and largely metal office, the spools of a tape-recorder revolved. On either side of the table sat Colonel Sergius and Captain Kodes. Both had headphones to their ears. In addition to the phones Sergius had a cigar, vodka and as close to a beatific smile as he was ever likely to achieve. Captain Kodes, too, was permitting himself the luxury of smiling broadly. Angelo, discreetly seated in a far corner, although he had neither phones nor vodka, was also smiling. If the colonel was happy, that made him happy, too.

XIII

Bruno returned from consulting the time-tables inside the Crau station. He said: 'There's a very convenient train for lunch. Meet me at the Kolszuki station at noon. You won't have any trouble in finding it – there aren't more than fifty houses in the village. Know where this place is?'

'There's a map in the glove-box. I've checked. I'll be there then.'

Bruno drove up the main street and parked the Volkswagen just opposite the lane abutting on the southern side of Lubylan. The street was not deserted – there were two trucks and a car on the south side of the lane, obviously parked for the night. It was a measure of the confidence in their security arrangements of those within Lubylan that they raised no objections to vehicles parking in such close proximity. Bruno made a mental note of this: there is no objection to the night-time parking of trucks in the south lane.

Bruno said: 'Now don't forget to tell Dr Harper everything we discussed tonight. And don't forget that, for the benefit of any innocent passers-by, we're just a couple of lovers lost in each other's eyes. Darling, darling Maria. That's for practice.'

'Yes, Bruno,' she said primly. 'We'll be married soon, Bruno.'

'Very soon, my love.' They relapsed into silence, their eyes fixed on the lane, Maria's all the time, Bruno's most of the time.

XIV

In the headquarters of the Secret Police Colonel Sergius was making harsh croaking noises in his throat. He was not choking on his vodka. Colonel Sergius was laughing. He indicated that Angelo should pour him another vodka, then indicated that Angelo should help himself also. Angelo refrained from crushing the bottle in his surprise, smiled his wolfish smile and swiftly complied before Sergius could change his mind. This was without precedent, an epoch-making night.

XV

Bruno turned suddenly, put his arms around Maria and kissed her passionately. For a moment she stared at him, dark eyes open in astonishment and surmise, let herself relax against him, then stiffened as an authoritative rat-tat-tat came on her window. She broke from Bruno's arms and swiftly wound down the window. Two large policemen, complete with the customary guns and batons, were bent down peering into the car. Uniforms and weapons apart, however, they bore no resemblance to the popular conception of the Iron Curtain policemen. Their expressions were genial, positively paternal. The larger of the two sniffed suspiciously.

'Very strange smell in this car, I must say.'

Maria said: 'I'm afraid I've just broken a phial of perfume. A drop is nice – but a whole bottle – well, it *is* a bit strong, I must say.'

Bruno, stammering slightly and with his voice sounding acutely embarrassed, said: 'What is it, officer? This is my fiancée.' He held up Maria's beringed left hand so that there should be no doubt about it. 'Surely there's no law—'

'Indeed not.' The policeman leaned a confidential elbow on the window-sill. 'But there is a law against parking in a main street.'

'Oh! Sorry. I didn't realize—'

'It's the fumes,' the policeman said kindly. 'Your mind must be all befuddled.'

'Yes, officer.' Bruno smiled weakly. 'Is it all right if we park behind those trucks?' Hopefully, he indicated the vehicles in the south lane.

'Certainly. Don't catch cold now. And, comrade?'

'Officer?'

'If you love her so much, why don't you buy your fiancée a bottle of decent perfume? Needn't be expensive, you know.' The policeman beamed and walked away with his colleague.

Maria, remembering her momentary yielding to Bruno,

said in a cross voice: 'Well, thank you. For a moment there I thought you had found me irresistible.'

'Always use your rear-view mirror. It's just as important when you're stationary as when you're driving.'

She made a face at him as he pulled the car into the south lane.

The two policemen watched them park. They moved out of eyeshot of the car. The larger man pulled a walkie-talkie microphone from his breast pocket, pressed a button and said: 'They're parked in the south lane by the Lubylan, colonel.'

'Excellent.' Even with the metallic distortion and the fact that his speech was interrupted by a series of whooping gasps – laughter was an unaccustomed exercise for him – Sergius's voice was unmistakable. 'Just leave the love-birds be.'

XVI

It took Bruno and Maria minutes only to establish that there were indeed ground-level guards. There were three of them and they kept up a continuous peripheral patrol, each making a full circuit of the Lubylan in turn. At no time was any guard in sight of the other two. As sentries, they were a degree less than enthusiastic. Not for them the continually roving, probing eyes, the piercing scrutiny of all that lay in their path of vision: with downcast gaze and trudging steps, they gave the impression of thoroughly miserable men, huddled against the cold and living only for the moment of their relief. There had been night-time sentries patrolling the Lubylan for ten, perhaps twenty years, and probably no untoward incident had ever occurred: there was no conceivable reason why it ever should.

From the two watchtowers they could see, the south-west and south-east ones, searchlights flashed occasionally and erratically along the tops of the perimeter walls. There was no discernible predetermined sequence to the switching on and off of the searchlights: it appeared to be a quite random process, its arbitrary nature dependent on the whim of the guard.

After twenty minutes Bruno drove off to the public convenience he had patronized earlier that evening. He left the car, kissed Maria goodbye as she moved into the driver's seat and disappeared into the depths. When he emerged, the grimy parcel with the old clothes and the amatol tucked under his arm, he was clad in his original sartorial glory.

— 9 —

PRECISELY AT noon on the following day Bruno was met by Maria at Kolszuki station. It was a beautiful, cloudless winter's day, crisp and clear and sunny, but the wind off the plains to the east was bitingly cold. On the twenty-minute journey out Bruno had passed the time of day studying his own highly-coloured obituary in the Crau Sunday paper. He was astonished at the richness and variety of his career, the international acclaim that followed him wherever he went, the impossible feats he had performed before Heads of State the world over: he was particularly touched to discover how kind he had been to little children. It contained just enough fact to make it obvious that the reporter had actually been interviewing someone in the circus, a person clearly possessed of a deadpan sense of humour. That it wasn't the work of Wrinfield he was sure: Kan Dahn appeared much the most likely culprit if for no reason other than the fact that he was the only person mentioned in the article apart from Bruno. The article, Bruno reflected, augured well for the morrow: the turn-out at the cemetery at 11 a.m. promised to be a remarkable one. Bruno carefully cut the piece out and put it together with the previous day's black-bordered obituary.

The inn Bruno had in mind was only two miles away. One mile out, he pulled into a lay-by, got out, opened the boot, gave a cursory examination to the tumbler's mat and the padded hook attached to a rope, closed the boot and returned to his seat.

'Both mat and rope are just what I wanted. Just let them stay there until Tuesday night. You have this car rented until then?'

'Until we leave here on Wednesday.'

They pulled off the main road, went some way up a narrow lane, then pulled up in the cobble-stoned courtyard of what looked to be a very ancient inn indeed. The head waiter courteously escorted them to a corner table and took their order. As he was finishing, Bruno said: 'Do you mind if we sit by that corner table.' Maria looked her surprise. 'It's such a lovely day.'

'But of course, sir.'

When they were seated, Maria said: 'I can't see any lovely day from here. All I can see is the back of a broken-down barn. Why the new table?'

'I just wanted my back to the room so that no one could see our faces.'

'You know somebody here?'

'No. We were followed from the station by a grey Volkswagen. When we stopped at that lay-by he passed us but then pulled into a side turning and waited until we had passed him, then he tucked in behind us again. Where he's sitting now he's directly facing our previous table. He may well be a lip-reader.'

She was vexed. 'It's supposed to be my job to see those things.'

'Maybe we should swop jobs.'

'That's not very funny,' she said, then smiled in spite of herself. 'I somehow don't see myself as the daring young girl on the flying trapeze. I can't even stand on a first-floor balcony, even stand on a chair, without getting vertigo. Fact. See what you're letting yourself in for?' The smile faded. 'I may have smiled, Bruno, but I'm not smiling inside. I'm scared. See what else you're letting yourself in for?' He said nothing. 'Well, thanks anyway for not laughing at me. *Why* are we being followed, Bruno? Who could possibly know we were out here? And who is the person they're following – you or me?'

'Me.'

'How can you be so sure?'

'Did anyone tail you out here?'

'No. I've listened to your lectures on driving mirrors. I spend more time looking backwards than forwards now when I'm driving. I stopped twice. No one passed me.'

'So it's me. And nothing to worry about. I detect Dr Harper's hand in this. It's what I take to be the old CIA mentality. Never, never trust anyone. I suspect half the members of espionage and counter-espionage services spend a good deal of their time watching the other half. And how is he to know that I'm not going to go native and revert to my old Crau sympathies? I don't blame him. This is a very, very difficult situation indeed for the good doctor. A hundred against one that that lad behind us is what it pleases Harper to call his man in Crau. Just do me one favour – when you get back to the circus train, go see Dr Harper and ask him straight out.'

She said doubtfully: 'You really think so?'

'I'm certain.'

After lunch they drove back to Kolszuki station with the grey Volkswagen in faithful if distant attendance. Bruno stopped the car outside the main entrance and said: 'See you tonight?'

'Oh, yes, please.' She hesitated. 'Will it be safe?'

'Sure. Walk two hundred yards south of the Hunter's Horn. There's a café there with the illuminated sign of the Cross of Lorraine. God knows why. I'll be there. Nine o'clock.' He put his arm round her. 'Don't look so sad, Maria.'

'I'm not sad.'

'Don't you want to come?'

'Oh, yes, yes, yes, I want to spend every minute of the day with you.'

'Dr Harper wouldn't approve.'

'I suppose not.' She took his face in her hands and looked deep into his eyes. 'But have you ever thought that now is all the time there may be?' She shivered. 'I can feel someone walking over my grave.'

'Nobody's got any manners any more,' Bruno said. 'Tell him to get off.' Without looking at or speaking to him again she let in the clutch of the car and moved off: he watched her until she disappeared from sight.

II

Bruno was lying on the bed in his hotel room when the phone

rang. The operator asked if he was Mr Neuhaus and when Bruno said he was put the caller through. It was Maria.

'Tanya,' he said. 'What a pleasant surprise.'

There was a pause while she apparently adjusted to her new name, then she said: 'You were quite right. Our friend admits responsibility for what happened at lunch-time.'

'Jon Neuhaus right as ever. See you at the appointed time.'

III

By 6 p.m. that evening the full darkness of night had already fallen. The temperature was well below freezing, a faint wind was stirring and patches of slowly drifting cloud occasionally obscured the three-quarter moon. Most of the sky was bright with twinkling frosty stars.

The lorry parked outside the truck-drivers' pull-up, three miles south of the town, was filled almost to capacity. From the low single-storey café came bright yellow light and the sound of juke-box music: the café was being heavily patronized, drivers entering or leaving at fairly regular intervals. One driver, a middle-aged man enveloped in the numerous swathes of his breed, emerged and climbed into his vehicle, a large and empty furniture van with two hinged rear doors and securing battens running along both sides. There was no partition between the driver and the body of the van: just that single seat up front. The driver turned the ignition, the big diesel thudded into life but before the driver could touch brake, clutch or gear he was slumped forward over his wheel, unconscious. A pair of giant hands reached under his armpits, plucked him from his seat as if he were a puppet and deposited him on the floor of the van.

Manuelo applied adhesive to the unfortunate driver's mouth and then set about fixing a blindfold. He said: 'I am grieved that we should have to treat an innocent citizen in this manner.'

'Agreed, agreed.' Kan Dahn shook his head sadly and tightened the last knot on their victim's wrists. 'But the greatest good of the greatest number. Besides,' he said hopefully, 'he may not be an innocent citizen.'

Ron Roebuck, who was securing the man's ankles to one of the parallel securing battens, did not appear to think that the situation called for any comment. There were lassos, clothes-lines, heavy twine and a large coil of nylon rope – the most conspicuous of all and by far the heaviest and thickest: it was knotted at eighteen-inch intervals.

IV

At 6.15 p.m. Bruno, magnificently attired in what he privately thought of as his pierrot's suit and the magnificent pseudo chinchilla, left the hotel. He walked with the unhurried measured gait of one for whom time is not a matter of pressing concern: in fact he did not wish to disturb the fulminate of mercury in the six explosive devices that were suspended from his belt. The voluminous nylon coat concealed those perfectly.

As befitted a man with time on his hands, he wandered at apparent random, following what would otherwise have been thought to be a devious twisting route. He spent a considerable amount of time in stopping and apparently examining goods in shop windows, not omitting the side windows at shop entrances. He finally sauntered round a corner, quickened his pace for a few steps, then sunk into the dark shadow of a recessing doorway. A dark rain-coated man rounded the same corner, hesitated, hastened forward, passed where Bruno stood concealed, then sagged at the knees, momentarily stunned, as the edge of Bruno's right hand caught him below his right ear. Bruno held him upright with one hand, went swiftly through his pockets with the other and came up with a snub-nosed automatic. The safety catch clicked off.

'Walk,' Bruno said.

V

The hijacked furniture van was about half-way down the south lane abutting the Lubylan, the last of five parked trucks. Bruno saw it at once when he halted, arm apparently cordially in arm with his erstwhile shadow, at the corner of the main street and the south lane. Bruno had deemed it prudent to halt because a guard was coming up the other side of the lane, machine gun shoulder-slung. From his general appearance the weapon was the last thing on his mind. Like the guards of the previous night he wasn't walking with a brisk military step, he was trudging along, wallowing in the unplumbed depths of his own frozen miseries. Bruno dug his automatic deeper into his companion's side, just above the hip-bone.

'Call out and you're a dead man.'

Clearly, the idea did not appeal to the prisoner. The combination of fear and the cold gave him the impression of one who was frozen stiff. As soon as the guard had turned the corner into the main street – he did not have the appearance of one who was about to glance back suspiciously over his shoulder – Bruno marched his captive down the line of parked trucks: once safely abreast of these they were hidden from the sight of anyone on the other side of the lane.

Pushing the man in front of him, Bruno moved out cautiously between the third and fourth parked trucks and glanced to his right. A second guard had just appeared round the south-east corner and was on his way up the south lane. Bruno retreated to the pavement. There was no guaranteeing that this captive would not suddenly screw his courage to the sticking point and, since, it was now safe, because free from observation, to have an unconscious man on his hands, Bruno repeated the earlier blow, although this time with considerably more force, and eased the man to the ground. The guard passed unwittingly by on the other side. Bruno hoisted his captive to his shoulder and carried him to the rear of the van just as one of the doors opened: someone had been keeping a good watch through the windscreen. Kan Dahn had the unconscious man inside in a second and Bruno followed.

'Is Roebuck on his way? To get that little toy for me from the train, and the cassettes?'

'On his way.' Kan Dahn jumped down followed by Manuelo, who hid behind the end of the van. Kan Dahn lay down in the middle of the lane, produced a bottle of Scotch from his pocket, poured a liberal amount over his face and shoulders and lay still, the bottle still clasped in his hand. His arm covered his face.

A guard came round the south-east corner and saw Kan Dahn almost immediately. He stood stock still for a moment, looked around warily, saw no danger and broke into a run towards the prostrate man. As he approached he unslung his machine-pistol and advanced slowly and cautiously, the barrel trained on the massive bulk. At fifteen feet it was unthinkable that he should miss. At twenty-five feet it was equally unthinkable that Manuelo should miss. The hilt of the knife caught the guard squarely between the eyes and Kan Dahn, courteously breaking his fall, had him inside the van in five seconds.

In another ten seconds Manuelo had retrieved his knife and retreated into his former hiding position while Kan Dahn resumed his recumbent position. Such was Bruno's faith in the two that he did not even bother to watch the painful proceedings but concentrated instead on the process of immobilizing, gagging and blindfolding the prisoners. Within six minutes there were five men lashed to the side of the furniture van, completely helpless and silenced, three of them already conscious but none of them able to do anything about their circumstances. The people of the circus are pastmasters in the art of tying knots: their lives too often depend on this very expertise.

The three men left the van. Kan Dahn had a pair of canvas shoes in a pocket and carried a finely chiselled but massive crowbar, Bruno carried a pocket flash, three bound poles slung from his shoulder, and a polythene wrapped and very peculiar packet in his pocket; Manuelo, in addition to a variety of throwing knives, carried a pair of rather fearsome-looking and heavily insulated wire cutters. The amatol explosives Bruno had left behind in the van.

They walked eastwards along the lane. Occasionally the moon shone through and their presence there was readily to be seen by anyone with eyes to see. Even so, they had no option other than to carry on as unobtrusively as they could – although it was questionable whether any close observer would have found anything unobtrusive about the crowbar, wire-cutter and poles. By the time they had reached the power station, some three hundred yards distant from the prison side of the Lubylan, the moon had slid behind some barred cloud again. There were no guards to be seen or heard, and the only form of protection appeared to be a heavy steel mesh mounted on ten feet hollow steel tubes, with one cross-railing at the top of one six feet up. The top railing was liberally festooned with very unpleasant barbed wire.

Bruno took the crowbar from Kan Dahn, pressed one end firmly into the earth and let the other fall against the mesh, at the same time taking two prudent backward steps. There was no pyrotechnical display, no blinding coruscation of arcs, sparks and flashes. The fence was not electrified nor had Bruno for a moment thought it would have been. Only a madman would put two thousand volts through a fence at ground level; but Bruno had had no guarantee that he wasn't dealing with madmen.

Manuelo began to snip his way through the mesh. Bruno took out his red pen and thoughtfully pushed down the end button. Kan Dahn looked at him curiously.

'Left it a bit late to write your last will and testament?'

'A toy Dr Harper gave me. Fires anaesthetic darts.'

One by one they stooped and passed through the hole Manuelo had made. Five paces they took and then they discovered that the lack of human guards was compensated for by the presence of canine ones in the form of three Dobermann Pinschers that came at them out of the gloom. Manuelo's knife flickered forward in an underhand throw and the leaping dog died in mid-air, the blade buried to the hilt in its throat. The dog jumping for Kan Dahn's throat found itself with one iron forearm under its lower jaw and the other behind its ears: one effortless twist and the vertebra snapped. The third dog did succeed in knocking Bruno down but not before the steel dart had lodged in its chest. The dog landed heavily, rolled over twice and lay still.

They advanced to the powerhouse itself. The door was made of metal and was locked. Bruno put his ear to the door and moved away quickly: even on the outside the high speed whining of turbines and generators was an assault on the eardrums. To the left of the door and about ten feet up was a barred window. Bruno glanced at Kan Dahn, who stooped, caught him by the ankles and hoisted him effortlessly: it was like going up in a lift.

The powerhouse was deserted but for one man seated in a glass enclosed control room. He was wearing what Bruno at first took to be a pair of headphones: they were, in fact, earmuffs for excluding sound. Bruno returned to earth.

'The door, please, Kan Dahn. No, not there. The handle side.'

'Designers always make the same mistake. The hinges are never as massive as the securing bolts.' He inserted the chisel edge of the crowbar between the door and the wall and had the door off its hinges in ten seconds. Kan Dahn looked at the bent crowbar in some vexation, grasped it in his hands and straightened it out as if it were made of putty.

It took them no more than twenty seconds, making no attempt at concealment, to reach the door of the control box. The duty engineer, facing rows of breakers and gauges, was no more than eight feet away, completely oblivious to their presence. Bruno tried the door. This, too, was locked. Bruno looked at the two men. Both nodded. With one scything sweep of his crowbar Kan Dahn removed most of the glass from the door. Even the ear-muffed engineer could not have failed to hear the resulting racket, for when Kan Dahn shattered a sheet of plate glass he did it *con brio*. He swung round on his swivel chair and had only the fleeting fraction of a second to register the impression of three vague silhouettes outside the control room when the haft of Manuelo's knife caught him on the forehead.

Bruno reached through the hole and turned the key. They went inside and while Kan Dahn and Manuelo immobilized the hapless engineer Bruno scanned the metal labels on the breakers. He selected a particular one and yanked the handle down through ninety degrees.

Kan Dahn said: 'Sure?'

'Sure. It's marked.'

'If you're wrong?'

'I'll be electrocuted.'

Bruno sat in the engineer's vacant chair, removed his shoes and replaced them with the pair of canvas shoes he used on the high wire. His own shoes he handed to Kan Dahn, who said: 'You have a mask, a hood?'

Bruno looked at his red and brown suit and mustard socks. 'If I wear a mask they won't recognize me?'

'You have a point.'

'For me, it doesn't matter whether I'm recognized or not. I don't intend to hang around when this lot is over. What matters is that you and Manuelo and Roebuck are not recognized.'

'The show must go on?'

Bruno nodded and led the way outside. Curious to see the duration of the effect of the anaesthetic darts, he stooped and examined the Dobermann, then straightened slowly. It appeared that Dobermanns had nervous systems that differed from those of humans: this Dobermann was stone dead.

There were several pylons, each about eighty feet high, inside the compound. He made for the most westerly of those and started to climb. Kan Dahn and Manuelo left through the hole in the compound mesh.

The pylon presented no problem. Dark though the night was – the moon was still behind cloud – Bruno climbed it with no more effort than the average person would have encountered with a flight of stairs in daylight. Reaching the top cross-bar, Bruno unslung the bound poles, undid the bindings, which he thrust into his pocket, and screwed the three pieces solidly together: he had his balancing pole. He stooped and reached out to touch, just beyond the retaining insulator, the heavy steel cable that angled off towards the south-east corner of the Lubylan. For a moment he hesitated, then fatalistically concluded that hesitation would serve no purpose. If he had switched off the wrong breaker then at least he would never know anything about it. He reached down and caught the cable.

He'd switched off the right breaker. The cable was ice-cold to the touch but, all importantly, it was not ice-sheathed. There was some wind, but it was slight and fitful. The cold was close to numbing but this was not a consideration to be taken into account: by the time he'd traversed that interminable three hundred yards he'd be, he knew, covered in perspiration. He waited no longer. Balancing his pole, he made his gingerly way along the insulator anchoring wire and stepped out on to the power cable.

VI

Roebuck took a couple of steps down towards the track, craned forward and peered cautiously fore and aft, saw no one in sight, descended the remaining steps, then left the train at a measured pace. Not that he had not the right to leave the train whenever he wished, nor even to be seen with what he had then, two canvas sacks clipped together at their tops and slung over his shoulders, for those were the containers he habitually used to transport his ropes and the metal pins he used as targets in his act: what might have aroused a degree of passing curiosity was that he left the circus train at a point four coaches distant from where he had his own quarters.

He climbed into the small Skoda he'd arrived in and parked it a hundred yards short of the Lubylan. He walked briskly on until he came to a small lane. He turned in here, crossed through a gate in a fence, jumped for and pulled down the spring extension of a fire-escape and climbed quickly until he'd hauled himself on to the roof. Crossing to the other side of the roof was akin to hacking one's way through the Amazonian jungle. Some arborealist whom Roebuck, in his total ignorance of central European horticultural matters, presumed to have been of some distant English extraction, had seen fit to plant, in earth-filled tubs or troughs, shrubs, bushes, conifers extending to the height of twenty feet and, incredibly, two transverse and immaculately trimmed privet hedges and one lateral one that lined the edge of the roof overlooking the main street. Even in this egalitarian society the passion for privacy was not to be denied. This was, in fact, the same roof garden that Dr Harper had remarked on their first trip from the station to the Winter Palace.

Roebuck, a latter-day Last of the Mohicans, parted the lateral hedge and peered across and up. Across the street and about fifteen feet above the elevation where he stood was the watch-tower at the south-west corner of the Lubylan. In size and shape it was very much like a telephone box, metal or wood for the first five feet then glass above. That it was manned by only one guard was clear, because a light was on inside the tower and Roebuck could clearly see the solitary occupant. Suddenly, a remote controlled searchlight, mounted about two feet above the top of the tower, came to life, stabbing along the western perimeter of the roof, but depressed so that it would not blind the guard in the north-west tower. The light died then came on again, this time playing along the southern perimeter, then again faded. The guard appeared to be in no hurry to put out his light. He lit a cigarette, then lifted what appeared to be a hip flask to his mouth. Roebuck hoped that the light would remain on: as long as it did the guard's night vision was virtually useless.

The curving spikes of the electrified fence were on a level with the base of the watch-tower. The distance, allowing for the angled increase of height, was about forty-five feet. Roebuck stepped back from the hedge, blessing the person whose sense of privacy had driven him to such horticultural lengths, removed the coil of rope from his shoulders and took about eight loops in his right hand. The free end of the rope had already been made into a running noose. The rope itself, hardly as thick as the average clothes-line, looked as if it might be fit for tying up a parcel but no more than that. It was, in fact, made of steel-cored nylon with a breaking strain of 1400 pounds.

He parted the hedge again and peered down. Kan Dahn and Manuelo were standing, apparently chatting aimlessly, at the corner of the main street and the south lane. The main street was empty of all life, except for passing cars, which were of no concern: not one driver in a thousand ever looks upward at night.

Roebuck stood on the parapet, swung the rope once round his head and on the second circle let it go. With what seemed a childishly simple inevitability, the rope snaked outwards and upwards and the loop settled over precisely the two spikes he had chosen. Roebuck did not attempt to draw the noose tight; he could easily have pulled it off the outward curving spikes. He gathered up all the remainder of the rope and threw it across the street to land precisely at the feet of Kan Dahn and Manuelo. They picked up the rope and disappeared along the south lane: the rope tightened and settled down on the base of the spikes.

VII

The first half of the journey along the power cable towards Lubylan Bruno accomplished without too much difficulty. The second part taxed all his powers, his innate ability, his reaction, his superb sense of balance. He had not appreciated that there was such a sag in the cable nor that he would be faced with so steep an upward climb: nor had he bargained for the increasingly frequent gusts of wind. They were slight enough, to be sure, but to a man poised in his precarious position even the sharp increase of five miles an hour in wind speed could have been lethal. As it was it was strong enough to make the cable sway in a highly disconcerting fashion. Had there been the most infinitesimal coating of ice on the wire he could never have made it. But make it he did.

The cable was clamped into a giant insulator held in place by two anchoring wires attached to the wall. Beyond the insulator, the cable looped upwards through another insulator in the base of a heavy switched breaker covered by a plastic hood. To switch off that breaker would nullify the danger that might be caused by someone discovering the power-station break-in and switching on the circuit that Bruno had already broken: but that twin-pronged switch, sunk though it almost certainly was in a bath of oil, might make enough noise on release to alert the guard in the south-east watch-tower, no more than ten feet distant. Bruno decided to leave it for the moment.

He unscrewed the balancing pole, bound it together and suspended it from an anchoring wire, unlikely though it was that he would be using it again. Getting over the fence of those outward curving spikes would be no problem. It was only about three feet above his head, and all he had to do was to hoist himself up to the top of the breaker and almost literally step over. But here was also the moment of greatest danger – the first time he would be completely exposed to observation.

He threw a loop of rope over a spike, hoisted himself up until he was standing on the breaker, his head at least four feet above the top of the spiked fence. The massive flat-topped wall was at least thirty inches thick. A five-year-old who didn't suffer from vertigo could have toddled around the top perimeter with ease; but the same five-year-old would have been suicidally open to the repeated and irregular probings of the watch-tower searchlights along the perimeter walls.

And, just at that moment when he was about to step over the curved spikes of the steel fence, a searchlight bloomed into life. It came from the north-east tower and the beam traversed the length of the east perimeter wall he had been about to mount. Bruno's reflex action was instantaneous. He crouched below the top level of the wall, holding on to the loop of the rope to keep himself from toppling outwards. It seemed very unlikely that the guard would pick up any object so small as the tiny bight of the rope round its anchoring spike and so in the event it proved. The searchlight beam moved away through ninety degrees, briefly traversed the north wall then died. Five seconds later Bruno stood on top of the wall.

Five feet below on the opposite side was the roof of the detention block. The entrance to the watch-tower had to be from there. Bruno lowered himself to the roof and made his crouching way along to the base of the tower.

A flight of eight angled wooden steps led up to the tower platform. As Bruno glanced upwards a match inside the tower flared and he had a glimpse of a figure with a fur hat and turned-up collar of a greatcoat lighting a cigarette. Bruno unscrewed the cover of the gas-pen and soundlessly mounted the stairs, putting his left hand on the door. He waited until the guard drew heavily on his cigarette, opened the door without undue haste, aimed the pen at the red glow and pressed the clip.

Five minutes later he arrived, via the detention block roof, at the north-east watch-tower. His stay there occupied him no longer than had his brief sojourn at the first tower. Leaving the second guard there as immobilized and silenced as the first, he made his way back along the east wall, lowered himself down to the breaker and gently pressed down the lever. The muffled thud could not have been heard more than a few feet away, for as he'd guessed the switch had been immersed in a bath of oil. He returned to the south-east tower, peered over the south wall and flashed his torch three times in rapid succession, then pressed it on and left it on. A recognition flash came from the south lane below.

Bruno doused his light, produced a considerable length of weighted cord from a capacious pocket and lowered it. He felt pressure come on the end followed by a gentle tug and immediately started reeling in the cord. In very short order indeed he had in his hands the other end of the rope that Roebuck had succeeded in attaching to the spikes at the south-west corner of Lubylan. He pulled it taut but not too taut – the steel core of the nylon ensured that the sagging factor would be negligible – and fastened it securely. He now had a rope that ran the full length of the outside of the southern wall, three to four feet below the base of the spikes. For an aerialist and high-wire specialist it was as good as a public highway.

It was a fifty-yard trip to the south-west tower and he made it in under three minutes. With the rope to walk on and the base of the curved spikes for support it was, for Bruno, a ridiculously easy passage. Once, but then only very briefly, he had to duck low when the searchlight of the watch-tower he was approaching traversed the south wall, but there was never any danger of discovery. And within a minute of his arrival at his destination a third guard had lost all his conscious interest in the immediate future.

Bruno pointed his torch down and signalled four times, this to let those waiting below know that he had arrived but to wait. There was still the final guard to be disposed of, the one in the north-west tower. It could well have been that the guards merely traversed their searchlights when and if the whim took them or there could have been some concerted arrangement, however irregular that may have been. In any event, he could not afford to arouse any degree of suspicion.

He waited until the remaining guard had made a couple of perfunctory traverses with his searchlight, dropped down to the roof of the research building – like its eastern counterpart it was five feet below the level of the wall – and made his silent way across. Clearly the guard had had no suspicion at all. Bruno made his way back to the south-west watch-tower, flashed his torch twice and lowered his weighted cord again. A minute later he was securing a heavy knotted rope to the base of the spikes. He flashed again, waited a few seconds and gave the rope an experimental tug. It was bar-taut. The first of his companions was on his way up. Bruno peered downwards to try to identify the climber, but the gloom was too deep to make positive identification: from the bulk of the shadowy figure it looked like Kan Dahn.

Bruno embarked on a more careful examination of the roof. There had to be an access hatch for the watch-tower guards, for there was no such vertical access in or near the towers themselves. He located it almost at once by a glow of light emanating from a partially covered hatchway close to the inner edge of the roof, about half-way between the north and south walls. The hatchway cover, vertically sided, curved through an arc of ninety degrees, whether to obscure the light from above, which seemed unlikely, or to give protection against the weather to the hatch below, which seemed more probable. Bruno hitched a cautious eye round the corner of the cover. The light came from a heavily meshed square of plate glass set in a hinged trap-door. Looking down, Bruno could see only a part of the bleak room below but what he could see was enough. There were four guards there, fully clothed, three of them lying, apparently asleep, on hinged canvas bunks, the fourth, his back to Bruno and facing an open door, playing some sort of solitary card game. A vertical steel ladder ran from the floor of the room to the side of the trap-door.

Gingerly, Bruno tried the hatch, but it was locked, probably bolted from below. The place might not, as Harper had said it was, be guarded like Fort Knox, but they certainly took every precaution against the most unlikely occurrences. Bruno moved away and looked down over a low parapet into the courtyard. There were no immediate signs of the guard dogs Harper had mentioned, but that did not preclude the possibility of their lurking in one of the several archways he could see, but that didn't seem likely: Dobermanns are inveterate prowlers. And there was no movement or sign of life in the glass-enclosed elevated passageway that joined the two buildings on the fifth floor level.

When Bruno returned to the south-west tower Kan Dahn

was already there. The ninety-foot climb hadn't even altered his rate of breathing. He said: 'How was the trip across?'

'A good performer always quits at the top. I can't ever top that, so I've just quit.'

'And not a soul to see you. Alas, life's little ironies. I mean, with an audience there, we could have cleaned up twenty thousand bucks tonight.' He appeared in no way surprised by Bruno's decision. 'The watch-tower guards?'

'Asleep.'

'All?' Bruno nodded. 'So there's no rush?'

'There's no time to hang around either. I don't know when the reliefs come on duty.'

'7 p.m. seems an unlikely hour.'

'Yes. But we haven't come all this way to take what looks even like a ghost of a chance.' He turned as first Roebuck and then Manuelo appeared in rapid succession. In contrast with Kan Dahn they appeared to be experiencing some difficulty with their breathing. Roebuck, the double canvas bag still slung over a shoulder, said: 'Thank God we go down that rope instead of up when we leave.'

'We don't leave that way.'

'We don't?' Roebuck paled beneath the tan. 'You mean there's another way? I'm not sure if I'm looking forward to that.'

Bruno said soothingly. 'A Sunday walk, that's all. Now, access. There's only one way in from the roof and that's locked.'

Kan Dahn said: 'A door?'

'A trap-door.'

Kan Dahn brandished his crowbar. 'Poof! No trap-door.'

'There are guards in the room below. One, at least, is wide awake.' He led the way half-way along the west perimeter wall, knelt, caught hold of a curved spike and leaned out over the main street. The others did the same.

'I know the geography of this place. That first window down – I want to get in through there.'

'That first window down,' Roebuck said, 'has got big thick iron bars protecting it.'

'It won't have in a little while.' Bruno knelt upright and produced the plastic packet from his pocket. He unrolled this to reveal two small polythene-wrapped packages. 'For iron bars, the ultimate persuader. Turns them into a form of putty near enough.'

Roebuck said: 'What kind of hocus-pocus is this?'

'No hocus, no pocus. You can apologize at your leisure. Every professional magician worth his salt knows about it. You can soften and bend practically any metal by smearing it with this stuff – oddly enough, with reasonable care, it doesn't affect the human skin. The plastic inside this polythene contains an acid that eats into the interstices between the molecules of metal and softens it up. There's an Israeli magician who says that given time and enough of the stuff he could bend a Sherman tank. Here we have only two iron bars.'

'How long does it take to work?'

'Five minutes should be enough. I'm not certain.'

Manuelo said: 'Burglar alarms?'

'Those I can fix.'

Bruno tied a double bowline, slipped his legs through them until they reached the top of his thighs, secured a bight round his waist and eased himself out and over the curving spikes. He lowered himself to the full extent of his arms while Kan Dahn took a turn of the rope round a spike; then he exchanged his grip on the spikes for one on the rope, and Kan Dahn eased him down.

With the rope round his thighs and waist, his feet on the window sill and one hand grasping an iron bar, Bruno was as safe as a man in church. There were four bars on the window, each pair about eight inches apart. He removed the two cylinders of plastic compound from his pocket, opened them half-way and, careful not to remove the polythene covering, wrapped the plastic round the middle of the two centre bars, closing and smoothing the polythene round each in turn so that the compound was again completely sealed off. He climbed the few feet up the rope to the metal fence: Kan Dahn reached down, caught him under the armpits and lifted him easily over the wickedly out-curving spikes.

He said: 'Five minutes. Manuelo, you'll come down with Kan Dahn and myself. Roebuck will stay here. And watch that canvas bag of yours – that's the last thing we can afford to lose at this stage of the game. Could I have the wire-cutters, please, Manuelo?'

Kan Dahn slipped into a double bowline, secured a bight round his waist, belayed the rope round three spikes – probably a sensible precaution for a man of his massive weight – and lowered himself down to the window ledge. He clenched a massive fist round each of the central bars and began to pull them apart. The contest was brief and unequal. The bars bent as if made from some inferior putty, but Kan Dahn wasn't content with just making a gap: he leaned some more on the bars and both came free from their anchorages. He handed them up to the roof.

Bruno joined Kan Dahn by means of a separate rope. Arrived opposite the window, he used his flash and peered through the glass. It appeared to be a perfectly innocuous office, bleakly furnished with metal cabinets, metal tables and padded metal seats. It certainly offered no hint of danger.

While Kan Dahn held the torch Bruno produced a roll of brown paper, unrolled it and pressed one side against a pane of glass. That side was clearly adhesive. He waited a few seconds then struck the centre of the glass quite firmly with the heel of his fist. The glass came away and fell into the room, making practically no noise at all. Bruno took the torch from Kan Dahn and, holding both torch and wire-cutters in the same hand, thrust his head and one of his arms through the hole he had made. He located the unconcealed alarm wires at once, severed them, reached up and opened the window catch and pushed the lower window upwards. Ten seconds and both he and Kan Dahn were inside the room: another ten and Manuelo had joined them. He was carrying Kan Dahn's crowbar with him.

The office door was unlocked, the corridor beyond deserted. The three men made their way along until they came to an open door on the left. Bruno signalled to Manuelo to move forward. He did so and, holding a knife by the blade, cautiously showed an inch of the hilt round the edge of the jamb. Almost at once came the sound of discreet tapping on the glass of the hatch-cover above, enough to alert the card-playing soldier but not enough to disturb the three sleeping men. The guard at the table looked up questioningly, and then it was over.

The hilt of Manuelo's knife caught him over the ear and Kan Dahn caught him before he even had time to strike the ground. Bruno picked up one of several guns stacked in a ramp and covered the three others with it. The last thing he wanted or intended to do was to use it, but the three men were not to know that and a man waking from his sleep is not going to argue with a Schmeisser machine-pistol. But they kept on sleeping soundly even when Kan Dahn unbolted the trap-door to allow Roebuck – and his canvas bag – down into the guardroom. Bruno took out his gas pen and advanced upon the three sleeping guards: Roebuck, armed with a suitable amount of rope, followed him.

They left the four guards there, securely bound and taped, three of them even more deeply asleep than they had been a few minutes previously. They bolted the trap-door, a probably unnecessary precaution, locked the guard-room door behind them and removed the key. Bruno said: 'So far, so good.' He hefted the Schmeisser he had borrowed from the guardroom. 'Let's call on Van Diemen.'

Kan Dahn paused in the passageway and looked puzzled. 'Van Diemen? Why do we have to attend to him first – or at all? You know where his offices and laboratories are. Why don't we go straight in there now, find out the papers you want – you're quite sure you'll recognize those—'

'I'll recognize them.'

'Then fold our tents and steal away into the night. Like the Arabs, you know. A classy job, smooth, slick and noiseless. That's what I like.'

Bruno looked his disbelief. 'What you would like is to crack every skull in the Lubylan. I can give you four reasons for not doing it your way and then no arguing – the change of the guard may be due at any moment. Time is not on our side.'

'The change of guard is all nicely asleep in the guard-room.'

'That may not be the change of guard. They may have to report to some kind of HQ at change-over. There may be an officer who carries out a routine inspection. I don't know. Reason one: what we want may be in his private quarters. Reason two: we may be able to persuade him to tell us where the papers are. Reason three: if his filing cabinets are locked

– and it would be astonishing if they aren't – we may make quite a noise in opening them up and his quarters are right next door. But reason four is most important. You should have guessed.' From their expressions it was apparent that no one had guessed. 'I'm taking him back to the States with me.'

'Taking him back—' Roebuck looked his incredulity. 'You've been through too much. It's your mind.'

'Is it? What the hell's the point in taking the papers back home and leaving him here? He's the only man who knows those damned formulas or whatever they are – and all he'd do is just sit down and write them out again.'

Roebuck said in slow comprehension: 'You know, that had never occurred to me.'

'Hadn't occurred to a lot of other people either, it would seem. Very odd, isn't it? Anyway, I'm sure that Uncle Sam can always find him a nice congenial job.'

'Such as supervising the development of this damnable anti-matter?'

'From what I've heard of Van Diemen, he'd die first. He's a renegade, you know that. It must have taken some awfully compelling political and ideological reasons for him to defect from West Germany to here. He'd never co-operate.'

'But you can't do this to a man,' Kan Dahn said. 'Kidnapping is a crime in any country.'

'True. But better than death, I would have thought. What do you want me to do? Have him swear on the Bible – or any handy Marxist treatise that we can lay hands on – that he'll never again reproduce any of those formulas? You know damned well that he'd never consent to that. Or just leave him in peace to write his memoirs – all about how to construct this hellish weapon?'

The silence was very loud.

'You haven't left me much choice, have you? So what would you have me do? Execute him in the sacred name of patriotism?'

There was no immediate answer to this because he'd left them without the option of an answer. Then Kan Dahn said: 'You have to take him back home.'

— 10 —

VAN DIEMEN'S door was locked. Kan Dahn leaned on it and it was no longer locked. It crashed back against its hinges and Bruno was the first in, Schmeisser levelled – it had occurred to him, not, fortunately, too belatedly, that, without some recognizably offensive weapon, they were at a distinct disadvantage – a wandering guard, seeing them apparently unarmed, would be sorely tempted to cut loose with whatever weapon *he* might possess.

The startled man, propped on one elbow and rubbing sleep from his eyes, had a lean aristocratic face, grey hair, grey moustache and grey beard: he looked the exact antithesis of the mad scientist of popular conception. His unbelieving eyes switched from the intruders to a bell-push on his bedside table.

'Touch that and you're dead.' Bruno's voice carried utter conviction. Van Diemen was convinced. Roebuck advanced to the bell-push and sliced the flexible lead with the wire-cutters.

'Who are you? What do you want?' Van Diemen's voice was steady, seemingly without fear: he had about him the look of a man who has suffered too much to be afraid of anything any more.

'We want you. We want the plans of your anti-gravity invention.'

'I see. You can have me any time. Alive or dead. To get the plans you'll have to kill me first. They're not here anyway.'

'You said the last two sentences the wrong way round. Tape his mouth and tie his hands behind his back. Then we look. For papers, keys, perhaps even one key.'

II

The search, which lasted perhaps ten minutes and left Van Diemen's quarters in an indescribable shambles, yielded precisely nothing. Bruno stood in momentary indecision. For all he knew, time might be running out very fast indeed.

'Let's try his clothes.'

They tried his clothes. Again they found nothing. Bruno advanced on the bound and gagged figure sitting up in bed, regarded him thoughtfully for a moment, then reached down and gently lifted the gold chain he wore round his neck. No crucifix for Van Diemen, no Star of David, but something that was probably even more precious to him than those could have been to a Catholic or Jew: dangling from the end of the chain was a bright and intricately-cut bronze key.

III

Two whole walls of Van Diemen's main office were lined with metal filing cabinets. Fourteen in all, each with four sliding drawers. Fifty-six holes. Roebuck was unsuccessfully trying his thirtieth. Every pair of eyes in the office looked at him intently. All except Bruno's. His did not leave Van Diemen's face, which had remained expressionless throughout. Suddenly there was a tic at the corner of his mouth.

'That one,' Bruno said.

That one it was. The key turned easily and Roebuck pulled the drawer out. Van Diemen tried to throw himself forward, which, if an understandable reaction, was a futile one, for Kan Dahn had one massive arm around him. Bruno advanced to the drawer, started leafing quickly through the files. He picked out one sheaf of papers, checked the other files, double-checked them and closed the drawer.

Roebuck said: 'Yes?'

'Yes.' Bruno thrust the files deep inside the inner pocket of his garish suit.

Roebuck said complainingly: 'Seems like a bit of an anti-climax.'

'I wouldn't worry about that,' Bruno said encouragingly. 'The climax may still be to come.'

IV

They descended to the eighth floor. Van Diemen had his

mouth taped and hands bound behind his back, for the prison staff lived there and it seemed highly likely that Van Diemen might have wished to call attention to their presence. There were no guards here, either asleep or awake, and no reason why there should have been: guards were expendable but Van Diemen's papers were not.

Bruno headed directly for the door at the foot of the stairs. It was not locked and neither were the filing cabinets inside, and again there was no reason why any of them should have been. Bruno began opening filing drawers in swift succession, extracting files, leafing through them rapidly and discarding them in turn by the elementary process of dropping them on the floor.

Roebuck looked at him in some puzzlement and said: 'A moment ago you were in one Godalmighty damned hurry to get out. What place is this anyway?'

Bruno looked at him briefly. 'You forget the note you passed me?'

'Ah!'

'Yes. Ah: "4.30. West entrance. No question. My life on it." They keep the prison records here.'

Bruno offered no further explanation to anyone. Suddenly he appeared to find what he wanted, a highly detailed schematic diagram with rows of names printed on one side. He glanced briefly at it, nodded in what appeared to be some satisfaction, dropped it to the floor and turned away.

Roebuck said: 'We are doing our mentalist bit again?'

'Something like that.'

They eschewed the elevator, walked down to the fifth floor, and crossed to the detention block by way of the glass-enclosed passageway. There was an admitted element of risk in this, but slight: the only people who might reasonably have been expected to have a watchful eye on that goldfish bowl corridor were the watch-tower guards and they were in no condition to have their eyes on anything.

Bruno halted the others as they reached the closed door at the far end of the passageway. 'Wait. I know where the guardroom is – just round the corner to the left. What I don't know is whether the guards will be patrolling.'

Roebuck said: 'So?'

'There's only one way to find out.'

'I'll come with you.'

'No. Nobody's recognized you yet. I don't intend that anyone shall. Don't forget that true trouper Roebuck is performing tonight. And Kan Dahn. And Manuelo. And not forgetting, of course, Vladimir and Yoffe.'

Manuelo looked at him in something approaching stupefaction.

'Your brothers?'

'Of course. They're here. Where else do you think they would have been taken?'

'But – but the ransom demands?'

'Courtesy of the Secret Police. So my brothers can perform with impunity. Nobody's got anything against them. How can they? They were just pawns, hostages for my good conduct. And do you think the police are going to admit they abducted them and sent ransom demands? Now that *would* cause an international uproar.'

Manuelo said complainingly: 'You do play cards pretty close to the chest.'

'It's one of the better ways of surviving.'

'And how are you going to survive any longer?'

'I'm getting out of here.'

'Sure. No problem. You just flap your arms and fly away.'

'More or less. Roebuck has a little gadget in that bag of his. I just operate it and a whirlygig should be here in about twenty minutes.'

'Whirlygig? Helicopter? From where, for God's sake?'

'American naval vessel lying offshore.'

There was no ready answer to this. Then Roebuck said: 'Very, very close to the chest. That means that you're the only one of us who's leaving?'

'I'm taking Maria. The police have recorded tape evidence that she's up to her ears in this.'

They stared at him in complete incomprehension.

'I think I forgot to mention. She's a CIA agent.'

Roebuck said heavily: 'Very, very, very close. And how do you propose to get her?'

'Go up to the circus for her.'

Kan Dahn shook his head sadly. 'Quite, quite mad.'

'Would I be here if I weren't?' He depressed the top knob of the black pen, slipped off the safety catch on his machine-pistol and cautiously eased open the door.

V

It was a prison just like any other prison, rows of cells on four sides of the block, passageways with four feet high railings bordering the deep well that ran the full vertical height of the building. As far as Bruno could see there was no one on patrol, certainly not on that fifth floor. He moved out to the railing, glanced up and then down the fifty-foot drop to the concrete below. It was impossible to be certain, but there appeared to be no one on patrol, nor could he hear anything. And prison guards, especially military guards, are not noted for the lightness of their steps.

Light came from a glass-fronted door about twenty feet to his left. Bruno pussy-footed his way towards it and peered in. There were two guards and two only, seated one on either side of a small table. Quite clearly they weren't expecting any senior officers or NCOs around on a tour of inspection, for they had a bottle on the table and a glass apiece. They were playing the inevitable cards.

Bruno pushed the door open. Both men turned their heads and looked down the uninviting muzzle of the Schmeisser.

'On your feet.'

They complied with alacrity.

'Hands behind your necks. Close your eyes. Tight.'

They wasted no time over this either. Bruno pulled out the gas pen, squirted it twice, then whistled softly for the others to join him. While they were immobilizing the two guards, Bruno inspected the rows of numbered keys hanging on the guard-room wall.

VI

On the seventh floor, Bruno selected the key numbered 713 and opened the cell door. The two brothers, Vladimir and Yoffe, stared at him in open disbelief, then rushed out and hugged him wordlessly. Bruno pushed them smilingly aside, selected more keys, opened up 714 then 715 and 716 in succession. Bruno, standing outside 715, smiled without mirth at his two brothers, companions and Van Diemen, who had moved up to join him.

He said: 'A rather nice touch, don't you think, to lock all the Wildermanns up together?'

The three doors opened almost simultaneously and three people made their way, two with very faltering footsteps, out into the passageway. The two who could not walk too well were old and stooped and grey, one who had been a man, the other who had been a woman, their prison pallor faces lined with suffering and pain and privation. The third figure had been a young man but was no longer young, except in years.

The old woman stared at Bruno with dull lack-lustre eyes. She said: 'Bruno.'

'Yes, Mother.'

'I knew you would come some day.'

He put his arm round the frail shoulders. 'I'm sorry I took so long.'

'Touching,' Dr Harper said. 'How very, very touching.'

Bruno removed his arm and turned round unhurriedly. Dr Harper, using Maria Hopkins as a shield, had a silenced pistol in one hand. Beside him, smiling wolfishly, Colonel Sergius was similarly armed. Behind them stood the giant Angelo, whose preferred form of weapon was a giant lethal club the size of a baseball bat.

Harper went on: 'We're not interrupting, are we? I mean, you weren't thinking of going some place?'

'We had that in mind.'

'Drop that machine-pistol,' Sergius ordered.

Bruno stooped, placed it on the ground, then, as he came upright, moved with lightning speed, grabbed Van Diemen and held him before him as a shield. With his other hand he got the red dart pen from his breast pocket, depressed the knob, and pointed it over Van Diemen's shoulder at Harper's face. At the sight of the pen Harper's face widened in fear and the finger tightened on the trigger of the silenced gun.

Sergius, no longer smiling, said viciously: 'Drop that. I can get you from the side.' Which was an accurate observation, but, unfortunately for Sergius, he had transferred his attention to Bruno while he was speaking, a period of about two seconds, and for a man possessed of the cobra speed and accuracy of Manuelo two seconds was a laughably long time. Sergius died unawares, the knife buried to the haft in his throat.

Two seconds after that both Van Diemen and Harper were on the floor, Van Diemen with the bullet intended for Bruno buried in his chest, Harper with the dart buried in his cheek. Angelo, his face contorted in fury, made an animal noise deep in the throat and leapt forward, his huge club swinging. Kan Dahn, moving forward even more quickly, and with astonishing agility for a man of his immense bulk, avoided the downward blow, wrenched the club from Angelo and tossed it contemptuously to one side. The struggle that followed was as titanic as it was brief, and the sound of Angelo's neck breaking was that of a rotten bough shearing under the woodman's axe.

Bruno put one arm round the violently trembling girl, the other round the stunned, terrified and uncomprehending old woman.

He said: '*Fine. Termine*. It's all over and you're all safe now. I think we should leave this place now. You won't really mind will you, Father?' The old man gazed at the prostrate figures and said nothing. Bruno went on, to no one in particular: 'About Van Diemen I'm sorry. But perhaps it's best. He'd really no place left to go.'

Kan Dahn said: 'No place?'

'In his world, yes. In mind, not. He was completely amoral – not immoral – in devising so fiendish a weapon. A totally unheeding, irresponsible man. I know it's a very cruel thing to say, but the world can well do without him.'

Maria said: 'Why did Dr Harper come for me? He kept saying something about his transmitter and tapes being missing from his railway compartment.'

'Yes. It had to be something like that. Roebuck here stole them. Can't trust those Americans.'

'You don't trust me very much. You don't tell me very much.' There was no reproach in her voice, just a lack of understanding. 'But perhaps you can tell me what happens when Dr Harper comes to.'

'Dead men don't come to. Not on this planet, anyway.'

'Dead?' She had no emotions left to register.

'Those darts were tipped with lethal poison. Some form of refined curare, I should imagine. I was supposed to kill some of their own men. Fortunately, I had to use it on a guard dog. Now a very dead guard dog.'

'Kill their own men?'

'It would have looked very black for me – and America – if I'd killed some of the guards here, then been caught red-handed. Their own men. People like Harper and Sergius are men without hearts, without souls. They'd shoot their own parents if it served their personal political ends. It was also slated, incidentally, that you should die. I had, of course, been instructed not to use the dart gun on Van Diemen on the pretext that he had a weak heart. Well, God knows he's got a weak enough heart now – Harper put a bullet through it.' He looked at Maria. 'You know how to operate the call-up on the transmitter – Roebuck has it in his bag there?' She nodded. 'Right, send the signal now.' He turned to Kan Dahn, Roebuck and Manuelo. 'Bring my folks down slowly, will you? They can't hurry. I'll wait below.'

Kan Dahn said with suspicion: 'Where are you going?'

'The entrance is time-locked so someone must have let them in. Whoever that was will still be there or thereabouts. You're all still in the clear. I want you to stay that way.' He picked up the Schmeisser. 'I hope I don't have to use this.'

When the others joined him on the ground floor some five minutes later, Bruno had already done what he had to do. Kan Dahn surveyed the two bound, gagged and for the moment unconscious guards with considerable satisfaction.

'By my count that's making thirteen people we've tied up tonight. It's certainly been an unlucky number for some. So it's up, up and away.'

'Indeed.' He asked Maria: 'You made contact?'

She looked at her watch. 'It's airborne. Rendez-vous in sixteen minutes.'

'Good.' He looked and smiled at Kan Dahn, Manuelo, Roebuck, Vladimir and Yoffe. 'Well, it's the van for us while you five make your own discreet way back to the Winter Palace. *Au revoir* and many thanks. See you all in Florida. Have a nice night at the circus.'

VII

Bruno helped his elderly parents and youngest brother into the back of the van, climbed into the front with Maria and drove off towards the rendez-vous with the helicopter. He stopped the van about thirty yards beyond the wooden bridge spanning the narrow fast river. Maria looked at the trees closely crowding on both sides.

'*This* is the rendez-vous?'

'Round the next corner. In a clearing. But I have a little chore to attend to first.'

'Inevitably.' She looked and sounded resigned. 'And is one allowed to ask what it is?'

'I'm going to blow the bridge up.'

'I see. You're going to blow the bridge up.' She registered no surprise and was by now at the stage where she wouldn't have lifted an eyebrow if he'd announced his intention of razing the Winter Palace to the ground. 'Why?'

Carrying his clutch of amatol explosives, Bruno descended from the van. Maria followed. As they walked on to the bridge Bruno said: 'Hasn't it occurred to you that when they hear the chopper's engine – and you can hear a chopper's engine an awfully long way away – the police and army are going to come swarming out of town like enraged bees? I don't want to get stung.'

Maria was crestfallen. 'There seem to be an awful lot of things that don't occur to me.'

Bruno took her arm and said nothing. Together, they walked out to the middle of the bridge, where Bruno stooped and laid the charges together between two struts on the side of the bridge. He straightened and surveyed them thoughtfully.

Maria said: 'Are you an expert on *everything*?'

'You don't have to be an expert to blow up a wooden bridge.' He produced a pair of pliers from his pocket. 'All you require is one of those to crimp the chemical fuse – and, of course, the sense to walk away immediately afterwards.'

He stood there thoughtfully and she said: 'Well, aren't you going to crimp the fuses, then?'

'Two things. I only crimp one fuse: the other charges will

go up through sympathetic detonation. And if I blow up the bridge now then angry bees will be out here immediately, perhaps with enough time to figure out a way to cross the river or find a nearby bridge. We wait till we hear the chopper, blow the bridge, drive round to this glade in the woods and use the van's headlights to light up the landing area.'

She said: 'I can hear the helicopter now.'

He nodded, stooped again, crimped a fuse, took her hand and ran off the bridge. Twenty yards beyond the bridge they turned round just on the moment that the explosion came. The noise was a very satisfactory one indeed, and so was the result: the centre of the bridge, a flimsy structure at best, simply disintegrated and fell into the river below.

VIII

The transfer to the helicopter and the flight back to the ship went without a hitch, the pilot hedge-hopping all the way to keep below the radar screen. In the wardroom Bruno was being apologetic to a rather stormy Maria.

'I know I fooled you and I'm sorry. But I didn't want you to die, you see. I knew from the beginning that most of our conversations were being recorded. I had to make Harper think that the break-in was going to be on Tuesday. He was all set to get us that night and that meant he would have got you, too.'

'But Kan Dahn and Roebuck and Manuelo—'

'No risk. They were in it from the beginning.'

'Why, you close, devious – but something must have put you on to Harper in the first place?'

'My Slav blood. Nasty suspicious natures we Slavs have. About the only place that wasn't bugged was the circus office back in the States. The electronic snooper that Harper brought in was an accomplice of his: this was designed to throw suspicion on the circus. If there was no internal circus contact then it *had* to be Harper. Only four people were really privy to what was going on – your boss, Pilgrim, Fawcett and Harper. Your boss was above suspicion, Fawcett and Pilgrim were dead. So, Harper. Aboard ship, Carter, the purser, wasn't there to make sure that my cabin wasn't bugged – he was there to make sure that it was. So was yours.'

'You have no proof of this.'

'No? He was in correspondence with Gydnia and he had fifteen hundred dollars in his cabin. New dollars. I have the serial numbers.'

'That night he met with the accident on deck—'

'Kan Dahn was the accident. Then Harper told me he had keys for Diemen's offices. He must have thought me a simpleton. You'd have needed a hundred skeleton keys to cover every lock. He'd keys for one reason only – he'd access to Van Diemen's keys. And he kept asking me about my plans for entry. I kept saying I'd play it by ear. So eventually I gave him all my plans – a tissue of lies – by giving them to you in your cabin. You may remember Harper suggested your cabin as a rendez-vous. And, of course, I didn't trust you either.'

'What!'

'I didn't *distrust* you. I just didn't trust anyone. I didn't know you were clean until you insisted that Harper had personally appointed you to this job. If you had been in cahoots, you'd have said your boss did.'

'I'll never trust *you* again.'

'And why were we followed by the Secret Police everywhere. *Someone* gave them the tip-off. When I knew it wasn't you, there wasn't anyone else very much to suspect.'

'And you still expect me to marry you?'

'I'll have to. For your own sake. After you've resigned, that is. This may be the day of women's lib, but I think all this is a bit too lib for you. Do you know why Harper picked you – because he reckoned you were the person least likely to give him any trouble. He was right. My God, it's never even occurred to you how Harper managed to drag Fawcett inside the tiger's cage without being savaged.'

'Well, since you're so clever—'

'He anaesthetized the tigers with a dart gun.'

'Of course. Maybe I should retire at that. You don't make many mistakes, do you?'

'Yes. A major one. One that could have been fatal for many people. I assumed that the red dart-gun was the same as he'd used on the tigers. It wasn't. It was lethal. If it hadn't been for that Dobermann Pinscher – ah well, it was fitting that he died at his own hand, so to speak. Hoist on his own petard, or those who live by the sword die by the sword or something like that.'

'One thing – among, seemingly, many others – I don't understand. This business of you having to take Van Diemen prisoner. Surely Van Diemen's almost certain ability to reproduce the formulas would have been foreseen by the CIA back in Washington?'

'It was foreseen. It was intended that I kill him with the lethal red pen. If not, Harper – who probably carried a vest pocketful of red pens – was slated to attend to him on Tuesday night, the supposed time of the break-in. He would have got off with it – he was as cunning as he was brilliant – and there would have been no one to testify against him. I would have been dead.'

She looked at him and shuddered.

He smiled. 'It's all over now. Harper told me a fairy story about Van Diemen's heart condition and insisted that I used the black gas pen against him. The need to use either did not arise. It was Harper's – and, of course, his masters' – intention that Van Diemen should survive. As I said, Harper died by his own hand – and Van Diemen by Harper's. Harper is totally responsible for the deaths of both Van Diemen and himself.'

'But why – *why* did he do it?'

'Who knows? Who will ever know? A dedicated anti-American? A million dollars on the nail? The motivation – or motivations – of a double agent lie beyond comprehension. Not that it matters now. Sorry, incidentally, that I jumped on you that night in New York – I had no means of knowing whether my family was alive or dead. You know, of course, why Harper sent us to the restaurant that night – so that he could have my stateroom bugged. Which reminds me – I must send a telegram to have Carter arrested. And Morley – Harper's bogus electronics friend who bugged my stateroom on the train. And now, I have a delicate question for you.'

'And that is?'

'May I go to the men's room?'

So he went to the men's room. There he extracted from his

inside pocket the papers he had taken from Van Diemen's filing cabinet. He did not even look at them. He tore them into tiny pieces and flushed them down the toilet.

IX

Captain Kodes knocked on the circus's office door and entered without invitation. Wrinfield looked up in mild surprise.

'I'm looking for Colonel Sergius, Mr Wrinfield. Have you seen him?'

'I've just arrived from the train. If he's inside he'll be in his usual seat.'

Kodes nodded and hurried into the large exhibition hall. The late-night performance was in full swing and, as usual, it was a capacity house. Kodes made his way along to the section of the seats opposite the centre ring, but there was no sign of Sergius. For a few moments he stood there irresolute, then instinctively, almost inevitably, his eyes followed the gaze of ten thousand other pairs of eyes.

For long moments Kodes stood stock still, as if petrified, his mind at first blankly refusing to accept the evidence of his eyes. But his eyes were making no mistake. What he was witnessing was the impossible but the impossible was indubitably there: two of the Blind Eagles were going through their customary hair-raising trapeze act.

Kodes turned and ran. As he went through the exit he was met by Kan Dahn, who greeted him in genial fashion. It was questionable whether Kodes saw him. He burst into Wrinfield's office, this time without the benefit of knocking.

'The Blind Eagles! The Blind Eagles! Where in God's name have they come from?'

Wrinfield looked at him mildly. 'Their kidnappers released them. We notified the police. Didn't you know?'

'No, I damn well didn't know!' Kodes ran from the office and into his car.

X

Ashen-faced and stunned, Kodes stood on the seventh floor of the Lubylan detention block. The shock of finding gagged and bound men both at the open entrance below and in the guard-room had been shattering enough: but nothing could have prepared him for the sight of the three dead men lying there, Sergius and Van Diemen and Angelo.

XI

A sure instinct led Kodes to the undertaker's emporium. He was hardly conscious of the fact that the lights were on in the front office. They were also on in the back parlour. He made his way to the coffin that had been so briefly occupied by Bruno, and slowly removed the lid.

Dr Harper, hands crossed on his chest, looked curiously peaceful. The hands held the large black-bordered box that had been cut from the paper that had announced Bruno's death.

XII

The admiral leaned back in his chair in his Washington office and stared in disbelief as Bruno and Maria entered.

'God! That suit!'

'Beggars can't be choosers.' Bruno surveyed his suit without enthusiasm. 'Chap in Crau gave it to me.'

'He did? Anyway, welcome home, Bruno. And Miss Hopkins.'

'Mrs Wildermann,' Bruno said.

'What the devil do you mean?'

'Holy matrimony. They give you a special licence for people in a hurry. We are in a hurry.'

The admiral contained his near-apoplexy. 'I have the outline of the past few days. The details, please.'

Bruno gave him the details and when he had finished the admiral said: 'Magnificent. Well, well, it took a long time before we could put it all together. Van Diemen and your family.'

'A long time.'

Maria stared from one to the other in puzzlement.

The admiral said briskly: 'And now. The plans.'

'Destroyed.'

'Naturally. But your mentalist mind isn't.'

'My mentalist mind, sir, has gone into a state of total shock. Amnesia.'

The admiral leaned forward, his eyes narrowing, his hands tightening on the desk. 'Repeat that.'

'I destroyed them without looking at them.'

'You destroyed them without looking at them.' It was a statement not a question. His voice was very quiet. 'Why?'

'What did you want, sir? Another mutual balance of terror throughout the world?'

'Why?'

'I told you why. Remember? I hate war.'

For long moments the admiral looked at him without enthusiasm, then he slowly relaxed, leaned back and astonished them both by laughing.

'I've a damned good mind to fire you.' He sighed, still smiling. 'But you're probably right on the whole.'

Maria said blankly; 'Fire him?'

'Didn't you know? Bruno has been one of my top, and certainly most trusted, agents for the past five years.'